I0647210

The Whisperer

The Children of Light - Book 1

Vicki Wootton

Stargate Publishing

The Whisperer

ISBN: 978-0-9950102-0-8 eBook

ISBN: 978-0-9780953-9-0 Print

Thank you!

I owe special thanks to Teri Saya, Pauline Van Havere, and Carlos Ruiz Checa for having the patience to read and re-read this manuscript. Many thanks for helping to correct errors and offering helpful suggestions for improvement. The responsibility for any overlooked errors is strictly mine.

Other books by this author

Novels

Where Have All the Young Girls Gone?

At War with Terror

Forbidden Worlds

Reluctant Warriors

Fatal Harvest

Non-fiction

Names of the World

1 – Leaving Home

Felindra

After helping her mother with some household chores, Felindra left the house and climbed up the slope outside the walls that surrounded their home. This was her favorite time of day and her favorite place to relax and meditate. It was late spring and the wild flowers were blooming in abundance in the long grass. The fragrance of the flowers and the scent wafting from the nearby orange orchard were entrancing, but what really captured her was the feeling of life all round, bees humming, birds singing, the rustle of tiny rodents in the grass, the contented murmurs of nearby cattle, and the whinnying and snorting of horses in the paddock. Sometimes, she imagined she could almost read their thoughts, especially the dogs and horses. She even received sensations from the little field mice and rabbits, not so much thoughts as feelings of alarm, or gratification when they found something to eat. She lay down in the grass in the shade of a tree and felt blissfully at ease and peaceful. This was her home and she loved it.

But she had to finish her lessons, so she roused herself after a while and stood up, brushing the grass and leaves from her knee britches. "Goodbye, little friends," she called softly. "Be safe!"

Daryan

When Daryan reached home, the first person he saw was his son.

"Father!" Darson darted out from the kitchen door as soon as he heard the clatter of hooves and rumble of wagon wheels on the cobbles of the yard. It was already after sunset, although the lantern light from the open door of their little house gave them enough light to work by.

"Hello, Darson. How do you fare this fine evening?"

"Hello, Father. I'm well, thank you, and you?"

Daryan couldn't help smiling. His son was so solemn and formal. Sometimes, he sounded like an elderly tutor. "I also am well. Would you like help with the horses?" Daryan replied, ruffling his son's hair. Darson was a sturdy boy of ten with light tan skin, caramel-colored eyes, and black curly hair that almost reached his shoulders.

His daughter, Felindra, poked her head out of the kitchen door. "Dadi's here," she called over her shoulder. "Welcome home, dadi." She dashed across the yard into his arms.

"You'd think I'd been gone a month," he laughed, "instead of one day." He planted a kiss on her forehead.

Felindra had thirteen years. Her hair was also black and curly, but her complexion and eyes were darker than those of her brother. She got her coloring from her mother, Parvana, while Darson looked more like his father.

"Need help with the horses?" she asked. Felindra enjoyed working with the intelligent horses.

Daryan had already removed the bridles and given them to Darson to put on the rack in the stable. "Would you like to rub them down? I'll get some water and feed."

"I'd love to." She turned and went into the little stable.

Meanwhile, Darson had clambered up onto the wagon and was rummaging through the things Daryan had brought back from Salispon. "What's this, dadi?" he asked, brandishing a cylindrical package.

"Nothing you need be concerned about. Leave it for now, but you can bring in a wheel of cheese. I'll take the flour. We'll leave the rest for tomorrow."

Daryan walked towards the open door with the sack of flour on his shoulder.

Inside, his wife, Parvana, was preparing their supper. The table was already set with spoons, ceramic bowls, and mugs. Daryan put the bag of flour down by the wall and turned to his wife. She left the stirring spoon in the iron pot and came to embrace him, then kissed him on the mouth. "You look tired, my love. Busy day?"

He nodded and pressed her against his body. Being home amidst the warmth of his family seemed to wash his cares away for a while and his body relaxed, shedding some of the tension he'd been carrying with him since hearing about the attacks in the north.

Parvana

From the moment Daryan stepped through the door, Parvana suspected he had something on his mind, but decided to wait until they were alone before saying anything that might upset the children. The two youngsters finally fell asleep up in the loft. Parvana and Daryan slept in the only other room in their little home, a small chamber under the loft, barely larger than a storeroom, but the door allowed them some privacy.

She reached out and took his hand as they lay waiting for sleep. "Is something wrong, my love?" she asked in a soft voice.

Daryan sighed and turned on his side to face her. "Aye." He hesitated, as if wondering how to break it to her, and then decided it would be best simply to tell her. "We're going to have to leave."

Parvana's heart lurched; she raised herself on one elbow to face him. "Oh no. What happened?"

"There are signs that *they're* back."

"You mean … *them*? What sort of signs?"

"I'm afraid it may be so, beloved. Some travelers at the inn were talking about things that had been happening farther north near the border. It sounded like their kind of evil magic."

3

"*Solas Naofa!* What sort of things?" A tremor went through her.

"What you would expect from the Dark Brethren. Attacks on travelers on the highways, children disappearing, unexplained fires and crop damage." He reached out and stroked her arm, which had broken out in goose flesh.

She moved into his arms for comfort and warmth. "I thought we had finally beaten them, but now... after all these years. When do we have to leave?"

Parvana offered no argument or second-guessing upon hearing this news. She knew too well the situation and the urgency brought on by these events. They had come to this village of Picobali outside Salispon eleven years earlier, following the last battle against their ancient enemy, when everyone in the League of Light had thought they'd been defeated for good. The followers of Oglestra, the Dark Brethren, the very epitome of malevolence, used evil magic and unspeakable rites in their attempt to destroy the Children of Light and gain control of their world.

Daryan and Parvana were both members of the League of Light, but since the last battle fifteen years earlier, they had settled down to live ordinary lives and raise their children. The children knew nothing of their parents' gifts or their past. To them, Daryan was a swordsmith, albeit a very special sword maker.

His swords were prized throughout the Duchy of Trethawynd for their power and perfection, and the nobility paid generously to acquire them. The price of one sword would keep his family through two seasons and so he only created four or five each year, even though the demand was higher. He worked in a smithy that opened into the stable yard, separated from the road outside by a stone wall; he didn't want observers asking question, even though his work was approved by the League. Truth be told, there was magic involved in his craftsmanship, but it was inadvisable for this fact to be known abroad. Although the use of Light magic, gifts bestowed upon the Children of Light by the Lord of Light Himself, had saved them from the previous attack by the Dark Brethren, ordinary people were still wary of it and suspicious of those who practiced any form of magic. That wasn't the only danger, or the most serious: The Dark Brethren had ways of tracking down Light mages, and killing them, so the less people knew about them, the less they could be forced to reveal.

Neither of the children had been initiated into the League. Gifts didn't usually become apparent until a child entered adolescence. It was obvious to their parents that they were gifted, but they had tried to put the children's odd feelings down to approaching adulthood. It appeared that the time was coming for them to be told. Felindra at thirteen, and Darson ten, were approaching the age of initiation.

"The day after tomorrow," Daryan said in answer to his wife's question. "I've bought supplies for the journey; it's all stored in the wagon,"

"So soon." Parvana sighed. "I suppose we'll have to spend all the morrow packing and preparing food for the journey. I'll have to bake plenty of bread. Is that why you brought the flour in? I take it we're going to the Monastery."

"Yes, my love. We have to get the children initiated as well." He kissed her gently and lay back. "We should sleep; we've some hard work ahead of us."

Daryan

The following morning after they'd broken their fast with quick bread, herbal tea, and stewed apples, Daryan remained at the table, pulling on his boots. "Come and sit down," he told the youngsters. "I have to talk to you about something before we help mother with the baking and packing. We're going on a trip."

"When? Where are we going, dadi? Darson asked, his eyes lighting up.

"We'll be leaving on the morrow, early in the morning. Now, what I am about to tell you must not be repeated to anyone around here, but it is time you knew." Daryan looked at his son and daughter, his children, more precious than life to him. They gazed back wide-eyed with expectation, but neither spoke.

He sighed as he reorganized the thoughts he'd already reviewed and reconstructed several times since the day before. "Firstly, our family is not what you know it to be. No that's not right. Let me word it another way: your mother and I, and you our children, are much more than the lives we have lived for the past dozen years."

Felindra, "What do you mean? What are we?"

Darson, "How?"

"I'm coming to that. Your mother and I are mages and members of the League of Light."

"*Solas Naofa!*" Felindra exclaimed, her eyes big with wonder. "Truly?"

"Indeed." Daryan replied. "You know what that means don't you?"

"Does that mean we're gifted, too?" Darson asked.

"Let's say there is a very good chance you are. But you need to be tested by an archmage at the Monastery to discern and confirm your gifts."

"Couldn't you and mami test us?" Felindra asked.

"We could, but we are not trained for that and might not make an accurate judgment. It is best to have it done by someone with the right training. You have probably been some experiencing strange or unusual ... how can I say this? ... perceptions, sensations. I know I did at your age."

The two youngsters looked at each other warily, neither wanting to be the first to admit to any such manifestations. Finally, Felindra gave in. "I sometimes think I can tell what the horses are thinking," she admitted shyly.

Daryan nodded and smiled at his daughter. He covered her hand with his. "How about you, son?"

Darson cleared his throat. "Nothing."

"That's fine son. You are a bit young." Daryan laid his hand on Darson's shoulder.

Parvana walked by carrying a bundle of linen. She smiled and nodded to them as she passed.

"I know this is a lot to take in at one time, but there is more. First, we have to leave the village because it might become dangerous for us here, but also because we'll be needed at the Monastery."

Darson interrupted, "Why must we leave, dadi? What danger is there?"

"There may be some very bad people looking for us, so I have to take you to a safe place. We're going to the Monastery of the League of Light in the Great Mountains, the headquarters of the Trethawynd division of the League. It's a holy place, but it is also a great center of learning. While I was in Salispon, I heard that there have been ... incidents ... that may have been perpetrated by the Dark Brethren. I fear they could be returning. The Dark Brethren are not just enemies of the people, they are also determined to hunt down and destroy the League of Light. We must get to the Monastery as soon as possible. We will be safe there and have time, we hope, to prepare for the struggle I fear is coming. You children have to be initiated—that is if you wish to; you are free to choose—and trained for whatever is to come. I'm sorry I've had so little time to prepare you." He stood up. "If your friends ask, tell them we are going to visit family friends if they ask. That's not an untruth; it just leaves out the details" He looked at his two children and smiled. "That's enough for now. There's work to be done."

Darson and Felindra went outside and through the gate into the field.

"What do you think?" Felindra asked her brother.

His eyes lit up. "It's great. Aren't you excited?"

"I suppose so, but I'll miss this place."

"We'll get to meet lots of new people, and Mami says there's a school. I can't wait to go to a real school. There's so much to learn."

***

They left at dawn the next morning with two of their horses pulling the wagon, the other two ridden by Parvana and Felindra, while Darson sat beside his father on the front of the wagon.

Daryan looked back at the village as they passed around a bend in the road, wondering how long it would be before they could return. Picobali looked so small and insignificant from this distance, but it was the place they'd called home for more than eleven years. They'd developed a bond with it and its people, this little cluster of small, rose-colored adobe houses lined up along a single unpaved road with a meeting hall, a blacksmith's forge, and one all-purpose store that sold everything from lamps to sewing thread, tools, and onions. The villagers' major source of income came from the surrounding orange orchards, vineyards, and olive trees.

2 – On the Road to Monastery

Daryan

By early afternoon, they reached the north-south highroad where Daryan turned south. The scenery changed slightly from the agricultural valley they were leaving to low rolling hills covered with yellowing grass, brightened by blue and orange wildflowers among the scattered oak groves. Grey-green spike-leaved aloe plants and other succulents grew along the margins of the road.

"How long are we going to stay there?" Darson asked his father.

"I don't know son. We'll have to see what happens when we get there."

"Is there a library there?"

"The biggest library in all Trethawynd."

Darson pondered this for a moment and then asked, "Will I be able to go there and see all the books?"

Daryan smiled. *My son the scholar!* "You will probably be allowed to use the public rooms, but I believe there are archives that are only accessible to the most learned scholars. How are your studies progressing?"

The Peshanar family had a limited number of books, mostly about the history and geography of their country, the life sciences, and a few sacred tomes devoted to *The Light*.

"I have been reading *The Path of Light*. It's amazing, the story of Solan and Alba. Father, are they really the Mother and Father of the Children of Light?"

"Indeed, son. We are all descended from them."

"So why do people have different colors? Even you and I are a bit lighter than my sister and mother. And I saw a man and woman once in Salispon whose skin was almost black."

"Good question. I think the answer lies in the fact that there were humans living in this world before the arrival of Solan and Alba, and they had evolved into many different races, but they were not as advanced as the Mother and Father. The children of Solan and Alba took partners from among the most advanced and intelligent members of each race. It was a great honor for the children of men to be able to mate with the Children of Alba, and most of them moved away from their native areas to set up new communities where they could develop civilizations that are more advanced. Do you know the purpose of their mission to our world?"

Darson thought for a moment. "Was it to teach us about the Light?"

"That's right, but there were other reasons also." He had his son's avid attention and was pleased by the boy's eagerness to learn. "One was the biological uplifting of the children of men, giving them greater resistance to disease, higher levels of intelligence, and physical improvement. Another thing they gave us was advanced agricultural and building techniques, better manufacturing methods, writing, and improved ways of governing society."

"It says in the book that they lived here for thousands of years. How could they live so long?"

"They were immortals, however, when they incarnated in material bodies, they had to eat the fruit of the Tree of Life to sustain their immortality."

"Oh." He pondered that for a second or two, and then said, "They must have had a lot of children."

"They did; they had hundreds of offspring, and their children had even more. They had to provide enough genetic material for the task of uplifting the children of men, but these births took place over a long span of time. Solan and Alba didn't age, and giving birth was easier for Alba than it was for mortal women."

"That's amazing," was all Darson could come up with in response. He obviously had a lot to think about. Suddenly another thought came to him. "What happened to the Tree of Life?"

"It was taken up with them when they left."

"They didn't die then."

"No, they returned to their home world when their task was completed."

"Do you think we'll ever see them again?"

"I believe there's a good chance we will when we pass on into the realms of Light."

"You mean after we die?"

"That's one way of putting it."

Daryan noticed a small cart pulled up on the side of the road. "It looks as if those people are in trouble. Whoa, boys!" Daryan cried, pulling on the reins to stop the horses. A young man and a woman stood beside the cart studying their horse's foot with expressions of bewilderment and dismay. The woman was holding a baby on her hip.

Daryan brought the wagon to a stop at the side of the road, and then climbed down and walked towards them. "Well met, brother, sister! Is there anything we can do to help?"

The couple looked surprised by the manner in which he addressed them. "Are you...?" the man stammered.

"Yes, I'm a brother in Light."

"But how did you know we're...?"

"I saw your medallions."

Both looked down at the small medallions hanging on chains from their necks.

"But you aren't wearing one," the man commented.

"Brother," Daryan replied, "it is wiser in these dangerous times to keep such symbols out of sight. But let me see if I can help with the horse; is there something wrong with its foot?

Daryan's whole family was now gathered around, watching. He saw Parvana move towards the woman with the baby and start a quiet conversation with her.

"Her shoe has come loose. It's a good thing we noticed it before it fell off," the young man said.

"Let me take a look." He lifted the horse's foot and saw the shoe hanging by a single nail. They were lucky, although even if they had lost the shoe, Daryan carried spares, along with a full box of tools. He turned and said to Darson, "Would you bring my tools, son?"

"I feel so useless," the young man said. "You see, we were summoned to the Monastery, but I don't know much about horses and such. The man we bought the horse from said they were well shod, so I didn't worry about it."

Darson put the heavy toolbox on the ground near his father.

"Thank you, son. Would you and Felindra give the wagon horses some water and a few oats while I'm doing this? Let those two graze," he added, nodding towards the saddled animals.

"Very well, father."

"I'm going to get everyone a drink and a biscuit," Parvana said, touching his shoulder as she passed on her way to the back of the wagon."

Daryan nodded. He lifted the horse's front leg and tucked it under his arm, making encouraging sounds to calm her as he put a few nails between his teeth and picked up his blacksmith's hammer. She was a docile little horse and he was able to complete the task quickly. When he'd finished, he stood up and gently stroked his hand up the front of her face, murmuring, "You're a good girl. You'll be fine now." He patted her on the neck and turned away to pick up the toolbox.

"I don't know what we would have done if you hadn't come along," the young man said.

"I'm glad we were able to help. I'm Daryan Peshanar, by the way," he added, offering his hand to the other man.

"My name is Nadi Farsan and this is my wife Lis and our daughter Vanelda." The young woman smiled shyly and looked down at her child.

"Well met, Nadi and Lis. We are going to the Monastery also. Would you like to travel with us? It would be safer if you were with a group; traveling alone can be dangerous sometimes."

Lis gave her husband a concerned look and nodded to him. "We would like that," Nadi replied. "I hope we won't hold you up."

"Not at all. It's always a pleasure to meet people, and we can help one another on the way. One more thing, Nadi, I would advise you to conceal your medallions. As I said before, these are dangerous times. It seems the Dark Brethren are returning. So far, the reported incidents have been mostly in the north, but they seem to be on the move again. They often target members of the League, so we don't want to make it too easy for them to identify us."

Nadi's face went as pale as ash. Lis held her baby closer, fear and dismay on her face. Nadi quickly tucked his medallion inside his shirt and Lis followed suit.

"I'm sorry," Daryan apologized I shouldn't have alarmed you; I doubt they have penetrated this far inland, but it pays to be cautious. Let's get on now; it will be dusk soon and I'd like to get to The Crossing before dark."

3 – Entering the Great Forest

Daryan

The sun had set by the time they reached the busy crossroads where the north–south highroad intersected the east–west road. The east–west road, which led west to the capital, DarSolas, followed the south bank of great Morvis River. This meant they also had to cross a stone bridge with two broad arches, wide enough to accommodate two wagons side by side. A town of sorts had grown up at this crossroads called simply The Crossing. It was devoted mainly to serving travelers, hence the dominance of services: inns, blacksmiths, stables, and purveyors of fodder for horses and food for travelers. There was also a travelers' rest on the south side of the bridge. It was to this facility that Daryan led them.

The Rest was a fenced area by the riverbank with room for about twenty-five wagons. A corral, opened on the riverbank side for the horses to graze and satisfy their thirst. Daryan drove his wagon to a space with enough room for it and the Farsans' cart. With the help of Felindra, he unharnessed the horses and led them to the corral. All the time she was working with the animals, Felindra murmured to them gently, pausing occasionally as if listening to their answers. After rubbing them down with pieces of old blanket dipped in the river, and ensuring that they had fodder, they returned to the wagon.

Lis had joined the group around the fire where she sat on a log to feed her baby, while Parvana cut up pieces of meat and vegetables to drop into a large black pot over the fire.

"Where are Darson and Nadi?" Daryan asked.

"They've gone to get water," Parvana replied.

Felindra approached her mother. "Mami, Shila has a pain in her stomach," she said softly.

"How do you know that?" Parvana asked.

"She told me."

Parvana looked surprised. "Do you mean you know what she's feeling?"

"I think so. I can sometimes feel what they feel, if I touch them. I could hear Soly's cat sometimes too, and the blacksmith's dog."

Parvana looked up at her husband, raising her eyebrows,

"Come, with me," Daryan said gently to Felindra. "Let's go and see Shila." He held out his hand for her.

Felindra looked a little confused, as if she'd broken some rule but wasn't sure what it was. She took his proffered hand.

"Did I do something wrong?" Felindra asked nervously as they walked away.

"No, daughter, not at all. Let's see what's wrong with Shila, shall we?"

They walked into the paddock and over to their horses, which had assembled in a group and were grazing on the grass by the river. They approached Shila, a chestnut filly.

Daryan stroked her side, and then ran his hands over her abdomen, pausing to press with his fingertips occasionally. At one point, the horse flinched at the pressure and kicked out. He dodged the foot and moved on to stroke her on the neck. "Good girl."

He turned to Felindra. "There is some tenderness. I wonder if it was something she ate."

"Maybe I can find out." Felindra laid her head against Shila's side and put her hand on her neck. "Good, Shila," she murmured. "We want to stop the hurt, but we need to know what caused it. What have you been eating, girl?" Of course, she didn't expect the horse to understand what she was saying, but vocalizing it enabled to her to transmit images from her mind. As she stood calmly beside the horse, continuing to stroke her gently, a compendium of plants began to stream through her mind in brief flashes. Most of them looked familiar and harmless, part of a grazing animal's normal diet, but one stood out. It was a spiky plant with blue flowers and broad hairy leaves. "That's good, Shila. Thank you." With a gentle pat, she moved away from the animal and turned to her father.

"It looks as if she ate some spikewort," she told him.

"It's no wonder she has a stomachache. At least it's not fatal, but she's going to have diarrhea for a while. There's not much we can do to help her, but we must remember to give her plenty of water tomorrow." He took her arm and led her down the riverbank away from the campsite where they sat down on the grass.

Felindra looked at him anxiously. "It's all right, love. I just wanted to talk to you away from strangers' ears. It looks as if you may have a very rare gift, Felindra. It's called Whispering, the ability to communicate with the higher animals. I don't think there's been another whisperer in Albasiny in many years."

She looked at him for a moment and then down at her hands, twisting them together in her lap. She didn't know what to say in response to her father's revelation. Finally, she looked up again and asked, "Do all the Children of Light have gifts?"

"It depends. It is more common in the offspring of mages, but there are gifted people among the general population. Ignorant or superstitious people often try to suppress it in their children, discouraging them from using the gifts; some even punish them. Many people are afraid of magic. They don't know the difference between Dark magic, which is evil and destructive, and Light magic, which can only be used for good."

"Do they ever attack mages and harm them?" Felindra asked

"It has been known to happen, especially in times of unrest and fear." He reached down the neck of his tunic and pulled up his medallion. "This is what all mages wear when they've completed their training." It was a red crystal in a gold frame. A small blue crystal was set in a protrusion at the bottom of the frame. "These crystals represent the gifts I have. The red is for relocation, and the blue is for enchanting."

She gazed at him with a look of sheer wonder. "What does relocation mean?"

"It means that, in an emergency I can move from one place to another very fast ... almost instantly."

"Can you go a long way?"

"No. It's limited to the visible area around me. I must be able to see where I will land so that I don't end up in the middle of a boulder, or up a tree. For example, if I saw a baby crawling towards a river bank several paces away from me, I could be there instantly to prevent it falling in."

"That's ... amazing. I never knew you could do that."

"There's one more thing you should know. Using magic, your gift, uses a lot of energy; it can strip the body of its life force if the user is not properly trained. Even with training, using a power like mine leaves me utterly exhausted and it takes time to recover. We use crystals to help us draw energy from the Light, which helps decrease somewhat the depletion of our own life force, but there's a limit to that, too. There's a lot of practice and self-discipline involved, and development of the wisdom to know when to stop."

"Will I get a crystal?" she asked.

"Probably. You are fortunate; you don't lose much energy with whispering, but it may be that a crystal could be used to reinforce the effectiveness of the gift." He rose from the grass and helped her up. "Let's go back; they'll be wonder where we've gone."

He continued while they walked back to the campsite. "Your apparent gift—communicating with animals—is extremely rare. It is highly valued among the Children of Light. I hope you'll decide to take the initiation and training when we get to the Monastery."

"Oh, dadi, I will. I'm so glad you told me about it; now I know I'm not a freak. I won't breathe a word of it to anyone until we reach the Monastery," she replied.

After they'd eaten, Daryan chose to brief everyone on what to expect during the remainder of the journey. He drew everyone into a close circle and spoke to them in a low voice so as not to be overheard by other sojourners at the traveler's rest.

"As you know, tomorrow we travel west towards the capital. By the end of the day, we will be in the Great Forest. The road will be mostly uphill—we're going into the mountains—and it will not be as well paved as the high roads. Once we enter the forest, we must be alert for other dangers. Most of the animals of the forest are harmless, but there are a few dangerous ones. Members of the cat family and some bears. Some of the cats are quite small, little bigger than domestic cats, but there is one cat that is very dangerous: the sabre cat. They have been hunted for many centuries for their pelts and teeth and are close to extinction, but there are still a few in the distant reaches of the forest. The only sound they make is a low throaty growl; it sounds a bit like distant thunder. The large cats rarely come down to areas where there are people, preferring to stay near the upland rivers and lakes to hunt. A wounded or starving mountain lion or cougar has been known to stray into human territory. That's when they are most dangerous. Then there are wolves; silver wolves normally hunt at night in packs. They are a lot bigger than the black timber wolf and very cunning and strong. You will hear their cries at night, but, like the bear, they don't usually attack people. The silver can grow almost as large as a donkey and is very quick, silent and ferocious." Daryan smiled reassuringly at his audience. "But the most dangerous creature of all is us humans. Sometimes bandits and outlaws lie in wait, ready to pounce on unwary travelers. However, I have a feeling that if we do encounter any of those, they will be in for a surprise. Now, let's get some rest. We have to be up at dawn tomorrow."

As they stood up and moved towards their bedrolls, Daryan beckoned to Nadi. "A word, brother," he said, drawing the young man aside. When they were out of earshot, he said. "It might be useful if we shared some information about our gifts. I'm a defender. I have two gifts; one is Relocation, and the other Enchanting. My wife is a Light-bearer and has a touch of Influence. How about you?"

"You are a very talented family," Nadi said admiringly. "I'm afraid we're not so gifted. I have the Life-sensor gift; Lis is a Healer and she's good at concocting potions. Do any of your children know their gifts yet?"

"My daughter is starting to tune in, but we won't know for sure until she's tested. Your life sensory gift could be useful in the Great Forest, Nadi. Are you able to discern between different types of life?" Daryan was not too familiar with this particular gift.

Nadi replied, "Well, between animal and vegetable, of course, approximate size of animals; I mean I could tell if it was a large or small animal. I can often tell something of its mood too. Whether it is predatory and preparing to attack or if it was frightened."

"That sounds very useful in our current situation. Does this work with people too?" Daryan asked, hoping to learn more.

"To a certain extent. Mostly it's a matter of discerning between benevolence, hostility or threat, and indifference. Our code of ethics forbids us to read people's thoughts, even if I could." Nadi stood still for a moment, alert. "I sense mild danger around here somewhere, maybe in that direction." He nodded towards a large red and black wagon closer to the river. There was no one in sight and no light showing. "Something dark," he added.

"Thank you, Nadi. We'll have to stay alert, although I doubt anyone will try something with so many people around. And we probably wouldn't be the targets, anyway. Sleep well, my friend." However, when Daryan folded himself in his bedroll, he made sure he had his sword close to hand.

***

Early the next morning the little group of travelers broke their fast with biscuits and dried fruit, washed down with water, and then packed their bedrolls into the wagon. The horses were brought and harnessed to their vehicles, or saddled.

Once everyone was settled in his place, Daryan clicked his tongue and shook the reins to start the horses moving, and they rolled out of the travelers' rest. On the road, he slowed the horses until Nadi was alongside, and called to him, "I think you should go in front, Nadi."

Nadi nodded and pulled ahead.

The scenery changed yet again to become farmland where many kinds of crops were cultivated, and pastures for grazing animals. The road, as befitted the main road to the capital, was paved with flat stone and well maintained.

Daryan was enjoying the ride. It was a lovely day and the countryside looked fruitful and at peace. Maybe the rumors of Dark Brethren were exaggerated, a few minor incidents linked together and blown up out of proportion. He hoped so. Nevertheless, he was looking forward to returning to the Monastery and seeing some of his old friends. He hadn't been there since the end of the Faldino War, so named for the location of the last infestation of the Dark Brethren and their minions, the werfolk, in a mountain range in the north of Trethawynd. After it was over, he had returned to the Monastery to regain his strength and reunite with Parvana, who had just given birth to their daughter. A few months later, they left for their new home in Picobali.

Parvana

As the sun rose behind them, it washed the fields in golden light. The mountains of the Great Forest formed a jagged bluish-grey band topped with white clouds across western horizon in the distance.

What a perfectly lovely morning! Parvana thought as she took in the scenery. She heard the approach of another vehicle behind her and dropped back behind their own wagon, leaving it room to pass. The vehicle was going much faster than their little convoy, the horses trotting, almost cantering. As it passed, the driver saluted her with his whip.

"Good day, my lady," he called with a friendly smile. She saw another man sitting beside him, a younger version of the driver. They were gone before she had a chance to respond, but she did have time to read the sign inscribed in gold letters on the side: *E Charnwell & Sons, General Merchandise & Provisions.*

My lady? He could hardly take her for nobility traveling as she was, so why did he address her in that manner? Maybe he was trying to flatter her, but why would he? What could he hope to gain by it? He seemed friendly enough, but there was something disconcerting about him. Being near him that made her feel uncomfortable. She gave a little shudder.

"Who was that, mami?" Felindra asked. "There's something creepy about him."

"I don't know, Felindra. A merchant from the capital I suppose. I've never met him before."

She moved back to the center of the road and watched the passing scenery. They were now going through an agricultural plain with grassy meadows grazed by healthy cattle and sheep. As the morning passed, the road started to climb, and small stands of woodland began to appear among the fields. This was the zone where agriculture was gradually encroaching on the forest. The farmers always left small copses as they cleared the land, using them for firewood, wild game, and windbreaks.

Just before midday, the great Morvis River made a turn to the south, as it passed around the mountain and the Great Forest. The road they were on crossed over a bridge to the other side and continued towards the high ground.

Felindra rode up beside her on Shila, just as the horse released a trail of liquid excrement behind her. Felindra quickly covered her nose with the edge of her cloak.

"How's she doing?" Parvana asked.

"She's had some cramps, but she's feeling a little better, mami. I think I should stop and give her some water, though." Felindra dismounted and took one of the hide buckets of water from the saddle and offered it to the horse. Shila drank thirstily, then raised her head and whickered, shaking her whole torso. Felindra gave her a pat on the shoulder. "Good girl. I'm glad you're feeling better. Next time, be more careful what you eat," she murmured to the horse and then remounted. The filly was very young and had not yet learned the wisdom of caution.

Parvana moved forward until she was level with Darson and Daryan. Darson was counting quietly, his head turning, eyes darting everywhere. She realized there was something odd about the *way* he was counting: "Five, six, thirteen, fourteen, fifteen, sixteen, seven, seventeen, eighteen, nineteen, eight, nine...."

She listened for a while, not wanting to break his concentration, but eventually, her curiosity got the better of her. She excused herself thinking it might relate to a gift. She and Daryan were always alert for signs of gifts in their children so that they would be able to guide them and refrain from doing or saying anything that might interfere with their development. "What are you counting?" she asked.

"Twenty-nine, thirty, twelve." He jumped as if startled. "Sorry, mami, I was counting birds."

"What kind of birds?" she asked.

"Ravens and hawks. There are a lot more ravens than hawks."

"You can count both at the same time?"

Darson nodded. "Why? Can't everybody?"

"I know I can't," she replied. "But I don't know about other people. I'm sorry I interrupted you,"

"That's all right. I think we are going to stop now anyway. I'm glad. I'm getting hungry."

Parvana watched the black and red wagon disappearing around the next bend and shivered.

Daryan

It was coming up to noon. The slope began to steepen and cleared land became scarcer than woodland. Before the afternoon was out, they would be well within the Great Forest. He recalled there was a wide stream up ahead, one of the many of tributaries the River Morvis. It was sheltered by trees that would be the ideal place for them to stop and rest the horses. As he rounded the bend just before the resting place, he saw the red and black wagon that had passed them, had stopped there. It was obvious they meant to stay for a while; the two men were unpacking eating utensils and food. Before he could make a decision whether to stop or go on by, the older man came to the side of the road and waved him over. He was a broad-shouldered man, a little taller than Daryan. His fleshy face was dark and florid with pox scars on his cheeks and forehead. He had a wide flaccid mouth and dark button eyes set too close together.

"Well met, friends," he called. "Why don't you join us in this beautiful spot? We were about to open a cask of Bartony Summer and would be glad to share a cup with you."

There really wasn't any reason to refuse such a gracious and friendly invitation without seeming churlish, so Daryan pulled over onto the grass. "Thank you, sir," he replied. "It is time to give the horses a rest."

Meanwhile, Nadi had stopped up ahead, and was looking back over his shoulder, an anxious expression on his face. "Come, Nadi, join us. I'm sure your horse could do with a rest."

He walked up the road to Nadi and put a hand on his shoulder. "Is it still bothering you?" he asked quietly, avoiding looking back at the strangers.

"I just don't feel comfortable near him," Nadi replied.

Daryan countered: "Could you try to bear with it for a little while? My curiosity is aroused. We may be able to discover what he's up to."

"As you wish, Daryan. At least we have them outnumbered if they start anything," he quipped.

"That's the spirit, but I doubt it will come to that." He turned back towards the wagon. "I should go and help Felindra with the horses. Follow me."

While Felindra and Daryan unharnessed the horses and took them to the stream, Parvana, with the help of Lis, set out some food: bread, cheese, and some dried apples from last year's harvest. Parvana also added a bowl of shelled nuts and a porcelain jar of honey.

"Come on, everyone, it's ready," she called.

"That's quite a splendid family you have," The older of the two men said as he walked across to their picnic site, carrying a small wine cask under his arm. He was wearing a simple but expensive-looking grey cotton shirt, matching formal trousers, a dark red mantle, and shiny black leather boots. "May I offer you some of this excellent wine? It's direct from Bartony vintners."

"Thank you. That's very gracious of you, sir. I'll take a sip." Daryan replied, holding out his wooden cup. "Have you been all the way to Bartony?"

"Indeed we have. We go up there twice a year to stock up on the summer wine. It sells very well in the capital, especially among the nobility."

Daryan took a sip and rolled it around in his mouth before swallowing. "It is indeed fine wine," he said to the other man. "Thank you, sir."

Daryan debated with himself whether to ask about the Dark Brotherhood rumors. Finally, he decided it would do no harm and the man's response might give him something useful.

"I hear they're having bit of bother up near the border. Sounds as if the Dark Brethren might be involved."

The man looked at him for a moment. "You hear of the occasional incident, but it's greatly exaggerated, believe me. We travel up there frequently, and we haven't seen anything out of the ordinary. Don't worry about it, my friend, it's nothing, probably just some bandit activity." He smiled and patted Daryan on the shoulder before turning to the rest of the group.

"May I have some, father?" Darson asked.

Daryan looked at Parvana and suggested. "Maybe a little drop in some water."

Taking her cue from Daryan, she poured some water into the cups of the children.

"It's my pleasure," the man replied. "May I?" he asked, before settling on nearby a boulder.

"Please, be our guest," Daryan replied. Once again, he had no choice and decided to be civil, although he was beginning to resent this intrusion into their peaceful journey. "Can we offer you something to eat from our humble table?"

"Just a morsel, thank you; we've already eaten." He leaned over the cloth and took a nut from the bowl. It would have been extremely bad manners to refuse.

"Allow me to introduce myself," he said. "I am Evaseen Charnwell, and that young fellow over there is my eldest son, Waldron. We have a trading company in DarSolas. Is that where you are headed?" he asked.

"Yes," Daryan replied, giving his children a stern look that said, *do not contradict me!*

"Are you, moving there?" Charnwell asked. "You seem to be carrying quite a load."

Daryan replied carefully, "No. I have a contract to fulfill and thought it would be a nice change for my family to accompany me."

"I see," said the Charnwell "Well, if you need supplies, be sure to look me up. We're easy to find, just off the central square on Via Palma. Ask anyone." He stood up. "Well, I suppose we should be on our way." He looked across at Nadi, who was sitting with his family a few spans away, as if seeing him for the first time. "I almost overlooked you, young man. You must try some of this summer wine."

Daryan watched Nadi as Charnwell walked towards him. Not wanting to offend the man, he didn't refuse, but when

Charnwell put his hand on Nadi's shoulder, the young man flinched as if he'd been burned.

"Pardon, sir," Charnwell said. "I didn't mean to hurt you."

Lis spoke up quickly, "My husband injured his shoulder a few days ago and it's still a bit tender." *She's a treasure,* Daryan thought, *a quick thinker.*

"No harm done," Nadi added.

"Farewell, friends," Charnwell called as he went back to his wagon where his son had already packed everything away.

As soon as they were out of sight, Daryan released a sharp breath in relief.

"What was that all about?" Parvana asked, giving her husband a puzzled look.

"Just a minute, my love." He turned to where Nadi and Lis were picking up their things and called to them, "Come and join us." When everyone was settled, he said, "Impressions, anyone?"

"I didn't like him," Felindra said.

"What made you feel that way?" Daryan asked.

"I don't really know. He just made me feel crawly." Felindra wrapped her arms around herself as if she felt cold.

"I think he was just pretending to be friendly," Darson said. "Dadi, why did you lie to him about where we are going? I thought we weren't supposed to tell an untruth."

"I'm sorry son. You are right about telling the truth, but sometimes you may have to bend it a little to avoid danger," Daryan explained, hoping his son would understand the subtle difference.

"You mean those men are dangerous?" Felindra asked. "I know I felt uncomfortable when they were here."

Daryan nodded his head. "I don't know if they are dangerous or not, but we must be careful from now on until we reach the Monastery. And, by the way, I shall be going to DarSolas sometime in the near future, so what I told him wasn't a complete fabrication." Daryan turned to Nadi. "What about you?"

"Could we talk about it in private?" Nadi replied. He looked quite shaken.

Daryan nodded in assent. "All right, everyone, time to pack up. We have a long way to go."

As soon as they were alone, Nadi took a deep breath and said, "I didn't think I should talk about this in front of the youngsters." He glanced sideways at the others and took another breath. "When he touched me, I felt evil. It felt as if a thick oily smoke flowed through his veins instead of blood. It was a terrifying feeling."

4 – Wolf Attack

Daryan

Late on the fourth day, the little caravan left the high road, which continued to follow the river around the south side of the mountain. They turned right onto a narrower, steeper path. The new road was only wide enough for one wagon. It wasn't as well paved as the high road, being composed of hard-packed earth and gravel with occasional larger stones and hollows where the soil had been washed away by rain. As it climbed into the mountains, the road meandered back and forth so it was never possible to see very far ahead. A darker coniferous forest gradually replaced the deciduous trees of the lowlands, interspersed with a few oaks and eucalyptus. In the darker places, the atmosphere felt gloomy and a bit sinister, although birds still sang in the trees, insects buzzed in the undergrowth, and the sun shone through gaps in the heavy canopy.

Just before the sun fell below the horizon, they came to an area where the trees and scrub had been cut back and the ground leveled to make a space for travelers to set up camp or break for refreshment. It was close to a swift-flowing creek, which became a small pond where it filled a wide bowl in the rock. The drainage from the pond poured through a hollowed tree trunk under the road to become a miniature cascade on the south side.

"This place is spooky," Darson commented, as he helped his sister remove the bedrolls from the wagon and spread them on the ground underneath. "It's like in those old stories about werfolk and evil wizards in the Legends of Time."

"But they're just old legends and children's fables," Felindra said. "There's no such thing as werfolk and evil wizards."

"I know," Darson replied. "I was just comparing."

Daryan and Parvana exchanged a look. Daryan was pleased with Felindra's assertion, even if it was not true. This was not the time to frighten the boy.

Once the horses were settled for the night, picketed on a narrow stretch of grass, the travelers sat around the fire in its circle of rocks and ate their supper.

"How much longer will it take us to get there?" Felindra asked.

"Just over a day," Daryan replied. "At the rate we've been going, we should be there by late tomorrow,"

"It's a long way," Felindra said. "The horses are tired and Tiki's leg is sore." Tiki was one of the stallions that pulled the wagon.

"Which leg? Show me." Daryan asked. "I'll take a look at it." He stood up and held out his hand to pull his daughter to her feet. The two of them walked over to where the horses were grazing in a clump of long grass. Felindra touched Tiki gently on the shoulder and put her head against the side of his neck. "Where does it hurt?" she murmured.

After a moment's silence, she looked up at her father. "It's his right front leg, just above the fetlock. He showed me how it happened when he trod on a big stone and twisted his foot."

Daryan crouched down on the horse's right side and gently palpated his lower leg. Tiki flinched and almost kicked him in the face when he touched a certain spot. Daryan stood up and patted Tiki's side. "Good boy!" He turned to his daughter. "He may have sprained a tendon. He'll have to walk tomorrow and Falcon will have to take his place. Let me talk to Lis. She may have some salve we can put on it, then we'll bind it."

"I haven't got a salve," Lis replied to his query. "But I do have some herbs that help bring down inflammation. We could make a poultice with some hot water. It might help."

While the poultice was being prepared in a small iron pot over the fire, Daryan walked around the campsite. He had a vague feeling of uneasiness, but he couldn't find anything to account for it. Everything seemed normal, crickets chirped, frogs croaked, and small animals rustled in the underbrush. Nevertheless, he decided to sleep with his sword by his side. He would also warn Parvana to keep a weapon handy.

When the poultice was ready and cooled off a bit, he bound it to the horse's lower leg with a strip of tough linen while Felindra stood by, calming him and keeping him from kicking.

Daryan put his arm around her shoulder and squeezed. "Good work, love. Your gift is already becoming useful. Now, let's get some rest."

Nadi

Nadi awoke with a start. He didn't know what had wakened him; he couldn't hear any unusual noise, in fact, there were no sounds at all apart from the breeze stirring the trees. The silence in itself was odd. He lay still for a moment, allowing his senses to wander. There it was! Some form of life approaching the camp. Whatever they were, they were all around the campsite. Then the horses whinnied nervously. Quietly, he rolled from under his blanket and stepped down from the bed of the cart. He stood still once again and a wave of something dark and menacing hit him. He scuttled rapidly towards Daryan's bedroll and shook his shoulder.

Before he could blink, Daryan was on his feet, standing before him with his sword pointing at his throat. Nadi had never seen anyone move so fast.

"Nadi, you startled me. I beg your pardon." He lowered the sword. "What's the problem?" Then he noticed the eerie silence and the restlessness of the horses.

"There's something out there," Nadi told Daryan. "And it's dangerous. I can feel it." To emphasize his assertion, the ghostly howl of a wolf echoed through the forest.

"Get Lis and the baby into the wagon," Daryan ordered. He was already waking his children. "In the wagon, all of you. No argument. You as well," he told Parvana. "And don't let anyone out!"

Felindra

"You may need me, dadi," Felindra said. "I might be able to tell you what they're saying."

"No, she mustn't," Parvana cried.

Just then, an answering call echoed from another direction and closer to the camp. Felindra called out, "Dadi, it said, something to the effect that they'd found us."

"All right," Daryan said, realizing she might be right about helping. "But get inside if they get too close. Parvana, stay ready to defend the wagon."

A whole chorus of howls erupted followed by one that was deeper and louder accompanied by a sharp bark. "*Kill!*" Felindra broke off with a sob.

"In the wagon!" Daryan shoved her towards her mother who bundled her into the back of the wagon. "Get in the wagon with them," Daryan ordered Nadi, "but keep your dagger ready." Daryan stood near the back of the wagon, sword ready and eyes scanning the perimeter.

"They're about twenty paces away," Nadi called. "They don't feel like real wolves; there's something..." Before Nadi could finish, a dark shape entered the clearing.

In a flash, Daryan slashed its throat with his sword. Another appeared, but Daryan intercepted it and brought it down. The clearing was filling rapidly with snarling grey bodies.

"How many?" Daryan called.

"Eight or ten," Nadi gasped.

Daryan moved like a whirlwind, slashing and stabbing, but more of the creatures kept coming.

Suddenly a brilliant light filled the clearing and a female voice called out, "Go back! You don't want to do this. We are not your enemies. Go back! We don't want to hurt you. Go back!"

The light illuminated a chaotic scene, Daryan tearing around the circle, moving in an eye-blink from one animal to the next stabbing and cutting. The yowls of the dying wolves filled the air and blood spattered all over him as he struck them down. Two of the wolves turned and slinked away, and then another followed. Daryan turned and saw another creeping up on the wagon. He flew towards the wolf and stabbed it in the shoulder. The animal howled in pain and rolled on its back as if in surrender. He lifted the sword to finish it, but Felindra cried out, "don't kill it!" Startled by his daughter's voice, he held back.

"I want to talk to it," she continued. "Maybe I can find out why they attacked us."

Looking around, Daryan saw there were no more attackers. He wiped his sword on the grass and stood watching her, ready to intervene if he sensed she was in danger. Parvana came and stood behind him. The light faded to a soft glow, just enough to see by. "Felindra is right;

normally, wolves don't act like this. Something must be influencing them," he said to Parvana. "I'd like to know how it happened, why they attacked us." The wolf, a young female, whimpered as she lay panting in the grass. Felindra knelt down beside the wounded wolf and put her hand gently on its haunch. The animal growled deep in its throat and bared its teeth, but made no move to attack her. The girl winced and gasped as a sharp pain burned through her shoulder. A weak thought entered her consciousness: *help me!* She had to remove her hand; the pain was too much for her to bear. "She's in terrible pain. Can't someone help her?" she cried.

"Wait a moment; there may still be more out there." Daryan countered. He turned to Nadi. "Are there any more?"

"I sense life, but it is damaged. I don't sense anything threatening," Nadi replied. "My guess is there are some wounded animals out there."

"All right." Daryan was staggering with fatigue, his breaths coming in rapid gasps. He had to cling to the side of the wagon to keep from falling.

Parvana followed him and fell against the wagon beside him, also gasping for breath. "Was anybody hurt?"

Daryan took a deep breath and let it out slowly. "No, thank the Light. We're lucky we had some warning from Nadi."

"I'm sorry my influence didn't work," she continued. "I'd forgotten how much it takes out of you."

"You did splendidly," he answered, putting his arm around her shoulder. "We couldn't have done it without your light, and a few of them did turn away." The couple slid down until they were sitting on the ground and closed their eyes.

As Nadi looked around, his eyes fell on Felindra and the dying wolf. "I don't sense any danger from it," he said to her. "Let me see if Lis has anything for the wound."

Lis had climbed down from the wagon and stood nearby soothing the baby.

"Let me take her." Nadi reached out towards the baby. "Do you think you could do something about that wound?"

Handing her daughter to Nadi, Lis gave the wolf an unsympathetic look. "I don't see why we have to waste our medicine on an animal that was threatening to kill us a few minutes ago."

"Please," Felindra begged. "It wasn't her fault. She's … I think she's been influenced by something, but it's wearing off now. I want to find out who did this to her."

"So do I," Daryan murmured.

Lis brought some clean cotton strips and a jar of salve from her cart. Before she could start working, Felindra connected with the wolf again. She was getting weaker, almost fading away. "This person wants to help you and make you feel better. All you have to do is be very still. Will you do that?" she whispered to the animal, illustrating her words with images.

All Felindra got was a breath of a thought brushing her mind, which she took as assent. The animal was frightened, but she seemed to understand they didn't intend to harm her.

When Lis had finished applying the salve, she made a pad of cotton and strapped it over the wound with strips wound around the shoulder and tied to the neck and leg. "That's the best I can do," she said rising to her feet. "Let her sleep and see how she is when she wakes up."

"I'll stay with her," Felindra said. "Just let me get my bedroll."

Felindra laid down her ground sheet and sat on it. She touched the wolf again and whispered, "I have to sleep now. I want you to stay close to me and don't run away. Will you stay?"

Although the wolf appeared to be sleeping, a faint trace of assent touched her mind. "You're a very brave girl. The Light will watch over you," Felindra said.

She lay down, covered herself with her blanket, and was soon asleep.

***

Felindra was woken by a warm tongue on her cheek. She opened her eyes and looked into the yellow eyes of the wolf. "Good morning," she whispered, smiling. Last night, she hadn't realized how massive this wolf was. Standing, her head would reach almost to Felindra's shoulder. *She must be a silver wolf,* she thought, trying not to allow her awe to get through to the animal.

The sun was rising over the mountain; the camp was waking and preparing for the day's journey. Felindra sat up and stretched. She felt amazingly light-hearted. "I'll see if I can find you some food and water," she told the wolf. When she patted the animal's head, she felt only a nagging ache from the wound in her shoulder. She stood up, picked up her bedding, and walked over to the wagon. To her surprise, the wolf stood up too and prepared to follow her. *Oh dear,* she wondered, *how are they going to take this development.*

"Good morning!" she called to everyone. "Don't be afraid. She won't hurt anyone. I think the enchantment or whatever it was has worn off completely now."

"How can you be sure of that?" Darson challenged her anxiously. "Especially after last night."

"Are you afraid?" she taunted.

"No. But it's a dangerous predator. Remember what dadi said; they're even more dangerous when they're hurt." Darson asserted, pulling back his shoulders and glancing nervously at the wolf.

The wolf whined and licked her hand, and then flipped her tail from side to side in a single wag. "Does that look dangerous to you? I'm telling you, she won't hurt anyone." Felindra grinned at her brother. "Pretend she's a big dog."

"I suppose you can read its mind, now?" Darson said skeptically.

Felindra looked at her father. He nodded. "As a matter of fact, I can ... well, just a little bit," she added to make it sound less arrogant. "Mami," she turned to her mother. "Have we got anything she can eat? She must be hungry."

"Just some dried meat. It's quite salty though," Parvana said.

"May I try a little piece?" Felindra asked, unsure whether they had enough to last until they reached the Monastery.

Parvana went to the wagon and rummaged through the boxes. She came back with a piece of meat the size of her fist and gave it to Felindra. "You should take it to the stream and soak it in water to get some of the salt out. She's probably thirsty too."

"Thank you, mami. Come on, wolf," Felindra called. "Let's get you some water."

The animal trotted obediently behind her, favoring its injured leg. While she washed the meat in the stream, the wolf lapped up some water. Felindra sat on the ground and handed over the meat. After sniffing it, the wolf took a dainty bite and swallowed it. Satisfied it was edible, she gobbled up the rest in a couple of mouthfuls.

"You know, wolf, I can't keep calling you 'wolf'," Felindra said. "I'll have to give you a name." The animal gazed at her and flipped its tail once. She thought for a moment and recalled the name of a princess in one of the children's stories she'd read when she was younger. She'd always like that name. "How do you like Ashala?" she whispered. The wolf gave a brief whine and licked her hand. "Good, you like it. I name you Ashala, the wolf princess!"

Daryan, who had followed her to the stream, spoke up, "You're going to be sorry when she leaves us; you're getting too attached."

"I can't help it, dadi. She really is a noble creature. Why does she have to leave?" Felindra said. She was already starting to feel a bond with the wolf.

"She will want to go back to her own kind. She has her own family and maybe even some children." Daryan explained.

Ashala stood beside Felindra, leaning against her side. She yawned displaying her long pink tongue and glistening fangs, a fearful sight, although they didn't frighten Felindra. She knew that animals lived by their own laws and that wolves were among the most ethical of beasts in their natural environment, away from human intrusion and interference.

"Was anyone hurt last night?" Felindra asked her father.

"I got a small bite on my arm, but it's not serious." Daryan rolled up his sleeve for her to see the bandage on his forearm.

"You were amazing," she said. "I didn't think anyone could move that fast." She stroked Ashala's head. "Would you like me to try to find out what happened last night?" she asked, suspecting that was why he had followed her to the stream.

"If you can. It would help us to know what the danger is and where it's coming from." Felindra received the impression something was bothering him as he said that.

"What are you worried about, dadi?" she asked.

"I was wondering what sort of an impact this gift of yours would have on your life. If it could lead you into danger."

"Don't worry about it, dadi, it's a wonderful gift; I'm really excited about it. You know how much I love animals," Felindra replied. She rested her hand on the back of Ashala's neck to make contact, and sent the question in the form of images.

Felindra was able to see, through the wolf's mind, a human male and some other, smaller creatures that had ventured into the forest and lured the wolves into a trap, and then the human had done something to their minds, compelling them to attack the campsite and kill all the humans. As an incentive, they were promised horses as prey.

"That's an abomination!" Daryan exclaimed when they were finished. "We'll have to hurry to reach the Monastery and warn the Grand Master of this."

"Do you think it was the Dark Brethren, dadi?"

"I'm sure it was. That's the sort of thing only they would think up, bending the forces of nature to their own perverted will."

"We'll win, dadi, I know we will. Nobody can defeat the Light."

He put his good arm across her shoulder and hugged her against him. "I think you should let her go now," he said gently.

"Must I?"

"It's the kindest thing you can do for her."

Felindra knelt on the ground and put her arm over the wolf's neck, being careful to avoid the wound. "You can go home now," she whispered with tears in her eyes. "I'll never forget you, Ashala; I hope I'll see you again."

The animal looked up at her and whined, and then she turned away and took a few tentative steps before stopping to look back.

"It's all right," Felindra said. "You can go back to your family." She turned away to return to the campsite.

Instead of leaving, Ashala walked around the campsite, visiting the body of each wolf that had been slaughtered during the night. She stopped and sniffed each one, making a little whining sounds at each body. When she came to a big male wolf, she lifted her head and howled, and then she sat down beside it and licked its muzzle. She raised her head and howled mournfully once more, and then she lay down and rested her head on her paws.

"What are we going to do about the bodies?" Parvana asked.

"There's nothing we can do. We don't have time to bury them all. There must be nine or ten of them."

"Seven," Felindra corrected. "I counted them while she was saying goodbye. We could bless them with the Light," she suggested. "Look at Ashala. She's mourning. That must have been her mate." She wiped a tear from her eye with her knuckle.

"Very well," Daryan agreed. "Then we must leave if we want to reach the Monastery by nightfall. I don't fancy camping out again, after what happened last night. We'll have to go much faster today."

5 –Arrival at the Monastery

Daryan

Everyone seemed nervous as the journey continued and the two men were armed with swords. In spite of it being a sunny day with a cloudless sky above, the forest seemed gloomy and forbidding. Every time a bird took off or a small animal rustled in the undergrowth, they tensed and looked around uneasily.

Tiki, the injured horse, was hitched by a long tether to the side of the wagon so that he could walk without the added weight of the wagon to strain his leg. Felindra rode Shila with Darson behind her. Parvana and Daryan were riding on the wagon with Parvana's horse helping to pull it. After a couple of leagues, the road became less steep. It widened a little and the trees were farther back from the road, opening it up to sunlight, which seemed to elevate everyone's mood and they began to relax.

Nadi brought his cart up level with Daryan and signaled him to slow down. Daryan leaned over so that he could hear what Nadi had to say.

"I sense a large animal up ahead, just around the bend. I think we should check on it before we continue. I don't sense any menace from it, but you never can tell."

"Thanks for the warning, Nadi. I'll go and take a look." He jumped down from the wagon, tucking his sword into its scabbard. "Wait here. I won't be long."

He jogged along the verge of the road, where he could drop out of sight if necessary. He slowed down and moved closer to the trees when he reached the bend and peered round the corner. There, in the middle of the road was the biggest bear he had ever seen. Standing upright on its hind legs, it must have been twice his own height. For some reason, he felt no threat, but he sensed the animal wanted him to come closer, as if it had been waiting for him. Daryan stepped out into the road and moved slowly towards it. Its fur was a rich golden color with patches of white around the muzzle. It stood watching him, unmoving as he approached. There was intelligence in its eyes, more than he would expect in a beast of the forest. After a moment, it growled softly and dropped to its four feet, and then turned and walked into the forest.

Daryan was stunned. He stood, unmoving, and stared at the place where the great beast had disappeared. *Have I been blessed?* he wondered, not knowing where that idea came from. *Was that the Guardian of the Forest? If it was, we have nothing to fear.* He turned and ran back to the wagon.

"What was it, Dadi?" Darson called.

"Just a bear," he replied. "It's gone now. Let's move on."

They rounded the bend and continued up the gentle slope until they heard the sound of water tumbling over rocks. When they reached the fast-flowing stream, Daryan took the wagon off the road and stopped near a grassy area. "We'll rest here for a while and have something to eat." He nodded to Felindra. "Would you like to help me get water for the horses? I don't want to unhitch them; we'll only be here for a little while." He reached behind him and retrieved two leather buckets, then jumped down and led the way to the stream. He

39

was still feeling lightheaded from his encounter with the bear, and a little elated.

While they were eating, he told everyone about his meeting with the giant bear.

"What's the Guardian of the Forest?" Felindra asked. "I've never heard of it.

"If you read more books, you'd know things like that." Darson said.

"Maybe you'd like to tell us, Darson," Parvana suggested.

"It's ... hmm, let me see... Yes, when the Light made all the beasts and the people, He realized that the beasts might be victimized by man because man has a larger brain and is much smarter, and so he set a great spirit to protect them. That's the Guardian of the Forest."

"I don't think we're smarter than animals," Felindra said.

"But we can make weapons to kill them," Daryan countered. "And we can build houses to protect ourselves."

"How does he protect them?" Felindra asked.

"When man goes into the animals' range to hunt them, it causes man's mind to become confused. Sometimes, he loses his way, or his arrow misses the target. He also warns the animals when man is near so that they can go another way. He tricks man's eye by camouflaging the animals so he can't see them," Daryan explained.

"But we still kill them." Felindra said.

"I know, daughter, but a lot more get away and survive. There has to be a balance in Nature. If one species became overpopulated, it would starve or die of disease, and man is part of Nature. We have a part in maintaining the balance. The problem is that some men go too far."

When they packed up and returned to the road, the sun had almost reached its zenith. Daryan calculated they had about seven hours left before the sun set. It looked as if they would make it by sundown, or shortly after. There was more daylight now as summer approached.

Felindra

Felindra felt tired. She was almost asleep in the saddle. Darson was counting again in his odd way. She couldn't imagine what sort of gift that could relate to. Maybe it was just an idiosyncrasy. She shrugged. The reason she had invited him to ride with her, apart from his not being too heavy for the horse, was to have someone to talk to, but all he did was count. She let go of the reins and stretched, then rotated her head to get the stiffness out of her neck, and wondered if animals had these sorts of problems. They always seemed so agile and supple. She yawned.

"Why do you keep fidgeting so much?" Darson asked irritably. "You've made me lose my count."

"Sorry. What were you counting?"

"I was counting all the trees with long leaves, the ones with short leaves, and the ones with red trunks."

"Three different kinds?"

Darson shrugged. "I have to practice."

"Why?"

"I don't know. I just do."

"Well, I'm sorry I distracted you. The problem is I'm feeling sleepy."

"Why don't you get down and walk? We're not going too fast."

"Can you manage Shila?"

"I don't see any problem. She's just walking."

She passed the reins over her shoulder to him and jumped down onto the road. She started to follow the horse, taking deep breaths of the bracing mountain air. It was so peaceful up here. The events of the previous night began to retreat to the back of her mind as she breathed the fragrant air, the pungent odors of pine and juniper, an occasional whiff of eucalyptus carried on a breeze. She saw berries were starting to ripen along the fringe of the forest. The sun poured golden pathways through the branches of the giant trees, *stairways to the Light.*

She heard rustling in the brush beside her, then a whine and soft bark. A wolf. She wasn't afraid, but she was curious. The sound wasn't threatening; it sounded more like a greeting, an announcement: *I'm here!* She wondered if it was one of Ashala's pack. Then a grey shadow became visible through the trees. After giving a little yap, the wolf's head appeared through the foliage of a bush. It came towards her slowly and stopped about two paces in front of her, wagging its tail. She saw by the torn bandage on its shoulder that the wolf had been trying to tear it off with its teeth. "Ashala! What are you doing here? Come."

When she bent and touched Ashala's head, she read a feeling of yearning and affection. Tears filled her eyes as she stroked the head. "You want to come with us?" The answer was an image of the two of them together, side by side. *Loyalty.* "I don't know if you'll be allowed inside the Monastery," she whispered. "But come." How could she refuse such an honor—acceptance by this noble creature, an offer of friendship?

The two of them began to run together up the road to catch up with the caravan while Felindra thought about how she would introduce Ashala to the horses, hoping she could convince them to accept her and not be afraid.

Daryan

They were traveling south-west now. The road had left the forest and on their right was a deep-drop off separated from the road by a strip of sparse grass and brush. On their left, the side of the mountain rose sharply with clusters of tenacious evergreens and shrubs clinging to its sides. As they rounded the bend, they saw the great golden orb of the sun about to sink into the sea beyond. When the Monastery appeared ahead, on the south side of the road, Darson gasped in awe.

"It's amazing," he cried. "That's where we're going?"

"That's the Monastery of the League of Light, son." Daryan replied. "We are probably going to live there for a while."

The road curved in an arc, following the edge of the massive cliff that dropped off to at least three hundred spans to the misty plain below. The mountains receded on the left leaving a small plain filled with orchards and fields, clusters of houses and storage buildings, and grazing livestock. The glint of water through the distant vegetation plotted the path of a small river running out of the mountain.

"It's the most beautiful place I've ever seen," Felindra said, pulling level with the wagon. "How could you and mother want to leave such a place?"

"There isn't enough room for everyone. Most of us had to leave and go home after the emergency was over. You are right though; it wasn't easy."

"So who lives here all the time?"

"In the Monastery itself, mostly the mages, archmages, teachers, administrators, and students. It's a school where all our children come to learn about their Gifts and how to use them. It also has a university where the nobility send their sons and daughters to be educated. The villages outside the wall are inhabited by support workers, the farmers, blacksmiths, weavers, tanners, and so on. It's like a city, all devoted to the Light and the Gifts of the Light."

"And it's got a big library!" Darson added joyfully.

It took them the best part of two hours to reach the Monastery gates, which were now illuminated by torches in brackets on the boundary walls. The edifice was monumental; easily the size of a small city, with thick stone walls, ten times the height of a man. The towers and turrets of buildings could be glimpsed, rising above the walls. The entrance itself was massive with a gateway wide enough for two wagons to pass.

Banners fluttered from the turrets and on poles above buildings. A large carved panel on each gate carried the same emblem as the banners: gold on an azure background: two cupped hands facing each other, supporting a gold circle between the finger tips with rays flaring out from it. The symbol of the League of Light.

The gates stood open and unguarded. The little convoy passed through into the outer yard and crossed a heavy wooden bridge supported by stone arches that fitted into the banks of a racing waterway. Across the bridge, they stopped in a much bigger yard paved with smooth cobblestones. Facing them was a four-story structure of smooth beige stone with multiple deep-set windows on each level. A defensive tower topped by a crenellated battlement rose from the middle of the roof.

On the left were workshops and stables. Most of the work had stopped for the day, leaving the area quiet, apart from the sounds of activity in the stable. Trees and flowering shrubs grew in the unpaved strips around the buildings to soften the starkness of the stonework. Off to the right, a wide pavement led to a magnificent building of white marble with a graceful tower on each side, and behind that, trees. Everywhere they looked, there seemed to be more buildings set among greenery and flowers. There were even flowering vines climbing the walls of the stables.

"It looks like a forest back there." Felindra pointed towards the white building.

"Indeed," her mother replied. "There's almost as much parkland and woods as buildings inside these walls."

"It's huge!" Darson exclaimed. "All these buildings and trees and stuff."

"You can get down now," Daryan said. "There'll be plenty of time for exploring after we settle in and get you registered for school."

He climbed down from the wagon and beckoned to Felindra and Darson. "Let's get the horses into the stable while your mother registers with the almoner."

They led the wagon and horses across the yard to a row of buildings on the left where they found a stable master, a tall young man with light skin and reddish brown hair.

"Welcome, friends," he greeted them. "I'm Lassiter. After you find I place to park your wagon, I'll show you where you can leave your horses. Let me help you with the harnesses." Daryan parked the wagon by the side of the stable, and then led the horses into the building. It was a long building with stalls for the horses along both sides. Along the center ran long troughs for feed and water, and on wall panels at intervals along the length were hung the tools for their care: brushes, clippers, liniments, soap and so on.

"You have an immaculate setup here," Daryan complimented the stable master. "I see you almost have a full house. There must be a lot of new arrivals."

"Yes, they've been coming in quite regularly over the past few days. It's not hard to guess something is afoot."

"It is that," Daryan replied. "Do you still have the paddock out back?"

"Yes, it's still there. We only keep the ones needed immediately in the stable, or those that are sick; the rest go out into the paddock. We put the new arrivals in here at first. We like to clear up any health problems they may have. Do any of these have ailments? I see that one has strapping on his leg."

"He turned his foot on a stone and the joint is sore. Father thinks he may have sprained a tendon," Felindra replied. "He's feeling better since we put a poultice on it."

Lassiter raised his eyebrows. "You like horses, don't you?"

"I like all animals. Their thoughts are simple and honest. Not like humans."

"You can tell what animals think?"

She looked at her father, who smiled and nodded. "I can feel what they feel when I touch them."

"That's a rare gift, child. I hope you develop it."

"I will. May I come back and visit?"

"Of course. You would be welcome any time," he glanced at Daryan and continued, "That's if you don't have more important things to do."

"Thank you. I have to go now," she said, anxious to find Ashala. "Oh, and I'm Felindra."

"It is pleasure to meet you, Felindra. I hope you'll come back and visit us."

Felindra rushed off to the main gate and found Ashala waiting for her under some bushes just outside.

Parvana

The almoner's office was in the temporary accommodation building, which faced the bridge over the moat and the main gate. Parvana entered a large lobby paved with white and pink marble, from which staircases ascended on either side. The walls were smooth whitewashed stone, hung with colorful banners depicting the symbols of the fourteen recognized Gifts. The door with the almoner's sign was on the right.

Inside the room, a middle-aged woman sat at a big wooden table laden with neat piles of documents.

"First, I need the names and ages of everyone in your party." The Almoner said after they'd introduced themselves.

It took less than a quarter hour for them to complete the registration. Once she was finished recording the information, the almoner continued with an explanation about the accommodation, "You can stay here in the rooms I've allocated for a few days while we find a family cottage for you, and then you can move into your own place. While you're here, you may eat in the refectory. You know where that is?"

"I think so. If it's still at the back of the building on this floor."

"That's right; it is. I hope you'll find everything you need. We'll let you know when your permanent housing is ready." She leaned back and pulled a cord on the wall behind her, and Parvana heard a distant bell tone. Almost immediately, a young man in calf-length green trousers and a short tan tunic hurried through the door. He looked about Felindra's age and wore the medallion of a student.

"Rafi," the almoner said to him. "Would you mind conducting Lady Peshanar to Swallow 25 and show her their quarters?"

The boy inclined his head in a shallow bow to Parvana. "Well met, lady. Follow me please." He turned and walked out of the room to the staircase.

She followed him up two flights and arrived at a floor marked by a plaque with a swallow painted on it. The sun was completely gone by this time and very little light entered from outside, but lanterns had been lit at intervals along the walls, one by each door. The doors were spaced about six spans apart, indicating that the rooms inside were quite spacious.

Rafi cleared his throat. "This is your suite," he said as he opened the door. He stood back and allowed her to enter ahead of him. "I hope you will be comfortable. If you need anything, please pull this and someone will come." He pointed to a braided rope falling from a small aperture in the wall by the door. "If there is nothing more, will you please excuse me? Oh I almost forgot; would you like me to send someone to show you to the refectory when you're settled?"

"I can find it thank you, Rafi."

"At your service, lady."

Parvana walked into the center of the large room and looked around. The floors were of light brown polished wood and the walls whitewashed plaster. There were two windows opposite the door overlooking an inner courtyard garden planted with trees and shrubs around a small flower-bordered lawn. In the center was a pool with a fountain. It was just as she remembered from her previous sojourns here, first as a student, then as a young wife and mage. She had worked in this building as a messenger and a cleaner when she was a student. She'd also worn the green and tan uniform of a novice. Things hadn't changed much it appeared.

She went around the room to check the facilities. At the end by the windows, there were two curtained alcoves, one on either side of the windows. She walked over, pulled back the curtain of the one on the right, and found it was a bedroom. The other alcove contained hygiene facilities.

A simple wooden table with four chairs stood in the center of the main room. And on either side, adjacent to the alcoves, were two cots each with a trunk beside it.

She'd just finished her inspection when the door of the room opened and Daryan came in. "How did it go?" she asked.

"The horses are in good hands," Daryan replied. "And I've found a porter to bring some of our gear up. I think we should give him a hand though, but I need to have a word with you before we go down."

"What's on your mind?"

"It's Felindra. I found her in the outer yard with that wolf. I don't know what to do. I don't even know if she's allowed to bring it inside the Monastery, although no one seems to have objected so far, but then, it's dark and there aren't too many people around."

"She seems to have really bonded with it," Parvana replied. "I doubt we'll be able to separate them, or even if we should try."

"I guessed as much.

"Not only are whisperers very rare, they're also very sensitive, so we need to handle the matter with great care. I'll have a word with her. Let's go down and see how they're getting on with the unloading."

6 – Felindra's Test

Felindra

Felindra and Parvana sat in a small room lined with six cushioned chairs. There were no windows in the room, but ample light came from a glass dome overhead. Opposite the archway through which they'd entered, there was a closed door.

"What's going to happen?" Felindra asked anxiously.

"I couldn't tell you, my sweet," her mother replied, taking her hand and squeezing it. "It's up to the examiner. Each one has a different technique depending on the candidate and his or her perceived gift. All I can tell you is that it doesn't hurt and there's no such thing as failing."

A woman wearing a dark blue archmage's robe came through the archway.

Parvana stood up. "Terábytha. How wonderful to see you again. And an archmage! How are you?"

"Parvana! My dear friend, you don't look a day older than when you left. I can't believe you have a daughter this age." She embraced Parvana and kissed her on both cheeks, and then she looked at Felindra. "Introduce us!"

"Yes. Come here, my love." Felindra stood, feeling a little nervous. "Let me present my daughter, Felindra Peshanar. Felindra this is my old friend Lady Terábytha."

"Welcome to the Monastery, Felindra. Such a pretty name." She glanced at Parvana and back to Felindra. "I think you are going to be very happy here; you're in for an exciting time." She took both of Felindra's hands in hers and squeezed them.

When Terábytha released Felindra, Parvana put her arm around her daughter's shoulder and said, "You should address her as Lady Terábytha or just lady. All archmages are addressed with honorifics, lady for women mages and sir for men."

"Thank you, Parvana. We'll get started now, and you and I will talk later." She turned to Felindra. "Come along, dear; let's go in the other room. And don't be nervous; it's a harmless little procedure and I guarantee when it's over you will feel wonderful."

They went through the door into a smaller room with blue fabric on the walls. With no windows or skylight, it was like walking into a box. Light came from four globes, one in each corner of the white ceiling. The only furnishings were a rust-colored rug on the floor upon which sat a small table with two padded chairs facing each other. In the middle of the table lay a round tray filled with indentations, something like an egg case. The indentations were lined with black velvet, and inside each hollow lay a faceted crystal. There must have been at least a dozen.

"Let's sit down and get comfortable," Lady Terábytha said. She sat on one of the chairs and indicated that Felindra should take the other.

"Comfortable?"

Not really, Felindra thought, but she nodded.

"Let's take some deep breaths before we start. Close your eyes and breathe in … hold it … breathe out. Now again."

They repeated the breathing eight more times before Lady Terábytha stopped. "All right. Now let's get started. I'm going to ask you some questions. Don't worry, they're just to assess the possibilities; there are no wrong answers. Ready?"

"Yes, lady."

"Good. Felindra, do you have an idea what your gift is?"

"Yes, lady, I think so."

"Tell me what it is."

"My mother told me it's called Whispering."

Terábytha's eyes widened with surprise. "Are you sure?"

"Yes, lady."

"Have you had many experiences or manifestations of this gift?"

"Yes, lady."

"Would you tell me about them?"

Felindra told her about the sick horses and the wolf, without revealing that Ashala was here with her.

"Extraordinary! It sounds as if you have an amazing talent, Felindra, a unique gift. How long have you known about it?"

"Well, I sort of felt something, like how they feel sometimes, mostly horses and the blacksmith's dog in Picobali, but it wasn't very clear. For about two years. I only found I could communicate with them while we were traveling here."

"Amazing! Forgive me for my enthusiasm, my dear, but … to think we have a Whisperer among us after all these years. You've no idea how exciting this is for the League. How do you visualize using the gift, Felindra?"

"I want to use it to help the League."

"Can you think of any specific ways in which you could use it?"

"I thought maybe I could tell when horses don't feel good and help the healers make them better. And maybe I could talk to other animals in the forest, wolves maybe, and get information about things that are happening, you know, if people are doing bad things." She looked at the archmage with sparkling eyes. "You know wolves are very intelligent and good."

"You like wolves, don't you?"

Felindra nodded.

"We don't really have a routine test for your gift; it occurs so infrequently, so we'll have to improvise. "Before we continue, are there any indications that you might have other gifts?"

"No, lady."

"We have to go somewhere else for the next step. Come with me."

Felindra followed Lady Terábytha back to the entrance. They left the building and crossed a lawn and small flower garden to a smaller building.

"This is one of the archmages' residences." Lady Terábytha informed her.

The building was constructed of brick covered in pale orange stucco. The interior walls were washed with light turquoise, and the floors were paved with white marble tiles. A glass dome over the entrance hall, which went up three stories, provided ample light and gave the whole building an airy coolness.

"This way," the archmage said.

Felindra followed her up two flights of marble stairs and along a hallway to the end door.

"This is where I live," Terábytha said as she opened the door. "Come in."

They entered a sunny room with windows on two walls overlooking the gardens, furnished in soft pastels. Padded chairs with embroidered cushions sat on either side of a white marble fireplace, on one of which a huge white cat stood up and stretched.

"Come here, Phoenix," Terábytha said. "I want you to meet someone."

The cat jumped down from the chair and strolled across the rug, and then weaved around the archmage's legs, purring loudly.

"Sit down, Felindra. Let's see what this young fellow has to say." She lifted the cat and put him in Felindra's lap, and then sat in the other chair.

Felindra put her hand on the cat's head and stroked down his back. Phoenix started purring loudly while extending and retracting his claws against her thighs. Although she could sense a blissful feeling of contentment from him, she lifted his front paws to keep him from pricking her legs.

"Well, he likes you." The archmage said. "Even I can tell that. But you have to be very firm with him when he starts doing that." She nodded to the animals' paws held in Felindra's hands. "He should have learned by now that it hurts when he sticks his claws into people. I've threatened to clip his claws if he continues to do it."

Felindra stopped stroking and rested her hand on the back of its neck. "Should I tell him that?" she asked.

"Oh, please do. It drives me crazy when I'm trying to relax."

"How are you feeling?" Felindra whispered. Contentment flowed from the animal. "He seems very happy." She turned her attention back onto the cat. "We love you, Phoenix, but it makes us uncomfortable when you stick out your claws like that."

The cat looked startled. He stopped purring and looked at her seriously, then across at his mistress."

"We aren't angry; we know it is your nature and your way of expressing contentment and affection. We still love you." Felindra hoped she was presenting the images to him in a way that he could understand.

The cat stretched out his legs along her thighs and rested his head on his paws.

"Well, look at him! It looks as if you conveyed the message without hurting his feelings," Lady Terábytha said. "You certainly have the gift. Ask him what his favorite food is!" she added.

She got a mixed response to food that seemed to be equal parts fish and chicken.

"Fish and chicken."

"Really? I thought he liked beef liver best."

"How about liver?" she whispered, and received a strong feeling of repugnance.

"He doesn't like liver; in fact, I think he hates it."

"Very good, Felindra, he does."

Felindra thought of something else she could ask. "Do you like playing outside?" She received an impression of running around on a lawn, jumping at butterflies with a feeling of great enjoyment. "He likes to be outside chasing butterflies," she said.

"Oh does he? I don't take him out much. I didn't realize how much he enjoyed it. Anything else?"

"Do you like swimming in water?" He replied with feeling of aversion and an image of being held down in a tub of warm water and covered with soapsuds. "He hates having his bath."

"Excellent. I think that's enough. You've convinced me."

"You mean we're finished?"

Phoenix followed them to the door, rubbing against Felindra's leg and purring. She could feel his longing to go out of doors. "He wants to go outside," she said.

"I'm afraid to let him out. I heard a rumor that there's a wolf living in the woods behind the palace."

Felindra felt contrite for not revealing Ashala's presence earlier. "Lady Terábytha, there's something I have to tell you."

The archmage closed the door again to keep the cat from escaping. "What is it, my dear?"

"The wolf. It's mine."

"Oh. What's it doing here?"

"She followed me all the way from the place we were attacked. She's so good and she won't hurt anyone. I thought if she stayed in the woods, it would be all right. She knows she's not supposed to hurt people or domestic animals; only to hunt the wild ones in the forest."

"How can you be sure she won't?"

"She knows if she does anything bad, she'll have to go away, and she's already lost her family, her mate and her cubs. We're the only family she has now. Please don't make me send her away." Felindra was close to tears.

"I'll talk to your parents and see what they say. Now, what about Phoenix? He wants to go out. Is he safe?"

"I could get her to recognize him as someone special. Then she would consider him part of the family. She thinks of everyone she's introduced to is her family, sort of like joining a clan. She would never hurt him then, and she would protect him as well if he were in danger."

"How would you do that?"

"All it means is familiarizing her with his scent. Would you like me to do it now?"

"What does he think about it?" She picked up the cat and held it in her arms.

Felindra stroked his head, but when she thought about the wolf, he hissed, his hackles went up, and his ears flattened on his head. She tried again after soothing him and thinking about playing in the grass, but he was still resistant. Felindra sighed and removed her hand. "I don't think he likes the idea," she said. "What I can do is go to her now, and let her get his scent off me, and then tell her he's a friend, and that she's not to hurt him."

"All right. I guess he'll have to stay in for now. Sorry, boy." She set him down on the floor and opened the door. This time the cat was not so eager to get out.

"You must come again," the archmage said. "I would like to see if a crystal would make any difference to your communications."

7 – School Starts.

Felindra

The next day, Darson and Felindra started their lessons.

Felindra, wearing the standard attire for students, long green smock and calf-length beige trousers, found the Junior Academy behind the temporary housing building. Expecting it to be another stone or brick building, like all the others she'd seen, she was surprised to find it was constructed of wood. Not in the crude style of log homes, but with smooth golden mora panels laid on timber framing. She found the room to which she had been assigned and looked in. There was only one other student there. She was sitting cross-legged on the floor with her eyes closed, appearing to be in deep meditation, but she heard the floor creak as Felindra entered and looked up.

"What are you doing?" the girl asked.

Felindra shrugged. "What are you doing?"

The girl tutted, sighed, and stood up. "I don't suppose you're going to go away." Her tone wasn't disagreeable, just rather matter of fact, as if she were commenting on the weather.

"I don't suppose I am," Felindra replied. "Why?"

"Oh, I thought I was going to be alone. Now you turn up."

"Do you want to be alone?"

The girl shrugged again. "I don't have any preference really."

"What's your name?" Felindra asked.

"My parents named me Vestani, but I prefer to be called Sama."

"Why?"

"It's easier to remember."

"Why? Do you forget your name?"

"I used to. What's yours?"

"Nothing as interesting as yours," Felindra replied. "Felindra."

"That's all right, I suppose. At least it's not Vestani."

Felindra realized she was beginning to like this girl's eccentricity. "Isn't there a teacher?" she asked.

"Sometimes. Sometimes we just study what we like, on our own. There should be another student, but I've no idea where he is. Shall we go outside?" She wandered over to the window that almost filled the outside wall and started to pull on a chain that came out of an aperture at the top of the frame. "You'll have to help me," she said. "When the window goes up, you have to pull down the props, see at the bottom of the frame?"

"What do you two think you're doing?" a supercilious male voice asked from the doorway.

"What does it look like? Sama replied. "You could help us if you're not above such things."

"Here, let me do it. You can't expect girls to be able to do such complex things."

"Well here you are!" they turned and saw a short, rather stout woman in a red mage's robe. "I see we have a new student." She walked to the window and took the chain from Sama. "Arnaz, pull out the props," and proceeded to raise the window while the boy ran outside to set the props into two holes in the paving, turning the window into a glass roof over the patio.

"Since you're all set on working outside, bring your cushions and let's get started." She picked up a low stool for herself and plonked it down on the floor outside the window.

When they were seated, she turned to Felindra. "New girl. Tell us about yourself."

Is everybody crazy here? Felindra thought with an inward sigh. *Well, I might as well join them.* "What do you want to know?"

The boy: "What's your father's name?"

Sama: "What's your gift, if you've got one?"

Teacher: "What do you want to learn from this class?"

Felindra pushed her hair back from her face. "First of all, I'd like to learn everybody's name. I already know Sama."

Slightly taken aback by her bold response, the teacher introduced herself. "My name is Tonia Alawalia. You may call me Lady Tonia, or Tonia." She looked at the boy and nodded.

"Arnaz Pashin."

"What's your father's name, Arnaz? Sama asked.

"Captain Mandras Pashin of the League of Light." He turned to Felindra. "Who's your father?"

"Why is that important to you, Arnaz?" Sama asked.

"I like to know where I stand."

"My father is Daryan Peshanar."

"Not Commander Peshanar?" Sama exclaimed with glee.

"Yes," Felindra replied indifferently. She was beginning to enjoy this game.

Arnaz glared at Sama, and his face became a bit redder.

"I think that's enough of introductions, don't you?" Tonia said.

"She didn't answer my question," Sama complained.

"Oh, very well," the teacher said. "What was it again?"

"I asked her what her gift is."

Felindra looked down at the floor, feeling heat spreading over her face and neck. "I'm a Whisperer," she said softly.

"A what?" Arnaz demanded crossly.

"She said she's a Whisperer," Sama yelled.

"I'm leaving." Arnaz stood up, picked up his cushion, and stalked back inside.

"I wonder what's upsetting him," Tonia said.

"He's miffed because somebody has turned up who outranks him, or should I say, his father?" Sama explained.

"But I'm not," Felindra protested. "I'm just an ordinary girl. And my father is just a swordsmith."

"I bet you're older than him too," Sama said with a wicked grin.

After that, they continued with a rather disorganized lesson about wildlife that drifted off into a bit of history, medicinal herbs, and recipes for cooking shellfish before ending with some gossip about one of the archmages. Tonia's easy-going style of teaching was nevertheless effective because it made the subjects more interesting, so the students paid attention. They pretty well had to pay attention because when Tonia realized they were off-track, she would stop in the middle of a sentence and say, "Now what was I saying?" and expect them to get her back on topic. Felindra enjoyed her first day of school, and felt that she and Sama might become friends. She had her doubts about Arnaz, though.

That night at supper, Daryan asked Darson about school.

"It was all right," he said. His eyes lit up. "They've got more books in our classroom than we had in our whole house at home, at least thirty. We can even borrow them."

"What did you learn?" Felindra asked.

"We did a lot of arithmetic, but it was too easy. I got bored with it. Then we talked about the mountains in the north and the people who live on the other side. Oh, I did learn something interesting ... a bit trivial but... Did you know the number nine has unique properties?" Without waiting for an answer, he continued, "If you add the digits in any multiple of nine and keep reducing them, they will always come to nine."

"What do you mean?" Felindra asked.

"I'll give you an example: say you multiply nine by seventeen, you get 153. Add the digits, 1 plus 5 plus 3 equals 9. It works with any multiple."

"That's very interesting, son," Daryan said. He turned to Felindra. "What did you learn?"

Felindra grinned, recalling how much she'd enjoyed her first day. "How to prepare shell fish in oil and vinegar, that the bark of willow trees is the source of a powerful pain killer, and that Duke Meril the third was murdered by his son, Meril the fourth because Meril the third wouldn't allow him to marry his cousin."

"That sounds like quite a list of topics," Daryan said. "It must be an interesting class."

"It is. I think I'll go back tomorrow."

"What are you going to be doing while we're in school, mami?" Darson asked.

"I'm going back to school," Parvana replied with a smile.

"You're going to school?" Darson's eyes lit up.

"That's right, Darson. When your father and I married, I had not completed my studies, especially in my secondary skill, then you children came along, and I didn't have much time to practice. I was tempted to use it on you when I was tired and you weren't behaving well, but I didn't think it would be fair to you."

"What is your second skill?" Darson asked.

"Conviction," she replied. "It's convincing creatures to do as you say, to obey commands."

"But we obeyed you," Felindra said.

"Most of the time. That's because you are good children, not because I used magic on you." Parvana said, smiling.

"And because you have a good mother," Daryan added.

Parvana smiled thanks to him. "We do not use my kind of gift lightly and never on those we love, those who trust us.

That would be infringing on their free will. It does come in handy in difficult situations, though, but it would be unethical to use it to take advantage of anyone. I would use it if one of you were about to get into a dangerous situation; for example, if I knew you were walking into quicksand, I would use my gift and command you to step back. That would be quicker and more effective than if I just warned you."

Daryan

After the children had settled down to sleep, Daryan and Parvana went down to the garden courtyard and sat by the fountain. They did this when they didn't want to be overheard. There was no real privacy in their suite with only a curtain separating them from the children.

"What do you think they'll decide about Felindra?" Parvana asked.

"Felindra's gift is unique, so there's no one to train her. It looks as if she'll have to work it out for herself for the most part. That doesn't worry me too much; she seems to be handling it very well, and I expect she'll get training in school on the ethics and hazards of using gifts, the same as everyone else."

"But what is she going to do? And how about the wolf?"

"There have been several suggestions put forward in the council. She could help animal healers with diagnoses. There has been a suggestion that the wolf could play a role in gathering information."

"You mean spying?" Parvana looked dismayed.

"If you want to call it that. I think it makes sense. The wolf ..."

Parvana interrupted, "Her name is Ashala; calling her 'the wolf' all the time seems a bit demeaning."

"All right, my love, Ashala. Now, where was I...? Oh, yes, Ashala could roam around, talk—or whatever wolves do to communicate—with other wolves and find out what's going on around here, and then she could come back and tell Felindra."

"That doesn't sound too dangerous, but I don't want Felindra doing anything that would put herself in danger."

"Of course not." He'd met with Archmage Plavan, the security chief, earlier, but he refrained from telling her Plavan's idea of having her read other animals, the horses of people they suspected of being enemies, for example.

"What about your trip to DarSolas? When are you leaving?"

"The day after tomorrow, early in the morning. We're taking Nadi with us. Having a life-sensor would be useful to warn us of danger."

He put his arm around Parvana and pulled her close, then bent and kissed her. "My beautiful wife, my treasure. I'll miss you."

"You'll only be gone a week," she replied, but she hugged him back and snuggled closer.

"That's the plan, but you never know with the duke. We have to maintain good relations with him and that may prove a bit difficult from what I've been hearing."

"What can he do? I mean to obstruct you."

"It's not so much him I'm worried about; it's that chancellor of his. There's something very menacing about him. I don't trust him. It's as if he has the duke under some sort of spell. The last time I was at court, the chancellor was very insistent about getting his point across, especially when it opposed any suggestions from the Monastery. And the sad thing is the duke backed him. He was never like that before this Gremulkin was appointed. This is one of the places Nadi will be useful."

"Can't you speak to the duke when he's not around?"

"I tried last time I was at the castle. The Duke won't discuss anything without Gremulkin being present. He seems frightened without him."

"I think you may be right. It certainly sounds as if he's under some sort of influence, a very powerful one by the sound of it."

"That aside, there's something else I want to discuss with you. I'd like to take Felindra and Ashala with us."

"What! You just got through telling me there is some sort of evil at work in the capital, and then you want to take our daughter there!"

"Hush, my love. You know I'd never put one of our children in harm's way. She would be well protected, and I won't bring her into contact with that man. I have another defender going with us, and I think Ashala makes a better bodyguard than anyone. They just might pick up something that will help us. Even a visit to the duke's stable might uncover something."

"But what about Ashala. Would she be allowed into the city?"

"I don't know. Maybe if we could persuade her to wear a collar and lead."

"I still don't like it," Parvana said.

"It would be a great experience for her, and she would have a chance to practice her skills. How about if we ask her? She may not want to go."

"And spring may not follow winter," Parvana said. She sighed. "All right, ask her, but I want to be there when you do."

Daryan raised his eyebrows. "You don't trust me?"

Felindra

Arnaz returned to school the next day, acting as if nothing had happened—that is, he was arrogant and surly, which appeared to be the norm for him.

They didn't open the big window because it was raining outside, so they sat in a circle on their cushions.

"How old are you?" Arnaz asked Felindra out of nowhere.

"Why do you want to know?" she responded.

"Just wondering. Fine with me if you don't want to tell me." He shrugged.

Felindra looked at him from under her eyelashes. He was quite a handsome boy, tall and slim with ear-length wavy black hair. His face was blessed with even features, nothing out of balance or misaligned. So why was he so disagreeable? "I have thirteen years," she replied "My anniversary is in three months, around the autumn equinox. How old are you?"

"I reached fourteen just before the spring equinox." He went back to fiddling with a stone he carried attached to a cord.

"Now that you've got to know each other better, would you mind telling me what we're doing here?" Sama asked

"We're supposed to be learning something," Arnaz replied. "If the teacher ever shows up."

Felindra turned to Sama. "Do you know what your gift is?" she asked.

The girl swiveled around on her cushion to face the window. "Look at that rain. I love the rain, don't you?"

"I take it you don't know," Felindra persisted.

"Of course she knows," Arnaz said. "She goes for training every afternoon""

"All right, since we're all in the mood for sharing our innermost secrets, it's farsight."

"Farsight? I haven't heard of that. What does it mean?"

"I can sometimes see things far away. I'm learning to control and focus it."

"You mean you can see things in faraway places?"

"Yes. And in time."

"Like things that happened in the past?"

"Sometimes. But I need something material connected to an event in order to see it."

"That's amazing!" Felindra said. "You sound as if you're much more advanced than I am. How old are you?"

"I have fifteen years. Your gift is pretty incredible. When do you start training?"

Felindra shrugged. "I'm not. There's no one to train me. I have to learn by myself, but Lady Terábytha said I should read some of the old books in the library written by other Whisperers." She glanced at Arnaz who was gazing at the rain, looking supremely bored. "What about you Arnaz. Are you training?"

"Not yet. I only just got tested."

"For what?" Sama asked. "If I'm not intruding on your privacy."

He shrugged. "Girls!" he muttered under his breath. "I'm not sure which is primary and which secondary. I tested for relocation and mastery of elements."

"Incredible! You mean you have two gifts that are equal in strength? That's unusual, isn't it?" Felindra said.

"I suppose so. I can only train in one at a time, and I can't decide which to start with."

"Which is the hardest to learn?" Felindra asked.

"Elements I suppose. Relocation seems to come naturally, so they say.

"My father's primary is relocation," Felindra told him. "Maybe you'd like to meet him and talk about it."

"We'll see." He seemed to be going inside himself again, like a mouse retreating into its hole.

Felindra decided to leave him alone. She looked around the room to see if she could find anything interesting, but apart from some pictures on the wall and a few books, she drew a blank. "Do we have to stay here if the teacher doesn't come?"

Sama shrugged. "Why, do you want to go somewhere?"

"I thought maybe I should go to the library and see if I can find a book to read about whispering." She stood up and smoothed her tunic.

Arnaz emerged from his mouse hole. "Hey, you're the wolf girl everyone's talking about aren't you?"

"I didn't know anyone was talking about it, but I do have a wolf friend."

"Where do you keep it?"

"She lives in the woods behind the Palace," she said, referring to the Grand Master's residence, the magnificent white marble building that also served as the administrative headquarters of the League. "Sometimes she goes out to the Great Forest to visit her friends."

"You mean she's just roaming around loose? Isn't that dangerous?"

"No. She knows how to behave. She's more civilized than many *people* are. Why? Are you afraid?"

"No, of course not, not with this." He pulled a dagger out of his belt.

"You're a fool," Felindra retorted angrily. "You try to use that on her and she'll rip your throat out."

"Hey! I thought you said she was civilized."

"I'm sorry," Felindra said. "It's just that, if they don't know how wolves behave, some people do rash things and get hurt. If she thought you were attacking her, she'd naturally defend herself and she's very strong. Look, why don't you come and meet her, then you'll see how harmless she is?"

"Hey, that's a great idea," Sama said getting up. "Why don't we, Arn? That's if you aren't afraid."

"I told you, I'm not afraid!" he got up and stomped out of the room, but he was waiting for them outside when they left the school building.

"What about Lady Tonia?" Felindra inquired.

"She'll find us gone, that's all, if she turns up at all. She can't expect us to sit around all morning waiting for her," Sama replied.

"Is she often late like this?"

"She has episodes. I don't know what of, but it's some sort of psychic thing, I think. She just has to be alone. She's quite nice really, and she's a good teacher, in spite of being a bit scatterbrained." Sama turned round and called Arnaz. "Are you coming?"

The three classmates went around the far side of the stables so that they could go past the paddock. Felindra looked for Shila, but she wasn't outside. *She must be in the stable getting ready for tomorrow,* Felindra thought.

"By the way," she said to her two companions. "I'm going away tomorrow. My father wants me and Ashala to go with him to DarSolas."

"Ashala?" Arnaz asked

"That's my wolf's name."

"Why do *you* have to go?" Sama asked.

"It's part of our training, mine and Ashala's. They are still trying to assess what we can do and where my gift will be useful."

"Lucky you," Arnaz said sourly.

"Arnaz! We can only use the gift the Light gives us. I can't help it if mine is different. At least you have two, and they're both pretty important." Felindra said to placate him.

They continued across the yard towards the Palace. About halfway across, Felindra let out a piercing two-tone whistle. They heard a gentle wolf howl in response. In less than a minute, Ashala came running across the yard, still favoring her injured front leg a little, although it was no longer covered with a dressing. She pulled up before Felindra and gave a little bark, then licked her hand. Her fellow students watched her with a look of amazement, Arnaz with his hand on his dagger, looking a bit nervous.

"She's so big," Sama said. "I didn't know wolves could get that big."

"She's a silver wolf," Felindra replied. She looked at them and smiled reassuringly, and then she squatted by Ashala and murmured to her, "I want to introduce you to my friends. Do you want to meet them?"

Ashala responded with a little whine and a flip of her tail.

"She says yes," she told them. "Sama, come here and hold your hand like this." She demonstrated by putting the palm of her hand under Ashala's nose. She had deliberately chosen Sama to be first because she sensed Arnaz was still nervous.

Ashala sniffed Sama's hand and then licked it, after that she gave a friendly yip.

"There, now she knows and you are friends," Felindra told her. "That was easy, wasn't it? Now your turn, Arnaz."

He came and stood by Felindra, cautiously extending his hand in Ashala's direction. The wolf snarled softly, but she came forward to sniff and lick his hand, and then she turned away and walked to the other side of Felindra.

"What's wrong with her?" Arnaz asked.

"I think she sensed you were nervous, that's all. Don't worry about it; she has your scent now, so she won't hurt you because you're my friend. You are, aren't you? My friend?"

"I'm getting soaked out here; I'm going home," Arnaz said. "Coming, Sama?"

"In a minute," she replied. She turned to Felindra. "Thanks, Felindra, and Ashala. This was fun." Sama said, and added, "I was thinking of going to the library. Would you like to go with me? Maybe you can find a book about your gift."

8 – The Wizard Gets a Mission

Monaltor

"You know what you have to do?" Monolta, the grand wizard, scowled at his son.

Barengush looked at his hands, clenched tightly in his lap. "You've told me enough times," he replied resentfully.

Monolta slammed his hand down on the table in the former Grand Master's study, making the candleholders and inkbottles shake. "I asked you a question! Now have the courtesy to answer me properly, instead of sulking like an infant!"

Barengush looked up into his father's angry face and quickly dropped his eyes to focus on the table between them. "Yes, father, I know what I must do."

"And I want you to see if you can control yourself for once. Only do what you've been told to do and don't go off into one of your ... I don't know what to call your little episodes ... if you were a child, I'd say they were tantrums, but you have eighteen years and should have learned how to control your impulses by this time. You're a wizard now; I expect you to act like one. You are to only use soft magic—spells—and leave the elemental stuff alone, unless it is absolutely necessary to the success of the mission." He stood up and pushed his chair back. "All right, you can go." He added, flapping a hand at his son.

Barengush stood up and walked to the door. He sighed and turned back to face Monolta. "Farewell, father," he said, not really expecting a reply.

Monolta grunted, then turned his back and walked over to the window. Two stories below, he could see the monastery workers—those who hadn't run away before the gates were locked—cleaning up some rubble from the attack. He watched them lifting stones from the wreckage and piling them up in a corner. Whenever a body was found, it was taken over and laid against the wall of an undamaged building. He had ordered them to burn the bodies and had reacted swiftly to their outcry of objections to the order by choosing a couple of the loudest dissenters and having them publicly strangled. You couldn't allow them to think they had any power at all. He was in charge now, and by Oglestra, he wouldn't allow any opposition, from either the monastery inmates or his own people, and that included his son. Ogryn relied on him to keep trouble from irrupting, and to assure their plan moved forward.

He looked up at the sky and visualized for a moment their victory. It might take a while, but with patience, endurance, and the blessings of Oglestra, they would soon control the whole of Albasiny. They had started now, and their progress so far was not insignificant. From this modest beginning, bigger things would develop. Just the thought of overcoming those spineless followers of Light filled him with satisfaction. To be free of all their restrictions, their useless principles and the moral constraints that limited the heights to which men could climb ... ah, the freedom, the possibilities....

A knock came on the door, interrupting his reverie. "Enter!" he snapped.

The door opened to admit one of the guards of the dungeons. "Grand Wizard, he would like to see you now." The man turned away without waiting for a reply. He knew Monolta wouldn't dare refuse such a summons.

Sighing, Monolta picked up his flat black hat and set it on his head, then he followed the guard down the stairs. He dreaded these meetings with the Disciple, the descent into the lowest levels of the monastery where no sunlight could reach. The air was dank and smelled of mildew. Just enough light to see was provided by a few candles set far apart along the damp stone walls. The cobbled floors were slick with mold, so you had to move carefully to avoid slipping and falling in the foul mess. But Ogryn shunned light; that's why he chose to live in these depths.

Eventually, they reached his cell, for cell it was, albeit a large cell, dismal and damp with little comfort. His table was a slab of smoothed stone standing atop other slabs laid on their edges. Even his elevated chair, if you could call it that, was made of stone. It hadn't taken him long to make himself at home in the monastery's subbasement. The only illumination in the room came from a single candle on the table.

"Well, Grand Wizard, what progress are you making? Report!" the creature said in his raspy voice. So vague and shadowy did he appear that Monolta sometimes wondered if he was a real person at all or some sort of simulacrum, but it didn't pay to act on speculation.

***

Sergeant Balend stood at the top of a hill in the small port of Toive on ValkonenMaa's west coast and looked at the scene below. What he saw was a group of around twenty werfolk being herded onto a coastal barge by several tough-looking individuals. "I'll be chucked!" he exclaimed. "Did you ever see such a sight?" he asked rhetorically.

His two companions, Dolan, and Solden—a defender and a mage—shook their heads. "I wonder where they're off to," Dolan commented.

"Hey, there's part of your answer," the mage said, pointing at the dark figure who'd just appeared from a structure on the deck of the barge. It certainly doesn't bode well for somebody."

Sergeant Balend had lost most of the people in his group by the time he reached the coast as they dropped off at different communities along the way, or branched off in other directions. Dolan and Solden had stayed with him so they could complete the mission they'd set out on. They were to visit towns and villages between the monastery and the coast to gather intelligence and link up with other people connected with the monastery, namely inactive League defenders and mages. Toive was their final stop and then they were to head for the capital.

"Let's go down and take a closer look," Balend suggested. "Then we'll have a meal and report in."

They sent periodic reports to the senior surviving archmage in ValkonenMaa, Perin Solvang, who had been visiting the capital at the time of the attack on the monastery. She had been the Chief of Communications at the monastery and had set up a provisional communications center in Mainio castle, providing a network to coordinate information as it was acquired from around the duchy. The ban on using telepathy had been lifted within days of the attack when they realize such a ban would hinder them more than the risk incurred in using the gift.

The trio, now wearing ordinary workers' clothing to make them less conspicuous, strolled down the steep cobbled street towards the docks. In addition to two coastal barges and a small freighter, about fifteen fishing boats were berthed at two narrow jetties off to one side. The boats had just returned from their day's fishing, and now the fishers were haggling with a small crowd of buyers along the wharf. Giving off a fresh fishy smell, tubs of seawater with live fish sat on the ground, and larger fish, already dressed, were arranged on top of boards laid across piled up boxes.

They sauntered along the wharf, inspecting the catches of the various fishers. Finally, Balend stopped at one makeshift table containing about a dozen fish that had already been cleaned. He recognized them as haddock by the black line along their sides and its size, which exceeded half a span. "These look tasty," he said to the fisher. "I'd buy a couple if I could find a place to cook them."

The fisher wiped his hands on his canvas apron and smiled. "They're the best catch on the west coast," he replied. "Fresh today. Traveling, are you?"

The Whisperer

"Yes," Balend replied without elaborating. "We haven't found lodgings yet, but we could surely make a meal of these."

"Well, you're in luck," the fisher replied. "See up there?" he pointed to the road above the wharf. "There's a woman up there who will cook them for you. That's the smoke of her cook fire."

"Well then, that's our problem solved. We'll take two. One for now, and one for tonight." As the fisher was placing the two fish in a burlap sack, Balend noticed him glance in the direction of the barge and scowl. "What do you think they are up to?" he asked, nodding in the same direction.

"Nothing good, I can guarantee that." The fisher handed over the sack and took the two silver coins Balend offered.

"Is this a regular thing?"

"There's been several … I've seen three myself."

"Where are they taking the little people?"

"I don't know. All I know is that they go south, and there's always one of them black-cloaks with them."

"You mean the wizards?"

The fisher nodded. He spat on the ground and fingered the Light pendant on a chain around his neck. "A curse upon them!"

"I wonder what they're doing with the little folk," Solden commented.

"They must have put a spell on them, or drugged 'em," the fisher replied. "Else they wouldn't allow themselves to be loaded aboard like sheep."

"You may be right," Balend said. "I wouldn't like to change place with whoever's on the receiving end of that lot."

9 – Journey to DarSolas

Felindra

It took a lot of persuasion to get Ashala to accept a collar, but she eventually gave in and allowed Felindra to fasten the loose strip of leather around her neck. For a while, she went around scratching it with a hind paw and shaking her head to loosen it, but after a lot of whispering and petting from Felindra, she settled down to the inevitable. In a way, Felindra thought it was a good idea, maybe not from Ashala's point of view, but it might make other people less nervous around her; when they were nervous it made Ashala agitated. The lead would be another matter, however, but she would deal with that when the time came. They'd had one made by one of the armorers from two long strips of cowhide sewn together with a loop at one end and a metal clasp at the other. For the time being, Felindra let the wolf play with it, getting used to its smell and feel, although she drew the line at chewing. Ashala had a thick piece of rawhide for that purpose.

On the morning of their departure, Felindra dressed in new riding trousers with leather patches sewn on the inner sides of the knees. She had on a long green tunic, as befitted a girl, slit at the sides, a pair of leather gloves, and leather riding boots. Her hair was tied in a scarf to keep it under control.

Once outside the building Felindra whistled her signal to Ashala, then headed for the stables with her father to get their horses. There, they met Othran, the other defender, and Nadi. They were all similarly attired, although the men's tunics were shorter than Felindra's.

Daryan said to Felindra, "We'll bring out the horses; you go and meet the wolf before she gets too close to the stable and spooks them all."

Felindra was riding Shila, the chestnut filly who was accustomed to Ashala, but the other horses were restless when she was near.

"Which way are we going?" she asked her father. "If I know the direction, I'll follow and try to keep Ashala away from your mounts."

"This way. Over the bridge and right along the inside of wall."

Felindra followed a few paces behind as they walked the narrow path along the interior side the wall. They went north almost to the end where the wall turned east. Instead of continuing on that path, her father led them into an angle of the wall where he grabbed torch from a barrel standing nearby and lit it with his lighter kit. The light revealed the gate of heavy iron bars, almost hidden in the surrounding foliage, when led to a ramp carved out of the rock that sloped downwards into the ground. After unlocking the gate, Daryan let them through and locked it behind them. The high-ceilinged tunnel was only wide enough for a single horse and rider. Daryan took the lead and Felindra came last. The rock walls were damp and mossy, but the air was fresh. After going down several paces, the ramp turned right and continued for a while, then turned left.

"We're outside the walls now," Othran informed her.

"How far down are we going?" she asked.

"It's a long way yet. We're going all the way down to the valley floor."

"Amazing! That is a long way."

Ashala trotted along dutifully beside Shila. "You're a good girl," Felindra told her. Ashala replied with a soft bark.

It took them the better part of two hours to navigate the ramp, zigzagging back and forth down to ground level. The tunnel ended in a blank wall of rock. In spite of it appearing to be a dead end, Felindra could feel a fresh breeze from somewhere. Daryan went to the wall and pulled down on an iron lever set into the rock. Rumbling and scraping, part of the rock face rolled to one side, letting in daylight.

In her excitement, Felindra urged her mount forward ahead of the others, eager to see what lay outside. She had never been to this part of the country before and had never even dreamed of such an unusual way to travel ... descending a mountain through a tunnel concealed behind a secret portal.

After they had all exited, her father found another lever hidden in a crevice behind a clump of bamboo. He pulled down on it and the rock ground its way back into place.

"There's no trail from here. This is a secret way into and out of the Monastery and we want to keep it a secret. If you ever need to use this entrance, remember two things, the bamboo thicket and the stream below us. There's a bluish-colored rock in the stream level with the opening." He turned his horse to face downhill. "Now we have to find our way through the trees until we reach a trail."

It was a relief to be back outside on level ground, although the atmosphere was noticeably hotter and more humid at this level. The vegetation was different too; there were fewer evergreens and more broad-leafed trees. Among the trees were ferns, bamboo, and vines that hung down from the larger trees. Some of the trees had flowering plants growing in the axils where the branches joined the trunks. The air resounded with the squawks of parrots and the excited shrieks of monkeys.

Ashala immediately took off to explore. A little while later, she heard a wolf howl from Ashala's direction followed by an answering call from farther away.

They crossed the stream after a short pause to allow the horses to drink, then continued south-west along its bank until they came to a track wide enough for a cart. Around midday, they stopped in a forest glade to eat some of the food they'd brought from the Monastery. The glade was filled with orange, red, and white wildflowers. The heat, the fragrance of

76

flowers, and the droning of the insects made everyone feel drowsy.

Ashala came back and flopped down beside Felindra. Felindra stroked her neck. "Why?" she whispered, thinking about the wolf calls. She received back an impression of being in strange territory and announcing her presence to the other packs in the area, plus an assurance she was only passing through. Felindra kissed her head. "You are so civilized," she said. "I wish people were more like you."

Ashala whimpered and licked her the back of her hand.

"Did you eat?" she whispered. The response was affirmative. The wolf rested her muzzle on Felindra's leg and closed her eyes. Several minutes later, she raised her head and growled deep in her throat, and then she jumped up and took off into the trees.

"Aren't you afraid you'll lose her?" Othran asked.

"No. She'll come back. She likes to go out and explore, meet new creatures."

"Time we were on our way," her father said.

They stood, picked up and packed their belongings, and then they remounted and continued down the trail.

"We should be reaching the high road soon; then we'll be able to make better time."

They'd barely gone a couple of paces when a terrifying, inhuman shriek filled the air followed by a wailing cry and the whimper of an injured creature, and then a yelp and a howl that Felindra recognized as Ashala's. She whistled for the wolf to come, and a few seconds later, she appeared. But there was something wrong. Blood ran down Ashala's side from three gashes, and she was carrying something in her mouth. Felindra jumped down from her horse as the wolf reached her and dropped what she was carrying at her feet.

Felindra shrieked and raised her hands to cover her mouth when she saw what was lying on the ground: A human hand cut off at the wrist. A child's hand. Before she could react, Othran was on the ground, sword drawn.

"That filthy beast. Look what it's done. And you thought it was tame. I'll kill the monster."

Ashala backed away and snarled at Othran, displaying her fangs, dripping with saliva.

"No," Felindra yelled. She threw herself over her friend. "She didn't do this. Let me talk to her and see what happened." She looked pleadingly at her father. "Don't let him hurt her, dadi. Look she's already wounded."

"Most likely by someone trying to protect the child it killed. By the Light, I swear…"

"Wait, Othran, Let's find out what happened before we do anything rash." Daryan came over and looked down at the hand. "This child wasn't killed recently. Look, there's no fresh blood, and it wasn't chewed off by an animal; that's a clean cut. Whatever happened to the poor child didn't happen recently."

"Then what were those screams?" Othran retorted.

"They weren't a child's cries. Let Felindra talk to the wolf and find out what happened."

Tears streamed down Felindra's face as she raised herself from Ashala's body. She saw the blood from the gashes in her fur had slowed to a trickle, so they couldn't be too deep or serious. They looked almost like claw marks. Ashala whined and licked the gashes. Felindra patted her head and rested her hand there. "What happened?" she whispered.

A creature, half man, half demon, carrying a sack over its shoulder. Pulling a curved knife from its belt with a hairy hand. Threatening Ashala. Ashala attacks, biting the arm with the knife. Creature drops sack, which falls open revealing human body parts. A little boy, cut into pieces. Creature attacks Ashala, raking its talon-like claws down her side. Ashala bites it again, shaking her head, fangs digging deep into the flesh, this time and almost severing the arm. Ashala hears Felindra's whistle, grabs one of the body parts and runs.

"Oh, Light save us," Felindra sobbed, feeling as if she was going to be sick.

"What, my sweet? Tell us." Her father put his arm around her and held her. "You have to tell us about it."

Trembling, Felindra falteringly related what she had received from Ashala's mind. She ended by saying, "You see; she didn't do it."

"How do we know she's not making this...?" Othran insisted.

"Enough, Othran!" Now Daryan was angry. "Can she show us where it happened?" he asked gently.

"Can I clean her cuts first?" Felindra asked. "They might get infected."

"All right, but hurry."

Felindra went to her saddlebag and took out a piece of cotton and some antiseptic lotion, and then she inspected the gashes. Ashala had already done a good job of cleaning them with her tongue, but Felindra needed something to occupy her while she calmed down from the shock of what she had witnessed. She poured some of the lotion on the cloth and dabbed it over the wounds. She gently patted the wolf's back. "Good girl. Now, show us the way to that creature!"

Ashala stood up and gave a little whine, and then started towards the trees, looking back once to make sure they were following.

Felindra took her father's hand. She needed comfort. She'd never seen anything so horrifying in her whole life and she was shaken to her core. It had taken all her self-control to avoid vomiting when she saw what Ashala revealed.

When she reached the place, Ashala let out a low moaning howl followed by a growl.

Daryan released his hand. "You stay here with the horses, love. There's no need for you to see this. You can call Ashala to stay with you. All right?"

She nodded, yes. She was glad he'd suggested it. There was no way she wanted to confront that creature or see the grisly remains of its victim. She whistled and Ashala came to her side, poking her nose into Felindra's hand. "Good girl," she murmured and started to cry.

Daryan

"It's alive," Nadi said. "But it's badly hurt."

"Good. Maybe we'll be able to get some answers from it," Daryan replied. He came to the edge of a small shady clearing and stood still, surveying the scene. The ashes of a fire. A sack with what looked like pieces of meat falling from it—that was somebody's child—his eyes filled with tears. *Imagine their pain.* Then he looked at the creature—a werman! What was it doing here? It lay on its side on the opposite edge of the clearing, inching itself towards the bushes as if it hoped to escape. Its right arm was badly mauled, as Felindra had described, almost severed just below the elbow. It whimpered piteously as tried to scramble away, obviously in terrible pain, but it was hard for Daryan to summon any pity for it. He assessed its appearance: about the size of a human ten-year-old; its skin was pale, covered with coarse black hair; it wore a filthy grey loincloth, but was otherwise naked. Its eyes were large and round, black and malevolent. Flat nose, wide mouth, and big ears, an adult male, although Daryan could not bring himself to refer to it as him or he. It snarled at him. "Kill me!"

"Oh no," Daryan replied coldly. "Not until you tell us everything. It's convenient that you know our language; that will make your interrogation easier." He was horrified by what they'd come across. The implications were dire and he needed to send a message to the Monastery as soon as possible.

He moved into the clearing. "Othran, will you tie something around its arm. I don't want it falling off when we move it. Tie its legs together, and watch out for weapons, especially its teeth and nails. Look at those talons!"

"What about its other arm?"

"Put a loop of rope around its neck and tie the other hand to it. That should hold it." He turned away from the clearing. "Wait here; I'm going to get a horse."

After wrapping up the bag with the child's remains and tying it to his saddle, Daryan and Othran rolled the creature into one of their groundsheets—they didn't want anyone to see what they were carrying—and tied it over the back of Felindra's horse. The creature shrieked with pain as they manhandled it, but the cries died down once it was on the horse; it must have lost consciousness.

Felindra rode behind Nadi, he being the lightest, but she had to tell Ashala to stay back because she made Nadi's horse jumpy.

"We'll have to go into Palgrigio and report this to the guardi," Daryan told them. "He'll probably hold on to this creature for us until we can get someone to interrogate it. There was a mage living there a few years back who may be able to help with the interrogation. We'll have to see if he's still there."

"It's going to make us late reaching the DarSolas," Othran said.

"It can't be helped. We'll have to stay the night here. There's a respectable inn where we could stay. We certainly can't carry this thing all the way to the capital. It would probably die on the way and we'd learn nothing."

"What about the wolf? They won't take kindly to us bringing a wolf into town."

"I've thought of that," Daryan said. "There's a healer in town, an old friend of my mother. I would like to leave Felindra and Ashala with her and her husband. I'm sure they'll understand."

Felindra and Nadi had moved in closer to hear the conversation. "You mean I can't stay with you?" Felindra asked.

"No, my darling. We are going to be busy, and you'll be much safer with them. I know they'll make you feel at home. It will be safer for Ashala too. If we left her outside roaming around, someone might put an arrow in her. Lady Isolda was a friend of your grandmother." He added to reassure her that she wasn't being left with complete strangers.

It was twilight by the time they reached Palgrigio and lanterns shone behind many windows and from posts on the streets. They had to cross a bridge to get into the town, but before they crossed, Daryan asked Felindra to put the lead on Ashala and walk with her.

"Keep her quiet," he said. "We'll try to pass her off as a dog."

"Mighty big for a dog," Othran said with a chuckle."

Felindra had tried to walk Ashala a few times on the lead, and the wolf hadn't made too much fuss after the first few tries, but it was clear she didn't like it. "This is to protect us, you and me," she whispered. "We'll take it off as soon as we get inside, I promise."

The town was surrounded by a high brick fence with a massive gate across from the bridge. The gate was already closed, but there were several guards watching from the walkway atop the wall. One shone a lantern on them and called out.

"Halt! State your business."

"We need to report an incident to the guardi," Daryan called back. "And we have a prisoner."

" Who are you?"

"We are emissaries of the League of Light on our way to DarSolas to consult with the Duke of Trethawynd."

"Wait there."

One of the double gates opened just wide enough to allow them to pass through. Daryan stayed back to conduct Felindra through. He watched her cross the ground outside the gates with Ashala walking sedately beside her.

The guard at the gate lifted his lantern. "What in a dark day is that?"

"That is my daughter and her dog."

"Dog, you say! Looks more like a wolf to me."

"Would a wolf be that docile?" Daryan asked. "Believe me she's as gentle as a lamb and makes no trouble. We thought it was a good idea for the girl to have a companion that would protect her and scare off malefactors."

"If you say so." The man scratched his head and stood well back as they passed. "You know how to find the guardi?"

"If it is in the same place it was five years ago."

"Hasn't changed."

"Well then, we'll be on our way. Thank you for opening the gate for us."

"Wait a moment. What about the prisoner you mentioned?"

"Oh, we've got him tied up on one of the horses."

"Oh, well… Go with the Light, sir."

"We'll drop Felindra off first. It's on the way," Daryan announced. He dismounted and led his horse by the reins. "Come on, love, walk with me." He held his free hand out to his daughter. She ran to his side, and he put his arm around her shoulder. "I'm sorry you had to go through this. I know how awful it is for you. I won't be able to stay with you when we get to the healer's house. Explain to them what happened. It might even help you to talk to them about it." He bent and kissed the top of her head.

They turned a corner onto a narrow lane and stopped at square little house with a flat roof. A light showed in the

Vicki Wootton

window. "Good, they're home." He turned to his two companions. "Wait here; I won't be a moment."

They went through the gate in the wall that surrounded a little garden and Daryan knocked on the door. He used a special pattern in the knocking to inform them that their visitors were from the League of Light.

The door was opened by an elderly man with silver hair and a drooping moustache. "Daryan?" he said querulously. "Come in, my boy. And who's this?" he added when he noticed Felindra behind her father.

"Well met, Ferland. This is my daughter, Felindra. Is Lady Isolda home?"

"Yes, come in and I'll fetch her. She's bottling some potions in the back." He turned away, leaving them in the doorway and went to the back room of the cottage.

Isolda, a tiny round woman, her beaming brown face mapped with wrinkles, came bustling to the door. "My dear boy," she cried reaching her arms up to embrace him. "Well met. Didn't Ferland invite you to come in?" she opened the door wider and saw the wolf attached to Felindra by a leather lead. Her eyes rounded and she clapped her hand to her mouth. "Oh, my!"

"She's quite safe, Lady Isolda. This is my daughter, Felindra, with her protector, Ashala. I'm sorry I don't have much time. I came to ask you if they could stay with you for tonight. Something rather dreadful has happened and I have to go and deal with it, so I don't have time to explain."

"Of course she can stay. She's very welcome. What about the wolf?"

"She's family, but I'm not sure if she can handle being indoors. Talk to Felindra about it. We just don't want her walking around frightening people or getting shot at."

"Very well. We'll work something out. You be off now and take care of your business. Your girl will be safe with us. Light guard your way."

84

Daryan

Thankful to have that settled, Daryan hurried to join his two companions. The body wrapped in canvas struggled and moaned miserably.

"It's coming around," Nadi said. "I hope we'll be done with it soon. I don't like the feel of it, or the stink."

"Just a little farther and we can get it off our hands." Daryan remounted his horse. "Speaking of feelings, do you sense anything especially bad about it?"

"Not really. Not the way those people we met on the road felt. My impression is that it's very frightened and in terrible pain."

"Interesting," Dayan said. He'd have to think about that some more. If it was allied to the Dark Brethren, surely Nadi would sense the evil.

They went back to the main street and turned left, then rode for a few more blocks and turned right. The guardi's building was about hallway down. It was a grim-looking structure of grey stone with deep-set windows barred with iron. Daryan dismounted and looped his horse's reins on a post, then banged on the door. Although there was light coming from the window, no one answered the knock. Daryan pushed up the latch, and the door opened into a dimly lit room with two lanterns hanging from the low ceiling. The only furnishings were a battered wooden table piled with papers and several chairs scattered around at random. A pair of scuffed boots lay on the floor by the door, and several chains and manacles hung from hooks on the wall. The guardi was obviously not a man devoted to order.

"Anybody here?" Daryan called.

A rustling sound came from an opening in the wall behind the table, and then a woman's face peered out. "Yes?"

"I need to see the guardi on urgent business," Daryan replied. "Is he here?"

A male voice called out from behind her. "What is it?" The man sounded put out, as if Daryan had interrupted something important; he came to stand behind the woman, tying the laces on his tunic, and scowled at Daryan.

"I have a prisoner outside and have to report a very serious crime. Shall we bring him in?" he deliberately referred to the creature as 'him' rather than 'it', not wanting to set off any alarms before getting it into the building.

"All right," the guardi said grudgingly. "Need any help?"

"No we can manage. Do you have a table or bench we could put him on? He's hurt, and we want to question him."

He heard a brief muted conversation between the guardi and the woman, then a door slammed. The guardi came in through a door at the back of the room. He kicked his boots over to one of the chairs, then sat down to put them on. "Would this do?" he asked, indicating the table covered with papers.

"I'd prefer something more private if you have it."

"Follow me." He rose to his feet with a groan and walked over to the back door. It led into a smaller room with two cells at one end and a bench down the middle about waist high. Hanging from the sides of the bench were four sets of manacles, two on each side. The wood showed signs of a good deal of wear—mainly gouges, brown stains, and scorch marks.

Daryan looked at it with a feeling of revulsion. It wasn't hard to guess its primary use. "Yes, this will suffice. I'll go and bring him in. And I'll need some water and a cup."

"Who are you?" he asked resentfully. The man was getting annoyed at being given orders in his own establishment.

"I'm Daryan Peshanar of the League of Light."

The guardi looked astonished for a second, before resuming his normal disposition, which seemed to be made up mostly of resentment at being asked to do anything.

"Thank you for your help, guardi. I'm sorry to disturb your evening but, as you will soon see, this is a very important matter and couldn't wait."

They untied their prisoner who was howling now and thrashing about. "Be still," Daryan told it. "All this noise and struggling is only making your pain worse. Give me a hand," He added to Othran. "We'll take him inside. Nadi, will you bring the bag?"

When they came through the front door with their prisoner, the guardi took one look and exclaimed, "*Sola Naofa*, what in darkness is that?"

"It's a werman. We suspect it's one of Oglestra's followers; that's what we want to find out."

"I hope you do," the guardi replied. "Do you need any help interrogating hi ... it?" He shook his head in disgust. "That's one of the ugliest specimens I ever laid eyes on. What happened to the arm?"

"He was attacked by a wild animal. We won't need any help, but thank you for offering." Daryan and Othran carried the prisoner into the back room and laid it on the bench. "Manacle its legs," he said to Othran. I'll put this chain around its chest."

The creature started to shriek. "Kill me, kill me...!"

"Oh, we'd like to, but first we are going to find out what you've been up to." Daryan picked up the cup that the guardi had set on the floor and dipped it into the pan of water beside it. He took a small package from the pouch on his belt, opened it and poured the white powder from it into the water. He swilled it around with his finger and went over to the prisoner. "Here, drink this; you must be thirsty from all that shrieking."

The creature began to throw its head from side to side, shouting, "No, no, no...'

"Give me a hand, please Othran," he requested. "Hold its head still, if you can get a grip on it; I'll pinch its nose."

Eventually they got most of the potion inside the creature. After a moment, it stopped moving and just stared at them with an aggrieved expression.

"What did you give it?" Othran asked.

"Just a powder to ease the pain in its arm and calm it down."

"I wouldn't give the thing anything. Let it suffer the way that little boy suffered."

"I want it to stay alive long enough for us to get some information. The way it was thrashing around, it could be dead before we get any answers. Watch it, and don't let that guardi near it. I believe he could be a bit of a loose arrow when he's worked up. I'm going to get the truth-seer now. I won't be long. Bring one of those chairs in if you're getting tired."

Daryan went out to the main room. "Now that's taken care of..." He took the sack from Nadi and handed it to the guardi. "Maybe you can deal with this. We found this with the prisoner."

The guardi opened the neck of the sack and staggered backwards when he caught a whiff of the decaying flesh inside. Then he looked more closely. His shaking hands released sack as if it had stung him, and the child's head rolled out onto the stone floor. Icy currents raced through Daryan's body when he saw this and it took all his self-control to keep from vomiting.

"*Sola Naofa* ... a little boy. How could anyone...? This is monstrous!" His complexion had turned an ashen shade of tan; his face was shiny with sweat.

Daryan felt remorseful about the way he had handled that. "Sit down, my friend, I'm sorry. I should have warned you. It was harsh of me to surprise you like that. May I know your name?"

"Brogal." The guardi took a piece of cotton from his pocket and wiped his face and hands.

"Brogal, have there been any reports of children missing in this area recently?" Daryan asked.

"A few. There always is. Most of them run away from home for one reason or another, but they usually come back once they find out how hard it is to survive out there alone."

"You're going to have to identify this boy so that you can inform his parents, but you know what to do without my telling you. I'll leave that to you. By the way, I would like to know how many children are missing and where they are from, if you can manage it. I want to inform the Council of Mages and the Grand Master at the Monastery. Do you have anyone to help you with the work?

"I've a couple of deputy guardis, and I can get my father to come in and help. He was the chief guardi before me."

"Good. I'm going now to find someone to help us interrogate the prisoner."

10 – Interrogating the Prisoner

Felindra

"Come inside dear, you're shivering. The cook fire is still going. You can get yourself warmed up."

"What about..." Felindra looked at Ashala.

"Bring her in as well, if she'll come."

Felindra knelt down and placed her arm over Ashala's back. "We have a problem," she whispered, envisioning the people around them in the town, the cottage and its closed rooms, a man with a bow shooting at her, Felindra being hungry and needing sleep. She gave an image of herself lying asleep in a bed with Ashala sleeping on the floor beside her. "What shall we do?"

Ashala gave a little whine. *Food.* Then she imagined going out to hunt and coming back, followed by a repeat of Felindra's image of them sleeping side by side.

"Good girl. You can go, but you have to be very quiet and don't let anyone see you." Ashala answered with a little woof and wagged her tail. Felindra patted her on the haunch, "Go on, but come back as soon as you've finished. And no chickens or sheep!"

A dark shadow leaped up on the garden wall and disappeared silently into the night.

I hope I did the right thing, she thought as she entered the cottage and closed the door. "She's hungry," Felindra told the old couple. "She is going to get something to eat, and then she'll come back and sleep."

"I hope she'll be all right," Isolda said.

"She wouldn't attack anyone would she?" Ferland added.

"She'll be all right," Felindra reassured them. "She lives inside the Monastery walls now and I don't think anyone is afraid of her." Felindra thought of the creature they'd found in the woods. Ashala had attacked it, but that was different; it was an enemy and had threatened her with a knife.

"Would you like to wash up, young one?" Isolda asked her.

"Yes please."

"Come with me."

She lit a small lamp opened the only other door and led Felindra into their bedroom. A washbasin and water pitcher stood on one of the chests with a pile of folded cotton towels beside it. "There you are. Come back when you are ready." She left the lamp on the other chest.

Refreshed, Felindra returned to the main room and sat on a chair between the cook fire and a table laden with a bowl of spiced beans, crisp corn bread, a bowl of fresh pineapple chunks and a glass of pale yellowish-green liquid.

"There you are dear, tuck in. That's limewater sweetened with honey in the glass."

Felindra broke off a small piece of bread, scooped up some of the beans with it and put them in her mouth, and then she broke down and cried. She covered her face with her hands and sobbed as if her heart would break, her shoulders shaking. She felt a hand on her back and a cloth being pushed into her hand. She grabbed the cloth and wiped her face, then blew her nose. "I'm sorry," she gasped.

"Dear child, you have nothing to apologize for. I understand you've had a very stressful day," The old lady's voice was soft and soothing. "Maybe talking about it might help. Do you want to tell me what happened?"

"I c-can't t-talk about it," she stammered. "It's t-too ... awful." She was shaken by another shuddering sob. She wiped her eyes again. *That little boy,* she thought, *that poor little boy.* She was sure that image would live in her mind for the rest of her life. *How can you forget something like that?* She tried some of the limewater, then another piece of bread dipped in beans, but she couldn't eat any more. "I'm sorry," she said. "I'm not hungry. Thank you for...."

"I can see you're exhausted. Why don't you come and lie down on the pallet? We can talk in the morning, if you're up to it." She led Felindra to the small bed on the other side of the room and pulled back the blanket. "Let me help you get your boots off."

Once Felindra was lying down, the woman pulled the soft wool blanket up over her shoulders. Before she left her, she asked. "What about when your friend comes back?"

"She won't make any noise. She may just scratch the door. I can let her in."

"Very well. May the Light bring you pleasant dreams, child." She stooped and kissed Felindra on the forehead.

Daryan

Daryan walked to the corner and turned right. There were more lanterns illuminating the main street, so it was easier for him to see his way. His stomach grumbled, and he realized none of them had eaten anything since their noontime stop. He brushed the feeling aside. Who could eat anything anyway, after what they'd seen today. He'd only walked a dozen paces when he saw someone walking towards him, a tall slim man with a billowing cloak. As the man approached a street lamp, he saw a light flash from something shiny and round on the cloak. A medallion, maybe? He walked a bit faster to meet him.

"Ashavan, is that you?"

"None other," the man replied in a pleasant baritone.

"I might have known you'd get the drop on me. Well met, old friend." The two men grasped each other's forearms in a greeting between friends.

"Likewise, Daryan. How are things with you?"

"On the whole, everything was going splendidly, that is until today. How much have you picked up?"

"Not much; only that you are here and need my help."

"Well I hope you're prepared for a shock." Daryan filled Ashavan in on the details as they walked back to the guardis' building.

Inside, Ashavan took off his cloak, folded it carefully and put it over the back of one of the chairs after wiping it first with a piece of cotton from his belt pouch. Ashavan had always been a sharp dresser, and tonight was no exception. He was wearing a deep turquoise tunic embroidered in gold thread over gold-colored trousers tucked into shiny black boots. He was a handsome man, tall and slim with a narrow nose, wide mouth, usually tilted in a smile, and dark, deep-set eyes. His dark brown, ear-length hair was now tinged with silver, which seemed only to enhance his good looks. At the moment, however, he was not smiling.

He grimaced and put his fingertips to his temples. "Ouch, that is a very nasty piece of work you've captured. Let's get this over with, Daryan. Lead on!"

Ashavan's talent was hard to fit into any of the usual categories of gifts. Basically, he was a telepath, but he could also pick up strong emotional currents, and once he latched onto one of these currents, he was able to put it into context by reading the circumstances surrounding the emotions. It was unfortunate for him that most of what he picked up was negative in nature, hatred, rage, fear, the cunningness of greed, the grinding resentment of envy. That is one of the reasons he'd chosen to live in this out-of-the-way community. On the whole, it was peaceful and once he'd become immune to the occasional drunken brawls and family conflicts, his life was fairly tranquil.

"Before we go in, I have a caution. I'd like to preserve this creature if possible. It's been a long time since we got hold of one, and we might be able to make use of it, if we could get it to the Monastery. Do you think you could help us with that?"

"I'll see what I can do."

His face screwed up in distaste when he saw the creature lying on the table. He took a pair of thin leather gloves from his belt and pulled them on, and then he went to the head of the bench. "Well, well, my wily little friend, what have you been up to? Have you been a naughty boy?"

Shrivel up and die in agony. My master will suck the marrow from your bones.

"My, my, that's not very nice." He put his gloved hands on the sides of the creature's head. "Now let's see what you've got inside this nasty little skull besides maggots, shall we?"

Kill me and get it over with, you rotting carcass.

"Oh, no, you're not getting off that easily." While the creature wasn't speaking or thinking standard Albasinian, Ashavan was able to understand the meaning behind the words that went through his mind by the emotions and images that accompanied them.

I no say.

"We'll see about that."

Don't think, don't think, don't think... bless the Master, bless the Master, don't think, don't think...

"That's not going to do you any good. What's your name?"

Nothing, nothing, nothing....

"I guess you must be too low to have a name. Only important people have names, don't they, and you aren't important; nobody cares about you, as you say, you're nothing."

I not nothing... I...

"If you are not nothing, then who are you?"

Axtya. I no say more.

Ashavan reached over and poked the injured arm. Axtya screamed. "I'd wager you would like to have something done about that arm. It must hurt a lot."

Tainted wolf! Fall into pit, you ... Wait 'til Master...my arm, my arm...

"What's this vaunted master of yours going to do against the Children of Light? He doesn't even have enough power to conquer our cattle."

You not know what he got. Our time come soon; you wait, you be sorry. We have all world and turn off Light forever. Master know what he doing.

"What, murdering helpless little children? That's for cowards and scum like you. Your master is nothing but a weakling and a coward. He will never win against the power of the Light."

You not know what he can do. He found new... Shut up, shut up, shut up...!

"What, a secret weapon?"

No, no, no. Shut up, shut up.… Pain, powerful burning throbbing pain.… *Leave me! Can't bear* .… *"Oooow."*

Ashavan winced and rubbed his right arm. "He's experiencing a lot of pain, I don't think we can go on with this much longer," he said to Daryan.

"Come over here," Daryan replied. They walked across to the farthest corner of the room. "Did you get anything useful?" he asked in a low voice.

"I'm not sure. He's getting desperate and the pain is beginning to cloud his mind. There's something about his Master, and I think he was hinting about a secret weapon, but I don't know what he meant."

"Do you think I should give it some more painkiller?"

"It might help, but then again, it might knock him out altogether. He's getting very weak."

"Try a bit longer while he's still conscious."

"Very well. But *I* may not be able to tolerate the pain much longer. It's quite fierce."

Back at the creature's head, he asked, "How would you like to be rid of that pain?"

Pain … bad, bad. Kill me…! He started to moan, then howl, rising to a piercing shriek.

"We can stop the pain, Axtya, and get a healer for your arm. Just tell me what your leader is planning.

No, no, no… Not know. Axtya screamed and started to thrash about, then stopped abruptly and lay still.

Ashavan put his gloved finger on the prisoner's neck and felt for a pulse.

"Sorry, I've lost him; he's still alive, though."

"All right. Let's all go outside and breathe some fresh air. We'll talk about what we can do." Daryan led the way to the door.

"The prisoner's passed out," Daryan informed the guardi. "We're going out for some fresh air. Please don't touch it, but let us know if you hear anything. By the way, I'm sure the League will compensate you for the extra work." *That should encourage him to cooperate.*

"Any comments? Ashavan?" he said.

"He's weak. If you don't do something about that arm, you're going to lose him completely."

"Why do you keep saying 'him'? He's not a person; he's just a thing." Othran said.

"I've been in his mind, Othran. He is a person, just not our kind of person."

"As far as I'm concerned, anything that kills and eats children is no better than an animal."

"Let's stay on topic, brothers." Daryan said gently. "What are we going to do with him?"

"Leave him to the guardi," Othran said.

"We could take him up to the Monastery," Ashavan suggested. "If he could survive the journey"

"That's what I think," Daryan said. "But first we have to do something about that arm. I think I'll get the healer to look at it."

"Why take him to the Monastery?" Nadi asked.

"They could operate on him in the infirmary and where he has a better chance to stay alive. We might be able to find a use for him if we can get him to work for us. I believe we can get a lot more information from him." He looked at his two traveling companions. "I know you're tired, so I suggest you go to the inn and get some supper and sleep. I'll take first watch with the prisoner. I'll come and wake you in three hours, Othran, to take over from me."

"Would you like me to stay with you for a while?" Ashavan asked.

"Yes, please. And there's something else I'd like you to do for us."

Ashavan and Daryan went back into the guardi's building. "Would you like to get some rest, Guardi? I'm going to stay and guard the prisoner. What did you do with the evidence, by the way?"

"I put the child's remains in an empty food locker until I can find the parents." The guardi seemed to resent Daryan referring to slaughtered child as evidence. He yawned and stood up. "Are you hungry?" he asked.

"I could certainly use a bite to eat, and something to drink," Daryan replied.

"All I've got is bread and cheese, and some wine."

"That would be very satisfactory," Daryan responded.

"I'll look in on Axtya," Ashavan said, following the guardi to the inner door.

Ashavan returned seconds later. "He's still out, but he is alive."

"Good. Let's sit down," Daryan suggested, pulling a chair over to the table.

The guardi returned with a chunk of cheese and a pile of flatbread on a pottery plate, and a large mug of wine. He pushed aside some papers on the table and put them in the space he'd cleared.

"I think I'll turn in now. It looks to be a busy day tomorrow," he said

Daryan reached into his pouch and pulled out a small gold coin. "Here, take this as a down payment on your compensation. And thank you for the food. I really appreciate your taking the trouble."

After the guardi had left, he pulled out a knife from his belt, cut a slice of cheese and rolled it in a piece of bread, then popped them in his mouth and chewed. Then he tried the wine and drank about half the mug. "Do you want anything?" he asked Ashavan, pointing at the food.

"No, thanks. I had a good supper before I left. What was it you wanted me to do?"

"I need to send a couple of messages. Do we still have a communication link in DarSolas?"

"Yes. I was talking with her only today."

"Good. I need to let the Duke know I've been delayed. Tell them there's been an accident, lame horse or something, and we'll not be arriving until late tomorrow. I don't want them to know about this situation."

"Don't tell me there's someone at the castle you don't trust." Ashavan said with a sardonic smile.

"Let's say I have reservations about the Lord Chancellor."

"Ah, yes. Lord Gremulkin. I think you may have cause. I've not been close to him, but I sense an air of ... shall we say malevolence? What else?"

Daryan nodded agreement. "I also want to send a message to Archmage Plavan. Tell him everything that's happened and ask his advice. If he thinks we should bring this ... our prisoner in, we'll need him to send someone with the gift of conviction. We don't want anyone to see us transporting the prisoner, or know where we are taking ... him. Oh, and tell them he'll need to get a healing team ready to take care of his arm. They'll probably have to amputate it; I don't see any way it could be saved, even with magic."

"What are you going to do with him until he reaches the Monastery? He needs urgent medical attention soon or he'll die."

"I'll get the healer to come and see what she can do. My daughter is staying with her tonight."

"And the wolf?"

"You don't miss much, do you?" Daryan smiled at his friend. "She's with Felindra."

"I'll go and get started on your messages. I'll do the Monastery first and tell you what they say." He moved one of the chairs over to the far side of the room, then pulled a small drawstring bag from under the neck of his tunic and emptied an orange and pink crystal into his palm.

Daryan ate the rest of the bread and cheese and drank the remaining wine, after which, he stood up and stretched. He was tired and knew if he sat still for any length of time, he'd fall asleep. He went to the inner door and looked in on the prisoner. The smell in the room was breathtakingly awful, a blend of excrement, sweat and decaying flesh. The creature looked so pitiful, lying there on the slab with his mutilated arm resting on his abdomen. His body was emaciated and his hair matted, showing patches of bluish-white skin underneath. Ashavan was right; this was a person. He felt remorse for his earlier attitude. He knew it had been his reaction to their terrible discovery. He ... Axtya, probably had a family, maybe even a wife and children. He didn't look very old, but it was hard to tell with such an alien creature who was about the size of a ten-year-old human child.

Daryan began to think about the werfolk. How had they become the way they were? Were they intrinsically evil, or had they been ensorcelled and corrupted by the evil Oglestrians, the Dark Brethren? He scratched his forehead and yawned. It would take wiser heads than his to puzzle that out. Nevertheless, he knew the werfolk and those who controlled them had long been a bane to the Children of Light. The battle had been going on for countless years, time beyond memory and written records.

The prisoner groaned and moved his head from side to side. His legs twitched and he frowned, then his eyes opened. He groaned again and moved his mouth as if he was trying to moisten it.

"Are you thirsty?" Daryan asked.

Axtya looked puzzled.

"Do you want a drink?" He mimed putting a cup to his lips.

"Water?"

"Yes, water."

Daryan removed another paper-wrapped package from his pouch and knelt on the floor to fill the mug from the pan. He emptied the white powder in and swilled it around. Although he was loath to touch the prisoner, he forced himself to put his arm under his neck and raise his head. "Here, water," he said, holding the mug to Axtya's mouth.

Most of it went down his throat, although a little spilled down his neck. Once the mug was empty, Daryan lowered his head. He watched the prisoner lying with his eyes closed and saw the muscles of his face relax as the drug took effect. He put the mug back on the floor and went out to the main room to see if Ashavan had anything for him.

"I'm waiting for them to wake up Plavan. I got the message to Avaya; she says she'll deliver it in the morning. You look exhausted. Why don't you try to take a nap while we're waiting?"

"I may do just that," he replied. He pulled another chair over to face one by the wall. He sat on one, his head resting on the wall behind him, and propped his feet up on the other. It was far from comfortable, but it was the best he could hope for this night.

***

Daryan awoke with a start and looked around. It took a few seconds for him to recognize where he was. Ashavan was standing in the open doorway, allowing a cool breeze to enter and clear the air.

"Did you get a reply from the Monastery?" Daryan asked.

"Oh, you're awake. Yes. Plavan agrees with your plan to bring the werman in. He's going to send down a team to take him up to the Monastery. They should be here in about five hours."

Daryan blew out a breath of relief. "Did I sleep long?"

"About two hours."

Daryan stood up and stretched. "Would you mind staying a little while longer? I have to go and wake up Othran to come and replace me. I gave the prisoner a potion, so you shouldn't have any trouble with him."

"No, go ahead."

After waking Othran and sending him on his way, Daryan bathed as best he could with a bowl of water and some towels, then he lay down on a bed and fell asleep.

Felindra

Felindra didn't remember letting her in, but when she awoke the next morning Ashala was asleep on the floor beside the pallet, her muzzle resting on the blanket near her hand. As soon as she realized Felindra was awake, she stood up and wagged her tail. Felindra sat up and wiped her bleary eyes with her knuckles, then swung her feet over onto the floor and patted the wolf. "You are a very good girl," she whispered.

Ashala licked her hand.

"You're awake," Isolda said. "I've only just woken myself, but Ferland is still snoring. How do you feel?"

"A bit better, thank you, lady. May I use your refresher?"

"Of course, dear. Out the door and around to the left."

By the time Felindra returned, Isolda had the fire stoked in the fireplace and a pot of water heating up.

"I'm going to cook some rice with dates and cream. Think you could eat some?"

"Yes, thank you. I'm starving."

Isolda gave her a glass of buttermilk to drink, then went to work on the breakfast. She chatted away as she bustled around, talking about the town, her healing, and her grandchildren. Felindra was grateful for the chatter. It required very little from her, and it distracted her from things she didn't want to think about.

Felindra and Isolda sat down at the table with their bowls of rice. The thick cream was in one bowl on the table and the dates in another, waiting to be added to the rice. Ferland poke his head around the door. "Mind if I join you?" he asked.

"Come in, man, and sit yourself down. I'll get you a bowl of rice." She made as if to stand up.

"Stay where you are, woman. I have hands, and they still work. I can serve myself." He winked at Felindra as he went over to the pot and picked up a bowl.

Felindra smiled. She assumed this was some personal routine they'd fallen into over the years. *People are so amazing in their different ways*, she thought.

"One thing I've been wondering," Ferland said as he put some butter on his rice. "About you and the wolf. How did that come about?"

Felindra told them about the journey to the Monastery and how she met Ashala.

"So you're a Whisperer?" he said. "That is truly remarkable. We haven't seen one in these parts in … in my lifetime, and that's a long time. My parents never mentioned any either, how about you Is?

"No, it must be at least a hundred years since the last Whisperer died," his wife replied. "You are a very special girl. You must take very good care of yourself, although I have a feeling that there will be many creatures looking out for you. Word spreads among the animals, you know."

'How did you first notice you could communicate with animals?" Ferland asked.

"It was on the road. I could tell when I touched one of our horses that she was not feeling well. She had a pain in her stomach."

"So what happened yesterday?"

"Ferland, maybe she doesn't feel like talking about it."

"It's all right," Felindra assured them.

She gave them a brief account of the events leading up to their arrival in Palgrigio, stumbling once when she got to the child's hand. "I wonder where my father is," she said when she'd finished. "He must be in a hurry to get on the road. We lost almost a whole day yesterday and the duke is expecting him."

"He'll be along," Isolda assured her. "I've known your father since he was a little boy, and if there's one quality that shines in his makeup, it's his devotion to the Light and defending His children. He will not allow yesterday's atrocity to go without redress. He'll be here as soon as he's able. He was probably tired after taking care of that business."

Daryan

When he awoke a couple of hours later, Daryan went directly from the inn to Isolda and Ferland's cottage. He felt much better now that he'd had some sleep. It looked as if the sun had risen within the last half hour; the sky was already changing from yellow to blue. The air smelled so fresh, it was a balm after events of yesterday, but he knew the freshness wouldn't last as the air heated up and the humidity rose.

Felindra, who must have been watching for him from the window, opened the door as soon as he was through the gate. She rushed out and hugged him, resting her head against his chest. "Are we ready to go?" she asked.

"Not yet. I still have a few things to clear up," he explained, kissing the top of her head. "How was your night?"

"I had a lovely sleep, and Ashala was very good. She didn't get into any trouble."

"That's good news. How are you holding up, my sweet?"

Felindra shrugged. "I still feel awful, but not quite as bad as yesterday."

"It will take time, but you *will* get over it, I promise you. And you know you can always talk to me about it." He gave her a hug and another kiss. "I have to speak to Isolda and Ferland for a moment. Where's Ashala?"

"She's sleeping under Ferland's fig tree. I told her not to go away."

"All right. I'm going to talk to Isolda now."

Once the courtesies were completed and he was seated with a mug of cold buttermilk and some sweet rolls in front of him, Daryan explained what he required of the couple.

After telling Isolda what he needed from her, he turned to Ferland. "I seem to recall you have the gift of conviction; is that so?"

"It is only a secondary gift and not very powerful," he replied.

"My wife has the same. Now, there will be various people at the guardi's building today who will have to be convinced that we weren't there and there was no prisoner. Do you think you could convince them?"

"I can try. This is important, yes?"

"It would be better if no one knew we had him, and in addition, we don't want anyone tracking them to the secret entrance. We have a defender with conviction coming to protect them while they travel to the monastery."

Ferland sighed. "I understand." He turned to his wife. "I think we should take the good guardi some of your summer wine, don't you, love?"

"That sounds like a good idea," she replied with a wink.

"Do you mind waiting here for a little while longer?" Daryan asked Felindra. "I promise you we'll be back in less than an hour."

"All right, dadi, but don't forget about Ashala. I don't know how long she'll stay asleep; she'll be restless when she wakes up."

"I know, Felindra; I will hurry."

Carrying the healer's case, he led the couple back to the guardi's building. When they arrived, Ashavan was gone, but two younger men, probably his deputies, had joined the guardi. The addition of Daryan and his two companions made the room seem crowded.

"Guardi," Daryan said, would you join me and Lady Isolda in the back room, please?"

Without waiting for an answer, he led Isolda through the inner door. The guardi followed, shutting the door behind him. He noticed Isolda fanning her hands and wrinkling her nose at the smell.

"Lady Isolda is going to take a look at the prisoner's arm," he said to the guardi. "I've been in touch with the Monastery, and they are sending a team to pick him up this morning. They should be here before long. I want to make it very clear that neither you nor your men are to tell anyone about this incident other than that we found the boys remains. Nothing about any prisoner. We are handling a very delicate investigation that could have repercussions throughout Trethawynd if this gets out. There are forces at work who seek to destroy the Children of Light, and we are trying to prevent that."

"I understand, sir. We are always happy to cooperate with the Monastery." He took out a rag and wiped his face. "Are we really in danger from the Dark Brethren?"

"There have been incidents and signs that they are on the move again, but it hasn't progressed very far yet. We want to stop this before it gets worse, and this prisoner may be one way to a solution. That's why we have to keep him hidden."

"I see. Is there anything else you need from me, sir?"

"Just keep everyone out of here until he's gone."

"I'll find something for them to do, don't you worry, sir."

"Hold on, I want to give you the rest of your compensation." He took four more coins from his pouch and handed them to the Guardi. "You've been very helpful, Guardi. Oh, I'd suggest you share some of that with your two men. And what about the young lady we saw last night? Was that your wife?"

The guardi looked a bit sheepish. "No, sir. She left right after you arrived. Well, if there's nothing else, I'll go and set the lads to work." He left, closing the door quietly behind him.

Daryan turned to see what the healer was doing. She had peeled away the rag that been used to wrap the injured arm and was swabbing the wound with some soft cotton.

"This is a disgrace," she said. "He is filthy. It's no wonder it's infected. He'll probably lose his arm. By the way, he seems to be sleeping well. Did you give him something?"

"I gave him a potion a few hours ago, powder of the poppy. I thought it would keep him from injuring himself."

"You can't fool me, young Daryan; I know your soft heart. You didn't want him to suffer. The pain must have been excruciating. It's a wonder he's alive. Your girl tells me her wolf did this."

"I'm afraid so, but she's not normally vicious. She had a just cause. He attacked her with a knife."

"I know, she told me." She spread green ointment over the damaged skin with a flat strip of wood wrapped in cloth. "There, that should clean it up a bit, but he will still lose the arm. I'll leave that up to the healers up top. I'll wrap some clean cotton around it and put a band around him to immobilize the arm, but that's all I can do." She finished working on the prisoner and started packing away her equipment. "Somebody should clean him up a bit. He's in a disgusting state."

"I don't have time, Lady Isolda. And I don't want any of those men out there near him." He picked up her case and led her to the door. "Let's see what everyone is up to."

The two deputies had gone and the guardi was sitting with his feet up on the table, reading a sheaf of papers. "I sent them to gather information about missing children. It should keep them busy until *that's* gone." He ducked his head towards the inner door.

"We're finished. I have to go now; I'm already a day late at the castle. I'm going to leave a Lieutenant Othran here until the team arrives from the Monastery. I thank you. You've been an enormous help, Guardi. This could have got out of hand and created a very nasty situation if you hadn't handled it so well and kept it quiet. Light be with you."

"Likewise, sir." He swung his feet down to the floor and followed Daryan to the door where Isolda and Ferland stood waiting with Othran and Nadi.

"Othran, I'd like you to stay here until the team arrives from up the hill, then you can follow after us to DarSolas. Nadi, would you mind collecting our horses and bringing them to the healer's house. I'm going to walk there with Isolda and Ferland."

Othran sat down on the step of the guardi's building looking gloomy and Nadi rushed off towards the stables.

"How did it go with the wine?" Daryan asked.

"I gave them a good serving each and had a talk with them. I may have convinced them that nothing out of the ordinary happened today. Do you think I should come back later? I could say I'm here to pick up the empty cask."

"Whatever you think, Ferland. I trust your judgment. If the team from the Monastery arrives and departs before the deputies come back, there'll be no problem."

When they arrived back at the cottage, Felindra was sitting on the doorstep with Ashala lying at her feet.

"Are you ready to go?" he asked.

"Very," she replied. "I'm starting to get sleepy again."

"Would you ask Ashala if she would find a way to get out of the town without being seen and meet us farther up the road? I'd like her to keep out of sight until we're clear of the area. There are too many people around and I don't want anyone panicking."

"I think she could. She went out to hunt last night and came back without any trouble."

After Felindra had communicated with her, Ashala jumped onto the wall and took off silently into the bushes behind the little house.

As soon as Nadi brought their three horses, they secured their packs and mounted. They waved goodbye to the old couple and turned towards the town gate and the bridge across the river.

"I hope I didn't forget anything," Daryan said. "I was so tired."

11 – Visit to Cavalcitas

Daryan

When they reached the outskirts of DarSolas, Daryan led them off the side of the road and stopped under a tree near a stream. The horses were let loose to drink and graze while they ate a late lunch. Othran caught up with them while they were there. He reported that the prisoner had been dispatched to the Monastery without any trouble. By the time they were ready to go on, the sun was closing in on the western horizon; it would be dark within the hour.

"I don't think we should stay at one of the regular inns in the town," Daryan said. "I'd rather not publicize our presence too broadly. I'm going to take us to the home of an old friend to see if we can stay there with him. It may mean sleeping on the floor or in the stable, but I prefer to be cautious until we know how things stand."

They turned off highroad onto a minor road that went westward around the northern edge of the city. After a while, they turned north into an unpaved track through some woodland. Eventually they reached a log palisade with a wide, solid gate. Since the gate was open and unguarded, they rode into the packed-earth courtyard. Three children between nine and thirteen years came running down the steps from the veranda of the sprawling adobe house that stood at the back of the yard. It was hard to tell whether the children were girls or boys as they all wore the same short trousers and tunics and had long hair flying our behind them. They rushed towards the visitors followed by three dogs, scattering a flock of chickens across the yard.

A woman standing at the top of the veranda steps, silhouetted by the light from inside was watching them. She descended the steps and went to the fence behind the house where she called to someone, and then she came to meet them.

"Well met" shouted the eldest child upon reaching them.

"Do we know you?" asked the youngest.

"Well met, all of you. We are friends of your father. Is he here?" Daryan said as he dismounted.

"He's in the back field with the horses," the eldest informed them, looking sideways at Felindra.

The rest of their party also dismounted and waited for the woman to reach them.

"Well met," she greeted them. "Have you come about the horses? I've told my husband you're here."

"No. I'm Daryan Peshanar, a friend of Andro from the Monastery."

The woman's face lit up with a smile. "Yes, he's spoken of you many times. Very well met, welcome to our home. Would you like to come into the house?"

"We would, but is there somewhere we could make the horses comfortable?"

"Of course. If you take them to the stable over there, the stableman will help you." She pointed to a long, low brick building on their left.

Just as they were moving towards the stable a tall man in riding clothes appeared from around the back of the house. "Ho, there!" he called. "By the Light, is that Daryan?" he broke into a run. When he arrived, out of breath, he grabbed Daryan by the forearms. "What are you doing here? I thought you'd settled down near Salispon. But welcome, welcome." Then he stopped and took a deep breath. "I still talk too much, as you no doubt can noticed."

"It's good to see you too, Andro, and hear you." Daryan replied with a smile. "A lot has been happening in the last few months. I'll tell you more when we get the horses settled. We were just taking them to the stable."

"Let me help you." He turned to his wife, "Valina, my sweet, why don't you take this young lady up to the house. We'll see to the horses. Is this your daughter, Daryan?"

"Yes this is Felindra."

"She's beautiful; you must be very proud of her," Andro said. "I see you've met my noisy trio."

Felindra walked over to her father and pulled him aside. "Are you going to tell them about Ashala, or shall I"

"I'll tell Andro and see how he takes it."

"I hope she'll be able to find us," Felindra said.

"Don't worry, dear girl, she'll show up. She's probably sharing her news with every wolf in the area."

"And gathering news for us."

"That too. Run along with Lady Valina, I'll catch up with you."

"Problems?" Andro asked.

"There may be, but I hope not."

"Sherdon! Are you in there?" Andro yelled as they reached the stable doorway.

A short man with a leather apron emerged from the darkness of the interior. "Yes, sir?"

"How many times have I told you to forget the 'sir' nonsense and call me Andro?"

"Sorry, sir... I mean Andro."

"Good. That's better. Can you help my guests settle their horses?"

"Very well, sir ... um ... Andro."

"Sherdon is new here," Andro explained, "Hasn't got used to my ways yet. My other man—he'd been with me for years—left to get married, if you can believe it, at his age!"

"I didn't know there was an age limit on marrying," Daryan replied.

"I'm surprised he can still..." he stopped, glancing around to make sure the children weren't within earshot. "You know what I mean. He must have all of seventy years. The new wife wanted to live near her children down in Algonia...." he stopped talking and looked apologetically at the visitors. "There I go again. You should stop me when I start to carry on." He slapped Daryan on the shoulder and turned towards the stable. "This way."

Daryan and the two men unbuckled the saddles straps and took them off, then removed the harnesses, and led the four horses inside.

"Leave them; Sherdon and the boys can do the rest. Come into the house, supper must be almost ready."

"You look as if you're doing well," Daryan commented, glancing around.

"Well enough. There's always a market for good horse stock."

"Do you specialize in any specific breed?"

"Mostly riding horses, but I've been getting some requests for warhorses lately. I'm thinking of buying a breeding pair of Destriers, if I can find any. Do you think there's a war coming?"

"Something's in the wind, but I'm not sure it will involve much traditional warfare. I'll tell you about it later. Before we go in, there's something else I should tell you."

"That sounds ominous. Good news, I hope."

"Oh yes, very good." Daryan smiled. "My daughter, Felindra, has a very rare gift. She recently discovered she's a Whisperer."

"That's wonderful. You must be very proud. How old is she?"

"She has thirteen years, fourteen in autumn. There's a catch, though. She's adopted a female wolf. They're inseparable, go everywhere together."

"Are you about to tell me she's brought the animal with her?"

"Well, yes."

Instead of being upset, Andro slapped his thigh and let out a loud laugh.

"What's so funny about that?"

"My best friend comes to visit me after how many years and brings a wolf with him! Is there anything else I should know? It's not going to eat all my poultry, is it? Or does it prefer young foals?"

"Nothing like that. She's a remarkable animal. Felindra saved her life and now she won't leave her side. She does everything Felindra tells her. She's been living inside the Monastery walls for more than two weeks, if you can believe that, and we haven't heard any complaints. If Felindra tells her you're a friend of her family—family seems to be important to the wolf—and not to kill any of your animals, she won't touch them, and she might even protect them from other predators. Yesterday, she discovered and helped us apprehend a murderous werman."

"She sounds like a super-wolf," Andro replied. "Where is she now?"

"She's around somewhere. Probably stopped off for a rest somewhere. We've ridden all the way from Palgrigio today. She'll let Felindra know when she's near, so don't be surprised if you hear her howl. I think Felindra has taught her not to hunt anywhere near people, so if she catches the scent of your family, she won't touch your livestock. You'd better warn your stable hands though; we don't want her frightening them off. Although I don't know how she will deal with the dogs, I'm sure she won't harm them."

"Amazing. Sounds very useful. Let's go in and eat something," Andro said, grasping Daryan's arm above the elbow. "I'll tell them after."

Felindra

After a supper of grilled chicken and fresh garden vegetables, Andro's two youngest children were sent to bed, and the grown-ups settled around the fireplace to talk about recent events.

Felindra went outside and walked around the perimeter of the homestead. She whistled a couple of times for Ashala, but received no response. *She'll come,* she reassured herself, but she was worried. It was now quite dark and thousands of stars sparkled in the heavens above. A blue-white sickle moon rose over the wooded hilltop, giving a little light. She heard the snort of a horse and followed the sound to the back of the house. A wide, low gate separated the stable yard from a meadow. Several horses stood near the gate. Their ears pricked up when they heard her approach and one whinnied. She climbed up onto the lowest bar of the gate and leaned over.

"Ho, horses!" she called softly. She plucked a tuft of grass from the edge of the wall and held it out to the nearest horse. It snorted and accepted her gift, crunching it into pulp before swallowing it. When Felindra stroked its neck, she sensed its mood of perfect contentment. Suddenly, all five horses tensed with their ears on alert and turned in the direction of the wooded hill. Then she heard the soft wolf call. With snorts and whinnies, the horses turned and galloped off in the opposite direction, down to the bottom of the meadow.

Felindra ran across the yard towards the main gate, whistling a couple of times. She heard a soft bark on the other side of the palisade. "Ashala! Follow me," she called. The gate was now closed and barred and she knew the bar holding it shut was too heavy for her to lift. "I'm here, sweet girl," she murmured. "Wait for me, I'll come and get you. Stay!" she hoped Ashala would understand her without the touching. The wolf made a little whining sound. *I'll have to get someone to open the gate,* she thought, walking away. She saw light glowing from the stable entrance. *Looks as if somebody is still here.*

As she walked across the yard towards the stable, a figure appeared in the doorway carrying a lantern. "Can you help me open the gate?" she called. *How am I going to convince whoever it is to allow a wolf into the compound?*

The door of the house opened letting out more light and Felindra saw her father and Andro descending the steps and walking towards her.

"Is there a problem?" Andro called.

"My... Ashala is here. I want to let her in."

"It's all right, Sherdon, I can handle this."

"Right, sir." The man gave him a curious look and went back into the stable.

"I have a lead for her." Felindra showed him the heavy leather strap. "I don't think she needs it, but..."

"Don't worry, Andro, she'll be fine, I guarantee it," Daryan reassured his friend. "Once she gets your scent and sees you with us, she'll add you to her 'pack'."

"That's reassuring," Andro replied drily. "All right, are we ready?"

When he opened a gap in the gate, Ashala stood still on the other side instead of rushing in. She whined softly, sensing the nervousness of the strange man. "There you are," Felindra cried, dashing out to hug her. "I've been wondering where you'd got to." Then she knelt beside the wolf, put her hand on her neck and whispered to her. Ashala gave a short yip and lowered her head to allow Felindra to fasten the lead. "We're ready," Felindra said. "May I bring her in now?"

"What did you say her name is?" Andro asked.

"Ashala," Felindra replied.

"Well met, Ashala. Welcome to my home." With that, he stood back to make room for them to enter.

There was a brief discussion about where Felindra and the wolf would sleep as they sauntered towards the house with Ashala attempting to make a thorough snuffling investigation of the ground as they went.

Daryan

Daryan and the other two men had been allotted a small room to sleep in at the end of the house. Valina had placed a pitcher of water and a bowl on a chest for them with a few towels. She'd also lain three pallets and blankets on the floor, and left a lantern hanging from a hook on the wall.

As they were preparing for sleep, Othran turned to Daryan. "I almost forgot, I have a message for you from Ashavan. He came back after you left and asked me to tell you this. He said 'while you were traveling to DarSolas, you came across evidence of a foul crime, a sack containing the body of a child. Suspecting the culprits might be wermen, you decided to investigate'. Why do you need to know this?"

"He sent a message to the castle for me telling them we'd be delayed and I told him to make up something as a reason for the delay. He wanted to make sure we were telling the same story, I suppose. That was clever of him; it is the truth about what happened, but without too many details. Now I can elaborate on it as I see fit if the duke asks. Incidentally, I don't want anyone at the castle to know we apprehended the killer. It's better to keep him and his whereabouts to ourselves for the time being. And be careful what you say around the chancellor. I'm not sure we can trust him."

Felindra

When her father and Othran came in, Felindra was sitting with Andro's children at the big table in the kitchen eating some beans with flatbread and cheese while Valina worked on a table nearby, kneading some dough to bake into bread. Felindra gave a gasp of surprise when she saw her father. Both he and Othran were wearing their formal defender regalia: dark blue fitted leggings tucked into shiny black boots, white tunics with gold braid around their stand-up collars, and white capes lined with blue satin. The emblem of the League of Light was embroidered on their tunics. Each man had a sword in a polished leather scabbard attached to his belt.

"My, you do look splendid," Valina said with a smile. "I haven't seen Andro in his regalia in years. I wonder if it will still fit him. Will you break your fast before leaving?"

"Thank you, lady." Daryan looked out of the window; the sun was up, but barely over the tops of the trees on the hill. "You are most gracious; we would be delighted, but not too much food, we don't have a lot of time."

She brought a basket of bread and two platters containing sliced meat and cheese to the table, adding a pitcher of summer wine and some mugs.

"By the grace of the Light, we bless this food, and bless this house and all who dwell in it." Daryan said, picking up a knife and tucking in.

12 – Meeting at the Castle

Daryan

It took them a little over an hour to reach the castle by the coast road that ran along the west side of DarSolas. The sparkling blue green of the ocean on their right as they rode down the highway created a feeling of tranquility for which Daryan was grateful. He wasn't looking forward to this meeting. They rode up the ramp that wound around the rocky crag upon which the castle was built until they reached the outer gate. The commander of the guard was waiting for them in his grey and red uniform when they reached it.

"Well met, sirs. I will inform His Grace of your arrival. Follow me."

"Thank you, commander." Daryan replied. He dismounted and handed his reins to the waiting stable hand.

"This way," the commander said, turning towards the bridge across the moat.

Once they'd crossed the bridge, they went under the open portcullis through the inner wall into a large courtyard, and then up a flight of stone stairs and through the main portal of the castle, two massive doors intricately carved with scenes from the history of the duke's family. They then continued along a stone-paved corridor to another set of doors, somewhat lighter than the outer portal, and through it into a large chamber. A long runner of sea green carpeting ran from the entrance to a raised dais upon which stood the two ducal thrones, the one on the left larger than the one on the right. Two carved wood tables ran the length of the hall, one on either side of the runner, with chairs facing the middle of the room. Illumination was provided by four tall windows on the right, and chandeliers hanging from the ceiling.

Several minutes later, they heard the tremulous voice of an old man answered by the gentle voice of another man as their footsteps trod slowly towards them. The duke entered room on the arm of an aging manservant. The servant helped the duke up the steps to the throne and then the duke shook him off irritably. "I can manage now, Mottle, I'm not dead yet." He grasped the arm of the larger throne and settled himself into it, wincing with pain as he bent his knees to sit.

The smaller throne beside him remained empty. His wife had died several years earlier and he had not seen fit to take another wife. He had two sons to succeed him and a daughter he had married off to one of the counts to ensure his loyalty. The duke looked around the hall and saw the three envoys from the Monastery. "You finally made it, I see. I thought you were supposed to be here yesterday." Without waiting for an answer, he twisted round to look back at the door. "Where's

Gremulkin? We can't start without him. Go and find him, Mottle. Tell him we're waiting."

Mottle was a cadaverous man dressed in a grey and red robe with a face that looked as if he had just eaten something unpleasant. This appearance belied the man's nature; Daryan knew him to be a kind and gentle man. He suspected that his expression might have had something to do with the activities of the people surrounding and influencing the duke. He'd served as the duke's steward for many years; as far as Daryan knew, since before Lord Valdor had been born.

Turning back to the visitors, he said, "Come forward." Daryan felt tremendous compassion as he looked at the frail elderly man. He looked to be in his ninetieth decade, thin and withered, wearing a long scarlet velvet robe trimmed with white satin, which looked rather incongruous on his shrunken body. Resting on his head was a slender gold circlet, and a heavy gold chain hung around his neck.

A movement behind the throne drew Daryan's attention, a dark figure in the shadows beside the dais, dressed in a black doublet and trousers. The man made a gesture with his finger across his lips. Darian recognized him as the duke's eldest son, but understanding the message, gave no sign he'd seen him. *I wonder why he's hiding.*

Daryan and his two companions walked forward and bowed to the duke. "Your Grace," Daryan said courteously.

"You're late," he answered in a high-pitched, querulous voice. "I expected you yesterday. Who's that with you?"

"Your Grace, allow me to introduce Defender Lieutenant Othran and Mage Nadi Farsan of the League of Light."

Before they could go on, a bustle in the doorway announced the arrival of Chancellor Gremulkin, followed by a sour-faced Mottle.

"Sorry to keep you waiting, your grace," he said half-heartedly. He rubbed his hands together and looked at the three men. "Let's get started."

Nadi and Othran bowed again.

The Chancellor stepped forward, glaring at Nadi. "What's your gift?" he asked brusquely.

Nadi coughed into his hand—the signal Daryan had arranged for him to use if he sensed something dubious about anyone they encountered. "Excuse me. It's nothing very impressive, My Lord; I'm a life sensor."

"Hm. Why did you bring him along with you?" he demanded of Daryan.

"The archmage of his class thought it would be an opportunity for him to gain some experience. He has only recently become a mage and lacks field experience." *Sorry about the demotion, Nadi.*

The duke cleared his throat for attention. "Bring them some chairs, Mottle. If we're going to talk, we might as well be comfortable, and order something to drink!"

The steward sprang into action, beckoning to a couple of pages and issuing them orders. One boy picked up two chairs ran back with them to set beside the visitors, then hurried back for another one. He arranged them in semicircle at the foot of the steps about a span from the dais. The other page disappeared through a side door and after a brief interval, brought back a large silver tray of carafes, pitchers and silver goblets.

"A table, get a table," the duke shouted at the other page. The boy's face turned red as he hurried over to the side wall for a small table to hold the drinks.

Mottle signaled for the pages to pour the drinks, once the table was set up. They took the first two goblets to the duke and chancellor, and then served the guests. Daryan thought the wine was rather sweet, but courtesy dictated he drink it. He noticed the chancellor grimace when he tasted the wine.

"Now," the duke said, setting his goblet down on the arm of his throne. "Let's get down to business. Mottle, bring me the paper."

While this was going on, the chancellor took the opportunity to inquire, "I understand you were delayed on the way here. Nothing serious I hope, nobody was hurt?"

"Yes, Chancellor, there was an incident that required our attention."

"What happened?" the duke chimed in.

"Unfortunately, Your Grace, we discovered a child's body in the woods."

"Oh my! That was unfortunate. What did you do?"

"Well, we found remains of a fire near the body, the ashes were still warm so we knew the villain could not have gone far. You are probably aware, Your Grace, that children have been disappearing throughout the duchy and people are beginning to suspect the werfolk are involved. Sightings have been reported in various locations. I thought this might be the work of werfolk and decided to investigate, see if we could catch them. There were no signs of horse tracks, so they must have been on foot."

"Or maybe they disappeared down a hole when they heard you coming," the chancellor said derisively. "You don't really believe those old woman's tales do you?"

"We have to investigate any unusual event that might endanger the people," Daryan replied.

"How did the child die?" The duke asked, determined to take over control of the discussion. "Are you sure it was murdered and not killed by an animal?"

"I'm afraid we are sure, Your Grace. The child's body had been cut into pieces and put in a sack. We think the creature had been eating part of it when it heard us and ran off."

There was gasp from behind the dais where the duke's son was still standing.

"Did you catch them?" the duke asked.

"Unfortunately no," Daryan replied. *Light forgive me for lying,* he prayed silently.

"So what took you so long?"

"We kept up the search until sunset, by then the horses were tired and hungry, so we decided to rest for the night at an inn and continue our journey in the morning. That's when we sent the message that we would be delayed."

"Message, what message? I never received any message. Do you know anything about it, Mottle?"

"Yes, Your Grace. It came while you were sleeping. Chancellor Gremulkin offered to bring it to you."

"Is that right, Gremulkin?"

"I must have misplaced it, Your Grace," he replied with a scowl. "I've had a lot on my mind recently, and probably got it mixed up with some papers on my desk. My apologies."

The mention of papers must have triggered a memory in the duke's mind. "Now let's get on with the matter at hand."

The duke turned over the paper Mottle had given him. Daryan saw that the printing on the page was so large, he could almost read from where he sat. *Poor old man must be losing his sight too*, he thought.

After scanning the paper, the duke said, "We are going to need more weapons from you."

"What kind of weapons?" Daryan asked.

"Combat weapons. Enchanted."

"May I ask for what purpose?

"Do I have to have your permission to arm my soldiers?" the duke replied crossly. "We are beset by enemies on all sides. We need to be able to protect ourselves."

"But we do not produce enchanted weapons for that purpose, nor do we mass produce them. I'm afraid the council would not permit such an order to be fulfilled."

The duke picked up his goblet and hurled it across the room, sending a spray of wine droplets in its wake. "Damn it! This isn't a request. We are ordering you to provide us with the weapons."

Daryan stood up. "I'm sorry, Your Grace, but I have no authority to change League policy and therefore I am impelled to refuse. If you wish, I will take it up with the council, but I know they will not grant your request."

Chancellor Gremulkin came forward. "Allow me, your Grace." He turned to Daryan. "I believe your own work, when you are not representing the League, is crafting and enchanting weapons, is it not?"

"That is correct."

"So why can't you, as a private citizen and craftsman, fill this order?

"Chancellor," he replied tightly, "Every weapon I produce is made to order for a specific person whom we know will not misuse its power and cause harm to innocent people. And each purchase is approved by the League. Therefore, I am unable do as you request. Not only would I be acting dishonorably, I would be betraying the League of Light and the people we protect. This may not mean a lot to you, but to us it is the purpose of our lives."

As Daryan was talking, the chancellor's face began to smolder with rage. His brows drew together, his lips turned white, and his eyes looked as if they would burst into flames. Daryan had never seen anyone so enraged.

"If that is all..." he started to say.

"All, all? Do you expect us to take your insults and innuendoes sitting down...?

"Gremulkin, get a hold on yourself," the duke shouted. "I will handle this. Commander, if that is all, you are dismissed."

With those words, the duke stood up and gestured to Mottle to come and help him.

"Gremulkin, come with me, we have to talk."

The Duke and his retainers left by a door behind the throne, Daryan noticed that the duke's son had already left. Daryan and his two companions went out through the door by which they had entered. Outside in the hallway, they were intercepted by the duke's son. "Quickly," he said, "come with me, you may be in danger."

Daryan hesitated for a second. He knew very little about this man, whether he could be trusted, but common sense took over. He might be leading them into a trap, although, he realized, they were already in a trap—the castle—and there was a chance the duke's son might get them out of it. The duke and Gremulkin could prevent their leaving if they wanted to, and maybe that's what they intended. If this man was leading them into another trap, they were still armed, and all he could see on the young lord was a sheathed dagger on his belt. He glanced quickly at Nadi who gave a faint nod. "All right, lead on, My Lord."

He led them through a narrow, barely noticeable door close to the one they'd just exited. This door opened into a narrow passage. "Ever wonder how servants move around without getting in the way all the time?" he asked, his voice just above a whisper. "Through passages like these. They run between the walls of the state rooms all over the castle."

"Why are you doing this, My Lord?" Daryan asked softly.

"I'll tell you everything when we get out of here."

He opened a door at the end of the passage and saw them through before following and closing the door again. To their surprise, he took out a small key and locked the door. "Now no one can follow us. This way leads to the cellars, down these stairs."

As they went down the narrow flight of stone stairs, the air became cooler and more humid. When they reached the bottom, they found themselves in a wide tunnel with walls made from blocks of cut rock. The floor was solid rock that had been laboriously smoothed. There were few lanterns to light the way, leaving large areas in shadow, but enough light to see the barrels and sacks of provisions and goods stored here. After a following the passage for few minutes, they came to a junction with a cross tunnel and heard voices echoing off the walls.

"Quickly, get back in here, behind the barrels. I'll see who it is. Don't move or make a sound until I get back." He felt around and picked a small wooden box, which he tucked under his arm. They heard his footsteps go away and after a few paces, stop. The voices—now identifiable as a man and a child—got louder; someone was coming in their direction.

"My Lord," the young voice said.

"Hello, Mion. What are you doing down here?"

"Cook sent my father down to get a sack of turnips so I came with him to help him carry them. Are they getting heavy yet, dadi?"

The duke's son laughed. "Like me. Her ladyship wanted a box of dried loofer eggs, so I said I'd get them for her."

"You could have asked one of the porters to fetch that for you, My Lord," the man's voice said.

"I know, but I like coming down here to cool off when it's so hot outside. Don't tell anyone, though. Let it be our secret."

"As you command, My Lord. Light be with you."

They heard a door slam in the distance and young lord's footsteps returning. "All right, it's safe to come out now. They've gone." He was still talking very softly.

They continued their trek though the cellars of the castle, around several more turns and down a few more steps until they came to an iron-barred gate. The duke's son had another, larger key to open this one. Once they were through, he locked it after them.

"This used to be the dungeons, but they're out of use now," he whispered.

They went down another, longer flight of stairs whose steps were made treacherous by slimy molds. The air had a musty smell, with a touch of sea air. A cool breeze came from somewhere ahead.

"Where are we going?" Daryan asked.

"This is another way out of the castle. My father showed it to me when I was a boy. Not many people know of it. It's supposed to be an escape route for the family if the castle can't fend off an attack. It comes out on the shore." He stopped to put down the box. "Won't need that any more. Loofer eggs!" he said with a chuckle. "My lady hates them."

They reached the final exit a few minutes later, but found it blocked by another barred iron gate. "Now this one may be a bit tricky; I don't have a key. Probably wouldn't work anyway, the lock's so rusty." He took hold of the bars and began to jerk the gate back and forth to no avail.

"Let's all try," Daryan suggested.

They all grabbed the bars and pushed, then pulled, but nothing gave way.

"This isn't going to work, My Lord. May I try something else?"

"Be my guest."

"Stand back!" Daryan drew his sword, held the blade to his forehead for a moment with his eyes closed, and then he stood back and struck the gate horizontally with it. There was a flash of light and the bars parted. "Once more," he said. This time he struck near the top. "Now pull them out."

The bars came away easily leaving a gap through which they could climb.

Felindra

After breaking her fast, Felindra spent the morning visiting the livestock—two fillies in the stable with their newborn foals who seemed to be doing well, although the new mothers had been alarmed by the smell of the predator. She whispered to them, trying to reassure them that her wolf wouldn't harm them. She saw three cows in the meadow with their half-grown calves. They must have been taken into a cowshed last night for she hadn't seen them in the field. She visited the horses in the field and found one who had a stomachache, which she reported to Andro.

"You could be very useful around here," he said to her when he heard about the horse. "I would never have known what was bothering her, although I knew she was cranky. I think I'm going to try to persuade your father to let you stay. Would you like that?"

"I would, but I've got my...."

"I know, your wolf and your family and your schooling. I understand, but if you change your mind, know that you would be very welcome here."

"Thank you. I'm glad I could help. May I tell you something?"

"Go ahead, child." He saw her frown. "I'm sorry, I forget you are a young woman and I shouldn't call you a child."

"It's all right. Everybody does."

"You know why? It's because children are so precious and we treasure them. We don't really want them to grow up and leave us. Childhood is so short. That even goes for my rambunctious brood. Now, you wanted to tell me something before I started rambling."

"I thought it was because I'm so small." She smiled and continued, "I had a talk with Ashala, my wolf, this morning. She's made friends with a wolf pack that lives nearby. I asked her to tell them not to hunt here and to look out for you and your family. They may be able to protect you a bit if anything happens."

"Oh, girl, you truly are a treasure." He folded her in his massive arms and hugged her. "I would never have thought of such a thing. Do you think it would work?"

"It might—the hunting part, at least—but they may want to meet you before they decide to protect you and your family."

"How would that work?"

"Well, with Ashala, she met each one and got their scents. She thinks they're part of her family now and would intervene to protect them if they were in danger. It might work if the other pack leader got to know you as the leader of your own pack, sort of like a treaty."

"What a precious person Daryan has brought to my home. I bless the day he appeared on my doorstep with you." He shook his head, for once at a loss for words.

Felindra blushed and ducked her head.

Daryan

They came out onto a strip of dry shingle about fifty paces from the reach of the incoming waves.

"Good thing the tide's out," the duke's son said. "We won't have to wade through wet sand and seaweed. I'm going to take you to a fisherman's hut just a little way along the strand. There we can sit and talk."

The hut was quite small, only about three spans by four. Besides a couple of bench seats, all it contained were some nets and a few fishing rods. It had a single door and a small window covered with scraped velum, which allowed in some filtered light.

"Sit down, gentlemen. We should start by properly introducing ourselves. I'm the eldest son of the Duke Ostran of Trethawynd; my name is Valdor. I think it would be less complicated if we stuck to given names. I remember you are Daryan and your fellow knight is ...?"

"Othran, My Lord."

"And I'm Nadi."

"Good. Now let's get down to explanations. I liked the way you put Gremulkin in his place, by the way. He's been asking for that for a long time." Valdor smiled at the recollection. "But it is dangerous to antagonize him, Daryan."

"I was just speaking the truth," Daryan said with a twitch of a smile. "I take it you two don't get along?"

"Not in the least. What he's done to my father is a crime. The man has much evil in him."

Daryan looked at Nadi. "The real reason we brought Nadi with us is that when he detects life, he is also aware of the nature of that life. Am I saying that right, Nadi?"

"It's more that … all life has light, and some lights shine brighter than others. Some are very dim, almost like dark smoke. The chancellor's light was like that."

"Interesting. Thank you, Nadi. You've confirmed what I suspected. Now, to continue. The way he wormed his way into our court was very suspicious for a start. Our previous chancellor died in a riding accident two years ago. That in itself was suspicious because he was an excellent horseman and in good health. I suspected foul play, but there was no evidence. Shortly after that, this fellow turned up with a letter of introduction from an old friend of father's, so we had to receive him out of courtesy to the friend. Almost before we could turn around, father had appointed him chancellor. Father has changed. It's hard to pin down exactly how, but his opinions and decisions are not as decisive or rational as they used to be. It was almost as if he'd lost his moral bearings. I believe the man has him under some sort of spell. It's not his age, his mind isn't deteriorating, he's as sharp as ever, it's just his … how can I say it? … his moral standards that have gone astray. As you can imagine, my brother and I are devastated, but we don't know what to do.

"It was Gremulkin's idea to order the enchanted weapons. Light knows what he intended to do with them."

"Do you think he might be in with the Dark Brethren?" Daryan asked

"It's possible. There have been a few suspicious incidents that no one can account for…" Valdor sighed. "We have to do something."

"Would you be able to get away from the castle? I mean go somewhere else."

"I couldn't leave without my lady and the children. There's no knowing how he would react if I left them behind. He could use them as hostages. I couldn't do anything that would endanger my family."

"What about your wife's family?"

"It's a thought, but their place is a bit isolated..."

"What I meant is what if you got an invitation to visit them, an anniversary or something? You could take your family with you, out of the castle. Where is their home?"

"North of here, about twenty leagues north of Palgrigio. Her father is the Count of Argento."

"That's good news. You would be safer there. Does the count have a sender?"

"I believe so."

"Excellent. You could send him a message explaining the situation, not all the details, and suggest he invite you all for a visit. We have an access road to the Monastery not far from there. I feel the council would be happy to offer you sanctuary while we investigate this man."

"I'll have to think about it carefully. What if something happened to my father? I'm first in line of succession, but he ... Gremulkin ... might try to do something to nullify that. Is there any way I can contact you?"

"Yes. There's a communications mage in DarSolas. She would send a message to the Monastery. If you address it to me, I'll see that it's attended to immediately. I'll tell you where to find her."

"Communications, you mean a sender?"

Daryan nodded. "That is correct. You know her?"

"Yes, I've used her services a number of times."

"Very good. Is there anything else," Daryan asked?

"That's about the gist of it," Valdor replied. "I'll set a visit in motion as soon as I've discussed it with Lady Dinaz."

"Now I'd like to know how we are going to get home from here," Daryan said. "We obviously won't be able to reclaim our horses from the castle."

"Where are you staying?"

"At a friend's place about an hour north of here. It's a horse ranch called Cavalcitas."

"Yes, I know the place. He breeds fine horses. About you getting back there.... As you say, it wouldn't be advisable to return to the castle for your own mounts. I could direct you to a livery stable in town where they'll provide you with horses. I'll have the grooms to bring yours down to the livery stable later and you can exchange them for the borrowed ones tomorrow."

"I think the horses sound like the best plan," Daryan decided. "My Lord, Valdor, I assure you that we are very grateful for your help and I know that what you have told us will be of great interest to the League. It would be good if you could come there yourself and talk with the council. Between us, we might be able to come up with a solution. Anything that threatens Trethawynd is also a threat to the League of Light."

13 – Lord Valdor

"The livery stable is not far from here; continue along the strand until you see an inn called The Star and Anchor; the livery stable is just round the corner and across the street from it." Valdor explained. "I'll have to get a horse for myself; I can't go back to the castle on foot, but we shouldn't be seen together. I have another errand to run so I'll get mine later. Go with the Light, my friends. I'll be thinking about what we've discussed. Expect to hear from me soon."

After the three men left, Lord Valdor sat for a moment to think over what he had learned from Commander Peshanar. Having someone to share his concerns with lifted a burden from him and he felt much lighter knowing he had someone to talk to who was as concerned as he was. The commander seemed like a dependable sort; he knew instinctively he could trust him. What their mage had told him about Gremulkin left him feeling both relieved and alarmed. Relieved to know his judgment was sound and he hadn't been wrong about him, but alarmed at the implications of having a person like that so close to the seat of power and having so much influence over his father. *Poor father.* Valdor sighed. From what he'd learned today, the duchy was in worse peril than he'd thought. It was definitely time for him to act.

He stood up and brushed the dirt off his clothes. Black might be a good color if you want to conceal yourself in dark places, but it was not very practical for moving through dungeons and secret passages. It wouldn't do for the duke's son to be seen in grimy clothes. *I suppose I could say my horse threw me and ran away. But why should I have to make excuses? I don't owe anyone an explanation for my activities. But he's bound to have spies, looking for anything he can use against me. I'll just have to make it up as I go along and hope for the best.*

In spite of his resolve, Valdor felt he should have a reason for being in town and decided he would buy a gift for his wife. That was innocuous enough. He walked north up the strand and turned right at the first street he came to, a cobblestoned way that led up a steep incline to the market district. There was a jewelry store at the top of the hill just before the market square that would do nicely.

Lady Hildina, the owner of the establishment, was standing at the open window where she served customers, talking to a young man. Valdor waited in the shade of the building next door while she handed the customer a small package and said goodbye, then he approached her.

"My Lord, well met," she greeted him with a warm smile. "What can I do for you today?"

"Well met, Lady Hildina! I want to buy a little gift for my wife. Nothing too ostentatious, maybe a bracelet."

"I've just had a new collection made, my own designs. Would you like to see them?"

Valdor looked at the tray of jewelry and selected a slender bracelet with amethysts set in silver filigree. He knew Dinaz would appreciate its simplicity. He paid for it and waited while the jeweler wrapped it in silk and placed it in a parchment envelope. "Thank you, lady, the Light be with you."

After completing his purchase, he went to the livery stable one street over. He didn't bother with an excuse; there was no need. The proprietor was away and had left a man in charge who didn't know him. He chose a black stallion, paid the fee and climbed in the saddle. "I'll have my groom bring it back tomorrow," he told the man as he departed."

Valdor went to his quarters as soon as he arrived at the castle and exchanged his clothes for something more suitable, and then he walked down the hall to his father's rooms.

"Is his grace in?" he asked the footman on the door.

"Yes, My Lord; he's with the chancellor. The chancellor said they didn't want to be disturbed."

"Did he indeed?" Valdor raised his eyebrows.

He knocked on the door, then opened it and entered his father's salon. "Good day father," he said, standing just inside the closed door.

"We missed you at the meeting?" the chancellor said before his father could answer.

"I wasn't aware I was needed at any meeting," Valdor replied coldly. "I'd like to speak to my father, alone, if you don't mind."

"Do we have to send the chancellor away?" his father asked plaintively.

"I want to discuss a private family matter, father."

"Oh, very well."

"I have some important matters to attend to anyway," Gremulkin said as he stood up. "I will see you later, Your Grace." He gave Valdor a venomous look as he passed.

If looks could kill, I'd be stretched out on the floor at this moment, Valdor thought. "Go with the Light, Chancellor," he said before the door closed. If Gremulkin was what he suspected, that should aggravate his already rancid mood.

"Come and sit by the fire, my boy," the old man said. The duke was sitting in a padded chair in front of a marble fireplace. A fire burned in the grate; even so, the old man's legs were covered with a lap robe, held in place by his gnarled fingers.

He kissed his father's hand before sitting down in the chair just vacated by the chancellor. "How are you, father?" he asked.

The duke sighed. "Let me warn you, son, old age is not for the weak."

"I'm sorry you are hurting, dadi."

"Oh, it's a little ache here, a little ache there, but it all adds up. I get tired so easily and I can never seem to get warm." The old man straightened up from his slumped position. "What have you been up to, my boy?"

Valdor smiled. His forty-third anniversary was coming up, but his father still insisted on calling him 'my boy'. "I decided to go into town and buy a gift for Dinaz."

"What's the occasion?"

"Nothing. I just want her to know how much I appreciate her."

"You're a good boy, son." Then his father laughed as he continued, "You should have heard that young knight tearing into Gremulkin. I thought he was going to pop a vein."

"You mean the defender from the Monastery?"

"That's the one. Really put him in his place." The duke's voice became more sober. "He outright refused to sell us any enchanted weapons. Said they only gave them to people who were approved by the League. The impudence of the young pup; implying we would misuse them."

"He probably didn't mean *you*, father. Besides, why do we need enchanted weapons?"

"Gremulkin says we should get some. I don't know what he wants them for. He say's we have to be prepared for the battle that's coming."

"What battle, everything seems peaceful enough to me?"

"I don't know. If I ask him anything, he just brushes me off."

"That man has far too much influence over you, dadi. I don't trust him or his motives."

"You want me to get rid of him?"

"I think it would be advisable, if you can."

"What do you mean by that? If I can! I can do whatever I want; I'm the duke." The old man shrank back down in his chair, looking fearful. "On the other hand ...." His voice sounded weaker all of a sudden.

"On the other hand what?"

"I don't know, son, it's a feeling, something pulling at me. I get frightened sometimes when I think about sending him away."

Valdor felt great pity for his father, a once strong, assertive man reduced to such a pathetic state. He got up from his chair and went to embrace the duke. Kneeling in front of him, he said, "don't worry dadi, I'll take care of things, I promise."

It's definitely time to take action, he resolved. *I must send a message to the commander.*

14 – Lost Horses

Daryan

Daryan and his two companions arrived back at Andro's farm about an hour before sunset. The only unusual event on the return ride was when Nadi started feeling uneasy shortly after they entered the woods near the farm. Even the horses were a little jumpy.

"It's different from a life impression, more like a cloud of darkness," Nadi explained.

"Can you pinpoint where it's coming from?"

"That's what is so strange about it; it seems to be all around, like cloud of evil."

"This is getting serious," Daryan said. "I'm puzzled; I wonder why it's in this particular location. I think we need to return to the Monastery as soon as we can and report everything we've discovered. I'm also eager to have another go at the prisoner, if he still lives."

Felindra was at the gate to greet them with Ashala sitting calmly at her side. Daryan noticed that all the poultry had moved to a far corner of the yard.

"Welcome back dadi! What happened to our horses?"

"It's a long story. I'll tell you when everyone is together."

Felindra's eyes widened as a thought came to her. "They weren't hurt, were they?"

"No, love, nothing like that."

The men dismounted from the borrowed horses and prepared to lead them to the stable.

"Look at your beautiful uniform. It's ruined. What happened? Were you in a fight?"

Daryan put his arm around her shoulder and squeezed. "Just a little adventure. It's part of the long story. Believe me it's worth waiting for, but I want to tell everyone together. Now, how was your day?"

She told him what she'd been doing, finishing with, "The animals aren't frightened of Ashala, now, but they don't like it if she gets too close."

"What about Andro's dogs? I notice they're not around."

He removed the bridle and saddle from his rented horse and put them on the rack.

"Ashala tried to have a talk with them, but they're too silly. They keep trying to attack her. But she just snarls at them and they run away. She thinks they are immature, like children, even the old one."

Dayan smiled. "It must be from being around children all the time."

After supper, Daryan had a long discussion with Andro and Valina, telling them of the new developments and the danger they had perceived as they were coming through the woods.

"I don't see what we can do," Andro said in frustration. "We don't even know the nature of the threat." He turned to Valina. "Have you seen anything?"

"Nothing material, just a feeling, as if something awful is going to happen." Valina had farsight, the ability to see events before they happened. "I'll take my crystal out and see if I can do a reading later."

"We have, or will have, an extra line of protection now, thanks to your daughter; she's brilliant."

"Oh? What's she been up to now?" Daryan glanced at his daughter and winked.

"She is recruiting the local wolf pack to defend us and our farm. That is, once I'm introduced to the pack leader." He smiled at Felindra. "Is everything ready?"

"Ashala has gone to meet them. She'll signal when they get near."

Later, when they were preparing for sleep, Nadi commented, "Your daughter and her pet wolf look as if they are going to win this struggle single handed."

"They will certainly be an asset." Daryan conceded. "I pray the Light she won't get hurt. She's much too young for so much responsibility. She needs to be with her friends and have some fun."

A wolf howled in the nearby woods. They heard two sets of footsteps leave the house, one heavy and one light. *I'm surprised Andro is taking this so seriously,* Daryan thought with a smile, *he's usually so skeptical. He must see something in Felindra. And there's no harm in making friends with the animals.*

"It's too bad we have to go back into DarSolas tomorrow." Othran said.

"No, it's good. Before we leave, I would like to have a word with the sender, warn her about what's happening."

"I wonder if the chancellor has any powers," Nadi, commented.

"What makes you say that?"

"Something Lord Valdor said about his father being under a spell."

"Could he be a rogue mage?" Othran suggested.

"It's possible, I suppose. This could be more serious than we thought," Daryan replied. *Something else the council should know about, immediately.* "I'll send a message in the morning from DarSolas."

***

The following morning, the team assembled outside the stable while the horses were being brought out. Felindra was to ride Shila, while the others mounted the hired horses.

Daryan, standing beside Felindra, said to her, "What do think of this idea? We don't want to take Ashala into DarSolas;

do you think you could ask her to go on ahead to Palgrigio and wait near the bridge?"

"That's a good idea, dadi. I'll talk to her." She knelt on the ground and whispered to the wolf for a moment. Ashala looked at her and licked her hand, and then she started walking towards the gate. She stopped halfway and looked back at Felindra. "Go on," she called. "We'll meet you on the road." In a way, she was relieved to be free of the anxiety caused by traveling with a wolf and always worrying about how people would react. *It must be stressful for her, too,* she thought.

Othran and Nadi took the horses to the livery stable while Daryan and Felindra went to the sender's house. Daryan was surprised to see how young she was, not more than eighteen, he guessed, and she lived with her parents who ran a weaving business.

Her father answered the door and led them through into a back room where Avaya was sitting working a loom.

"A client for you, my dear," he announced. "From the Monastery."

"Thank you, Father." She looked a bit surprised to see them, but she put down the shuttle on her stool and led them out the door. "Well met," she said. "Please follow me. We have to go upstairs."

"My name is Daryan Peshanar and this is my daughter, Felindra."

"I'm Avaya." She looked at him more directly and then asked, "Are you Commander Peshanar?" Daryan smiled and nodded. "My father often speaks of you. He was a defender in the League of Light."

"I didn't recognize him. Where did he see action?"

"I think it was in the south, Algonia?"

"Ah, well, our paths probably never crossed in that case. I was in the east, mostly around Coringe."

"What can I do for you, sir?"

"I would like to send two messages, the first one to the Monastery. Address it to Archmage Plavan. I've written out the message. Now this is a confidential message. No one outside your household should know of it, however, you may show it to your father as your family might be threatened, also."

"Our sendings are all confidential, sir, but thank you for the permission."

Daryan nodded. "I know how discreet your work is and I appreciate it, but I cannot leave you unprepared if there is trouble. The second message is to Toma Ashavan in Palgrigio. Here it is." He handed her a slip of paper with the note informing Ashavan of their pending arrival and asking him to contact the guardi to arrange a meeting.

"Would you like to wait downstairs while I send them?" Avaya asked. "I'll show you where you can sit."

She led them into a small kitchen furnished with a wooden table and four chairs. It had a cooking fireplace in one corner and one wall was lined with shelves containing utensils and containers of foodstuffs. They could hear someone moving around in the next room and then footsteps coming towards the kitchen.

"I thought I heard someone." The man looked a few years older than Daryan. He had dark skin, curly black hair and dark brown eyes. His muscular shoulders and arms showed he was a man who did heavy physical work on a regular basis. "Waiting for an answer?"

"That's correct. And for our friends to come back with the horses. I'm Daryan Peshanar from the League, and this is my daughter, Felindra."

"Welcome." He squinted at Daryan and his eyes lit up. "You wouldn't be *Commander* Peshanar, would you?"

Daryan smiled, "Yes."

"Oh, this is an honor, sir. I never thought I'd get to meet you in person." He hesitated and looked around. "Where are my manners? May I offer you some refreshment?"

"A small drink would go down well. Water would be fine, thank you," Daryan replied. "May I know your name, sir?"

The man put some mugs on the table and produced a pitcher of summer wine and one containing a milky fluid. "I'm Sasan Humaya, formerly defender of the League of Light. Would you like summer wine or buttermilk?"

Daryan raised his eyebrows. "Buttermilk would be refreshing. Same for you, Felindra?" She nodded. He turned back to Humaya. "Will you join us, sir? I would like to ask your opinion about something."

"I'm at your service, sir, but please call me Sasan." Sasan pulled out a chair and sat down at the table.

"I'm sure you must know a merchant called Evaseen Charnwell."

"Yes, I've had some dealings with him," Sasan replied cautiously, looking sideways at Daryan.

"We met him on the road when we were traveling to the Monastery. I was wondering if you have any sort of feeling about him."

"To tell you the truth, sir, he gives me the creeps. Not that he's dishonest or anything, but ... I don't know how to explain it ... there seems to be something sinister about him, if you know what I mean. My wife, Sady, and my daughter don't like him. If we have any dealings with him, I have to take care of them. He buys a lot of cloth from us, though, and always pays his bills on time; I'll say that for him."

"Tell me, Sasan, have you ever seen him with the duke's chancellor? You know the chancellor, don't you?"

"Oh, him! Nasty piece of work, that. Come to think of it, I have seen them talking a couple of times. Once he was in the emporium when I delivered some linen. They had their heads together mumbling away about something."

140

"Good. You've been very helpful, Sasan. I have to agree with your assessment. I'm doing a little investigating for the council. I'll be returning to the Monastery tomorrow. If you ever need to contact me about this or anything out of the ordinary you see or hear of, ask your daughter to send me a message."

"I will, sir. It would be an honor to help in any way I can."

"Oh, and there's something else. The message I'm sending to the Monastery has some information in it that you should see. I've told your daughter she may show it to you."

"Thank you, Sir." Sasan looked a bit mystified, but refrained from asking any more questions.

Light footsteps came down the stairs and Avaya entered the room. She was carrying two sheets of paper, one fresh and the other the crumpled page he'd given her.

"This is the response from the Monastery, sir. Sir Ashavan just said he would take care of it and see you tonight. Shall I give this to my father now?"

"Yes, go ahead." He took a coin from his pouch and laid it on the table. "And this is for your excellent service."

"Oh, we couldn't possibly take it sir," her father protested.

Daryan smiled at Avaya. "Maybe your daughter would like a new sunhat, or a box of iced almond drops. Go on, please take it."

"Thank you, sir. I hope we will see you again. Go with the Light." With a little bow, she put the coin in her belt pouch and disappeared in the direction of her workshop.

"And we should go too, young lady," Daryan said to Felindra. "I wonder what's keeping our friends."

After saying farewell to Sasan, they left the shop and turned down the street towards the seafront, leading Shila by her reins. After a few paces, they saw Othran and Nadi walking towards them, but no horses.

Seeing their unhappy faces, Daryan picked up his pace. "What's wrong? Where are our horses?"

"Lord Valdor sent a page with a message. It seems the chancellor has impounded our horses and won't let them out of the castle grounds," Othran informed him.

"*Solas Naofa!* It seems almost as if he's trying to provoke us into a confrontation. Well, we will not be provoked." Daryan sighed. "Let's go back to the livery and see if they will lend us some more horse. It will probably cost us a pretty pile of gold."

"One of us could ride Shila back to Andro's farm and see if he could lend us some of his," Felindra suggested.

"That's a good idea," Othran said. "I'll go."

"No, it better be me," Daryan said. "I can persuade him more easily than anyone, with the possible exception of this young lady. The three of you can start walking and I'll meet you with the mounts. And please take care of my daughter. If anything happens to her, you'll have to answer to Ashala." He paused and looked up at the sky. "I should be back in an hour at the most."

He mounted the horse and took off at a gallop.

Felindra

Othran looked frustrated at his forced inactivity, but Nadi took it in his stride. "Let's walk," he said.

They started back up the north road, which was bustling with commerce. Carts and people on horseback passed in both directions, but they were one only ones walking. The road was lined on both sides with adobe dwellings, many with bananas and corn plants growing in their gardens, and a few gardens had date palms. There were also many small businesses along the roadside: several fruit and vegetable vendors, a blacksmith, a furniture maker, and finally, a roadside stand selling drinks.

"Anyone thirsty?" Othran asked. "I'm a little parched. Let's stop for a few minutes." Without waiting for a response, he went to the vendor's stand and sat on a stool.

"What'll you have?" the vendor asked. She was a small woman with sunbaked skin and short grey hair. "I've got fresh summer wine, freshly pressed fruit juices, or dark and light ale."

"I'll take a light ale, if you please," Othran replied, placing a silver coin on the stand.

"What kind of fruit juice do you have?" Felindra asked.

"Orange and pineapple, mango and guava, or grape."

"May I have a small mango juice, please?"

"Coming up!"

"What about you, Nadi?" Felindra asked.

"I'll take some summer wine." He too produced a silver coin.

The woman put their drinks in front of them and collected the coins, seeming satisfied with the amount, but offering no change. "Are you on foot?" she asked. "It's not very often we see people walking along this road."

"Well we are," Othran replied grumpily.

"We lost our horses," Felindra explained.

"How lost? We're they stolen?"

"Something like that," Nadi interjected before Felindra could be drawn into more discussion of the matter.

"Did you report it to the Guardi?" the woman asked.

"Not yet, we will, though." Nadi continued in the role of spokesperson for the group.

A man pulled his cart off the road and came over to the stand. "A nice big tankard of ale, please Sami," he ordered.

"Coming right up. How are you today, Ferdan?"

"Somewhat fair," he replied gloomily.

"Got a problem?"

"Aye. I went all the way into town to pick up a load and only half of it was ready. Now I'll have to come back again tomorrow for the other half."

She looked speculatively at Othran and Nadi, and then said, "You think you've got problems. You ought to hear the trouble these poor people have. They had their horses stolen and now they have to walk all the way to … where did you say you were going?

"Just up the road a little way. It's not far," Nadi, replied. "Really. Our friend has gone to get some more horses for us; he should be along any time now.

The man turned round and looked at them a moment, before making up his mind. "I could give you a lift, until you see your friend," he offered. "There's plenty of room in the cart. It's too hot to be walking in this weather."

"Thank you, sir, we would be pleased to accept your kind offer," Othran jumped in before Nadi could refuse.

Once the driver had swallowed the last of his ale, he returned to his cart. "Hop in," he invited, letting down the tailgate. "Need a hand, miss? Steady now. You can sit on those bales. It won't do them any harm. Right, then." He snapped the tailgate back into place and jumped up on the box. "Hold on now."

"Isn't this better than walking?" Othran said, settling back against a bale. He sniffed. "What is this stuff, anyway? Smells a bit fishy to me."

"It's seaweed," the driver said.

"What do they do with it?" Nadi inquired.

"I sell it to an old herbalist. He uses it to make some sort of medicine."

"He must make a whole lot if he uses this much."

"He sells it by the barrel to healers and medicine men. I bring him about thirty bales a month."

144

"He must be making iodine. It cleans wounds so they don't become infected. My wife uses it to clean cuts and grazes."

"That's interesting," the driver said. "I never thought to ask before. I wonder if it works on animals as well."

"I would think so. Animals get infections the same as people," Nadi said.

"What does your wife do; she some sort of medicine woman?"

"She's a healer. Just starting out."

There was silence for a while and they watched the scenery go by. Suddenly, Nadi stiffened.

"What is it?" Felindra asked anxiously.

"I don't know. There's something in the woods, something dark and cloudy." He murmured softly so as not to alarm the driver. "I sensed it yesterday as well when we got close to the farm.

Felindra shuddered. "What do you think it's doing?"

"It feels as if it's watching us."

"Is this your friend?" the driver called.

They turned and looked forward. A man on a horse leading three others was riding towards them. "It looks like him. Would you like to let us out when we get closer?" Othran said.

The driver slowed down, then stopped the cart. The three travelers climbed over the tailgate and jumped down into the road. He was about to pull away when Nadi called out to him. "Wait a moment!" and ran up to the front of the cart. He took a coin from his belt pouch and handed it to the driver. "Thank you, driver, you've saved us a lot of walking. Take this for your trouble."

"It was no trouble, young sir. You gave me someone to talk to and I learned something new. I'd say that's a fair exchange. But I'll take it anyway, since I lost half my cargo. The blessings of the Light upon you all." He smiled and touched his forehead, and then shook the reins to get his horse moving again. He saluted Daryan with his whip as they passed each other.

"Dadi!" Felindra called running up the road to meet him. "Good, you got the horses! Ashala must be all the way to Palgrigio by now."

"Yes, it is getting a bit late. Valina packed us some food, but I think we should ride on for a while. I don't like the feel of this place."

"Yes, I know, Nadi was just talking about it. He calls it dark life."

Daryan looked at her for a moment, a very serious expression on his face. He glanced at the woods and shuddered. "Come on, pick your horses," he said. "You can have Shila again, Felindra."

They mounted up, turned north and galloped away. After about half a league, Daryan led them onto a side road going east. "A shortcut," he explained.

15 – Return to Monastery

Daryan

The road veered gradually to the north again, so they continued until they reached the river. Daryan looked up at the sky, noting that the sun had passed its zenith. "We can rest here. Let's take care of the horses and then eat something." The horses were taken to drink at the river, wading in knee deep so that the riders could sluice water over them to cool them before they went to graze along bank. The four travelers made themselves comfortable in the shade and ate the substantial meal Valina had packed: cold chicken, tomatoes, cheese, and bread, grapes and bananas. She'd even included a small keg of summer wine, which they had to drink by passing it around, sucking it through small glass pipe stuck in the bunghole.

They were just packing up to resume their journey, when they heard a wolf call from somewhere nearby. Felindra sat up, rubbing her eyes. The call came again, closer. Ashala! She put two fingers in her mouth and whistled. In seconds, the wolf was in their midst. She yipped when she scented Felindra, ran to her and licked her cheek as if they'd been parted for days. "Hey! I'm pleased to see you too, but let's not get carried away, girl."

The men stood up and picked up the cloths in which the food had been wrapped. They took them down to the river and wet them to wash the sweat and dust off their faces and arms. Once everyone was mounted, they walked the horses upriver to the bridge and crossed over, then they continued north at a sedate trot.

"I think we've made up for most of the lost time," Daryan announced, so we can take it easy and spare the horses for a while. I don't think we'll be there before sunset, but it won't be long after."

"This time tomorrow, we should be at the Monastery," Othran said. "I can't wait."

"Barring unforeseen incidents," Daryan said.

Felindra was the first to notice something. "Hey, what's that awful smell?"

Nadi turned his head around until he located the source. "It smells like rotting vegetation, and it's coming from over there."

Daryan spotted a patch of black in one of the fields. They rode around the neighboring meadow for a closer look.

"Eeuw, that's horrible," Felindra said, clamping her lips together.

Daryan dismounted and moved closer for a better look. It was a grain field, but half of the ripening grain was turning into a foul-smelling black mush. "Don't touch it," he said.

"And don't get any on your boots. It looks like black rot. This is serious; it could spread like wildfire. We'll have to inform the authorities and have them burn the field. If it spreads, it could wipe out the whole harvest. I wonder where it came from." He looked around at the other fields and shook his head. "That's strange; it's the only field infected. We haven't had this problem in Trethawynd since the last upheaval."

"How do you know about it, dadi?"

"I saw it once before when we were fighting in the east. It caused a famine that wiped out a two percent of the population. I don't ever want to see anything like that again." He remounted and led them back to the road.

"Does it affect other plants?" Nadi asked.

"It mostly attacks grasses, but even that would be a disaster. Almost a third of our food comes from grain, and we use it as fodder for most of our domestic animals too, so that would be another big chunk out of our diet."

"How does it spread?" Othran asked. "A patch like this seems too random and isolated to do that much harm."

"Maybe that's what they use the Werfolk for," Nadi said. "They're small enough to get around without being noticed. It would only take a small patch to start it.

"That's true," Daryan replied. "It spreads very fast. In a couple of days, this patch could spread to all the fields around it. It dries into a powder under the hot sun, which becomes airborne to be spread by the wind. Let's get on." He slapped the side of his horse with the rein to bring its speed up to a canter.

"Don't you think we should burn this to keep it from spreading?" Othran asked.

"I would, but we'd be trespassing on someone's land, as well as risking a wildfire that would spread faster than the blight. It takes precise action by people experienced in this sort of thing, to prevent replacing one hazard with another. It's a tough call. If we knew who owned this field, we could tell him about it. Look out for a dwelling. We can stop and tell whoever lives there about it and if it's not the owner, he can pass it on. That's the best we can do, I'm afraid."

They arrived at Palgrigio a little after sunset. Daryan sent everyone to the inn to get a meal and rent some rooms. Felindra let the wolf go off and explore, with usual reminder about humans and domestic animals, even though she was confident Ashala had absorbed that rule by now. Daryan, in spite of his exhaustion, went on to the guardi's building.

The guardi was sitting with his chair back against the wall, front legs tilted upwards and his feet on the table. A single lighted lamp stood near him on the table. When Daryan closed the door, he jumped, lowered his feet to the floor and let the chair snap back into its upright position.

"Well met, guardi. You look as tired as I feel."

"Yes, it's been a busy couple of days. I was lucky if I got four hours sleep altogether. I received your message. What can I help you with, Commander?"

Daryan dragged one of the wandering chairs to the table and plopped himself down on it. "I won't keep you long. I'd like to hear how your investigation is going. We are on our way back to the Monastery and I want to give them as full a report as I can. Have you made any progress?"

The guardi sighed and reached for a sheet of paper. "We found the family of the little boy. It seems his mother was hanging out her washing on the clothesline the last she saw him. He must have wandered off. His father is a hunter and sometimes the little fellow tried to go after him. They're a nice young couple; he was their only child, but she looked as if she had another one on the way. They are devastated by what's happened to their son. I don't know how anyone can survive something like that, losing a child and in such a horrible way."

"Yes, it's a terrible tragedy. My heart goes out to them. We'll try every possible way to get to the root of it."

"But you've got the killer."

"Yes, but we need to know why he did it, find the reason for his actions. Werfolk wandering around the countryside killing children is not a common occurrence. Something is making them do this. Any more reports on missing children or sightings of werfolk?"

The guardi looked at his paper. "We've only covered the area in our jurisdiction, but five children have gone missing from this area, four little boys and one girl, all under six. Also, a hunter came across the corpse of a little girl, but it was so chewed up and decayed, it was hard to tell how she died. It could have been wolves. Several people have reported seeing what they describe as dark little men; they think they're demons."

"How many sightings?"

"Seven in all. We are putting signs up warning people to be on the lookout for anything unusual."

"Good. I know you'll warn people not to let their children out of sight. You might ask the local Light Society to caution people about it. They are the group that has contact with the most people."

The Light Society was an organization dedicated to the spiritual leadership of communities and teachings of the Light. They held regular social gatherings aimed at fostering spiritual values, and played a part in supporting and comforting those in need.

"We're already working on that."

"Do you think it might be time to call on the regional leaders to take part in this?" Daryan suggested.

"The count, you mean? I don't think it's that serious yet, but it might be a good idea to send him a report. If this is happening in other jurisdictions, it would help coordinate our effort."

"Excellent idea. I assume you are referring to the Count of Argento?"

The guardi nodded. "Yes, that's him."

"Now, one last thing and I'll let you retire for the night. On our way here today, we came across a grain field that appeared to be infected with blight. If it's what I think it is, it would be disastrous if it got out of control. Is there any authority that deals with this sort of thing?"

"Again, it might be a matter for the count. It's his county and anything that goes wrong in it is his problem. What do you think is causing it? And where exactly is it?"

"It's about five leagues south of here, across the river on the east side of the road. It looks like Black Rot to me."

"Light help us if it is," the guardi said. "I'll send someone down to burn it tomorrow."

"I already notified the farmer who owns the field, but it might pay to get a report from him. Anything else I should know?" Daryan asked, praying there wasn't.

"No, I think that about covers it."

"Well, I'll be off. If anything comes up you think we should know, you could send a message to the Monastery through Sir Ashavan. Light be with you, guardi."

***

They started out the next morning feeling refreshed after being able to bathe, sleeping in real beds, and breaking their fast with cooked food. It only took them two hours to reach the secret entrance to the Monastery, and by noon, they were home. Daryan noticed the activity in the courtyard, surprised at the increase since they'd left, wondering what was happening.

When he crossed the threshold of the transient dormitory building, the almoner came out of her office as if she had been waiting for him to appear.

"Well met, commander," she greeted him with a smile. "You must have had an eventful trip. You seem to have stirred up quite a wasp's nest while you were away."

"I did?"

"Yes, sir. I suppose you noticed all the people out there."

"Yes, I wondered what they were doing here. Where did they all come from?"

"Something serious must be happening. They've been sending messages all over the duchy, summoning mages to come in and bring their families. But that's not what I wanted to see you about. There's going to be a council meeting at two hours past midday. They want you and your team to be there. Your daughter included."

"Very well, lady, we'll be there. That'll give us time to eat our midday meal. And I'll need to locate Othran."

"If you hurry. I'll send a page to find Lieutenant Othran when the time comes. Oh, and one more thing, your housing is ready. Here's the address. It's near the back wall, just past the parade ground. You can move in any time."

"Thank you, lady. My wife will be as pleased to hear that as I am." Daryan took the stairs two at a time eager to see his family. He was disappointed when he found no one there except Felindra, who was changing into her regular clothes, lightweight cotton trousers and tunic. "Where is everyone?" he asked her."

"Probably down in the refectory," she replied. "I'm going down now. See you down there."

After splashing some water on his face and arms, he changed into clean clothes, grabbed a writing board and graphite stick, and hurried back downstairs

Parvana was waiting in the hallway leading to the refectory. She flew into his arms; he lifted her, spun her around, kissed her, and let her down. "Now that's what I call a welcome! How are you my love?"

"Happy to see you safely home. I even missed you a little bit."

"Only a little. I'm disappointed."

"Don't be. I'll show you how much later."

"That's my girl. I missed you too, a lot."

"Let's go and eat. I heard you have to go to a council meeting."

They went into the refectory where Darson was sitting with Felindra. Nadi was there too with his family. After kissing his son and greeting Lis, he spoke to Nadi."

"Have they told you we have to go to a council meeting this afternoon?"

"Yes. One of the pages just brought me a note. I don't know why they want me there."

"Because you have an important contribution to make."

Daryan helped himself to plate of grilled fish and took it to the table. "I've got some good news, too," he said as he sat down next to his wife. "Our house is ready. We can move in whenever you want to."

"That's wonderful. Do you have the address?"

Daryan felt for his belt pouch and realized he'd changed his clothes and left the almoner's note in his travel attire. "I left it upstairs in my belt. If you can't find the note, you can get it from the almoner if you're eager to start moving right away."

The council meeting was held in the council chamber in the white palace. The room was cool because all the east-facing windows down the left side were open to let in a refreshing breeze from the valley beyond the wall. The white marble floor and the sky blue walls also had a cooling effect. A long oval table stood down the middle of the room with twenty seats arranged around it, although only the fifteen at the far end were occupied by council members. The vacant chairs at the bottom end were left for the testifiers, petitioners, and witnesses invited to give reports. Two rows of seats, along wall opposite the windows, were occupied by non-council members interested in the proceedings. Looking round the room, it seemed to Daryan every archmage in the league was there.

Othran was waiting for him just inside the door.

"Take a seat, commander," Grand Master Bar-tori Algoran said, indicating the empty seats at the end of the table opposite him. "Your colleagues too."

Commander! Things must be serious if he's using my rank, Daryan thought. He bowed to the Grand Master and sat down in the seat facing him at the opposite end. He placed his writing board and graphite on the table and looked up.

The Grand Master, a tall, wiry man with nut-brown skin, white hair and beard, shuffled some papers on the table and cleared his throat, and then he looked up and focused his penetrating brown eyes on Daryan. "We'd like you to give us a full report of what you've learned on this expedition," he said. "How would you like to proceed?"

"Grand Master, honorable councilors, I've broken it down into three categories." He straightened his writing board, on which he had made some notes during lunch. "My meeting with Duke Ostran, the apprehension of the werman child-killer, and other matters of concern that may need attention. Which would you hear first?"

"I'd like to hear about that creature you sent us," a woman councilor said.

"Patience, Lady Jostrin, I think the situation with the duke needs more urgent attention," the Grand Master said calmly. "Go on, Commander, tell us about that."

Daryan consulted his notes where he had written the name Gremulkin and underlined it twice. "May I be frank, Grand Master?"

The Grand Master nodded. "I would expect nothing less. Continue."

"To be quite honest, I fear for the duke's safety." Some of the people on the side benches gasped. "For one thing, he is old and frail; he did not appear to be in the best of health. In addition—and this is where I fear the danger lies—I feel he is being unduly influenced by his chancellor, Gremulkin. While

I was there, I had an opportunity to speak in confidence with the duke's heir, Lord Valdor. He thinks the chancellor holds his father in thrall. He told me that Gremulkin arrived at the castle suddenly, under unusual and suspicious circumstances, one being the sudden accidental death of the former chancellor.

"The other thing that aroused my suspicion was the demand for enchanted combat weapons. When I told them their request could not be fulfilled and why, the chancellor flew into a rage and the meeting ended. The duke knows the circumstances under which we sell enchanted weapons and I doubt he would ask for them to be mass produced, knowing that our arms are matched to the individuals who will wield them. That's why I concluded that it wasn't his, but Gremulkin's idea. The duke's son, Lord Valdor, confirmed this later."

Daryan went on the tell the council about their escape from the castle with the help of Lord Valdor and the impoundment of their horses, as well as his recommendation that Lord Valdor remove his wife and children from the castle and find somewhere safer to live.

"I took Mage Farsan with me on this trip because he had exhibited keen perception in several other incidents and I thought his gift might be helpful. It was, on a number of occasions. Nadi, would you mind telling the council your impressions of Chancellor Gremulkin?"

Nadi cleared his throat and stood up. "Grand Master, honorable councilors," he gave a little bow. "When I was within close range of the chancellor, I felt uneasy, as if something were not quite right. Then something darker, more frightening emanated from him. It was as if his light, his living essence, was dimmer than normal. I've been trying to find an explanation or a way to describe this phenomenon—I'm not very advanced in my gift—so I thought 'life is light, but his was dark, so I called it 'dark life'. There is an element of evil to it, I believe. The same thing happened when we were camping at Crossroads and met a merchant. His light was 'dark' too."

"That's a good assessment and analogy, Mage Farsan. I think you've made it clear to everyone. Thank you." The Grand Master turned to Daryan. "Go on, Commander."

"My recommendation is that we investigate Gremulkin, find out where he came from, and if he does use magic, where he learned it."

"This sounds like the buildup to a serious situation, Daryan continued. For one thing, with all the reports we're receiving about incidents involving werfolk and other attacks, it looks as though the Dark Brethren are preparing for another offensive. It is imperative that the duchy has strong leadership and the current situation with the duke does not bode well. If this Gremulkin is allied with the Dark Brethren, we could have a disaster on our hands.

"I couldn't agree more. Thank you, commander. Now, before we finish with this matter, are there any questions?" the Grand Master asked the councilors."

There ensued another hour of questions, during which Daryan was able to elaborate on his other concerns. When the questions finally ended, the Grand Master stood up. "Thank you all. Since this matter took rather more time than expected, I am going to call a recess. I think Commander Peshanar might like to spend some time with his family after his absence. We will assemble again on the morrow at two hours after sunrise. Thank you, councilors. Commander, would you be able to spend a few minutes, maybe half an hour, with me in my office around sunset this evening?"

"I'm at your service, Grand Master."

16 – Lord Valdor 2

Valdor

Valdor glanced up when he heard his father's laugh. Anger filled his blood when his eye fell on the Chancellor sitting on his right hand side, his eyes roving over the people sitting around the table like a predator surveying for prey, trying to decide upon which one it would pounce, which would prove it the choicest morsel. The eyes peering out from beneath the black brows settled on him, paused for a moment, and then moved on to Dinaz before passing on to his two children. The chancellor nodded ... the slightest twitch of his neck, and resumed his conversation with the duke.

Valdor had completely lost his appetite, but he forced himself to put another piece of venison in his mouth and chew it, although he could have been eating paper for all the satisfaction he derived from it. He was sure Gremulkin knew about his rescue of Daryan and his two companions; how he knew, Valdor couldn't guess, unless the cook's daughter had said something about seeing him in the cellars. He kept his eyes on his plate, afraid that if he looked up, he would see those hateful eyes on him again. *We have to get away from here*, he thought, *my family isn't safe. But how can I leave poor father at the mercy that hyena?* Daryan was right though. As long as his family remained in the castle, they could be held hostage against any action he took. If he could get them somewhere safe, he would be able to act more freely. It was his duty to the people of the duchy to rescue the duke from the power Gremulkin wielded over him. Valdor had made up his mind. He turned to his wife.

"Have you finished, my love?" he murmured.

"Almost. I would really like to try a little of the flan, though.

He put his hand over hers. "I want to get out of here," he said softly. "Would you help me?"

Her eyes met his. "*Him* again? Say no more. What would you like me to do?"

"Could you feign a headache?"

Her forehead wrinkled with pain. She put her hand over her brow and groaned. "This pain; it's getting worse. Do you mind if I go back to our rooms?"

He got up and helped her stand. With his arm supporting her back, he turned to his father. "Your grace, would you pardon us? My lady is not feeling well and wishes to be excused."

"Of course, my boy. You poor dear," he said to Dinaz. "Would you like me to send my physician?"

"I'll be all right, Your Grace, I just need to take a potion and lie down for a while." She still kept the pained expression on her face as she turned to the two children. "Come with us. It's getting late and I'm sure you must be getting sleepy."

"Oh mother," fourteen year-old Varan, the eldest protested. "I'm not tired and I haven't eaten my pudding."

"Do as your mother asks, Varan. We can get a servant to bring some to your room. You too Jilly." Valdor said quietly but firmly.

"Oh, very well, father."

His hand still on his wife's back, Valdor escorted them from the hall, leaving behind an ominous silence. He dared not look back, but he could feel the chancellor's menacing glare on his back. They walked down the wide carpeted hallway, at this time of evening aglow with candles and lamps, and turned the corner to the slightly narrower hall that led to their suite.

"My lord," A footman opened the door for them and held it while they entered. "Is there anything I can do for you, my lord?"

"Yes, Firton, would you send to the kitchen and have them send up some pudding for my son and daughter and some flan for my lady?"

"I'm at your service, My Lord."

Once the door was closed, Valdor turned to his two children. "I apologize for taking you away from your dinner," he said to them. "Someone will bring you your pudding to your rooms."

"Is something wrong, dadi?" Varan asked. "Is mother all right?"

"She's fine, son, just a little headache. Just go along with what I say for a little while, even if you don't understand why. It will all become clear to you soon."

The boy's eyes crinkled with concern, but he knew better than to ask more questions. He was very much aware of the tensions in the castle and his father's unhappiness with the situation. "Very well, dadi, don't ...." He stopped as if he had been about to say something indiscrete.

Valdor put his hand on his son's shoulder and squeezed it affectionately. "All right, you're excused."

"Go with the Light, dadi and you, mami."

"Blessings of the Light on you both." He kissed Jilly on her cheek. "Sleep well."

The salon, while not as big as his father's, was just as richly appointed with red and gold rugs on the marble floor. The walls were white stone, softened by gold lantern brackets and embroidered wall hangings worked in rich colors. Comfortable padded chairs were arranged in front of the big marble fireplace. Three tall windows overlooked an ornamental garden below. At the height of their summer glory, the scent of roses, peonies, and jasmine filled the air. Several pools, one with a fountain in the center glittered in the lantern light. The glass doors of the window were opened to allow a cool sea breeze to enter, carrying with it the fragrance of the garden.

Dinaz was standing by the window, looking down upon the garden. "It's a beautiful night," she sighed. "If only life were as serene as this view."

Valdor came up behind her and put his arms around her waist, leaning his chin on her head. "You look lovely in that outfit," he told her.

She was wearing a knee-length tunic of pale yellow lawn over filmy aquamarine trousers and a gauzy headdress of yellow silk held in place by a braided gold circlet, which set off her black hair and olive skin to perfection.

He turned her to face him and kissed her. "Shall we take a walk in the garden?" Valdor wanted to talk something over with her, but he didn't trust even his own suite not to have spies listening in on their conversations. He knew well about the servant's passages between the walls. He and his brother and sister had often played in them as children, sometimes overhearing grownups' conversations. It was safer to talk about anything private outside in the open.

"Just let me get a wrap and I'll be with you." She dashed off to the dressing room to get it herself rather than summoning her maid who would probably be eating her supper right then. She returned with a light shawl around her shoulders. "Ready!"

When they reached the gardens, the couple strolled hand in hand to far boundary and back before sitting down on a bench near the fountain. Valdor noticed a footman watching them from the doorway, but his was a familiar face, a man who had been at the castle since Valdor was a young man. He was watching over his lord, waiting to fill any requests he might have. His being there somehow made Valdor feel safer; his presence would discourage would-be eavesdroppers.

"What did you want to talk about?" Dinaz asked.

"After Gremulkin's abominable behavior the other day, I feel we may be in danger."

"But surely he wouldn't dare..."

"My love," Valdor interrupted squeezing her hand. "I am afraid he might. He has father under his control, what's to stop him trying to attack me? No, dearest, please listen to what I have to say. I want to get you and the children away from the castle. My greatest fear is that he might use you and the children to threaten me and try to coerce me into doing what he wills. I won't allow that."

"But surely the guards will protect you."

"I don't know if you've noticed, but he has been gradually changing the castle guards since he came here. He even appointed a new commander of the guard, dismissed the old one for what he called negligence. He didn't dare have him executed, as I am sure he would have liked, because my father was fond of him. Even though father protested and defended the commander, Gremulkin had his way. Now it looks as if the majority of the guards are his and the loyal ones are afraid of him."

"I didn't know that. I'd noticed a few new faces, but I thought it was normal turnover. I understand why you want us to leave, but where would we go?"

"The best place I can think of is your family estate. I doubt even Gremulkin would dare attack the count. At least I hope he wouldn't. The idea for us to leave must come from outside. An invitation or some such thing. I suggest we send a message to your father asking him to invite us to come for a visit. Maybe your mother could be sick, something along those lines. It has to be something urgent and innocent so that he wouldn't have an excuse to stop us."

"I can't believe he would have the nerve. You are the Duke's heir."

"All the more reason," Valdor replied. "He knows I suspect him, and I don't like him. With me out of the way, there would be nothing to stop him taking complete control."

"How can we do this?" Dinaz asked. "I could go into town to shop, and ask the sender to transmit a message. Do you think we can trust her?"

"Absolutely. She's a member of the League of Light. But I think I should send it."

"It's father's name day next week. It's perfectly natural for me to send greetings. I could buy him a gift as well while I'm in town."

"Very well. What would you say?"

"Let me think." She paused for a moment, considering the best way to word a message. "How about this: Dearest father, fond greetings on your name day. Need to see you urgently. Please invite us to come. Must be urgent reason, family member sick or...? Your loving daughter, Dinaz."

"I think that should get it across to him. I'm glad you didn't mention danger and you managed to get 'urgent' in twice. I'll go with you. I want to send a message to Commander Peshanar at the Monastery."

"Isn't it a little odd that there's no sender in the castle?" she commented. "I thought all the nobility employed them.

"We had one, remember? But he left shortly after Gremulkin arrived on the scene and father hasn't been able to persuade the Monastery to appoint a new one. Doesn't that tell you something is wrong here? When I think about it, we have *no* mages from the League at the castle. There always used to be two or three around. Father was rather fond of them, and he knew he could trust them. Poor father; he's got nobody now, except me. I won't desert him, but I must get away from the castle in order to help him. I'm powerless here."

"Where could you go for help?"

"The only place I can think of is the Monastery."

"What about your brother?"

"I'm not sure about Evanar. We've never been particularly close. Father paid much more attention to me when we were boys and I think he resents that. He was very attached to mother; she adored him and it was a terrible blow to him when she died. Besides, he's never here for more than a few days at a time. He seems to care about hunting more than what's happening here at home. I wouldn't be surprised if

Gremulkin has been trying to influence him, though. What better way to take over than to get rid of me and name Evanar heir? Then Gremulkin would be able to maintain control, not just of the castle, but the whole duchy.

"I see what you mean," she said taking his hand and leaning her head on his shoulder. She sighed. "I really hope it isn't that bad. I'll miss the capital. Shall we go in now?"

When they arrived at the hallway leading to their suite, they encountered Gremulkin reading a document standing close to one of the lamps. He looked up when they approached. "Well met, My Lord, is your headache better, My Lady?"

"Yes thank you, chancellor. A little fresh air always helps. Go with the Light."

He scowled, but in a flash turned it into a somewhat sour smile.

Once they were in their suite with the door closed, Dinaz whispered to her husband, "Do you think he's checking up on us?"

"Undoubtedly."

17 – Planning a Response

Daryan

"Your report has us very concerned," the Grand Master, said. "Yours is not the only one we've received. Almost all of our centers throughout the duchy have reported strange events, all of them dangerous and threatening in some way. I wanted to discuss with you what steps we can take to counter these attacks. Do you have any suggestions?"

"Yes, Grand Master, I have a number of ideas, but before we talk about them, may I know the extent of the threat?"

"Of course, Commander. I'll give you a brief summary of the incidents that have been reported, and there's a written report you can take with you to get the details." He stopped and rummaged through the papers on the table. "Where is that ... ah, this is it." He picked up a sheaf of papers tied together with a ribbon and handed them to Daryan, then continued. "There have been reports from Pontirav that packs of wolves and individual bears have been attacking people, mostly hunters and travelers on the roads, but some wolves have even invaded isolated farms and destroyed livestock. In Salispon—your area, I believe—there have been incidents of sickness among the livestock killing many swine and cattle. Apparently fish in the Morvis and other rivers are dying. We hear from Zinawar that not only are the fish dying, but the waterfowl too. In some places, they say the surface of the water is covered with the rotting carcasses of birds and fish. Down in Algonia, people, mainly children and the elderly, are succumbing to an unrecognized bleeding disease."

Daryan rubbed his forehead. "It's worse than I thought. What about werfolk? Are they connected to any of this?"

"We can't prove they are responsible, but there has been a great increase in sightings everywhere these event take place. And the disappearance of children continues. That is the most tragic and most urgent of the things we have to deal with."

"I..." Daryan shook his head. "I am astonished at the extent of it. It's hard to know where to start. I agree that we must put a stop to the taking of children, with all haste."

"What do you think would be the best approach, Commander?"

"We have a problem here in that we are unsure what action the duke will take, whether he will deploy his defenders. With or without the duke, we must bring the counties into this. They have their own militias, which they can use to protect their people, but their approach needs to be coordinated. I suggest we dispatch senior defenders to each county to work with the local militia in formulating plans for patrols to protect the local people and hunt down werfolk and strangers acting suspiciously. We would have to contact the counts first of course and get their agreements."

"As you say, the situation in DarSolas makes this complicated," the Grand Master said. "This is the really the duke's jurisdiction, but if, as you say, he is incapable of handling it, there is really no other authority aside from ours that is capable on a duchy-wide level. We cannot take this responsibility without first communicating with his grace, however, to find out if in fact he is willing and able to take charge. What I propose is to send another emissary, a team of archmages, to consult with him and to offer our services. They would be able to assess the situation, and I doubt the chancellor would dare to take any action against them. You would be invaluable to such a mission, but I would not want to put you in such a risky situation. You are too valuable to us here."

"Thank you, Grand Master, I understand, but I would not object if you wanted me to go." Daryan thought for a moment. "There's one other thing I should mention: Lord Valdor. I fear he may also be in danger. It's not too far-fetched to suppose that the chancellor might be influencing his younger brother, Lord Evanar, in order to supplant Valdor. During my conversation with him, I suggested he take his family away from the castle and find them a safe place to stay. I was hoping he would come here once they are safe. I am expecting a communication from him once he decides what to do."

"Yes. He is an honorable man. It would be disastrous to Trethawynd if he were lost. Please, when you hear from him, tell him I would welcome him here for a conference on the overall state of affairs, including his personal situation."

The arch mage looked out of the window and saw it was quite dark outside.

"One more thing and I'll let you go; we can continue this tomorrow." He went on to talk about the importance of strengthening the Legion of Light. After he'd finished, the Grand Master stood up. "I'll let you return to your family now, although we barely touched all the things that need action. We can continue tomorrow after the council meetings. Light be with you."

"Thank you Grand Master, you also."

18 – Incident at Cavalcitas

Andro Haro

One of the children screamed, "Dadi!"

Andro and Valina woke instantly, as parents are wont to do when their children are in danger. Andro saw a red glow from the window and heard a cacophony of noise outside, the screams of horses, men shouting, wolves howling, dogs barking.

He grabbed his knife and ran for the door. His three children were standing by the front door looking scared, the two younger ones crying. "The stables are on fire!" "The horses...!" "Dadi, what's happening?"

"I want you two," he fluffed the hair of the two youngest children, "to go to your mother and do exactly what she tells you while I find out! Olind, you come with me."

Andro and his eldest son ran out into the yard. The stable was in flames, but it looked as if Sherdon had brought most of the horses out; two mares and their foals were huddling by the far fence, the mares tossing their heads, eyes bulging in terror. His stable master was trying to lead a bucking stallion out of the stable.

"Sherdon!" he shouted, to get his attention. "Open the back gate and let the other horses in. Leave that one; he'll come out of his own accord."

He watched to make sure the man understood and did as he'd asked, then turned to thirteen-year-old Olind. "Would you go around the walls and look for breaches?" He turned and grabbed a pitchfork from the ground. "Here, take this to protect yourself. Come back and talk to me when you're done."

"What shall I do if I find a breach?"

"Let me know."

The dogs were running around in every direction, barking madly and trying to jump the wall. Outside the walls, it sounded as if a battle was taking place between demons from the abyss and a pack of wolves. Haro climbed up the steps to the top of the wall and looked out. It was a wolf pack all right, about twenty wolves chasing down an army of wermen armed with long knives and spears. Even though greatly outnumbered, it looked as if the wolves were winning. As he watched, he saw a huge wolf—it must have been the pack leader—take one of the creatures by the throat, shake it and toss it aside, then go on to the next one. It was a rout; the creatures racing for the tree line pursued by a pack of wolves. He climbed down, went to the back gate and walked into the meadow to assess the damage there. One of his prize mares was lying on the ground, unable to get up, screaming in agony from a long deep gash in her abdomen. He went to her and cradled her head in his arms, murmuring comforting words as he took his knife and severed the artery in her neck. He jumped back quickly to avoid the fountain of blood that followed; nevertheless, his tunic and trousers were soaked.

Back at the gate, he saw Olind and Sherdon trying to calm the other horses and drive them through into the paddock. He went back into the yard and looked at his stable. The flames were dying down, having consumed all the flammable material inside—hay, blankets, wooden roof beams and stalls. The building itself was still standing although the brick walls were blackened with soot. It looked as if he would have to refit the interior completely.

Olind came to join him. "It's awful, dadi. How can anyone to something like this?"

"The thrice-cursed Dark Brotherhood has no mercy for man or beast. Nothing is too evil for them." He wiped his face with the bottom of his tunic, leaving a streak of blood on his forehead. "How are the walls?"

"I found a few of the logs burning, so I took some water and dowsed them. They're still smoking, but it'll die down now they're wet."

"Good thinking, son. Anything else?"

Olind shook his head. "No breakthroughs or anything like that." He looked around the yard. "Dadi, what was all that noise with the wolves?"

"You remember when Commander Peshanar and his daughter were here, and she introduced me to the wolf leader?" Olind nodded. "Well, it paid off. That was the wolf pack attacking the creatures responsible for all this."

"Wow ... wow! Did they get them all?"

"Almost. Some of them ran away, but the pack went after them."

Sherdon joined them. "Did we get them all out?" Daryan asked him.

The man wiped a black stained rag across his face, leaving a trail of soot mixed with the sweat. "I sorry, Sir Andro, there was one trapped at the end of the row, the little roan mare. Beams fell from the roof, all ablaze, and I couldn't get past them. We've lost all the tack and most of the hay as well. What could have caused this? Who would do something like this?"

"I don't know, Sherdon, but I'm going to find out." With his hands on his hips, he looked around the yard. "We've a lot of work ahead of us. For now, fill some troughs with water for the horses. We can do the rest after we've had some sleep. Thank the Light the wolves took care of the attackers. I'm going to look around outside again." He turned to Olind. "Go in and tell your mother everything is all right now. Then you can go to bed. Thanks for the help, son. Sleep well!"

"Watch out for those wolves, sir."

"Sherdon, I'm not concerned about them; they're on our side."

"You mean that girl...?"

"She may have had something to do with it."

"Well bless me!"

Taking a lantern, Andro did a complete circuit outside the wall. He saw one dead wolf, and dozens of dead werfolk, looking just as repulsive as he remembered them from past encounters. They'd have to burn the bodies tomorrow when the extra stable hands would be around to help. The only breach in the wall was where the stable butted against it. It looked as if the raiders had thrown burning torches over onto the stable roof and the fire had spread along the wall, but the damage was minor.

He would have to send a message to Daryan at the Monastery on the morrow to report the incident.

Back inside the paddock gate, he spoke once again to Sherdon. "I'm going to leave this gate open so that the horses can get out to the pasture. They'll be able to sense if there's any danger and go out by themselves when they feel it's safe, meanwhile, make sure those two mares have some hay if there's any left."

"There's a couple of bales down at the end where the fire didn't reach."

"Have you got somewhere to sleep?"

"I'll manage, sir."

"You're welcome to sleep at the house, Sherdon. I need you to be rested for the morrow. I'm going to stay on watch, but first I have to reassure my family, so wait for me, then I want you to rest."

"Light bless you, sir."

19 – Planning

Daryan

The meeting with the Grand Master was dominated by news from ValkonenMaa.

"The whole monastery?" Daryan exclaimed. "Things are even worse than I'd feared. How about survivors?"

The Grand Master sighed and smoothed a pile of papers before him on the table. "There are some, but they are scattered all over the duchy. From what I hear, they're converging on the capital to plan a course of action. Most of them have taken shelter at the duke's castle. There's no news of the Grand Master apart from the fact that he disappeared during the attack; it's not known whether he was taken prisoner or is in hiding, although I feel that if he were in hiding, he would have contacted someone by now. My fear is that he may no longer live."

"I hope you're wrong, Grand Master. It would be a terrible blow to the League, and a tragedy if those fiends have killed him. About those who escaped, should we invite them to join us here in Trethawynd?"

"I've already let them know they would be welcome if they want to come here, but my feeling is they will be more concerned about protecting their own people. We'll more likely end up sending them our help." The Grand Master took Daryan's report from the table. "Let's get to this, shall we?" he said.

After they'd finished discussing a variety of topics relating to Daryan's trip to DarSolas, the two men took some refreshment. It was another lovely late-spring day with a cloudless sky. The Grand Master's study in the east tower of the white castle, looked out upon fields of burgeoning crops—grain, fruit, and vegetables—spread to the distant tree line.

"It looks as if we'll have a bountiful harvest again this year," the Grand Master said, turning from the window. "I believe you have a couple of ideas to discuss, Commander. Would you like to begin?"

"Yes, thank you. They may seem a bit unusual, but these are unusual circumstances. I'm not sure whether the first one will work, but I feel it's worth a try. It's about the prisoner, the werman. I'd like to have some time with him to find out if we can turn his capture to our advantage. That's why I wanted him kept alive. First, I'd like to try to get more information out of him about why he was here and why they are abducting children. I don't think we would be violating any ethical constraints if we used our powers to this purpose." He looked questioningly at the Grand Master who replied with a nod of his head.

"There are a number of psychological techniques we could apply, along with our gifts. If we succeed with that part, I would like to try to turn him into an agent, to go among his own kind and get information for us."

"They'd probably kill him the minute they see him," the Grand Master said.

"Well, sir, he would be executed by us for what he did to that child, so I feel we would be giving him a chance of survival, narrow though it may be."

"Very well, commander, you have our approval. But you have many other duties to perform, so you will only be able to pursue it in your spare time."

"I understand, sir. My second proposal concerns my daughter, Felindra." Daryan went on to elaborate on the ways in which her gift could be useful, particularly having Ashala gather information for them from other creatures in the forest, particularly wolves.

"That's a very interesting proposal, Commander. I will think about it and bring it up with the council. It is marvelous to have a whisperer among us. Maybe the Light chose this as an auspicious time for her to come among us. However, we must keep in mind that she is still very young and her gift comes at a cost in emotional and psychological stress. We don't want her to wear herself out. She needs to take part in other activities and continue with her education. After being in the field and witnessing events like those on your last trip, she needs time to recover her equilibrium."

"I'll make sure she gets it, Grand Master. Thank you for your concern."

"Thank you, commander. I'll let you go now. You've given us something to think about. I'll let you know as soon as we decide something. Go with the Light."

20 – Daryan Visits Axtya

Daryan

"How's he been behaving?" Daryan asked the defender who escorted him.

"It's got some pretty disgusting habits, filthy creature."

"What's he been doing?"

"Well for one thing, it likes to throw its excrement at us, and it keeps asking for rats."

"He must be feeling pretty powerless. I suggest we put one of those disposal units in for him to use. That way the excrement will be processed before he can get his hands on it."

"If it will use it. It's just as likely to do it on the floor."

Daryan ignored the comment. "As for rats, they may be a part of his normal diet. There's nothing intrinsically wrong with rat meat, even though we may think it's disgusting, but when you've nothing else to eat.... They live in caves and there's not much food to be found there. Anyway, we're going to start working on him today to see if we can make something of him. Oh, and I'd appreciate if everyone stopped referring to him as 'it'. If we are going to get his cooperation, we need to make him feel like a person, not a thing."

They came to the door of the room that held the prisoner. The Monastery didn't have a prison or detention cells, so Axtya was being kept in a storeroom in the basement of the defenders' quarters.

A strange droning nose came from within the room.

"What's that noise?" Daryan asked the defender.

"Oh it ... *he* does that all the time. I think he's singing in his own disgusting way." He opened the door and the droning stopped.

It was a clean room with a small window near the ceiling. To look out, the prisoner had to stand on a stool. The stone walls were painted grey and the floor was covered in stone paving. The furniture consisted of a child-sized pallet and a small table with a stool. Several garments hung on wooden pegs near the bed. A bucket with a lid in the corner served as a receptacle for body wastes.

Axtya was sitting on the floor with his back to the opposite wall, rocking back and forth. He looked clean and didn't smell as bad as he had when Daryan had last seen him. His right arm was still encased in a thick bandage that started at the elbow and covered it almost to the shoulder; the hand and forearm were gone. The werman had been kept in the Monastery infirmary for two days after the amputation surgery, until they were satisfied that the infection no longer endangered his life. He was now wearing a pair of child's blue knee trousers that almost reached his ankles, and a child-size blue shirt. The werman was still not a very attractive sight by human standards, but Daryan didn't feel the revulsion he'd previously felt. In fact, he seemed rather pathetic. A flicker of recognition showed in the werman's eyes when he saw Daryan, but otherwise, there was no change in his expression, which was one of dull hopelessness.

"Well met, Axtya. You remember me don't you? I'm Commander Daryan. I see your arm is getting better. How do you feel?"

No answer, just a scowl.

"I would like you to come upstairs to one of our leisure rooms so that we can have a chat. I'm sure you'd be interested in what is going to happen to you. I know you don't want to spend the rest of your days in here." Daryan said, trying to sound encouraging without being patronizing. The hardest thing was trying to talk to him as an adult and not a child. "Shall we go?"

"Kill me."

"Why should we kill you after we've gone to all this trouble to save your life?"

"No care."

"Why don't you come and hear what we have to say? We might be able to make your life more interesting than it is sitting down here doing nothing all day. We might even be able to let you go free."

"No care. Dead now." He raised the stump of his arm.

"We can *make* you come with us, but I would it prefer if you made the choice. While we're there, we can talk about the kind of food you like and other things that might make you more comfortable." He still wasn't sure the creature understood what he was saying.

Axtya sighed, stood up slowly and walked towards the door. This was the first time Daryan had seen him upright, walking. He really was a small person, his head barely reaching Daryan's chest. When he walked, his body rocked from side to side.

Daryan stepped out first. "This way," he said, starting slowly down the hall towards the staircase. Axtya followed him passively, his expression showing no curiosity. The defender followed behind. When they reached the ground floor, Daryan turned into a small room with a couple of tables and some chairs. Someone had left a pile of books on one of the tables. The window facing the garden was open allowing a gentle breeze to cool the air. Two other people were sitting at one of the tables with a pitcher and some mugs in front of them.

"Sit wherever you like Axtya."

The little man looked around the room and scowled at the two people seated at the table. "Who?"

"They are here to help with your interview. The young lady is Marwin, and the man is Jovan. We are all interested and learning more about you and discovering how best we can help you, and how you can help us."

"Hear think. Stupid." He spat on the floor.

"Please sit down somewhere. I don't feel comfortable sitting while someone is standing."

Axtya climbed up onto the chair farthest from the other people, but instead of sitting on it, he knelt and looked out the window.

"Would you like to tell us something about yourself?"

"No! No help."

"Do you have a family? A wife? Children?"

"Shut up, shut up, shut up." He covered his ears with his left hand and right stump.

"Where is your home? You must miss your home and your family."

"*No talk.*" He almost shrieked this time.

"I have a wife and two children. How many children do you have?

No answer.

"That little boy you killed had a mother and a father. He was their only child."

"No kill."

"You didn't kill him? Then who did?"

"Axtya no kill." He shook his head vehemently.

"But he's dead. So who do you think killed him?"

"Father."

"No, that's not possible. He loved his little boy. He wouldn't kill him."

Axtya got down from the chair and walked to the door. "Go now."

"You want to go back to your room? But what about telling us what kind of food you like?"

"RATS!" he shrieked and left the room.

The defender went to stop him, but Daryan said, "Let him go. Follow him down and see if he goes back to his room."

"And if he doesn't?"

"Let him go, but watch him."

After they had left, Daryan turned to the other two and said, "I didn't handle that very well did I?"

"No, it was good," Jovan replied. "Touching on emotional topics can elicit some interesting responses."

"Let's go over what you got," Daryan requested.

Marwin, who was a defender and an empath, replied first. "A great deal of hostility, a nagging feeling of dread, fear, plus an underlying sadness and longing."

"Anything else?" Marwin shook her head. "Thank you, Marwin. Jovan?"

"When you asked about his family, I got an image of a female ... werwoman? ... She was wearing a short grey skirt made of what looked like animal skin. Two children, very young—it's hard to tell their age by size—but I'd guess under five years. They were naked ... both boys. They were in a small dark room, a cave or tunnel, I would guess. The light came from an oil wick in a stone bowl."

"Ah, so he does have a family."

He nodded. "About the murder of the little boy, I think he was telling the truth. I don't think he killed him."

"Did you get any indication of how the body came into his possession?"

"Nothing definite, just a flash of his seeing the bag under some bushes."

"Anything else?"

"He really does like rat meat. I felt him longing for it."

Daryan sighed. "I suppose we'll have to get some for him. I'll send a message to some of the farmers to catch a few and send them up. Unless there's anything else, that's all for today. Thank you for your help."

When Daryan got back to his office, there was a message for him. *Messages received from Lord Valdor and Andro, Communication Mage Divora.* He took the note and rushed over to the communications center on the ground floor of the white palace.

Inside was a circular bank of crystals on pedestals with a mage sitting by each of them. The student mage who sat closest to the door didn't appear to be occupied when Daryan entered, so he spoke to her. "I have a message to see Mage Divora."

"Yes, she's over there." She pointed out an older woman on the other side of the circle who had both hands on the crystal in front of her and looked as if she was listening. "I think she's receiving right now, but you can go and see her as soon as she's finished. Would you like some tea?"

"That would be very nice. Thank you."

"Come over here and sit down." She led him to a small table by the wall and poured him a mug of hot tea, and then returned to her station.

He sipped the tea until he saw Divora take her hands off the crystal and stretch her arms above her head. She looked over at him, picked up a small writing board, and stood up.

"Commander Peshanar?"

"Yes, archmage, I received your message."

"Well met, commander. Let's go in here where we won't be disturbing anyone." She opened the door into a small room furnished with a table and several chairs.

"Which one do you want to hear first?"

"Give me the bad news first."

"It's from Andro Haro: Cavalcitas was attacked last night. No lives were lost, no human lives, that is. Lost two horses and the stables were destroyed by fire. The attackers were werfolk, and here's the amazing part: a pack of wolves came to their rescue and killed many of the attackers. He wants you to know that everyone is well and say thank you to Felindra and Ashala. Do you want to send a reply?"

"Thank the Light no one was hurt. No, lady, no reply. Now, what did Lord Valdor have to say?"

"Gremulkin seems to be consolidating his power and Valdor fears for the safety of his family. He is waiting for an invitation from Count Yima and intends to leave as soon as it arrives. Says he fears the chancellor may try to influence his brother. He asks whether you can suggest a place where he can stay until things are settled. He adds that if you send him any messages, tell Mage Avaya, to give them only to his personal footman, Firton. He will send Firton into town frequently to check with her. That's about it," she finished off. "I'll take these summaries and erase them now," she added. "Unless there's a reply."

"Not at this moment. I need to consult with the Grand Master before I have an answer, but thank you." He left the communications center and went up the stairs to the tower vestibule, where he spoke to the mage on duty. "I'd like to have a word with the Grand Master. Would you find out if he has a few minutes to see me, please?"

"I'll check for you, commander." She got up from her chair and went through a door behind it. A couple of minutes later, she returned. "Yes, commander, you may go up."

Daryan went through the door to another hall with a white marble staircase curving up around the right hand wall. Two flights up, he came to the Grand Master's suite. A page opened the door for him. The Grand Master was standing by the window looking out over the farmlands. He turned when he heard Daryan's footsteps crossing the floor.

"Commander! What can I do for you? Have a seat."

Daryan waited until the Grand Master was seated before taking the chair opposite him. "I just received a message from Lord Valdor and thought you should know about it, Grand Master."

"Yes, go on."

"As I mentioned yesterday, he is planning to leave the castle and go to the Count of Argento's estate. As you know, the count is the father of Lord Valdor's wife, so they are going to use the relationship as an opportunity for a family visit. In his message, Valdor mentioned that he might be in need of sanctuary if things deteriorate at the castle. I was hoping we could offer him such a place."

The Grand Master cupped his chin in his hand while he thought for a moment. "Personally, I would be delighted to welcome him here, but I foresee complications if we offer him sanctuary. We would be placing ourselves in a position contra to the constitutional government of the duchy. Our charter forbids our becoming involved in political matters. That's how we've survived all these years. Once we start intervening on one side or another in disputes of this sort, the authority of the duchy could, and probably would in the current situation, post grievances against the Monastery, and might even resort to military intervention. We cannot change our obligations to our brotherhood, no matter how compelling the reason."

"I understand, Grand Master. Would there be any problem if he visited the Monastery as a guest for a few days while he sorts out what he is going to do? We need not talk of sanctuary."

"Only if we issued a formal invitation through official channels. For that, he would need the consent of his father, the duke."

"What do you think are the chances of it going through?"

"Not very promising, but if you and he, wish it, I can arrange it for an invitation to be sent to the Castle."

"Would we have to have a reason for an invitation?"

"Oh, I think we could find one, the graduation of apprentice mages, or something like that."

Daryan smiled. "Should I send him a message about the idea?"

"Let's not rush into it. I'll let you know what I decide."

***

Daryan climbed the stairs wearily and opened the door to their suite. He found Parvana sorting through some of their clothes.

She put down the tunic she was folding and came over to kiss him. "How was your day?" she asked. "You look tired."

"I didn't achieve very much today. It's so frustrating when everything you want to do comes to naught." He looked around, suddenly realizing how quiet it was. "Where are Felindra and Darson?"

"They're out somewhere with friends. I'm glad they're making some friends." She went to the table in the middle of the room and picked up a pitcher. "Would you like something to drink?"

"No thank you. I have a better idea." He put his arm around her shoulder and led her into their sleeping alcove. "It's not often we have the place to ourselves," he said, kissing her neck as he untied the fastening of her tunic.

After the children were asleep, Daryan and Parvana walked in the garden.

"We'll have more privacy when we move into our new home," Parvana said.

"Have you seen it?

"Yes. I went over there today. It's a good place. I think we'll move in tomorrow, if I can get some help with the boxes and chests."

"I'll take care of it, my love. Is there a road to take the wagon?" Most of their household belongings were still sitting in the wagon behind the stables.

"Yes. There's a path that looks wide enough. We could bring it here first to load our clothes and things, and then take it all in one trip."

"Good. I'll arrange for some men to come and unload for you. I'm looking forward to having our own place again, and I know you are."

They walked on, hand in hand, doing one more circuit of the garden. "What sort of problems?" she asked.

"What?"

"You were saying earlier something about nothing going according to plan."

"Oh, that. We'll find a solution."

"Would you like to talk about it?"

They turned at the end of the walk and retraced their steps. "I had a message today from Lord Valdor. He more or less hinted at looking for a sanctuary where he can get away from the influence of Gremulkin. I talked to the Grand Master and he said we can't get involved in political affairs."

"Is it that bad?"

"Valdor thinks so. I got the impression he's afraid of what the chancellor may do next."

"Why can't he stay with his father-in-law?"

"I don't know. It might put the count in conflict with his liege lord, the duke. It would probably be as perilous for him as it would for the Monastery to offer sanctuary. I suggested inviting Valdor here as a guest so that we could talk about it. He said he'd consider it."

"There, you see, some way out of the dilemma may be possible. You inferred there was more than one problem."

"It's that werman. I don't seem to be getting very far with him. He refuses to talk to us ... after all we've done for him! It's not as if we're mistreating him. Other agencies would torture him to get at the truth." Daryan felt a twinge of guilt; what he'd already done to the werman might be considered a form of torture. He had certainly given Axtya no reason to trust him.

They sat down on a bench by the fountain. "I have an idea! How would you like to meet him?"

"I suppose I could. What's he like?"

"I'd rather you made your own judgment about him than color your opinion with my feelings. It would be very helpful if you could come to our next session and practice your persuasion techniques on him."

"When?"

"How about tomorrow?"

"I thought we were moving tomorrow. I suppose we could see him first and take care of the move afterwards. If we start early enough, we should be able to manage it. I don't know how successful I'll be, but I'm willing to try."

"Don't forget that during the wolf attack; most of your energy was devoted to bringing light, but you persuaded some of the wolves turn away. This time you can concentrate it all on your persuasive powers." He took her hand. "I have complete confidence in you, mother of my children and most superior woman."

21 – Lord Valdor Goes to Argento

Valdor

As soon as he arrived back at the castle, Valdor went to his father's suite. The old man was sitting before the fire with a robe over his legs, as usual, and a glass of warmed wine in his hand. Gremulkin was standing by the hearth with his back to the window.

"Come in, my boy," the duke greeted him. "Have a seat. Would you like some spiced wine?"

"No, thank you, father. How are you feeling?"

"Oh, not much better. I seem to spend most of my time sleeping these days. Leaving all the work to poor Gremulkin."

Valdor looked at Gremulkin. "Oh, I'm sure he can handle it, father. But if you ever need my help, you have only to ask."

"Thank you, son, I'll keep it in mind. Now, I'm sure you didn't come to discuss my health. What can I do for you?"

"I am always concerned about your health, father." Valdor willed himself not to give Gremulkin an accusatory look. "I came to tell you I'm going away for a few days. Dinaz's grandmother is dying and she wants to see her granddaughter one last time"

"Lady Consella? I'm distressed to hear that. She was a great beauty in her day. A remarkable woman. Used to visit us all the time, always made a big impression with the young lads. I think she liked coming here and receiving all that attention." He stopped, deep in thought for a moment. A brief smile tugged at the corner of his mouth. "Ah well, can't dwell on the old days. Of course you must go, my boy. When will you leave?"

"Early tomorrow, I hope."

"You'll need an escort, My Lord. Would you like me to talk to the guard commander and arrange it?" Gremulkin asked. He smiled, but it was not an attractive smile.

"Thank you, Chancellor; I've already taken care of it."

"As you wish, My Lord. Please give my condolences to Lady Dinaz."

"Thank you, Chancellor. I will." *Why does he always make me feel so inadequate?*

"With your permission, father." He bent to kiss his father's cheek.

"Go with the Light, my son. And give my condolences to Lady Dinaz."

Valdor let out a long breath once the door was closed. *That went better than I expected,* he thought as he hurried down the hall to his own suite. *Naturally, he would want to choose my escort. I'd as soon put my family in an alligator pond. I wonder what he was looking so pleased about. Does he want me to leave?*

***

An impressive entourage, befitting the heir to the duchy, left the castle shortly after sunrise the next morning. A coach and a baggage wagon, escorted by six of Lord Valdor's personal knights, and four defenders chosen by Valdor from the castle garrison. Lady Dinaz rode in the coach with Jilly, her personal maid, and Jilly's governess. Valdor, his secretary Imali, and son Varan rode horses. Three pages rode on the baggage wagon with two knights and two defenders riding ahead and behind the column, while the other two knights rode on either side of the coach.

It saddened Valdor to be leaving his home, not knowing when he would be able to return. Of course, if the duke sent for him, he would have to return, but he would never voluntarily go back as long as Gremulkin was there. He could do nothing to protect his father and the duchy from within the castle now that Gremulkin has sunk his talons in so deeply. It would be folly, not knowing whom to trust and whom he'd corrupted. The chancellor's control over the duke was insidious. Even old retainers could be under his control;

all Gremulkin needed to do was persuade his father to order them to obey the chancellor.

As they entered the town of DarSolas, Valdor turned to his secretary, who was riding just behind him. "Imali, would you ride ahead to the sender's premises and see if there are any messages?"

"As you wish, My Lord. I'm on my way."

But there was no message. Valdor sighed. Maybe there would be one at Argento. He wondered why he hadn't heard anything from Daryan

The first night, Lord Valdor's entourage set up camp, erecting their tents on the banks of the River Stelgo just outside the village of Kist north of Palgrigio. They had made good time the first day, but the road began to climb north of Kist, and it was slower going.

Next day, they crossed the mighty Devin River that flowed westward from the mountains. Once over the river, they had to circumvent the Great Swamp. This forced the road to take to the foothills of the mountain range. They had left the farmland behind and were now traveling through forest. The road began to twist and turns as it edged through the foothills. Although the road didn't run very high up the incline, it seemed that travelling along the side of the mountain was more difficult than actually climbing it would be. There were frequent ravines and wild rock-strewn streams to cross on wooden bridges, barely wide enough for a wagon. Most of the time, there were precipitous drop-offs on the left and steep mountainside on the right. The trees on this terrain were sparse and did little to alleviate the heat or smell from the swamp below the road.

"Is it much farther?" Varan asked. "I'm so hot and these flies are killing me."

"It's not much farther, son; we should be there before nightfall. See, the road is starting to descend now."

"I'll be glad when we are past this stinking swamp."

The road was now only a few spans above the swamp on the left, affording them a symphony of wildlife sounds, the shrieks of waterfowl, the belching grunts of alligators, the chirruping and croaking of frogs. Clumps of trees stood on knee-like roots above the water, which was coated with green scum and veiled in mist.

Suddenly a thunderous boom came from above, followed by a heavy rumble traveling down the mountain towards them, sounding like a dozen wagons racing at full speed. The sharp cracks of branches snapping off trees added to the din. Clouds of birds took to the air screeching.

So startling and confusing was the noise that all Valdor had time for was to shout to his son, "Go back!" before a shower of massive boulders fell on the road in front of them.

They heard horses and people screaming, but the cloud of dust raised by the avalanche of rocks and debris blocked their view of everything in front of them. Valdor and the escorts were off their horses and rushing forward as the dust settled, but they were too late. The coach carrying his wife and daughter was gone. All that remained in their place were the badly mutilated bodies of one of the knights and his horse. Valdor looked around, stunned. Everyone still alive seemed dazed, numb with shock.

Valdor looked down over the edge of the road. The crushed coach was lying on its side in the murky water; nothing moved within. Even the two horses, still harnessed to the coach lay twisted into unnatural positions, motionless. Valdor saw a sinuous movement under the water slithering towards the coach and gagged.

"We have to go down there," he shouted, trying to get his escort to start moving. "Someone might still be alive." Tears of frustration and fear ran down his face.

"My lord, you should stay here. It's too dangerous. We'll go," Sir Arvand, one of his knights, said.

"No! It's *my* wife, *my* daughter. I have to get to them out."

"I know, My Lord, and I'm devastated, but our primary purpose is to protect you. I can't permit you to risk your life. I insist that you stay here. Your son needs you right now." Arvand had been in service of the duke for more than twenty-five years—since they were both boys—and was devoted to the family. "Please don't force me to restrain you, sir," he said gently. "We'll get to them, I promise you." He turned to the other knight and said, "Take care of his lordship, Karan."

While he had been arguing with Arvand, Valdor saw that four defenders and two knights were already climbing down the rocks, accompanied by Imali and the driver of the baggage wagon. He could feel anger building up inside him. "Can't someone do something about that horse?" He yelled, pulling his sword from its scabbard and rushing down the road to where the wounded horse lay screaming and struggling to get up. He could see that both its hind legs were crushed.

"I'll take care of it My Lord," Karan said, coming up behind him. "Stand back please, My Lord." He drew a long dagger from his belt and rapidly slashed the artery in the horse's neck. Its thrashing and screaming faded as its lifeblood ran out onto the road.

Valdor noticed the bodies of two pages lying by the supply wagon, innocent young boys, their bodies crushed by falling rocks. *What more?* He looked around at the mayhem on the road, and then glanced back down towards the swamp.

Valdor suddenly remembered his son; he should be with him. It was Varan's loss as much as his own. "Where's my son?"

"He's sitting over there, My Lord, on that rock."

The boulder on which Varan sat was sheltered by an overhanging rock. He walked to his son, followed closely by Karan. The knight's eyes were constantly moving up and down the road, up the mountainside, and down at the swamp, determined nothing more would threaten his lord.

Valdor went and sat down next to his son who was valiantly trying to stifle his sobs. He put his arm around the boy's shoulder. "I'm so sorry, son."

"Why?" Varan took a clean square of cotton from his pocket, wiped his face and blew his nose.

"This trip... I didn't ... How could I know this could happen?"

"But we had to go," Varan said. "Mother's grandmother is dying."

How would he explain that lie to his son? Valdor was drowning in despair. He put his head in his hands, trying to block everything from his mind, but it was impossible.

"Are mami and Jilly...?" Varan asked in a squeaky voice. He cleared his throat.

"I don't know, son. Men are down there now, trying to free them from the coach. We'll have to wait until they come up."

Varan got up and walked to the edge of the road "What's taking them so long?"

"Lord Varan, you must come away from there," Karan shouted, running after the boy and grabbing him by the arm. "You must stay in the shelter."

Valdor joined them. "Do as he say's son. Come over here with me." *No one could survive that,* he thought as he looked down on the scene below. *All this because I was too cowardly to face Gremulkin. Damn his rotten soul!* But he couldn't sit still, doing nothing. He stood up, crossed the road again and looked down. He sensed Karan behind him.

The men were waist deep in the muddy water, prying panels loose from the coach and peering in through the gaps. One man climbed on the side that was facing up and leaned in the window. He shook his head and climbed down. The men left the coach and gathered in a group apparently discussing what to do next. One of them looked up at him and quickly away. It was obvious from their demeanor that they hadn't found anyone alive. His wife and daughter were gone in a

flash, their serving women with them. All because of *him* …
that accursed chancellor! *And my own cowardice,* he added

The men reached the top of the embankment and pulled
themselves up onto the road. They were covered in mud from
head to toe, pieces of weed clinging to their clothing. Sir
Arvand came to his side. "I'm sorry, My Lord, but …" he
coughed and cleared his throat. "… there are no survivors."

A whooshing came from above, so fast that no one had
time to even duck. An arrow embedded itself into the side of
the baggage wagon.

"Take cover!" Arvand shouted, grabbing Valdor and Varan
and shoving them down beside the wagon.

Some of the men took shelter under the rocky shelf below
the mountainside. After a moment, one of the escort guards
put his head out to see where it came from and another arrow
flew past, just missing him.

"It's a good thing they're such bad shots," Arvand said,

"The horses!" Valdor exclaimed. "We have to protect them
or we'll never get out of here."

Two horses were still harnessed to the baggage wagon,
but the riderless mounts of Valdor and his escort had
wandered down the hill and were now grazing on some
vegetation at the side of the road.

"Ben," Arvand said to the wagon driver who was crouching
by the front wheel. "Can you get those horses moving without
getting shot?"

"I can try. I just have to take them by the reins, but
someone will have to pull out the chock." He pointed to the
thick wooden wedge under the back wheel that kept the
wagon from moving. "Problem is they might shoot the
horses."

"We'll have to risk it," Valdor said, "Make them go as fast
as you can until they are out of range. I don't think whoever
is shooting is a very good shot."

"As you wish, My Lord."

The driver, ran in a crouch to take the reins of the nearest horse. "Now!"

"Be ready to run with it, My Lord," Arvand said and pulled out the chock by its rope handle.

The wagon would have moved down the slope by itself once the chock was removed, but Arvand wanted them to run, not dawdle. Ben gave a sharp tug on the harness and the horse started up slowly as its partner took a moment to get in step, then they were off at a gentle trot. Valdor, his son, Sir Arvand and the secretary kept pace with it running in a crouch. Two more arrows were released, but they missed the horses; one embedded itself in the wagon's canopy.

As soon as the wagon was out of range, Ben jumped up on the box and tried to set the handbrake with one hand while pulling on the reins with the other to get the horses to stop.

"Would you mind getting the other men down here?" Valdor said to Sir Karan. "Be careful; I don't want any more casualties."

"I wonder how many there are up there," Sir Arvand said, looking up the mountainside. "We may learn more about who they are when we look at the arrows. There may be something distinctive about the fletching and the way they're made that could give us a clue."

"Good, that's something we need to know," Valdor added. "Listen, Arvand, we have to get word to the count. Get him to send a rescue party. Can you pick one of the men to ride to Argento? We can follow as soon as it's safe to move."

"Very well, My Lord, I'll send Linwal."

As soon as the defender was dispatched, the remainder of the party started to move cautiously down the road, sheltering wherever they could, leading their horses on foot. After going around a couple of bends and hearing nothing more from above, they mounted and started at a trot towards Argento. Valdor looked back over his shoulder as he turned the bend in the road, as if expecting to see his loved ones behind him. *They're behind us all right,* Valdor thought bitterly, *and always will be now.* Tears pressed his eyes painfully, attempting to escape, until he relaxed his control over them and allowed them to be carried away by the wind. Eventually, he took out a handkerchief to wipe his face.

Valdor was riding beside his secretary. "You realize, Imali, that we might have thought it a natural disaster if they hadn't started shooting at us. That seems to me a very stupid tactic."

"Unless they wanted us to know. I think they really wanted to get you; that's why they used their bows. It's just bad luck that they got the coach instead." Imali had been with Valdor for fifteen years. He was more than a secretary; he was a friend and companion. They still played cards and went hunting and sailing together.

"It might have been bandits," the knight on his other side said. "Just taking advantage of the situation."

Valdor was silent for a while. The pain of his loss and his guilt gnawed at him unbearably. *How am I going to face the count and countess? Will he blame me? He has a right to; it was my fault... I have to leave Varan with them and go back after the burial. But where will I go if I can't go to the Monastery...? What I should do is go back to DarSolas and confront Gremulkin... Dinaz! Jilly! Life will be so empty without you. Oh, Light, help me; please help me.*

***

Count Yima of Argento pushed himself back in his chair, trying to get comfortable. He'd been troubled with sore joints in recent years and was never able to sit in one position for long. He was a short rather stout man with receding hair and a bushy moustache that seemed designed to compensate for the loss above.

"Would you like a footstool, my dear?" Lady Roshan asked.

"Bring me a footstool, Bennis," he said to the footman. He raised his feet and allowed the man to place the padded stool under them. "Ah, that's better. Thank you."

The count and Lady Roshan both had red-rimmed eyes from weeping over their daughter and granddaughter. The dreadful news was still sinking in, but the count couldn't talk about it anymore.

"What's this trouble you're having?" he asked Valdor, who'd been sitting still as a statue, slumped over before the fire.

"It seems so trivial after what happened, My Lord Count." Valdor replied, straightening up. "Although I fear it may be connected to what happened today. I have no proof, that's the problem."

"If it is, I certainly want to hear what you have to say. Would tell me about it? I need to make sense of this awful...." he shook his head and sighed.

"As you know, my father's former chancellor, Mauban, died in an accident a couple of years ago, and suddenly Gremulkin turned up. It's too much of a coincidence." Valdor told his father-in-law about the adverse changes the chancellor's activities had brought about at the castle. "Father's health has declined rapidly since Gremulkin came, and he's very weak. I don't know how long he'll be with us, I'm afraid."

"Yes, I've heard something about the man. Sounds like a very unsavory character, if you ask me," the count said.

"Poor Ostran. I can't imagine him being weak. He was such a robust, energetic man. Do you think we should pay him a visit, my dear?" the countess asked her husband.

"We'll talk about it after the internment of our daughter," he replied. "Go on, Valdor. What else?"

"Everything came to a head last week when a delegation came from the Monastery at the request of my father, at the chancellor's bidding, I'm sure. He does things now that he never would have before and seems afraid to go against Gremulkin's will." Valdor went on to describe the incident.

"That's outrageous," the count said with a scowl.

"There's worse," Valdor continued. "He impounded their horses. Oh yes, there's one more thing: one of the mages with Commander Peshanar is a life sensor. He said he could sense some sort of evil force coming from Gremulkin. He called it dark life."

"It all sounds very irregular, I'll admit. And he is obviously a very unpleasant fellow, but you're going to require something more solid to take action."

"I realize that, My Lord. I was hoping you could offer me some guidance."

"I'll think about it, son, but right now, I must go to bed." He struggled to his feet and hobbled to where Valdor was sitting. "Don't worry, my boy, we'll get to the bottom of this and if this Gremulkin fellow has anything to do with what happened today, I'll rally every county in the Duchy of Trethawynd to support the duke and oust the fellow. Let me sleep on it, if I can get any sleep after today." He squeezed Valdor's arm.

"Light be with you, Lord Yima."

22 – Axtya Talks

Daryan

Daryan was feeling optimistic as he descended the stairs. He knocked and opened the door to Axtya's room, expecting him to up and dressed, ready to go out, but the little werman was lying naked on his cot with his good arm over his eyes.

"Good morning, Axtya," he said. "Are you sick?"

The werman slowly uncovered his eyes and turned his head to look at Daryan. "Sick here," he said, thumping his chest with his left fist.

"In your heart?"

"Heart. Yes."

"What can we do to help?"

"Kill me."

"You don't really want to die, do you? What about your wife and children? Do you really want to leave them without you to support them?"

Axtya's head drooped as a tear leaked out of his eye. He rolled over and buried his face in the blanket.

"Would you like to go outside?" Daryan asked.

The werman raised his head and turned sideways to look at Daryan. "Out there?" He sat up and looked at the window.

"Yes, out there? I thought you might be tired of being in here all the time."

"I go."

"Well put some clothes on and we'll go now."

Daryan sighed. *The things I have to do to get him to talk, when, in reality, I'd like to strangle the wretched creature.*

When he was dressed, Daryan led him up the stairs. They had decided to dispense with guards and locked doors. There was nowhere the prisoner could go, and today Daryan planned to tell him that Ashala was out there.

"Before we go outside, there's someone I want you to meet."

The prisoner backed away, looking suspicious and afraid.

"Don't worry; we're not going to hurt you. It's my wife." He opened the door to the room in which they'd met the day before and beckoned to Parvana, and Jovan from the previous interview. "We're going outside."

Axtya watched from a distance as they came out into the hallway, still on his guard. They towered over him, obviously making him feel uncomfortable and at a disadvantage.

"Axtya, I would like to introduce you to my wife; this is Parvana. And you remember Jovan."

"Well met, Axtya," Parvana said with a smile.

He looked her in the eyes and, although he didn't reply, he seemed to relax a little.

Daryan led the way to the outer door with Axtya close behind him and the other two following. The door opened onto a large paved yard, but at the side was a pleasant grassy area with some trees and wooden benches. This green area bordered on the magnificent gardens of the white palace. "Shall we go and sit down on the grass?" Daryan asked, "Or would you like to walk around for a while?"

"Walk."

"I want to ask you some more questions, but first, I want to warn you about something. Don't try to run away. Do you remember the wolf that found you? She's here somewhere."

Axtya froze, cradling the stump in his left hand. He looked terrified and the skin under his hair turned even whiter. "She won't hurt you as long as you're with somebody she knows, but if you run, she'll come after you. Do you understand?"

He stood still, cradling his stump with his remaining hand, his whole body trembling, his large eyes gazing at Daryan.

"N-no wolf." He stammered. "Go..." he pointed back to the building they'd just left.

"I promise you, she won't hurt you."

"No! Go back," he shrieked and turned to run back to the building, glancing nervously over his shoulder as he went.

Parvana ran after him and stopped him by stooping in from of him. "Please stay with us, Axtya. You'll be quite safe. Come on, walk with us."

He blinked, looked at up her dubiously, and then at the two men, before he reluctantly changed direction. He followed Parvana, obviously very nervous, eyes darting from side to side. Parvana looked at Daryan and smiled.

After walking for a few moments, Daryan asked, "Tell us about your family, Axtya. I know you miss them."

"No!"

"Axtya," Parvana said. "I wish you would tell me about them. Do you have any children?"

"Two. Man-child."

"Two boys. You must miss them. What are their names, and what is your wife called?"

"She G'rag, boys Rega and Brotz." He looked up at her with watery eyes. "No more," he pleaded.

"Why did you leave them and come to Trethawynd?" Daryan asked. *Now we're getting somewhere,* he thought. He wanted to hug his wife.

"No!" Axtya shouted. "No more."

"Please tell us," Parvana said.

"Man come, say Lord Oglestra send. Say we clean world of Light. Light evil. Be blessed by Lord Oglestra."

"Was it a man like us, or a werman?" Daryan asked.

"NO!

"Tell us, Axtya. Was he like us or like you?"

"Look like you and wer."

"You mean he looked like both werfolk and human?" he gave Jovan a surprised look. Jovan nodded.

"I say!"

"Do you know his name?"

"Ogryn."

Hmm, both races, Daryan thought. *I've never heard of such a thing. Is it even possible?* "Where is your home?"

"In big wall. Cold, snow."

"How did you get here?"

Axtya shook his head.

"How did you come to Trethawynd, Axtya?" Parvana asked.

"In cave. Man come. Big animals pull cave. Cave go over wall."

Cave? Daryan looked at Jovan. "Wagon," Jovan whispered.

"What did the man look like?"

"Big man. Big hair." He stroked his own chin.

This is going better than I expected. Maybe I'm pushing my luck, but I have to ask. "Why do you eat children?"

"No, no, no."

"Axtya, tell us why."

"Man, Ogryn, say make big strong like him. Axtya no eat!" He became agitated. "No more! Go back."

"Very well," Daryan replied. "We'll go back."

They gave Axtya a honey and butter bun when they got back inside and told him he was free to go. He looked at them dubiously and went towards the stairs.

"Where do you think he'll go?" Parvana asked.

"To his room, probably. I'm sure of one thing; he won't leave the building. Ashala was the one who damaged his arm. You did a great job out there, by the way. Thank you, my love. Now let's hear what Jovan has to say. Did you get an image of this creature, Ogryn, the two men with the wagon?"

"I think I should go back and start packing if you don't need me anymore," Parvana interrupted, giving him a quick peck on the cheek. "You can tell me later."

Ah yes, moving day. Daryan accompanied her to the door, and then turned back to Jovan. "What did they look like?"

"The images are not very clear, more like impressions. The first one, Ogryn, did look like a hideous crossbreed of wer and human. The main differences were his height, slightly taller than the werman, and his eyes which were small, like obsidian beads. The older man with the wagon was dark skinned with dark eyes and was fairly well dressed. He was almost certainly a Trethawyndian,"

"Could you guess his age?"

"Not really, but I got the impression he was neither young nor old, with somewhere between forty and fifty years, I'd say."

"Very good. What about the other?"

"Young, probably in his twenties, tall and muscular. He was dressed all in grey and had a heavy woolen cloak with red lining. Dark. Also a native of Trethawynd."

"What about the wagon?"

"It was big, red and black, and it seemed to have something painted on the side in gold, but he couldn't discern what it was. It had a high rounded top and was pulled by four horses."

"I can guess who that is," Daryan murmured to himself. "One more thing. I suppose that when he said 'wall' he meant a mountain range?"

"That's the picture I got. Some of the mountains had snow on their peaks."

"Anything else?"

"I think the werfolk must have been drugged some of the time. Everything went out of focus and faded periodically. Also, it must have been a very uncomfortable ride, cold and bumpy with very little provided for their comfort beyond food and water."

Daryan sighed and sat back in his chair. A picture was starting to form. What they needed now was to fill in some of the missing pieces.

23 – Gremulkin Chats with Lord Evanar

Gremulkin

The duke had gone to his rooms. He'd been complaining of not feeling well and had not been able to finish his evening meal. This left only Gremulkin and Lord Evanar at the high table. Although there were a few guards still sitting at the lower table, they were enjoying their wine and making so much noise, they wouldn't be able to hear anything said by anyone else.

"More wine, My Lord?" the chancellor offered Evanar the carafe.

"Thank you, chancellor." The young man held out his goblet for Gremulkin to fill.

Evanar was a smaller version of his elder brother, with the same light brown skin and dark brown hair. He also sported a small pointed beard in contrast with Valdor who was clean-shaven.

"Father seems to be getting very weak," Evanar said.

"I fear so, My Lord. It's a pity. He was such a vigorous man. Old age is like that, one day you're in top form and the next ..." He shrugged. "It comes to all of us in time." He ate some more cake and took another sip of wine.

"How do you feel about your brother's closeness to the Monastery, My Lord?"

"I wasn't aware he was close to them."

"He's been awfully ... shall we say friendly? ... with the commander of the League Defenders recently. Oh it's probably nothing, but it does concern me that he might be unduly influenced by this man, Daryan Peshanar."

"Commander Peshanar, yes, he's a bit of a national hero. I'm sure it's just friendship. The Monastery is strictly forbidden from becoming involved in civil affairs; I do know that."

"The fellow was here a week ago, while you were away. The duke had sent for an emissary from the Monastery to discuss weapons. He wanted to order some enchanted weapons. The man downright refused. He was most disrespectful and insulting. We had to take your father to his rooms, he was so upset."

"Did he indeed? Did he give a reason for refusing?"

"Some nonsense about ethics and not taking mass orders for weapons."

"Has my brother had any more contact with him?"

"I'm sure he has. Someone saw them talking on the strand shortly after the meeting. They were acting quite furtive."

"I'll have to have a word with him when he gets back," Evanar said. "See what they're up to."

"I wouldn't mention it if I were you, My Lord. We'll just have to keep an eye on them both. As you say, it's probably nothing. I am concerned about your father's health, though. If anything happened to him, which fortune forbid, it wouldn't do to have the mages interfering in duchy matters. They've got far too much influence as it is."

"As you say, Chancellor. Have you spoken to my father about it?"

"I wouldn't want to bother him with it without proof of wrong-doing, My Lord."

"Well, I have to go. I have someone waiting for me. Light be with you." Pushing his chair back, he stood up, then picked up his glass and drank the remaining wine in one swallow. He left the room without noticing the chancellor's sour look.

Young cockerel, Gremulkin thought. *I don't know which of the two is worse. This one would be easier to handle though. Valdor is much too serious.*

24 – Valdor's Investigation

Valdor

The count had a sender at the castle—the niece of one of his gardeners—through whom Valdor was able to send a message to Daryan about the ambush of his family. The count's comments about requiring evidence had sparked an idea and he wanted to find out if Daryan or the League could help him with it. He would have to leave as soon as his wife and daughter were laid to rest. Sitting around thinking about it was doing neither himself nor Trethawynd any good. It was time for some action.

The count's men had gone with some of Valdor's knights to the site of the attack and brought back the bodies from the wrecked coach, along with others who had been killed by the rockslide. The interment ceremony was held the next day in the Chapel of the Light, the count's private chapel, where and Dinaz and Jilly were interred together in the family vault.

Valdor waited anxiously for a reply from the Monastery, pacing in the garden, walking around the parapet of the castle walls. Once more he realized he was neglecting his son whose loss was equally as devastating as his own, if not more so. He found the boy in the stables with his horse.

"Ah here you are," Valdor said, walking out of the sunshine into the shade of the building.

"Father! I thought you were busy. I was going to take Chappi for a bit of exercise. Would you like to come?"

It broke Valdor's heart to see his son trying so hard to keep his emotions under control. "Varan, my son, I am never too busy for you. Remember that. All you have to do is find me. I'm sorry if I've neglected you. I have so much on my mind … but that's no excuse. Yes, I would like to ride with you, but only for about an hour. I'm expecting a message from the Monastery."

Once their horses were saddled, they mounted and walked them down the slope to the castle gate and out into the village. Valdor heard another horse hurrying to catch up and turned to see who it was. "Arvand. I take it you are coming with us."

"Yes, your lordship. I can't allow you to go out unprotected. The duke would have my head if anything happened to you or Lord Varan."

All three were wearing white stoles of mourning over their shoulders. As they ambled down the village street, people came out to watch them, some giving little bows as they passed. A woman called out, "The Light bless you, Lord Valdor!"

Valdor smiled bleakly with a nod of acknowledgement and waved back.

When they reached the farmland on the other side of the village, they gave the horses their heads and cantered down a path through the fields, scattering many startled sheep as they passed. They came to a stop at a stream and waited while horses drank. Valdor could see that Varan wanted to talk about something, so he dismounted and nodded his head. "Out with it. I'm listening."

"Dadi, what's going on?" Varen also slid down from his horse.

Valdor checked to make sure Arvand was out of earshot. "First of all, tell me what you think it is."

"I don't know anything, father. I thought we were coming because mother's grandma was dying, but she doesn't look ill. The only other thing I can think of is that it has something to do with Chancellor Gremulkin. I've seen how angry you are every time you see him, even when someone mentions his name. Is it something to do with him?"

"That's what I want to find out, Varan. I'm angry because of what he's doing to your grandfather. I am going to find out what he's up to, but I need to tread carefully. If he knew I was investigating him, you and I would be in danger too. I want you to stay out of it. I don't want anything to happen to you. I'm going to leave you with your grandfather for now, until I feel it's safe for you to return home. You'll be safer here for the time being."

"As you wish, father. It's nice and quiet here. Sometimes I was afraid at the castle in DarSolas."

"Why? Did anything happen to frighten you?"

"No. It was just the atmosphere. It seems so heavy and dark sometimes, as if something bad could happen at any moment." Varan glanced at the sheep in the meadow and then back at his father. "Do you think *he* had anything to do with what happened on the road?"

"I honestly don't know, son. But I'm determined to find out, I promise you that. And if he was involved, I'll take action. I'll be going away, tomorrow and I don't want anyone to know where I am. I won't tell you where I'm going, but it will be a safe place, I promise you. I want you to promise me while I'm away you will be very careful. Don't go anywhere without an escort. I'll talk to your grandfather about it. The worst thing that could happen would be for you to become a hostage, or worse. It would tie the hands of those who will be working to solve this disaster. Do you understand?"

"Yes, dadi. I'll be careful, I promise."

"That's the spirit. I don't like having to frighten you like this, but you're almost a man now and I'm confident you can deal with it. You have to behave like a man. That means being responsible for your actions and thinking before you act. Now, anything else you would like to ask me?"

"Yes, there is one more thing. May I continue my swordsmanship training while I'm here?"

"Of course. I'm glad you mentioned it. I'll ask your grandfather if you can have lessons from his best swordsman. Would you like to learn archery too?"

"Oh yes, dadi, I would. I was going to ask you about it."

"Then you shall have that too. I hear the archers of Argento are very skilled. You'll be learning from the best. Now, shall we go back?"

They turned and retraced their steps, trotting across the meadow and out into the village.

"I'm glad we had this talk, Varan. Remember, any time you want to ask me anything, don't hesitate. We're in this together now."

After washing his hands in the basin in his room, Valdor went down to the hall and helped himself to a mug of summer wine from a tray on the sideboard. He took it over to a chair by the open window and sat looking out at the garden.

"Lord Valdor?" The soft female voice startled him out of his reverie. He looked up and saw it was the sender, Daylin. "A message has arrived for you, My Lord."

"Would you like to sit here and tell me?"

"Thank you, My Lord." She perched on the edge of a chair and leaned towards him. "My lord, the message is a bit long and complicated; I'm afraid I might forget something or get something wrong if I give it to you verbally. I could give it to you directly, just as I received it, if it would please you."

"Really? I haven't heard of that. What does it entail?"

"Not many mages can do it. I have been blessed by the Light with this extra gift. I could put it in your own mind exactly as I read it from the mind of the sender."

"What would I have to do?"

"I will hold my crystal in my hand and you cover it with your own hand. That's all. Would you like to do that?"

Valdor thought for a moment. He didn't like the idea of anyone having access to his thoughts, but she seemed like such an innocent girl. *If you can't trust a member of the League of Light, whom can you trust?* "Very well, Daylin. Let's try it. Oh before we start, who sent it?

"It's from the Monastery, My Lord."

She held out her hand to him with an orange crystal resting in the palm. He placed his hand over hers and, like the gentle brush of a feather, the whole message was there in his mind. He looked at her for a moment. "That's all?"

"Yes My Lord. That's all." She smiled sweetly at him as she withdrew her hand with the crystal.

"Thank you, my dear."

Already the words of the message from Daryan were going through his thoughts.

We can meet. Wear ordinary clothes so as not to be recognized. Bring escort, two men only, for protection, also wear ordinary clothes. All armed. A mage from Palgrigio, friend of mine named Ashavan, will meet you at dusk tomorrow, day 27, at Palgrigio Bridge and escort you to secret entrance to Monastery. Will meet you at entrance. Have advised Grand Master of your tragedy. Sends his sincerest, most heartfelt condolences at the loss of your loved ones, as do I. He commits the League to helping find those responsible for this outrage. The blessings of the Light upon you, My Lord. Daryan.

Valdor went over it again in his mind. He didn't need to memorize; the message would be there in his mind permanently now. *Action at last!*

***

Just before sunrise the next day, three horsemen left the castle of Argento. They looked like ordinary men dressed in plain garments of browns and beige. Two of them wore brown cloth caps on their heads each sporting a green feather. Although all of the men wore swords, they also carried bows on their backs and had sheaves of arrows fastened to the horns of their saddles, looking like huntsmen setting off for a day's hunting in the forest. They rode at an easy pace down the village street and continued out to the high road where they increased their speed to a canter. The road curved upwards in a southeasterly direction and then straightened out to due south after about a league. As the sun came up over the mountaintops, the color of the sky became soft azure and the water in the swamp changed from a murky brown to an opaque greyish green.

When they arrived at the site of the rockslide, Valdor stopped his horse, removed his cap, and sat with bent head for a minute, and then he looked around. Most of the debris had been swept away down the slope into the swamp, but patches of dried blood still showed on the rough surface of the road. It would take a good rainstorm to clear that. Sir Arvand and Sir Karan, the two knights, stood at a respectful distance until he was ready to move on.

"Light help us," Valdor murmured as he replaced his cap.

They rode on, making two more rest stops before reaching Palgrigio. The sun had passed its zenith hours earlier and was now low in the west.

"We made good time, My Lord," Sir Arvand said.

"Thank the Light," Valdor replied. "Now we have to find our guide." He had explained the general plan to Arvand before leaving, without revealing their final destination.

The town of Palgrigio was on their right on the other side of a narrow, slow-moving river.

"Ah, there's the bridge." Valdor shaded his eyes and squinted at it, but couldn't tell if anyone was there. "Do you see anyone?"

"There's a man on a horse coming out of the gate," the younger knight pointed out. "He's coming towards the bridge."

"Let's go on and see if it's him." Valdor said.

They rode slowly to the bridge and waited for him to reach them. He was a tall slim man in a black cloak over black trousers and black leather boots.

"Daryan's friends, I presume?" Ashavan stated in his mellow voice.

206

"We are," Valdor replied. "You must be Ashavan."

"At your service, My Lord." Ashavan ducked his head in a bow. "If you will follow me, I'll take you on a little excursion into the forest."

"Lead on, my friend," Valdor replied.

As the sun fell below the horizon, it became increasingly difficult to see where they were going on the trail through the woods. Arvand took a torch from his pack and lit it, then rode up beside Ashavan to help light his way. They were surrounded by music of the night: the hoot of an owl, the screech of monkeys, the sudden scream of a small animal fallen prey to a night predator, the distant howl of a wolf, all with a counterpoint of chirping cicadas and croaking frogs. Ashavan led them away from the trail after about an hour and struck out through the trees in another direction. At one point, he stopped and asked if anyone had another torch he could use. Sir Karan took one from his pack, lit it, and handed it to him. Ashavan led them on a meandering route through the trees, with frequent stops to get his bearings and, after about an hour of going back and forth for about am hour, they came to a stream.

"Now comes the easy part," Ashavan told them "We just follow the stream."

"I don't know how you got us to this point without getting lost," Valdor said. "You must be an expert tracker."

"Something like that," Ashavan replied enigmatically. "And I've taken this route many times, but I confess, it's much harder by night."

After following the stream for a while, he paused and turned towards a boulder that reflected purplish grey in the torchlight. "Here we are," Ashavan stated. "It's a bit hard to find in the dark when all colors look alike. Let's rest the horses and allow them to drink. With your permission, My Lord."

"You're in charge now, sir," Valdor said. "This is your territory."

They took their horses down the bank and waited while they drank from the stream.

Valdor dismounted and walked upstream a little way, followed by his escort. "I'm only getting a drink," he told the two men.

"Nevertheless, My Lord..."

"I know. You have your duty. I thank you. You should have some too. It's been a long ride."

Once their thirst was satisfied, they went back to their mounts and found that Ashavan had crossed the stream and was climbing up the scrubby bank opposite. He continued until he reached a sheer wall of rock that was so high, it seemed to disappear into the sky. They followed him across and waited while Ashavan went to a clump of bamboo, where he reached behind it and manipulate some sort if mechanism. A loud grating sound turned their attention to the rock face and they watched in astonishment as a slab of rock that had seemed an integral part of the mountainside began to move to one side, revealing a large opening like the entrance to a cave.

"In we go," Ashavan said cheerfully, climbing back on his horse.

When they entered the opening, they could hear the sound of hooves approaching from above and, after a few seconds, Daryan appeared.

"Well met, My Lord," he said to Valdor. He dismounted and walked over to Valdor.

"Well met, Commander. You've no idea how pleased I am to see you, my friend." Valdor touched Daryan's shoulder.

"Likewise, My Lord, but I wish our meeting were under happier circumstances."

"I know, but the fact that the League will help me in this lightens the pain somewhat."

"With your leave, My Lord." Daryan turned to Ashavan. "Well met, Toma. Thank you for stepping in at such short notice. Are you going back now?"

"I think I'll come up with you. I don't fancy going back through the woods alone in the dark. It will give me an opportunity to catch up with some old friends. But first I'll close the entrance." He returned to the wall by the opening and pulled the lever down. The rock rolled back into place.

Daryan remounted his horse. "Are we all ready?" he asked.

They began the long silent climb up the switchback ramp to the upper level and the Monastery.

Valdor was exhausted. He and his men had been on the road for almost sixteen hours, only stopping for two short breaks along the way. It was obvious the horses were tired as well; they toiled slowly up the slope with their heads bent low, their breathing labored and their coats lathered with sweat. He couldn't think of a solution for their fatigue other than to keep moving and hope it would end soon so they could all, man and beast, rest.

At last, after almost an hour, they came out of the tunnel into the cool air of the higher altitude, and onto a path that led along the Monastery wall. They paused for a moment to allow Valdor and his men to get their bearings.

"This is amazing," Valdor said. "I had no idea you could reach the Monastery this way. We're actually inside the Monastery walls?"

"Indeed, My Lord. Come, I'll take you to your quarters."

They dismounted and followed the wall around, leading the horses by their reins, until they came to the bridge that led into the Monastery's inner yard. Grooms who had been alerted to their pending arrival were waiting to relieve them of their mounts and take care of them.

"My lord," Daryan said to Valdor. "I've arranged for your men to be accommodated in the defenders' quarters, with your approval. We have pages on duty at all hours if you need to send for them. I can assure you and your escort that, with our extraordinary security, there is no fear of intruders. With your leave, My Lord, I'll have someone show them to their quarters."

"That's very thoughtful of you. I'm sure they will be well taken care of."

Daryan beckoned to a page who was waiting in the doorway of the transient residence to take care of the two knights, and then he turned to Valdor. "I imagine you are ready for a rest, My Lord. The Grand Master has made a suite available for you in what we call the white palace, if you'd like to come this way."

"Lead on, commander."

After bidding Ashavan good night, the two men walked towards the white building.

"It's not officially called the white palace," Daryan explained, "but most people refer to it that way because of the white marble used in its constructed. It's really the administration center, although the Grand Master also resides there, in one of the towers. You see, at the back?" he pointed out a square tower above the roof of the great white building. "Your suite will be in the west tower, My Lord, the one on the right. There is activity on the lower floors at all hours, but it's quite peaceful in the towers."

"It's a beautiful building. I wish we could replace that awful castle of ours with something like it."

As they approached the steps up to the entrance, a grey shadow slinked around the side and ran at Daryan, stood on its hind legs with paws resting on his shoulders, and licked his face.

Valdor jumped back in shock and drew his sword, his heart pounding as he watched in disbelief.

"Down, Ashala," Daryan said crossly. "Down." She uttered a little whine and backed off, her tail between her legs. "It's all right," he said to her, "But that was very rude. Now go back to your woods. I'm going to have a word with Felindra about this. She's going to have to teach you better manners.

"I'm terribly sorry about that, My Lord. And just after telling you how safe it is here."

"Was that really a wolf? I thought it was going to tear out your throat."

"It's my daughter's friend. It's a long story and I'm sure you can wait for it until another time. I can assure you, though; she's quite tame, with people who offer no threat to her family, which is just about everyone who is a friend of Felindra."

Valdor restored his sword to its scabbard and wiped his face as he followed Daryan up the steps.

The suite was on the second floor of the tower and Daryan regretted having to ask the duke to climb more stairs, but at least he would soon be resting. Daryan opened the door and ushered him inside. The main salon was furnished with soft chairs and tile-topped tables, windows filled the east and west walls, and there was a marble fireplace on the wall opposite the entrance. Upholstery, curtains and rugs were all in rose and various shades of orange, complementing wall hangings of aqua, blue and violet.

"What a beautiful room," Valdor said, taking in the details.

"Thank you. I hope you'll be comfortable. Before I leave you, I'd like to point out the bell pull." He went over to the wall beside the fireplace and pulled it. "We've arranged for two pages to be at your disposal all the time; they will rotate, of course, throughout the day. They will be able to provide anything you may need. The bell pull will summon them."

A knock on the door announced the arrival of two young men, of around sixteen dressed in the page's uniform of green and beige. They both bowed to Lord Valdor. "We are at your service, My Lord," the smallest on said. "My name is Benig and my friend is Tavor."

"It's a pleasure to meet you Benig and Tavor," Valdor replied. "I'll be with you in a moment if you'll just wait. How about showing me the rest and then I can get settled," he added to Daryan.

"That door leads to a small library," Daryan pointed to the door on the left of the fireplace, "and the other one is your bedroom. There's a refresher in a little closet inside." Daryan opened the bedroom door for Valdor to look around. "Is there anything else you'd like to know?"

"Food. I confess I'm a little hungry, and I'd like to bathe."

Daryan went back into the salon. "Boys, his lordship needs hot water for bathing and a light supper. Please bring the water first." He watched as the two boys dashed away to fulfill the request. He went back to Valdor. "They'll take care of you," he said. "I expect you would like a change of clothes as well. I'll order something suitable to be brought up for you in the morning."

"What are we doing tomorrow?" Lord Valdor asked.

"We've planned a meeting with the Grand Master in the morning to decide what we can do for you, and to make plans for the day after. I'd like to set out the following day to investigate the incident that killed your wife and daughter. I thought you might like to take some leisure after the meeting is over. I can show you around the Monastery and its surroundings, if that is your wish of course. If there's anything else you'd like to do or see while you're here, please let me know. I think I can leave you in the capable hands of the pages now. If you want to contact me, please ask a page to take a message. With your leave, My Lord." Daryan bowed.

"Thank you Commander, you have been most helpful. Light be with you."

Daryan

While Daryan was having breakfast with his family prior to leaving with Lord Valdor, he noticed Felindra was looking a bit edgy. "What is it, daughter? I can tell you have something on your mind."

"Don't you think we should take Ashala to help with the search, dadi?"

"I think we can manage," Daryan replied. "We are taking three very capable mages with us. I wouldn't want to keep you away from your studies.

"But dadi, she can find out things that they might miss. She can go where the mages can't go and talk to the other wolves. She'll be really helpful, I promise you!"

Daryan glanced at his daughter, noting that she was already wearing her going-on-an-expedition clothes instead of her student's tunic and culottes. "There is some merit in what you say, but I would feel uncomfortable taking you somewhere that is potentially dangerous, not to mention away from school. However, if your mother says you can go," he turned away from Felindra and winked at Parvana, "I'll consent to having Ashala along with you as her chaperone."

"Oh, mami, please let me go," Felindra begged. "Ashala hasn't had an outing for so long!"

"Yes, it must be at least ten days since you got back from the last one. All right, you can go, but listen to your father and don't go off on your own anywhere."

"Why does Felindra always get to go with you, father?" Darson asked.

"Daryan leaned across the table and whispered to his son, "It's Ashala we really want, but I can't talk to her, so we have to take your sister to interpret for us." Not really believing his son would be taken in by it, but hoping it would ameliorate his feelings of being left out. *I'll have to find some way to compensate him,* Daryan thought. *Maybe he'd like some weapons training. I'll have to remember to ask him.*

They left the Monastery by the main gate, Valdor and Daryan accompanied by two mages, five defenders and Valdor's two knights, plus Felindra and Ashala. Daryan had provided light armor for Valdor and the knights, and a leather jerkin for Felindra, although all she really needed was Ashala, who would be her best armor if she were in danger.

They set out along the trail that followed the curve of the mountain range above the lowland plain.

"I think this would be a good place to stop for the night," Daryan announced at sunset. "We'll be sheltered by the rocks and there's water for the horses. What do you say, My Lord?"

"It looks like a fine place to me," Lord Valdor replied.

"Who's going to find some firewood?" Daryan asked.

Immediate, all the Legion defenders turned towards the trees. "Don't all go," Daryan told them. "We need help putting up the tents. I suggest Valmar and Tarbin get the firewood and the rest of you help out here" Valmar and Tarbin were the two youngest defenders, barely out of their teens. "And don't try to use your swords to cut wood. We have an axe for that."

"Yes sir. What about the wolf?" Tarbin asked.

"Don't worry about her," Daryan replied. "She won't hurt you. Speaking of the wolf, I haven't heard her for a while. Do you know where she's gone, Felindra?"

"She's probably exploring or visiting friends," Felindra said. "Remember, we're in her territory now. Do you want me to call her?"

"No, don't worry about it; she'll return when she's ready."

25 – Gremulkin Takes Over

Perin, the duke's footman woke with a start and straightened up in the chair. The fire had burned low in the hearth and it was chilly in the bedchamber. He groaned as he stood up, feeling as if every bone in his body ached. *His grace is right,* he thought, *there's no joy in growing old.* Perin was almost as old as the duke. *Better light another candle,* he thought. He went to the fireplace and added a few more sticks and a couple of logs, then picked up a twig and took flame from the burning embers. He went to a table by the wall and used it to light a tall candle in a brass holder. "That's better," he mumbled to himself. "Let's take a look and see how he's sleeping."

Usually the duke slept badly, waking several times in the night with aches and pains, to relieve his bladder, or because of bad dreams. He'd been very quiet this night; he must have been or Perin would never have fallen asleep. "It's good he's had some rest," he murmured. "Needs it, poor old soul."

He went to the bedside and held up the candle to look at the duke's face. *He looks so peaceful, Light bless him.* He noticed that there wasn't a flicker of movement in the duke's face, and then it occurred to him that he couldn't hear the duke's normally ragged breathing. He leaned over and laid his cheek against the duke's mouth and nose. Cold as marble, no air, no movement at all.

"Light save us," he said to himself. "He's gone. Light rest his soul."

He touched the duke's hand, which was lying on the coverlet. It was cold as marble.

"And I was asleep," he mumbled to himself. *But what good could I have done if I was awake? I couldn't have saved him. I could have called the physician. Lot of good he'd have done. It's not been the same since the healer was sent away. He used to take good care of the old duke. Kept him healthy and fit, never sick a day, until* he came on the scene. *It's all his doing!* "But to think, he died all alone." Tears slid down his wrinkled face. *All alone. His family should have been with him. I should get Mottle. He'll know what to do.*

Perin took out a square of cotton and wiped his eyes, and then he took the large candle and quietly left the room.

He went through the salon and out into the hall. Mottle's small bedroom was next door to the duke's suite so that he would be nearby if the duke needed anything. Perin walked down the hall and knocked on the modest door, then poked his head in.

"It's me, Mott, Perin. Are you awake?"

"I am now. What's the matter Perin?"

"It's his grace. I want you to come and look at him."

"What time is it? It's the middle of the night," He sat up and saw the look on Perin's face. "Has something happened, Perin?"

"I think he's gone, Mott."

"*Sola Naofa!* Are you sure?"

"Well... Why don't you come and look?"

Mottle confirmed that the duke really was dead, but he sent for the physician anyway.

"We'll have to tell the chancellor," the physician said. "Will you send someone?"

Mottle and Perin looked at each other; Mottle scowled and Perin shivered. "You go," Mottle said to Perin. Being of lower status than Mottle, Perin reluctantly set off to the Chancellor's suite.

Gremulkin arrived in a black satin night robe and swept over to the bed. He looked at the duke, and then turned to the physician. "You've verified his demise?" he said.

"Yes, chancellor."

"Very well. You can go." He turned to Mottle. "Arrange to have the body prepared for the lying-in-state. I have other things to take care of." He flounced out of the room as quickly as he had entered.

"Cold-hearted son of the dark one," Mottle growled.

"You never said truer words," Perin agreed.

Gremulkin

Gremulkin went himself to wake Lord Evanar. Without waiting for the footman standing watch outside the door, he knocked and opened it. The only lighting in the salon came from a candle on the table near the door of the bedchamber. Gremulkin opened the door again and looked out. "Bring me some light." The footman came inside and lit one of the table lamps.

"His lordship said he didn't want to be disturbed, Your Excellency," he said.

"Never mind that," Gremulkin growled. He started towards the door of the bedchamber, but the footman hurried past him.

"Allow me to announce you, sir," he pleaded.

"Not necessary. I know the way."

"But..."

"Out of my way."

Gremulkin elbowed the footman aside. After a cursory knock on the door, he opened it. The first thing he noticed, in the brightness of the many candles burning around the room, was a trail of hastily discarded clothing between the door and the bed, men's and women's clothing. His eye followed the trail to Lord Evanar's naked body sprawled facedown across the equally unclothed body of a young woman on the bed.

With a snort of disgust, he went around to the uncluttered side of the bed and cleared his throat. "My lord," he said emphatically.

Lord Evanar twitched and rubbed his nose, but didn't wake up.

"Lord Evanar, you must wake up," Gremulkin said even louder.

This time Evanar turned over and his eyes squinted open. "I thought I said I didn't want to be disturbed... oh it's you

Chancellor. Couldn't it wait?" He sat up and pulled a loose corner of the sheet over his lap.

"No, My Lord, it cannot wait. I want you to put something on and come out into the salon. I've something to tell you. Something a little more important than this." He waved his hand around the room with a look of distaste,

"Who do you think...? Oh, very well. I'll be there in a minute. Send my footman for some tea, would you?"

Gremulkin was fuming when he went back into the salon. The footman was still dithering inside the outer door, obviously caught in the dilemma of whom he should obey. He feared the chancellor more than he feared his lordship, although his lordship held precedence as a member of the ducal family.

The chancellor looked at him, a grimace of disgust on his face. "Order his lordship some tea. Better bring some sweetbread with it. Go along now, and hurry." He waved the footman away.

Gremulkin sat down on one of the chairs and started to make a mental list of what needed to be done. He had to seize control while he had the chance, but how? His major problem was Lord Valdor ... no, he would be Duke Valdor now ... he was the biggest obstacle. If only his ambush had worked, he would be rid of him and Lord Evanar would be the regent. Irresponsible as he was, he would be so much easier to control. Then the whole of Trethawynd would be in his hands. He cursed himself and he cursed Waldron for the clumsy way he handled things.

The door to the bedchamber opened and Lord Evanar came out wearing a peacock blue satin robe.

"What's this about, Gremulkin?" he said irritably, running his hand through his hair.

"Sit down, My Lord. I have some bad news."

Evanar took a chair opposite the chancellor, storing away the fact that the chancellor had not shown him the courtesy of standing when he entered the room.

A knock at the door announced the arrival of the footman with the tea.

"Put it on this table," Gremulkin ordered him, indicating a small table between himself and Lord Evanar. "Then wait outside."

The footman hesitated, glancing at Lord Evanar, before setting the tray down.

"Thank you, Tallo. That will be all," Lord Evanar said. "Now, chancellor, what is so important that you have to wake me in the middle of the night?" he asked after the footman had closed the door.

"I thought you might like to know that your father has died," Gremulkin told him bluntly.

"But... Light help us. Can I see him?" Evanar put his hands on the arms of his chair and leaned forward, preparing to stand

Gremulkin gestured for him to remain seated. "I suggest you wait a while, My Lord. The body is being prepared for the lying-in-state. It would be better if you waited until it ... he is ready. Why don't you have some tea?"

"What about my brother. Has a message gone to him?"

"We would not be able to reach him if we sent a message," Gremulkin said. "I sent a courier two days ago to find out when he'll be returning, but he couldn't be found. He seems to have disappeared."

"But that's preposterous; how can the heir to the dukedom disappear?"

"As I said, nobody knows where he is. I have a feeling the Monastery has a hand in this."

"But why would they take him?

"I didn't say they'd taken him. I suspect he went voluntarily."

"But why?"

"I'm sure he has his reasons. Don't forget his mind is in a turmoil after losing his wife and daughter like that. He can't be thinking very clearly."

"Maybe he went there for solace," Evanar said. "I'm going to send a message to the Monastery about my father. If he's there, he'll surely return home. He needs to be here for father's memorial service, and his investiture."

"Don't worry yourself about that, My Lord. I'll take care of it; I'll make it an official announcement. Meanwhile, you will have to stand in as regent for him until he returns, or young Lord Varan gets back. I'm going to send a company to Argento to bring him back to DarSolas. If Lord Valdor doesn't turn up, he will be the duke."

"What do I do?"

"Well, first of all I suggest you send that young lady home." Evanar scowled at him. "Then get yourself cleaned up, put on your ceremonial uniform and go to the hall to stand vigil over your father's remains."

"You will keep me posted, Gremulkin?"

"Of course, My Lord."

"Poor father."

26 – Valdor becomes the duke

Daryan

The following morning, they were up at sunrise. The tents were taken down and bedrolls put away while the two mages and two defenders prepared smoked fish, bread, and fruit to break their fast.

"We should reach the location today," Daryan assured Lord Valdor as they mounted their horses.

"I pray we find an answer," Valdor replied.

Felindra came up on her horse. "Excuse me, My Lord," she turned to Daryan. "I have some information," she said

"May we hear it?" he replied.

"Of course, father."

"We can talk as we ride. My lord, would you like to ride with us?"

"I'd be delighted to ride in such charming company," he said, looking at Felindra with a sad smile.

He misses his daughter, Daryan thought. *I don't know how he holds himself together. He's a stronger man than I am.*

"Ashala was visiting what remains of her pack last night. They told her about a man who came into their territory recently. They recognized his smell. It was the same man who enchanted the pack and sent them to kill us."

"By the Light, another piece of the puzzle," Daryan exclaimed. "She's becoming quite an asset."

"Did they give her any idea about where he was going or what he was doing?" Lord Valdor asked.

"He had some other creatures with him, many, and they did not smell like men. Their scent was unfamiliar to the wolves. That's not exactly how she described it, but it's as close as I can get. She didn't smell them, so she couldn't tell me if they were the same as the werman we caught. They went that way," she pointed to the northwest. "To the big rock that used to be there."

"Used to be?" Daryan asked. "How long ago? What happened to it?"

They had to go single file for a little way as the path narrowed to pass between two large trees. When they could ride side by side again, Felindra said, "I didn't ask her that. I can ask her now if you like. She's following us over there in the trees."

"We can wait until we stop for a break," Daryan replied. "But it would be interesting to know.

About two hours later, they stopped to rest at a mountain pool where a stream had become blocked by forest debris and stones, leaving only a thin stream running out of it to trickle down the mountainside.

Felindra took her horse to the pool, left her there to drink while she moved a short distance from the others, and whistled for Ashala. After a short discourse with the wolf, she returned to the horse and remounted.

Back on the trail, she rode beside her father again. "The rock was there the last time she was here. It was a favorite spot for the pack. They used to go there and have group howls. They said the man and the other creatures did something to it and it disappeared. It made a lot of noise."

"Group howls?" Daryan exclaimed.

"It's a wolf thing," Felindra explained. "I don't really know what it's about, but it sounds to me a bit like singing together. It makes them feel close."

"The rock disappeared! That must be it," Lord Valdor said. "I wonder how far it is."

They reached the site of the disappeared rock close to sunset. As soon as they arrived, Ashala gave a yelp and took off. "It sounds as if she's found something," Felindra said.

While the team set up camp for the night, Daryan and Lord Valdor looked around, paying special attention to the place where the rock had been. It showed evidence of a major struggle. Broken tree branches and piles of earth and stones littered an area around a huge hollow in the ground. Walking round it, they saw that it extended all the way to the edge of the mountain face where it dropped off to the valley below. Far below, they could see the sinuous road running along the edge of the Great Swamp. A trail of broken trees and flattened scrub fell directly from the hollow to the road below.

"This looks like the place," Lord Valdor said.

"I agree," Daryan replied. "But I think we'll have to wait until morning to do a complete investigation. It's almost too dark to see anything. Shall we go back now, My Lord? You must be getting hungry; I know I am and I smell something very appetizing back there."

As they sat around the fire eating their supper, one of the mages said, "Something bad happened here, can you feel it?"

"Yes. I sense something dark and evil. A lot of pain and suffering," the other added.

A while later, just before they settled down for the night, Ashala returned. She went round the back of the group to Felindra and dropped something on the ground.

"What's that?" asked one of the defenders.

"I don't know," Felindra replied. "It looks like a bunch of bones."

The defender took a burning stick from the fire and brought it closer. "Ugh, it's a hand, and it smells awful." He broke off a large leaf and used it to pick up the object.

Ashala sat back, watching them, her tongue lolling halfway out of her mouth and her ears up.

"It looks like a child's hand and it still has bits of flesh and hair on it. What kind of child has hair on its hands? And look at those talons! Commander, take a look at this." He got up and took it over to Daryan.

Felindra followed him. "Ashala found it," she told her father.

Daryan took the proffered hand and examined it. "Thank you, defender. It looks like the hand of a werman. There's nothing we can do tonight. Leave it by that tree, away from the fire. We'll look at it in the morning. I suppose she'll take us to the place she found it?" he added to his daughter.

"She will," Felindra replied. "Same as she did last time." Events were starting to repeat themselves and that made her very uncomfortable. "May I sleep in your tent, dadi?" She didn't want to be alone, even with Ashala around.

Daryan

Everyone was up before the sun crested the mountains, eager to find out what had happened there. After a quick breakfast, Daryan and Lord Valdor had another look at the site, followed by an entourage of guards and mages.

"This confirms my suspicion," Lord Valdor said. "This is the place. Now what we need is to find out how it happened."

"It was obviously not a natural event." Daryan replied. "There's too much damage on this side of the hollow. Look here, it looks as if shovels were used. And all these footprints; the ground is well trampled."

"And I think some of those thick branches must have been used in an attempt to pry the rock loose. See how they're mashed at the ends."

"My Lord, commander," Flamond, one of the mages interrupted them. "There was dark magic used here."

"How can you tell?" Daryan inquired.

"I can feel it, in the soil, in the rocks."

"I don't suppose you can tell what type it was, can you?"

"Not specifically, but it was a power of great force."

"I heard what sounded like a loud clap of thunder or an explosion just before the rocks came down," Lord Valdor said. "Do you think they used an explosive force to blast the rock free?"

"That's possible, My Lord." Flamond replied. "It was probably elemental magic, lightning or some such."

"Well, that solves one mystery," Daryan said. "Now we need to find out who they were. It's obvious there was more than one person, and they were probably accompanied, if not led, by a dark wizard. Could you and Delara keep looking around here, see if you can find any clues to their identity? I'll leave some defenders with you to help. There's something else I have to look into."

Daryan went back to the campsite, picked up the skeletal hand and went to look for Felindra. He found her with the horses, moving from one to another, stroking and whispering to them. He smiled. "Are they all happy and comfortable?" he asked.

"They are feeling a bit nervous," she replied. "They don't like it here. I was trying to reassure them"

"I don't like the feeling either. The sooner we finish this and get out of here, the better I'll feel. Do you want to call Ashala and see what she found?"

"I'll call her. She's probably sleeping somewhere nearby."

Felindra whistled and a minute later, the wolf appeared, nosing her way through the bushes. She took the hand, still wrapped in a leaf, from her father and gave it to Ashala to sniff. "Go find it," she whispered. "And find us a path." She didn't want her to lead them through thickets and brambles, which to her were not serious hindrances, but were almost impossible for humans.

The sun was now over the mountains, sending shafts of golden light through the leaves. It was such a beautiful peaceful place, with the birds singing and insects humming, it was hard to imagine anything evil could violate such serenity. It was in such surroundings that Daryan usually felt closest to the Light. He sighed. *What is happening to our beautiful world? What sort of evil is infecting it? Why? Who is responsible? We will find them and we'll eliminate them,* he vowed.

"I can smell something," Felindra said.

"Wait here," Daryan told her. "I'll take a look. We must be close to whatever it is." He had a suspicion; he'd smelled that stench recently.

Ashala came back to see what was holding them up.

"I'll go ahead with her," he said to Felindra. "You wait here while I look. I'll send her back to stay with you. I'll let you know when I reach it."

Daryan patted Ashala on the head. "Come on, show me!" she licked his hand and trotted ahead. The first thing he noticed was the humming of flies, clouds of flies. He almost vomited when he saw the scene in the clearing. He pressed the bottom of his tunic over his mouth and nose before he advanced for a closer look. There were about a dozen wermen tied to trees and shot with arrows. Each body had at least three arrows piercing it. They had all been savaged by predators and many were missing eyes, hands and feet, and strips of flesh from the meatier parts of their bodies, and now covered in clusters of maggots.

He spat out the mouthful of saliva produced by nausea, and turned away, shaking his head sadly. They could do nothing for the poor creatures. Nature would continue to take care of the remains. He went back to Felindra.

"Let's go back." He put his arm around her shoulder and moved forward towards the campsite.

"What did you find, dadi?"

"I found out who did all the digging. Now, they're all dead."

"Who were they?"

"Werfolk, but they weren't killed by werfolk. Humans were involved in this. I think malevolent humans are using the werfolk, tricking them into coming here to help them in whatever they're planning."

"Like killing Lord Valdor's wife and daughter?"

"Exactly. Now we have to find out who they are and why they're doing it, and stop them."

When they reached the campsite, it was in turmoil; the mages and defenders were standing around in groups quietly talking to one another, looking as if something dreadful had happened. Delara was sitting alone on a rock, wiping tears from her face. Alarmed, he looked around for Lord Valdor.

"Where's his lordship?" he asked.

Several people pointed or nodded towards his tent. "In his tent," Sir Arvand replied. "He's just received some bad news."

Daryan went to the tent flap and called, "May I come in, My Lord?"

He heard Lord Valdor clear his throat. "Yes, enter."

Daryan pulled aside the flap and stooped to go inside. Lord Valdor was sitting on his sleeping pad, elbows on knees, face resting in his hands.

"My lord. Has something happened?"

Lord Valdor cleared his throat again and raised his head. "Yes, commander. My father has died," he replied in a thick voice.

The news hit Daryan like a shockwave. He felt the urge to go to Valdor and embrace him, but he forced himself to hold back, not knowing if it would be an acceptable gesture. In the space of less than a week, the poor man had lost his wife and daughter, and now his father. His life was shattered! How do you endure something like that? He still felt the urge to comfort and went to kneel by the man he was beginning to think of as a friend. He put his hand on Valdor's shoulder.

"My lord, I don't know how to express how much I feel for your sorrow, the terrible tragedies that have befallen you.... All I can say is that I have the highest regard for you, and offer you my genuine brotherly love. I am ready to do anything in my power to help you and only await your command."

"My dear friend," Valdor murmured. He leaned his head on Daryan's shoulder and wept, while Daryan kept his hand on Valdor's back, patting a few times.

After a moment, Valdor straightened up and wiped his eyes with a cotton handkerchief. "I'm sorry, but enough of this, there are things I must take care of immediately."

Daryan stood up. "My lord, may I ask..." He suddenly realized that the man before him was now the Duke of Trethawynd "... I mean Your Grace, how you found out about it?"

Valdor stood up and straightened his clothes. "I suppose I *am* the duke now, Light help me." He combed his hair back with his fingers. "It appears that my father's chancellor sent an official message to the Monastery with the news, and they sent it on to me through your mage, Delara."

"We have to get you back to the capital as soon as possible, Your Grace."

"I agree," the duke replied, but first I would like to send a message. "Could you ask Delara to come in and take it, please?"

Valdor

The message he sent was to his father-in-law, the Count of Argento. He requested that his son, Varan, be dispatched immediately to the capital with an escort, at least six of his most trusted men and the knights who had stayed there to guard Varan.

"I'll wait for a reply," he said to the mage-sender. "Please find me when you have it. Thank you."

"As you command, My ... Your Grace."

Valdor left the tent and found his escort, Sir Arvand, standing outside the flap. "Ah, Arvand!"

Arvand bowed low. "Yes, Your Grace? May I offer my heartfelt condolences?"

"Thank you, Arvand. I think I'm going to appoint you Commander of the Trethawynd Defenders when we get back to DarSolas. There are going to be many changes made."

Arvand bowed again. "I'm deeply honored, Your Grace."

"Where's Commander Peshanar?"

"He was over there a moment ago. We're breaking camp. Shall I go and find him, Your Grace?"

"Come with me. We'll both go"

As they walked past the fire ring towards the trees, the mage, Delara, intercepted them.

"I have a reply from the count, Your Grace,"

"Good." He turned to Arvand. "Would you go and find the commander and tell him I'd like a word?" He turned his attention back to the mage. "Let's go over there." He was aware that everyone was watching him making him self-conscious; he needed some privacy, so he conducted her to some trees on the edge of the clearing.

"What does he have to say?"

"The count says that a delegation arrived this morning from the chancellor, reporting that you, Your Grace, are missing, and whereabouts are unknown."

"The nerve of the man!" the duke exclaimed. "Go on."

"They told the count that they'd been ordered to escort the new heir, Lord Varan, back to DarSolas. The delegation consisted of six members of the castle guard. The Count says he will only release Lord Varan to you, Your Grace, and was waiting for your instructions. He asks do you still want Lord Varan to go as you instructed in your earlier communication."

"Let me think for a minute." What were the implications of this new development? If he sent Varan back to DarSolas, even with an escort of trusted men, including three of his own knights, Gremulkin's men could easily ambush them on the road and try to take his son, or even kill him, believing they must obey the chancellor's orders. It wasn't very likely, but he couldn't be sure it wouldn't happen. Best not to expose him to the risk, though. "Here's my answer," he said. "Tell the count that my son should stay there until I say it is safe for him to return to DarSolas. Under no circumstances should he leave his grandfather's custody until I send for him personally. Oh, and add 'if possible, detain the men sent by Gremulkin until I decide what to do with them.' Tell my son I am fine and I send my love. That will be all, thank you, Lady Delara."

"I'm honored, Your Grace."

Daryan walked into the clearing. Seeing him, the duke left the trees and walked over to meet him.

"There is so much to do," he said. "Are we ready to leave?"

"Yes Your Grace. I'll bring your mount."

"No, no. I'll go with you."

On their way back to the Monastery, the new duke had a long talk with Daryan. He'd had so much responsibility dropped on his shoulders, he didn't know what to do first. He didn't know whom to trust and he had no confidants with whom he could discuss his concerns, but he instinctively trusted Daryan.

"May I speak frankly with you, my friend?" he said while they were out of earshot of the rest of the entourage.

"Of course, Your Grace."

"I was impressed by the way you handled Gremulkin that day at the castle. It showed me you are an honorable man. That's what impelled me to help you get away. I feel I can trust you."

"Thank you, Your Grace. I...."

"It's all right, Daryan." How could he put it? *Follow your instincts*, he told himself. "Daryan, I call you my friend, and I truly mean what I say. There are so few people I can trust; it's good to meet someone I know I can rely on. I used to have many friends who enjoyed coming to the castle or my visits to their homes, but since Gremulkin came on the scene, they seem to have drifted away. Either that or he deliberately drove them away in an attempt to isolate me. That's why I need a real friend. I need a confidant, someone I can discuss things with, who will give me good council, someone off whom I can bounce ideas. I wish I could make you my chancellor, but I'm not sure it would be allowed."

"You have already done me much honor, Your Grace. It would a great privilege to be your friend."

"Well you can start by not calling me 'Your Grace' when we are having a private conversation. My name is Valdor. The title puts up barriers between us; I would prefer us to be like brothers."

"As you wish Your Gra ... I mean Valdor."

"Right. I'm not sure what my greatest problem is right now, but most of them seem to revolve around Gremulkin. The first thing I'm going to do is get rid of him. He'll not get *me* under his spell as he did my poor father. I'm not fooled by him and I want him out of the castle, although I'm not sure how I'll accomplish that. I can dismiss him, yes, but forcing him to leave may prove more difficult. More than half the castle guards are his men. He could hold my loyal servants hostage as well. That's another thing. I'm going to have to completely restore the guard, get new men and try to return some of the old ones he got rid of. But that's another matter." He looked across at Daryan. "Feel free to interrupt if you have any comments. I'm just thinking out loud."

"I too see Gremulkin as your number one problem."

"Yes. Once we get rid of him, we can start putting things back together. Let me tell you about his latest outrage. He sent a delegation of his guards to Castle Argento to bring my son back to the city, claiming he thought the 'new heir' should be in the safety of the castle. I told the count not to let him go, and to detain the men he sent. I had originally intended Varan to return, but not with Gremulkin's men as his escorts. I can't put his life at risk while Gremulkin's people are around. The poor boy's been through enough."

"A wise decision ... Valdor."

"I have to bury my father and then there's my investiture to arrange, and I'll need more staff, a new chancellor, I can't think what else. It will be a difficult transition with none of the old staff around to guide me." He rode on for a while, deep in thought. "In the old days, we always had mages around the castle, I liked that. I think I'll hire some to fill the vacancies that will be left by Gremulkin's people when I'm rid of them. You know he drove away our old healer and brought in his own physician. I wouldn't let him near my family; I prefer to send for someone from the town if anyone was sick. I wouldn't be surprised if he and Gremulkin were responsible for my father's demise."

"Do you really think so?"

"You've been away a long time, but I'm sure you remember how full of life my father used to be. He could outlast men half his age. His decline was too rapid for it to be natural. In two years he changed from a strong vigorous man to the way you saw him the last time you came to the castle."

"I know. I was shocked by the change. He was barely recognizable as the old duke. I'm so sorry, Valdor. You know I will be happy to help you in any way I can."

"That means a lot to me, Daryan. It really does. I pray the Light will sustain us all; we have a difficult road ahead of us." He turned and looked away through the trees on his right, passing a fingertip over the corner of his eye and clearing his throat.

***

By midday the following day, the investigatory team was coming round the curved road leading to the Monastery.

"If you wish, Your Grace, I will arrange a meeting with the Grand Master. Maybe he can give us some guidance for the coming days."

"I thought the League would not become involved in the political matters of the duchy," Duke Valdor replied.

"That is true, but given the evidence that dark magic has been used against you, the ordained leader of our people, it is possible he might wish to investigate and perhaps provide you with protection against it. After all, with magic involved, it affects the League as well as the ordinary people, and we must protect all the people of Trethawynd."

"Very well. But I must leave at dawn tomorrow for the capital. I dare not be away any longer."

27 – Return to DarSolas

Daryan

By the time the duke's entourage came in sight of the city of DarSolas, the sky had taken on a dark pall. Low clouds churned above the city like smoke, turning the daylight to dusk, although it was less than three hours past noon.

"It looks as if something's burning, something big." Sir Arvand, who was leading the procession, said to the Daryan beside him.

"You're right. Look south, beyond the city," Daryan replied. "See that reddish glow?"

"Sola Naofa!" Arvand exclaimed. "It's the castle!" He turned his horse and went back to where the duke was riding in the middle of the column. "Your grace, it looks as if the castle is on fire."

"Light preserve us. That's impossible! Are you sure, Arvand?" Without waiting for a reply, the duke urged his horse forward to the brow of the hill. When he saw the smoke and red reflections in the clouds, he turned and looked for Daryan.

Daryan rode up and joined them. They stood for a moment staring at the sight.

"What are we going to do? Arvand asked.

"We have to go and find out what's happening down there," the duke replied, urging his horse into a gallop.

The rest followed and quickly surrounded him; protecting the new duke was their first responsibility. When Daryan signaled, urging him to slow down, he slowed to a trot and looked at Daryan. "Yes Commander?"

"Your grace, I don't think we should rush into something potentially dangerous. We should send a reconnaissance party first to assess the situation. We don't want to barge into something lethal without any knowledge of what we're up against. It must have taken something very powerful to set the castle on fire, a very strong force. For all we know, Trethawynd has been invaded. We are too few and need to conserve our strength until we know if we can handle it."

The duke sighed. "You're right. We'll do as you suggest."

"I shall lead a team of investigators, Your Grace." Daryan chose four League defenders and Byarshan, one of the duke's guards, to go with him. He also decided to take the two mages, leaving the two knights, Sir Arvand and Sir Karan, to protect the duke.

"There is an inn about half a league down the road called The Golden Lyre; it's a good place. I suggest you wait there and I'll meet you there when I return."

"Thank you, Daryan." Valdor grimaced. "I hate being left out, but I'll concede to your superior experience. Light protect you, commander; hurry back."

The Fort of DarSolas was situated near the eastern edge of the town, close to the cotton mill, which was built to take advantage of a rapid flowing river that passed through the norther edge of the city. The team reached the gate of the fortress, which was closed and guarded. From the noise of activity inside the walls, it was obvious that the fort was on high alert.

Daryan introduced himself and his companions to the guard at the gate. "We'd like to speak to the commander. Tell him we're here on behalf of Duke Valdor to investigate the situation at the castle and we would appreciate any information he can give us."

"Very well, commander." He looked up at the top of the wall and called, "Permission to open the gate, Lieutenant? They've come from the new duke."

"Permission granted," the lieutenant replied after looking them over.

The commander arrived moments later with another officer.

"Captain Gauri at your service, and this is my assistant, Sergeant Danghar he said. He led them into the fort to a ground floor room filled with tables and chairs. "Take a seat." He pulled out a chair from one of the tables and sat down. Daryan and his men followed suit.

"The officer at the gate said you were from the duke? I understood from the castle that he was missing."

"Not at all, Captain. Naturally, after the tragic death of his wife and daughter, he felt he needed some seclusion in which to recover, so he went to the Monastery. He also wanted to investigate what caused the rockslide that killed them, and to find out whether it was an accident or deliberately started. He's quite safe and was on his way to the castle to lay his father to rest when we saw the smoke and flames. We thought it would be prudent to have him wait somewhere safe while we found out more about the situation, and I thought you might have some information." Daryan took a sip of water. "What can you tell us about the castle?"

"Not very much, I'm afraid. As soon as we became aware of the attack, I sent half my garrison to investigate and help the castle defenders—we had to keep some back to protect the town, in case we also were attacked. I haven't heard anything from them so far."

"I notice you said 'attack'. Are you sure it was an attack and not an internal rebellion? I know there has been some unpleasantness up there for some time. Maybe those loyal to the duke have had enough and took this opportunity to rebel against the newcomers."

"I don't know, Commander. The ferocity of the attack and the amount of damage inclines me to believe it was an attack from outside. Where would servants and guards get the kind of materials or skills to cause such damage? It's not easy to set a stone building on fire."

"I agree. Thank you for the information, Captain. We'll go and see what we can find."

Daryan and his team continued through the town, which appeared to be undamaged, though it looked virtually deserted.

"I want to check on something before we continue," Daryan said. "This way." He led them though several half-empty streets to the central square and looked for Charnwell's establishment. He spotted it on the opposite corner and rode over. As with all the other businesses in the square, no lights showed inside and many of them were shuttered. He dismounted and peered in through the glass door panel, but detected no movement within. He noticed a sign card in one of the windows.

———

Closed for renovations
Reopening at Harvest Moon
We apologize for the inconvenience.

———

Just as I suspected, he thought. *He must have known what was coming and left.*

"That's it," he said and got back on his horse. He led them down the street where Avaya and her family had their business. A glimmer of light came from the back room so he dismounted and knocked on the door.

A shadowy figure came through the doorway from the back and walked towards the street door. "Who is it?" a man's voice asked.

"Commander Peshanar. Is that you, Sasan?"

After some sliding of bolts, the door opened and Sasan Humaya's beaming face appeared in the gap. He stopped smiling when he saw the crowd with him. "Commander, I'm so glad to see you. We don't know what to do. Come inside." He opened the door wider.

"I can't, Sasan, I don't have time. We have to find out what's happened at the castle. Do you have any idea?"

"All I know is someone or something attacked the castle. The townsfolk say it was demons; whatever it was, it was something powerful. Everybody seems to be panicking and running away. I don't know what we should do."

"Is Avaya here?"

"Yes, she's in the back. Shall I get her?"

He went back inside and soon Avaya appeared in the doorway. "Hello, commander, can I help you?"

"Yes, Avaya. I want to send a message to the Monastery. Are you ready?"

"Just tell me; I'll remember."

"Tell them the castle has been attacked and occupied by forces unknown. Castle in flames. Townspeople alarmed. No damage to town so far. Rumor of attack by demons. Duke is safe. Peshanar. Would you repeat it back to me, please?"

After she repeated his message verbatim, he added, "You may add your own impressions to the message and anything unusual you see. I must be off now. Light go with you."

"Blessings of the Light on you too, Commander Peshanar."

Daryan remounted his horse. "We'll take it slowly," he told the others, "look around for a while, and then see if we can get a closer look at the castle."

They checked other parts of the town, which seemed strangely deserted, and then went to the harbor. The smell of smoke was more noticeable here. An ocean-going cargo carrier sat in the last berth at the far end of the wharf, and two coastal barges were tied up closer to the shore. Lights glowed in some of the portholes of the cargo carrier, but the barges appeared to be deserted. The whole place had an abandoned look.

Daryan turned and looked along the waterfront. Lights showed from a tavern facing the docks, so he led his team there. Maybe someone had seen something. There wasn't much noise coming from inside, a shout, a short burst of laughter, and then silence. "Not much happening here," he said to his team. "Let's leave it for now and see what we can find at the castle."

As they turned south towards the castle, they met two very tired-looking Knights followed by about twenty defenders, some in the duke's colors, gold, black and red with his emblem, a golden falcon holding a sword in its talon. They all looked exhausted and bedraggled, their uniforms in tatters. Some of them were wounded, those without horses using staves and broken branches for support, their injuries wrapped in crude, bloodstained dressings. They were covered in soot, on their skin, their clothes and armor, even on the bandages.

"Well met," Daryan greeted them. "You're the duke's men, aren't you? I'm Commander Peshanar of the League of Light. Duke Valdor sent me to assess the situation here. Who's in charge?"

A tall slim man with a bandaged arm came forward. "The duke is here, alive? The chancellor said he'd been killed. Thank the Light!" He turned in his saddle. "Did you hear that men, the duke is alive?" The other soldiers raised a ragged cheer, too weak to shout. The officer wiped his face with a sooty rag. "I'm Captain Laurin. Well met, Commander. We thought everything was lost, but if the duke still lives...."

"We need to get you to somewhere you can rest and get medical attention. You can tell us about everything later. I suggest you go to the fort."

"That's where we were heading. Most of us are from the fort, but some of these men are from the castle garrison; the few who managed to fight their way out."

"Have you a healer?"

"We lost our healer during the retreat."

Daryan shook his head sadly. *How many more losses would there be...?* "I'm sure there'll be one at the fort. Would you like me to send anyone with you?"

"I think we can make it, but thank you. I just hope there's food waiting for us and some hot water."

"I'll see about finding another healer and check in on you before we leave town. The duke is not far away and I know he'll be anxious to see you too. Blessings of the Light on you captain, all of you. We have to finish our inspection, and then we'll follow you."

Daryan turned back to his own team. "Archmage, could you check and see if there's a healer in the area, please? They may need him or her at the fort to help treat the wounded."

She went to a quiet corner and took out her crystal. After a few minutes, she returned and she reported to Daryan, "There's one at the north end of town. He'll go directly to the fort."

They continued up the hill to the castle. Thick smoke was still issuing from the ruins, so it looked as if the fires were still smoldering inside. After looking through the castle gate and seeing the devastation, Daryan turned away. "Let's go back to the inn," he said. "There's nothing we can do here."

It was close to midnight by the time they reached the Golden Lyre. Light was shining from all the windows on both levels. It was an old building with stone walls on the lower level and plastered brick above. They rode through a side gate into the stable yard and, after disposing of their horses, entered the inn through large double doors made of stout hardwood studded with iron.

Daryan went slowly up the broad staircase to the upper level. Sir Arvand was sitting on a comfortable chair outside the first door. The knight stood up as Daryan approached. Daryan drew him away from the door, not wanting to disturb the Duke if he was sleeping. "How is the duke?" he asked Arvand.

"He's tired, commander. It's best he rest. At least in sleep, he can escape for a while. What's happening in DarSolas?"

"The town hasn't been damaged, but the people are uneasy. They've heard a rumor that demons have attacked the castle and think they might be coming for them next. We couldn't get into the castle, but it appears to be smoldering still. We didn't go beyond the gate, but from what we saw, it looks bad. A lot of damage and many dead. Some of the guards got out, with the help of the town garrison. There are many wounded returning to the town fort, so I've arranged for an extra healer to go there and help.

A door opened behind them, "I thought I heard voices. Ah, you're back, commander. Come in and tell me what you've found out."

"Shouldn't you be sleeping, Your Grace?"

"Who can sleep with all this going on? Come in and sit with me, Daryan, you look exhausted, you too, Arvand. I'll order something to eat. Arvand, be a good fellow and ask the landlord to send up some supper for Commander Peshanar."

Daryan followed the duke into his room. It looked quite well appointed, at least to Daryan who was used to sleeping in a tiny room at the Monastery or a tent in the open air.

"Have a seat, commander."

The duke sat on the edge of the rumpled bed, so Daryan pulled one of the chairs away from the table and sat down, trying to stifle a yawn. He looked at the duke for a moment, noticing the dark patches beneath his eyes, and his rumpled hair that looked as if he'd spent the evening running his fingers through it. He'd removed his outer clothes, and now wore only his shirt and rather crumpled trousers.

"How are you, Your Grace?"

Valdor sighed and combed his hair back with his fingers. "I've been better. Tell me about DarSolas and the castle."

"The city is fine; the main damage is at the castle."

There was a knock on the door and Arvand came in followed by the landlord himself carrying a large enameled tray. He placed it on the table and bowed to the duke. "Your Grace." Then he unloaded the plates and dishes onto the table together with two carafes. "This one is wine," he said, "Very fine wine from Zinawar, and the other is our best ale." He bowed again and backed towards the door.

"Thank you, landlord," the duke said as he walked away.

"It's an honor to serve you, Your Grace, gentlemen." He bowed his way out and closed the door behind him.

"He's obviously very impressed to have you here," Daryan commented.

Valdor gave a weak smile. "Eat something, my friend, you too, Arvand. I think I'll have a little of the wine."

Daryan gave him a summary of the situation in DarSolas while he ate. Valdor and Arvand drank some wine and picked at the cheese and fruit.

When they'd finished, the duke said, "I can see you're tired, Daryan. I'll let you go to rest now. We can talk in the morning." He yawned. "I may be able to sleep now."

"I just realized, Your Grace, you don't have a valet or footman. I'll see what I can do to find someone tomorrow. Can you manage for tonight?"

"I think I can get a nightshirt out of my pack, and pour a bowl of water to wash, but thank you. He turned to address Arvand. "Why don't you get a defender up here to stand guard while you go to your bed? It's been a long day and we may be even busier on the morrow."

That's what makes a good ruler, Daryan thought as he closed the door. *Concern for others and consideration for the people who serve him. They'll never let him down and he'll be able to count on them in a crisis*

28 – Making plans

Valdor

Duke Valdor of Trethawynd rode into DarSolas at the head of his entourage on a rainy morning three days after leaving the Monastery. At his side were newly appointed Commander Sir Arvand and Commander Peshanar. They turned right at the paper mill, and stopped at the gates of the fort. The guards on duty at the gate jumped to attention when they recognized the duke and quickly opened the gate.

Both guards bowed as he entered. "Welcome, Your Grace," one said.

"Shall we summon the captain?" asked the other

"Well met, defenders," the duke replied. "Yes, please send for him. I need to talk to him."

When the he made to dismount, a man jumped forward to hold the horse's bridle.

By then, several other people had appeared from different directions, men in tattered clothing, many of them exhibiting signs the battle they'd fought: bandaged wounds, crutches, healing cuts, burns and bruises.

As Duke Valdor ascended the steps to the barracks building with Daryan and Arvand, the captain emerged from the building.

He bowed to the duke. "Captain Gauri at your service, Your Grace. Please, come in out of the rain. We can go to the officers' hall if it pleases Your Grace."

"Thank you captain, that sounds perfect, but first I want to say a word to your men." He turned round in the doorway and faced the men in the yard, feeling a little nervous and hoping it wouldn't be too obvious. This would be his first public address. "Loyal defenders, I want to tell you how grateful I am for your support and the courage you demonstrated in your attempt to save the castle. I see many of you are wounded. I know you are receiving good medical attention, and I pray for your speedy recovery. Bless you for your courage and loyalty.

"There are some difficult days ahead for all of us and I am going to be relying on you for your continued service in restoring freedom to our homeland and overcoming the dark forces that beset us. Now, I think you should find shelter from the rain. The blessings of the Light upon you."

The men in the yard raised their hands and cheered. "Light bless the Duke," someone shouted and the rest took up the salutation. The duke smiled and waved to the men one last time and turned to enter the building.

Sitting at the table in the officers' hall, with a mug of cool summer wine, Valdor asked Captain Gauri. "How many able men do you have now, Captain?"

They talked about this for a few moments and then the duke asked, "Have you sent anyone to the castle to investigate the current situation?"

"Yes Your Grace. A team left this morning. I expect they will be back before dark."

"Good." He looked at Daryan and Arvand. "Do you have anything to add?"

"Yes, Your Grace," Daryan replied. "I wonder if we could talk to some of the men who escaped from the castle and get some idea of what happened up there from the inside. It all seemed so chaotic and horrifying, what we were able to see; I'd like to have some idea of the reality."

"Splendid idea," Valdor said. "Captain, could you send for a few of them, including one of rank?"

"Defender," the captain summoned one of the men guarding the door. "Would you tell Captain Laurin the duke would like to see him, and ask him to bring a couple of his men?"

"Immediately, Captain."

"Captain Laurin is the most senior of the escapees, Your Grace."

"Do you think it would be helpful to have a mage present to get a picture of what they report, Your Grace?" Daryan asked. "Defender Farah can see images of the incident in the mind of the person as he describes it. She might be able to pick up something."

"Not without their permission, Commander, but we can ask them if they would mind."

The guard returned with Captain Laurin and two of his fellow escapees. The captain had one arm wrapped in a swath of bandages, supported by a sling, and one of the men walked with a crutch, the other had a bandage on his upper leg and a patch over his eye.

"Come in captain. Take a seat over there, please." The duke pointed to three empty chairs on the opposite side of the table. When they were seated, he continued, "Captain, defenders, I want to express my gratitude for the sacrifices you made defending the castle, and my admiration for your bravery. We lost many fine defenders in this tragedy—most of them your friends and comrades—and I mourn their loss with you."

Captain Laurin stood up and bowed. "Thank you, Your Grace. It is an honor to serve you."

"This is Commander Peshanar of the League of Light," the duke continued. "He suggested that we have a mage present to see if she can clarify the images of things you describe. I'm asking if you would consent to her presence."

The captain and the two men exchanged glances. One man shook his head and muttered something to the captain. "Defender Fremond wants to know if that's mind reading, Your Grace."

"Commander." The duke deferred to Daryan for an answer.

"In a way it is, defender. The mage sees a picture in your mind of what you are describing. She pays no attention to anything else, and even if she inadvertently did catch a thought, she would never reveal it to anyone. That's part of the mages' code. There's nothing to fear."

The man still didn't look convinced.

"We are asking your permission, not ordering you to allow it, defender. If you have doubts, we will not force you," Daryan explained. He looked over at Farah, the mage. "Would you mind leaving for a moment, Lady Farah?"

As she stood up, Defender Fremont interrupted, "It's all right. I don't mind. It's giving me nightmares, what I saw. I don't think I could find the words to...."

"Thank you, defender. Is it all right for you as well?" he asked the other two.

"We're fine," the captain said.

"Thank you. I'm grateful. The mage will help us get an image of some of the details that might be missed in a verbal report; she might even pick up something you may not have noticed consciously." Daryan said. "Now, Captain, what was the first thing that happened; how did you become aware that something was wrong?"

The Captain rubbed his cheek. "It was the screams, Your Grace. We heard screams coming from inside the hall, then people started fleeing out the door, servants, guards, everyone inside was trying to get out, all screaming, terrified. Then they started coming out with horrific wounds, as if they'd been slashed with sharp knives. I rallied the defenders to go into the hall and find out what was happening and help the people get out. I and some other men went to the kitchens. We had to force out way through those fleeing. When we got there, it was a shambles. Blood everywhere, dead people on the floor, some of them with their hands or feet cut off." He looked mournful and baffled. "Why would anybody do a thing like that? They were cooks and scullery maids, even two little pages."

Everyone sat looking down at the table, waiting for the Captain to continue, but he seemed unable to speak.

"Did you see any of the attackers?" The duke asked.

"I did, Your Grace," Defender Fremond replied. "We was going down the stairs to the servants' quarters when one o' them demons started coming up towards us. It looked raving mad, as if it wasn't frightened of us at all. There was more behind it. We had our swords out, ready, and then the man next to me sliced down the middle of its head. There was hundreds of them, coming out of the servants' passages and up the stairs from the cellars, screaming and slashing at anything that moved. They even cut down the cook's cat. We killed a few of them, but there was too many. We turned and ran. I'm sorry, Your Grace." He added with tears on his cheeks. "I swear they was demons from the abyss. No man could have stood up to them."

"There is no need to apologize, defender. As you say, no one could have done more than you did. Anything else?" the duke asked Captain Laurin.

"They started setting fire to everything, furniture, curtains, clothes, books, anything that would burn. They must have poured oil or tar over everything because the smoke was black and smelled like burning coal oil. We pulled as many people out as we could, but we were overcome by the smoke and the raging demons.

"Did you see or hear anything of my brother, Lord Evanar?"

"No Your Grace. One of the footmen we rescued said he'd seen Lord Evanar with the chancellor going down the cellar steps. He thought it odd at the time, but it wasn't his place to ask questions, he said."

"What about my father, the duke?"

"He was still lying-in-state, Your Grace. They set fire to the Hall of State. There was nothing we could do, Light rest his soul." The captain rubbed his eyes with the balls of his thumbs.

Duke Valdor sighed and massaged his forehead with his fingertips. He took a gulp of wine and shared a look with Daryan.

"How did you escape from the castle?" Daryan asked.

"We went out the back entrance, intending to go through the barracks, but they'd set fire to them, as well as the stables and the workshops. When we saw all the fires, we found our way to the gate by circling along the inside of the wall. I ordered the men to come down from the walls and to fight our way out. They must have put bowmen up onto the roofs because flaming arrows started raining down on us when we tried to reach the gates. Not many of us made it out." Captain Laurin shook his bowed head, and then he looked up, his eyes glistening. "We didn't see them coming, Your Grace. Who would have thought we would be attacked from inside the castle?"

"Be at peace, captain. Nobody is blaming any of you. We were betrayed by someone on the inside who had discovered another way in, and I think I know who it was." He turned to the two defenders. "Would either of you like to add anything to the captain's account?"

"I was on duty by the royal apartments when I heard them coming up the stairs. I didn't fancy my chances if they caught me, so I went into one of the servant's passages next to the old duke's ... Light rest his soul ... by the late duke's sleeping salon." He flicked a look full of misery at Duke Valdor, and then continued. "I recognized his voice, that devil ... pardon, Your Grace ... the chancellor. He was leading them and was telling them where to look. I don't know what they were after, but it must have been something valuable. They was talking, sort of urgent like. 'Hurry up' ... 'stop wasting time'... and so on. Then I heard a lot of bumps and things crashing about. I decided to get away from there and took the servants' stairs down to the main floor."

"Thank you, defender. It's very useful to have an eyewitness report that the chancellor was one of the ringleaders. Did you recognize anyone else?"

"No, Your Grace. At least one of them had a Valkonen accent though."

"Did any of you see any dark wizards? They'd probably be wearing black robes." Daryan asked.

One of the defenders shook his head, but after thinking a moment, he reported. "I didn't see him, but one of the footmen—he'd escaped through the servant's passage—told me he'd seen a tall man dressed in black, shooting fire in one of the ducal apartments."

"Anything else?" The three men looked at one another and shook their heads. "Well, I'll let you get back to your rest. Thank you for coming to talk to us. If you think of anything, please, no matter how trivial it may seem, we'd like to know about it. I'll let you know what we are going to do as soon as it's decided. Until then, rest up and regain your strength. We have much work before us if we are to defeat this enemy. The Light be with you," the duke concluded.

When the three men had left, Valdor turned to Captain Gauri. "I think we should allow the wounded men to go home and spend time with their families, if they have the means, or alternatively, bring their families to them here. It would be good for their morale and speed their recovery. What do you think, captain?"

"Most of our men are local recruits, so it shouldn't be too difficult, but we'd be leaving ourselves short if they attack the town."

"We won't decide until the men get back from the castle. If they've been gone this long, it could mean they were able to get inside, so the attackers must have left." He was reluctant to put into words the alternative reason they'd not returned yet; that they might have been killed. Then he turned his attention to the mage. "Lady Farah, what impressions did you get?"

"They actually gave very good descriptions of what they experienced. First, there were definitely werfolk. But what they missed when talking about it was that there were some men with them as well. Maybe that didn't register consciously in the general confusion."

"Would you be able to describe any of them?"

"Only impressions. My impression is that at least one was northerner with fair skin and light hair, dressed in black. And I noticed a typical Trethawyndian, brown skin and dark hair. The archers on the roof were definitely human, although in all the smoke, it was hard to get details, but they were built more like humans, taller and standing straighter. The images came and went in a flash, so it's hard to be more specific."

"Anything more?"

She leaned back in her chair, frowning with concentration. "When he talked about bringing the men down from the walls, I could swear there was a blond man in a black robe up there, crouched in a corner but, as I said, it was just a flash. That's all I think."

"Thank you, lady."

29 – The castle

Valdor

Valdor stood by the window of the officers' hall, looking out at the wet parade ground below. The rain had stopped and the clouds had begun to disperse, leaving the air fresh but humid. He knew that once the clouds were gone, the hot weather would return with a vengeance and was thankful for even this brief respite.

"The men are here, Your Grace," Captain Gauri announced.

Valdor turned and looked at the two men who had entered and were standing by the door, waiting for his attention. "Come in and sit down, you look tired."

"Thank you, Your Grace," the more senior of the two replied, bowing to the duke and glancing at the chairs by the table.

Seeing that they were waiting for him to sit first, Valdor pulled out a chair in the middle of one side and gestured for them to sit opposite. Daryan and Sir Arvand sat on either side of him, and Captain Gauri sat at the end of the table.

"First of all," Sir Arvand said, "May we know your names?"

"I'm Lieutenant Prylon, and this is Sergeant Janara."

Arvand made a note on a paper in front of him. "Thank you. Lieutenant, would you give us a brief rundown, please?"

"It was the most … awful … thing I ever saw … absolutely horrifying." He paused and straightened his shoulders, then continued. "We dismounted and secured our horses outside the main gate, and then we went back inside. There were bodies everywhere, many of them burnt beyond recognition, and all the wooden buildings were burnt to the ground. The stone buildings were covered in soot and most of the windows were broken." He stopped and looked at Daryan again as if looking for guidance.

"What did you find inside the building?"

"We split up into two groups—one with Sergeant Janara and one with me—and went inside the hall. We had to climb over bodies, sir." His voice wavered. He coughed into his fist. "Excuse me, Your Grace. I sent the sergeant to look around on the ground floor and I took the first. Everything was destroyed, everyone dead. It looked as if they'd taken hatchets to the wood paneling of the doors before setting them alight, and the walls must have been attacked with pickaxes. Everything that wasn't burnt was slashed to shreds. I don't know what the rooms were, but they looked as if they had been very ... opulent."

"The ducal apartments," the duke said, closing his eyes for a moment. "Thank you, lieutenant. Help yourselves to the drinks," he added, nodding at the tray near the middle of the table holding pewter drinking vessel and some carafes. They each took a mug and filled it with water.

"What about you, sergeant, what did you find?"

"It was the same as the lieutenant said, Your Grace. Everything was a shambles, burnt or destroyed."

"Did you have time to look in the cellars?" the duke asked.

"Yes, Your Grace," the lieutenant replied. "That's when we heard the shouting and banging in the walls. We couldn't understand where it was coming from; there was no door or any opening we could see, but a woman's voice called, 'there's something blocking the door', so we looked around and saw a heap of barrels and casks. After we moved them aside, a panel in the wall opened and they came out."

"Who were they?" the duke asked.

"There was a woman and a little girl, and four defenders. The woman said she was one of the cooks."

"Falisha and Mion," the Duke said. "Thank the Light they're safe. Are they all here?"

"Yes, Your Grace."

"Good. I must talk to them. What else did you see?"

"Nothing was burnt down there, but there was a mess of broken boxes and barrels, stuff spilt on the floor. It looked as if some of the stores had been dragged away; there were drag marks on the floors and some grain that must have come from a torn sack."

"It sounds as if they've looted the whole place. Which way did the drag marks go?"

"We followed them for a long way, until they went down a stairway to the level below. We didn't go any farther, Your Grace. It was getting late."

"You did well, sergeant, lieutenant. If you've nothing to add, I'll let you go to rest now, with our thanks."

When the two defenders had gone, a few comments were exchanged, but it was obvious they were all tired. The garrison captain turned to the duke.

"I've arranged for some rooms on this floor to be cleaned up and restocked for you, Your Grace, and I've also appointed a young defender who used to be a gentleman's valet to attend you. His name is Arkad. If you would like to follow me."

"I am very much obliged to you, captain. I'm sure everything will be fine. What about Commander Peshanar and his crew?

"We've prepared a room on this floor, adjacent to your own, for the commander and Sir Arvand. There's a room for the mage as well. The others have accommodations on the ground floor in the regular barracks."

Valdor stood up and stretched. "It's been a tiring day. I'm ready for bed." He yawned as he followed the captain from the room.

DarSolas Defenders

Corporal Danghar and two defenders walk down the dark street, checking doors and looking into dark corners and alcoves. Although many of the street lamps were unlit, they could see fairly well with the portable lantern carried by Defender Stervin.

"It's quiet tonight," Stervin commented. "I wonder when people that left will come back."

"*If* they come back you mean," Charok replied. "It's *too* quiet if you ask me. I like to see a bit of nightlife. The only tavern I've seen open is the one by the docks."

"Wait!" Corporal Danghar said. "Look at that window. There's no glass in it." He looked up at the discrete sign by the door. "Wouldn't you know ... the jeweler?"

"How did they get all the glass out without making any noise?"

"They could have made plenty of noise if we wasn't here," Charok replied.

"Bring the lantern so we can see inside," Corporal Danghar ordered.

In the light of the lantern, they saw smashed showcases and broken furniture, but not a single sparkle from a gemstone. "It looks as if they've cleaned her out," the corporal said.

"Look over there," Stervin blurted. "Fire!"

Then somebody screamed. "Come on, Charok, you're with me. Stervin, get back to the garrison and get help."

As Stervin ran off in the opposite direction, Charok and Danghar ran towards the fire. They rounded a corner onto a street that led to the main square and saw one of the businesses on the corner of the square blazing. Some of the palm trees surrounding the square were also on fire. A short distance away, the body of a man lay in the street. It looked as if he'd been slashed across the neck with a sword or sharp knife.

"Over there," Danghar shouted. "See it?"

Vicki Wootton

The sound of horses' hooves faded into the distance. By the time Charok looked where he was pointing, they were gone. "What was it?"

"Light if I know. It looked like a little tot, but different, more like one of them demons. This man must have tried to grab it but it rode away on the horse."

"Do you think it was them did this?" Charok asked.

"I wouldn't be surprised. I told you they was still around," the corporal replied.

"This fire is getting out of control," Charok said. "I don't see how it can burn so strong after all that rain."

"Smell anything?"

"You mean besides the smoke? You're right! Smells like tar."

"Well if somebody doesn't come to put it out soon, the whole square's going to go up."

"Shouldn't we try to put it out?"

"With what? We don't even have a bucket." Corporal Danghar retorted. "Let's take a look at the man."

They went across to where the dead man lay and examined him in the light of their lantern. "That's Sammy," Charok exclaimed. "Poor old Sammy. Just trying to protect his shop. Those devils!"

The shop that was burning was a purveyor of pottery and kitchenware. *Everything for the Home* was how Sammy's sign described it.

The sounds of horses drew their attention from the dead man. Charok quickly blew out the lantern and they both retreated into a nearby doorway. The horses slowed down and came around the corner.

"It's the sergeant," Danghar said, leaving the doorway and going to meet the newcomers.

That night, four buildings burned to the ground in the market square and six other suffered fire and smoke damage.

Several other businesses had been broken into and robbed of all their valuables and three more people had been killed by the robbers. A woman, who had escaped by hiding in a water closet, had identified the attackers of her dairy and the killers of one of her cows as demons. "But there was a man telling them what to do," she added.

Daryan

"I have to go to the castle," Valdor told Daryan the next morning. "I need to find something."

"Couldn't someone else go for you?"

"No, I have to do this myself. I'm the only person alive who has the key now. Besides, we'll have to see about cleaning up the mess and disposing of the dead."

"Very well. I'll put together some people to go with us. Most of the town defenders are busy with what happened last night. I'm hoping more defenders from the Monastery will arrive today."

"Thank you, my friend. We'll also need a small cart to carry things back. I'll go and change; it's going to be a dirty job. Let me know when you're ready to go."

Daryan found five members of the castle garrison fit enough to accompany them. It was preferable to have men who were familiar with the place. Along with three of his own defenders, he felt they would be enough to protect the duke. The mage Farah was going along too in the hope she might be able to get some sense impressions from the site.

While they waited for the duke, Daryan thought of something that had been hovering in the back of his mind. He turned to the five castle guards. "Were all of you in the guard before Gremulkin came?" he asked.

They looked at one another for a moment and all nodded. "Yes commander, we were all part of the 'old guard' as we call ourselves," the sergeant replied.

"How did you get along with the ones appointed by the chancellor?"

Looks of aversion lit the guard's faces. "We didn't," one of them answered. "We knew they was spying on us and we had to be careful what we said around them. We tried to keep to ourselves as much as we could. A lot of our friends got sent away for one reason or another, always with some trivial excuse, a minor infraction."

Another man interrupted him, "I knew all along, as soon as he sent our old commander away, that he was planning a takeover, building up his own little army ... but who could we tell?"

"What did these other guards, Gremulkin's men, do when the attack started?" Daryan asked.

"They disappeared," the sergeant replied tersely. "I saw a lot of them riding out the gate before the attack even started, led by the new commander. I've no idea where they went, but I'd sure like to get my hands on them."

On the way to the castle, Daryan told Valdor what he'd heard.

"It's no wonder the castle fell so easily." He sighed angrily. "It gets worse and worse; the sheer unrelenting treachery ... It's beyond belief. I should have realized what was happening and acted long ago. Looking back now, it seems so obvious."

"It's not your fault, Valdor. You can't blame yourself. How could you have deserted your father? I'm sure your presence was a comfort to him. You couldn't have fought Gremulkin from inside the castle, not with the power-base he'd built up."

"I know," Valdor replied. "But I could have done something. I should have approached the Monastery with my suspicions a long time ago."

They hitched the horses and the donkey cart to some trees outside the gate, and then tied masks over their faces, leaving only the eyes uncovered, and then they went inside.

"Sola Naofa!" Valdor exclaimed when he saw the carnage. "My poor people. They didn't deserve this. I swear by the Light, Gremulkin will pay for this."

Daryan saw tears in his eyes. "You were right about him all along. What I don't understand is why he did this." He gestured to ruins of the castle.

"I have an idea," Valdor replied. "But I hope I'm wrong. That's what I want to find out. We must go to my father's rooms."

Two of the castle guards led the way up the damaged staircase and along a broad hallway, littered with bodies and debris, to the ducal suite. The duke took the lead once there were inside the salon, which was a shambles of shattered glassware, and broken tiles. Everything that was flammable— carpets, furniture, draperies, wall hangings—was burnt.

"Through here," he said, leading them into the duke's study.

All the books, pictures and ornaments had been destroyed, some by fire and some by sheer brute force. Valdor went to the fireplace and walked from one side to the other, testing the stone blocks of the chimney. "Oh, no," he cried in dismay. "Your dagger please," he asked Daryan.

He slid the dagger blade into a groove between two of the blocks and pressed it sideways. With a scraping noise, the block slid out, revealing an intricate locking device. He took a large ring from his finger and pried the garnet from its setting. He then put the ring in a hole in the lock and turned it. Several blocks slid aside leaving a gap as wide as a door.

"Bring a light."

One of the defenders passed him a lighted torch and he went inside. "Just as I feared," he uttered in despair. "Everything's gone. He must have persuaded father to tell him about the vault, and taken his ring from his body after he died."

He came out of the opening, wiping his face with his mask. He didn't even bother to put the stone back in the ring and return it to his finger; he just shoved them in his belt pouch. "There's nothing more we can do here. I must check another place. I hope he didn't find that one as well. We have to go to my rooms now."

Valdor's vault was a slightly different design from his father's, but when he entered his bedroom, he saw the marble floor tiles broken and scattered around, exposing a hole in the floor. It was obvious it had been plundered as well.

"We're finished," Valdor said. "Just as I suspected; this was why he attacked the castle."

"But what did he take?" Daryan asked.

"The treasury of Trethawynd. All our wealth. My father's vault contained most of the gold and silver bullion, our jewels and other priceless treasures. Nobody but he and I could open it. He always called me to help him when he needed to go in. My own vault had my wife's jewels, a fortune in gold and silver coins, and some items of historic value like my great grandfather's enchanted sword." He pressed the heels of his hands against his temples and then combed his fingers through his hair. "I don't know how we are going to pay our defenders. We won't be able to repair the damage, arm our soldiers, anything." He wandered out of the bedroom and looked one last time at the ruined salon then went to the door. "There's one last place I want to check."

They followed Valdor down two flights of tiled stairs to the cellars. At the bottom of the stairs, Valdor took a torch from one of the defenders, and then he unlocked a door on the right and entered a small, wood-paneled anteroom. He closed the outer door and turned to the one facing them. This one didn't have a lock, latch, or any other way of opening. "Wait. I have to think about this. It's been a long time since I was down here. Hold this." He gave the torch to Daryan and started pacing back and forth; he then began to count the squares in the paneling. "I think I've got it." He went to the right hand wall and pressed a panel near the top on the left, then another in the middle, then he crossed to the opposite wall and pressed three more in various positions, finally, he turned around and pressed two more on the opposite side.

With his eyes closed and his palms pressed together, he counted, and then pressed two more, one on each side. He returned to the center of the chamber and waited. With clicks and rumbles, the tiles he'd touched slid back into their original positions. "Blast it!" he exclaimed. "I'll have to start again. Have you got something to write on?" he asked Daryan. "I should have written down the pattern I just used, so I don't waste time repeating it. But we can note the next attempt, just in case..."

"Go ahead."

"All right, this time we'll work together. Ready?"

When the second attempt didn't work, Valdor sighed and massaged his face with his palms. "It looks as if I've forgotten it," he said.

"Don't give up, Valdor," Daryan said. Let's go outside for a few moments and get some fresh air. If you stop thinking about it for a while, it might come back to you. This is important to you, is it not?"

"Yes, it is. It's my last hope."

"Is there a garden, so we don't have to go back to the courtyard?"

"There is, but I don't to waste any time. Let me try again. You took my mind of it for a few moments and now I feel more confident. I was beginning to feel too tense and that always leads to errors. Ready?"

Valdor started to work once more on the code that would open the inner door. This time a low rumble came from the door and it slowly began to slide to one side. "Thank the Light," he said with a deep sigh. "I was afraid I'd never remember it. Now let's see.... Bring the light please."

Holding the lighted torch, the duke took a step inside. "Come with me, Daryan."

At first, Daryan thought it was an empty room, but then he noticed there was a gap at one end of the facing wall. He followed Valdor to the opening and saw a larger room on the other side of the wall.

"Don't go any farther," Valdor said quickly, putting his arm in front of Daryan. "There's a trap. I have to disarm it." He looked around at the stone blocks of the wall and finally chose one. He pushed it inward and took out his dagger. He did something Daryan didn't see with the dagger and produced a click. "There, that should do it." As he withdrew his hand from the gap, the stone moved back into place. "Just to be sure..." he went back out to anteroom and asked one of the guards, "Would you find something heavy, a sack of grain or a small barrel?"

The guard returned carrying a sack of onions. "Would this do, Your Grace?"

"Perfect. Thank you."

"I'll take it," Daryan offered. He took the sack followed Valdor back into the small room and closed the door.

"I'll show you where to put it."

Daryan followed the duke into the inner room.

"Right there, throw it on the floor just inside the doorway, and then step back quickly." Daryan did as asked and nothing happened. "Very good, perfect, thank you. It's disarmed. Now, let's see if there's anything left."

They walked around the screening wall into a larger room lined on two sides by shelf-like apertures carved into the rock walls. One wall was blank. Three of the apertures on the other walls contained large ingots of gold bullion, about fifty in all, but Valdor was obviously disappointed. "It's not much. These shelves used to be packed. I can't imagine where it's all gone." He walked over to a pile of sacks leaned against the blank wall. "More coins," he told Daryan. He counted the sacks and nodded his head. "All right. Would you help me carry some of these into the outer room? We'll take them back to the garrison. I imagine we can manage two each."

They moved eight of the bags of coins to the other side of the wall. They dragged the bags out to the door where the guards were waiting and gestured for them to be carried up the stairs to the main door.

When they reached the courtyard, the duke instructed the sergeant and two of the defenders to bring the cart. "You can load these bags and guard them until we return. The rest of us will go back down and bring up what's left."

They returned to the garrison with the loaded cart, the contents covered with canvas sheets. Valdor asked the captain if there was a secure vault, in which he could store the gold until he decided how it was going to be used. He lifted one bag of coins and handed it over to the commander. "These are to cover your costs for the next few weeks, and pay the men," he told him.

30 – Aftermath

Valdor

The following morning, the new duke addressed the citizens of DarSolas on a common near the fort. Although only a few people turned up, the ones who came welcomed him enthusiastically. He made a short speech to reassure them that he was working on solutions to the problems besetting the duchy and everything would return to normal in the near future. His objective was to show himself to the people and allow them to see that he was fit and working on the situation.

Back at the fort, Valdor changed into something comfortable and went to meet Daryan and Sir Arvand in the small common room between their bedchambers. It was a gloomy room walled in stone with two narrow windows, a small wooden table with chairs and benches. Two lanterns hanging over the table from the ceiling beams supplemented the meagre of light from the windows.

"I'm sure I'm overlooking something," Valdor grumbled as he pulled out a chair at the end of the table. "There are so many things to think about. I need my secretary, and a new chancellor, someone to help me organize everything."

"Did you send for the tailor? You'll need something to wear tomorrow," Sir Arvand reminded him.

An investiture ceremony was being held the next day to formally instate the new duke. It was to be at the DarSolas Temple of the Light, along with a memorial ceremony for the old duke. There would be none of the normal pageantry for these ceremonies, just the formalities to make everything official.

"What about your son, Lord Varen?"

"I'll have to send for him along with the knights I left at Argento. I would also like to have Gremulkin's men that are being retained there brought with them. We need to question them."

A knock came on the door and Arkad, the defender who was acting as the duke's valet, poked his head around. "There's a young woman downstairs who says she has a message for the commander.

"Did you get her name?"

"Yes, sir. It's Avaya."

"Ah, the sender. Would you bring her up, please?" Daryan said. He turned to Valdor as the door closed. "This should be the answer to the one I sent earlier about your accommodation."

A light knock on the door announced the arrival of the sender.

Daryan let her in. "First let me introduce you to Duke Valdor, and then we can sit down and hear the message."

"I'm honored, Your Grace," Avaya said with a slight bow.

"We've met before," Valdor replied. "Welcome, Avaya. Take a seat."

She sat down on the edge of a chair across from Daryan. "The message is from the Grand Master of the Monastery. I have taken the liberty of writing it out for you, Your Grace. If you have any questions, perhaps I may be permitted to assist you."

She handed two leaves of paper to the duke written in neat legible script. He took the two pages and read them through, and then he handed them to Daryan.

In view of the destruction of the castle in DarSolas, the Duke of Trethawynd is welcome to reside at the Monastery of the Light at his convenience until such time as he is successful in acquiring alternative accommodation. We are in the process of preparing one of our buildings for his grace's sole use. We are prepared to provide any domestic staff he may require for his comfort and to enable him to fulfill his purpose as the ruler of Trethawynd. The building provided will be considered the sovereign territory of Trethawynd, rather than part of the Monastery, and will have such security as his grace considers fitting. A signed copy of this agreement in documentary form will be available at the Monastery. We look forward to receiving his grace and hope that these arrangements will prove beneficial to Duke Valdor and the people of Trethawynd.

The duke smiled, "Thank you, mage. That takes care of one of my most serious problem. It seems clear enough. Would you mind staying for a while? I have some more messages to send." He turned to Daryan. "Sounds very legalistic, doesn't it?"

"Oh, we have legal specialists at the Monastery. I think he worded it that way for your benefit in case anyone should accuse us of trying to influence you." Daryan stood up. "I'll leave you in peace to send your messages."

The first message Valdor sent was to his father-in-law, the Count of Argento. The two–part communication requested his help in influencing the other counts to send help to the duke in order to increase the defense forces of the duchy. Secondly, he asked the count to have his son and all his knights and defenders currently at Argento meet him at Palgrigio the following evening, together with the men Gremulkin had sent to bring back his son. The second message was to the Grand Master, thanking him for his agreement and advising him of his planned arrival two days hence.

The valet interrupted again with the news that the tailor had arrived. "I'm almost finished," he told Arkad. "Bring him up."

"Thank you, Avaya. I like the discreet way you handle things."

"Thank you, Your Grace, but I'm no different from any other sender who was trained at the Monastery."

31 – Return to the Monastery

Daryan

Duke Valdor left the DarSolas fort early in the morning accompanied by Daryan, Sir Arvand, and five defenders from the Monastery. The rest of his entourage was taking a wagonload of supplies by road along the river, around the south side of the mountains and then back up the road to the Monastery. One of the defenders was sent ahead to reserve rooms for the night at the inn in Palgrigio, anonymously, simply registering them as a merchant with his guards. Valdor didn't want to publicize his presence in the area yet as it might cause complications.

They arrived at Palgrigio early in the evening. After crossing the bridge over the river, they stopped and looked around. Greensward covered the ground from the riverbank to the town walls and a few cypress and willow trees lined the riverbank.

"This looks like a good place for the guards," Daryan said. "They could set up camp by the trees close to the bridge."

"I agree." The duke nodded.

Daryan instructed the five defenders from the Monastery who were to stand guard outside the walls and watch for any suspicious-looking persons approaching the town.

"Now I feel more secure," Daryan told Valdor. "Not that I expect trouble, but it pays to be wary. Shall we proceed, Your Grace?"

The rode through the open gates and Daryan led them to the inn halfway down the main street. Lanterns were being lit as the sun finished its final descent. The last golden tints of sunlight were reflected on the undersides the inky clouds that were piling up in the west.

"It looks as if there's a storm coming," Valdor commented. "I hope it holds off until my son gets here."

People on the street eyed them curiously, as they rode through the town, but no one recognized the duke, although they obviously suspected he was someone important. When they arrived at the inn, Daryan spoke to Valdor, "I warn you, it's not very fancy, but it's clean and the food and service are good."

"I can guarantee it will be a lot better than my home in the castle," Valdor replied with a sad smile.

Daryan talked to the landlord while the others waited near the stairs. "Well met, landlord. We're the party that reserved the rooms earlier today."

"Well met, sir; I'll show you the way myself. Would the distinguished gentleman like water to bathe before we bring his supper?"

"That would be excellent. Thank you. The gentleman's son will be joining us later this evening."

He signaled for Valdor to join him and they followed the landlord up the stairs. A narrow hall ran across the top of the staircase. The landlord turned to the right and opened the door to a room facing the front of the building. "This is our best room, Sir. The count himself stays here once in a while and this is the room he occupies."

"Thank you, landlord. If the count is satisfied, so am I. This will suit me very well" Valdor replied, going past the landlord into the room. "Arvand, would you arrange to have the bags brought up, please?"

"Would you like to see the other rooms?" the landlord asked Daryan.

"Yes, please."

He opened the door next to the duke's room and lit one of the lanterns, and then crossed the hall and unlocked two more doors, each containing two narrow beds. "If that's all, Sir, I'll make arrangements for the water and food to be brought up." The landlord returned to the stairs and disappeared below.

Daryan returned to the duke's room. Arvand, who had been carrying the leather bag full of gold coins, was massaging his shoulder. The duke was sitting on one of the two chairs by a small table. Apart from the bed, which was barely wide enough to accommodate two people, the only other furniture, apart from the table, was a small chest with a lamp on top. But the room was clean and looked as if it had recently been whitewashed, and there were shutters on the inside of the two small windows that overlooked the street.

"I'm afraid there's not much room," Daryan apologized.

"It's only for one night," Valdor replied. "Are they going to bring us something to eat?"

"Yes, Your Grace, and some water for bathing."

"That will be very welcome. I can't wait to get these boots off."

"Let me help you, Your Grace," Arvand offered, kneeling in front of the duke.

"Do you think the commander of my defenders should be doing the work of a valet?" Valdor asked.

"These are extraordinary times, Your Grace. Anything I can contribute to your wellbeing adds to my satisfaction."

"Go on like this and you could end up becoming the Commander General of Trethawynd."

Daryan could see they didn't need him, so he decided to go on to his next task. "I'm going downstairs now to get something to eat, and then I'll go out to the bridge to keep an eye out for Lord Varan. I'll send one of the defenders back to help keep watch here," he added.

On the way downstairs, he passed two women carrying pails of steaming water, followed by a boy hauling a wooden tub over his head.

Daryan sat down at one of the tables and ordered a plate of spit-roasted chicken and some boiled potatoes with butter. The chicken was cooked to perfection with a coating of thyme and ground peppercorns. After he'd washed it down with a mug of ale, Daryan stood and went to the door. As he opened it, he came face to face with Ashavan who was just reaching for the latch.

"Up to your old tricks. I see?" he greeted his friend.

Ashavan smiled and made a bow. "Isn't it more convenient than your having to go looking for me every time you need me?"

"Who says I need you?"

"What are you doing here?" Ashavan countered.

"Walk with me. I'm just going to the gate."

The two men set off at a leisurely walk. Daryan looked at his friend, who, as always, was dressed as if he were on his way to a ball, Dark green trousers with a purple mantle over a pale green shirt, and a purple cloak lined with pale green velvet.

"You enjoy dressing up, don't you?"

"My sartorial splendor is an expression of my creative nature. After all those tedious years at the Monastery, wearing those dreadful beiges and blues," he shuddered dramatically, "I need something to brighten up my life. Besides, it does no one any harm."

"I don't understand why you chose to live in Palgrigio. It seems a bit dull for a man of your taste."

"Oh it has its advantages. I do have some friends you know, and a social life. It's quiet; the townspeople leave me alone, and treat me with respect. I think I also give them some entertainment; my unusual attire seems to amuse them. It's handy for the Monastery as well, should if I feel the urge for a change of scenery."

"I didn't mean to imply... I'm sorry, Ashavan. I just wondered that's all. Besides, look at me. I buried myself in Picobali for ten years. That's hardly a hub of excitement."

"What are you doing here?" Ashavan asked.

"I'm bringing the duke to the Monastery. He's staying at the inn overnight. We're meeting his son here and taking him with us. Lord Varan has been staying with his grandfather at Castle Argento. I'm going now to watch for his arrival."

The gate had been closed, but the guards let them out through the small side gate.

"Excuse me a moment, I have to talk to one of my men."

Daryan went towards the five defenders who were sitting on the grass around a fire eating their supper. As soon as they saw him, they all stood up.

"It's all right, carry on. I just want to speak to Valmar."

Valmar put his cup down on the ground and came over, "At your service, Commander?"

"Would you mind taking your things and going back to the inn. I want someone to help guard the duke. You can report to Sir Arvand. I'll be along shortly as soon as the other party arrives."

He watched as Valmar emptied his cup and put it in his pack, and then hurried towards the town gate.

Daryan turned his attention back to Ashavan "I take it you're caught up on what's been happening in DarSolas."

"I expect I am. Did I hear correctly that there was an attack in the center of the town? Buildings burnt down. That's the last I heard."

"Yes, it's true, but I'm sure it's been greatly exaggerated. It was hardly a raid, more like large-scale robbery. A couple of merchants were killed and some merchandise stolen. They, whoever they were, set fire to a shop and it spread to several other buildings. Nevertheless, the townspeople are very nervous and some have left, not that I blame them. The garrison is being beefed up and there are more night patrols. What's going on around this area?"

"We've been hearing about raids from the sea on coastal villages. It sounds like burn and plunder, then back to their ships or boats, whatever they use."

"That needs looking into," Daryan said. "Do you have any idea of the extent of the attacks? Are people being killed?"

"Yes, from what I've heard, and buildings destroyed, by fire mostly, livestock either slaughtered or driven off."

"This is serious. I'll have to inform the duke ... one more thing we'll have to take care of. They have chosen their strategy well. Virtually disabling the duke and destroying a large number of his defenders so that he has neither a roof over his head nor the ability to resist. And they've isolated him from his people, because no one knows where he is or how to contact him when they have anything to report. However, that problem is being remedied; we're working on getting him settled in his own command center at the Monastery."

"It's not an enviable position to be in, especially having to take on the leadership of the duchy after so many personal losses. Well, if there's anything I can do, I'd be only too glad to help." Ashavan offered.

"You're already helping, Ashavan, but I do have an idea, something you'd be good at. We need an intelligence network, people to report unusual events that could be associated with the Dark Brethren, but more than that, we need a center where all the reports could be assembled and assessed. We can't form a coherent strategy without having the big picture of what they're up to and where they are. What do you say?"

"Interesting. An intriguing idea. I could do it. I have contacts all over Trethawynd whom I could ask to do some snooping, check rumors and so on. Would I need to be at the Monastery?"

"I'm not sure yet. I'll have to discuss it with the duke and see what he says. He may already have plans of his own, but I'll let you know. How would you like to go up to the Monastery with us tomorrow?"

"I could do that, yes." Ashavan suddenly became alert, holding his hand up for silence. He turned to face the north and frowned.

"What is it? Is something wrong?" Daryan looked in the same direction, to where the road disappeared around a bend, but it was too dark to see anything but shadows.

"I'm not sure. There is some sort of disturbance, but I can't tell...."

"Is anybody hurt?"

"Possibly, but it's not clear."

"Let's go." Daryan ran to defender's horses, untied a couple and quickly saddled them. As he was doing this, he called to the defenders on watch. "Felgar and Liries, come with me. The rest of you stay here and stay alert!

They mounted quickly and followed Daryan and Ashavan as they galloped across the bridge and onto the road north. Just before they reached the next bridge, they saw torchlights ahead and a crowd of people milling around. He dug his knees into his horse's sides to make it go faster.

For a moment, it was difficult to tell what was happening. He looked for someone he knew and saw one of the duke's knights walking towards him. Relieved to see the man didn't appear to have been in a fight, Daryan jumped down from his horse to meet him.

"What happened?"

"That carriage," he pointed to a vehicle lying beside the road on its side, where most of the activity seemed to be taking place. "It belongs to the count's steward. It was attacked on the road."

"Was anybody hurt?" Daryan asked.

"The steward and his wife are dead, and their driver, but there's a child. She survived. I think the attackers must have heard us coming and fled before they could finish the job."

"It makes no sense. Why would anyone want to kill a steward?"

"I don't know, commander. Everything seems to be falling apart, as if somebody wants to demoralize us and destroy our society and our faith in ... everything we take for granted."

"Is the young lord all right?"

"Yes. He's over there with the escort."

Daryan looked where the knight pointed and saw a group of knights and defenders. "Good. Where's the child? How's she doing?"

"She's over there with the lady defender. I think she's in shock."

Daryan turned to Ashavan and signaled him with a nod to go and join them. "See what you can find out." He returned his attention to the knight. "Let's sort this out, shall we?"

Daryan walked around the small crowd for a moment. "First, we should get Lord Varan to his father," he said. "Two knights and two of the defenders can accompany him and..." he paused and looked around again. "Is the secretary here?"

"Yes commander, he's with the boy."

"Good. As I was saying, we should send Lord Varan and the secretary, with the escort, straight to the inn in Palgrigio."

While the knight was sorting that out, he strolled over to where Ashavan was talking to the female defender and the little girl. "How's she doing?" Daryan crouched before the child who looked about seven years. She had her finger in her mouth and appeared to be biting it quite hard. *She's having a hard time holding herself together,* he thought. There were tears drying on her cheeks and her eyes were glazed over, almost as if she were in a trance. He stroked her hair. "You're safe now. We're going to take care of you," he said softly. She seemed to look right through him as if she was completely unaware of his presence.

"I think we need to get her away from here," the defender stated.

"I concur," Ashavan added.

"All right, I'm sending the duke's son on to Palgrigio; they're almost ready to go. I suggest you ride with them. Take her to Lady Isolda. She's better able to help her than we can. The guards at the gate can direct you to her house. Shall we?" he said to the defender.

She picked up the little girl and took her to one of the horses, then handed her to Ashavan while she mounted. He lifted the child into the saddle in front her and went to get his own horse.

When the duke's son and his party had left, Daryan checked on the remainder of the people while thinking about how to deal with the bodies in the carriage. "There's not much we can do for them," he said to one of the knights, nodding towards the carriage. Then there were the prisoners, the Castle guards Gremulkin sent for Lord Varan. "We'll have to report the incident to the Guardi in Palgrigio, of course, but otherwise.... We have to get the prisoners to the fort in DarSolas. His grace wants them there for questioning. I'll leave the rest to you."

"Kellen," the knight introduced himself. "We'll have to stop for the night to rest the horses, he added."

"They'll make it to Palgrigio won't they?"

"That's where we were planning to set up camp, Commander. Now they've had a little rest, it won't be a problem."

"How about the prisoners. How have they been behaving?"

"Much as you'd expect, surly, belligerent, abusive. Would you like to have a look at them? We've got them all chained up inside the supply wagon."

"No, I think I'll forgo that pleasure for now, thank you. I would like to have a look at the ambush victims, though. May I have a torch?"

The knight handed Daryan his own torch, and then mounted his horse. "We'll be on our way then, but I expect we'll meet again. Have you any idea what the duke's plans for us are?"

"He is going to set up headquarters at the Monastery and is sending most of his men, and knights, up there. There's already a group on its way there now by the high road. He'll probably send orders for you to stay at the garrison in DarSolas until the prisoner problem is settled. You've had the pleasure of their company longer than anyone has, so you may be the best person to interrogate them. Now I have to go and examine the victims." He nodded towards the coach. "Farewell."

Daryan carried the torch over to the ruined carriage. The driver's boy was pierced by two arrows, one through his right arm and one through the neck, but the steward and his wife had both been hacked to death with swords or some other type of sharp blades. He looked a little closer at them and gagged. The attackers, whoever they were, had started to hack off their hands before being interrupted. Both victims still had their jewelry, gold chains and a necklace, plus valuable rings on their fingers, so the motive for the attack didn't seem

273

to be robbery. He looked through the baggage on the back of the carriage, using his dagger to cut through the leather straps securing the trunks. One trunk contained a small casket of jewelry and a leather bag of gold coins. Daryan removed the valuables and went back to his horse where he placed them in his saddlebag. He then took all the jewelry being worn by the murdered couple and added them to the contents of the casket. They now belonged to the steward's heirs—if they proved to be his property and not the count's—and he didn't want to leave them for some passerby to carry off.

"Light be with you on your journey," he murmured to the departed couple as he turned away to mount his horse.

The following morning while the duke and his retinue were having breakfast, Daryan went to the home of Isolda and Ferland.

"Well met, Daryan." Isolda greeted him with a kiss on the cheek. "Come inside."

"Well met." He hugged the old lady and returned her kiss. "How's the little girl?"

"She's sleeping. I had to give her a potion. It's going to take a while for her to recover, if she ever does. I don't understand what the world is coming to, first that poor little boy and now this harmless little soul. Why are things like this happening?"

Daryan sighed. "Something has awakened the Dark Brethren, Lady Isolda."

"It looks as if we are going to have another fight on our hands. Well, you can count on Ferland and me, to do anything we can. Although I hope I don't have to see more of these poor unfortunates. Oh, I almost forgot, your friend left a message before he went home."

"Ashavan?"

"That's right. He says he's coming with you and will tell you what he's learnt on the way."

"I'm glad to hear that. I have another favor to ask of you, lady. Can I leave these items with you for safekeeping?" he showed her the leather bag and jewelry casket. "They may belong to her parents, unless he was carrying them for count. I'm on my way to tell the guardi about the incident." He handed her the bag and casket. "I have to be off now, Lady Isolda. Keep well; Light be with you."

"You too, dear boy. What's going to happen to this poor little girl?"

"We'll contact the Count of Argento. Her parents were on his staff. Do you think she could stay with you for a few days?"

"Of course. Now you be on your way and the Light go with you." She patted his shoulder and opened the door for him.

Daryan was glad Ashavan had chosen to accompany them to the Monastery. He knew that, in spite of his foppish appearance, Ashavan was a skilled swordsman. In actuality, apart from the secretary—whose name he had discovered was Imali—they were all armed and capable of defending themselves if they were attacked. He wasn't sure of Lord Varan, but by the muscular development of his upper body, he must have had some weapons training.

On the ride to the secret entrance, Daryan rode beside Ashavan and talked to him about the attack of the previous night. "Did you find out anything about the attackers?" he asked.

"I couldn't ask the girl anything, of course, but I was able to monitor a little of what was going through her mind." He looked sideways at Daryan. "Not prying, just seeing if I could pick up any clues."

"I understand. What did you get?"

"Her mind seemed to be going in a loop, the same sequence over and over. She wakes up—apparently, she was sleeping under a blanket, lying on the seat next to her mother—woken by the screams, especially her mother screaming next to her. She's afraid to look out and see what's happening and keeps her head under the blanket. Everything goes quiet and she peeks out. She sees a hairy little man standing in the carriage opening, looking off into the distance. He'd holding a big thick blade—the kind they use to cut down weeds—covered in blood. Then he jumps down and disappears. It was the blanket that saved her. The killers didn't know she was there."

32 – New Palace

Valdor

Bar-tori Algoran, the Grand Master, was waiting to greet Duke Valdor when he arrived at the Monastery. The Grand Master was wearing his ceremonial robes, only brought out for the most significant occasions; a long white robe of heavy woven silk inset with vertical panels of deep azure blue and embroidered in gold around the hem, cuffs and neckline.

The duke dismounted and, with his son by his side, walked forward to meet the Grand Master. The row of archmages standing either side of the Grand Master all bowed as he walked towards them

"Welcome, my brother," the Grand Master said, coming forward and making a bow. "Welcome to your new home Your Grace." He grasped the duke by the shoulders and kissed him on both cheeks."

Valdor returned the gestures, including the bow—he and the Grand Master were equals, although they served different entities and had different functions; the duke served the people and was guardian of their material wellbeing, while the Grand Master served the Light and supported the people's spiritual welfare.

"Brother indeed, Grand Master. I cannot express adequately how much your help means to me and our people.

When I had no roof to shelter me, you offered me a place wherein I could rest and recover my strength to continue the fight. I will be forever in your debt."

"This is *our* fight, Your Grace, and together we shall triumph, with the guidance of the Light."

Valdor put his hand on his son's shoulder and looked down at him, then at the Grand Master. "May I present my son Varan."

"Welcome, young lord," the Grand Master said. He stepped towards the young man and embraced him. "You've been through a terrible few weeks and born your sorrow and suffering with courage and grace. Be assured that your loved ones have now embarked upon the eternal journey towards the Light and I pray that the pain of your loss will pass, leaving you a stronger man."

"Thank you Grand Master," Varan replied. "You are most kind. I will remember what you said." He stepped away and bowed, then looked at his father.

"Well," the Grand Master said. "You must be getting anxious to see your new home. If you would kindly come with me, I'll show you the way. He stood beside the duke and took his arm to point him in the right direction. "It's over there on the other side of those trees. It's one of the older buildings, but it was restored about eighty years ago and is in excellent condition. I hope it will prove adequate for your needs. It's not as commodious as the castle, I admit, but we have made every provision for your comfort. If there is anything else we can provide, you only have to inform us."

They parted ways with the archmages and continued on a broad paved walkway through the trees—mixed ficus and mahogany interspersed with a few avocado—and came out on a broad meadow. Across the meadow stood a building unlike any Valdor had ever seen. He stood dumfounded as he took in the details. The building was in the form of a ziggurat, constructed of stone blocks covered with pinkish beige plaster. Each story was set back from the one below, and each level had a garden planted on the terrace, which stood above the roof below. Plants trailed over the terrace walls giving the whole building a delightfully airy and graceful appearance. The glimmer of windows could be seen at the back of each terrace.

"It is absolutely magnificent," Valdor exclaimed. "I never imagined such a place could exist. Thank you Grand Master. We are indeed in your debt."

"I'm gratified that you like it. We've renamed it for you. It is now called the "Palace of Trethawynd." The Grand Master said with a smile. Go ahead and look around. I've appointed a steward and a few footmen and valets until you can get your own people here.

They started walking across the grass towards the palace.

"The building has its own kitchens and all the other conveniences. Painters and carpenters are still working in some parts of the building, but that should not cause too much inconvenience. Your personal rooms are ready. Ah, here is the steward now. I'm going to leave you here and allow you to settle in. Any time you feel you need someone to talk to, let me know; I'd enjoy sitting down with you and sharing a little conversation. Light bless you, Your Grace." He started to walk away, and then turned back. "His name is Barastin, the steward. You may keep him as long as you need his services."

"Thank you, Grand Master."

He watched the Grand Master walk back across the grass until he heard the rustle of footsteps approaching from the other direction. Valdor turned around and saw the steward was waiting.

"Your grace." The steward bowed low and straightened up to stand at attention. He was a young man, not much over twenty by his appearance, wearing black culottes and black shirt with a red tabard.

"You must be Barastin. Well met."

"Well met, Your Grace. I'm honored. May I show you around the palace?"

The rest of his party, all but Daryan, had reached the palace and disappeared inside while he was talking to the Grand Master, and he was eager to join them. "Yes, Barastin. Do you think you could lay on a light meal for us? I know I'm getting hungry, and I'm sure the others are too.

"Very well, Your Grace. Would you like to refresh yourself first?"

"That would be good, and call all the others from wherever they've got themselves. We'll all eat together."

"As you wish, Your Grace."

"Tell me something Barastin; is everyone at the Monastery gifted?"

"No Your Grace, not all. The pages are ... the ones that run errands; they're student mages. Many of the service people are from the villages. My father and mother manage the inn in Alba, the main village. Many of us prefer to stay and work in the Monastery when there are no jobs for us in the villages, rather than going somewhere else. You know like, when someone has too many sons to take them all into the family business, we can always find work here." He stopped talking and touched his mouth. "I beg your pardon, Your Grace; I didn't mean to talk your ear off."

"What you tell me is interesting. I have so much to learn about our people, and you are helping me by filling in details like that." *That might be a good way to recruit defenders and staff for the duchy, men and women without hereditary prospects.*

They had arrived at the entrance to the palace. Valdor paused for a moment to look at the portico, which was roofed over with glass, supported by delicate marble columns, carved in a spiral pattern, on either side of the door. The doors were smooth polished wood of a mellow golden color with wrought iron fittings. Two wrought iron gates stood open outside the doors.

"This is one of the most beautiful buildings I've ever seen. You are very fortunate to live in such an extraordinary place."

"I do feel blessed, Your Grace." He opened the door and allowed the duke to precede him into the foyer. "This way, Your Grace, the main dining hall is on the first floor." They climbed the stairs into a wider hallway, running from left to right. "The refresher is this way, next to the dining hall. Would you like to eat on the terrace, Your Grace? It's nicely shaded at this time of day."

"Very well, Barastin."

A beautiful wrought iron table with a tiled top was brought out onto the terrace and laid with a white linen cloth and silver utensils, and then the food was brought out by the steward and two serving women. The duke took his place at the head of the table so that he could see everyone with Daryan facing him at the other end. The food laid out on the table looked and smelled so appetizing it was hard to resist. There were platters of broiled fish and cold chicken, spiced beans in tomato sauce, large bowls of raw vegetables cut into bite-sized pieces, with a variety of sauces. Several baskets of small crisp cobs, still warm from the oven, were scattered along the table, with cheeses, fruit, butter, honey, jugs of fruit juice and carafes of wine.

"All the food here was produced in our own fields and gardens and is brought in fresh every day," Barastin, who had taken a position in the doorway, informed them proudly.

"Even in winter?" Valdor asked.

"Whenever possible," the steward replied. "We have glass houses for tender varieties like tomatoes."

"Thank you, Barastin. You've been most helpful, and this looks like a splendid feast. We'll call you if we need anything more."

They helped themselves to the food and ate for a while, savoring every mouthful, before they turned to talk.

"I never thought I would enjoy eating raw vegetables," Sir Arvand commented. "But they're quite tasty, especially with this sauce. What do you call this?" he held up a chunk of a round white vegetable with a dark green rind.

"That's cucumber," Ashavan replied. "It's good as a coolant in hot weather. You just take a piece and rub it over your skin."

"How do you learn stuff like that?" Daryan asked his friend.

"My mother is an herbal botanist."

"Is that a gift, sir?" Lord Varan asked.

"I think it's part of her being a healer, but she certainly has a way with plants, especially healing herbs.

"Is she here at the Monastery?" the duke asked.

"Not permanently, but she comes here occasionally for conferences. She and my father are at the Faldino Monastery in the north east."

"Daryan was telling me you might be able to help us with intelligence," Valdor said to Ashavan after they had all finished eating.

"I would like to try," he replied. "I have a network of contacts all over the duchy who could send me information about their regions."

"That sounds like just the sort of the thing we need. Up-to-date information is critical. We must find out the scope and nature of all these seemingly random events in order to settle on a way to combat them." He stood up. "Shall we move to another room where we can start making some plans?"

"There's a hall on this level we could use, or another on the fourth level, closer to your own quarters, Your Grace," Imali said.

"Which do you think would be best, Imali. You know more about these things ... meetings and conferences and the like."

"I think the one on the fourth floor would be best," the secretary replied.

"Good, we'll go there. You know, I haven't even seen my quarters yet! I think I'll change into something more comfortable before we meet. Why don't you all take a break, rest, look around, whatever you want to do. We'll start in half an hour. Could you show us the way, Imali?"

The five men and the boy climbed the three flights of stairs up to the level where the ducal family would live ... currently a family of two. Their personal rooms were on the east side of the building with views overlooking the valley beyond the Monastery walls, the farms and villages, and the forested mountains in the distance There was a large salon with a bedroom on either side overlooking the terrace. Each bedroom had a private refresher room opening off it. The duke's bedroom had cream-colored floors and walls with brightly colored wall hangings and rugs. The bed, which rested on a marble slab, had a deep aquamarine cover and was surrounded by diaphanous white curtains hanging from brass bars. A large chandelier from the center beam of the sky-blue ceiling.

Valdor splashed some water on his face and changed into a causal robe and sandals, then went back to the salon, where he found Varan waiting for him. Valdor went to him and drew him close in an embrace. "How are you feeling, Varan?" he let him go and stood back to take a real look at his son. He'd changed from his travel clothes into a blue tunic over loose dark green culottes. More than anything, he noted the change that had come over his son in the past weeks; his face seemed thinner and he had shadows beneath his eyes. He also looked older, more mature.

"I'm well, father. How are you?"

"The truth? I feel overwhelmed by everything that's been happening. I wish I could get some perspective on things and

282

find a way to solve all the problems, or at least some of them. I miss your mother and Jilly terribly—I know you do, too—I miss my father, but I just don't have time to mourn them. I think moving here and having a more or less permanent place to work and gather our forces will help." He put his arm around Varan's shoulder. "And I've got you to help me now. Want to sit in on our meeting?"

Varan's eyes lit up. "I'd like that. Thank you, father."

Imali was waiting in the hallway outside the door. "Ready, Your Grace?"

"Lead on!"

Imali led them around the corner and into an identical hallway with doors on one side, and windows opposite, overlooking the atrium in the center of the palace. "Look down there! Isn't that beautiful?"

Varan followed his father and together, they looked down at the scene below. It was at least a hundred and fifty paces from end to end, and almost as wide, divided into small individual gardens that were planted with flowering shrubs, miniature fruit trees, and ferns. There were benches at intervals along paths paved with terra cotta tiles. In the center was a fountain surrounded by a square pool with blue and gold tiles. Valdor noticed that some of the beds in one corner were bare, and saw garden tools and some potted plants resting in a small wagon nearby.

"Look father, there's a peacock!"

"I see it. There's another." Valdor pointed out another bird identical in form to the first one, but with brown feathers instead of glorious blues and greens. "She must be his mate," Valdor explained.

"Why is she a different color?"

"I'm not sure, but it must have something to do with being inconspicuous when she's sitting on her nest. Like camouflage to hide her from predators. Most female birds are quite drab-looking compared with their male counterparts."

The doors of a room halfway down the hall were open and Valdor could hear men's voices from inside. "Come on, we shouldn't keep them waiting."

His three advisors, who were standing at the open windows to the terrace, turned when he entered. "Shall we get started? My son is going to sit in. It's never too early for him to learn about our work. Sit down everyone. Imali, why don't you sit next to me and take notes?"

He looked around the table at his two most trusted associates, Sir Arvand, the commander of his defense forces, and Daryan, his liaison with the Monastery and his friend, and Ashavan, a newcomer and unknown factor so far, but with the potential to being a valuable member of the team. "Thank you for your patience. I'll keep this meeting short; I know you probably have other things to do. I think we should start with an analysis of the problems and some suggestions of the actions we can take. Sir Arvand?"

"Your grace, we need to recruit more men for our forces. I know you are appealing to the counties, but I think we should also have a duchy-wide call to arms in every town and village."

From the corner of his eye, Valdor could see Imali busily writing everything down. "I agree. I would like you to make an assessment of our needs and come up with a plan for recruitment," he replied. "Daryan?"

"When we do get more troops, they will have to be organized into working units. My suggestion is to have League defender mages in each unit to supplement the defenders' skills with their special gifts. The Grand Master considers that this problem as much a threat to the League of Light as it is to Trethawynd, so working together makes sense."

"Would you bring this up with your council, Daryan? I agree we must work together. Perhaps League defenders might train with the new recruits too, or help train them, so they get used to one another. Now I'd like to ask Sir Ashavan what he can do for us."

Ashavan stood up. He'd found time to change out of his travel clothes and was now wearing an orange floor length cotton robe with a mage's orange medallion on a gold chain. He also had a floppy turquoise cap with a white feather on his head, which Daryan knew were not part of any uniform.

"Your grace," he bowed to Valdor. He went on to elaborate on the proposal Daryan had made on the way to the Monastery.

"Very good, Ashavan. Would you go ahead and start acquiring the contacts and creating the network? We need to know the extent of the threat as soon as possible. Is there anything we can provide for you to make your task easier?"

"There is, Your Grace, but the Monastery would have to supply some of it. I'll need at least three communication mages to receive messages. It would also be useful for us to have our own quarters—work and living quarters. The room in which we work needs to be isolated from areas of major activity that would distract them and disturb their concentration."

"I'll talk to the steward and make sure it's set up. I'm sure we'll be able to find a suitable place for you in such a large building. Make a note of that please, Imali." He pulled Imali's book around and read his notes. "We've covered recruitment, coordination and intelligence. Can you think of anything else that we should start working on?"

"Yes, Your Grace," Sir Arvand replied. "Two things both of which have to do with the troops and logistics. We'll need healers and medical supplies, and catering to feed everyone. That involves the acquisition and distribution of food supplies and cooking equipment, and the training of cooks."

The duke smiled. "Another task for you to plan."

"With your permission, Your Grace, I might need a little help with this work."

Valdor smiled. "Then, we'll have to find some officers and defenders who can help you."

Daryan stood up. "May I suggest getting help for Sir Arvand from the Monastery? I can find out if you like."

"That's an idea," Valdor replied. "Yes, go ahead. Talk to Arvand about what he needs." He looked around the table and stood up. "I think we've made a good start, so I'm going to stop now. Oh, one thing more: I see from this discussion that you will all need offices and rooms for your staffs, so I will consult Barastin, the steward, and see what he can arrange. All right, let's finish here and get on with our work. We'll meet again tomorrow morning. I'll make sure there is food and drink for you to break your fasts."

Daryan came around the table to intercept Valdor before he left. "May I have a private word, Your Grace? It concerns Lord Varan."

"Very well. Why don't you come along to our suite and talk about it? Coming, Varan?"

"No thank you, father, I think I'll go outside and look around." He obviously hadn't heard what Daryan had said to his father.

"If you see a wolf on your travels, don't be afraid. She's people trained and friendly."

Varan looked at Daryan suspiciously, as if he were teasing him. He turned to his Valdor. "Is that true, father?"

Valdor smiled. "It is son, don't worry about it. The wolf belongs to Daryan's remarkable daughter, Felindra. With any luck, you might see them together."

Once they reached the duke's apartments, they went out on the terrace to talk and sip glasses of chilled fruit juice.

When the server had gone, Daryan said, "Have you thought of his lordship's continuing education? We have excellent schools here with first rate teachers. I think he might enjoy it, and the company of people his own age might help him adjust to his changed circumstances."

"That's a great idea. I didn't realize they took ungifted children in the schools here."

286

"Many noble families send their children here for schooling. They know the level of academic learning is high, and I think some secretly hope that the magic will rub off on their offspring."

"Does it?"

"On occasion, yes. I believe there are many latent gifts in our people just waiting to be awoken. Parents probably brush them off as childhood idiosyncrasies or attempts to gain attention."

"Speaking of children, isn't it time you went home to your family? There's one advantage to working here, you'll be able to see them every day from now on."

"For that I am grateful. There's one other thing: my son, Darson, has an unusual talent. We aren't sure if it will develop into a recognizable gift, but I think we might be able to use it in our work."

"What is this ability?"

"He has an amazing facility with numbers. He can count and keep track of several different sequences of numbers at the same time. For example, he can count up the three different species of bird simultaneously and not lose his count of any of the categories."

"That is amazing. Either he's gifted, or a genius, or both. How old is he?"

"He has ten years right now. He's also very serious and bookish. Seems to enjoy acquiring knowledge."

"I can see several areas in which he might be helpful, but he's very young. I wouldn't want to deprive him of his leisure time or the company of his friends."

"Oh, don't worry about that; he seems to spend most of his leisure time reading. I don't even know if he has any friends. I've been away so much lately, I've lost track of what they're doing. I could bring him over one afternoon and let him talk to Sir Arvand. It doesn't take him long to count and do the calculations."

"All right. I don't see what harm it would do," Valdor said. "Now go home. I know you're dying to see your family." Valdor stood up and sighed, then went to the window and gazed out over the distant farmland, although he didn't really see it.

33 – Felindra Meets Varen

Felindra

Felindra was thinking about how much their lives had changed since coming to the Monastery, especially for her father. Two months ago, he had been a swordsmith in a small, insignificant village where the most exciting event was the Festival of Light every midsummer. Now he was the personal friend and advisor to the Duke of Trethawynd. Her reflections were brought to an abrupt halt when a huge grey shape flew out of the woods and knocked her to the ground.

"Ashala, haven't I asked you not to do that?"

In reply, the wolf held her down with its front paws and licked her face.

"All right, I'm pleased to see you, too. Now let me get up!" Ashala backed off and stood wagging her tail while Felindra got to her feet and brushed leaves and debris from her clothing. "What have you been up to?"

Ashala gave a little yelp so Felindra put her hand on the wolf's back. "You want to tell me something?" Felindra received images of people walking through the grounds of the Monastery and entering a building. "New people?"

Ashala looked up at her and gave a wag of her tail. "You want to meet them?" this time the response was a tail-wag and a yip. "I don't know if I can do that, Ashala. They are very important people—leaders of the pack—but I'll try. Let's go for a walk."

Ashala's idea of going for a walk was trotting ahead at a rate that forced Felindra to run in order to keep up. After doing a circuit of the gardens around the white palace and a turn through the woods, Felindra stopped to catch her breath. They'd come to the trees at edge of the meadow in front of the duke's palace. She sat down on the grass just outside the tree line and looked across at the building, hoping to catch a glimpse of the illustrious new residents, but no one came in view. Ashala flopped down beside her and licked her arm, then settled with her muzzle on her paws.

"That's quite an impressive pet you have there," a young male voice said.

Ashala raised her head and snarled. Felindra rested her hand on the wolf's neck. "Don't do that, Ashala, it's all right," she scolded. She turned to see who had spoken and saw a boy of about her own age with light tan skin, straight brown hair, and amazing grey eyes. "Well met," she stood up. "I'm Felindra."

"Well met, Felindra, my name is Varan"

"Lord Varan! The duke's son?"

"That I am," he replied, with a sad smile.

"Shouldn't I call you 'lord' or something?"

"Not if you want us to be friends." He looked at the wolf, who was now standing watching him. "Does it really understand what you say?"

"In a way," Felindra responded. "She gets the images from my mind when I say something to her, but I don't think she understands words." Felindra paused for a moment and put her hand on Ashala's head. The wolf wagged her tail. "She says she wants to be introduced."

"How?" he brushed back a lock of hair that had fallen over his forehead.

"You can pet her or hold your hand near her nose. As long as you're with me, when she gets your scent you will be her friend. To her, all her friends are like members of her extended family."

"That sounds like a real privilege," Varan replied. He wiped his palm on his tunic and held his hand towards Ashala. She sniffed it, and then licked it and wagged her tail. Varan pulled away quickly and wiped his hand again.

"There, you're her friend. Now she will greet you when she sees you and protect you if you are in trouble. You don't ever have to be afraid of her. She will never hurt you; that is unless you hurt another of her friends. Pat her on the head to show you accept."

"I'll remember that. She's amazing. You're amazing," he said. He reached out his hand and touched Ashala's head; when she didn't move, he stroked her and received a tail-wag in reply. "You're Commander Peshanar's daughter aren't you?"

"Yes. You've probably been seeing more of my father than we have lately. I'm glad your father decided to come and live here so he doesn't have to keep going away."

"I know what you mean." His voice faltered and he looked away.

"Oh, I'm so sorry," Felindra cried. "I'd almost forgotten. You must be feeling terrible, losing your mother and sister like that. I don't know how you bear it." She put her hand on his upper arm and stroked it gently. "I wish there were something I could do to...."

He covered her hand with his. "Thank you, Felindra. There is something. Would you be my friend? I don't know anyone my own age and...." He withdrew his hand and moved away a step. "This is stupid. How can I ask a complete stranger to be my friend, just like that?"

"No, Varan, it's not stupid. I'd be honored to be your friend and to prove it, would you like to come and see where I live?"

He suddenly brightened up. "I'd have to tell my father where I'm going or he might be worried."

"All right. I'll wait here for you."

"No, come with me. Have you seen the palace before?"

"I haven't been inside, but I saw them working on it for the last few days."

"Come on then." He held out his hand to her.

"Just a minute, I have to say goodbye to Ashala." She patted the wolf on the head. "You've been a good girl, but I have to go now." Ashala whined, then turned and loped off into the woods.

They walked across the meadow together and into the palace.

"This is an amazing place," Varan said. "Everything is so beautiful. There is so much to discover and so many conveniences we never had at the castle.

He led her inside the building and up the stairs. "We're on the fourth floor," Varan said.

At the top of the stairs, they turned towards the duke's quarters. Just before reaching the door, it opened and her father came out. "Father! You're here!"

"Yes, I believe I am." He turned to Varan. "Excuse me, My Lord, is she with you?"

"She is, commander. I met her outside and brought her in to see the palace. I met the terrifying wolf too, and I believe I am now part of her pack."

"Splendid. If you'll excuse me, My Lord, I'm off to see my family."

"Light be with you, commander. Do you want your ... I mean Felindra ... to go with you or can she stay awhile?"

"She can stay if she wants to, but first I must greet her properly; it's seems like weeks since I last saw her." Daryan held out his arms and Felindra rushed to embrace him.

"Welcome home, dadi. Tell mother I'll be home in time for supper."

"His title is 'My Lord,' or 'Lord Varan'," Daryan whispered in her ear, "and the duke is 'Your Grace'".

She looked for Varan and saw he'd walked a couple of paces away, closer to the door.

"But he said I could call him Varan because we're friends," she whispered.

When Daryan had left, Varan asked, "Does this mean you aren't going to show me where you live?"

"Oh, it's not very interesting. We can go there any time." She thought her parents might like to have a little privacy.

"That's fair. Come in and meet my father." He held out his hand to her and opened the door to the suite.

"I've already met him, Felindra replied. "They needed Ashala to help with the investigation, so I had to go with them to keep her out of trouble. I'd like to greet him though."

It took all Felindra's self-control to avoid gasping in awe when she saw the salon. The beauty of the style, the colorful furnishings and wall decoration astounded her.

The duke was seated at a table on the terrace, just outside the glass doors. "Can you spare a moment, Father?"

Valdor stood up and came inside. "Of course I can for you."

"I've brought Felindra to say hello."

"It's my pleasure, Felindra," the Duke said, holding his hand towards her, palm up.

"Thank you Your Grace." She brushed her fingers across his hand.

He really is a nice man, she thought. *Varan's nice too.*

34 – Preparing for the Coming Conflict

Daryan

"Are you sure you're all right with this?" Daryan asked his son. It was late afternoon and he was taking Darson over to the palace to meet the duke and some of the new Defense Committee—the title they'd just adopted.

"Of course, father. It's what I enjoy," Darson replied.

"Well, some of the stuff you may be dealing with could be very disturbing."

"I'll try to keep it abstract, just concentrate on the numbers."

"You're a smart boy," Daryan said. "If it gets to be too much for you to handle, stop."

"I will, father, but I'm sure it won't come to that."

"And I don't want you to become so impervious to the horrors you'll be exposed to that you are desensitized."

"What does that mean, dadi?"

"It means becoming indifferent to the pain and suffering of others because you are so used to seeing and hearing about it. You somehow have to work out a balance between abstracting the facts and keeping your sensitivity and sympathy for those who suffer."

"All I have to do is count the numbers, not what they mean. It's like when I count flowers or trees, I don't judge whether they are beautiful or useful, just how many there are."

"I hope you're right," Daryan replied. "We'll try it for a while and see how it works out. I don't want you to spend more than two hours a day on it. And I want you have time to do other things, play with your friends, or go to the library. If you start losing sleep, you'll have to take a break, or stop altogether."

They'd walked to the palace by the paved walkways from the school instead of through the woods and over the field. They passed through one of the Monastery's beautiful gardens on the way.

"Here we are," Daryan announced

The guard on the door saluted and held it open for them. As he passed the guard, he decided to introduce his son. "I'd like you to meet my son, Darson. He may be coming in once in a while to help the committee."

"Well met, Darson. Good to meet you."

"Thank you, sir," Darson replied with a tilt of his head.

They climbed the four flights of stairs up to the duke's residential level and turned left towards his private suite.

"That's four levels and eighty-four steps we've climbed," Darson informed his father. "Each step had ten tiles, that's eight hundred and forty tiles."

"That's a lot of tiles," Daryan replied. "Don't forget, you call the duke 'Your Grace' or 'sir', his son, Lord Varan, is addressed as 'My Lord'."

"I won't forget," Darson replied irritably, this being about the fifth time his father had reminded him.

The footman at the door opened it and announced Daryan, then allowed them to pass into the salon. The duke was, walking towards them from the terrace."

"Welcome," he greeted them.

"This is my son, Darson, Your Grace."

"It's a pleasure to meet you, Darson."

"Thank you Your Grace," he replied shyly. Being a stickler for formality, he stood stiffly, his hands at his sides and made a small bow.

The duke smiled. "Come out on the terrace and have some fruit juice while we talk."

They followed him outside to a table upon which was a pile of paper, weighed down by a large brass paperweight, and a tray with glasses and several flasks.

"Help yourselves. The red stuff is pomegranate; the white, lemon water; and the green is lime and something, I forget what."

Daryan picked up the flask of lime mix and offered it to the duke.

"All right, I'll try it."

"How about you, son?"

"Could I have some mixed with pomegranate, please?

Once each had a drink in front of him, the duke looked at Darson. "When did you first become interested in counting?" he asked.

Darson thought for a moment. "When I was very small, I used to count my blocks. My father made them for me and painted them all different colors, so I counted the colors."

"All at the same time?" asked the duke.

"Not at first. I was only just learning to count, but later, I began to count two colors, then more."

"How old were you then?" the duke asked.

Darson glanced up at his father. "I had about three years, I think." Daryan nodded.

"That's remarkable. You have a unique talent, like your sister. Now would you mind trying something for me? You can count from the written word, can't you?"

"Yes, Your Grace."

"Good. Here, see what you can do with this." He handed Darson, a sheet of paper.

Darson read it carefully, his lips moving as he read, then, after about four minutes, said, "859 long swords, 915 short swords, 1095 shields, and 981 bows."

"That's incredible!" the duke exclaimed. "All from reading a page of text. Look at it, Daryan!"

Darson handed the page to his father. It was a report from the garrisons of their weapon strength, with the type and number of weapon listed by garrison. "Good work, son," he said, patting Darson on the shoulder.

The duke took up another page and handed it to Darson; Daryan read it over his shoulder. The numbers Darson had given were identical to the summary on the paper. Darson looked at the two men and ducked his head, focusing at his hands holding the glass of juice.

"Do you want to take him down to meet Sir Karan and Ashavan? I'm sure they can find work for you, Darson."

"Thank you, Your Grace. Come on, son; let's go to see some more of my friends."

Darson quickly finished the remains of his juice and stood up. "Thank you, Your Grace; it was an honor to meet you," he said with a short bow."

"The pleasure was mine, Darson. Light be with you."

Valdor

Two days later, the Defense Committee met in the fourth floor meeting room to discuss the results of their various tasks. The committee had been expanded to include Plavan, who was responsible for the security of the Monastery, and Sir Karan, the knight who had been put in charge of the duke's personal guard.

"Let's begin with the damage reports," the duke said. "Ashavan, what have you come up with?"

For the next two hours, the committee discussed the situation in Trethawynd and planned the courses of action and remedies.

"Does anyone else have any questions or observations about the commander's suggestion to send out patrols?"

"Would the units have bases from which to operate, and if so, how many groups do you suggest for each base?" Sir Karan asked.

"I think that's something we'll have to work out," the duke replied. "Or should I say *you* will have to work out between you."

"Why not have a string of bases along the border and coastlines with communicators to warn of situations that need attention and at least two teams at each base, one for rapid response to emergencies, and the other for routine patrols of the area?" Sir Karan suggested.

"I agree," Daryan replied. "I do have some concern about the border region, though. It is mountainous and heavily forested. Hard to traverse. We wouldn't be able to patrol everywhere."

"Surely we wouldn't need to. If we can't access the area, they probably won't be able to either," the duke countered. "Just the populated areas. No one could cross those mountains either way except at the pass. There's no other way through, unless they can fly. We should concentrate on populated areas and around the pass. Let's work on that and get the patrols ready as soon as possible. I'll leave it up to Commander Peshanar, Sir Karan, and Archmage Plavan to work out the details, but we must be ready to move at the beginning of next week.

"There's something else I want to bring up. I know it's traditional for a national leader to lead his troops into battle, but if, as you suggest, there will not be a major battle, at least not soon, I have decided to go on a tour of the duchy." He saw several people looking ready to object and held his hand up. "No, let me finish, please. For one thing, the people of Trethawynd don't know me as they knew my father, and it would be good for the people's morale to know that they do have a leader and that the leader is concerned for their safety and wellbeing. Therefore, at the end of next week, I propose to begin visiting as many communities as I can and talking to the people and the local leaders, starting in the north where there are the most problems. I would like to use this as an opportunity to reassure them and tell them of the steps we are taking to defend them, and to gain their support.

"Now, I think we've done enough talking; now it's time to start taking some action. Thank you all and know that I appreciate what you are doing. Light be with you."

Daryan

Later that evening, Daryan and Valdor were sitting on the terrace outside the duke's salon, sipping chilled wine. They'd been talking about the meeting and the plans for implementing the patrols.

"I've been thinking," Daryan said. "We had coastal patrols at one time. What's happened to our navy?"

"That's one of the things Gremulkin got his hands on. He talked father into selling off the boats to raise gold for the treasury." Valdor's face darkened and his fists clenched in an attempt to control his rage. "One more thing we have to thank him for," he added in a strangled voice. He cleared his throat and continued, "It's not as if we needed more gold. The treasury was healthy enough. No, I think he was planning to leave us defenseless the whole time he was there. He knew just when to strike and how leave us too helpless to respond. He was already planning to abscond with our treasury and selling the boats meant more gold for him to take."

"Don't worry, my friend, he'll pay for it. They can't win and when we've beaten them...."

"I know." Valdor sighed. "I live for that day. I go to sleep at night thinking of ways to make him pay for what he's done to my people, my family." He poured himself some more wine and took a few swallows.

"But we should be discussing the patrols." He looked at some notes from the meeting. "They'll need transport for their supplies, and extra horses," Valdor said.

"I suppose we'll have to buy some," Daryan replied.

"You know what that means don't you? The gold retrieved from the castle will tide us over for a while, but it's not going to last very long at this rate and we're two months away from receiving the assessments from the counties."

"Could you get a loan?" Daryan suggested.

"From whom?"

"The Monastery. I believe our treasury is quite healthy. Why not approach the Grand Master? He knows of your circumstances, that your treasury has been plundered. And besides, he said himself that this battle concerns the League as much as the duchy."

Valdor stood up and went to the balustrade, rubbing the back of his neck. "Do you realize how humiliating it is, having to ask for help like that?" He turned around and looked at Daryan.

"I can imagine," Daryan replied, "but sometimes … I'm sorry, I shouldn't be preaching to you."

"No, please continue. I'm asking for your advice."

"What I was going to say is that for the greater good, we sometimes have to … put aside our personal feelings and do what must be done."

"You're right, of course. Do you really think I could get a loan from the Monastery?"

"To tell the truth, I don't know, but I believe it is possible. You … all of us … are in a very difficult situation and have nowhere else to turn, so we have to try."

"How do you think I should proceed? Should I send a message to the Grand Master asking for a meeting, or would you go to him and ask him?"

"I think both options would work. He's not a terrible stickler for protocol, but I think a formal request in writing would be appropriate. I could also go to him and explain the problem, if you like."

"I'll get Imali to write a request for a meeting and have one of the pages take it over."

"There is another source we could approach," Daryan said. "The queen herself."

"I've sent messages to our ambassador in Sola Regis asking him to bring it to her attention, but I haven't received any response from him yet."

"That's odd. How long have you been waiting for a reply?"

"The first message went out two weeks ago and I sent another two days ago."

"It sounds to me as if something is wrong. Maybe he's sick, or gone away somewhere. You may have to send someone from here to find out what's happening."

"Yes, I can see I'll have to do that if I don't hear from him soon. This is too serious to waste time on. I'll have to decide who to send. One more problem, eh?" He picked up the carafe. "More wine?"

"I think not Valdor. I should be going home for supper."

"Very well. Oh, I wanted to tell you we're all very impressed by your boy. He's quite brilliant. And Felindra is a lovely girl. My son is quite taken with her. I'm glad he's making friends. It's hard for someone in his position; people his own age are often either too intimidated by his rank, or resent him for his imagined privileges. He starts going to classes next week. I hope it works out for him; he's been so lost since the ... incident."

"Most of our students get along with one another quite well, no matter what their background. It's not uncommon for the child of a cook to be friends with the son of a count, and in your son's case, a duke. Gifted children are unusually sensitive and aren't often cruel because they really know what it feels like to be hurt or misunderstood. Of course, there are a few eccentrics, but they don't really harm anyone."

Daryan was about to turn and go back through the salon when he thought of something else. "Have you thought of appealing to the other dukes, especially the Duke of

ValkonenMaa? After all, the attacks are coming from his duchy."

"Before I do that, we should contact the survivors from the ValkonenMaa monastery and find out what the situation is there. We also need to find out the status of the duke, whether or not he's been corrupted, as my father was. It wouldn't do much good appealing to him if he was. I'll talk to Ashavan and ask him if he can find out. It would be a good thing if he were free of their influence. We could work together to eradicate the problem. I'll do that immediately. Thank you for the suggestion. There is so much to think about, and working without a chancellor is a real handicap. I don't know what I'd do if I didn't have you to discuss things with."

35 – Taken

Felindra

Felindra strolled into the classroom and dragged a cushion out onto the veranda where Arnaz was already seated. "You're early," she commented, dropping the cushion on the floor and plopping down on it.

"Better early than never," he replied. "Hey, have you heard the news?"

"I don't know. It depends on what news you're talking about."

"We're getting a new teacher."

"Has something happened to Lady Tonia?"

"I heard she's in the infirmary."

"Why? What happened?"

"I don't know, but she must be seriously ill."

"Poor Tonia. We'll should go to visit her after class."

Arnaz shrugged.

"Do you care about anything?" Felindra asked.

"There's nothing we can do about it, so why get worked up?"

"Ho!"

"Ho, Sama! Bring a cushion out here," Felindra called. "Arnaz says Tonia's sick. We're getting a new teacher. Oops," she added when she saw a man coming through the classroom doorway.

She and Arnaz stood up and went inside the classroom.

"Well met," the man greeted them. He was a short, thickset man with short black hair and beard. "I'm Archmage Shah-lin Farhg and I am replacing Lady Alberthaw who is retiring from teaching due to ill health. I also want to announce that we are getting a new student who will be arriving in a few moments. Before we start the class, I would like to know your names, and if you choose, your gifts." He pointed to Sama. "You are?"

"Sama," she answered. "My real name is Vestani, but I prefer to be called Sama. My gift is far sight."

"Well, met, Sama! You have a precious gift."

His response to Sama raised Shah-lin in Felindra's estimation. He wasn't going to be too stuffy.

He looked at her next. "I'm Felindra," she replied. "My gift is whispering."

"Well met Felindra."

Her estimation of him rose a notch higher. He didn't even raise his eyebrows when he heard about her gift.

"I'm Arnaz Pashin," Arnaz said. Before the teacher could respond, he continued, "May we know how we should address you, sir?"

"Well met Arnaz. You may call me Shah-lin, sir, or if you forget that, Archmage."

The new boy appeared in the classroom doorway alongside a palace footman. Felindra's heart skipped a beat when she saw who it was.

"Here is our newest student. Come in and meet the other students, My Lord. I'm the teacher, Shah-lin Farhg."

Felindra noticed Arnaz's eyebrows go up.

Varan came just inside the door. She could see sweat on his flushed face. *Poor Varan. I know what it's like to be singled out and treated like someone who's different.*

"Welcome, my lord; come in and meet the others." Farhg gestured with his hand for Varen to sit with the other three.

"Please, sir, could we dispense with honorifics? I'm just a student and would like to be treated the same as everyone else. My name is Varan."

"As you wish, m... Varan."

"Please excuse me a moment, Archmage." He turned to the footman who had accompanied him. "You may go, Inders; I'll find my own way back. Thank you."

"Since this is also my first day as teacher, we are introducing ourselves," Shah-lin said. After introducing him to the other three, he invited everyone to go outside and sit on the verandah.

Varan brought his cushion and placed it near to Felindra. He smiled at her as he sat down.

"I would like to start today by finding out what you already know. This isn't a test, it's just a way of gathering information so that I can plan our sessions without a lot of duplication. First, perhaps you could start by telling me what sort of schooling you have received so far. Sama?"

"When we lived in Zinawar, my mother taught me to read. After that, I learned from books until the Community of the Light started a school there. I went there for about four years, and then we came here."

"What sort of things did you learn?"

"The history of Trethawynd and the League of Light, nature studies, some plant lore, things like that."

"Thank you, Sama. Do you like to read?"

"Sometimes, if I'm interested in the subject."

"What subjects interest you?"

"I like to read about famous heroes, and about the wars against the Dark Brethren."

The teacher nodded. "How about you, Arnaz?

"I've lived here all my life," Arnaz replied. "We have a house in the village, so I've been going to League schools all the time. I've studied science and mathematics, military studies, history, some geography."

"Excellent. Thank you."

The information gathering continued until it was time for the noontime meal.

"I'm going to let you go now," Shah-lin told them. "You are free this afternoon while I do some planning, but I have an assignment for you. I want you to write something for me about yourselves. Anything you would like to share; it can be about your family, things you have done and experienced, your hopes for the future, how current events affect your lives. Please write at least two pages, and bring them me tomorrow. There are no marks for this.

Felindra saw Varan grimace and felt pang of sympathy for him after his recent experiences.

"Now let's take the cushions inside and close the window, then you may leave. Light guide you."

The four students stood outside the school building, undecided about what to do next.

"What do you think?" Arnaz asked.

"About what?" Sama asked. "You have to be more specific, Arnaz."

He shrugged. "The new teacher."

"He seems all right to me," Felindra replied.

"He's better organized than Tonia," Sama said.

"You can't blame her if she was ill," Felindra said. "I think it's going to be interesting."

"What about you, Varan, how do you feel?" Arnaz asked. "It's a bit different from having a tutor I expect."

"Yes, it is. Now I can meet other people my age and make some friends, I hope," he said, looking down at the ground.

"We're all your friends," Felindra said. "I have an idea, why don't we all go to the refectory in temp housing and have something to eat. I expect my mother and brother will be there, so you can meet them. I don't know about my father, though; he's always busy with something."

"Good idea," Sama replied. "Let's go!"

"I'd have to let my father know where I am," Varan said.

"You can send a page with a message from the building," Felindra told him. "Please come."

"I'd like to," he replied.

Arnaz shrugged, but he followed them anyway.

I wonder where Ashala is, Felindra thought as they walked to the refectory. *She's usually here to meet me when I get out of school.*

Felindra was relieved that they were serving something more substantial than the usual stew or beans. Platters of grilled chicken and mushrooms, and potatoes roasted with herbs were being kept warm over charcoal burners on the sideboard, and on the table was the usual assortment of fresh vegetables, crisp bread, and beverages.

Parvana and Darson joined them soon after they sat down It was an enjoyable meal and conversation as they all became acquainted.

"We should do this more often," Parvana said as they were getting ready to leave.

"I agree," said Varan.

"Do you want to come and see where I live?" Felindra asked Varan. "It's by the east wall, not far from your palace."

'I think I should be getting back. My father might be worried about me."

"Very well, if..."

She shot to her feet startled. "What was that?"

Everyone stopped moving and listened. A wolf's howl.

"That's a distress call," Felindra said. "She's calling for help. I have to go to her; she might be hurt."

Before anyone could ask questions or stop her, Felindra was out the door and racing towards the bridge over the moat.

The other students ran after her. When they reached the outer gate, two guards stepped out to stop them when they saw that one of them was the duke's son.

"We can't allow you to go outside the wall, My Lord." Both guards converged on him and took his arms, giving Felindra an opportunity to sneak past. As she passed the guardhouse, she snatched up a lance that was leaning against the wall and took off in the direction of the call. Another cry rent the air, so pitiful and heart-rending. She whistled to let Ashala know she was coming, and kept running along the outer wall off the Monastery to the forest on the south side.

"I'm coming, sweet girl!" she called.

Ashala barked once and moaned again.

There was something forbidding about the last call, almost as if she didn't want Felindra to come to her. She heard her snarl, and bark again, a threat signal. But how could she not come to the aid of her closest friend? No, she had to help her; Ashala wouldn't abandon *her* if *she* were in trouble.

She raced through the trees, jumping over rocks and fallen branches, skirting undergrowth. The snarling, definitely hostile, continued; Ashala was obviously in trouble. Felindra came around the trunk of a giant tree where she thought the noise originated, but couldn't see her. A low whine made her look up. *Oh, Light save us!* She saw Ashala caught in a trap, hanging from a tree limb in a big net. There was an arrow sticking out of her haunch.

Felindra wiped away tears and looked around. How could she have been caught like that? Surely she would have scented the strangers who'd set the trap. Something didn't make sense. Ashala knew she was there and snarled again. "I know, sweet girl," she whispered. She held the lance ready to use and stepped out into the clearing, edging forward slowly across the open space.

"Drop the lance," a male voice ordered.

Felindra spun around and saw a tall light skinned blond man holding a bow with the arrow pointing at her.

Ashala's snarl became a steady rumble.

Felindra knew she couldn't win; an arrow was faster and more accurate than a lance. She placed it on the ground. "Please, let her down. She's hurt," she begged. Tears started to flow down her face. "I'll do anything you want if you bring her down and let me help her."

"You'll do anything I want whether I let it down or kill it," he said coldly. "Come and get her," he called to someone else.

Another man appeared from the bushes. The second man was darker than his companion. He looked familiar, someone she'd seen before somewhere. He grabbed her, tied her hands behind her back, and then roped her ankles together. The Nordic shoved her towards the other man. "Here, take care of her while I deal with the animal.

"No, don't hurt her, please...." She thought for a moment. "Ashala, family. Family!" she concentrated on an image of wolves, her pack.

This time Ashala howled several times.

"It's going to bring the whole Monastery down on us. Let's get out of here," the blond man shouted.

"Shall I kill it?" the dark man asked.

"Forget about it. Let's get going." As he said this, he pointed the arrow at Ashala and let it go.

Felindra heard a yelp of pain and screamed. The two men dragged her away by her arms into the trees. Then she heard another howl. Ashala was calling to her pack.

Daryan

Daryan and several defenders, accompanied by Duke Valdor came running to the gate. They were followed by most of the duke's staff and guards, including the two knights, Sir Arvand and Sir Karan. Varan and his fellow students were still standing with the gate guards.

"What's happened?" Daryan demanded.

"Your daughter, Commander, she ran outside after the wolf." The gate guard replied. He turned to the duke. "We had to restrain Lord Varan to keep him from following her, Your Grace."

"You must go after her; she's in danger, I know she is." Varan cried.

Daryan turned to two of the guards from the palace. "Go to the stables and tell them to prepare some horses. Quickly, now."

"How many?" one asked.

"Eight," Daryan replied.

"That's not enough," the duke complained.

"I'm sorry, Your Grace," Daryan said, guessing the duke's intention. "We cannot permit you to endanger yourself. I'm sure your knights agree. You must stay here. This could be a move against you, a trap. Let us handle it."

Sir Arvand went to the duke's side. "I agree, Your Grace. The commander can take care of it."

"Oh, very well. But keep me informed," the duke replied. "Come on, Varan; let's go back to the palace. The Light go with you, commander, and keep Felindra safe," he added to Daryan.

Daryan and the League defenders followed the duke and his escort back across the bridge, and then veered off towards the stables.

He took aside Felgar, one of the League defenders. "I'd like you to go to the white palace and find us two mages. A healer, and Ashavan or Lady Farah. Get them horses and tell them to follow us; and make sure they're well-armed."

The grooms led the horses from the stables and men mounted up. Just as they were turning to leave, he saw Nadi walking towards the residence. Daryan urged his horse forward and called, "Ho, Nadi!"

Nadi turned and saw Daryan riding towards him and took a few steps forward to meet him. "Well met, Daryan."

"I need you, Nadi; we've got a horse saddled. Can you come?"

"But what...?

"Felindra has disappeared outside in the forest and we need help tracking her."

"What about the wolf?"

"That's the problem, Nadi. She was going after the wolf, said it had been hurt. Would you help us track them and warn us of danger?"

"Of course. I'm at your service any time you need my help."

As Daryan and his team left the Monastery, they heard the weak howls of a wolf coming from the left. After a moment, other wolf calls were heard from several different directions. The feeble call, barely a moan, came again from the left.

"It sounds as if she's getting weaker," Daryan said. "They must have used her as bait to lure Felindra out and then left her to die."

Nadi, who was riding beside him, responded. "What about those other wolf calls? It sounds like a whole pack."

"It probably is," Daryan replied. "I think she was calling them to come and help her."

"Will they attack us if we're close to her?"

"I don't think so. Felindra seems to have conscripted the whole pack, what's left of it, to help protect us. Let's hope Ashala lives. She's the only way we can communicate with the wild creatures. And, more importantly, it would break Felindra's heart if she were killed."

"I sense life over there to the left. It's very weak, though. Whatever it is, it's in severe pain."

"That must be Ashala. Come on, let's find her."

They came to the clearing and saw the injured wolf hanging in the net suspended between two trees.

"Two of you continued tracking my daughter while I handle this." Daryan pointed out two defenders.

When they were gone, he approached the trapped wolf. "Stay back. I'll deal with her; she knows me best."

As he rode towards the trap, he heard a soft whine from Ashala.

"It's going to be all right," he said softly. "I'm going to get you down." He looked at the two arrows, one piercing her flank and one through her ear. If the one in her flank hadn't pierced any vital nerves or blood vessels, she might survive. The one in her ear was just a painful nuisance, although it was probably very tender.

He studied the net and saw that it was held to the branches by twisted vines. It should be easy to cut down. The problem would be supporting the heavy wolf as they lowered her, without hurting her more. "Nadi, would you give me a hand? We'll need your horse. She's probably more familiar with you than any of the others."

"I'm going to cut the rope. I want you to hold your side of the net and I'll take the other, then we'll lower her gently to the ground."

The horse didn't like being so close to a wolf and started to fidget, but Daryan pressed his knees against its side to make it hold still. "Steady your horse," he instructed Nadi.

This won't work, he thought. *We'll end up dropping her and probably killing her in the process.* "I want two of you men to help on the ground. Dismount and stand between our horses and get ready to take the weight when I cut the rope. We'll help from the saddle. Don't drop her on any account, and watch out for the arrows."

All the time they were getting her down, Daryan kept murmuring assurances, hoping he was getting through to her.

Eventually she was on the ground. Daryan cut away the net with his sword and left her lying where she was. "I'll cut the arrow from her ear, but there's nothing more we can do at the moment." He patted Ashala's head and whispered. "I have to go now find Felindra, now." She licked his hand and rested her head on her paws.

Another wolf called closer now, and several others answered.

"Come on, men, let's go."

They followed the trail until they caught up with the two defenders who'd gone ahead. Darian could see immediately that Something was wrong. The two men were turning their horses in circles instead of advancing, looking very frustrated.

"What's wrong?" Daryan asked. "Why have you stopped?" Then felt it. It was as if they were pressing against some sort of invisible substance that they couldn't penetrate.

"What do you think it is, Nadi?" Daryan asked.

"I don't know," he replied. "They must be blocking us with some sort of warding spell."

"Can we go round it?"

"Let me try." Nadi turned to the right and started walking, then came to an abrupt halt after a few paces. He turned right again but the barrier seemed to continue all the way around them, blocking their way in every direction. "We're surrounded by it," he reported, scratching his head in bewilderment.

"Let's see if we can force our way through," Daryan suggested.

Felindra

Felindra was sick with terror, and her heart pounded so rapidly, she was afraid it would break down. Tears streamed down her face unchecked at the thought that Ashala might not survive. Had that last arrow killed her? She couldn't be dead; such a brave heart couldn't stop beating. Her single-minded loyalty and courageous spirit were incomparable. One thing Felindra was certain of: Ashala would give her life for her. *I wonder if I would have the courage to risk my life for her. Light, don't let her die! Please don't let her die.*

They dragged her roughly through the forest, not bothering to avoid roots poking above the ground; pinecones and stones tore at her legs and feet. The front of her culottes was worn through from its rough journey over sharp obstacles. Now the unprotected skin of her knees was being scraped raw. The men who were dragging her obviously had no empathy for her pain, but maybe if she appealed to their practical side.... There was a slight possibility, but she had to try.

"We could go a lot faster if you untied my legs and let me use my feet."

The two men who were dragging her let go of her arms, allowing her to fall flat on her face. She turned her head sideways, spitting out the particles of leaf and dirt.

"I said untie my feet!" she repeated.

One of the men kicked her in the side. "Keep on like that and we'll have to gag you." She couldn't tell which one it was, all she could see from her position was his boots.

"It's stupid to keep my feet tied up," she said defiantly. "I could run a lot faster than you can drag me."

Her heart skipped when she heard the swish of a knife being drawn from its sheath, but was relieved when she felt a tug on the rope and it fall away, freeing her feet. The man grabbed her arm, painfully wrenching her shoulder as he pulled her upright. Her knees gave way and she almost fell to the ground again, but he caught her in time.

"All right, walk!" the dark man snarled. He was obviously upset about her suggestion, especially that it had shown more common sense than he'd shown himself by tying her feet. "And from now on, keep your mouth shut."

Felindra stumbled forward, but managed to stay on her feet; the circulation was returning to her feet, making them tingle, but the abrasions on her legs and knees were more painful. She was starting to get sharp stabbing pains through her shoulders from having her arms wrenched back behind her. She wished her hands were free so she could wipe her eyes and nose. She looked down and saw her culottes were torn in two places over her knees revealing raw, bleeding grazes covered in dirt and debris. If only she could brush the dirt off her knees.

Felindra staggered along painfully for a while, urged along by pushes and jabs on her back. Eventually, they reached a clearing where three horses were hitched to trees, grazing. The blond man hauled her up onto one of the horses and turned away. She looked down at him and asked, "How do you expect me to hold on with my hands behind my back?"

He turned back, scowling fiercely and pulled out his knife. Reaching up, he cut the rope binding her hands and allowed her to bring her arms forward. She couldn't get a grip on the reins, her hands were so numb.

The blond man turned to his companion. "I need some more rope," he demanded, holding out the short piece he'd just cut. "We'll have to tie her to the saddle or something so she doesn't try to get away."

Once they had her settled to their satisfaction, they set off again through the trees.

It wasn't too difficult for Felindra to guess who her captors were, but why were they doing this? What could they hope to gain from abducting her? A hostage, maybe? Yes, that made sense; they must want her as a hostage.

"What is it between you and that wolf?" the blond man asked her, riding up closer to her left side. She hadn't heard him coming and his sudden question startled her.

"She's my friend."

"How can you be friends with a dumb animal? Wolves are natural born killers."

"Wolves have more ethics and courage than some humans I could name."

"What's that supposed to mean?"

"They only kill out of necessity, for food; they don't go around killing innocent people. They don't corrupt other species and make them do their dirty work. And they're loyal to one another."

"Shut your mouth and hurry up. We haven't got all day."

"Where are you taking me?"

"I told you to shut up!" Something hard hit her in the back. She cried out in pain and, if she hadn't been tied to the horse, she might have fallen off.

"Come on, get moving!"

Felindra rode on miserably through the seemingly endless forest. After a while, the trail started to go downhill, a slight incline at first, but the gradient was getting steeper. The path changed direction so that they were now going diagonally across the slope as they descended. Felindra thought she could hear wolf calls from behind her, but couldn't tell if they getting any closer.

Daryan

"We can try. It's not a physical barrier," Nadi replied. "I think it's supposed to work on our will so that we don't want to go past it. Its purpose must be to confuse us and make us waste time so they can get away. We need believe we can get through it."

Daryan urged his horse forward into the barrier. It was like trying to force his way through a heavy glutinous substance, but he made some headway. The others followed.

As they pushed their way through, they heard wolves calling behind them, and then the rustle of vegetation and the trod through it. "Be on your guard," Daryan warned the other men. "They probably mean us no harm, but be ready in case!"

The horses started to snort and toss their heads, and it needed strong hands and reassuring strokes to keep them going.

Daryan needn't have worried, the wolf pack hesitated when they reached the men but, after sniffing in their direction, they continued right past as if the barrier weren't there.

"Must be Ashala's pack. That was what she was calling for. Poor creature I hope the healer has reached her by now. Littes, would you ride back tell Felgar to wait there in case the healer needs help, and then bring the other mage here."

The wolves howled ahead of them. They were in full pursuit of the felons now and pity them when they caught up with them.

It was getting a little easier now to shove their way through the barrier and after a few more minutes, it was gone, although an atmosphere of foreboding still lingered in the air.

A call from behind alerted them to the arrival of Ashavan and Littes.

"What's happening?" Ashavan asked Daryan.

"Nothing much. A pack of wolves is pursuing them and we're following their trail. Can you get anything on them?"

Ashavan fingered his crystal and closed his eyes. "There are two men. One of them has very strong magic powers, but I can't get a fix on what his particular gifts are; he seems to have several. I'm wondering if he's a multi. I hope not, because if he is, we've got a real battle on our hands."

"Argh!" Ashavan suddenly recoiled and pressed his fingers to his temples, as if he'd experienced a sudden, severe pain. He kept his eyes closed and massaged his forehead.

"What is it?" Daryan asked, alarmed.

The mage flinched again. "Whoof! That was bad," he gasped. "I'm afraid we're up against something very powerful. We may have to protect ourselves against it. Will you all try to ward against it as strongly as you can? I'll try to set a defensive ward around all of us, but I'm not sure it will be enough if he sends another blast like that. That was aimed specifically at me, but he could target any one of us, or all at once, given his strength."

"You'd think it would take a lot out of him to use his powers like that," Daryan said.

"You would, wouldn't you?" Ashavan replied. He must have done something to reinforce himself before he started out."

"How could he do that?"

Ashavan massaged his forehead again and let out a long breath. "There are ways. The practitioners of Dark magic have some foul ways of reinforcing their power, the vilest being the fresh blood of someone they've just killed."

Daryan shuddered. "You mean they drink blood?"

"So I've heard."

Daryan was speechless; his stomach felt as if it were about to revolt.

They continued their pursuit, using what they knew of warding protection. All mages, no matter what their gifts, were taught warding against malicious spells, although some were more adept at it than others.

Suddenly, they heard wolves yelping, obvious cries of pain. Then their cries changed to wails, which gradually died out until there was only silence.

SEE NOW WHAT YOU ARE FACING, FOOLS! It blasted into Ashavan's head with a force that almost unseated him, leaving him momentarily breathless and dizzy.

"Even I felt that," Daryan gasped. "This is worse than I thought. What are we up against here?"

KEEP FOLLOWING US AND YOU WON'T SEE THE GIRL ALIVE AGAIN!

"Stop, everyone," Daryan ordered. "We have to think about this. There must be some way we can fight it, but I don't know what it is. I'm going to find out, though."

"I'm going to try something," Ashavan said.

He closed his eyes and concentrated for a moment. "Damn! I almost had her."

"What were you doing?"

"I was trying to contact your daughter. I almost got through to her, but he shut me out as soon as he detected me."

"Do you think she felt you?" Daryan asked.

"Just for a flash, but we couldn't exchange any information."

YOU'VE BEEN WARNED!

Daryan's horse suddenly bucked, and then it screamed and dropped to the ground with blood pouring from its nose and mouth. Daryan's heart pounded in terror. Never had he encountered such power. He lay on the ground, his right foot trapped under the heavy body of his horse, trying to catch his breath and summon the strength to free himself. He was able to loosen his left leg from the stirrup and bring it over against the back of the poor creature. With everyone else trying to raise the lifeless animal and he pushing against it with his left foot, he managed to free his trapped right foot.

"NEXT TIME IT WILL BE ONE OF YOU, COMMANDER!"

"I think we should do what he says, Daryan," Ashavan urged. "She's still alive, and I don't think they'll harm her unless we do something to annoy them. We should go back to the Monastery and consult the council. It sounds as if he dealt with a whole pack of wolves in one blow. We wouldn't have a chance against such power. I hate to give up like this, but we can't handle it on our own. We need something stronger."

36 – The Dark Wizard

Daryan

"The first thing we need to know is what they want," the Grand Master said. The emergency meeting had been called as soon as Daryan and his team arrived back at the Monastery. They were now in the meeting room on the fourth floor of the duke's palace. "I don't think your daughter will be in danger until we respond to their demands. Until then, we have to plan on several fronts. First, we need a contingency plan in the event that we don't concede to their demands.

"We also need to bolster our defenses against a major dark magic attack. We should also plan how we can defend people outside the Monastery. I'm sorry, Commander, I know your daughter is the one in imminent danger, but we have to look at the threat to the whole of Trethawynd. If there are more wizards as powerful as he is, we'll have a real fight on our hands. I assure you we will do everything in our power to get her back safely. This situation has suddenly taken on a more sinister and lethal aspect. Anyone who has the power to disable and even kill a whole group of animals is much more dangerous than we expected. And if Ashavan is correct, this one may even have multiple dark gifts. He could be the Dark Wizard reincarnated."

"I understand, Grand Master," Daryan said softly, although in his heart he was protesting strenuously against any delay in rescuing her. He knew the Grand Master was right, but that was no balm to his personal pain and the threat to his family. Now he had an inkling of how the duke must have felt after the attacks on his family. "I don't understand how they can develop such powerful magic," he added.

"This was before your time, but there was an incident in the north up near Bartony about forty years ago. A group of wizards came over the border and destroyed a small logging village. Killed all the people and animals. We managed to capture one of them. He'd used too much of his power, leaving him very weak, so he couldn't keep up with the others ... a youngster, no more than seventeen. At that age, they don't know their limits and tend to be reckless with their use of power. Anyway, to answer your question, Commander, we found out from him that they absorb the life force of other creatures to fortify their own."

"That's horrible," Daryan exclaimed. "You mean they kill animals so they can use powerful magic? How? I mean how do you take the life force of another creature?"

The Grand Master sighed. "It was hard to get all the details; the young wizard didn't really know how it worked. All he could say was that they had a ceremony in a secret cavern with their leader officiating. It involved sacrificing the creatures and a lot of ceremonial mumbo-jumbo. And it wasn't just animals they used; in this particular ceremony, they were wermen. Apparently the higher the level of the creature, the more powerful is the force and werfolk are almost human."

"That is pure evil," Valdor said. "Did you discover the reason for that attack?"

"As far as we could make out, it was a training exercise for novice wizards." The Grand Master went back to his notes and looked through them. "I think we should get on with the purpose of this meeting, which is how do we respond to these attacks and prevent further occurrences?"

"I hope you have some way of bolstering the defenses here, because I confess, I'm at a loss. I wouldn't know where to turn. We can't deploy all our forces to defending one place," Valdor said.

"Oh we have a few things in reserve for such occasions," the Grand Master replied. "For one thing, we can array our warding defense to protect everyone within these walls from magic attacks. I wouldn't want to use it except in extreme circumstances. The energy needed for such an effort comes at a great cost, and the result would not justify such a cost at this time. There's one thing in our favor though; there can't be many wizards with such enhanced powers, and he can't be everywhere at once. If we could keep track of his whereabouts, and any others we encounter, we'd know where to concentrate our efforts."

"How do you think they will make their demands known to us?" the duke asked.

"Oh, I'm sure they'll choose something unexpected and dramatic to get our attention," Daryan replied. "It may or may not involve magic, but you can be sure it will be something very nasty. That seems to be their way." *My poor girl, what must she be going through? She'll be so frightened. At least Ashala will survive, thank the light. I wish I could let her know that; it might give her some comfort.*

"What do you think they'll demand?" Daryan asked.

"It is sure to be something related to me," Valdor replied. "They'll probably want me to surrender to them in exchange for your daughter. I suspect Gremulkin has plans to put my brother in my place."

"We can't permit that," the Grand Master stated emphatically. "Under no circumstance will you surrender to them."

"But that child's life is in danger. I can't allow another innocent girl to die to save my own life. I'm sorry, Grand Master, but if it's a choice between her and me, I will give myself up."

"If you do that, you'd be giving all of Trethawynd into the hands of the Dark Brethren." The Grand Master replied. "We can't allow that, and we won't, much as we admire your courage and honor. Trethawynd needs you."

"What about the tour I was planning? We were going to leave on the morrow."

"That would be very inadvisable, given today's attack. It seems obvious that you are being targeted again."

"I don't want to make this a conflict of authority, but surely I'm free to make my own decisions in that regard," Valdor insisted.

"And normally you would be, Your Grace, but when the entire realm is at risk, it is our duty, as the Defenders of the Light, to prevent anything that may result in the triumph of the forces of darkness. Therefore, it is imperative that you remain under our protection, much as I regret such a decision. If we lose you, there is no one to rule in your place until your son comes of age, and by then it would be too late and he'd have nothing to inherit."

"I won't give up my efforts to rescue my daughter,"

"I agree, Commander, that's our top priority at the moment. But we need to find out where she is in order to rescue her," the Grand Master said. "We'll assemble some of our strongest telepaths to try to contact her, including you, Ashavan."

"That goes without saying, Grand Master," Ashavan replied. "I'll do everything in my power to help bring her back."

As the meeting drew to a close, Valdor looked at Daryan. "You should go home to be with your family, Daryan," he advised.

How am I going to break this to Parvana? She'll be devastated, but I can't keep it from her.

37 – The search for Felindra

Ashala

Ashala raised her head and sniffed the air. The wound in her side ached, but when she tried to examine it, she found it bound tightly with cloth. She moaned and lowered her head again, resting it on her front paws. She knew there was something she should be doing, but didn't have the strength to get up and attend to it. She whined softly and closed her eyes.

Ashavan

It was early evening. Ashavan, Farah and Delara sat together in one of the lounges of the mages quarters. They sat with closed eyes, holding their crystals and concentrating on Felindra. Their minds reached out to the girl. Farah was holding in her hand one of Felindra's sashes that Daryan had provided, hoping it would enhance her ability to link with her.

Ashavan mumbled under his breath, "Felindra, where are you?" He received a vague awareness of her presence among barely discernable impressions of passing trees.

Who's that? The response was faint was.

Ashavan. Where are you? He held his hand out to Delara so that she could link with him and strengthen the connection.

In the forest. They've put me on a horse; I'm tied on.

Felindra...! He listened for a moment. "It's no use. I've lost her."

"Well, I don't think she's badly hurt," Delara said. "I didn't sense a lot of distress, did you?"

"She's not comfortable. She's in pain, but it doesn't seem too severe." Ashavan looked at Delara "Anything else?"

"She's still in the forest," Delara said. "We should be able to find them without too much difficulty."

"Don't count on it," Farah interjected. "I just saw her being led somewhere on horseback by two men. One of them was a dark man, probably a local; the other was big and light-skinned with fair hair, and very powerful magic."

"We'll have to move quickly if we're going to catch them," Ashavan said. "Did you sense anything that would indicate where they were or what time of day it was?"

"I saw them near the sea. They seem to be moving down a slope towards the water, and I thought I caught a glimpse of the end of a boat. It looks like twilight, but I couldn't tell if it was dawn or sunset, only that the sun is below the horizon. Let's hope it was dawn; that would give you more time."

"I'm off to get Daryan," Ashavan said, standing up abruptly. "Would you mind staying available? We might still need your help."

Daryan

Daryan was lying on the bed holding Parvana in his arms, unable to sleep because of the roiling furnace in his stomach. Parvana had completely gone to pieces when he told her about Felindra, sobbing inconsolably and moaning Felindra's name, over and over. He'd barely had time to comfort Darson and see him to his bed before having to return to his distraught wife. Now she was finally sleeping, thank the Light.

He heard a soft knock on the outer door, as if someone were trying to attract attention without making any noise, a futile undertaking. He heard Darson pad across the floor to answer, then a whispered conversation. As gently as he could, Daryan disentangled himself from Parvana and went over to the chest to get his trousers. The door was pushed open and Darson's head appeared.

"Are you awake, Father?" he whispered.

"I'm coming," Daryan replied softly.

He walked out into the day room with his boots in his hand, closing the bedroom door behind him. Ashavan was standing just inside the door. Daryan beckoned to Darson to follow him and led Ashavan outside. "What have you found out?" he asked Ashavan.

"We have an idea where she is," Ashavan said. "Farah used her farsight." He told Daryan what Farah had seen.

While he was listening, Daryan was putting on his boots. "Would you get my cloak and sword belt? They're by the table," he asked his son. "Be as quiet as you can. I don't want to wake your mother."

Darson came back after a few seconds and gave him his cloak and the other equipment.

"Now go back inside and try to get some more sleep," he instructed the boy. "Tell your mother what we talked about when she wakes up and, son, stay with her today. She's going to need someone. I have to go and find your sister."

Daryan hugged his son and kissed him on the forehead.

Felindra

Felindra woke with a start. She was lying on a hard surface that rocked steadily up and down. The damp air was so cold she was shivering violently. Her shoulders and knees ached relentlessly. She looked up and saw the dark sky strewn with stars that seemed to rock with the rhythm of the floor. *It's a boat!* she realized. *Oh Light they're taking me away on a boat. They'll never find me.* Stifling a sob, she tried to get more comfortable, but she could only move about a hand's-breadth. Her wrists were tied in front of her, with the ends of the rope secured to the sides of the boat. If only she could move her arms, she could wrap them around herself for warmth.

She moaned softly. *Ashala. My poor sweet girl. I hope you're all right.* Tears ran down the sides of her face, adding to her discomfort as they pooled in her ears. *Where are they taking me?*

Daryan

"IF YOU WANT THE GIRL BACK ALIVE, YOU WILL BRING US THE DUKE. TELL YOUR MASTERS. THERE WILL BE NO NEGOTIATION."

Daryan reeled from the shock of the blast in his mind.

"DO YOU UNDERSTAND?"

I understand, evil one.

"GO. DO AS I DEMAND."

You won't get away with this! The light always wins. He'll put an end to your kind.

"HA HA HA! SHE WILL NOT LIVE MUCH LONGER IF YOU DON'T HURRY, FOOL."

"Did you hear that?" Daryan asked Ashavan.

"I did indeed, my friend. We must hurry."

"Is he close by?"

"It's hard to say, he could be anywhere. Telepathy is not restricted by distance; however, my direction sense tells me he is north or northwest of us."

"I'll round up a few defenders to go with us. Would you like to go to the stables and ask them to ready some horses? Are you coming with us?"

"Most assuredly," Ashavan replied.

"We'll need eight horses, and a spare one for Felindra to ride when we find her."

Daryan urged his horse forward followed by the rest of his team of four defenders with various skills, plus Farah, Nadi, and Ashavan. The sky was still resplendent with stars and a half moon when they left the Monastery. The torches they carried enabled them to jog through the forest at a fair rate, but not fast enough for Daryan.

After they'd ridden for about three hours, the sky began to lighten. As the sun came over the horizon, the sky changed to gold. Rays of light filtering down through the leaves, painting them with golden halos and showering the forest floor with gold medallions.

Daryan's fear that they might not be in time to rescue his daughter made him oblivious to the surrounding beauty. The trail ahead seemed clear enough, although it was narrow. If they rode single file, they could go faster. He slapped the reins and his horse broke into a gallop. He heard the others coming along behind him and kept up the speed, veering left and right to avoid obstacles.

Felindra

Felindra opened her eyes and saw the sun was rising. Already, she thought. Has it been that long...? *Ashala! Where are you, girl? Are you all right? I'm sorry... They must be so worried. Poor mother. Father will come after me, I know. He's probably getting close now... But how can he find me in a boat on the sea? I know he's got mages, Ashavan ... so why aren't they reaching me? Is something blocking them?* The thoughts tumbled through her mind in a random turmoil.

She turned her head sideways and looked at one of the men in the boat with her. She knew him! He was one of the two men who'd passed them in the big wagon on the road to the monastery. *He might be the one who made the wolves attack us.* All she could sense of the other one was that he was very angry about something and he kept moaning as if he was in pain.

Sensing her attention, the man said malevolently, "not so proud now, are you? We've got great things in store for you, girl," he added, gloating. She realized he had a northern accent; she'd been too terrified yesterday to notice it. "Are you ready?" he asked. She tried to swivel her head to see him, but he was directly behind her.

"They're almost here. Get ready to drop the sail."

Another vessel floated into view, coming up on the landward side. It looked much bigger than the one she was in. She watched the man lower the sail as they maneuvered into position beside the other vessel. Two sailors reached out and grabbed the side of their boat, pulling it close until their sides were touching.

"Cut the ropes," the northerner ordered.

His partner stooped and slashed the rope anchoring her bonds to the sides of the boat. "Stand up," he ordered roughly, grabbing her arm. She gasped as searing pain ripped through her damaged knees and she almost collapsed. "Come on; stop whining, you're not hurt that bad." Still holding her biceps in a vise-like grip, he dragged her over to the side of the boat.

The two men on the other vessel leaned over and grabbed her by the arms. "We've got her," one of them said. "Come on girl, climb over."

Felindra was determined not to speak to any of them. She wasn't going to give them the satisfaction of showing how frightened and uncomfortable she was. She knew if she asked them anything, they would probably mock her helplessness. And she certainly wasn't going to beg. She firmly resolved and impressed upon her mind that they were evil, followers of the Dark One and not worthy of her attention. The Light would win. She only had to be patient. *But oh, how I wish it could be over. I don't know if I'm strong enough to do this. Light, help me, please!*

She lifted one leg shakily, feeling the scabs on her knee tearing and blood trickling down her leg. She rested her foot on the higher gunwale of the other boat, and then with the help of the men holding her, pulled herself up. She felt very wobbly once she was on the deck and looked around for something to sit on, but the two mariners continued to guide her roughly across the boards until they reached a small structure near the stern.

"In here," one of them said. "Sit down over there." He indicated a full sack leaning against the wall of the cabin, or whatever the structure was called. The other man had left, and this one stood in the doorway watching her as she sat down. The sack was filled with something knobbly, like rocks, only not quite so hard. She thought they might be potatoes. "Stay there," the man ordered. "Don't go wandering around or we'll have to tie you up again." With that, he left.

Daryan

It took them until almost noon to reach the high road, where they stopped to rest the horses.

"Can any of you find her?" Daryan asked the mages who were clustering around him.

"There's a very faint trace. It's like trying to see in heavy fog." Farah replied.

"Damn!" Ashavan cursed. "They must still be blocking her, holding her inside a psychic cloud."

Daryan sighed and turned to Farah. "Anything else?" he asked.

"Nothing that will help, I'm afraid. I think we may already be too late. I sense her at sea on a boat. It seems to be heading north. The trouble is I can't get a fix on the time … whether it's a farsight into the future, or happening right now."

"What's your best estimate?" Daryan asked, knowing he was grasping at straws. Fire surged in his stomach and he saw Ashavan wince.

"It's just a guess, commander, but I'd say they're already at sea. I'm sorry I couldn't do better"

Daryan's shoulders sagged. He grasped the saddle on his horse and rested his head on it. *What am I going to do? What am I going to tell Parvana? Light help me.*

Ashavan came over and rested his hand on Dayan's shoulder. "We'll overcome this, Daryan," he said softly. "It's a setback, but I don't believe they are going to harm her. I've been trying to make sense of it all, and it's my guess now *she* was the target of the attack all along. I think they wanted her because of her gift. That demand from the wizard was just a distraction."

"How can you know that?" Daryan massaged his stomach. "It could just as well be a ploy to get the duke."

"Think about it, my friend. Is it logical that they would go to such elaborate ends to take a hostage to threaten the duke? They could have threatened his brother who is already their hostage. No, I think they want Felindra."

"What you say makes sense, but why threaten to kill her if the Valdor doesn't surrender to them?"

"That could be just another tactic to confuse us. I get the impression this boy likes to play games."

"But what good would she be to them? There's no way they could make her work for them. She just wouldn't, especially after what they did to Ashala."

Ashavan sighed. "I don't know. Maybe they want to find out more about the gift, perhaps to find a way to duplicate it." Ashavan stepped back. "Do you want to continue to the coast, or shall we go back?"

"I'm going to go on. I think everyone else should return to the Monastery. I'll go on alone. I know you've been up all night and you must be exhausted."

"I don't think you should go alone. At least take a couple of defenders with you."

"I'll go with you too," Farah said. "You might need me." Farah was a robust woman, tall and slim, approaching her fortieth year. Daryan had always considered her levelheaded and reliable. There was no mage he liked to work with more than Farah, except perhaps Ashavan.

Daryan continued down the high road to the coast with Farah at his side and the two defenders following.

When they reached the shore, they left the road and rode down towards the water. Daryan crested a dune and pulled his horse up short. "Solas Naofa!" he cried. "What in darkest hell happened here?" He jumped down from his horse, heart pounding, and walked up a sand dune to look more closely.

"Light preserve us!" one of the defenders cried as he reached the top of the dune. "This is monstrous! Could one person have done this?"

Daryan walked slowly along the strand, examining the bodies. If it weren't for their scorched shields and scraps of clothing that still clung to their bodies, they wouldn't have known who they were, but there was little doubt these badly charred corpses were DarSolas defenders.

Tears welled in Daryan's eyes. *They beat us at every turn,* he thought as a spike of pain pierced his right temple. Too late to rescue Felindra, and now these poor souls. His dejection turned into rage. *They are not going to get away with this! I'll make them pay for it with my dying breath if necessary!* he vowed, hands compressing into fists. He turned round and saw Farah, whose face was as pale as ivory. "What do you make of this?" he asked.

Farah wiped her eye with her knuckle. "It's beyond me," she replied, shaking her head. "How can anyone do this to fellow human beings? It's unimaginably evil."

Daryan patted Farah's shoulder. "This is another example of what the Dark Brethren of Oglestra are capable. Can you tell anything about what happened here, and was Felindra present when it happened?" He prayed she had been spared seeing such an atrocity. It would be a devastating event for anyone to witness, but with her sensitivity, who knows what it might do to her.

Farah stood with her eyes closed, her face twitching with emotions as she concentrated. "As far as I can reconstruct it, it looks as if the defenders came upon the abductors as they were getting into the boat. One of their arrows struck the wizard and he turned back, raging. It seems as if he lost control completely and used the full force of elemental fire. Your daughter may have been out of sight in the boat, which was sheltered behind that big rock."

Daryan glanced at the rock and sighed. He rubbed the side of his face as another spike drove through the side of his head. "Can you send a message to the fort in DarSolas and tell them what happened here?"

"I will, commander."

He looked around at the two defenders who had walked down to the shore. "There's nothing more we can do here; they're gone," he said. Defeated, he dragged himself back to his horse and mounted. "We might as well return to the Monastery."

38 – Attacks in the west

Count Yima

Count Yima woke with a start. He sniffed the air; something was wrong! He shook his wife's shoulder to wake her. "Do you smell smoke?"

"What's the matter? Why did you have to wake me? I was having a lovely dream," she replied drowsily.

"I said can you smell smoke? Oh never mind; I'll find out for myself."

"I can't smell anything but the lavender in my pillow."

The count went to the window and drew aside one of the heavy curtains. He couldn't see anything unusual, just the garden and, on the other side of the wall, a meadow rolling towards the edge of the forest. He turned away and went back to the bed to put on a warm robe and some sandals. He was interrupted by an urgent knock on the door, and then the door opened to admit his guard captain.

"My lord, forgive me for intruding, but you must come quickly."

"What is it Quentin?"

"My lord, there's been an attack. There's fire everywhere, houses in the town, barns and stables. All the haystacks are on fire and the grain fields."

"By the Light! I knew I could smell smoke. Come on; let me see what's happening." He pushed past the captain and hurried from the room.

The count's rooms opened off a gallery above the great hall. The view he saw through the tall windows of the hall was very different from the one from his bedroom. Clouds of smoke rose above the castle walls; the sky was filled with smoke reflecting the redness of the fires below.

"This is a disaster!" the count exclaimed. "What has been done so far?"

"I sent half the guards into the town to investigate and help the victims," Quentin replied. "I've ordered the gates to be kept closed and posted the other half to defend the castle."

"What about looking for the attackers? Have they gone?"

"We believe so," Quentin replied. "Half the guards I sent out have been ordered to make the attackers their first priority. I'm waiting for reports from them now."

"Carry on. I have to get dressed," the count said. "Oh, and send some more men out. If they're gone, we can manage with less guards here." He looked over the railing of the gallery and called for his footman, "Bennis! Come up here; I need you."

The footman arrived just as the count was tying the waistband of his trousers. "Go and find Daylin for me. I have to send a message."

Count Yima finished dressing and went down the stairs to the hall. He grabbed a sweet roll from one of the baskets on the table as he passed and walked towards the outer door. He heard a young female voice behind him. "My lord, you sent for me?"

"Ah, Daylin. I have a message to send. Let's go and sit down at the table. Have you broken your fast?"

"No, My Lord. Thank you for asking, but I can eat after I've sent the message.

"Good. All right, are you ready? This is to my son-in-law, Duke Valdor. Send it to the Monastery."

The count's message was brief, as he didn't yet have much information. While Daylin was sending it, he grabbed a mug, poured some hot tea for himself and took a peach from another basket.

Dozens of families were left homeless and destitute. Loss of life and injuries were heaviest in those areas on the perimeter of town where many houses were built of wood.

"Get the people who are injured and those who've lost their homes into the castle," the duke instructed the guard captain. "We'll find room for them somehow, even if it means putting them in the guard barracks. And we should have some tents we can use as well. And make sure they get some hot food."

"As you wish, My Lord."

The attackers had come in and done as much damage as possible and disappeared as quickly as they'd begun. A large portion of the harvest was destroyed in the attack, and some of their livestock slaughtered or stolen. Along with the destruction of property and loss of life in the town, several farms in the surrounding area had also been fired. *Typical of those cowardly devils,* the count thought. *Well, we'll have to see about that. They'll be sorry they picked on this town.*

Back at the castle, he sent for the captain. "I have received a message from the duke and he has promised to send down a few more men, League defenders, and some mages," he informed Quentin. "We are going to form some defensive squads, some Monastery forces with some of our own. They'll patrol the area from the coast the mountains.

Andro

Although the work on the new stables had been progressing satisfactorily, Andro kept the horses in the meadow behind his house to allow them room to exercise and graze. They had just finished mowing the second field and were now moving the hay into the yard. Once that was done, they would move the herd into the field they'd cleared. Satisfied with the day's work, he washed his hands in a trough and went inside for his evening meal.

Andro finished eating and wiped his mouth. "That was delicious as always, my love," he said, pushing away from the table.

"Where are you going?" Valina asked.

"Just checking on everything. I won't be long."

"Can we come?" his youngest son asked.

"Olind can go if your father approves, but you two have to finish your lessons and prepare for bed." Valina replied.

"But I've finished my…"

"Not another word," Andro said. "Your mother says no and she is right." To take the sting out of it, he kissed his son on the forehead and ruffled his black curly hair. "Sleep well, son; Light watch over you."

He opened the door onto the porch, lit a torch from the basket, and, accompanied by Olind, started his inspection of the gates and walls. Once they were sure everything was secure, they checked the stable and said goodnight to Sherdon, whose living quarters were attached to one side, and then started towards the meadow to check on the horses out there.

All at once, the dogs started to bark and race madly around the yard, trying to get out. Then he heard alarmed cries from the horses in the paddock. As soon as the gate was opened, the dogs raced through barking frantically. Andro rushed after them through the paddock gate, with Sherdon and Olind close behind him.

The dogs headed for the woods at the bottom of the meadow, but the horses were moving up the slope towards the forest, milling around, snorting and stamping. Even in the twilight, he could see the whites of their eyes.

"What in the world's happened to them? They look terrified?" Andro walked towards the unsettled animals, hoping to be able to calm them, but as he approached, they backed away from him and neighing in anguish. Then one of them fell to the ground, foam seeping from its mouth and nostrils. He rushed over to get a closer look, hoping to find what was causing the distress. Its eyes were rolled back in its head and its sides heaved as it gasped for breath.

"There boy, what's the matter?" He stroked its neck, at a loss. He didn't know what was wrong or what to do for it. The poor creature was obviously suffering. Then he noticed something black sticking out from its chestnut pelt. He brought the light closer, took it between his fingertips and pulled it out. It was a small spike about the size of a large thorn, with a groove down one side. Andro sniffed it and, by the sweetish acrid smell, he realized it must have been dipped in poison.

Andro looked around to find his son. "Check the others," he shouted. "Look for spikes in their pelts and pull them out quickly!"

He turned his attention back to the fallen stallion. It gave a deep, whooping sort of cough and its head flopped to the ground, its breathing stopped. Andro looked around at the other horses. Several of them were already down on the ground, and many of those still standing were wobbling on their feet. He saw Sherdon and Olind examining two others. His eyes locked with Sherdon's and he shook his head.

Andro walked over to him. "Did you see what it was?" he asked, holding up the spike.

"Aye, I saw it. Poison! They've been poisoned." Sherdon wiped the back of his hand over his eyes. "Who would do such a thing? These poor creatures have done nothing to deserve this."

"Who set our stable on fire last time?"

"You think it's the same people?"

"Who else? I hope their souls rot in the deepest abyss." Andro stood and surveyed the damage. What was he going to do? He didn't know where to start.

The dogs came running back across the field. The large black hound whined and tried to scratch its shoulder with its hind leg, but couldn't reach whatever it was. Andro noticed the other two dogs were equally distressed, one was chewing at something on its front leg and the other was rolling on the ground trying to dislodge something from its back.

"Quickly," Andro shouted, "The barbs. Get them out before it's too late."

He grabbed one that was worrying its leg and searched for the telltale spike in its fur. When he found it, he pulled it out and put it in his pouch to keep the dog from trying to eat it. Olin took the one rolling on its back and turned her over. It was easy to see the spike in her short white coat and he had it out in an instant. He saw Sherdon examining one in his hand and patting the big hound.

"Let's hope we got them in time."

"Aye" Sherdon spat on the ground. "We've lost the horses though. I'd like to get my hands on whoever did this. They'd wish they never was born."

Andro nodded in agreement. "Let's check up in the woods; some of them might have been able get away and may be hiding in the trees."

The three men walked up the slope, checking the fallen horses as they went. None of those in the field had survived, even the colts from the spring foaling were dead. They continued up into the trees and walked deep into the wood without finding any survivors.

"It's no good." Andro said. "Let's go back. We can look around again in the morning. They may have gone deeper, but we'll never find them in this darkness. Would you mind counting the dead ones, see how many, if any, are missing?"

Suddenly they heard screams from the house and saw flames rising from one of the walls. He could see flames through the windows and smoke from the roof, indicating that the fire was spreading rapidly through the interior. The hay in the meadow they'd just finished mowing was also on fire. Andro ran to rescue his family. He saw Valina bundling the children out the door and off the verandah as he ran down the hill towards them.

"Come on, run!" Andro urged them when he entered the yard. "Over by the well." At least by the well, they'd be close to water and as far from the walls as possible.

Haro sat down, his back to the well coping and his arms around his wife on one side and two younger children on the other. He looked for Olind and saw him dragging himself through the gate from the meadow, head lowered, shoulders slumped, looking completely defeated.

The bitterness of loss and helpless feeling fogged Haro's mind. *What are we going to do?* Everything he'd worked for in the last ten years was gone, destroyed. His house a burnt out shell, his stock gone—the only things left standing were the palisade and the half-finished stables, which were mostly undamaged, as if the monsters who did this left them to mock him. Even the palisade was smoldering in places. A whine and a warm tongue licking his hand brought him back to the present. He opened his eyes and saw the white bitch. Behind her was the big hound, his head drooping and his tail wagging faintly, as if he didn't have enough energy to be more enthusiastic.

"Where's Bruey?" his son Micah asked.

"Oh, he'll come when he's ready," his mother replied. "He's probably off chasing monsters." She pulled herself up from the ground and brushed the dust off her culottes. "We should find somewhere to sleep," she said. "Let's take a look at the stable and see what we can make of it."

There was a pile of horse blankets in the finished part of the stable, and plenty of hay, from which they could put together some reasonably comfortable beds.

Once the three children were settled, Andro said, "I'm just going to take another look around. Want to come with me?" He held out his hand to Valina, then picked up one of the torches from its bracket on the wall and together, they went outside. "I won't lie to you. This is bad. Very bad. It looks as if we're finished."

She squeezed his hand. "How bad?"

"As far as I can tell in the dark, all the horses are gone. Whoever did this must have used blowpipes to shoot them with poisoned darts; I can't..." he broke off for a moment and stood still. "Did you hear that?"

"You mean a horse whinnying? Yes, I hear it."

"Wait here while I go and find it," he said, thinking to spare her the sight of all the dead horses.

"No. I'm not standing out here alone in the dark; I'm coming with you."

The two dogs who'd followed them out of the stables trotted after them as they ran through the paddock gate into the pasture. They found one of the mares with a colt by the edge of the trees at the upper end of the pasture. Both animals were nervous and agitated when Andro and Valina approached them, backing away, snorting and tossing their heads. The colt threatened to run when the dogs came up. "Would you hold the dogs back?" He asked Valina.

Once she had the dogs calmed down, Andro turned his attention back to the two horses. He knew the colt would follow the mare, so he tried to calm her first, speaking to her in a soothing tone, gradually moving in closer. Once she allowed him to touch her, he stroked her neck.

"We'll have to bring them back to the stables," Andro told his wife. "If we can get the mare moving, the colt will follow. He turned to the mare and faced her. "Come on, old girl, let's go home," he said confidently. He then turned and walked away, looking back over his shoulder to see if she would follow, but the mare just stood there. "I think she's waiting to see what you do, so follow me," he said to Valina.

Eventually they got the two horses back to the stable, filled a trough with water and gave them some hay. Although the compound walls were now breached in several places, Andro didn't think they would stray far. The smell of death and smoke would deter them and they would feel safer with the people who fed them."

"What are we going to do?" Valina asked.

"I don't know. I think it would be safer for us—especially for the children—to go to the Monastery. It's time we contributed something to this war."

"What about clearing up around here?" she asked. "All the dead horses."

"We haven't got enough hands to bury them," Andro said. "I'm exhausted. Let's try to get some sleep. I can't even think straight anymore."

They weren't allowed to sleep for very long. The barking dogs woke them just before sunrise, although they didn't sound as lively as usual.

"There's someone at the gate," Olind, their eldest son called from the stable doorway.

Andro dragged himself up and staggered outside, yawning and rubbing his eyes. He was confronted by a small band of defenders, identified as town garrison by their crests.

"Well, met, sir," the leader, a sergeant, greeted him. "I see you've had some trouble." He looked around at the wreckage that was almost visible in the predawn light.

"You could say that," Andro answered. "How did you know?"

"We were patrolling along the coast road when we met someone who'd seen the flames. We got here as soon as we could. What happened?"

"Well, for one thing, someone, or some things, poisoned all my horses. They're out back there in the paddock where they fell." He gestured towards the back gate. "Then they set fire to my home and anything else they could reach."

"Is there anything we can do, sir?"

Andro rubbed the back of his neck and shook his head. "I wouldn't know where to start. We have horses to bury. We have to sift through the rubble of our house to see if we can salvage anything. We need to find something to eat, at least for the children. That's in the short range, in the longer range we will need to decide whether we can stay here or where we can go if we decide not to."

"Do you mind if I make a suggestion?"

"Go ahead, sergeant. It's too much for me to deal with at this moment."

"You're obviously exhausted, sir, and you have a family to think of. My suggestion is that you allow us to escort you all to the fort where you can report what happened. Then you have something to eat and rest up for a while."

"But what about cleaning up here?" Andro was on the verge of despair.

Sherdon came over to where they were talking. "I can start here, Andro, and the two hands can help me when they get here. You go along with the defenders and take the family somewhere safe."

"What do you think, my love?" Andro asked Valina.

"I think it's a good plan. You can always come back when you've had some rest."

"How many horses did you lose?" the sergeant added.

"Nineteen altogether."

"That's an awful lot of digging to bury them all," the sergeant said. "Maybe you should think of burning the carcasses. I'm sure the garrison could spare a few men to help, but it would be better if the children weren't here."

Andro looked around for his children and saw them at the well drawing up water for the dogs and the two horses. "Very well, we'll do that. How are we going to transport everyone?"

"I see you've got two horses, Sir. I thought we could leave two of our men here, you and your lady could ride their horses, and the children could share your two. Would that work for you?"

"I'm not sure if our horses would take riders right now. They were very traumatized by the events last night, but we can try them."

It turned out that the mare allowed herself to be saddled, but the colt refused adamantly. They ended up with the two smaller children on the defenders' mounts with their parents and Olind on the mare. The colt, of course, followed its mother.

39 – Refugees

Daryan

On their way back to the Monastery, Daryan and his team met a trio of wolves. At first, Daryan was surprised they didn't fall back to avoid the humans, then he recognized Ashala by the now-tattered and soiled dressing on her haunch.

He dismounted from his nervous horse, stroking its neck to sooth it, and crouched by Ashala. She flicked her tongue at his hand his face and uttered a soft whine. He stroked her head and told her, "You shouldn't be walking around with that wound; you should be resting." He tried to think of a way of conveying to her what had happened to Felindra, but didn't need to. She must have felt it in his mind. She raised her muzzle and howled an agonizing cry of loss and rage. The other two wolves joined her.

"Come back to the Monastery with us and allow yourself to heal. We'll need you to be strong for Felindra. You can help us find her, but only if you're well enough." As he spoke to her, his hand on her head, he tried to visualize what he was telling her.

Ashala lay down on the ground with a whimper and rested her head on her paws. Her two companions licked her face and then lay down beside her.

"She probably didn't understand a word I said," he said to Farah.

"You'd be surprised," Farah replied.

Back at the Monastery, Daryan went to his home, dreading having to give the bad news to Parvana

By now, the pain from his stomach had spread upward into his gullet, and even his guts were becoming embroiled with spasmodic cramps. *Light, how am I going to tell her? A* pain shot through his chest. He stopped for a moment and tried to take a deep breath, but even that caused a pain across his midriff. *I can't afford to be ill; there's too much to do.* Hand massaging his chest, he continued towards his house.

***

After talking to Parvana and trying to reassure her, Daryan managed to eat a bowl of soup and drink some soothing herbal tea, but he was exhausted. *I can't go on like this, especially if I'm going to be ill every time something unexpected happens. It's too much for any man.*

A knock on the door announced the arrival of a page. "Commander, the Grand Master and Duke Valdor request your presence at the new palace," she informed him when he opened the door.

Daryan thanked her. He sighed and went back inside to change into some clean clothes. He found the Grand Master and the duke waiting for him in the vestibule of the palace, sitting together on a padded bench.

"I apologize for keeping you waiting, Your Grace, Grand Master."

"You look terrible, commander," the Grand Master greeted him. "I take it you haven't been able to find your daughter." He stood up. "Are you ill?"

"No, Grand Master, I'm fine, it's just worry about my daughter and lack of sleep," Daryan replied. He gave them a brief summary of their search for Felindra.

"My heart goes out to you, my friend," Valdor said, getting to his feet and putting his hand on Daryan's shoulder. "I can imagine how helpless you must be feeling."

"I think we can postpone this meeting until tomorrow," the Grand Master said. "If that's agreeable with you, Your Grace."

"Yes, of course," Valdor replied. "Go home, Daryan and get some sleep. We'll see you in the morning."

"What is the meeting about?" Daryan asked.

"Just tying up some last-minute matters. We're having a farewell ceremony tomorrow morning for the men and women who are leaving for their postings around the duchy," the duke replied. "The Grand Master thought you might like to address them before they leave."

Felindra

Felindra was woken by the sound of angry male voices. She blinked and looked around, wondering what time it was and what they were quarrelling about. She couldn't hear what they were saying, but Their voices sounded like the two men who had abducted her. She sat up and realized someone had draped a blanket over her while she was sleeping. She stood up and went to look out of the opening, but she couldn't see anyone on the deck. It was twilight now. She must have slept the afternoon away after eating the mashed beans and hard bread they'd given her.

The shouting seemed to be coming from somewhere below the deck. Suddenly, the sound of a crash came from below, followed by a shriek of pain.

I hope they kill each other, she thought, *wrapping her arms around herself. It's so cold, and I'm dying of thirst. No! I'm not going to cry and feel sorry for myself. It wouldn't do any good. I have to gain their respect, then maybe they won't … what? Hurt me. They certainly don't have* my *respect.* She reached for the blanket and shook it out. It was dirty and didn't smell very pleasant, but it was all she had so she wrapped it around her shoulders, clasping it in front with her hand. *I wonder where they're taking me. I hope it's not to ValkonenMaa. That would be much too far for Ashala to find me … all those mountains to cross. Poor Ashala; I wonder how she's doing. I miss her so much.*

She saw a shadowy figure emerging from a square hole in the deck, but it was too dark to identify him. *I wish they would tell me something.* The man came towards her and stopped a pace away. She recognized him, the dark skinned trader from DarSolas.

"How's your friend?" she asked, determined to get the first word in and lead the conversation. "He must be very angry about the arrow." Her lips twitched in a smile. *Serves him right for what he did to Ashala.*

"How do you know about that?" the man snarled. "Someone's been talking?" She saw him clench his fists as if he wanted to strike someone.

"I'm not stupid," she replied. "I saw it, even though he tried hard to keep out of sight. I hope it hurts."

"You'd better watch your mouth, girl."

"Or what? You'll punish me?"

He went back down the deck towards the opening and returned with a lantern so that he could see her better. "Who untied you?"

"What difference does it make? It's not as if I'm going to jump overboard and try to swim back to shore. I can't even swim." By now, they were well out of sight of the coast. "Where are you taking me?"

"You'll find out."

"So why did you come out here? Getting lonely down there in that hole? Or did your brave leader send you away?"

"I've warned you!" he turned and walked away again.

"Where's my supper?" she shouted after him. "And I need some something to drink."

Daryan

Daryan had not slept well; the discomfort in his stomach was causing nightmares. He went into the kitchen alcove, poured himself a glass of buttermilk, and grabbed a chunk of cheese and some flatbread. He sat down at the table and ate slowly. He'd discovered that having some food in his stomach alleviated the discomfort somewhat.

Parvana appeared in the doorway. "You had a bad night," she said. "How are you feeling? She didn't look so good herself, with dark shadows under her eyes and no sign of her usual sparkle. Even her hair looked sad.

"It's fine now I've eaten something." He stood up and wrapped her in his arms, kissing the top of her head. Her hair smelled oily, as if she hadn't washed it recently. "How are you holding up?" he held her away from him and saw her eyes fill with tears. "I know, my love. It's unbearable, but we'll get her back, if I have to cross mountains and seas. They'll find out they've picked a fight with the wrong man. Sit down; I'll make you some tea."

"I should make something for you."

"I already ate."

"What did you have?" Daryan told her. "You're going to need more than that. How about some cold chicken? And I'll make you some herbal tea. I know your stomach's hurting."

Without waiting for his reply, she went into the Kitchen alcove and began to prepare a meal.

He was sipping his tea when he heard a knock on the door. "I'll get it," he called.

Daryan opened the door and was surprised to see Andro Haro standing there.

"It's good to see you, my friend! What are you doing here?" He realized something was wrong; Andro was not his usual hearty self. He seemed exhausted and dejected. Daryan put his hand on his shoulder and ushered him into the house. "Come inside and have something to eat with us. Tell me what's happened!"

Andro sighed and patted Daryan's shoulder as he passed him.

"Parvana, you remember my old friend Andro Haro, don't you?" he closed the door behind Andro. "Andro, this is my wife, Parvana."

"Well, met Andro," Parvana said. She pulled out a chair from the table. "Have a seat; I'm just preparing some food.

Daryan sat down and looked at his friend. Andro looked as if he'd aged ten years since they'd last met. "I can tell something bad has brought you here. Tell me about it."

"I've lost everything," Andro said with a deep sigh. He went on to describe the events of the last three days while they ate, and then Darian told Andro about Felindra's abduction. Andro sighed. "We're a sorry-looking pair, aren't we?" he said. "I don't know how you keep going with such catastrophe hanging over you. I thought my problems were bad, but at least my family's all right. What are you going to do now?"

"I'm going to work 'til I drop to get my daughter back from those fiends. They'll be sorry they ever tangled with me, I swear."

"I'm with you there, brother. In fact, that's the reason I came to the Monastery. It's time we started fighting back, and I want to be in the forefront of the battle."

Darson came from his room as they finished talking and sat down at the table.

Daryan introduced him to Andro. "How are you this morning, son?" he asked Darson.

Darson grimaced and shrugged his shoulders. "Not so good," he replied. "I wish Felindra was here."

"We all do," Daryan replied. "Don't worry, we'll get her back." He stood up, but as he did, another sharp pain hit him in the stomach and he doubled over.

"What is it, Father? Are you hurt?"

"Nothing, it's nothing, son. Just a little twinge."

"You should see a healer, Parvana said. "There's too much to do to risk your being ill."

Daryan released a breath and moved away from the table. "Now, I have a meeting to attend and I don't want to be late." But his wife's words went to his heart. He should really find out what was wrong with him, if only for the sake of his family. He admitted he was carrying a heavy load of responsibility, but he'd handled responsibilities before with no problems. He looked at Andro. "Would you walk with me? I have to go to a meeting with Duke Valdor."

Andro thanked Parvana for the meal and then joined Daryan at the door.

"You know, your wife's right," he said as soon as they were out of earshot. "You're carrying too many burdens for one man, trying to be everywhere and do everything yourself. I remember the headaches you used to get the last time."

"I know," Daryan said, with a sigh. "I just need to get something for my stomach. I'll do it after the meeting with the duke. But that's not the reason I wanted to speak to you. Were you serious about joining the fight?"

"I came here because I want my family to be safe, for one thing, and I think they are safer here than at Cavalcitas. And yes, I want to get back into the League, help rid Trethawynd of this menace once and for all ... that is if you have a place for me."

"We can use every willing hand we can get and you are one of the best qualified men I know. How would you like to work with me? I could use somebody to take some of the burden."

"That sounds like an excellent offer. But would I be able to see any action? The way I feel right now, I want to break a few heads."

"I'll have to think about it. We can talk it over together, but we do need someone to do inspection tours of the troops we have in the field. Where are you staying, by the way?"

"We're here in temporary quarters right now, but I'm hoping we may be able to find a cottage in the valley we can rent."

"I have an idea, though. I pretty well have control over structure of the League defenders, so I can assign you. If you are going to be working with me, you'll also be liaising with the Duke's staff, so I think a meeting with him would be helpful. Why don't you put on your uniform—you did bring it?

Andro shook his head. "Lost in the fire, I'm afraid. It probably would have been too tight anyway," he said, patting his stomach.

"We'll get something for you." Daryan replied. Maybe you can go over to the defenders' building and find the quartermaster. Whatever you wear, come over to the duke's palace in about an hour and I'll show you around."

"Where is his palace? We only arrived last night."

"You remember the ziggurat?" They had arrived at the meadow in front of the palace.

"Of course. Who could forget the most beautiful building in Trethawynd? Very nice. I wager he won't want to leave it when the conflict is over. I know I wouldn't. All right, I'll see you soon."

40 – Sending out scouts

Daryan

A small platform had been erected on the edge of the parade ground. The Grand Master, Duke Valdor, Sir Arvand, Daryan and the duke's son, Varan, stepped up onto the platform and faced the troops before them.

The Grand Master moved to the front of the platform. "Before you leave on your missions, his grace Duke Valdor of Trethawynd would like to say a few words to you."

Valdor gave a short speech of encouragement, followed by Darian. When Daryan had finished, he looked behind him at the Grand Master, who stepped forward to take his place.

"Before you go, I would like everyone to join in prayer.

Dear Lord of Light, Creator of universes, Maker of worlds, Light of our souls, great is our love for you and greatly thankful are we for your bounteous gifts. Your blessings uplift us and ennoble our lives. Your love enriches our souls and lightens our hearts. Without you, oh Divine Father, our lives would be as cold ashes. We, your children, praise you, oh Lord of Light. You are ever in our hearts and in our thoughts. Your perfect Spirit lives in our souls, guiding us in the paths of virtue and honor.

Lord of Light shine upon us in this time of adversity. Guide us in using wisely your divine gifts. Help us defend your children against the enemies that now assail us. In Your Holy Name, we beseech You to strengthen us that we might conquer the evil arrayed against us and, by Your will, we shall prevail. And when this mortal life in the flesh has run its course, may we dwell with You in Your Glorious Halls of Light forever in eternal bliss.

Eternal Lord of Light be with us now and forever. So be it, as it truly is."

"So be it, as it truly is!" the crowd echoed.

"Now the choir will sing a song of praise. *Hear now, beloved Father."*

Several cords were struck on the lutes, then flutes joined in, followed by the voices of children, men and women in perfect harmony. When the singing finished, the people began to disperse quietly.

When everyone was gone, except for himself and Ashavan. Daryan turned to his friend. "I don't know about you, but I'm exhausted and hungry. Would you like to join me and my family for a meal?"

"I would indeed, Daryan, but I am so tired, I don't think I could stay awake long enough."

"Thank you for your help yesterday; I wouldn't have got through it without you, my friend."

Felindra

In spite of being told not to move, Felindra went to the opening of the shack and sat on the deck. She had been freezing all night, and she hoped the sunlight might help her thaw out. She sat there, exhausted, sore, and thirsty, her head resting on the doorpost. *Maybe I should break down and ask for something,* she conceded. *It doesn't look as if they care whether I live or die.* The crewmen didn't seem as hostile as her two captors were. The next time one of them passed her on the deck, she called softly, "Excuse me." He looked at her and veered in her direction. "Could I have some water?" she asked.

"They didn't tell me to give you anything," he replied.

"Did they tell you not to?" she asked. "I haven't had anything to drink since midday yesterday. I don't think they'd be very pleased if I died of thirst."

"Aye," he replied, wiping his hands on a rag hanging from his belt. "I suppose they've got other things to think about right now."

"What things?"

"The big fellow. He got an arrow in his neck. Didn't you know?"

Felindra smiled. *Serves him right. I hope it kills him ... Forgive me Light; I know I shouldn't wish someone bad fortune, but he really is evil.* "How bad is it?" she asked.

"I don't know. The kid moans and complains, but he doesn't look that bad. I think he just likes to..." he looked over his shoulder. "I'll get you some water."

He left her and went behind the shack, returning a moment later with a tin mug. "Here. Anything else?"

"Lots of things," she replied with a smile. "Some warm clothes, something to clean my sore knees, and maybe something to eat. Oh, and I'd also like to go home to my family."

He stared at her for a moment, then gave her the water and went away.

The she saw a head appear out of the deck. The head rose higher and gradually one of her captors came into view, the dark one.

He walked towards her, scowling. "I thought you were told to stay inside."

"I was cold," she replied. "I need to be in the sun. Besides, what harm can it do? It's not as if someone is going to fly over and rescue me, is it?"

"You've got a smart mouth," he said. "Don't give us any trouble."

"Or you'll ... what? How's your friend?" she asked, hoping to annoy him.

"Why don't you keep your mouth shut?"

"Hey," she continued. "Do you think I could have something to eat?" *I don't know how I dare to talk to him like that. Maybe because I have no respect for him.*

He turned abruptly and returned to the opening in the deck. He scowled at her again before he disappeared from view.

Daryan

Daryan had a restless sleep, plagued with bizarre nightmares, and when he woke up two hours after midnight, the burning in his stomach had risen up to his throat. His whole gullet was on fire. Parvana moaned in her sleep. At least she was sleeping, but probably having bad dreams too. He crept quietly from the room, picking up his clothes as he went, and tip-toed to the Kitchen alcove where he poured himself a cup of water. Maybe that would put the fires out. He sat with his elbows on the table and his head resting on his clasped hands. *What are we going to do?* He'd been over and over it, unable to come up with a plan to get Felindra back. He was in charge of the League of Light defenders; he couldn't just go off on a personal mission, no matter how important it was to him. He'd have to get help. But from where, who? He went through all his friends, trying to decide which ones could be spared to help him. Then he recalled the meeting scheduled at the palace and decided to go back to bed and try to get some more sleep.

***

"Come in, Commander," Duke Valdor greeted Daryan when he entered the conference room. "I hope you are rested."

"Thank you, Your Grace." Daryan sat down and reached for a glass of water, to quell the fire in his stomach.

"I understand from Ashavan that you've found out something about the people responsible for your daughter's abduction. Would you like to tell us about it?"

"The wizard we are dealing with uses elemental magic—fire and lightening—and shows an impulsive recklessness. I would guess he is not very mature and hasn't developed the self-control of an adult. He also displays powerful telepathic and spellbinding abilities. Apparently, he was hit by an arrow from by of the DarSolas defenders and that's what set him off. I believe his is probably one of those responsible for the devastation at the castle as well. We also believe that Evaseen Charnwell was involved in the abduction of my daughter and that the Charnwells are closely aligned with Gremulkin."

"I agree," the duke replied. "Gremulkin is close to the heart of the attacks; I'm sure of it." Daryan gasped and held his breath as a sharp pain stabbed through his stomach.

"What is it, Daryan? Are you ill?"

"It's nothing, Your Grace, just a little indigestion."

"You should see a healer; we can't afford to have you out of action."

"I will."

"Today?"

"Yes, Your Grace, after we finish here."

"You've got too many responsibilities, commander. You need someone to shoulder some of the burden."

"I have someone in mind, Your Grace. A former captain in the League has come to join us. He's an old comrade of mine and a good friend."

"I'd like to meet him."

"You already know him, Your Grace. It's Andro Haro from Cavalcitas."

"Good, I look forward to seeing him again."

"I don't know if you've heard about the attack on the horse farm at Cavalcitas."

"Oh, no! How serious was it?" There was a touch of fear in the look Valdor gave him. "Is that why he's here?"

353

"Yes, they arrived last night. From what he told me, everything was destroyed, house burned down, horses killed, all the work of the past ten years, gone in a flash."

"That's terrible news. I can imagine how he feels. What about his family?" Valdor replied.

"They're safe, thank the Light." Daryan paused for a moment, thinking, and then continued, "I've asked him to come over and meet everyone.""

"When do you expect him?

"He could be downstairs now. I'll go and check."

Daryan went down to the palace kitchens to get some herbal tea to settle his stomach. He sipped it slowly and felt some immediate relief, but it still felt as if it might erupt again at any moment. He went outside and saw Andro waiting for him, now wearing the standard defender uniform with a captain's insignia on his tunic.

"I see you found something to wear. The duke's waiting for you. Are you ready?" Daryan asked.

"I'm looking forward to seeing him again," Andro replied, inadvertently echoing Valdor's sentiments.

"How well do you know him?"

"Oh he used to come and look at the horses occasionally. He's bought several from me."

"Of course, the horses. All right, let's go up. The meeting room is on the top floor."

At the end of the meeting, Valdor stood up and turned to Daryan. "Now, if that's all, I want you to go now and see a healer. You can use the palace healer if you wish. His rooms are on the third floor. One of the pages can show you the way."

"I will, Your Grace." Daryan unconsciously pressed his hand against his stomach, which was still on fire. He said goodbye to Andro on the third floor and went to find the healer.

He found the door with the glowing hand symbol of healing and knocked. It was opened by a tall thin man wearing a green smock. "Ah, a patient!" he said with a smile. "Come in and make yourself comfortable ... here use this chair. You have come to consult me about a health problem, haven't you?" he asked looking at Daryan hopefully.

"I have," Daryan replied. "Nothing serious, but I thought I should have it checked." Daryan sat in the chair indicated next to a table covered with instruments in glass trays, bottles and jars of potions and salves, and a pile of clean cotton cloths. "It's my stomach."

"Where do you feel the worst discomfort?"

"Here, mostly," Daryan replied, touching the area just below the middle of his ribs.

"You say mostly. I take it there is discomfort in other areas as well."

"Sometimes I feel burning up here too, especially when I lie down." This time he indicated a region from his stomach up to the middle of his neck.

"I see. I'm just going to perform a deep examination of the area. You won't feel anything except possibly a slight tingling."

After finishing the examination, the healer smiled. "You'll be relieved to know it doesn't seem to be anything serious. There is some inflammation in the lining of your stomach, and a slight amount up in the gullet. It's caused by an excess of digestive juices, which are very acidic."

"What causes the excess acid?"

"Usually it's caused by stress, but also eating the wrong things, foods with excessive fat contents, for example.

"People have different ways of handling stress. Those who keep it bottled up inside and try not to let anyone see how much they are affected by stressful events often react as you have."

"Is there anything I can do about it?"

"Oh, yes. I can give you some medicine to relieve the symptoms. I must point out that if you go on the way you are going, you could develop erosions in the stomach, and that would be even more painful. If the erosions start to bleed, you'd really have a problem, so I urge you to follow my directions. Another thing; how much time do you spend in recreational activities with your family?"

"Not very much," Daryan responded with a twinge of guilt. "To tell the truth, I haven't seen much of my family lately, except my daughter."

"Recreation and time spent with loved ones can alleviate many of these problems."

41 – Diplomacy

Valdor

Duke Valdor came forward to greet the Grand Master. " Welcome, Grand Master. Thank you for coming. Would you like to sit on the terrace?"

"Yes, Your Grace, that would be a delightful treat. I've always liked this building. I used to come up here sometimes to get away from people and just think."

"What will you have to drink?" He nodded to the page to pour some for everyone.

Valdor started by introducing the Grand Master to Imali. "Allow me to present my secretary, Ferland Imali. I've included him in this discussion because he may be involved in what follows." He took a sip of his fruit juice and continued. "The reason I asked for this meeting is to discuss something that I think might involve the League, and also to seek your advice. Since my father's death and the default of his chancellor, I'm working in the dark ... learning as I go, so to speak. I rely on counsel from people I know and trust. I don't have time to appoint another chancellor, although I do have someone in mind." He glanced at Imali and continued: "All the records and archives of the duchy have been destroyed, so I have nothing to look back on for historic examples and procedures." He emptied his glass and put it down on the table. "Now, I will get to the point of the meeting. I would like to reach out beyond our borders to discover if we can get help from other rulers."

"I understand your predicament, Your Grace. You are in a very difficult position. As for records and precedents, you are welcome to consult our library, which probably contains much of the information you seek. I could loan you the use of one of our archivists to do research for you. We have a vast amount of historical information, not only about the League of Light, but also much concerning Trethawynd and places beyond. If you accept my offer, I will send someone to discuss it with you, or your secretary, and find out specifically the information you need."

"That's very gracious of you, Grand Master. I'm mostly concerned with diplomacy at the moment. I'd like to send diplomatic missions to some of the dukes of neighboring duchies, and to Queen Zenobia herself, but I want to make sure we follow the correct protocol.

"Now, I'll get to the reason I'm consulting you. I thought you might be able to reach out to whoever is now leading the League in ValkonenMaa to find out how bad things are there."

"I'm afraid the situation there may be worse than it is here," the Grand Master replied. As for Yoldys, they haven't reported any problems so far, although, knowing our predicament, they are taking precautions. I believe a diplomatic mission to the Duke of Yoldys might receive a favorable response. After all, if Trethawynd falls, they'd be next."

"Now, what would you think of my idea of appealing to the Queen?"

"It's the diplomatic thing to do, Your Grace. After all, it's her kingdom that is being attacked. That's one of the reasons the duchies pay tributes."

Valdor stood up. "That's what I wanted to know. I should tell you that I have been unable to contact our ambassador in the capital. He has failed to respond to several messages I've sent. I suppose the first thing I would like your archivist to find out is about the protocol for appealing to the monarch, and diplomacy in general."

"I'll have her get to work on it immediately, given the urgency. I'm sure you want the envoys to leave as soon as possible." The Grand Master stood up, ready to go.

"Thank you Grand Master. I appreciate your help. I won't take up any more of your time; I know you have much to do.

"I will get an archivist working on your information; you will probably hear from her by the end of the day. Now, I bid you good day."

Imali

"What's the Queen like," Imali asked the duke a few days later.

"I only met her once, when I was a child with about seven years. She was Princess Zenobia then. She was accompanying her father, King Olvano, on a tour of the duchies. All I recall is that she was a pretty girl, with a slight build and long black hair. She seemed a little shy to me." Valdor replied.

"How old was she then?"

"About fourteen, I think, but the courtiers treated her as an adult."

"So she's quite young. What about her husband, the prince consort?"

"Prince Felidorn; he's the son of the Duke of Yoldys, as you probably know. That may work in our favor, if we appeal to the duke for assistance." Valdor folded his hands on the table in front of him and looked at Imali, who was sitting opposite. "Are you sure you're ready? Do you need anything else?"

"No, I think I have everything. The gifts are packed in one of my trunks; I have my 'regalia' and your letter, I can't think of anything else. Oh, and I've got my copy of the Protocol for Ambassadors, which I shall study on the ship."

"Very well," Valdor stood up and pushed his chair back.

Imali rose rapidly to his feet as the duke moved around the end of the table. He grasped Imali's upper arms. "I'm sure you'll perform your assignment splendidly. Go in peace, my friend, and the Light guide you."

"I hope so," Imali replied. "Light be with you."

***

Imali set out on horseback the next morning with two knights, and a small horse-drawn cart to carry their trunks. They had a long ride ahead of them to the east coast port of Bailuchi, where they would take a ship south to Sola Regis, the capital of Albasiny. Nevertheless, it was quicker to go by sea than overland through Yoldys.

Eight days after leaving the Monastery, they were on board a ship heading across Solan Bay towards Solar Regis, the capital, which was located in the Royal Province of Regio. The ship was a small coastal freighter that ran from northern ValkonenMaa south to the capital and beyond. With three masts fully rigged and a good wind, they could expect to reach their destination in two to three days.

Being the only passengers, Imali and the two knights each had his own small cabin. The three men preferred to spend most of their time on the deck, watching the ever-changing vistas as they passed a varying coastline. Within a day, the shoreline scenery could change from agricultural land to forested hills to desert.

"I didn't know it could get this hot," Sir Bryon complained, wiping his face and neck with a kerchief.

"You should come over here in the shade," Imali advised him. He'd found a place to sit in the shadow of the sails.

"I wager that if I do move, the wretched boat will change course again and the shade will be gone." Nevertheless, he got up and moved to the crate next to the one on which Imali was perched. He looked towards the stern. "What's Kevan doing?"

The other knight was leaning over the side of the ship, engrossed by something in the water below, his arms moving occasionally from side to side.

"He's probably fishing. I saw him a while ago playing with a hook and line."

"I hope he catches something for our supper. I could do with something fresh for a change. It seems to me that all they serve on this tub is hard bread and salted meat." Sir Bryon said.

"It won't be long now. We should be there by morning." Imali replied. "Then you'll be able to choose whatever you like to eat."

"As long as we don't run into a storm."

"Has anyone ever told you you're a pessimist?" Imali asked with a smile.

Sir Bryon shrugged. "What are we going to do about the ambassador?"

"We'll go directly to the embassy after we've found a place to stay and had a meal. At least we can make an effort to be courteous while we see where he stands. Normally, he would be the one to present us to the Queen as the duke's special envoys, but given the lack of communication since the old duke died, I'm not sure about his attitude to Duke Valdor."

"Do you think he may have been Gremulkin's man?"

"It's possible; nevertheless, we still have to follow protocol."

The following morning, just before midday, their ship docked at Sola Regis. The weather was torrid this far south, made even worse by the high humidity, although a light sea breeze ameliorated it somewhat. The aroma of tropical vegetation, and rotting fruit competed with fish, seaweed and tar to overwhelm their sense of smell. The quay was lined on one side with warehouses and other related businesses, and wharfs extended in either direction. The city, the largest city in Albasiny, rose up on a gentle slope beyond the port. The lowest levels were filled with the crowded housing of the poor, tradesmen, and workshops with few niceties such as provisions for waste disposal. Almost all the streets on this level had sewage and wastewater running down the gutters, and piles of rotting trash being picked over by bony dogs, and occasionally, a beggar in rags.

The buildings on the higher levels were mostly white with red tiled roofs, some with towers and spires, spread across in terraces amongst ample vegetation Above all, at the peak of the hill, stood the royal palace, a massive though elegant structure. The walls surrounding it were grey stone with lookout towers along the top; behind this, the actual palace shone like a jewel. Constructed of white marble, it rose in tiers similar to the duke's palace at the Monastery, although on a much grander scale. Imali assumed that the royal palace was probably the model for the other one.

There were dozens of drays lined up along the quay, waiting for cargo, but Imali bypassed those and chose a small cart for their baggage. During his negotiations with the carter, he asked about a suitable inn.

"Depends where you plan to do most of your business, sir," the woman replied.

"Is there an embassy district?"

"Well, there's a few embassies close together in one part of the city. I suppose you could call it an embassy district. Let me think... Yes, sir, I think you would find the Mittalane to your liking."

"Very well," Imali said. "Now we have to find a livery stable and hire some horses."

"There's one over there, the little blue place next to the big red building."

"I see it. Thank you. Can you see to our baggage from the Flying Gannet? You can use this to identify it." He handed her the wooden disk with a number stamped on it that he'd received when the baggage was taken on board. "There should be five trunks."

"Very well, sir. Do you want me to take it to the inn, or would you like me to wait?"

"Wait for us. We'll ride along with you; that way we won't get lost.

As the woman had promised, the hotel was very much to their liking. It was a stucco building with a small garden fronting the street. Large houses behind high walls lined the street, plus a few high-end shops selling jewelry, clothing, and expensive wines. Inside a wrought iron fence of the inn was a courtyard with a few tables shaded by ficus trees, and a wide tiled path to the entrance. Everything inside the inn was designed for coolness: the white plaster walls ornamented with painted tiles, the high ceilings, the seating upholstered in tropical colored linen, and the fired clay tiles on the floor.

"Are you sure this isn't too grand for us?" Imali asked. "She must have taken us for royalty, although I don't know how, dressed the way we are."

"She probably gets a commission for bringing people here, in addition to your generous tip," Sir Bryon informed him.

"I'm disillusioned," Imali replied. "I thought she detected our superior status."

"Ha!"

A man in dark blue livery, decorated with gold, approached them. "How may I serve you, sirs?"

"We would like accommodation for three days." Sir Kevan had decided to take over the formalities, sensing that Imali may be a little out of his depth.

"Would you like one room, or three individual rooms, sir?"

"What do you think," Sir Kevan asked the others. "We have a lot of planning to do; should we stay together?"

"Why not? If the room is large enough and has three beds."

"Very good, sirs. We have just the room. Would you follow me, please?"

"Can we have our trunks brought up?" Sir Kevan asked. "And we'd like water for bathing. We want to change into some fresh clothes."

As soon as the door closed on the servants, Imali turned to his friends. "Don't you think it's a bit expensive?"

"Don't worry about it," Kevan responded. "We'll share the costs, and we saved a lot by taking one room. After all, we have to keep up appearances."

Once they'd cleaned up and put on some suitable attire, the three men left the inn in search of a place to eat. "The meals at the inn are probably a bit expensive," Sir Kevan had advised them. "It's better to find somewhere less luxurious, and while we're at it, we can take a look around.

They found a tiny seafood place after wandering for half an hour. The tables were set out on a patio separated it from the street by a low brick wall. Only the cooking facilities were roofed over.

"This is so good," Kevan said when he took his first bite of the delicate, flaky white fish. "I hadn't realized how much I missed seafood at home." Fish from the rivers of Trethawynd had become rare, and ocean fish was very costly.

"Now we have to find the embassy, I think we should go as soon as we've finished eating," Imali said.

"You do realize that most people here take siesta after their midday meal," Sir Bryon informed him.

"I don't care. The situation is urgent. I'd like to see the Queen tomorrow and get this business settled. We have to know if we can count on the ambassador to back us up, or if he is going to make difficulties for us."

They left the restaurant and strolled casually back the way they'd come, taking time to look in shop windows and admire gardens. Most of the residences were kept out of sight behind high walls, but some of them had flowering vines growing over their walls in glorious gem-like shades of blue, purple, orange and pink. There were small gardens at some intersections, just a bit of grass with a fountain in the center surrounded by flowers.

"These people really know how to put on a show," Imali said. "I've never seen anything like it."

"They're rich, and the capital attracts the best in all the crafts: gardeners, architects, decorative artisans." Sir Kevan replied. "Not only that, there has been relative peace here for more than half a century. They've had time to make it pretty."

It's a pity they can't spend something on the poor wretches living at the bottom, Imali thought. He'd been horrified at the conditions on the lower levels, but felt it wouldn't be wise to comment on it.

They turned a corner and found what they were looking for halfway down the street which had, among the residences, several buildings with discreet signs by the gates announcing that they were embassies. They were all of foreign countries except for the smallest, which was Trethawynd. The emblem of the duchy was posted on a brass plaque beside the gate.

Imali pulled a chain hanging from an aperture in the wall. They waited half a minute, but no one answered, so he pulled it again. He knew it was working because he could hear the bell clanging inside the building. Still no response.

"I warned you," Sir Bryon said.

"I don't care. I'm going to keep ringing this bell until someone answers. How long do these siestas last anyway?"

"Not more than a couple of hours, usually less, just through the hottest part of the day."

"Well I think they've had plenty of time. See, the sun's already descending." He tugged the bell pull again and waited, watching through the wrought iron gate for any movement inside.

Finally, the front door opened and a small, dark-skinned man looked out. Seeing the three men at the gate, he came out. "Sorry, sirs, the embassy is closed."

"I insist that you admit us," Imali said. "We are on an urgent mission for the Duke of Trethawynd. There is no time to lose."

"The ambassador is sleeping, sir," the man replied.

"Then I suggest you wake him up."

The poor man stood there twisting his hands together, torn between facing the ambassador's wrath and the helping the obviously important visitors from his employer's superior. Finally, he decided. He came over and unlocked the gate, waited for them to enter and relocked it. "Come this way."

He led them through the door into a vestibule, which had a tiled floor and was furnished with a small table and some chairs.

"Be seated, gentlemen," he said. "I'll see if he's awake." He left them and disappeared through a door on one side.

"What do you think?" Sir Bryon asked.

Imali shrugged. By now, he was convinced the ambassador would not be much help.

42 – Inspection tour

Andro Haro

"Farewell, my friend. Light be with you," Daryan called as Haro joined the rest of the team outside the stables and mounted his horse.

The team was led by Sir Baramen—one of the duke's knights—and Commander Haro, representing the League. It included three mages with various skills, two defenders from DarSolas, and two from the Monastery. Two pack animals carried their supplies, mostly food and camping equipment.

Now they were finally on their way. Andro felt a tremor of excitement, the feeling he recalled from years ago when he and Daryan had served together in another conflict. This time however, there was also a touch of trepidation. He had a family now. What would become of them if anything happened to him? They would be taken care of by the League, but he knew from personal experience that no one could replace a father. His own father had died in a boating accident when Andro was seven and he remembered how devastating it had been for him and his sister, not to mention their mother. *I'll just have to be extra careful that nothing happens to me,* he thought.

They spent the first two days travelling east to Salispon. Much of the rural area around Salispon had an abandoned look about it: shuttered houses with no smoke from the chimneys; fields scarred black by fire, now being reclaimed by weeds, and fields left unharvested. When the road ran close to the river, they caught the stench of rotting fish and birds; there was no sign of living waterfowl.

"This is devastating," Sir Baramen, said, looking around at the ruined fields.

Andro was sickened by the sight. "This is unforgivable. We'll add it to our report, although I'm sure they already know about it."

"Yes, but not the extent of the damage. From the weeds and new growth, these look like old attacks."

Occasionally, they passed a farm or smallholding where men and women were tending their crops and gardens. There were still a few sheep and cows grazing in the fields, and chickens pecking around the yards.

"At least some of the people stayed, or came back. They're going to have a lot of work cleaning up the mess and revitalizing the land, Light help them," Andro commented, thinking about his own holding. I don't know how they're going to clean up the river, though."

"They'll probably have to let it clean itself, although there are plenty of crows consuming the carrion," Sir Baramen replied. "That will help a little, but it's a long river and everything downstream is going to be polluted as well. There won't be much fishing this year. By the look of it, they mean to exhaust our food supply and destroy the livelihoods of our people."

"They want to weaken us," Andro said. "If this is what's taking place this far south, I can't imagine how bad it must be farther north."

After spending a night in Salispon, they continued east to Zinawar, the county seat of Coringe.

As they rode through the small town, lanterns were being lit outside the inns and livery stables. A few shops that were still doing business and most of the houses showed light in their windows. With only a few people on the street, it all looked so peaceful, almost as if there were no troubles in the duchy. About halfway along the main street, Sir Baramen pointed out an inn. "This is a good place to have a meal and spend the night."

"So you're familiar with the area?" Andro asked.

"Yes, my family's estate is a little south of here. It's too bad we don't have time to visit them; I think you would be interested in our horses. My family's been breeding them for over a hundred years. They're a rare stock imported from Anjiu Mir bred with our own Seguines."

"That sounds like an interesting combination. I'd like to see them. Maybe we could stop on the way back."

"Do you think you'll return to horse breeding when this is over?"

"I'd like to, but there will be a lot of work to do to restore Cavalcitas. I don't know whether I'll be able to do it, then there's the cost of buying new breeding stock." Andro sighed at the sheer magnitude of it.

Andro and the inspection team continued to the coast the next day and spent some time in the port of Bailuchi, visiting the town garrison and talking to the guards, then going down to the harbor to speak to the harbormaster and some mariners from a couple of the ships that were in port.

They discussed their findings over midday meal at the inn nearest to the docks. "What have we got?" Andro asked rhetorically. "A ship fire of unknown origin, could have been an accident, or not. The only thing suspicious about that is the fact that it carried supplies for our people in the north."

"Don't forget the tar," Sir Baramen reminded him. "The black smoke and a strong smell of tar. Do supply ships usually carry large quantities of tar?"

"I think they use some tar to protect the timber," Andro replied, "but I would think it's more the sort of thing builders use."

"The refugee camp outside town is another sign. All those poor people driven from their farms, and businesses," a female defender added. "I wonder what they are going to do."

"It's hard to tell. They will probably scatter and lodge with relatives, or try to fit into other communities until it's safe for them to return to their homes," Andro said. "Whatever they do, it's going to be a hard winter for them what with food shortages and being homeless." He knew what that felt like, but realized he was more fortunate than they were, having the Monastery to fall back on.

They continued to move north along the Great South Road, talking to people and noting the damages they saw. The most telling sign was the steady flow of refugees going south, some with little more than the clothes they were wearing, some carrying bundles on their backs, leading children and the occasional sheep or goat. The lucky ones had carts in which to carry their belongings and provide transport for the sick and elderly.

Late in the afternoon, after passing through a deserted stretch of road, they saw an old man sitting on a cart whipping an emaciated donkey with a leather strap.

"My good man," Andro said, dismounting from his horse. "Why are you punishing that poor creature?"

"She won't move, damn her" the old man said angrily.

"Do you not think she might be tired and hungry? Is it right to do that to a poor creature who has served you faithfully and never complained or asked for anything other than a little fodder and water to quench her thirst?" Andro went over to the little donkey and laid his hand on its head, which was drooping almost to the ground.

The old man dropped the strap and tears began to roll down his face. "I've lost everything. They killed my wife and my dog, took all my sheep, and burned my house to the ground. There's nothing left but old Flo and me. I didn't mean to hurt her; I was mad with rage at my fate."

"I understand, friend," Andro said. "Do you have any food?"

The old man wiped his eyes with the sleeve of his dirty smock. "No. I was going to try to trap a rabbit or bird, but..." he shook his head and gazed into the distance, looking beaten down and hopeless.

"We were going to stop for a bite to eat in a few minutes, so we can rest the horses. Would you like to join us? We passed a little stream a while back; maybe we could go back there to water the horses there while we eat."

The old man seemed to remember he was a civilized man, not a tyrannical brute created by anger and despair. "That would be most kind of you, sir. I thank you." He climbed down from the cart and took the rein of the donkey, ready to move.

"Wait a moment, friend, I'll get some water for her before we move." He went to one of the packhorses and removed a leather bag of water. When he held it under her nose, she drank a little, then raised her head and shook it, after a moment, she took some more.

Before parting from the old man, they gave him two of the leather water bottles and a small package of dried meat and some bread.

"I felt sorry for the poor old man," Andro said as the mounted his horse. "But there was no cause to take out his anger on an innocent animal."

"You're fond of animals." Sir Baramen commented.

"I am that. My experiences of the past few months have given me a great deal of respect for our four-legged brothers."

"Would that have anything to do with the Commander's girl and her wolf?"

43 – The queen responds

Imali

The three men from Trethawynd had finally settled down for the night. The lights were out, except for a single candle on top of one of the chests and, judging by their even breathing, the two knights were asleep, but Imali was playing over in his mind the meeting with the ambassador, worrying over the implications of their conversation.

They had sat in the waiting hall of the embassy for many minutes before the ambassador appeared. They'd stood up as he entered. He was a short, chubby middle-aged man with greying hair, wearing black trousers and a gold over-tunic with the crest of Trethawynd emblazoned on the left side. He didn't smile when he greeted them, although he did refrain from expressing his displeasure at having his siesta disturbed.

"Well met, gentlemen. How may I be of service?"

Imali stepped forward and gave him gave a slight bow. "Well met, ambassador. I'm Fernad Imali. I have the honor of being appointed special envoy to Queen Zenobia by Duke Valdor of Trethawynd. My two companions are Sir Bryon and Sir Kevan in the duke's service. I regret the urgency of our mission has caused you inconvenience, but in accordance with protocol, it was necessary for us to introduce ourselves to you before approaching her majesty. Since we must see the Queen as soon as possible ... tomorrow we hope ... we needed to find out what assistance you can give us in this matter." Imali looked at his two companions and back at the ambassador. "May we sit down, sir?" he asked.

"Of course," the ambassador replied sourly, pulling out a chair by the table for himself.

Imali noticed he didn't offer them any refreshments, although elementary courtesy would have made such an offer obligatory. *Maybe he doesn't think we are important enough; he's treating like tradesmen.*

The ambassador cleared his throat. "We, the Queen and I, do not recognize Lord Valdor as the rightful Duke of Trethawynd."

"How could that be possible?" Imali was shocked. He looked at Bryon and Kevan. Kevan had gone pale, but Bryon's features were noticeably darkened and his fists were clenched on his lap. "Valdor is the legal heir of the old duke."

"He was," the ambassador replied. "We feel that the tragedies he suffered, losing his father and his wife and child, followed by the destruction of the ducal residence have unbalanced his mind. We recognize his son, Lord Varan as the true duke, and Lord Valdor's brother, Lord Evanar, as regent until Duke Varan comes of age."

Both Bryon and Kevan stood up, knocking back their chairs, with fury in their eyes, their fists clenched at their sides. Imali knew that if they'd carried weapons, they would have been drawn.

"That's absurd," Imali replied calmly. "Duke Valdor is perfectly fit in mind and body. There is nothing preventing him from leading his people to victory over the Dark Brethren. He is at the center of all our planning and strategy..."

"Be that as it may," the ambassador interrupted. "He is not serving the people of Trethawynd as he should. He should be out, leading them in the battle, showing himself to the people, not hiding out in the Monastery, taking orders from the Grand Master. This cowardly behavior does not serve the duchy. For all the people know, he could be a prisoner of the League, a puppet."

"That's not true!" Sir Bryon could no longer control himself.

"Is this one of Gremulkin's schemes?" Sir Kevan added.

Imali put up his hand to silence them. "Mr. Ambassador, I am shocked at the misinformation you are disseminating. As Sir Kevan suggests, this sounds like something we would expect from former Chancellor Gremulkin. Lord Evanar has not been seen since the attack on the castle and we strongly suspect he is in the hands of Gremulkin and other traitors."

The ambassador stood up. "I see no point in continuing this conversation, sirs. I suggest you return to your lodgings and prepare to leave. I will give you until midday tomorrow to find a ship that will return you to Trethawynd. If you are not gone by then, I will announce to the Royal Guardians the presence of traitors to the crown, and you will be arrested." He led the way to the door and opened it for them, then, realizing that the gate was locked, called for the doorman. He left them standing in the courtyard and went back inside, slamming the door behind him.

"What are we going to do?" Sir Bryon asked.

"He's the traitor," Sir Kevan said vehemently. "He should be executed for treason."

"I think he's being controlled by Gremulkin. I recall that he was appointed shortly after Gremulkin became chancellor. Do you think he was bluffing about the Queen not recognizing Duke Valdor as the true duke?"

"Probably. The whole case he presents against Valdor sounds too farfetched to fool anyone as intelligent and well informed as the Queen." Bryon replied.

What are we going to do? Imali ruminated. They couldn't return to Trethawynd without completing their mission; they would look like fools and be admitting they were, as the ambassador implied, traitors. *I'll have to communicate directly with the palace and hope the ambassador hasn't influenced the Queen with his ridiculous accusations.* With a sigh, he rolled over on his other side and closed his eyes.

A loud knock at the door of their room roused the three men. Sir Bryon was first on his feet. Tucking his dagger under his arm, he picked up the lighted candle and went to the door. After sliding the bolt back, he opened the door. He barely had time to see them before three men forced their way into the room. By then Imali and Kevan were also up. Kevan went for his sword, but was stopped by a knife at his throat in the hands of one of the men.

"I wouldn't do that, sir," the man warned.

"Who are you?" Imali demanded angrily.

"We're members of the Royal Palace Guard," one of them replied.

One of guards was carrying a lantern and in its light, they could see the uniforms of the three men. Dark blue fitted trousers and gold-trimmed blue tunics with the royal coat arms in gold across the chest. One of them had a stripe on his cuff, which Imali took to indicate he was an officer. There was little doubt in his mind that they were who they claimed to be.

"What's this about?" he demanded.

"We received a report that three traitors to the realm were lodging here and we've been ordered to take you to the palace for investigation," the officer replied.

"But we're not..." seeing the look in the guard's eye, he tried another tack. "We are special envoys of the Duke of Trethawynd. If you'll allow me, I can show you our credentials."

"All in good time, sir. Right now, we want you to get dressed and accompany us to the palace."

"Does that mean we're prisoners?"

"That is your status at the moment. Now, no more question. Get dressed please."

The three guards stepped back to the door to give them room, keeping eyes on them all the time to make sure they didn't try to conceal any weapons on their persons.

"What about our trunks?" Imali asked. "We have valuable gifts for the Queen..."

"We'll take care of that, don't worry. Now, let's go. And don't make any trouble; we don't want to have to restrain you."

The three guards took one of them each by the arm and led them from the room. They descended the grand staircase to the entrance, passing no one on the way down. Outside on the street, they were surprised to see their hired horses saddled and tied to the horse bar with those of the guards.

"Mount your horses," the officer ordered. "We are going to restrain your hands so that you don't try to escape. Then we will proceed to the castle."

The guards tied rope around the wrists of Imali and his companions, securing each to the ring on the front of the saddle. Their hands were free to hold the reins, but the restraints didn't allow them much range of movement.

They set off up the hill to the palace, the senior guard leading and the other two following behind the prisoners.

What in the name of the Light is going on? Imali wondered. Had the ambassador broken his word and reported them to the palace already? *But they aren't treating us badly; in fact, they've been rather gentle and courteous, considering our alleged crime. I'm sure if they thought we really were traitors, they would have roughed us up quite badly by now.*

The gate in the outer palace walls opened as they approached and, as soon as they had passed through, closed again with a solid thud. The sun was coming up, casting a glow in the sky over the palace in front of them. They were in a smoothly paved yard with outbuildings lined along the inside of the outer wall.

The three guards dismounted and cut the ropes binding them to the saddles. "You may dismount now."

They climbed down from the saddles and stood waiting for the next move. Several other guards came by and looked at them.

"Are these the traitors, captain?" one of them asked.

"Be on your way, defender, and stick to your own business," the captain replied harshly, far more harshly than the tone he had used with them, the prisoners.

The guard slinked away, scowling.

"This way," the captain ordered them. He started to walk across the yard, but not to the main gate of the palace. They walked along the wall to the right of the gate until they reached a smaller, iron-plated door. The captain took a key from his belt and opened the lock, then pushed the door inward. "Go ahead," he said, holding the door open.

After passing through several passages where people were busily going about their duties, they climbed a flight of stairs to a wider hall, where the captain opened a door and escorted them inside.

"I'm going to leave you here for a while. Someone will come to talk to you shortly, in the meantime, just sit quietly and wait. You may help yourselves to the refreshments." He left, closing and locking the door behind him.

"It doesn't look much like a prison," Sir Bryon commented as he looked around.

The room was a clean, though very plain, with white plaster walls, a beamed ceiling and tiled floor. A small window on one wall looked out upon another wall with a matching window about three paces away. The room contained three long wooden tables with benches on both sides and a sideboard by the end wall containing serving bowls, plates of bread and cold meat, plus several jugs. Eating utensils, mugs and bowls stood beside the food.

"Not like a prison at all," Bryon reiterated. "More like a servant's dining hall."

"It probably is," Imali replied. "At least it's not a dungeon."

"Maybe they want to soften us up before they start interrogating us," Sir Kevan added.

"A very unusual technique, if you ask me," Bryon said. "I don't know about you, but I'm hungry. Let's see what they have to eat."

Bryon and Kevan made two contrasting figures, Kevan was tall and thin with straight black hair, light brown skin and a short beard, while Bryon was shorter and more solid with wide shoulders and muscular arms and legs. From the south of the Kingdom of Albasiny, Bryon was the darkest of the three.

They filled their plates with bread and sliced meat, and poured fruit juice from the jugs, then sat down at one of the tables to eat.

"How long do you think we'll have to wait?" Bryon asked.

"As long as it takes, I expect." Kevan laughed.

"It's not funny," Bryon replied. "We could be in serious trouble."

"Well we'll face it when it comes. What's the point in wasting energy on something that might not happen?"

They sat for a time after eating making desultory conversation, anxious, but strangely unafraid. Each of them had different feelings about what had happened or would happen. Kevan was furious at the ambassador's betrayal; all he wanted was a chance to make him pay for it. Imali was worried about being unable to complete Valdor's mission—he couldn't imagine returning to Trethawynd without bringing good news—he felt it was better to be imprisoned here in Sola Regis than let his friend down. Bryon expected that any moment, the door would open and they would be dragged down to the dungeons and tortured.

When the door did finally open, they all looked up with feelings of dread, anticipation, and hope. They were surprised by the sight of the man standing in the doorway. Judging by his dress, he was an important court official. He wore a long robe of deep blue with gold—real gold by the way it gleamed—trim at the neck and cuffs and a medallion with the royal coat of arms hanging on a heavy gold chain from his neck. He wasn't a tall man, but his bearing was so poised, it gave him stature. He had a narrow face, a light complexion, yellowish-brown eyes, and a long thin nose.

"Well met, gentlemen. I apologize for the way we had to bring you here," he said in a deep voice. "There was no other way we could proceed without tipping our hand. If you will come with me, I will give you a full explanation. And have no fear; we don't for a moment think you are traitors."

"But why...?" Sir Kevan started to ask.

"All in good time sir. Once we reach the receiving room, all will be made clear. We don't want to discuss this in public hallways."

With an immense feeling of relief, Imali fell in behind the courtier. Whatever was going on was obviously not against them.

"Forgive me, sir, I didn't introduce myself. I'm Dar Osgand, Chancellor to Her Majesty Queen Zenobia."

"It is a great honor to meet you, sir. My name is Fernad Imali, private secretary to Duke Valdor." *Chancellor!* Imali thought, *the most powerful person in court after the Queen herself. They are taking us seriously, after all.*

They went up another flight of stairs much grander than the one they'd previously trodden, and at the top, found themselves in a wide, marble tiled gallery with walls covered in woven silk of a subtle greenish-blue, almost jade, color. The doorways they passed were massive with double doors in the rarest woods and trimmed with gold; even the wall sconces appeared to be made of gold. The gallery was separated from a central atrium by a waist-high stucco wall with pedestals supporting plants at intervals. After walking down one side of this gallery and halfway along another, the chancellor came to a door, outside which stood two footmen in livery of the same royal colors as the chancellor's outfit.

"Lord Chancellor," they said simultaneously and bowed to the distinguished gentleman. They immediately opened the doors to the room and stood back at attention while the Chancellor Dar Osgand led his guests inside.

It was a large bedroom with two massive beds, luxurious tables and chairs, but what caught their eyes immediately were their trunks sitting on benches at the foot of the beds.

"This is one of the royal guest rooms. I will leave you here to refresh yourselves and change your clothes. If you brought anything special to wear at court, I suggest you don it. I will send someone to fetch you in half an hour. The bathing facilities are through that door." He indicated a door in the right hand wall, and then he turned and walked out the door held open by a footman.

The three men from Trethawynd looked at one another for a moment, smiled, and turned to unpack their ceremonial garments from the trunks.

After washing in the bathing facility, they donned the garments they'd brought for the occasion. Imali had fitted white trousers and a high-necked white tunic embroidered with the crest of Trethawynd and gold braid on the collar and cuffs; the two knights wore their white dress uniforms, also displaying the crest across the fronts of their tunics, ceremonial swords and black boots.

"I think we look all right," Imali said after a last look in the mirror and a quick pat to his hair. "Now the gifts," he opened a small chest and produced two packages bound in gold cloth, one was long and slender, and the other was the size of a small jewelry casket. He handed them to the two knights to carry.

They didn't have to wait long before a footman opened the door to admit a woman. "Well met, gentlemen," she said with a nod. She wore loose culottes of filmy silk with a long tunic of sky-blue silk trimmed with white lace and a white satin sash; her dark hair was piled up on her head in an elegant style of curls and jewels. She appeared to be in her middle years. After looking them up and down, she said, "If you will follow me, Her Majesty is ready to see you now." With that, she turned and exited.

They followed her down the hallway past palms in stone planters, doors with footmen at attention outside, and a flurry of courtiers who eyed them curiously, and servants who kept close to the walls with their eyes focused on the marble floor.

The woman led them around a corner and stopped in front of a larger door trimmed with elaborate gold filigree. The two footmen opened the door for them to enter.

"This is her majesty's private audience chamber. If those are gifts you are carrying, may I suggest you place them on the table in front of her chair, but first, would you mind telling me what the packages contain?"

"One is an enchanted sword, my lady, from the Duke of Trethawynd ... it hasn't been tuned to anyone yet ... and the smaller one is a gift from the Grand Master of the Trethawynd League of Light. I believe it is a crystal having certain properties with which I am unfamiliar, although I think it has something to do with relaxation and well-being."

"Thank you, envoy. I'm sure our mages will be able to identify its effects." She then introduced herself. "My name is Anahita Kurav. I am her majesty's principal lady-in-waiting. Now we will await her majesty. Please stand over here. When she appears, bow, but don't speak until she does. Answer her questions as concisely as possible, and please don't elaborate unless she asks you to."

She led them to stand about three paces in front and to the side of the Queen's chair, and then she left the room by the door behind the chair. They looked around the room while she was gone, taking in the row of floor to ceiling windows down the wall facing the outside of the palace. The windows had roll-up shades, which were currently open. Outside they could see a terrace, similar to those in the duke's palace, but much wider and furnished with palm trees and flower boxes with dazzling arrays of flowers growing in them. Among the plants were several small fountain pools and round tables surrounded by comfortable chairs.

The door behind the Queen's chair opened again and a liveried footman entered. "Make way for Her Gracious Majesty, Queen Zenobia of Albasiny," he announced.

He stood back and the Queen entered. Imali and the two knights bowed low and then stood at attention.

Imali was surprised at how tiny she was, barely reaching the shoulders of her lady-in-waiting, Anahita Kurav. She was also very slender and, was it not for her black eyes, which told of experience and wisdom, she might be taken for a much younger woman. She was simply dressed in a white linen gauze robe, topped by a knee-length mantle of pale violet. A simple plaited gold coronet rested on the translucent veil that covered the dark curly hair that fell to her shoulders. She couldn't be called beautiful, Imali thought, but she was certainly very striking. She would probably gain more attention than traditional beauties, even if she were an ordinary citizen and not the queen.

Kurav accompanied her to the largest and most ornate chair at the table, and helped arrange her clothing when she sat down. She then stood at her right shoulder. Another young woman had entered behind the Queen. She was tall with remarkably pale skin and blue-eyes, her hair, which fell below her shoulders in glossy waves, was light reddish brown.

The queen peered around the back of her chair. "Come in, dear, and sit beside me." She indicated the chair on her left. Queen Zenobia's voice was high and bell-like, not at all like the voice of a mature woman.

The girl ducked her head and sat down. "Thank you, your majesty. I am honored," she said softly, with a slight foreign accent.

"Now let's get to our business," the Queen said. "Gentlemen, would you please be seated at the end of the table?"

Since the table only had eight chairs, including the Queen's, they would not be very far away from her. They bowed to her again. "Thank you, Your Majesty. We are greatly honored by your graciousness." Imali answered. As he was the spokesperson, he pulled out the chair at the foot of the table.

"Would you start by introducing yourselves?"

"My name is Fernad Imali. I have been the confidential secretary to Lord ... and subsequently Duke Valdor of Trethawynd for fifteen years. On my right is Sir Bryon, and on my left is Sir Kevan, Knights of Trethawynd."

She dipped her head at them, and then looked down at some papers on the table in front of her. Before she could say anything more, the door opened again and the Lord Chancellor entered. He moved in front of her, to her right, so she could see him and bowed. "I apologize, Your Majesty, something came up that I had to attend to."

"Was it anything to do with this business?"

"Yes, your majesty, indirectly. If you will permit me, I would prefer to discuss it with you later, although I can assure you that everything went as planned."

"Good," the Queen replied briskly. "Sit down, for goodness sake, Dar. You know I don't like to be hovered over."

Once he was seated, she spoke again to the envoys. "You are probably wondering who this young lady is," she said with a fond smile at the person in question. "Allow me to introduce my foster daughter, Princess Carylis of Traesbern. Princess Carylis is the heir to the throne of Traesbern. She attends many of my meetings to observe how we proceed with courtly business here in Albasiny."

The three men raised themselves in their seats and bowed to the princess.

She smiled shyly at them then resumed watching the Queen.

"Now, about our business. Before we go on, I feel we owe you an explanation of our handling of the situation. I'll let my chancellor explain." She gestured to the chancellor with a slight smile.

Osgand angled his chair slightly so that he could face them without turning his back on the queen. "We needed to get you safely to the palace without alerting your ambassador. He has been under observation since the incidents started in

Trethawynd when the ducal castle was destroyed. We have reason to believe that he is under the influence of former Chancellor Gremulkin, and have observed a number of suspicious characters entering and leaving the embassy. Our agents found one of these people snooping around the inn where you were staying. He was taken into custody and brought here for questioning last night and he revealed that the ambassador was planning to have you assassinated if you did not leave Sola Regis this morning. He wanted to prevent you communicating, by any means, with her majesty's government. Shortly before we arrived at your lodgings, the ambassador was taken into custody and the embassy was closed under royal seal. With your consent, we will search the embassy and question the staff, seeking evidence of his treachery. If the ambassador has indeed joined the Dark Brethren, he faces execution as a traitor to the Sovereign and the Nation of Albasiny." The chancellor stood up. "Envoy Fernad Imali, as the senior representative of His Excellency the Duke of Trethawynd here present, we are asking you for your formal consent on the duke's behalf to pursue this inquiry."

Imali rose to his feet. "Your Majesty, Lord Chancellor, as you may guess, these events have taken us by surprise. I beg leave to consider your request and to consult His Grace before I respond." He smiled apologetically. "I pray you will take into consideration my lack of experience in diplomatic matters and allow me a little time."

The chancellor looked at the Queen, who smiled and nodded her head. "Her Majesty has graciously assented to your request, Envoy Imali." The chancellor sat down again.

"Thank you, Your Majesty." Imali bowed and resumed his seat.

The queen lifted the papers from the table in front of her. "We have read Duke Valdor's request," she said, then smiled. "However, we need a little more time to study it and talk it over with our council. You may now return to the inn and await our response." Seeing Imali's disappointed expression, she continued, "This does not mean we are turning down the request; we just need to discuss how best we can respond to it. Perhaps, while you are waiting, you can think over the matter of the ambassador."

As the Queen stood up, everyone else at the table rose and bowed to her. She left the room followed by the princess, and the lady-in-waiting. When they had gone, the Lord Chancellor came over to their end of the table.

"I see you are a little bewildered," he said to the three men. "Don't worry; you'll receive an answer by tonight. Her Majesty has to consult the Marshal of the Albasiny Royal Defenders and the Grand Master of the National League of Light in order to decide how much help she can send and the logistics involved. She is well aware that if Trethawynd falls to the Dark Brethren, the rest of the nation would be in peril. As you may perceive from the matter of your ambassador, they are already at work in the capital.

"Come, I will have a footman conduct you out to the place where you can pick up your horses. Your trunks have already been sent back to the inn."

Before he could leave, Imali had a question for the chancellor. "Lord Chancellor, we will need to find a sender to communicate with Duke Valdor. I am wondering if there is one you could recommend."

"By all means. You may use one of the palace mages. I will ask the footman to take you to the senders' suite on your way out."

"Thank you, Lord chancellor. You have been most helpful."

The chancellor accompanied them to door and instructed one of the footmen to conduct them to the sender's suite. The mage senders were in a large room farther along the hall. There were three of them, two men and one woman. Once inside, Imali explained what he needed and one of the two men responded.

"Sit down here, sir and tell me the message you wish to send." He indicated a chair next to his communications crystal.

"I want to send to the Duke of Trethawynd. His sender's name is Cybele and she is situated in the Palace of Trethawynd at the Monastery of the League."

"I will try to contact her, but if I cannot, we will be obliged to link with the Monastery communications center where they can forward it to his grace."

"Will I be able to wait for a reply? It may take a while."

"As you wish sir, I will emphasize urgency in the message. Now what is your message?"

Imali tried to make the message as succinct as possible while including all the relevant details. Apparently, the sender had been sending while he dictated the message because he looked up from his crystal a moment after Imali had finished talking.

"You may wait over there," the sender said, nodding toward the chairs where the two knights were sitting.

The communications room was very quiet. Thinking they might disturb the senders, Imali gestured towards the door. "I think we'll wait outside, so we don't distract you," he said to the sender who had served them.

The footman who had brought them here stood outside the door. He came to attention when they came out. "We have to wait for an answer," Imali explained. "We'll just have a look around if that is permitted."

"I will accompany you, sirs, so you don't get lost."

They walked slowly down the gallery, avoiding the people hurrying past by staying close to the atrium wall, looking down at the scene below. The atrium was an indoor garden planted with palms, miniature bergamot trees, and exotic flowers.

"We'd better not go too far in case there's a reply," Imali said.

"What do you think it will be?"

"Oh I expect Valdor will leave it to the Queen to decide what to do with the ambassador. Much as he dislikes the death penalty, he won't want the Queen to think he's weak." He walked to a bench near the atrium wall. "Let's sit down over here and wait."

They sat down on the long marble bench and watched the people passing by, enjoying the fragrance wafting up from the garden below. After a while, they realized the aroma of food was beginning to overpower the flower scents. A team of servants appeared wheeling an elegant cart piled high with covered dishes, followed by a second with hot and cold beverages, dishes and eating utensils, all moving towards the Queen's suite.

"The smell of all this food is making me hungry," Sir Bryon stated, rubbing his middle. "I'm starving."

"Me too," added Sir Kevan.

"It won't be long now," Imali said. "I imagine they have to do some running around at the Monastery."

At last, the door to the communications center opened and the sender looked out, nodding to them. They went back inside where he was waiting with the reply from the duke.

"Would you like it directly, mind-to-mind, or would you prefer a transcript?"

"Both if you don't mind," Imali replied. "And will you send a copy to her majesty, please?" He sat on the chair by the sender and put his hand on the crystal. The answer was in his mind instantly. Then the sender gave him a rolled up sheet of what looked like very expensive paper or vellum. "Here's your transcription, sir."

"Thank you," Imali replied.

As soon as they were outside the door, Kevan asked Imali what the duke's reply was.

"As we expected, leave it to the Queen."

Imali unrolled the paper and skimmed through it, then tucked it in his belt pouch, trying not to crease it.

"We're ready for our horses now," Imali said to the footman who had been standing patiently outside the door. *It's fortunate he has a tranquil nature,* Imali thought; *he probably spends most of his time standing around waiting.*

This time, instead of taking them to a side door, the footman led them to the main entrance of the palace through a grand hall lined with marble pillars and gold lamp holders. It was furnished with long sofas upholstered in deep turquoise velvet and small gilded tables, the refined ambiance brought to life by potted palms and flowering plants.

They rode away from the palace, their moods completely changed from their early morning arrival when they hadn't known what to expect and had feared the worst. Arriving at the inn, they went directly to their room and were gratified to see their trunks were waiting.

"I don't know about you," Imali said to his companions, "but I feel quite pleased. I think our mission will be successful. Apart from that, I'm hungry. Let's change into something less formal and find a place to eat."

They decided to look for a different restaurant this time and went in another direction. "There must be a place that does traditional Regio food," Kevan said. "I hear it's very good. It will probably be a long time before we are here again, so we should make the best of our stay.

"I don't care where we eat, as long as it's soon," Bryon replied.

"Over there, see?" Imali point across the street, near the next corner. "House of Regio, Fine Foods."

"Good, let's try it." Kevan said, dashing across the street in front of a wagon. The other two waited for the wagon to pass and crossed over more sedately.

It must have been a good restaurant, judging by the number of patrons, all in expensive clothes. They waited in the entrance, not knowing if there would be a vacant table and not wanting to push their way through the crowded tables without a direction. A tall woman wearing loose red culottes and a cream knee-length tunic with the restaurant's insignia on the breast approached them.

"At your service, gentlemen," she said with a warm smile. "I'm Teralina."

"It looks as if you're busy today," Imali said to her. "Do you have room for three more?"

"We certainly do, sir. We're always busy at this time of day, but we are prepared for it. If you'll follow me…"

She led them to a staircase in a corner at the back of the room and up to the next floor. Here was another layout similar to the one downstairs, though a little less crowded and noisy. It had windows opening onto a terrace with a couple of tables set up outside.

"Would you like to sit outside? It's less windy than usual today."

After looking at his companions, for consent, Imali said, "We'd be delighted."

Sitting outside, they had a good view of the street and could watch the wheels of commerce turning below. The motley crowd in the street seemed to have two things in common; they all appeared to be prosperous, and they were all in a hurry. It was a surprisingly multicultural crowd too, with the costumes of many countries: long robes, baggy pantaloons, skin-tight trousers, short breeches, all with a variety of vests, blouses, tunics and jackets. However, it was the head gear that really set them apart, varying from several styles of turban, skullcaps, flowing veils for women, to multi-colored headbands, and floppy hats with feathers. There were also many racial types, ivory skinned with narrow black eyes, reddish brown hair and skin, dark-skinned with black hair; a good proportion of them had the pale skin and light hair that characterized people from northern climes, commonly called Nordics.

When Sir Kevan inquired, they were told that the traditional dish of Regio was something called Javelina Supreme, small steaks of tender meat grilled with spicy sauce and served with the roasted sliced roots of a tropical plant called taro, with onions and tomatoes. Javelina, they discovered was a variety of brown-haired pig that lived in the tropics. Imali found it a little too spicy, but the effect was somewhat alleviated by slices of iced fruit.

"Well that was one of the best meals I've ever tasted," Sir Kevan declared when he had finished. He emptied his glass of chilled guava juice and stood up. "Shall we go?"

"I'm glad you liked it," Imali replied. "We've just used up most of our food budget for the trip."

"Oh don't worry about that," Kevan responded, "We'll help you pay for it, won't we, Bryon?"

"If you say so," Bryon replied. "How much?"

"Oh, one should be enough, for now." Kevan took a small gold piece from his belt pouch and gave it to Imali.

Sir Bryon scowled at Kevan and produced another, which he also handed over.

They walked around for another hour and then returned to the inn, where Imali penned a letter to the Queen to verify the reply he'd received from Duke Valdor regarding the ambassador. He wrapped it in a sheet of parchment and sealed it with his own sigil.

It was almost sunset when a courier from the palace arrived. He brought a large box wrapped in gold cloth, and presented Imali with a bleached leather envelope containing several documents, one of which was addressed to him personally. After handing his message for the Queen to the footman, Imali gave him a silver coin and saw him off, and then he sat down to read his message. It was from the Lord Chancellor.

"We're booked for passage on a royal carrier that leaves port at dawn tomorrow," he told the two knights.

"That's nice," Kevan replied. "Did he say anything about what help the Queen plans to give us?"

"Not in detail, but some of it will be going with us tomorrow. There'll be a unit of twelve Royal Defenders under a captain and one sergeant, complete with horses and equipment. Also ten cases of weapons and armor, a dozen extra horses, tack, and two grooms. They're also sending six League defenders and three mages with us. According to the Lord Chancellor, this is just a preliminary contribution to assess the situation and report back."

"It must be a large ship to carry all that," Sir Kevan commented.

"It must," Imali agreed. "There's also a whole package of documents for Duke Valdor and the Grand Master. He patted the leather portfolio."

"It sounds as if everything is taken care of and we have a little free time. Now, what are we going to do for the rest of the day?"

"Stay out of trouble, I hope," Imali said with a grin. "I would love to shop in the bazaar, but I don't have enough coin, so we'll have to find some other way to entertain ourselves."

"I know what we can do this evening," Sir Kevan said. "They have demonstrations of martial arts at the arena. The performers are from many cultures from around the world. It's fascinating to see the variety of fighting and defensive techniques."

"No bloodshed, I hope," Imali said.

"Oh, no. As I said, it's just friendly demonstrations of their arts by skilled fighters, but occasionally someone may get hurt accidentally, not often though."

44 – Felindra at ValkonenMaa Monastery,

Felindra

The ride from the port to the Monastery was utterly miserable for Felindra. The only good thing about it was that she had a horse to ride, but it was not a healthy horse. The poor creature was so old, she seemed to have aches and pains all over her, especially in the joints of her legs. Although her escorts, the dark man from the boat—whom she'd finally discovered was named Charnwell—and two strangers, continually urged her to hurry, she refused to cause the horse more discomfort than she already suffered and made frequent stops to allow the horse to rest, increasing their anger.

To make matters even worse, it had started to rain again and she was shivering in the cold air.

"If you don't get a move on, one of us will ride the old nag, and then we'll see how fast she'll go." Charnwell threatened.

"She's in pain," Felindra protested. "Don't you understand? She shouldn't even be ridden in her condition. If you try to force her to go faster, it will kill her."

"And how do you know all this?" he asked.

"I can feel her pain," Felindra replied, dismounting to offer the horse some water. "She has barely any strength at all. Even my weight is too much for her."

The other two men laughed. "She expects us to believe she knows how the animal feels."

"You'd better believe," Charnwell snarled. "She's got a gift. But that doesn't mean she can slow us down."

"You'll be slowed even more if she drops dead and I have to walk," Felindra retorted. "Can't we stop somewhere and exchange her for one that's not so sick?"

"You think we're wealthy merchants?" one of the other men replied.

"I think one of you is," she replied.

She remounted the old horse, stroking her neck and whispering, "I'm sorry. I'll try not to make you go too fast."

The road steepened and became much rougher, with holes and large stones to contend with. The poor horse staggered, wheezing and heaving, groaning pitifully. Finally, Felindra said, "I'm not going to ride on her anymore." She dismounted and went to the front of the horse. The poor creature's breath was flecked with blood. She took the bit from its mouth and removed the bridle.

"What are you doing?" Charnwell shouted. "You can't do that. We'll never get to the next town..." he grabbed the reigns and went to mount the horse.

"Wait," Felindra cried. "You'll kill her."

"We'll see about that. Mert, put the bridle back on." The man called Mert jumped down from his horse and grabbed the bridle from Felindra. Meanwhile, Charnwell had hauled himself up into the saddle.

The horse let out a weak moan as her legs gave way and she fell sideways, dumping Charnwell in the mud. The horse lay on her side, wheezing and whickering with pain, her eyes bulging as she tried to get up, but it was no use; she had no strength left. Felindra knelt on the ground beside her, trying to comfort her by talking to her—visualizing a grassy meadow by a stream on a sunny day—while stroking her face and neck. The poor creature was barely conscious. Felindra looked up angrily at Charnwell and the other two men. "Are you satisfied now?"

"Can't you make her get up?" Charnwell asked.

"I warned you. Don't you understand? She's dying," Felindra cried, tears filling her eyes.

The horse drew a final painful breath and her head sank to the ground. Tears ran down Felindra's face as she patted her one more time. *At least the poor creature isn't suffering,* she thought. *I hope she finds herself in a kinder place.*

They used two of the other horses to drag the carcass off the roadway. By this time, Charnwell was enraged. "Where did you get that useless piece of horseflesh?" he raved at one of the men. "Couldn't you find something that was at least alive?"

"It was my grandma's," the man replied sheepishly.

"Well I hope she's in better shape than her horse," Charnwell said.

"She's not," he replied. "She died last week."

"Oh, that's so touching," Charnwell sneered. "Grandma's gone and poor horse dies of grief. So where's the money I gave you?"

"I was going to give it back to you."

"You'd better, otherwise, you might end up joining your old granny. "She's going to ride with you now," he said, glaring at Felindra. "I'm beginning to wonder if you're worth all this trouble. Get on behind him."

"I didn't ask you to kidnap me," she replied. "I'd be quite happy to be sleeping in my own warm bed right now instead of stuck in this freezing place without warm clothing." It looked as if the man expected her to sit in front of him, but she made it clear she would sit behind. She didn't want him groping her. She hauled herself up behind the saddle and put her arms around him to keep from falling off. After a while, she realized she was absorbing some of his body heat and was starting to warm up a little. Unfortunately, she also had to endure his dreadful smell. She probably smelled almost as bad herself; she hadn't been able to wash herself the last few days, although she'd been too cold most of the time to sweat very much.

Monaltor

The room was dimly lit by blue light from a few candles set around the tabletop. The stone block walls did nothing to reflect the light; rather, they seemed to absorb it. Even the furniture conspired to create an atmosphere of gloom, most of it made of dark wood and black iron. Ogryn, the disciple of Oglestra, the Fallen One, sat in a high chair at the massive stone table. He had been reading in the light of a single large candle when Monaltor, the Grand Wizard entered.

"I want to talk to you about, Barengush, your son," Ogryn, the mortal leader of the Dark Brethren, said to Monaltor. "He's getting out of control. Maybe we shouldn't have trusted him with this."

"I realize he's reckless and impulsive, your magnificence. The boy has always been hard to control, but I'd like to point out that he is creating a lot of chaos in Trethawynd, and he is bringing us the Whisperer. Isn't that what we wanted?"

"True. But he's got himself hurt now. That allows them to see that he is vulnerable. If they think we can be easily damaged, they will be less reluctant to fight back. And look at the way they are building up their defenses, in spite of the duke's base of operations being destroyed and his treasury confiscated."

"It's that damned Monastery, Legion of Light indeed! It won't be long before we put out that light forever."

"That's as maybe," his superior responded. "But we have to stay with the plan. We can't have people going off and making independent attacks. The killing of the duke's family was going too far. Things like that only reinforce their determination to fight us."

"I believe that was Gremulkin's idea. It did demoralize Valdor for a while, and isolate him from his supporters."

"Not for long. Now he has the Monastery backing him."

"Do you want me to recall Barengush?" Monaltor asked.

"Yes. And I've been thinking about how we can use the duke's brother. Tell your son to bring him here."

"As you wish, your magnificence."

Ogryn picked up the manuscript he'd been studying. "That's all."

Monaltor backed out of the room, only turning away when he was out the door. It was not respect that prompted this behavior; he was afraid of being attacked from behind, unlikely though that seemed. Deep down, he didn't really trust Ogryn. He wiped the sweat off his face with the sleeve of his robe and started up the rough stone stairs to the main floor of the dungeons. For some obscure reason, the great Disciple preferred to keep his chambers below ground level, and to keep the light so dim that it barely illuminated the surroundings well enough to keep one from bumping into things. And the blue lights emphasized the gloomy, cold atmosphere; *creepy,* was the way Barengush described it.

That boy, he thought. *What am I going to do with him? It's entirely his mother's fault; she always indulged him too much. The witch forced me to kill her; she was ruining the boy. He sighed. Now I have to recall him. He's going to hold that against me too. Damn it, I'm his father. He has to be disciplined for his own good. He must learn that the Dark Brethren have to be taken seriously, and magic powers are not playthings.*

Barengush

Barengush had been left, with a small sailboat, at one of their hideaways up the coast from DarSolas instead of continuing on the barge to ValkonenMaa. The cave had been stocked with emergency supplies and was sometimes used as a refuge between actions. His decision to stay behind had caused a dreadful row with Charnwell, but he, Barengush, was in charge. He just hadn't felt up to seeing his father until he recovered his strength. He brushed the scar on his neck with his fingertips. It was still there; a finger-length ridge of hard keloid tissue that still burned and throbbed. *Damn their rotten hides; they'll pay for this,* he fumed. He tried to move into a comfortable position, but it was impossible in this stinking cave. His straw mattress was perpetually damp and lumpy. The stink from the swamp permeated the air, making it barely breathable. At high tide, seawater came to within two paces of his mattress, leaving stinking seaweed and dead shellfish all over the floor when it ebbed. Everyone had deserted him ... that weasel Gremulkin and his toady, Charnwell, had gone back down south. Just to relieve his misery, Barengush sent a small fireball toward the entrance of the cave.

GET BACK HERE AND BRING LORD EVANAR! IMMEDIATELY!

Yes, father, he replied with a sigh. *You realize I am injured. It might take me a while to organize things.*

WELL GET STARTED!

What's this about?

YOU'LL FIND OUT WHEN YOU GET HERE.

Barengush got up from the mattress and shook the dust and debris from his robe. On second thoughts, he decided to take if off. The pain of raising his arms to pull it off almost made him give up, but he needed to be agile and couldn't move around freely with the thing flapping around his legs and catching on everything. He stood for a moment deep breathing and swallowing the nausea caused by the pain. He rolled the robe into a bundle and added it to the contents of his pack, some matrix stones, and two vials of medicine, plus some moldy bread. He stepped into his boots, fastened them, and then added a sword and a dagger to his belt.

He looked out to sea and nodded his head. It looked like a calm day with a light breeze and a few small clouds on the horizon. A good day for sailing! The small boat was pulled up under a tree a few paces from the cave mouth. He threw his pack in, untied the rope that anchored it to the tree, and started to pull it down the slope towards the water. It was a lot harder than he'd expected because the bow kept catching on roots and stones, but once he had it out in the open, it slid easily through the sand into the water.

It took most of the morning and all afternoon to reach the place where Evanar was being held. That was another thing that infuriated Barengush; the duke's son, the prisoner, had better accommodation than he had. When he came in sight of the jetty, he saw larger boat anchored there. Charnwell? Or Gremulkin? He sighed. *I suppose I'll find out soon enough.* He dropped the sail and climbed out onto the jetty. After tying the rope to an iron ring, he started towards the cabin hidden among the trees north of DarSolas. Built of timber planks, it was what the Charnwells called their hunting lodge. Barengush was exhausted; all he wanted to do was lie down in a comfortable bed and sleep, but now he had another complication to deal with.

Barengush pushed open the door without knocking and stood in the opening to take stock. It was Gremulkin. He might have known.

"Come in, boy. Don't be shy," the former chancellor said disdainfully. "We were expecting you."

Barengush scowled at him. "How did you know I was coming?" He could have bitten his tongue the moment he said it, but he couldn't take his words back now they were out.

"How else. Your illustrious father sent me a message."

"What do you want?" He looked around for somewhere to sit, but Gremulkin was using the only comfortable chair and Lord Evanar was sitting on the narrow bed. His only choice was a wooden stool or the floor. He dragged the stool over to the side and sat on it, leaning his back against the wall.

"How were you planning to travel to ValkonenMaa? Not that toy you used to come down here, I hope. Or didn't you think that far ahead?"

"Look, Gremulkin, I'm tired and I'm in pain, so cut the pig swill." He glanced at the table, but it was bare apart from an unlit lantern. "Is there something to eat around here? And I could use a drink."

"If you hadn't been so hotheaded and impulsive, you wouldn't be in that condition," Gremulkin said. "There's some food and water around the corner there. Help yourself." He pointed to an alcove at the back end of the room.

Barengush got up and went slowly to see what was available. "How's his lordship?" he asked as he passed Lord Evanar. "Can I get you anything, My Lord?"

Evanar shook his head. He didn't look too happy, either. His clothes were rumpled, as if he'd been wearing them for weeks, and his hair was oily and uncombed. With his pallid skin, his dull lifeless eyes, and the way his clothes hung on him, he looked as if he'd given up hope. *Not happy at all,* Barengush thought. *Never mind, we'll see how you like my father's accommodations.*

He found some bread wrapped in a cotton cloth, and a hunk of yellow cheese. He cut a chunk off each and put them on a wooden plate, then poured himself a mug of water from a large metal cask. At first, he'd expected wine, which was what he needed, but that would have been hoping for too much. He carried them to the table, dragged his stool over. Before he started eating, he took some medicine from his satchel and swallowed a mouthful with water to combat the pain.

"What were you saying about a boat?" he asked Gremulkin.

"I've brought something more suitable. There's a three-man crew waiting out there, probably sleeping somewhere."

"Why do we need such a big boat? There's only two of us."

"I'm afraid not," Gremulkin replied. "I'm coming with you. You don't think I'd allow the future Duke of Trethawynd to travel unescorted, do you?"

Lord Evanar groaned, but made no comment.

Felindra

After the horse died, they had stopped at an inn in the next town. It was far from being a comfortable place to rest, and the food was barely edible, but Felindra had been so tired she'd managed to sleep. All they had been given was a small, not very clean room with pallets laid out on the raw wood floor, and a thin blanket to cover them. As they were leaving the following morning, the woman who owned the inn had drawn Felindra aside and presented her with a rough wool cloak. "You'll freeze to death in that flimsy outfit," she murmured, shaking her head. "Men!"

Before Felindra could reply or thank her, Charnwell had dragged her outside. "I warned you not to talk to anybody," he snarled. "We've got you a horse," he added, pointing to a small grey filly. "I hope this one suits your superior taste. Now, let's get going!"

They arrived at the ValkonenMaa monastery just before sunset. The rain had stopped, but the wind raked her with icy fingers, making her grateful for the cloak, threadbare though it was. They rode into the monastery yard and left the horses with a stableman, and then Charnwell and his helpers escorted her inside. Evidence of the battle that had been fought here only a few weeks before was still evident everywhere she looked. The scorched walls and doors, broken stone and plasterwork, and the general air of neglect were depressing. She tried to imagine how it must have looked before the attack. There were signs of the former elegance in details like the wall sconces and scrollwork borders along the walls. Even through grime and litter, it was possible to see that the polished stone tiles on the floors must have been quite beautiful.

Charnwell sent the other two mariners off somewhere before leading Felindra to a large ornamental door halfway along the hallway. He knocked and pushed it open, revealing a spacious room furnished with soft chairs, an enormous desk and two walls of shelved books. The somber-looking man seated behind the desk glowered at them.

"I've brought the girl," Charnwell announced pushing her forward.

"So I see," the man growled. "Look at her! I can't believe you let her travel across the duchy in that state. Don't you have any sense at all? Don't you think people might be suspicious?"

"I didn't think…"

"That's obvious." He leaned back in his chair and tugged a bell pull on the wall. "What happened to her? Why has she got blood and scabs all over her legs?"

"She fell down, sir."

There was another knock on the door and a small elderly man poked his head in. "You sent for me?"

"Yes. Take this girl and get her cleaned up and into some decent clothes. "And don't let her out of your sight. If she gets lost, it will be on your head."

"Come with me, child," he said gently, indicating the doorway with his open hand.

As the door closed behind them, Felindra could hear the angry voice of the man continuing to berate Charnwell. *Good,* she thought, *he deserves it. He's so stupid.*

45 – At Sea

Evanar

Gremulkin found Lord Evanar leaning against the bow rail, gazing down into the water. He sighed when he sensed Gremulkin behind him, but didn't turn round to acknowledge him. He was stunned by recent events, but he couldn't think of any way to get out of this situation. He couldn't even decide what his role was, prisoner, hostage, or just the tool of Gremulkin's ambition to control Trethawynd. Gremulkin was holding out the promise of the dukedom, but Evanar knew he only wanted a puppet to advance his own power. There was no way he wanted to usurp his brother's position. What Gremulkin didn't seem to grasp was that, in spite of his seeming life of pleasure-seeking and self-indulgence, Evanar loved his brother. His life may have seemed trivial and self-centered before their father's death, but that was mostly because he had felt so useless, without a role to play in the governance of the duchy. It had been his way of compensating for the boredom of his life. In part, he blamed Gremulkin for that situation. Until Gremulkin came to his father's court and had himself declared chancellor, they had been a close-knit family, he, his brother and their father, but after Gremulkin took control of the old duke, Evanar and Valdor had been shut out of the day-to-day responsibilities of running the duchy. Even when they wanted to talk with their father, Gremulkin was always hovering in the background, waiting like a spider to jump in and divert the duke's attention from any suggestions they made. It was different for Valdor; he'd had a wife and children, but Evanar had nothing, no one.

Evanar blamed Gremulkin for everything that had befallen his family. His father's sudden death, the assassination of Valdor's wife and daughter, the disasters that had befallen Trethawynd, and especially the destruction of the castle. He was sure the chancellor was behind all of it.

"A nice day for sailing, My Lord," Gremulkin said when he realized that Evanar would not acknowledge him voluntarily.

Evanar grunted and spat over the rail. "For you maybe," he said after a moment, still not turning round. "It's never a nice day for a prisoner."

"Don't talk like that," Gremulkin cajoled him. "You should be happy. Before long, you'll be the Duke of Trethawynd."

"Why doesn't that make me feel any better?" Evanar said.

Gremulkin patted him on the shoulder. "You'll feel differently, My Lord, when you are the Duke."

I don't think so, Evanar thought, *not with you pulling the strings. And whatever you may choose to believe, I will never betray my brother. I'll play along with your scheme, but the moment I have a chance, I'm done with you.*

Once he'd heard Gremulkin's footsteps recede, Evanar turned around to watch the activity on deck. Some young men—mostly the blond Nordic type—were practicing their moves, some dueling in pairs, two others working on unarmed tactics. Another couple was practicing shooting arrows at a target set up in the stern. He watched for a while, wishing he could join in with them, even though they were rehearsing for the conquest of his duchy. It was months since he last went hunting and he was getting out of practice, but Gremulkin wouldn't allow him to have weapons, as if he could do any harm surrounded as he was by armed fanatics and all this water.

A blond head appeared on the companionway from the lower deck, and the loathsome Barengush emerged from the stairwell. Evanar knew that he was one of those responsible for the fires that had burned the castle; the young fool had boasted about it enough times, and Evanar would never forgive what he'd done. He had heard talk among his travelling companions that the boy had received a sound reprimand from his father, the grand wizard, and he would now be supervised by a more mature wizard, whose job it would be to train him and curb his violent impulses.

Evanar noticed the young men stopped their activities when Barengush walked past them and watched him with loathing in their eyes.

Barengush was followed by the minder, the wizard Belmar Darksen.

The moment he saw Evanar the boy turned and approached him. "I see they've let you out of your cage," he sneered.

"I'll leave you to play by yourself," Evanar replied. "Mind you don't hurt yourself." He heard someone snicker as he turned away from the bow and strolled along the guard rail. *Damn*, he thought as he walked away, *I shouldn't let him get under my skin like that. There's something about him that really destroys my self-control. It makes me sound as immature as he is.*

Evanar sat down on a keg. He didn't want to go below yet, even though there was a chill in the wind. He'd been given new clothes to wear, but the cloak was unlined wool and did little to cut the blasts of cold air. He'd been forced to stay in his cubbyhole—it would have been a stretch to call it a cabin—and Barengush had not been far wrong when he referred to it as a cage. It was about three spans by two with one small porthole that didn't open, and contained nothing but a pallet on the floor. He had to ask someone to let him out when he needed to use the privy. Some way to treat a prospective duke! A taste of things to come? He was kept confined for the first two days of the voyage, and then allowed to go on deck at will, once they were out of sight of land and closer to the border. They thought this would prevent him from knowing where they were heading, but everyone was discussing the preparations for upcoming invasion. He knew they were heading for ValkonenMaa.

As always, he was thinking of ways to escape. It would be no use trying until they left the boat, however. He leaned over the rail and watched the other vessels in the small flotilla. He knew they were making good time by the way the wind filled the sails. He sighed and turned around. Resting his back against the bulwark. Every time he closed his eyes, his mind went back to that dreadful day...

The day that had started with being woken after a night of inebriation and lust to be informed by Gremulkin that his father had died. From there, things went downhill rapidly. Following the chancellor's instructions, he'd dressed and gone down to the hall to stand vigil over is father's body.

His father's remains, garbed in his robes of state, rested on a plinth in the center of the hall. Nine large candelabra stood around the plinth and provided the only illumination in the hall. All the furniture, tables, benches and chairs had been moved back against the walls and the window curtains had been drawn to shut out the daylight. He stood at the head of the stand and watched a parade of staff and people from the town walk slowly by to pay their respects. Some of them brought flowers and laid them on the body of the old duke.

By midday, he was getting very hungry and tired from standing, so he ventured out to the family dining hall to see if he could get a bite to eat. As he sat alone at the table with his feet up on a chair, he thought he heard shouts and screams coming from far away. A footman rushed in followed by two of the castle guards.

"We're being attacked, My Lord!" the footman said.

One of the guards pushed the footman aside. "Come with us, My Lord. We'll conduct you to a safe place."

"I don't want to go to a safe place when my castle is under attack. It's my duty to defend it. Take me to my quarters so that I can change into something more suitable, and then we'll find the guard commander and get his report." Evanar's head began to ache.

"The chancellor's orders are for us to get you to safety," the guard protested.

Just then, Gremulkin entered. "It's all right, defender, do as his lordship asks. I'll come with you so that I can explain what is happening."

"Yes, it's about time someone told me what's going on."

"The castle is under attack." Gremulkin told him.

Loud booms, sounding as if they were coming from inside the castle, cause walls to shake and loose items to rattle and fall. He could hear people screaming, which was more even alarming. "I don't understand. How did they breach our defenses so quickly?"

"It seems they found a way in from the strand, some kind of secret tunnel that leads into the cellars. We're managing to hold them down there for the time being, but I don't know how long we can keep them back."

They arrived at Evanar's quarters and he quickly shed his ceremonial robes and put on some thick linen pants and a tunic. He went to a chest and took out a chainmail vest, but before he could put it on, Gremulkin interrupted him.

"You won't need that, My Lord," he said. "We have to get you out of the castle to somewhere safe."

"But it's my duty…"

"Your duty is to stay alive," Gremulkin insisted. "You are the only family member we can locate at this moment, so you have to be alive to secure the succession. Come along, My Lord, and bring a cloak."

The two guards stood beside him, one on each side, close enough to make him feel like a prisoner with no escape. He took a wool cloak out of the chest and laid it over his arm, then started to move towards the door, feeling more as if he was being abducted rather than rescued, but he was helpless to resist the armed men who bracketed him.

He could smell smoke as they walked towards the service stairs and descended to the ground floor. He was taken to a side exit that led to the stables where three horses were waiting, saddled and ready to go. As they rode towards the gate, he saw smoke coming from some of the ground floor windows, and the screams were becoming louder and closer. Tears filled his eyes as they rode out through the gate.

"Who are they?" he asked Gremulkin. "Who's attacking us?"

"I don't know, My Lord, but there are a lot of werfolk among them and some Nordics, so my guess is it's the Dark Brethren from ValkonenMaa."

"But why? I don't understand."

"That's what we'll have to find out."

And now he knew the full extent of Gremulkin's treachery, and the plans of the Dark Brethren to take over Trethawynd.

46 – Daryan recruits Axtya

"Feel like helping me with a little project?" Dayan asked Ashavan.

"It depends, doesn't it?" Ashavan replied. "Do I have to get dirty? This is my best robe." He smoothed his hands down the gold-trimmed turquoise robe.

Daryan grinned. Pure Ashavan! "No, you don't have to get dirty; in fact, you might find it an interesting challenge. If you have some free time, that is."

"A challenge, eh? That appeals to me, as you no doubt know. I'm ready when you are."

Daryan led the way to the defenders' building and down the stairs to the basement level.

"Ah, the little monster! What have you planned for him now?"

"He's changed quite a bit. You'll hardly recognize him. He's a bit depressed; but who wouldn't be in his situation? He's making progress learning Albasinian, though. Ah, here we are." Daryan knocked and then pushed open the unlocked door to Axtya's room.

The little werman was sitting at his table with some blocks, arranging them to form a picture. He looked up when Daryan and Ashavan entered, and then dismantled the project he'd been working on. He brushed his hands together and mumbled, "Stupid."

"How would you like to come outside with us?" Daryan asked.

Axtya shook his head. "Demon wolf."

"The wolf is sick," Daryan replied. "She's been hurt by the wizard and can't walk." He was stretching the facts a little, but felt it was in their best interest if he wanted to get the werman outside. "There's something I want to talk to you about. If you agree with our proposal, we may be able to take you back to your home."

Axtya slid down from his chair and walked towards the door. He looked quite spruce in the clean children's garments. It was obvious this had encouraged him to take care of his personal hygiene as well ... that and having a couple of grilled rats inside him.

Ashavan shook his head and smiled at Daryan as the werman went past them into the hallway. Daryan shrugged. "It's worth it, believe me," he said.

Once they were outside, Daryan and Ashavan sat on a bench under some trees while Axtya sat on the ground in front of them, scraping the earth with a piece of wood while waiting to hear what they had to say.

"I would like you to work for us," Daryan started. The werman scowled. "We will not ask you to do anything dangerous. All you need to do is tell us what you know about the wizard and help us find him."

"Why?" Axtya gouged the ground.

Daryan looked at Ashavan who shrugged his shoulders. "Tell him."

"He's taken my daughter and I want to get her back."

Axtya was still for a moment and then looked up at Daryan, his big eyes swimming. "Axtya know how feel."

"Have they taken your children?" Daryan asked.

Axtya nodded his head, his eyes drifting towards the trees.

"It looks as if we can help each other," Daryan said. "You help us find my daughter and we will help you find your children."

Axtya nodded again. "When we go?"

"Soon," Daryan replied. "We need you to get some training in self-defense, and you will need to learn some other skills as well before we leave."

Daryan nodded to Ashavan, pointing him to the building, and then they both stood up. "I'll make some plans for you," Daryan said to Axtya. "I'll let you know when you can start your training." The two men walked away, leaving him where he was.

Daryan looked back over his shoulder and saw Axtya stand up, and glance towards the trees and then back at the building, a look of confusion on his face.

"What do you think?" Daryan asked Ashavan.

"He's certainly warmed to you," Ashavan replied. "He seems to trust you now. He's heartbroken about his family; he misses them a lot. I think he'd do anything to get back to them."

"I'd like to start a training session with him tomorrow. It might be a bit difficult to find a good match with a trainer, so I was wondering if you could sit in on a session and see how he reacts. Maybe you could give us some pointers on how we can make it work, review his reactions, and the trainer's. It would be useless to try it unless he and the trainer respected each other."

Ashavan shook his head and chuckled. "The things you get me into."

47 – Evanar Arrives in ValkonenMaa

Evanar

Gremulkin, Lord Evanar, Barengush, and two of the seamen arrived at the monastery near sundown, having disembarked the previous morning and continued their journey on horseback.

While they waited for a lackey to take them to Barengush's father, Evanar looked around at the neglected grounds of the monastery. Where there was grass, it was knee high and yellow from lack of water. Flowerbeds held dead plants among the flourishing weeds, and litter lay on the ground everywhere he looked. He shook his head sadly at the deterioration. He couldn't believe the former occupants would keep it in such squalor.

Evanar felt completely defeated and demoralized. What was Gremulkin up to, bringing him here? Whatever it was, he wanted no part of it. The pillage and destruction of his father's castle and the horrifying deaths of the people inside still haunted his dreams, when he managed to sleep. He hadn't had a decent meal since the day Gremulkin took him away from his home. When they remembered to give him something to eat, it was often dry bread, day-old fish or meat, or cheese so dry it was almost impossible to bite into or cut with a knife, if he'd had a knife. All he'd had to drink was water, always tepid and not very fresh. He yearned for a glass of wine and some fresh fruit. And Gremulkin had the audacity to call him *the future Duke of Trethawynd,* such pathetic mockery. The former chancellor had no intention of sharing power with anyone, should he succeed with this rebellion.

Evanar scratched his arm, then his leg started to itch. One of the consequences of being locked up in the cabin was fleas. The bedding had been infested with them. *If only I could have a bath and some clean clothes,* he thought, *and something fresh to eat.*

"Take us to the Grand Wizard," Barengush demanded when an old man appeared from one of the buildings near the stables,

"As you wish, young wizard," the old man replied. He had the light brown skin and greying black hair of a native Albasinian. "This way." He turned and shuffled off towards a large building at the far end of the yard.

"Why hasn't anyone been working on these gardens?" Barengush asked. He wasn't really concerned, but he liked to demonstrate his assumed superiority.

"Everybody's gone," the man replied. "There's nobody left to do the work."

"You haven't left."

"I'm too old to go out and try to start a new life."

"Has everyone gone, all the mages and servants?"

"Yes. Everyone that could get away, left during the attack, all the servants, the mages and the defenders."

That's odd, Evanar thought, *the wizard was here; he must know what happened. Maybe that's all for my benefit, a way of telling me it was no use expecting to be waited on. Young fool.*

Since he wasn't manacled and appeared to be part of the group visiting the Grand Wizard, Evanar decided to pose a question of his own. "Do you think you could find me some clean clothes and a bath? I've been travelling a long time and would like to clean up."

Gremulkin and Barengush glared at him, astonished by his audacity. Gremulkin recovered first. "That's a good idea," he said. "Maybe we should all freshen up before we see the Grand Wizard. And we'll need accommodation as well. We'll probably be staying here a few days."

The old man stopped and scratched his head, looking around at the various buildings. "Well, I suppose you could have some rooms in the mage's quarters. That's over there." He pointed to a smaller building on the right. "Let's go and have a look, shall we?"

Evanar almost smiled. He might be on the verge of getting what he'd asked for. Things were looking up. If he could to talk to the old man alone, he might even be able to get a message out.

The old man held the door open for them to enter the building. "What do they call you, my friend?" Evanar asked with a smile as he passed.

"My name is Dominel, sir."

"Well met, Dominel. I'm Evanar of Trethawynd." Evanar put his finger over his lips as he said this.

Dominel's eyes widened, but he said nothing, only nodded.

"What are you doing?" Barengush growled. "Come and show us some rooms."

They were each given a separate room. Evanar was disappointed, but not surprised, when Gremulkin told one of the mariners to watch him. He was not going to be left alone.

Evanar closed the door behind them. "You might as well sit down," he said, nodding towards a chair.

"I'll have a look around first," the man replied. He was a hefty man, a hand taller than Evanar, with skin reddened by constant exposure to the sun and wind, wearing heavy canvas culottes and a blue shirt under a leather jerkin.

A small area of the room was partitioned off in one corner. The seaman peered around the partition, and then walked around the room, opening drawers and cupboards; once he was satisfied, he sat on the chair nearest to the door. Evanar looked behind the partition and saw a large copper tub raised above the floor on some bricks. It had a spout coming out of the wall with a pump handle above it.

Evanar poked his head around the screen. "Do you know how to work this thing?" he asked the seaman.

The man sighed and got up. "I can see you haven't done anything for yourself before." He entered the small space and went over to the pump. "You have to pump the water in," he said as he demonstrated by lifting the lever and pressing it down. After a clank and a spitting noise, a gush of water came out of the spout. "See, it's simple. Any fool could work it."

Evanar managed to control his temper at this lack of respect. He couldn't get on the wrong side of any of them because he never knew who might be persuaded to help him eventually. "Thank you," he said. He went over to the pump and pumped some more water into the tub. "It's very cold," he said to the seaman.

The man came back to the tub, kneeled down and looked underneath, and then he stood up, wiping his hands on his trousers. "You could heat it up if there was any wood in the firebox, but it looks as if you're out of luck; box's empty."

"Isn't there any by the fireplace?" Evanar asked. He followed the other man back to the main room. There was none there either. "I suppose I'll have to bathe in cold water, then." He reluctantly went back to pumping.

There was a knock on the door. Evanar went out to see who it was. The seaman had already opened it to admit Dominel, who was holding a pile of clothing. "This is the best I could find, My Lord," he apologized. "There's some towels to dry yourself and some soap as well."

"Splendid, Dominel. I'm very grateful."

"Is there anything else you need, Sir?"

"I don't suppose you could find some firewood?"

"Coming right up, sir," Dominel replied. "There's plenty in the room at the end of the hall if you run out." He looked pointedly at the seaman as he said this, but the man stared straight ahead as if he hadn't heard.

When Dominel returned with the wood, he asked, "Would you like me to try and get those boots clean, My Lord?"

"I don't want to put you out, my friend; I'm sure you have a lot to do. I'll give them a rub with my dirty clothes. But thank you for offering."

"I hope you're not up to something," the seaman said when the old man had gone.

"You saw the whole transaction. Did you detect anything suspicious?"

The seaman shook his head. "You never know," he replied. "Why don't you go and finish cleaning up?" he added.

The door opened minutes later and Gremulkin looked in. "Are you ready, My Lord?" he asked, a touch of mockery in his tone.

"I'm almost finished," Evanar replied. He came out from behind the screen and sat down on the bed to wipe the dirt off his boots with his dirty undershirt. He felt so much better now, even though the clothes brought by the old man were not up to his usual standard; brown wool culottes with a blue cotton tunic, some stockings and some clean under-drawers. He'd even included a thick wool cloak. Evanar had torn a length of braid from his old tunic and used it to tie back his wet hair. Once the boots were as clean as he could make them, he put them on and tied the laces. "There!" He stood up. "Ready to go."

"This way, My Lord," Gremulkin said in a friendlier tone than he'd been using recently.

Barengush was waiting by the door scowling and rattling the door latch. "At last!" he growled. *He really should learn to control himself.*

Outside, a stiff wind was blowing through the pines. Evanar was grateful for the cloak and pulled the hood over his wet hair. The dark sky above them sparkled with stars that provided little illumination, making the torches carried by Dominel and Barengush necessary, even with the wind making the flames flutter and waft incessantly, threatening to extinguish them as any moment.

The three men, accompanied by the two seamen, followed Dominel across the yard to the large building where the Grand Wizard was waiting. It was constructed of granite blocks, rows of narrow windows on three levels, and a tower on the right side. Not a very attractive building but imposing in its own way. There had once been flowerbeds and shrubs along the front, but they were now shriveled up and brown. *It's a pity,* Evanar thought; *they would have done a lot to soften the bleakness of the building,*

When they reached the door, Dominel asked them, "Do you wish me to go up with you and announce you?"

"I know the way," Barengush replied curtly.

Dominel climbed up the steps to the double doors and held one open for them to pass through. Inside the building was almost as gloomy as the outside. Evanar couldn't even tell the color of the walls in the light provided by one sconce. It was a little better after the old man lit a few more from his torch. The walls were covered in cream tiles, which showed paler patches where hangings had been removed. The only decoration now was a border of blue tiles at elbow height. The floor looked as if it hadn't been swept or washed in months, and the wall tiles were stained with soot and other marks that looked ominously like blood in some spots.

"This way," Dominel said, heading for the staircase. He started climbing the stairs in front of them, breathing heavily from the exertion. At the top of the first flight, he paused to rest.

"We'll be here all night at this rate," Barengush grouched. "I just told you I know the way. You can go."

"As you wish. I'll bid you good night now, if there's nothing else." He bowed to Evanar, and mumbled "My lord." but ignored the others.

Evanar noticed the old man's lack of respect for Barengush and Gremulkin; he'd never once used an honorific when addressing either of them. He wondered if they'd noticed.

By the time they reached the fourth floor, Evanar and Barengush were out of breath. Evanar knew the reason for his own lack of stamina; he'd been confined to the cabin for weeks and allowed very little exercise. Most of the time, he'd been chained to the bedframe with a chain long enough for him to get food and water, and use the makeshift latrine.

Barengush went first and knocked on the door, and then he opened it and called out, "We're here, father," sounding as if he was unsure of his welcome.

"You two can wait in the hall for us," Gremulkin told the two seamen. "We won't need you for a while."

"Come inside and shut that blasted door before I freeze to death," a voice from within called

Good to see you, too, Evanar thought and grinned. It appeared Barengush was a chip off the old block; he could see now where he got his temperament.

His first view of the grand wizard surprised him. He couldn't have been much older than Valdor and, were it not for his scowl, he would have been quite handsome. He wore his straw-colored hair shoulder-length, his features were well proportioned, a wide, thin-lipped mouth, a straight narrow nose and a high forehead; his eyes were dark, although in the dim room light, it was hard to tell their color. Barengush didn't resemble his father where looks were concerned, although he might have looked more attractive without the constant sour expression or mocking smirk on his face.

"Come closer; let me get a look at you," the grand wizard said, beckoning with an elegant hand. They approached the big table behind which he sat, Barengush a bit more slowly than Gremulkin and Evanar. "So, we meet again, my friend," he said to Gremulkin. "Welcome home. You've done a remarkable job in Trethawynd, and in such a short time. Sit down and be welcome," he added.

"It is an honor to serve, My Lord." Gremulkin replied, pulling out a chair from the table and sitting.

"Barengush, will you stop fidgeting. I'll deal with you in a moment. I just want to greet our guests first."

Evanar almost felt sorry for the young man, obnoxious though he was. He wondered if his father always humiliated him in public. It might account for some of his behavior. He must always be trying to win his father's approval.

"Welcome to ValkonenMaa, your lordship."

Evanar neither smiled nor replied; he merely moved his head down and up, once.

"You seem displeased, sir."

"That's putting it rather mildly," Evanar replied. "How would you respond if someone killed your father, utterly destroyed your home and massacred your entire household, then locked you up in a flea ridden cabin for weeks without any decent food, no means of performing the most basic hygiene, and no news? I don't have the slightest idea what is happening out there," he nodded towards a window. "Wouldn't you be a little 'displeased'?" Evanar watched the grand wizard's face as he spoke. He didn't seem the least bit put out by Evanar's outburst, apart from a quick movement of his eyes towards Gremulkin and back to Evanar, his expression didn't change from its look of bland indifference.

"Yes, well, we'll have to talk about that another time. We shall meet again very soon, and discuss what plans we have in store for you. For now, you may go back to your quarters while I discuss some important matters with Gremulkin and my son."

With fists clenched, Evanar tried hard to hide his feelings, his anger and outrage at being brushed off so casually. It added insult to injury after what he'd been through and what they may still 'have in store for him'. Without another word, he turned and made for the door. He knew he must look almost as disgruntled as the young wizard.

Before he closed the door, he heard the grand wizard say, "Well! Come over here and sit down, Barengush. I think you've got some explaining to do."

Felindra

Felindra was accommodated in a bare, narrow room on the ground floor of one of the smaller buildings. She found out from the old man who seemed to be the only servant in the place, at least the only one she'd seen, that this room had been a store room, which he'd cleaned up and furnished with a narrow cot and small table. He'd also put an old, threadbare rug on the floor by the bed so that she wouldn't have to put her feet on the bare stone floor. In addition, he'd supplied her with some clean clothes to wear—female undergarments, woolen culottes and shirt, with some comfortable stockings and leather slippers. Although the garments were a little on the large side, they were comfortable and kept her relatively warm. He'd even sneaked in a few books for her to read to alleviate the boredom of being alone all day, locked in and not allowed outside. She kept those hidden under the mattress. He brought her meals three times a day and kept her water pitcher filled.

She was slumped on the bed, reading one of the books in the light of a small oil lamp on the table beside her, when she heard a noise in the hallway outside her room. It sounded like several people coming towards her door. She detected at least two male voices, although she couldn't make out what they were saying. She quickly concealed the book under her blanket and leaned back with her eyes closed, taking deep breaths to ease her sudden fear. She sighed with relief and relaxed when they went past her door, wondering who they were and what they were doing here.

She got up and looked out the window. The rain had stopped, but there was nothing to see except the wall and the dense evergreen forest beyond. The starry sky did little to alleviate the gloom. Occasionally, she heard a dog bark and wished she could touch it. It wasn't Ashala, but she really needed to talk to some creature, and dogs, though not as intelligent as wolves, were good companions. *Oh Ashala,* she mourned, *are you all right? I miss you so much. I don't know what they're going to do to me. Why do they keep me locked up all the time? What do they want from me?*

She went back to the bed and retrieved her book. It was a scientific treatise on celestial navigation, not very interesting to her, but it would probably fascinate Darson. She wasn't interested in things related to sailing and the sea, especially after her recent experience, and wondered why the old man had picked it for her. He may not be able to read, she realized. Maybe he'd chosen it because of the illustrations. She'd have to ask him if he could find a book about animals.

Her eyes blurred and her head sank to her pillow. She was almost asleep when she heard a gentle knock on the door. She recognized the old man's knock. "Come in!" she called.

"How are you tonight, Miss Felindra?" he asked as he poked his head around the door.

"I shouldn't complain, Dominel, especially with you taking such good care of me, but I wish I could go outside. I miss talking to the creatures in the woods. Anything interesting happening?"

He came in and shut the door, then carried a metal jug of water over and placed it on the table beside her. "I can't help you to go outside," he said regretfully, "but I do have some news." He beamed as if he was offering her a delectable treat. "Some new people arrived today.

"I thought I heard people going by my door. Anybody interesting?"

He nodded and leaned closer to her. "One of them is Lord Evanar, the Duke's youngest son," he whispered. "He was in a terrible mess, just like you were when you arrived here. I had to bring him new clothes and help him fill the tub for bathing. I don't know how long they've been keeping him prisoner, but they haven't been taking very good care of him. He's nothing but skin and bones, poor fellow."

"So now they have two hostages," Felindra said thoughtfully. "I wonder what they are going to do with us." She thought for a moment and then continued. "If you overhear anything, you will let me know, won't you, Dominel? I can't bear not knowing what's happening."

"That I will. Would you like me to tell Lord Evanar you are here? Maybe I it would cheer him up to know there's someone from home nearby." He picked up her empty water container, and then hesitated. "Two others arrived with his lordship: someone called Gremulkin—nasty-looking fellow—and the grand wizard's son, Barengush. He didn't look too good either, apparently he's been wounded, but he's always a grumpy one, even when there's nothing wrong."

Felindra nodded. "That's interesting. Thank you, Dominel. And be careful; I'd hate you to get into trouble. I've seen how nasty they can be. Light protect you."

48 – Inspection tours

Haro

Andro's team was about twelve leagues north of Bailuchi, approaching the town of Spartis, when they came across a remarkable sight. A whole meadow had been turned into an impromptu settlement. At first, it looked as if a fair was being held, but as they got closer, it became apparent that it was not a place of celebration and trade, but more the scene of grief and loss. Canvas tents had been set up in three neat rows, and a small wooden building constructed near the entrance to the field. When Andro saw several women in long blue robes and white veils among the dejected people, he realized it was run by Sisters of the Light. The sisters were originally an offshoot of the League of Light, but they had opted for independence when they decided to admit lay people and non-mages, to their organization.

"Refugees," Sir Baramen declared.

"It looks like it. Let's go and talk to them," Andro replied. "They'll probably have some useful information."

The team dismounted and walked along the rough path into the field. "Spread out and talk to the refugee, see what you can find out," Andro told the men and women of the team.

Andro decided to talk to one of the Sisters and looked around for a likely candidate. He spotted one woman who stood out from the others; she was tall and poised, with an air of authority, as if she knew what she was doing and would do it with diligence and devotion.

"Excuse me, Sister, I'm Commander Andro Haro of the League of Light and this is Sir Baramen in the duke's service. My colleagues and I are on a fact-finding mission for the Duke of Trethawynd. Would you care to give us some information about what's happening on the East Coast?"

She shaded her eyes from the sun with her hand as she looked at him. "Well met, Commander Haro. I'm Sister Clarony. Would you care to go somewhere less exposed? The sun is very hot today."

They went to sit on a wooden bench by a table sheltered under a tarpaulin-draped wooden frame.

"I'm going to see what I can find out from the refugees," Baramen said. "An honor to meet you sister." He bowed and wandered off in the direction of the tents.

"Water?" Sister Clarony asked, pointing to a covered jug on the table. Andro nodded and she half-filled two mugs and gave one to him.

"Thank you, Sister." He gulped down half the mug's contents, in spite of the water being lukewarm. "How long have you been here with this camp?"

"Two weeks. Our local headquarters are in Spartis. Once we became aware of the plight of these poor souls and saw how many there were—the numbers were increasing by the day—we knew we must do something to ease their misery."

Andro nodded. "What will happen to these people?" He looked around at the milling throng, old and young, men and women, and most of all, children. Some of them showed signs of injuries with bandages, scars and bruises on their arms and faces; some used staves to support them as they hobbled around on one leg because the other leg was disabled in some way. He even saw an old woman being wheeled around in a wheelbarrow, and several lying on pallets, in the shade of tents.

"It's hard to say. If ... *when* we win this conflict, they will be able to go back to their homes, but even if they do, they will have lost their harvest and will have to rely on other sources for food and fodder. The majority of them are grain farmers, who aren't known for their great wealth. It is very hard for them. We can show them how to cultivate food plants that grow through the winter, and in addition, we will provide them with seeds and tools. But that will only be possible when they get back to their own farms. Some of them find temporary work here, helping local farmers with their harvests.

"We'll advise the Monastery and the duke of these problems, and maybe they can contribute to your efforts."

"Thank you captain. We already receive some support from the Monastery, but we can always use more." She stood up and smoothed her robe. "Would you like to walk around with me? There is so much to do; I daren't take too many breaks." She started towards a large tent close by. "Another thing we provide is a healers' tent where we treat injuries and illnesses. But there's one injury—the most serious, in my opinion—that doesn't respond easily to treatment, that's the wound to their souls."

"That's true, unfortunately," Haro replied. He knew from firsthand experience. "If I would not be in the way, I'd be grateful for a brief tour to see what you're up against."

"What's your background, commander?" she asked as they walked towards a big tent on the other side of the entrance.

"I was a defender in the last conflict, and then I bought some land and started breeding horses while I raised my family. It was a beautiful farm; we were very happy there."

"You say 'were'. What happened?"

"We were attacked one night. They killed almost all of our horses and burned down our home. We didn't have the resources to rebuild. That was the second attack and we'd barely recovered from the first one. So I went back to the Monastery to see if I could help."

"I hear so many stories like that, sadly. I hope your family is safe."

"Oh, yes, I made sure of that. You can replace buildings, but nothing can replace a child. They're at the Monastery."

She stopped outside a larger tent. "Here we are; this is our healers' tent. I have to check on some things here if you'd like to come with me."

One side of the tent was rolled up, leaving it open to allow natural daylight and fresh air to enter. Four pallets lay at the far end—only two of them occupied— while at the front were some stools and a table holding implements of the healer's trade, including jars of salves and bottles of potions. One man was sitting by the table attended by a female healer who was carefully cleaning what appeared to be burns on the man's legs.

"Good morning, Serily. Do you mind if I speak to him?"

The healer shook her head and asked the patient, "You don't mind, do you?"

He looked at them, then back at the healer. "Whatever you will, my lady."

"I told you, Afran, you don't have to call me that. I'm just a healer." She nodded to Clarony and Andro.

"I'm Sister Clarony, and this is Commander Haro from the Monastery. Would you like to tell us what happened?"

Afrin winced as Serily dabbed his injured leg with cleaning solution. "That stings ... took me by surprise," he said. "I was cutting grass in my hay field. Suddenly fire came streaming out of nowhere and set it all alight. It was like magic. It burned so fast, I ran to the gate of the field as quick as I could, but

422

my legs still got burnt." He looked down at his legs, which appeared to have lost a whole layer of skin, from the knees down, leaving them raw and oozing.

"Did you see or hear anything else?" Andro asked.

"I could hear some devilish babble, then a man saying, 'That's enough, let's get out of here'." The man thought for a moment, frowning. "He had a funny accent, maybe Valkonen."

"They didn't do any other damage?"

"No. you see, a band of defenders arrived. That's what frightened them off."

"What about your family, no one else hurt?"

"No. My mother didn't even know anything was happening until she saw the smoke and flames in the field."

"Why did you leave?"

"I didn't want anything to happen to my mother. She's not very old, but she has arthritis and doesn't get around so good. We'd been hearing rumors about attacks on farms, people being killed, buildings set on fire. They take the livestock and all the food they can find. We brought our cow and the donkey with us. We haven't got much else to lose."

"Thank you, Afrin. Light bless you."

Sister Clarony took him to the other end of the tent where a corner was screened off. They could hear a woman moaning softly and gasping for breath. "How's it coming, Jinna?"

"Not long now," a woman's voice responded.

"The young lady behind the screen is having a baby," Clarony explained. She gestured to the two occupied pallets one was a woman who appeared to be sleeping. The other a boy of about fifteen with his leg splinted and covered with bandages.

"How's the leg, Van?"

The boy shrugged. "I don't hurt so bad now I got the medicine. I wish I didn't have to lie here. I want to go outside."

"What happened to you?" Andro asked.

"It was stupid. My brother and me climbed up into the loft in the barn when we heard the people screaming. We could see out through a hole in the wall. A lot of them little demons running around with spears and a man in black clothes telling them what to do. They had a cart and were filling it up with all our merchandise, bags of corn and beans, smoked meat, oil; they was taking everything. They tied up old Corsovin and his wife and shoved them into the trees by the road, and then they started setting fire to everything. When they got to the barn and set it off, we waited for them to leave and got out of there. But we couldn't get to the ladder to climb down, so we had to jump. That's when I broke my leg. My brother had to drag me out; I couldn't walk!" He finished on an indignant high note.

"Where's your brother now?"

Van waved towards the opening. "He's out there somewhere, probably looking for girls." He sounded disgusted.

"Was this your farm?"

"No. It was the merchant's place. We just worked there."

"What happened to them, the owners?"

"We found them in the woods and untied them. Old Corsovin had a bruise as big as an apple on the side of his head, but I don't think the old woman was hurt. She was squawking like a hanging turkey, though. We untied them and helped them get their other cart, the one they kept in a shed in the woods, and came here."

"So everyone got away alive, that's the main thing," Sister Clarony said. "I expect you'll be able to get out of here after midday—we'll give you a staff for support—but you do need to rest for a while, get your strength up."

They went back outside where Andro thanked the sister and went to find Sir Baramen and round up the team. It was approaching midday and they needed to move on.

49 – Felindra Tested

Felindra heard the footsteps of several people coming along the passage and quickly tucked the book she'd been reading under the mattress. A key rattled in the lock and the door crashed open revealing the two people she least wanted to see, Barengush and his father, Monaltor. She wasn't too upset to see Barengush looking pale and decidedly uncomfortable. He looked as if he'd lost some weight since she'd seen him last.

"Come with us!" Monaltor ordered.

"Where?" Felindra asked.

"We'll ask the questions. And stop wasting my time."

Felindra sat on the edge of her cot and put her boots on, and then she grabbed her cape. There was no telling where they might be taking her, so she might as well be prepared for whatever was to come.

They led her out of the building, but instead of going to the main building where Monaltor had his office, they continued past it and through some piles of rubble to a small field surrounded by a crude fence, packed with horses. Nearby, she noticed several burnt out buildings that had not been cleared and wondered if they ever intended to finish clearing the rubble from their attack.

She returned her attention to the horses. They milled around nervously, kicking and snapping at one another, radiating an atmosphere of stress and extreme discomfort. There was an overpowering stench of urine and feces. The droppings had been trampled into foul-smelling slurry, soaking into the hay that had been thrown in for fodder. She was sickened by the sight, close to tears, but too angry to let them show. She turned to Monaltor. "How can you leave them like this? They need more room. You can't overcrowd horses like this. Don't you know anything? They need space to move around in and exercise. Can't you see their food is being fouled with their droppings? Look at them, they're so stressed out, being packed in like this, it's a wonder they haven't broken out and gone on a rampage."

"We didn't bring you here to listen to your opinions," Monaltor snarled. "We want to see what you can do with your power. Go closer and talk to them!"

Felindra looked around and spotted a clump of grass out of reach of the horses. She pulled up a handful and went over to the fence. She chose a small filly that was being squeezed against the barrier by a large stallion, and put the grass under her nose. Instead of taking it, the horse snorted and tossed her head. Before she could prevent it, the stallion leaned over and grabbed the grass from her hand. Felindra put her hand on the filly's neck. It flinched, but couldn't get away from her. She stroked it gently and whispered, "Don't be afraid. I won't hurt you. How do you feel?"

Waves of fear and pain emanated from the animal, and a yearning to get out and move about. She felt closed in, almost suffocating. She was hungry, too. Being small was a disadvantage when competing for food.

She turned angrily to Monaltor, fighting back tears. "What kind of people are you? These animals are suffering. They're hungry and frightened, and they're in pain. You have to give them more space! They are getting to breaking point. If you leave them like this much longer, they'll start killing one another."

Without thinking, she rushed forward, grabbed the iron bar that held the gate shut and snapped it sideways to open it. The animals burst out of the enclosure like timber being released from a logjam. Barengush and Monaltor were so completely startled, they barely managed to dodge aside and avoid being trampled. As the horses ran past her, Felindra noticed some of them were limping and others had bloody patches on their coats. She watched them scatter throughout the grounds of the monastery and wondered if the gates were open so they could escape into the forest.

She was frightened when, she realized what she'd done. Oh, Light, help me. I did the right thing, didn't I? And I'm not sorry.

Once the horses had all departed and they could reach her again, Monaltor and Barengush rushed over and grabbed her by the arms. "What have you done, you stupid little wretch? You'll pay for this. How are we going to get them back?"

"Ouch, you're hurting me," she said, trying to free her arms. "I won't stand by and see the Light's creatures suffering. You're the ones who should be punished for the way you were treating them. If you make them a more inviting place to rest, they'll come back." She tried once more to pry Barengush's hands from her wrist, then she looked up and saw a brief grin twitch his lips and he let her go.

"So you're the expert, are you?" Monaltor sneered. "Think you know better than your elders and betters."

"In this case I do," Felindra replied defiantly. "I know how they feel. I can *feel* what they feel. They need room to exercise, they need to be washed, and they need clean fresh food."

"Come on, we've got work to do." With his steely grip on her arm, Monaltor dragged her back to the main building, where he stopped and looked around. "Barengush, go and round up some men to get those horses under control, then get a small animal and bring it to the lab."

"Are you going to try to put them back in that enclosure?" Felindra asked.

Monaltor turned on her, smoldering with rage, and thumped her hard in the face with his closed fist, sending her reeling. She would have fallen if he hadn't been holding onto her. She was stunned, too shocked to react at first. No one had ever hit her before. She hadn't even considered such a possibility. Then she felt the pain. Her cheekbone throbbed, sending burning pain throughout her face and ear. Even her teeth hurt. She raised her free hand to her cheek and felt something sticky. When she withdrew her fingers, there was blood on them. This time, she was unable to fight back the tears.

Monaltor threw open the door of the building and dragged her inside. "Come on, stop dragging your feet," he snarled. "Because of your stupid behavior, I'm behind schedule. Up the stairs."

She stumbled up the stairs after him, followed by the two guards who'd been in the background all the time she was out of doors.

Felindra said nothing, recalling her resolution to avoid letting them see any weakness.

He finally let go of her arm and let her move under her own power. She had no illusions that he did it for her sake. He probably felt uncomfortable dragging her around and was satisfied he'd made his point. He was in charge. *For the moment,* she thought, *but he'll find out...*

When they reached the second floor, Monaltor turned left into a wide corridor with doors at intervals along its length. He glanced over his shoulder once to make sure she was still with him. *As if I had a choice,"* she thought bitterly. She comforted herself with the thought of what Ashala would make of him. *Forgive me, Light, I know I shouldn't be vindictive, but there are limits, and one is hurting blameless animals.*

He unlocked the third door from the staircase and entered the room, waiting for her to follow. "You two wait out here," he told the two guards as he closed the door.

Still cradling her bruised cheek in her hand, Felindra glanced around the room and found it looked much like the others, although the furniture had been arranged in some sort of order. One notable element was a work bench, about waist-high to an adult, upon which were arranged a variety of what looked like laboratory equipment; mortars and pestles, flasks, a couple of spirit burners, and several glass contraptions she couldn't identify. There were still some books on the shelves around the room, but far fewer than in the other rooms. Instead of books, many shelves contained arcane pieces of equipment for what purpose she couldn't guess, but she had a feeling they didn't bode well for the objects of their use, man or beast.

"Sit down over there," Monaltor order her, waving his hand towards a wooden armchair standing next to a heavy table apparently being used as a desk, given the untidy piles of papers and implements scattered on its surface.

She sat down warily, dreading what was going to come next. She held her palm over the swelling that had developed on her cheekbone. It still throbbed, but the warmth of her hand was comforting. *It probably needs something cold to reduce the swelling.* She felt so helpless. She watched the wizard walk along the shelves and pick out a few things, among them a handful of wires with disks attached to their ends.

"While we're waiting for my son," Monaltor said. "I'm going to run a few tests." He brushed aside some of the papers on the table and put the equipment in their place.

Felindra's heart began to race. She licked her dry lips and tried to summon up some saliva for her parched throat. She wiggled back in the chair, as if she could put some distance between them. "What sort of tests?"

"Just keep quiet and let me get on with this," he snarled. "And stop fidgeting. He attached some of the wires to screws on the outside of a square wooden box, and then brought the other ends over to her and tried to attach them to her scalp. "Dammit, too much hair. I'll have to cut it out of the way."

"You can't cut my hair," she shrieked, trying to stand up and get away from him. "Leave me alone!" He was blocking her way with his body and she didn't have a hope of getting past him, so she put her arms up to protect her head.

"Sit still and don't keep making a fuss!" he said coldly. "When you make trouble for me, you make trouble for yourself." He took a dagger from his belt and tested its edge. Not satisfied, he went over to the bench and scrabbled around for a whetstone.

The moment he took his eyes off her, Felindra was out of the chair and across the room to the door. She pulled it open and came face to face with the two men guarding it.

"It's no good trying to run away," Monaltor said, applying the side of the blade to the stone. "Bring her back," he ordered the guards, "And one of you stay here to hold her still."

She watched warily from her seat, with the guard's hand firmly on her shoulder, as the wizard continued sharpening the blade. Finally, he seemed satisfied tested it by slashing a sheet of paper. He wiped the blade on the paper and turned his attention back to her. "Hold her still, now ... hold her head! This won't take long."

Before he could go continue, they heard a dog barking outside in the hallway. From the high pitch of its yelps, Felindra assumed it was either a very young dog, or a small breed. Barengush entered the room holding a squirming puppy in his arms. "Will this do?" he asked.

Monaltor gave him a sour look. "Are they getting the horses back?" he asked, ignoring his son's question.

"I got as many men as I could find," Barengush replied. "What are you doing?"

"I'll ask the questions," Monaltor snapped. He turned to Felindra. "We can finish this later. You go and wait outside the door," he added to the guards.

"What do you want me to do with this creature?" Barengush asked.

"Let her hold it." Once the dog was in Felindra's arms, he continued. "Remember what I told you?" With a sigh, Barengush nodded his head. "All right, get ready. And don't get carried away!"

Felindra wasn't paying much attention to the wizard's conversation with his son; she was busy comforting the puppy after Barengush's rough handling. It was responding with tail wags and licks wherever it could find some bare skin. She was surprised when Barengush stepped behind her and placed his hands firmly on her head. "What are you doing? Don't touch me!" She tried to shake him off, but his grip was too strong, his fingers were digging into her scalp and tangled in her hair.

"Sit still and do as I say," Monaltor ordered her in a tone that brooked no dissent. "Now, talk ... or whatever you do ... to the animal."

Felindra didn't see any harm in this. Holding it gently between her hands she started to send out mental feelers to the dog's mind along with a sense of well-being, which was difficult, considering her circumstances.

Suddenly, she sensed something alien in her head as if insects were crawling around her brain and burrowing on her mind. Pressure built up inside her skull until she lost all sense of the animal in her lap and its frenzied yelps. The pressure increased to the point where she felt as if her head would explode. When she tried to push back, to force it out, a massive shock careened through her, like a flash of lightening. She screamed and everything faded into darkness.

50 – Return to Trethawynd

Imali

The royal carrier was indeed a big ship, approximately twice the size of the one on which they had arrived in the capital. It had three great masts, two equipped with double sails, and a main mast carrying three. The horses and all their supplies we stowed below deck where cabins for the crew were also located. The officers and Imali's team were accommodated in airy cabins along the middle of the deck.

The queen's defenders disembarked at Pershoni, on the border between Trethawynd and the southern Duchy of Yoldys. They intended to ride across country to the Monastery and review the situation in the south. They left behind one of the supply wagons, half the horses and two grooms to travel with Imali back to the Monastery.

***

Imali and his team rode through the gates of the Monastery just before noon five days after leaving the ship at Bailuchi. They left the wagons, horses and extra grooms in care of the stable master. Imali and the two knights went straight to the palace. Word of their arrival had already reached the duke and he was waiting for them with Commander Peshanar and Sir Arvand in his private meeting room on the fourth floor.

"Welcome home. I understand you had a successful mission," Duke Valdor greeted them. "Sit down, help yourselves to a drink, and tell me about your trip."

"First, Your Grace," Imali said, after helping himself to some fruit juice. "I have this letter from the Queen. I don't know what it contains, but I believe it will answer many of your questions." He handed the sealed document to Valdor, who broke the seal with his ceremonial dagger, unfolded it and spread it on the table before him.

The five men waited while he read the two-page letter, observing his expression change from smile to frown and then become passive. Once he had finished, he looked up and smiled at them. "Well, apart from the news about the Ambassador Tovina, it looks promising. I suppose we'll have to appoint another ambassador now, so if any of you have any suggestions, I'd be glad to hear them" *It would be an ideal post for my brother,* Valdor thought, *if only...*

Sir Arvand spoke up first. "I take it the Queen is sending help, Your Grace?"

"Yes, Arvand, she certainly is." He turned to Imali. "Would you like to tell me about the ones who travelled with you?"

Imali gave a quick summary in answer to the duke's question.

"So, until the main body arrives, I take it the ones who came with you are acting independently." Duke Valdor said.

"It appears that way, but once they arrive here, I expect they will fall in line with our defenses. Did the Queen give any details of the additional help we can expect? The Lord Chancellor alluded to forthcoming resources."

"Indeed, she did," Duke Valdor replied. "She is preparing to send a whole company of Royal Defenders, to be led by the prince consort, Prince Felidorn, himself. She also pledges to see that they are fully equipped. In addition, she is putting two patrol boats and their crews at our disposal to patrol the east and west coasts. We can also expect a small amount of gold to help cover our expenses."

"That sounds like a good contribution," Sir Arvand commented. "I expect all our own defenders will have to come under the prince's command."

"I believe so, but our League of Light defenders will probably remain more independent, and continue to be led by Commander Peshanar, working in coordination with the Royal Defenders. Having one central command is for the best in the long run, so that we can put up a coordinated response to these attacks, instead of fielding scattered groups acting independently."

"Is there any indication of when they will arrive, and how they will get here?" Daryan asked.

"According to the Queen's letter, they will be leaving the capital in five days and will march overland, which means they should reach the border of Trethawynd in about fifteen days, if all goes well."

51 – Felindra Detected

Ashavan

"What is it?" Daryan asked, alarmed at Ashavan's sudden recoil in the middle of their conversation.

Ashavan gasped in a deep breath, as if he'd been under water. "That was powerful; I'm surprised you didn't feel it," he replied. "A very powerful shock wave and I think it's connected to Felindra."

"What do you mean? Is she all right? Was it that accursed wizard?"

"No, not him. I think it came from her."

"Felindra? How could that be? Can you contact her and find out?"

"I'm trying." Ashavan closed his eyes and concentrated. After a couple of minutes, he shook his head. "No, I can't get through to her. They must be warding." He didn't tell Daryan what really alarmed him; it might have cost her life. *No, it couldn't be that; maybe she was just unconscious. It's reasonable after such a tremendous release of power. No, I'll leave it at that for now and hope I can reach her later.*

Ashala

Ashala raised her head with her ears pointed forward. She whined and let out a brief howl, and then stood up, shook her whole body and took off for the gate leading to Great Forest. It was time to go and find Felindra.

Monaltor

Monaltor gasped, still reeling from the shock, and darted across the room to check his son, who'd been thrown against the far wall. Assuring himself that Barengush was still alive, he opened the door and yelled at the guards, and then he turned to Felindra. She was lying on the floor where she had landed after the power surge—the little dog cowered beside her, licking her face and whining softly. Felindra was unconscious as well. *Damn,* he thought, *what in the depths happened? Which of them was responsible? If the girl has a power like that...* He was at a loss for a response to that possibility. *It's enough that she has the gift of Whispering, but if she has the power of* Repel *as well, nobody will be able to control her. But if she does have Repel, why didn't she use it to protect herself before, when they took her? It doesn't make sense; you can't suddenly acquire new powers. I'm going to have to tell Ogryn about this, if indeed, she was responsible. I can't imagine Barengush causing it and harming himself.* "Get help," he yelled.

Two guards and several mages answered his call. The mage who entered the room first, looked from one body to the other. "What happened?" he asked. "Are they dead?"

"No, they're not dead. And I don't have time for idle chatter. Three of you take my son to my office. The rest of you, take the prisoner to her room and make sure the door is locked when you leave. Fergon, you guard her door; I don't want any more trouble from her. I'll deal with her later." *If I can,* he added to himself. *Who knows what we are dealing with here?*

52 – Felindra's New Gift

Felindra returned to consciousness with a ferocious headache. She slowly turned her head to see where she was, but the pain flashed so powerfully, it all but blinded her. *What the...? Oh, Light help me, I can't move!* She realized she was going to be sick. She took several deep breaths to quell the nausea as her mouth filled with saliva. *Get up. Find bowl.* Summoning every iota of willpower she could muster, she placed one hand on the mattress and slowly pushed herself up, and then swung her legs around to the floor. She pressed her fingertips into her temples, but it didn't help. The nausea was worse now that she'd moved. She knew she couldn't prevent herself from vomiting, but Lord, not on the floor. She saw her washbowl on the table less than a pace away and gently raised herself up until she could stand, and then lunged towards it and gripped the bowl with both hands, just as her stomach erupted. She vomited until there was nothing left to come up but a bitter taste. When she bent to put the bowl on the floor, a flash of agony smashed into her head, causing her lose her grip. She slowly raised herself, tears flooding down her face. She picked up a cloth and wet in the water pitcher to wipe her face.

Oh, Light, what can I do? I've made such a mess, and now I need to drink something. Her drinking cup was at the other end of the table. She moved a pace to her left to grasp it, and then passed it to her right hand and dipped it in the water pitcher, knowing she wouldn't have the strength to pick up the pitcher.

Why do I feel so awful? She staggered back to her bed and sat down to drink the water, hoping it wouldn't make her sick again. She wanted to lie down, but she was still holding the cup, and she knew from her previous experience with the bowl that it would be agony to bend and put it on the floor, so she took another couple of sips, and lay down with it still in her hand.

She must have slept after that, because the next thing she knew was sound of the key turning in the door. She opened her eyes a crack and peered through her lids. The door opened and she saw the one person she didn't want to encounter at this moment, Monaltor.

"What's that appalling smell?" he walked farther into the room, saw the bowl, and then turned around and went out again. "She's been sick," he said to someone outside. "Get that mess out of here, and then send the healer."

"What's wrong with you?" He scowled at her from the doorway, not sounding the least sympathetic. "You're no use to us if you're sick."

436

Felindra felt so ill, she abandoned caution. "I don't want to be useful to you," she said in a low, raspy voice. "Why don't you leave me alone?" She closed her eyes again and rested her forearm over them.

"You're going to have to change your attitude, girl, or we may have to take more stringent actions with you. We've treated you well so far, hoping you would cooperate willingly. We gave you a comfortable room with a proper bed and everything you need, when you could be sleeping on filthy straw in a cold dungeon. Any more nonsense like this ... releasing the horses and what you did to my son ... and you will be moved. Your food won't be as edible down there either, what you'd get of it.

I wish he would just shut up and go away. Tears pressed painfully at her eyelids, exacerbating the pounding in her head. *I've never felt so sick in my life. Oh, mami, I wish you were here. All I want is to be back with to my family. Light, help me ... please help me.*

"What's the problem, Grand Wizard?"

Felindra opened her eyes halfway and saw a man with long white hair in the doorway.

"Ask her," Monaltor replied.

The man crossed the room and stopped beside her bed. "You don't look very well," he said, clearly not averse to stating the obvious. "What's the problem?" He sounded gruff and not very friendly or sympathetic.

Felindra cleared her throat. "My head hurts, and I've been sick."

"What have you been doing?"

This questioned puzzled Felindra. "I don't know what you mean."

"Something must have caused it. I want to know what it was."

"I was in the lab with *him* and his son. The son was trying to read my mind, touching me when ... I don't know what it

437

was … I just felt pressure building up in my head, and then everything went blank. That's all I remember."

"So you lost consciousness. I see. Has this ever happened before?"

"No, never."

"Hmm. Well." He stroked his beard and closed his eyes for a moment. "Well, let me see…"

"Get on with it, man" Monaltor interrupted. "Can't you give her something? I need her to be fit."

"Right. Let me see what I can find." He placed a hand on each side of her head and closed his eyes again.

The smell of his breath, onions and fish, made the nausea return. "My bowl," she said. "I'm going to be sick again." The healer jumped away from her and looked around for a receptacle, but it was too late. She leaned over the side of the bed and vomited on the floor. This time she brought up mostly water and something yellow and extremely bitter.

"Oh, for Oglestra's sake, give her a potion." Monaltor was losing his patience, not that he ever had much to lose in Felindra's opinion. He was always in a hurry, complaining about wasting time, but giving no hint as to what was so important.

"Right," the healer responded. "I'll have to mix something. I don't have anything prepared."

"Well, get on with it."

Monaltor herded the healer out the door and followed him. "He'll be back," he said. "And I'll send that man to clean up."

Thank the light, Felindra thought, *that's one way to get rid of them.* She closed her eyes, trying to relax, and waited for Dominel. I hope he brings some water; I need to wash. What a mess!

Dominel arrived before the healer came back. He'd brought a clean bowl, also a mop and pail of water to clean the floor.

"I'm sorry to make such a mess," Felindra said. "If I wasn't feeling so awful; I'd clean it up myself."

"Don't you worry none, miss, I cleaned up worse than this. You just concentrate on getting better," Dominel said as he squeezed the water out of the mop. "What have they been doing to you?"

"Oh, they were doing some experiments and something went wrong. I may be the one who caused it. I think Monaltor's son was hurt worse than me."

"That's something. Not that I'd wish ill on anybody, but those people are accursed." He mopped over the already cleaned floor and then put the mop back in the bucket and carried it to the door. After placing it on the floor outside, he came back in. "I brought you a clean bowl so you can freshen up, but I'll have to fetch some more water. I'll get some clean blankets, too, while I'm at it, and some clothes. I'll be back in a few minutes."

**

Finally, they'd all gone. The potion the healer had given her was starting to relieve the pain and nausea; she'd had a good wash and was now resting in a clean bed. *Thank you, Light.*

Something had woken her from a soothing sleep. It wasn't a noise; it was more like ... Light! She opened her eyes and saw a woman in a dazzling white robe standing across the small room. Felindra wasn't afraid, just surprised. The woman glowed with warmth and compassion. Apart from her height, which well was above average, the thing that drew Felindra's attention most was the brilliant stone set in the silver band around her neck. It seemed to radiate light.

"Greetings, Felindra," the woman said in the most soothing voice she'd ever heard.

Have I passed on? Surely, she is not of this world.

"No," she said. "You are still in the material world."

Felindra sat up straighter and leaned back against the wall. "Who are you?"

"I am a servant of the Light, a messenger," she replied.

"Are you an angel?"

"No, I'm just a messenger."

"Where are you from?"

"I come from another level of existence, the plane you will reach once you relinquish your material raiment, but that is distant in time. What I have to tell you is about something much more immediate." Felindra listened with her lips parted and eyes wide. "You are a very special person, Felindra. You have been chosen for great things; that is why the Light has endowed you with special gifts." She smiled at her. "I see you are puzzled."

"Yes, um ... what can I call you?"

"My name is not important. You may call me Messenger."

"I'm wondering what gifts you are talking about. As far as I know, I only have one gift."

"Yes, I know, a very remarkable gift, by the way. It appears you have just manifested another gift, although you may not truly appreciate it yet, given your reaction to it. You have the gift of Repel. Using it is how you ended up in the state from which you are currently recovering."

"Repel? How does it work, what does it do? I don't think I want to use it if I end up this sick every time."

"It's a very useful gift to have when you are in perilous situations, when your survival is at stake. It needs training and practice, but unfortunately, that in itself requires a degree of endurance. The reason it affected you so strongly this time is that you were unaware that you had the gift and its use was unexpected. You reacted reflexively to something that your instincts perceived as threatening. Now that you are aware of it, you can learn to control it, but, as I said, you need to be trained. There are those at your Monastery who would be able to guide you."

"What sort of training?"

"You will have to learn how to control your mind through various exercises so that you can assess in a split second whether something is truly lethal and use the appropriate response. For example, your life was not in danger from the event this morning. You reacted from fear."

"What kind of exercise? Would I have to use the power?"

"No. The exercises are designed to train your mind and speed up your reaction times. It requires certain stimuli to which you learn to react swiftly and appropriately. The exercises are repetitive in order to hone your responses gradually until they become second nature to you. What else would you like to know?"

"You said I was chosen. What does that mean?"

"That will be revealed to you when the time comes."

"Are there any other ... chosen?'

"Not at this time."

"What am I supposed to do?"

"Just carry on with your life as it is until you are called." The Messenger drew closer. "May I touch you? Nothing I am about to do will cause you any discomfort."

Felindra believed that the person would not harm her, but was puzzled and intrigued by her intention. "Yes."

The Messenger rested her hand on the top of Felindra's head and a glorious feeling of warmth and peace flow through her. She stepped back. "You should feel much better now," she told Felindra. "I will also give you the gift of telepathy to help you in your current situation and throughout your chosen life journey." She took the sparkling gem between her palms and tilted her head forward, the light from the stone radiated from her hands, towards Felindra, reminder her of the League of Light symbol.

A warm, tingly feeling went through Felindra's mind, leaving a feeling of intense clarity, almost as if as if she had been seeing everything through a mist before and now it was cleared away. *I wonder if this is how all telepaths feel,* she thought in wonder. "Thank you, Messenger, I feel wonderful." Felindra smiled.

The messenger returned the smile and ducked her head. "I will leave you now, but remember that the Light will watch over you always. You are indeed blessed, Felindra." She turned towards the door and faded out of sight.

Felindra had a strange feeling of loss when she was gone. She lay for a moment, savoring the peace, the release from pain, and thinking about what she had told her. *Why me?* she wondered. *There's nothing special about me.* She thought about her life to this moment. She was an ordinary girl, not perfect by any means, although she knew her parents were good people, devoted to serving the Light. They had led her and her little brother in the direction of the Light, and everyone in her family had faith in Him. *Maybe that's what it takes, but there are thousands of people like me. I wonder if it has anything to do with my whispering gift.*

Enough of this; it's time to get up and do something. The only problem with feeling so good was being confined to this room. Felindra needed to be outside in the woods, among the creatures she loved and whom she considered her friends. She got up off the bed and looked around. I need a wash, she thought, and some clean clothes. The kind old man had brought a small wooden chest containing a variety of clean garments. She raised the lid and sorted through the contents, then pulled out some undergarments, a wool tunic with matching pants, and a pair of wool socks. She then filled the bowl with water, took off her soiled shift and washed herself thoroughly, and then quickly rubbed the cold water off with a clean cotton towel. Once she was dressed, she sat in the chair and wondered what to do next.

Felindra realized something was tugging faintly in her mind. She tried to focus on it, curious to find out what it was. After a moment, she realized she could hear a jumble of voices. *Am I going mad? Or could this be the telepathy the Messenger promised me? If it is, it's a bit confusing. What am I supposed to do? Maybe if I focus on one voice. No, I have a better idea!*

Felindra closed her eyes, gathered all her energy and willpower into linking with Ashala. Even before this new gift, they'd been able link without touching, but would it work over such a great distance?

53 – The Royal Council Meets

Queen Zenobia

Queen Zenobia looked around the table at her counselors, one by one. "As you are aware, our nation is again threatened by the Dark Brethren. They seem to have sunk their talons firmly into the two northern duchies, ValkonenMaa and Trethawynd. Every day, the situation grows worse. We can't have that. It hasn't reached Yoldys or the capital province yet, but if we don't act now and stop it before it gets worse, we could be next. I've called you here today to discuss what can be done to put an end to the situation. Marshal Tiburon, what are your thoughts on the matter?"

The marshal stood up and bowed to the Queen. "Your Majesty, we cannot leave the capital without adequate defenses, but I believe we could send a company of three hundred defenders to help in the north. Given the terrain and nature of the attacks, I don't think more would improve the situation. May I also suggest that we deploy four of our war ships to carry troops and materiel more rapidly to the troubled areas, and to deal with enemy shipping? I suggest one on the west coast and three on the east."

"Thank you Marshal." She turned to the chancellor. "What do you think, Lord Chancellor?"

"It depends, Your Majesty, on our goal in this conflict. I assume we want to wipe the Dark Brethren completely from Albasiny, or do we just want to put down the current rebellion?"

"We must get rid of them once and for all this time. Even if it means rooting them out of every mountain stronghold, cave and cellar in ValkonenMaa. It is only ... what, fifteen years? ... since their last incursion and they're back seemingly as strong as ever."

"In that case, Your Majesty," Chancellor Osgand continued, "We may need more defenders than Marshal Tiburon is offering."

Marshal Tiburon stood again. "If I may, Your Majesty, until we can assess the total situation—how many Trethawynd can be put into the field, and the full nature of the attackers' forces—it might be a little precipitous to send more than one company immediately. Once we have a better picture, we can increase the number of fighting men where they are required. It would take a little time to raise a larger force at this moment, but I believe we could have them ready in about two months, once we know how many are really needed. Not only do we have to bring in forces from other parts of the realm, we also have to supply them with weapons, food, transportation, and so on."

"That sounds reasonable to me," Queen Zenobia replied. "Now, Admiral Mushafa, are we able to have the ships ready that Marshal Tiburon suggested?"

The admiral bowed. "We could, Your Majesty. We have two ships patrolling the west coast, and another one in for repairs at this moment. Perhaps we should extend the patrols as far as ValkonenMaa, and refit the one that's in the shipyard for troop transport."

"How long would that take?" the Queen interrupted.

"At least three more weeks," the admiral replied. She nodded. "We have four ships currently plying the east coast which could be brought into port within days and used for transports. There are also six patrol boats, four of which could extend their range as far as ValkonenMaa immediately. Their crews could be augmented with more defenders and weapons."

"Very well. Excellent. We would like you, Admiral Mushafa, and Marshal Tiburon, to consult together with the Prince and plan how you are going to proceed, remembering that we must work quickly." The two men stood up and bowed their assent to the Queen. The prince consort remained seated beside her. "Good. Carry on then and please send us a report outlining the steps you have taken and the plans you will be implementing."

The queen turned to address the National Grand Master of the Legion of Light. "What plans do you have, Grand Master?"

He was an elderly man, tall and thin with slightly stooped shoulders, light brown complexion, with long silver hair and beard. "Your Majesty," he bowed his head in her direction and continued. "Naturally, the League of Light also has much at stake in this conflict and we are preparing accordingly. Before the week's end, we will be dispatching a team of our most skilled mages and defenders to assist in this conflict. So far, we have managed to assemble just over seventy, but more are coming from outlying regions to answer our call and once they arrive, they will likewise be dispatched to Trethawynd. The corps comprises about two thirds defenders, and one third mages of various skills, predominantly healers."

"How do you plan to deploy, once you arrive in Trethawynd?" the Queen inquired.

"Our people will coordinate their activities with the Trethawynd Legion of Light, and with His Highness the Prince Consort, in order to be placed where they will do the most good. They will be departing by ship in five or six days and expect to disembark in Bailuchi within five days of departure. They will be in constant contact with the Monastery of Trethawynd and with His Royal Highness. He nodded to the prince consort. "And if our people are required farther north, they will continue with the ship."

"Well, it seems as if you have everything worked out splendidly," the Queen replied. "I know we can leave everything in your capable hands, and yours, Marshal Tiburon and Admiral Mushafa. Now, if there is nothing else, I think we may return to our duties. I thank you for your hard work and pray the Blessings of the Light guide you."

The queen turned to address the chancellor. "Chancellor Osgand, I would like you to discuss this matter with Treasury and ensure sufficient funds are released to cover the immediate expenses, and that plans for future outlays are implemented. We can meet again in my private audience room to discuss this further."

54 – The Royal Troops Arrive

Prince Felidorn

Prince Felidorn straightened up and pulled his shoulders back. He couldn't permit the men to see him slouching in his saddle, no matter how exhausted he was; he was supposed to set an example. At least it was a little cooler since they'd crossed into Trethawynd and started up the mountain road to the Monastery. It was being constantly in the saddle that was so tiring. They'd done the last thirty leagues without a break, changing horses when their mounts became tired, eating in their saddles, and only stopping when necessary for personal reasons. The country through which they had traveled was deceptively peaceful, apart from some damage along the River Morvis, which they'd crossed a few hours back. They were now deep into the Great Forest and closing in on the Monastery.

He turned to the commander riding beside him. "We're almost there. I don't know about you, but I could use a cool bath and a comfortable bed."

"I agree with that, Your Highness. I hope they have accommodation for all of us."

"I'm sure they will. This is one of the great monasteries of Albasiny, and one of the oldest. They may even have a few vacant buildings. I've heard they treat guests very well; good food, luxurious accommodation."

They turned the bend in the road that brought the Monastery and its surroundings into view, which was especially impressive with the setting sun bathing everything in pink and gold.

Prince Felidorn pulled the reins to slow his horse and looked around. "My word, this is magnificent. I'd heard it was spectacular, but wasn't prepared for such splendor. Look at the view over there," he indicated the drop-off on the right. "You can see almost see the ocean, and all those little settlements!"

They continued around the crescent-shaped edge of the drop-off and turned left towards the Monastery that nestled on the edge of the forest.

The Duke of Trethawynd was waiting to greet him, accompanied by the Grand Master of the Monastery, a man in the uniform of a commander of the League of Light, and a knight of Trethawynd.

Duke Valdor came forward and bowed to the prince. "Welcome to Trethawynd, your royal highness. I'm Duke Valdor,"

"Thank you, Your Grace, we're very gratified to be here."

The prince made as if to dismount, but Valdor forestalled him by taking hold of the reins. "You don't need to dismount, Your Highness. It is a little distance to the palace and you can ride there if you wish."

"That's very thoughtful of you, but we've been riding all day and I'm sure my men would like to stretch their legs. I know I would. Do you want us to leave the horses here?"

Valdor beckoned Daryan to his side. "This is Commander Peshanar of the League of Light. He will make sure your horses and equipment are taken care of."

Daryan bowed to the Prince. "I'm honored to meet you, Your Highness. Leave them to me."

Prince Felidorn dismounted and invited the commander to join him so that he could introduce him to the knights in his entourage. "This is Commander Peshanar. He's going to help us find our way and get ourselves settled. Commander Peshanar, this is my aide, Commander Kaniz. Are the men all being quartered in the same place?" he asked Daryan.

"No, Your Highness. There is only room in the palace for the officers and your personal staff. I'll explain everything to Commander Kaniz. I expect you would like to get to your quarters now."

The Duke took over again and introduced the prince to the Grand Master and the two knights, then started walking with them to his palace.

Daryan

The following morning, a meeting was held in the Duke's personal meeting room on the fourth floor. Prince Felidorn led the meeting as the ranking person present. Duke Valdor sat on his right and the prince's aide, Commander Kaniz, on his left, while Daryan, Sir Arvand, Imali, and Grand Master Algoran filled the other seats.

"Before we start planning a course of action, would you mind outlining the current situation, Your Grace?" Prince Felidorn asked Duke Valdor.

"As you wish, Your Highness." He went on to describe their current progress. When it came to placement of troops and enemy presence, he called on Daryan. "Would you like to point out the distribution, Commander?" he asked Daryan.

Daryan stood up and walked to the map where he proceeded to explain the deployment of personnel. He went on to define the present situation. "We have people all over the duchy gathering intelligence and relaying it to us, keeping us up to date on the situation as events happen." He added.

"How many troops do you have deployed in the areas under attack?" the prince asked.

It was past midday before they finally completed their planning and settled on a strategy that seemed to suit everyone. Just as everyone was about to leave, the prince looked at a note handed him by Commander Kaniz. "I hear you have a whisperer at the Monastery."

"We did have," the Grand Master replied. "Unfortunately, she is no long here. I'll let Commander Peshanar explain.

"She's my daughter—but I'm afraid she's been abducted by an enemy wizard."

"That's terrible news!" the prince replied. He looked genuinely shocked. "Do you have any idea where they've taken her?"

"We believe she's somewhere in ValkonenMaa."

"Are there any rescue operations in progress?

Daryan shook his head. "No, your highness; we feel it would be futile unless we knew precisely where she is. Our resources are stretched so thin, and it would take a substantial number to penetrate unknown and probably hostile territory. I would go after her myself if I thought I could succeed, but I can't leave my responsibilities at such a critical time." Daryan's hand automatically moved to his waist as the burning started again.

"It certainly is a dilemma. I don't know how you continue to function under so much stress," the Prince replied. "And your devotion to duty here is admirable. How old is she?"

"She has fourteen years, Your Highness. Or she will have in two days."

"She's so young. I know this is difficult for you, Commander, but rest assured, we will do everything in our power to help with her recovery. It won't be long before we are in ValkonenMaa, and I'm hoping you'll be with us." Prince Felidorn then addressed Duke Valdor. "Well, we'll leave it for now. We were planning to leave here tomorrow at sunrise. Is that enough time for you to prepare, Your Grace?" he asked Valdor.

Valdor thought for a few moments. "It should be," he replied. "If not, we'll ride after you and catch up on the road."

After the meeting, Daryan left the building swiftly and walked over to the woods across from the palace. Once out of sight of the building, he took a bottle of stomach medicine and took a good swallow. He massaged his stomach as if trying to facilitate the effects of the potion and then started walking through the trees.

He suddenly was brought to a halt by something tickling his mind. It felt familiar, like something buried in his memories that he knew but couldn't place, and then he heard a faint voice in his head say, *Dadi?*

Felindra! By the Light! Is it really you? He wasn't used to communicating this way; he wasn't a telepath, but it was happening.

Dadi. I'm all right. I'm fine. I love you, dadi. Tell mami I love her, and Darson.

I will, my darling, I promise. Where are you?

At the ValkonenMaa monastery.

What are they doing to you?

Nothing. Don't worry, dadi, the Light is protecting me. I think they are a bit afraid of me. How's Ashala?

I haven't seen her for a while. I think she's gone back to the forest.

Maybe she's coming to find me. I hope she's all right. I have to go, dadi, someone's coming.

We're all thinking about you and sending our love, my precious girl.

Daryan let out a breath and wiped the sweat off his brow with his sleeve. *Was that real? It's hard to believe. I'll have to talk to Ashavan, find out if people can suddenly develop telepathy. I have to believe it really was her and not some trick of my mind.* He started walking again, veering off towards the white palace where the mages were usually to be found.

55 – Haro in the North

Haro

Andro Haro and Sir Baramen had joined up with one of the teams sent out earlier in the conflict, a mage, two Trethawynd defenders, and four League defenders. After visiting the Faldino monastery to pick up some supplies and send home a detailed report, they turned west, aiming for Bartony and the central high road. The road was narrow and badly maintained. It traversed hilly country and was heavily forested—this forest was the second most extensive in Trethawynd, surpassed only by the Great Forest in the west. Sometimes, they were able to rest for the night in a logging camp, most of which were abandoned now, their workers having been conscripted to join the Trethawynd Defenders, or had fallen to attacks by the Dark Brethren. When there were no logging camps or dwellings where they could bed down for a night, they were forced to camp out. Fortunately, the weather had been dry and warm so far.

***

Andro woke with a start, wondering for a moment what had roused him, there was no noise; in fact, it was unnaturally quiet. Then he smelled smoke. He got out of his bedroll, put on his boots, and crawled out of his tent to look around. He couldn't see any flames or fire-glow, and it was too dark to see smoke. He walked over to where the defender on watch was sitting on a boulder.

"It's only me, Haro," he said softly to the defender. "I thought I could smell smoke. Have you noticed anything?"

The man stood up and turned in a circle, sniffing the air. "I think I do, sir, but it's very faint. It must be a long way away."

"I guess I'm very sensitive to fire these days. Maybe someone's lit a campfire," Andro suggested. "Well, keep your eyes and ears open."

He returned to his tent, trying to decide if the smell was getting stronger. Now that he was alerted to it, it would be too easy to imagine the worst. He pulled off his boots and lay down again, but was unable to sleep. He was too aware of the damage fire could do. The memories of the attacks on his farm invaded his mind, increasing his anxiety. Finally, he got up again and went outside to sit on the log beside the cold fire pit they'd used before bedding down. Before long, Sir Baramen came out of his tent, yawning and stretching his arms above his head. He came over and sat down beside Andro.

"Couldn't sleep?" he asked Andro.

"No, I kept imagining I could smell smoke. Can you smell anything?"

Baramen turned his head and sniffed the air. He shrugged. "Maybe, I'm not sure. It could be the smell of last night's cooking fire. I don't have a very keen sense of smell."

Andro looked up at the sky. The three-quarter moon was dropping below the tree line to the west. "It's almost dawn," he said. "We might as well start the fire here and heat up something to break our fast."

The rest of the company joined them a few at a time, aroused by the noise they were making and the smell of food cooking. Soon the sky started to lighten and a glow in the east made it easier to see. Two of the defenders went into the trees to check on their traps and returned with a squirrel and a small rabbit.

"Hardly worth bothering with," one of them commented, holding up the squirrel. "This poor little creature wouldn't feed a child."

"You could put them in the pot with some vegetables and grain to make a stew," Andro suggested.

The two defenders set about skinning and chopping up the two little animals while another cut up some vegetables and put them in a pot of water over the fire. In ones and twos, members of the group went into the woods to use the makeshift latrine and wash in the stream. By the time they had taken down the tents and packed all their gear, the sky was noticeably brighter and the food was ready.

Andro noticed that the horses staked out by the stream were becoming restless. He could hear them snorting and pawing the ground, then one of them whinnied. They could sense that something was wrong and were getting edgy. He looked around above the tree line and saw a grey pall over the sky to the north. Now that their cooking fire had been dowsed and buried with a layer of earth, he could also smell the smoke of burning vegetation.

He walked over to Baramen, who was putting on his armor. "Can you smell it now?"

Baramen sniffed. "Yes, it's much sharper now."

"Look over there." Andro pointed north.

"Light help us. A forest fire?"

"Looks like it."

"What can we do?"

"There's nothing much we can do apart from alerting the authorities. If it gets out of control, with these dry conditions, it could destroy huge areas of forest." Andro omitted mentioning the destruction of wildlife, which meant a great deal to him, although other people might think them less important. He turned to the rest of the team who were ready to leave. "Let's get the horses and move out. I'd like Lady Divora to ride with me. I need to send a message."

A petite woman with short dark hair detached herself from the rest of the band and, kit bag slung over her shoulder, walked with him to get her horse. Andro helped her with the saddle and secured her equipment, stroking the animal and murmuring soothingly to keep it calm.

"It's the smell of smoke that's making them restless," he said as he mounted his own steed. "Are you ready to send?"

"Yes, sir. Go ahead."

After sending Andro's message to the Monastery and the town watch in Bartony, the closest community to the fire, Divora fell back to the middle of the group.

Andros gradually became aware of a rumbling sound in the direction of the fire. The noise became louder as it drew closer, and then flocks of birds flew over their heads, all kinds of birds, falcons, ravens, grouse, pheasants, and swarms of smaller birds like sparrows and thrushes.

"It's the animals running from the fire. We'd better take cover in the trees or we'll be run down. They're panicked and they won't be able to stop." He turned around and called to the rest of the group, "Get behind the trees, there's a stampede coming our way."

Once in the shelter of a large tree, he dismounted and stood beside his horse, which was becoming increasingly jittery. He soothed him by talking to him and stroking his neck.

"Is everyone in cover?" he asked Sir Baramen.

"It looks like it," Baramen replied after looking around. "They're almost here," he added.

As they watched from their sheltered positions, a panting, heaving mass of animals burst out of the woods on the north side, prey and predator together. The animals were forced to act unison and forget for a moment their fear of and hunger for one another. The larger grazing animals were in the lead, deer and elk, followed by wild cats, wolves, foxes and bears, while a swarm of smaller animals struggled to keep up. The stampede barely slowed as it crossed the road. For a short time, they were surrounded by animals running for their lives, the sound of the thundering hooves and panting breath too close for comfort. It took several minutes for them to pass. Some of the smaller animals, rabbits, raccoons, and squirrels, had stopped at the road and were cowering in the undergrowth or climbing trees.

After the animals had passed, the team continued west along the road through a litter of broken vegetation and droppings left by the terrified animals. After several hours, they stopped at a stream to water the horses and have something to eat, and then continued, hoping to reach Bartony before nightfall.

On their right, the fire was close enough to hear the crackling as vegetation was consumed and see the sparks rising from the burning woodland. The thick smoke made eyes water and throats become congested. As long as they could keep the horses to a slow trot, they were able to keep them from panicking, even so the were restless, snorting and shying away from the fire. When the road turned southwest, they moved farther away from the burning region and, after a while, they dismounted for a rest break at a stream.

Andro was by the stream, refilling his water bottle when he heard a thunk followed by a scream of pain. He stood up and looked around. One of the defenders was on the ground with an arrow piercing his shoulder. "Get down, everyone!" he shouted. He fell to the ground behind a boulder and took his bow off his back. "Where did it come from?" he called.

As if in answer, a stream of arrows came from the south and south east of the clearing. Grunts and screams announced the injury of more members of the team. This time, however, arrows started to fly the other way. He heard one of the League defenders shout, "STOP FIRING AND SURRENDER!" using his command power. There was a lull in the enemy's action and a few men came forward and dropped their weapons on the ground, but the others continued to attack.

Andro turned to the two closest defenders. "Let's try to circle around them, but be careful. We don't want any more casualties."

They crept forward on their knees through the undergrowth, and spread out to the right of the attackers. Suddenly, an arrow shot through the air and lodged in Andro's upper arm, and then another caught him in his buttock. He gasped at the pain and collapsed on his face in the grass. He heard a man laugh over to his left. "Another one down. They fall for it every time!" he called to one of his cohorts.

Andro didn't hear anything else; he'd passed out.

"What happened?" he groaned as he regained consciousness. He was still lying on his face on the ground.

"You were shot, Commander," the healer replied.

"I know that," he responded grumpily. "Where's Sir Baramen?"

"He's awake, sir" the healer called.

Baramen came over and knelt on the ground beside him. "How do you feel?" he asked.

"How do you think I feel with an arrow in me behind? Bloody awful. I don't understand why I passed out. It's not that serious, is it?" Andro growled. "Where are we and what's the situation?"

"It was probably the shock, that made you faint, Commander, or the pain," the healer interrupted. "I'm going to have to cut the head of this arrow out. It doesn't appear to have gone in too deeply, but it will still hurt."

"Can't you anesthetize him?" Baramen asked.

"There's not very much powder left, I could use some of it, but there are other wounded."

"Never mind that," Andro growled. "Just get on with it."

"As you wish, Commander." He looked at Baramen. "Could you steady him, Sir? Put your hands on the sides of his torso about halfway down."

Baramen shifted his position and placed a hand on either side of Andro's waist. "Like this?"

"Good," the healer replied. "We'll soon have it out, Commander. I'm going to start cutting now."

The moment the knife entered his skin, Andro bucked and groaned loudly, then he fainted again. When he came to, he was resting on his side to protect the arm from which the other arrow had been removed. This had been an easier wound to treat because the arrow had gone right through, so they were able to cut the head off and draw the rest of it out from the other side. The wounds were covered with antiseptic ointment now, and secured with bandages and the healer had gone on to help someone else.

"You haven't answered my question," Andro said to Baramen.

"I was too busy holding you down; besides, it would have been no use talking to you when you were unconscious. Could you repeat it?"

"I'm sorry, Baramen. I just hate being helpless like this. I feel so stupid, being shot in the behind of all places. It was such an obvious trap, too. I don't know how we fell for it. What's the status?"

"They've gone; we chased them off. They must have been a small band of stragglers. We got two of them with our arrows and now they're prisoners."

"What about the ones who surrendered?"

"We've got them as well, three of them."

"Good. I leave it to you to interrogate them; I don't feel up to it at the moment. What about our casualties?"

"Four with arrow wounds, none too serious. We're still at the stream, Andro, and we may have trouble transporting everyone."

"As long as they can ride, they should be all right if we take it easy."

"What about the ones who can't sit on a horse?" Baramen said, giving Andro a meaningful look.

"I'll manage somehow. I think we ought to send a message to Bartony and ask them to send someone to meet us. It's getting dark and we aren't going be able to travel very fast like this. I fear the ones that got away might bring back reinforcement and attack us again." He struggled to get his right knee under him; he didn't dare to put pressure on his left leg, the side that was injured. "Help me stand up, Baramen."

The knight grasped his right arm and steadied him as Andro straightened his leg and rose to his foot. He put his left foot on the ground and got a sharp burning pain in his buttock and all the way down his leg. He cried out and swiftly raised it again.

"Put your arm around my shoulder and see if you can hop on one foot."

"It's a good thing both wounds are on the same side." After a couple of hops, Andro stopped. Pain shot through his leg and arm with every jolt. "It's no good. If you could get me to that boulder, perhaps I could sit on the edge of it." They struggled across the short distance to the boulder and Andro lowered himself gingerly until he was resting on his right buttock. "That should do it." He uttered a sound, half sigh and half groan. "Would you tell Lady Divora to send the message to Bartony, please?"

Eventually, all the injured were placed on horses, a couple had to double with an uninjured comrade because they were unable to sit without support. Andro, to his great chagrin, had to lie face down across his horse's back with Sir Baramen beside him in case he slipped.

It was completely dark by the time they met a group of defenders from Bartony leading a wagon.

"Well met, sir," their leader greeted Baramen. "Any more trouble on the road?"

"No, thank the Light, sergeant," Baramen answered. "I take it the wagon is for our injured?"

"Yes, Sir. We've put a few pads in the bottom for their comfort. Do you want us to start helping them down?"

"Yes please. Be careful with Commander Haro. He's got a quite painful injury."

The wounded were quickly transferred to the cart where they were covered with blankets against the cold wind blowing from the north. Once they were all settled, they began the return journey. Before long, they reached the top of the ridge above Bartony and started down the road into the town.

The streets of Bartony were so crowded, they had to force their way through the multitude that seemed to be out in unusual numbers for the hour. In addition, far more than normal numbers of defenders mingled with the crowd.

"Where did all these people come from?" Sir Baramen asked the sergeant.

"Well, sir, a lot of people have come in from the surrounding areas for protection from the dark ones. Everyone's heard about them and the terrible things they do. Some of them escaped from places that were attacked—it's not right, attacking helpless people the way they do. And we just heard the Prince Regent is on his way with a big army from the capital. I don't know where everybody is going to stay. There's no room in the town. They'll have to set up tents and bivouac outside. It's going to get cold soon, and I feel rain coming, too."

"Thank you, sergeant. I'm sure they'll sort it all out when the prince gets here," Baramen replied when the garrulous sergeant stopped for a breath. We are prepared to camp outside, but our people could use a good meal and I'd appreciate it if our wounded could be given a place to recuperate."

"We can put the injured men in our infirmary; it's almost empty right now. We haven't been attacked yet, but we're expecting it any day. The rest of your crew can find beds in the barracks, except the lady, of course. Is she your healer?"

"No, she's our sender. We'll keep her with Commander Haro and myself."

In spite of the overcrowding, they managed to get everyone accommodated and given a hot meal. Andro was to share a small room, containing little more than two narrow beds, with Baramen. The mage Divora had an even smaller room nearby. Both rooms looked as if they may have been servants' quarters, but they were still better than sleeping on the ground in tents.

As Andro and Baramen were settling down for the night, Lady Divora knocked on their door. Baramen slipped out into the hall to hear what she had to say, not wanting to disturb Andro who was already lying face down on his bed with a blanket over him. "What is it, lady?"

"I've received a message for Commander Haro from Commander Peshanar, sir."

"Could I give it to him?" Baramen offered. "He's lying down."

"Yes, sir. The commander wants Commander Haro to return immediately to the Monastery. He's needed there."

"I see. Could you send a reply?"

"Yes, Sir."

"Tell Commander Peshanar that Commander Haro has been wounded. Say it's not serious, but he is experiencing a lot of discomfort at the moment—no need to go into details; just say they are arrow wounds—and he will return as soon as he is able to travel, which we estimate could be two or three days. If there's a reply, bring it to us in the morning. I'd like him to rest as much as he can. Thank you, lady. Oh, one more thing: would you ask if we should continue with our survey, or wait here for further orders?"

The order came the next morning for Haro to stay where he was and that Commander Peshanar would be arriving in less than a week.

56 – Felindra Talks to the Wizards

The door opened and Monaltor came in. Felindra sighed inwardly. *Now what? I suppose I'll have to face him, not that there's a choice.*

He looked surprised to see her up and dressed in fresh clean clothes. "I see the healer's potion worked for you."

"Yes," Felindra replied. "I feel much better."

"We have to talk about what happened yesterday. Come with me to my office. It's much more comfortable there." *Comfortable for him, maybe, he wouldn't have to stand while I'm sitting down.*

"I was just waiting for Dominel to bring my midday meal."

"This won't take long. You can eat when you get back."

Yes, when everything is cold, she thought, but there was no point in arguing with him; he had the upper hand ... for the moment.

She followed him across the yard to the main building and up the stairs to the room he called his office. When he was seated behind the desk, he pointed to one of the chairs. "Sit!"

She could sense a smoldering anger under his apparent calmness, and perhaps a touch of nervousness.

"Now, tell me about this talent of yours, this ability to repel. How long have you had it? Do you use it often?"

"I didn't even know about it until it happened yesterday. I didn't do anything intentionally; it just happened when your son tried to pry into my mind. I didn't want to hurt anyone, and I certainly didn't want what it did to me. I've never felt so ill in my life."

"So why did you do it?"

"I told you, *I* didn't do anything. I had no control over what happened."

"Will you do it again? *Can* you do it intentionally?"

She glanced up at him. His face showed no emotion, but she sensed his unease. "I don't know," she replied. "I think it depends on what happens."

"What do you mean?"

"I mean it was probably caused because something frightened me. My mind must have thought I was in danger."

"What could possibly have frightened you? No one was threatening you or hurting you."

"I felt someone pushing me in my mind, trying to take over and make me do something bad."

"You mean my son."

Felindra nodded. "Is he all right?" she asked.

"He's recovering," Monaltor replied with a scowl. "What do you care?"

"I feel sort of responsible. I know I didn't do it intentionally, but... Can I see him?"

"No, of course you can't. It's none of your business."

"I just thought it might cheer him up to have a visitor. That's what we do when someone is sick."

Monaltor gave her a scornful look and shook his head. He stood up and walked to the door to speak to the guard outside. "Take her to my son's room and stay with them. Don't let her try anything." He turned to Felindra who had followed him to the door. "Go with him. And don't stay too long or cause him any more pain."

As if you care.

Barengush's room was not much bigger than hers and didn't have any much better furnishings. She was surprised because, being the Grand Wizard's son, she had expected him to have much better accommodation. He was lying on his bed with an arm over his eyes. "What is it now?" he asked, without removing his arm.

"You've got a visitor," the guard announced.

"What! Who is it? Someone else want to poke at me? Leave me alone."

"No, it's the girl."

Barengush uncovered his eyes and turned towards the door, wincing from the pain in his head. "What do you want?" he asked. "Come to gloat over what you did to me?"

"No. It made me just as ill as you seem to be, and I certainly didn't mean to hurt you. I just came to see if you were all right."

Barengush grunted. "How did you get past my father?"

"I didn't have to; he allowed me to come."

"All right, now you've seen me, go away and leave me alone. You've done enough damage already. And how is it you've recovered so quickly?"

"A gift of the Light."

"Oh, don't give me that excrement."

"It's true. If you have faith in the Light, miracles can happen."

"Sure. If you believe that, you'll believe in flying horses next."

"I'm the proof. You can see me here, now, perfectly recovered. I was just as sick as you."

"You probably weren't affected as badly as I was."

"You should have seen me. I was blind with the pain in my head and I vomited every time I tried to move. Let me ask you something. Can your Oglestra perform miracles the way the Light can?"

"Look, I don't want to get into a theological debate. Just go away and leave me alone."

"Did that healer give you a potion to take?" Felindra persisted.

"Much good that did me," Barengush replied scornfully.

"Would you like to try an experiment?"

"What sort of experiment?"

"Nothing that will harm you. Just let me touch you and see if I can call on the Light to help you."

"Oh Lord, give me strength," he moaned. "Yes, do it, if only to prove how deluded you are."

Felindra glanced at the guard who was watching and listening to everything. *I have to ignore all distractions,* she told herself; *just concentrate on what I'm doing.* She went to where she could reach Barengush, trying to ignore the putrid miasma that surrounded him. *Did I smell this bad? Poor Dominel,* she thought. She closed her eyes. *Please help me, Light. I have complete faith in your love, but I don't know if what I'm doing, or trying to do will work without Your help.* She reached out and touched Barengush's shoulder, then closed her eyes again and tried to visualize a great purifying light moving over him. *You will feel much better,* she said mentally, directing the thought to him.

After a few moments of concentrating the Light on Barengush, she stopped and opened her eyes. Hardly daring to look at him, she removed her hand from his body and stood back. Finally, she did look and saw him staring at her. There were tears in his eyes, which he dashed away quickly. His color seemed better, at least his face looked a little pinker than it had, but she was still afraid to ask him.

"What did you do?" he demanded, but much less aggressively that before.

"Do you feel any better?" she asked tentatively.

He scowled at her. "You sound as if you don't believe in your own Light,"

"Of course I do, but if it was against His will, He wouldn't have helped me. Tell me; do you feel any better?" she was starting to lose her patience with him. She was trying to help him and all he did was mock her.

"His will, eh? Oh, my, that's a handy way out." He moved his head from side to side and shrugged his shoulders. "I suppose so. I do feel a bit better. Not completely healed, but better than I was. Satisfied now? Go away and leave me alone. I want to think."

A wave of sheer love and warmth flowed through her. *Thank you Light.* "All right, I'm going. Do you want me to come back later?"

"I'll find you if I want to see you. Goodbye!"

"I think you need to be outside getting some fresh air and exercise. I could go with you if you like."

"Get out!"

He was beginning to sound like his old self, so she left him to deal with what had just happened. She was sure that his father would find out before long. *I wonder what he'll do,* she thought, with far less anxiety than such a prospect would have caused a few days ago.

***

Felindra was not surprised a couple of hours later when she heard a key unlocking her door, although it was

Barengush who poked his head in, not his father. When he saw her sitting on her bed, he came right in. "I thought I'd go outside, get some air. You can come with me if you like."

She noticed he was looking much better and had changed into clean clothes. "Does your father approve?" she asked.

He scowled at her. "I don't have to get his permission. I can make my own decisions."

"Good," she said. "I'd love to go outside. Just let me put my boots on and get my cloak.

"What happened to that little dog?" she asked casually as she laced up a boot.

"How would I know? It probably went back to its owner."

"Whose was it?"

"Some old woman who works in the kitchen. What do you care, anyway?"

"In case you haven't noticed, I like animals. She was a sweet little thing. I hope she's all right." Another thought occurred to her. "What happened to the horses?"

"They're still around somewhere."

"They weren't put back in that awful pen, where they?"

"As far as I know, they're still loose on the grounds. The gates are kept closed now so they can't get outside the walls."

"That's a good idea. They wouldn't fare so well in the woods. They should find enough to eat around the grounds, and who knows, they might even clear some of the weeds."

Barengush gave her a surprised look, but only grunted in reply.

They left the building and stood for a moment deciding where to go. "Can we go out in the woods?" she asked.

"Why?"

Felindra shrugged. "I like being among the trees and wild animals."

"I don't think it's a good idea to go outside the walls," Barengush replied. "There's a sort of garden behind this building—it's bit of a mess—but there are some trees. You might even find some horses to talk to."

They reached the so-called garden, which was a mess of weeds and dead flowers, the ground muddy from the recent rain, mottled with hoof prints, although there were no horses in sight.

"Can I ask you something?" she said as they started to walk down one of the paths.

"Like what?"

"Do you people really worship Oglestra?"

"What do you mean 'you people'?"

"Well, I don't know what you call yourselves. We call you the Dark Brethren, but what do you call yourselves?"

Barengush shrugged. "Oglestrians, I guess."

"You mean you don't know?"

"I don't care. I don't care about any of that religious stuff."

"So why are you fighting for them? Why do you want to make everything dark?"

"It's the way I was raised. I just do what my father wants me to do." He was beginning to sound annoyed at the direction the conversation was taking. "Can we talk about something else?"

"But I'm interested and I'd like to understand. Why is your father a follower? I mean, there has to be a reason. You don't suddenly wake up one day and say 'I'm going to be an Oglestrian'."

"His ancestors always hated the Light. It's something that happened a long time ago, maybe hundreds of years, and was handed down from father to son. When our people, the Nords, first settled here in ValkonenMaa, the followers of the Light were fanatical about their religion and persecuted anyone who didn't believe what they did. They used to raid our settlements and murder everyone who worshiped so-called pagan gods and wouldn't convert. They burned whole towns and took all their livestock and possessions." Barengush's voice rose in indignation. "They tortured people too to make them recant their beliefs and turn to the Light."

"But that was a long time ago. Things have changed. I know we did terrible things too, but we're not like that now. Why keep up old vendettas? What started it in your family, anyway?"

Barengush shook his head. "The village where this ancestor lived was raided by the rabid priests, but one little boy escaped by hiding in a root cellar. Had to watch his whole family and all the neighbors being herded into the empty granary and burnt alive. Everyone, his mother and sisters, his father and even his baby brother. We are descended from this boy, who swore and made his children swear, that they would get vengeance on the followers of the Light whenever they had the chance. The boy was taken in by a follower of Oglestra who treated him kindly and introduced him to the faith."

Felindra was silent for a while when he'd finished talking; thinking about what he'd told her. It was true that you can't force people to believe something and what those ancient priests did was monstrous. It seems the Oglestrians of that time had learned that the right way to influence people was to use kindness and love, not brutality. Then she said, "That's a terrible story. It's hard to believe that Children of Light could behave like that." She stopped walking and faced him. "But we're not like that now. There have been so many reforms since those days and I believe that such atrocities would be impossible today. I mean, look at how fast you recovered when I asked the light to heal you."

"I know," he replied, walking past her. "I didn't say I want to follow them. I don't give a flea's fa... um ... I don't care about Oglestra and his followers. It's just..."

Felindra walked faster to catch up. "It's your father, isn't it?"

Barengush shrugged kicked a stone out of his way. He wouldn't look at her and just walked ahead.

"I'm sorry if I made you feel uncomfortable," she said. "Do you love him?"

"What sort of a stupid question is that?" he replied angrily.

Touched a tender nerve there, Felindra guessed. "I'm just trying to understand."

Barengush scowled at her.

"Why do you hate him? He's your father, isn't he?" she couldn't understand anyone not loving his father.

Barengush stopped and face her, his fists were clenched and his face red. For a moment, she thought he was going to strike her. "He killed my mother!"

She put out a tentative hand to offer comfort, but he brushed it aside. "I'm sorry. I shouldn't have pried like that. Shall we go on?"

"I abducted you! Dragged you away from your home and family, and hurt your pet," he yelled. "Doesn't that mean anything to you? Don't you hate me for it?"

"No, I don't hate you. You were doing what you thought was right, I suppose ... following orders." She raised her shoulders. "And anyway, I may have gained something from the experience." She thought for a moment before continuing. "You always seem so angry. I have a feeling you're not very happy with your life."

"What is this," he snarled. "You trying to convert me?"

"No. I wouldn't presume to... It's just that I don't like seeing you so miserable." She looked at him, trying to decide whether to continue. "There's just one more thing I want to say, then I'll stop. The Dark Brethren can't win. Darkness can never obliterate light. It can cast a shadow over light, or cover it up, but the light is always there ... ready to shine again. But when light shines on darkness, the darkness is banished."

"Can we talk about something else, or should we just go back inside?"

"I miss my family," Felindra said. "This week is the anniversary of my birth, and we always celebrated it together."

Barengush looked at her. "How many years do you have?" he asked grudgingly.

"Fourteen," she replied sadly.

"You're just a child," Barengush said. "But when you talk, you sound older."

"That's because I have loving parents who treat us with respect, as if we were people, not an inferior species."

Barengush scowled. "We?"

"I have a little brother."

"Oh." He turned towards the building. "I think we should go back. It's getting dark."

As Felindra slowly followed him back, she reached out for Ashala.

Ashala

Ashala lay in a shallow hollow under a screen of foliage. She woke suddenly sensing something touching her. She stood up, instantly alert, and shook herself. She sniffed the air and then let out a soft howl. *It was her!* She wagged her tail for the joy she felt in the presence of the most important being in her life. Her friend, her sister was there!

My precious girl, I miss you so much. I am far away, girl, but we will be together soon. I want you to do something for me, Felindra continued. Ashala barked her consent. *Can you find the Guardian of the Forest and ask if he can help us?* Ashala received images of the attacks by the Dark Brethren, concentrating on those that affected animals, and then the image of Ashala, standing in a sunny forest glade, communicating with a great golden bear.

Suddenly Ashala sensed someone else near her precious person and snarled, and then the link was severed. Ashala lowered her head, dejected, and then she raised her muzzle and howled.

Felindra

Barengush shook her arm. "What are you doing? You looked as if you were leagues away."

The sudden interruption cut off her link with Ashala leaving her dazed and with a terrible feeling of loss. *I'll have to try again when I'm alone*, she thought. *I hope she understood what I was asking of her.*

57 – To the Dungeons

Felindra

Felindra had finished all the books Dominel had brought for her, even the ones she'd found inscrutable or boring; those she had skimmed through several times in the hope that understanding would develop through repetition. Now she had nothing else to do but think, but she had a lot to think about.

A key scraped in the lock and the door flew open, crashing against the wall, and Monaltor barged in, looking furious. Felindra sat up, anxious but not terribly afraid. *I can handle it,* she told herself.

"What have you been telling my son?" he demanded. "I won't have you telling him all that Light trash, messing with his mind. I forbid you to go near him! You think your precious Light can protect you. Well, we'll see about that." Before she could answer, he turned to someone behind him. "Take her."

Not knowing where they were supposed to take her she stuck her feet into her boots and grabbed her cloak. Before she even had time to wrap the cloak around her shoulders, two guards took her arms in steely grips and dragged her to the door. "Where are you taking me?" she asked trying to control the fear in her voice.

"You'll see," Monaltor replied. "Or should I say you won't see … not a thing! Now, hurry up; I have important things to do. I can't waste my time on you."

They dragged her to the door at the end of the hallway, the one she'd often wondered about, and opened it onto a staircase. The guards thrust her down the stone stairs so violently, she was afraid she'd lose her boots. "I can walk, you know," she said to the guards. "You don't have to be so violent. I'm hardly going to try to escape from two such big strong men."

Neither man said anything, but after looking at each other over her head, they allowed her feet to touch the steps. They continued down the stairs, the air becoming more and more chilly and dank. The light faded to near-blackness until Monaltor lit a torch.

"You'll find out just how impotent your vaunted Light is down here," Monaltor sneered. "He won't be able to penetrate the place I have in store for you. You'll find out just how easily dark can defeat light."

"I notice even you have to use his gift to light your way," Felindra retorted.

Monaltor pushed her violently in the back and she would have fallen down the steps if the guards hadn't been gripping her arms. As it was, one of them stumbled and barely caught his balance in time to prevent himself falling.

Finally, after descending into the bowels of the building, they reached the bottom. The stairs didn't go any farther. The air had become so cold, Felindra shivered. She still had the cloak clutched tightly in her hands. If she was going to remain down here, she would need it and she was determined not to let it go.

As they dragged her along the wide corridor, she took note of the stone walls and the patches of greyish-green slimy mold that appeared to be sliding down from the beamed ceiling. Everything was made of stone except for the beams and the doors that lined the hallway. The wooden doors were reinforced with iron bands. *What is this?* she wondered. *It couldn't be storerooms; it looks more like some sort of dungeon.* She shuddered. Without the torch, it would be pitch dark. *Oh, Light, don't let them leave me down here, please.*

"Well, little princess of Light, let's see how you like this. He won't be able to help you down here. This is our world, the world of darkness."

For once, Felindra was lost for words. She was afraid. Clutching the cloak tighter against her body, she watched him take out a large key to unlock one of the doors. "There you are, welcome to your new home. Enjoy it." He opened the door outward and gestured to the two guards to take her inside. "I'll let you have one look at your new accommodation before I take away the light." He gave her a sickly smile, his eyes triumphant.

"You're quite a man, aren't you?" Felindra retorted. "You've only proven that you can defeat one helpless girl, with the help of two strong men."

Monaltor's face changed from smiling triumph to smoldering rage. "Put the chains on her and close the door!" he ordered the two men.

They dragged her into the cell and attached manacles to her legs and wrists, then pushed her to the wall and linked the other ends to a ring driven into the bare rock. They left, slamming the door shut behind them, and then the key scraped in the lock, which turned with an audible click. She was left in complete darkness, but before the light was taken away, she's managed to see a few details. The room had a smooth stone floor, but the walls were the same damp stone. There was no window or any other opening apart from the small grill in the door a little too high for her to see through.

She'd also noted the straw-filled pallet on the floor in one corner, and a bucket at the other end. *I hope I'll be able to reach the bucket,* she thought, moving cautiously away from the wall until she touched the wall opposite. *At least it's a long chain, but I'm going to have to be careful I don't trip over the bucket.*

The manacles on her ankles and wrists weren't too tight, but the friction caused by movement was going to chafe after a while. *They probably didn't have any my size,* she thought derisively. *I wonder if I can get out of them.* She wrapped the cloak around her, thanking the Light that her captors allowed her to keep it, and then she sat down on the pallet and started to test the wrist manacles. *Good, I can get out of them, but I'll have to be careful they don't see them.*

"Oh Light, what am I going to do?" she prayed. She realized that the room was gradually filling with low intensity light, which seemed to emanate from the walls. Not only did it enable her to see, it also provided a modicum of warmth. "Thank you Light."

Felindra lay down on the pallet, trying to ignore her hunger pangs. She hadn't eaten anything since midday and it must be after sunset now. *I wonder if they're going to bring me some food.* Wrapping the cloak around her, she turned onto her side, and closed her eyes.

A fumbling with the lock of the door woke her. She turned over to face it and realized that the light had gone from inside the cell, although whoever was outside had a torch. The door opened slowly and Barengush poked his head in, putting his finger over his lips to warn her not to make any noise. He quickly entered the cell and closed the door.

"What are you doing here?" she asked softly. "I thought you were not supposed to talk to me."

Barengush shrugged his shoulders and frowned at her. "Yes, you've brought a whole load of misery down on my head with your stupid talk about the Light,"

474

"So why did you tell your father?"

He shrugged again, as if trying to convince her—and himself—that the subject was too trivial to bother with, but she could see the hurt in his eyes. "I don't have much choice in the matter. He seems to know my every thought and action."

"Aren't you afraid he'll punish you for coming down here?"

Barengush ignored the question and pulled a small package wrapped in a clean cloth from inside his tunic. "Here, I've brought you something to eat." He handed her the package.

Felindra took it and opened the cloth. It contained a large hunk of bread, some cheese, and a ripe tomato. She looked up at him. "Thank you Barengush. I was getting a bit hungry." She took a bite of the bread. "Did *he* send you?"

He appeared startled by her question. "No, of course not. If he even knew I was here he'd...I don't know what he'd do, but it would not be pleasant."

"Then you are very kind, and brave. Why are you doing this?" She took a bite out of the tomato and wiped the juice off her chin.

"I want to get away from here," he said in a low voice. "I thought maybe we could help each other. You want to escape, don't you?"

"Of course I do, but I was hoping the Light would come up with something."

"Is that how you live your life, waiting for the Light to do something?" The old sneer was back. "I would have thought you'd have enough gumption to find a way on your own."

His reply stung Felindra; it touched too close to home. Why was she suddenly expecting the Light to do everything for her? *Forgive me, Light.* "You're right," she replied. "Do you have a plan?"

"Yes, but we'd have to move fast. Once they find out what I'm doing, all the demons in the abyss will break loose. It's good that you have your boots and cloak. You'll…" Barengush suddenly doused the torch and stood back against the wall by the door.

Felindra heard the footsteps in the hallway, coming towards her cell door. She quickly wrapped the remains of her food in the cloth and tucked it under the cloak, and then sat back against the wall.

"Why isn't this door locked?" a male voice asked. The guard opened the door and looked at her suspiciously. "Has someone been here?"

"Not that I know of. I just woke up."

"I saw a light," the guard persisted.

Felindra shrugged. "I don't know what you mean. Listen, if you think someone is here, come in and look around. There's nowhere anyone could hide. And another thing. I need some water."

The guard frowned at her and slammed the door. He turned the key in the lock and pulled on the door handle to make sure it was locked this time.

Barengush wiped some sweat from his brow. "That was quick thinking," he said. "I almost wet my … um … when you told him to come in and look around. What would you have done if he'd taken you up on it?"

"I'm sure you would have thought of something. I thought that if I said that, he'd think I had nothing to hide."

"We have another problem now," Barengush said. "The door's locked. How are we going to get out? Damn!" He punched one fist into the palm of his other hand

"I thought you had a key."

"I do, but there's no keyhole inside the door."

"Maybe he'll come back with some water, and then we can overpower him and tie him up."

"You'd do that?"

Felindra couldn't see the expression on his face, but his tone told her he was surprised by her suggestion.

"I don't mean hurt him. I won't do anything that would harm him."

They continued to sit in the pitch darkness, Felindra on her mattress and Barengush on the floor with his back against the wall beside the door. Finally, Felindra thought of a question. "Do you have a plan for escaping?"

She heard him sigh. "Well, I know a secret way out of here that would take us outside the wall. But after that...."

"It's a start," Felindra replied. "That would mean we'd be on foot, no horses to ride. I might be able to get some help from animals in the forest."

"Shh! I hear something."

He'd barely finished warning her when a key rattled in the lock again and the door flew open, bringing with it a current of decay and dank air, but no light. Felindra cringed back against the wall although she could see nothing of the shadowy figure in the doorway, apart from its glowing eyes.

"Ogryn!" Barengush's voice was a barely audible squeak. Felindra was chilled by the fear it carried.

"Yes," the voice snarled. "We're going to have to do something about you, boy. You don't seem to be able to learn discipline. Up to now, I've left it to your father, but I think it's time I took a personal interest in you. Now, get out of here."

There must have been a light somewhere down the hallway, because Felindra saw the shadow move aside and Barengush slink out. "Go with the Light, Barengush. Keep a pure heart."

Felindra was driven back by an icy blast from the doorway. She couldn't move, she couldn't even cry out, she was totally paralyzed. *Light?*

A blanket of warmth fell over her. *Have no fear, child. I'm with you.*

"I'll deal with you later, girl," Ogryn said. "You can stay here until I decide what to do with you." The shadow moved back through the doorway and she heard him snickering as he slammed the door.

"I need some water!" Felindra croaked. She was so dry, her tongue seemed glued to the roof of her mouth and her lips like onion skin.

58 – The Battle Goes North

Daryan

The three armies—the League of Light, the Defenders of Trethawynd, and the Defenders of Albasiny—under the prince's command reached the town of Bartony five days after leaving the Monastery, in spite of the rain, which had begun as they passed through Crossroads. Several fields outside Bartony had been prepared to receive them. They were provided with firewood, water barrels and cooking stations to make it easier to set up camp. Once the tents were erected and food procured to feed them, the men and women settled in to make themselves comfortable, eat a meal, maintain their weapons, and have much-needed baths, albeit with cold water from the river that ran by the town.

When Dayan was confident his people were settled in, he went directly to the Bartony watch headquarters inside the town. His first undertaking was to see his friend, Andro.

Haro was alone in the small room, lying on his side on the narrow bed, eyes closed, although his face was far from relaxed; his teeth were clenched and his brows drawn together in a frown. Daryan leaned over and gently shook Haro's shoulder. "Wake up, Andro."

Haro's eyes opened and he blinked. "Daryan!" he said in a gravelly voice. "I wasn't sleeping, just resting my eyes. I thought you were Baramen. When did you get here?"

"Just arrived, about an hour ago. I came to see you as soon as our people were settled at the campground. So what's this mysterious injury of yours?"

Andro grimaced and rolled down the blanket.

"Ouch," Daryan said when he saw the dressing. "It's no wonder you didn't feel like riding. How's it coming along?"

"The healer says it's getting better, but it doesn't feel like it. To me it feels as if it's getting worse."

"Can you walk?" Daryan asked.

"Yes, I can manage that. They've provided me with a staff to take the weight of the injured side. Why?"

"There's going to be a meeting this evening with the prince and all the commanders. I thought it would be good if you attended. If you feel up to it."

"Of course I'm up to it. Just because my behind is messed up doesn't mean I'm totally incapacitated." Haro said petulantly. "I need to do something to take my mind off it, that's all!

"I'm sorry, Andro, I didn't mean to imply..."

Haro sighed. "No, I'm the one who should apologize. I shouldn't take my frustration out on you."

"Better me than someone who can't fight back." Daryan grinned at his friend.

Daryan stayed with Andro until it was time for the meeting, sharing their recent experiences, bringing each other up to date. At the appointed time, they walked slowly together to the room where the meeting was being held. At least thirty people were milling around inside creating a lot of noise as each one tried to be heard above the others. It quieted down the moment the prince appeared and everyone rushed to find a chair.

It seemed that at least half the people in the room were aides, secretaries and other support staff. They took their places behind the chairs of the officers they served. He saw that Valdor had arrived. He was seated next to the prince with Sir Arvand beside him and Imali sitting on a stool behind them. Daryan found a small table, just the right height for Andro to perch on, and dragged it over beside him.

Prince Felidorn placed a sheaf of papers on the table and looked around, waiting for everyone to settle down. Once there was silence, he said, "Well met, comrades. Let's get started. First, I would like to call on Commander Peshanar of the League of Light to give us a summary of the current situation. Commander!"

Daryan knew he would be asked to speak, but he was taken by surprise when the prince called him first. He stood up, gathering his thoughts; he hadn't had time to make any notes. "First of all, let us welcome Prince Felidorn to Trethawynd!" Everyone in the room responded in his own individual way, a cheer, some clapping, drumming on the table. Daryan held up his hand to stop them. "Now, let's get to the matter at hand."

Daryan somehow managed put together a coherent summary of events before handing over to the next speaker.

The meeting seemed as if it would never end, with everyone adding his own ideas as to how they should proceed. But finally, once decisions were made, they all left to return to their own troops and sort out the logistics of the plan. It was decided that the Prince Felidorn would go north into ValkonenMaa while the Trethawynd armies would split up into companies containing both duchy and League defenders and branch out towards the east and west. Their mission was to round up the invaders as far as the border of ValkonenMaa.

Haro

As Daryan and Haro were about to leave, the Prince Regent intercepted them. "Commander Haro?"

"Your highness," Haro replied. "How may I be of service?"

"I was thinking of how I might be of service to you, the prince replied. I understand you've been wounded."

"Yes, Your Highness, but it's getting much better. I assure you, it will not affect my ability to do my duty."

"I know, Commander, but I'll wager you would welcome a little relief from your discomfort. I'm proposing to have my personal healer see if he can do anything to help."

"That's very gracious of you, Your Highness."

"So it's settled then. I'll send him to you as soon as he can be located."

Haro was summoned to another room for the consultation. Apparently, the healer had set himself up here and was using it as a clinic. When the healer examined Haro's wound, he noted redness and swelling in the surrounding tissue, which was unhealthily warm to the touch. He put his hand gently over it and closed his eyes for a moment. "I think I know what is causing you so much discomfort, commander," he told Haro. "There's a small piece of debris in the wound that has infected the area around it. I'll have to remove it, and then we'll see if we can make it heal a bit faster."

"Anything that will help make me more useful," Andro replied. "I feel like such a fool, trying to lead my defenders and unable to sit on a horse."

"Well, I think we can remedy that," the healer replied. "I'm going to have to reopen the wound to clean it, but I'll try not to cause you too much distress." He rested his hand on Andro's head for a moment. Andro began to feel very relaxed and a bit drowsy. Overall, it was a pleasant feeling. He could feel the activities of the healer as he opened and cleaned the wound, but for some reason, he was indifferent to it. Once it was over, the healer applied a salve, and then he rested his hand once again on the area. Andro felt a warmth deep in the muscle. He imagined he could almost feel the flesh growing together. "There, that should do it. I've removed the infectious material and knit most of the tissues together, but I advise you to stay off it for a day in order for it to heal completely. And put some padding on your saddle for a few days. I can give you some cotton wadding from our supplies, if you need it. In a few days, you should be as good as new."

"Thank you, healer. I can't tell you how relieved I feel." Haro took a deep breath, rearranged his clothing, and stood up, miraculously free of pain for the first time in days.

Daryan

It took all the next day for the various groups to prepare and start out on their operations. Daryan and Sir Kevan were to command the northwesterly division, while Haro and Sir Baramen were leading the ones heading east. The prince and his forces left in the morning, and the other two groups departed a little after midday. Duke Valdor was staying in Bartony to coordinate the activities of the Trethawynd armies, keeping reserve defenders with him, ready to go to the aid of any group that needed bolstering.

The rain that had died down overnight started up again at twilight, not a serious downpour, but a misty drizzle, which was nonetheless irritating and limited their vision to a distance of about twenty paces.

"This is too miserable," Sir Kevan commented after they travelled about three leagues. "We might as well stop and make camp. At least we could stay relatively dry in our tents, and I don't know about you, but I'm getting hungry."

"I agree," Daryan replied, "It seems fairly peaceful around here, so let's look for a suitable location."

***

When they awoke the next morning, the rain was pelting down. They had no choice but to wrap themselves in waterproof capes and continue, hoping it would it wouldn't last all day.

"We're not going to be able to see much in this weather," Daryan said. "Is there a town or village anywhere close? There might be people there who can give us some information."

Kevan reached for the pocket inside his cape and withdrew a map. "I'll have to stop under a tree to look at it, so the ink doesn't run," he said. He found a dry spot under a large fir tree and unfolded the map. "There's a small town about three leagues on. Maybe there's an inn where we can get a meal, and while we're there, we can talk to some of the citizens."

"I doubt there'll be one an inn large enough to hold all of us." There were over a hundred defenders and mages in their combined unit. "We'll have to find a sheltered spot outside the town where they can rest while a few of us look around the town."

The scene that met them when they arrived was not very promising. Several buildings along the road outside the town were burnt-out shells; all the timber destroyed, leaving only scorched stones and piles of sodden ash. The town was surrounded by a log palisade, which might protect it from predators and bandit attacks, but which would have been inadequate to stop a concerted attack. The logs were charred and the gate hung from its hinges, but it showed signs of habitation—home-fire smoke rising from some of the houses inside the palisade.

"The rain must have prevented a worse disaster," Daryan said. He sat on his horse and looked around for a moment. "There's a small river over there with some cleared land. Let's set up there for a while and prepare something to eat. It looks as if the rain's letting up finally so we may even be able to light a cook fire."

"Shall we leave everyone here and head into town?" Kevan suggested.

"You go. I'll stay here. I want to contact the Monastery and find out if there's any news about my daughter."

While Sir Kevan and two duchy defenders went into town, Daryan asked Lady Farah if she could get in touch with Ashavan at the Monastery. The news was not encouraging. Ashavan had not been able to contact Felindra, but he knew she was alive. "They must still have her under a warding spell," was Ashavan's explanation.

Sir Kevan returned after about an hour and reported. "It was just a small band of attackers, mostly Nordics and a wizard. They burned the buildings outside the wall, killed a couple of shepherds who were trying to protect their livestock, and took off with some sheep and goats. Then they lobbed a few fiery brands over the wall, but they didn't cause much damage, a stable and a small warehouse were scorched and they injured a man and a child, plus two horses. They have a pretty good town watch that rallied as soon as they heard the alarm and chased them off."

"No prisoners?" Daryan responded.

"They caught one of them. The fool's horse had bolted and he couldn't get away fast enough on foot."

"What are they doing with him?"

"He's locked up in a watch cell."

"I think we should take him with us. We might be able to get some intelligence out of him," Daryan replied. "You get something to eat and I'll go into town to get him."

Once the prisoner was secured, they packed up their belongings and moved out. The prisoner, a sullen man of around thirty years with brown hair and grey eyes, rode on one of their spare horses with his hands tied in front of him and his feet manacled to the stirrups. Daryan rode beside him with Lady Farah on his other side to monitor the interrogation.

"You're from ValkonenMaa, aren't you?" Daryan said.

"It's no good asking me questions," the prisoner replied in a sullen tone. "I'm not telling you anything."

Daryan glanced across at Farah who nodded. "All right, let's leave that as a yes. Who sent you?"

This time the prisoner didn't even bother to answer, but Daryan was not too concerned. "Why are you here? What do you think you're doing?"

Another sullen silence. "I hope you realize that the lady beside you can probe your mind and find the answers. I'm just paying you the courtesy of allowing you to answer my questions voluntarily."

The prisoner looked at her and back at Daryan, a wary, almost frightened expression on his face. "Damned magic! Lucky for me, I can block it."

"Oh, you have a gift, do you?"

Farah shook her head, no.

"I think you're bluffing. Let's start again. What's your name? Surely, you don't mind us knowing that. Tell me who you are."

The man shook his head, his lips pressed together.

"How do your people interrogate prisoners? I'll wager it's more brutal than this."

The prisoner shrugged, but his face grew paler.

"How did you get here?"

No answer other than a headshake.

"Why are you here?"

Nothing.

"Oh well," Daryan said. "We'll leave it at that. You're probably too unimportant to give us anything useful anyway, so I won't waste any more of my time on you." He jerked his head sideway, signaling Farah to join him and rode ahead, leaving other defenders to watch over the prisoner.

"What did you find out?" he asked Farah when they were out of earshot.

"Quite a bit actually," she replied. "His bluff about blocking was just that. All he did was keep repeating the same words over and over in his mind, but he couldn't keep it up for long and things started to seep through.

"What words?"

"'Don't think, don't think....' Let me tell you what I got. His name is Pervil; he came on a boat from an east coast town and landed just south of Faldino. All I could understand about the person or persons who *sent* him was that they were somehow connected to Oglestra. He seemed a bit confused about that. The reason they came here is somewhat confusing too. I got the feeling he didn't completely understand their motives. I think he is a minor follower of Oglestra, or maybe just an opportunist, and was going along with whatever their leaders decided to do, hoping for a share of the plunder."

"I wish we could find out more about why they abduct people, especially children. I have a feeling there's something very sinister about that."

"Do you want to ask him more questions?"

"Not right now. I'd like to let him ponder his situation a bit first. He probably thinks we're powerless because with haven't tortured him, or he might expect we'll do that later. The longer we wait, the more anxious he'll get. I'm going to talk to Sir Kevan about it now, Thanks for your help, Farah."

She smiled and inclined her head. "It's what I do; I want to help whenever I can."

59 – ValkonenMaa

Felindra

After Ogryn slammed the cell door, a loud click told her it was locked, leaving her in complete darkness. She could still feel the warmth of the Light and soon the walls started to glow faintly again. When it became light enough for her to see objects, she finished the food Barengush had brought.

She thought for a while about the creature who had just visited her and wondered who he was and what part he played in things. There was something extremely menacing about him. He was much more terrifying than anyone she'd encountered so far. He didn't seem human somehow, with those eyes that glowed in the dark, and the smell of him ... it was as if he breathed noxious fumes. She shivered and rubbed her arms.

What am I going to do now? I wish Barengush had had time to tell me how to get out. She shrugged. *It wouldn't have done me much good anyway with the door locked. I'm so thirsty. Are they going to let me die of thirst?*

No, child. I'm with you. Close your eyes and rest; much work lies ahead.

Felindra realized there was moisture in her mouth; she was no longer thirsty, but her eyelids were drooping. *Thank you, Light.* She curled up on the pad, pulled the cloak over her and fell asleep.

She woke later and sat up, stretching her arms and legs to loosen the muscles. In the light that still glowed in her cell, she saw a metal canister on the floor inside the door. Beside it was a paper-wrapped package. Curious, she got up and went to investigate. She picked up the canister first and felt liquid sloshing inside. Opening the top, she sniffed it. *Water! I wonder who brought them. Did they see the light? No, it would have faded when the door opened.* She picked up the soft package and took it and the water over to her pallet. *Just a little sip.* She put the canister to her lips and tilted it so that some of the water went in her mouth. Apart from a slight musty taste, it seemed all right. She took another sip and swallowed it, and then she unwrapped the package. It contained some mashed beans in a disk of soft flatbread. After tasting a morsel, she took a good bite and chewed it slowly. It was tasteless, but it was food. She wasn't very hungry after eating Barengush's snack, so she rewrapped it and put it on the pallet, covering it with her cloak. There was no telling when they would bring more, so she had make it last.

She started to wonder about time; she didn't even know if it was day or night. Next, she tried to extend her senses outside the cell to see if she could reach anyone, but for some reason she failed. *Rats' tails! They must be warding me. What's the use of having the gift of telepathy if I can't use it? I want to see if Ashala has done what I asked and find out where she is. And I need to talk to Barengush about getting out. My family.... I feel so useless, sitting here. I know I should be doing something.*

Patience, child. Everything proceeds according to plan. You need to rest and gather your strength for what is to come.

I feel fine, Felindra responded.

Stay here for a while longer and communicate with your friends and family.

But I can't get through the warding.

It is gone now, child.

How am I going to get out of here?

You will be shown a way.

Are you the Light, or the Messenger?

I am your guide, but the Light protects you.

Then, she sensed that she was alone again, although the warmth remained. *I should do what she says.*

Ashala first. She reached out again, focusing on the wolf and conveying her love. An image appeared in her mind. Felindra imagined hearing her little yip and soft bark. *Where are you, my precious girl?* Ashala relayed an image of the surrounding forest. It was daytime and she'd just finished a meal.

Did you see the Great Bear? Felindra asked.

She picked up an image of Ashala in a position of submission in front of a massive golden bear. The bear towered over her for a moment, and then dropped to all fours and approached her, sniffing and grunting, then it backed away and sat down.

Is he going to help us? Felindra added.

Ashala relayed images of many different types of animals, rodents, birds, and predators, all watching the activities of humans as they went about their daily activities.

It looks as if they are watching over us, Felindra thought. *You did well,* she sent to Ashala. *How are you feeling? Is your wound healed?*

Images came of Ashala wagging her tail and licking the injured hip, and then she started to run through the trees.

Where are you going now?

Felindra received a very clear image of herself and Ashala together. *She's coming to find me,* Felindra thought as tears filled her eyes. *I'll be waiting, girl.*

She left Ashala and she stopped to think for a moment. *I should try to contact Ashavan. He'll be able to pass on information to everyone.* She closed her eyes and pictured him as she'd last seen him.

Felindra? Is it really you? When did you become a telepath? Sorry I should give you a chance to answer, shouldn't I instead of pelting you with questions.

It's all right, she replied, excited by actually being in contact with him. *I'll tell you everything, but first I want to know about my family and what everyone is doing.*

They exchanged news and information for about half an hour. The only thing Felindra omitted from her account was the visit from the Messenger. She didn't feel she could convey it properly, nor did she understand enough about it to explain it to anyone else.

Finally, she reached out to contact Barengush, but he seemed to be surrounded by a cloud of fog. *What could be causing that?* she wondered. *Is it a ward, or is he unconscious?* She didn't want him to be hurt because of her. Maybe his father had done something to punish him. She lay down on her pallet and thought about it. *He couldn't be dead, could he? No, no matter how evil he is, surely Monaltor wouldn't kill his own son. But he killed his mother, and what about Ogryn?* That was something else altogether. She wouldn't put anything past him. Evil radiated from him in murky waves that contaminated everything around him.

Daryan

After sleeping and waking several times, Daryan finally managed to fall into a deeper sleep. He'd been running Ashavan's message from Felindra through his mind, trying to find a clue as to her safety and the possibility of being able to rescue her. Now that he was getting closer to the border, he was even more determined to find her and bring her home. It was the thought of her being locked in a dungeon that bothered him the most as his mind tried to imagine the conditions she must be enduring. Had she been truthful about that when she said it wasn't too bad? Were they giving her enough food and water? Was it filthy and filled with vermin? Did she have proper sanitary facilities? Finally, he'd taken a dose of his stomach medicine. He was exhausted from riding all day through rain-soaked forest on road that was partly washed away by the rain.

He woke up suddenly, managing to keep himself from twitching as he tried to detect what had awakened him. Then he heard it again, a soft whine. He looked towards the opening of his tent and saw a familiar silhouette against the dawning light. "Ashala!" he said softly. It had to be her. No other creature would approach him this way. "Come here, girl."

As the wolf advanced into the tent, she made a little yipping sound, and then he felt her coarse fir against his arm and her warm tongue licking his cheek. He pushed her gently away and sat up. "What are you doing here?" he asked, running his fingers through the ruff on her neck. He hardly expected her to understand him, but he had to acknowledge her in some way.

She wagged her tail and whined again, looking up at him. The light outside was increasing as the sun rose.

"It's Felindra, isn't it?" He made an image of his daughter in his mind, hoping she would understand. "Are you going to find her?" The image of Felindra and Ashala together.

She must understand something of what he was saying because she wagged her tail again.

"Go and find her," he murmured. "I'll be following you." He concentrated on the image of a map with the location of the place where she was being held. He realized it would probably mean nothing to her, but he had to offer her something. "Go and find her," he repeated, pointing towards the north and giving her a final stroke on the head.

She wagged her tail again, yipping softly, then turned and left the tent silently.

Suddenly, he heard a commotion outside. Men shouting, "Get it!", "Where's your bow!" "Damned predator!"

He leaped up from his pallet and rushed outside. Several men, mostly duchy defenders were rushing around going for their weapons as Ashala crept into the surrounding bush.

"Stop!" he shouted. "Leave her alone. She's won't hurt anyone."

"But it was in the camp," one of the sergeants, called back.

"It's all right," Daryan replied. "She came to see me."

One of the officers came out of his tent to see what was causing the excitement. "To see you, sir? I don't understand."

Daryan sighed. "I know her. She's my daughter's friend. She's gone now, so you can carry on. We'll be leaving as soon as we've broken out fast."

60 – A Prisoner's Revelations

Daryan

The rain had finally stopped, although the ground was still soggy underfoot and the evaporating moisture enveloped everything in mist. Daryan decided to interrogate the prisoner again during the midday break. Most of the troops were eating standing up except the few lucky ones who'd found boulders or logs to sit on.

"Will someone please bring the prisoner, and ask Lady Farah if she'll attend?" He waited as a couple of men moved away in different directions. They returned immediately with Farah and Pervil, the prisoner, who was still manacled.

"Sit here," Daryan said to Farah, standing up from his boulder and going to lean against a tree trunk. "I'm sorry to interrupt your meal, but I want to try to get some more information from him."

"It's all right, I've almost finished." She sat down and continued to eat the food, some meat wrapped in a piece of rolled-up bread, she'd brought with her.

"Have you eaten?" Daryan asked Pervil.

"Yes," the man replied sullenly.

"I just want to clarify a few things we didn't get to yesterday. First, do you have a family?"

"Why do you want to know?"

"Just answer the question."

The man shrugged and looked away.

Daryan looked at Farah and she nodded. "Very well; you do have a family. Are they in danger from the Dark Brethren? I mean can they be used as hostages to make you obey them?"

The prisoner looked up, surprised. "I don't know. There's a woman and she has a daughter ... not mine. I don't know if they would go after her. She moves around a lot, so it wouldn't be easy to find her. Why would they bother about me, anyway?"

"I just wanted to be sure," Daryan replied. "What about your parents?"

"My father's a fisherman. They live on an island off the east coast."

"What would you do if I decided to let you go?"

The man looked at Daryan, his eyes wide and mouth open. "No, don't," he said.

"What are you afraid of?"

"They'd kill me."

"How do you know that?"

"They killed my friend. He met a woman and stayed with her a night. They, the wizard, burned him. Said he was a traitor, an enemy spy. He wasn't, I knew that, but I was too scared to say anything."

"I see," Daryan replied, suddenly losing his appetite, thinking about the casual brutality of their enemies. He massaged his stomach, which had started to grumble again. "All right, we'll keep you with us, but you'll have to work. We can't feed you for nothing. You'll have to help with the cleanup of campsites, and digging latrines, things like that. But be warned, if you step out of line in any way, we will release you to fend for yourself. And believe me; our own people won't be feeling very friendly towards you if they catch you, that's if your friends don't get you first."

"I'll do the work, sir. I won't make no trouble, honest," he replied hastily, and rather desperately.

"Right. Now there's one more thing I'm curious about. Do you know why they kidnap people and take them away?"

The man looked down at his feet appearing very uncomfortable. "I don't know."

Daryan looked again at Farah. "He knows something," she said.

"What do you know about it?" Daryan asked again. "We can tell you know something."

"I don't ... I don't want to think about it. It's probably just a rumor anyway, things men make up to..."

"Come on," Daryan insisted. "This is very important. We have to know what is happening to our people. Tell us what you know, or what you think happens."

"It's the wizards," Pervil said reluctantly.

"What's the wizards?"

"They use them."

"How? What do you mean, use them?" Dayan had a feeling of dread, as if he was going to hear something so appalling, he'd wish he hadn't heard anything about it.

"They kill them."

"Why?"

Tears formed in Pervil's eyes. He turned his face away from Daryan and Farah. "We didn't know they were going to do that. It's something to do with their magic. After they cast one of their spells, it uses up all their energy and they need to get it back quickly so they ... they take them away where we can't see them, but one of the men saw it one time, accidental like."

"Go on! Saw what?"

"They took a little b...boy and cut ... cut his th...throat. Then the wizard d...drank the blood. This man said the wizard suddenly became strong, full of life and energy. Before, he'd been drooping with fatigue. They say children's blood is more ... powerful." Pervil wiped his face with his sleeves and looked around at his captors. "We didn't know, I swear. They just told us they were being taken to work for us in Valkonen." Daryan looked at the man for a few seconds before adding, "Where were your ... people going when they left the village where you were captured?"

"They went that way," he replied, pointing towards the northwest.

"The same way we're going. Maybe we'll run into them, then."

Dayan looked around and spotted a sergeant. "Take him away," he said. "Remove the manacles, he's not going anywhere. Put him on cleanup detail." He walked out of sight around the tree and took a deep breath, then reached in his pocket, took out his medicine bottle, and swallowed a mouthful.

61 – Daryan Goes West

Daryan

As Daryan was riding along the next day, thinking about his last interview with the prisoner, it occurred to him that he might have found the solution to something that had been puzzling him for quite a while: Why did they massacre all the wermen after causing the rockslide that killed Valdor's family? Obviously, such a massive use of destructive power would severely drain the wizards' energy. If they could use the deaths of werfolk to restore their power...

"Do you know where Axtya is?" Daryan asked the sergeant riding behind him.

"He's probably hiding in the wagon, too scared to come out. Do you want me to get him?"

"It's all right," Daryan replied. "I can talk to him when we stop for our midday meal."

He found Axtya sitting alone in the back of a supply wagon chewing on a piece of dried meat. "Why don't you come out and get some exercise?" he asked the werman.

"Man people not like me. Say I commander's pet," Axtya said, his big eyes were full of sadness.

"Don't worry about them; they don't know any better, but they do know they must not hurt you. I want to ask you something. Do the dark wizards kill your people very often?"

Axtya looked at him for a few seconds as if Daryan had said something offensive. "Sometimes," he murmured.

"Do you know why?"

"They crazy."

"Does anything happen when they kill someone?"

"Not know!" Axtya turned away from Daryan. "No more."

"I'm sorry. I don't want to upset you," Daryan said. "I'll change the subject. Do you know where we are?"

Axtya looked back at him, brows drawn together in a frown. "Yes. We in forest near big wall."

Dayan smiled and decided to word it another way. "Would you be able to find your way home from here?"

Axtya sighed. "Not know."

Well that was a waste of time, Daryan thought as he went to find his horse.

They had been travelling for two days and, other than the attack on the village on the first day, hadn't seen any signs of the invaders apart from some burnt patches of forest. The people they'd met in those areas were alert to the possibility of attack and were being very cautious, many of them carrying weapons, and never going anywhere alone. Some of the people, especially those with families, had escape plans in case they were attacked, plans which included leaving caches of food and clothing hidden outside their villages, and they now posted watchmen at night to sound an alarm if they sensed anything suspicious.

The road they were travelling became harder to navigate as they climbed higher into the mountains and the constant turns and switchbacks slowed them down considerably. A wheel on one of the supply wagons broke when it fell into a deep rut and hit a rock. They lost a couple of hours transferring the supplies from the disabled wagon into the one remaining. It would have made it heavy for the horses to pull, had one of the drivers not found a way to extend the rigging so they could harness two teams.

After this delay, Daryan and Kevan were anxious to make some progress, but it wasn't easy given the twists and turns, and the rough condition of the road. As they came around a bend, they heard a rumbling noise beyond the next turn.

"Stop! Everyone stop!" Sir Kevan cried, pulling on the reins. The horse's ears flattened and it snorted in alarm, stopping so suddenly, it almost threw the knight.

"What is it?" Daryan asked.

"Sounds like a rockslide to me. Another damned delay." He turned and looked back at the rest of the team and picked two men. "Corporal Doneti, take a defender and scout ahead. And be careful."

***

The two men rode cautiously around the bend, their eyes darting in all directions as if expecting an attack at any moment. They saw a massive pile of rocks blocking the road about seventy paces ahead. The moment they started to move closer, more rocks plummeted down from the shear rock wall on their right. One of the smaller rocks hit the defender's head, knocking him off his horse. Corporal Doneti stopped abruptly under some trees and dismounted, and then he crept back to where his comrade lay, keeping under the shelter of roadside foliage. "Laron, are you all right?" he said, kneeling on the ground beside the fallen defender. He could see his chest rising and falling, so he knew he was alive. The corporal leaned over and shook his shoulder, at which, Laron twitched and gasped in a deep breath, and then his eyes opened. "What happened?" he asked the corporal, squinting up at him.

"You tell me. One minute you were beside me and the next you were gone." He noticed some blood matting Laron's hair.

"Your scalp's bleeding. Looks as if you were hit on the head. Can you get up?"

Laron examined his head with his fingers and grunted when they came away with blood. "Help me up."

Doneti reached out and grasped Laron's hand and drew him to his feet. "Your horse's gone, so you'll have to ride mine. Can you manage that?"

***

They're taking a long time," Daryan said. "I'd better see what's happened to them." He urged his horse forward and moved slowly up the road, staying close to the sheltering trees along the right hand side. He saw a horse grazing on the foliage beside the road. *What the...?* A moment later, the corporal appeared supporting his companion on the other horse. The one on horseback seemed to be injured.

"What happened, Corporal?"

"There was a rock slide, Commander," he replied. "Blocking the whole road. Laron here must have been hit by a falling rock."

All of a sudden, rocks and arrows started flying from the hillside above. None of them found a mark, but there were a few near misses. "We'd better get out of here," Daryan said, turning his horse back down the road. "Keep to the side," he added needlessly. *It's a good thing we didn't all go barging ahead; that would have been a disaster.*

"They're up there on the ridge. They shot a few arrows at us," Daryan told Kevan when he arrived back where the rest of the team was waiting.

"Is the road passible, apart from the rockslide?" Kevan asked.

"No. Even if we could get to it, it would take too much time and effort to clear it. We'll have to find a way to get around it."

"How about going up through the woods and getting behind them?" Kevan suggested.

"It would be quite a climb and we wouldn't be able to get the supply wagon up there."

"We could leave it down here with some guards. This might be an opportunity to clear out a whole mob of them."

"We could give it a try," Daryan replied, although something made him feel uneasy about the plan.

Once they had climbed higher into the forest, they found there was less undergrowth so there was more room to maneuver among the massive sequoias and pines.

"We should be right above where they attacked us," Kevan said. "Let's spread out and surround them."

Using hand signals, Daryan passed on the suggestion, and then turned back to Kevan. "I don't like this," he said, looking around. It's too quiet, and the trunks of these trees are thick enough to conceal an army."

"I see what you mean," Kevan replied. "And there should be some noise from birds at least." He turned his horse southward. "I'll go and see how they're getting on over that side."

Daryan followed the defenders on the other side as they proceeded down the slope towards the place where the enemy should be, above the rock slide. With hand signals, he indicated they should spread out more. The silence was unnerving, no voices, no clanks of armor or the snap of broken twigs. Daryan was becoming increasingly disconcerted. He suspected their attackers had moved and could be anywhere. He looked among the defenders and mages and found Nadi. From the frown on his face and closed eyes, he appeared to be listening or concentrating on something that disturbed him. Daryan rode closer and touched his shoulder. Nadi started and opened his eyes. "Can you sense anything?" he asked in a whisper.

Nadi moved closer to him and murmured in his ear, "I sense dark life, but it seems diffused, as if it were all around us, not just down there."

"That's a bad sign. Can you sense individual life signs?"

"There are specs of dark animated life all over." He raised his hand and swept it in an arc from north to south.

Lady Farida was coming towards him looking agitated. "They're not down there," she said softly when she reached Daryan. "They're all around us."

"Quickly, send a message to all the telepaths to take cover and spread the word." Dayan turned his horse and moved towards a large tree. "Take cover," he yelled. "Take cover! We're surrounded."

The words were hardly out of his mouth when he heard a horse scream. This was followed by human screams and curses. Streams of arrows flew from all directions, some of them missing their targets, the horses, but many bringing down riders. The defenders could take shelter behind trees, once they had found out the direction from which the attacks were coming, but the poor horses were more vulnerable and bolted the moment they lost their riders.

Daryan decided to leave his horse and go on foot to face the attackers. The situation was almost impossibly chaotic, trying to command an army that was spread out all over the place, concealed among the trees that prevented him from knowing where they were. He had to trust their instinct and training to do what was needed. The arrows had stopped after the initial barrage, so the defenders were able to steal closer to the enemy positions. Moving from tree to tree, they advanced through the woods, but there seemed to be no one to confront. Suddenly a flock of ravens flew in and landed in some of the trees, screeching stridently and flapping their wings. This initiated another barrage, this time aimed at the birds.

"Come on," Dayan called to the people around him. "I think the birds have found them." He drew his sword and rushed in the direction of the ravens' perches.

Daryan noticed a movement ahead, someone dashing from one tree trunk to another. He charged after him and confronted a man in ragged dark-colored clothing, his eyes wide with fear. He had a bow over his shoulder and a long, vicious-looking knife in his hand. "Drop the knife and I'll let you live," he said. The man pointed the knife threateningly at Daryan and crouched ready to attack. "We haven't got time to play games, Daryan said. "Now, or you die!"

The man dropped the knife without taking his eyes off the Commander's sword. Dayan turned to an approaching defender. "Tie him up and then follow me."

Screams and shouts continued to echo through the forest as people from both sides encountered one another. Daryan kept moving through the trees, occasionally picking off one of the enemy. He heard a thunderclap over to his left and a flash of brilliant light followed by screams. A wizard! Daryan relocated again to bring himself closer to the site and found the mangled forms of a man and a woman, burned to death.

"Aha, the famous commander!" a mocking voice called out. "You want some of this?"

Daryan moved again without hesitation, hoping he would land behind the wizard, but he'd been seen. He moved again to the other side and ended up standing right behind the wizard. Without hesitation, he slashed the neck of his enemy, creating a fountain of blood from the wizard as he fell dead at his feet.

"One down," he said. "Now let's find the others."

While they were searching and fighting through the trees, they heard deep throaty growls followed by screams that ended abruptly. *That sounded like cats,* Daryan thought. *I hope they're not attacking us.*

Once there was no more enemy to fight, the two commanders gathered everyone together and addressed them. "That was not one our best-planned encounters," Sir Kevan said. "But you conducted yourselves admirably. Now we have to search the area for casualties. Anything you'd like to add?" he asked Daryan.

"While we search the area, some of you should collect the horses, if you can find them. We'll need them to transport the casualties. Be careful of enemy wounded. They might still have a trick or two left."

"Should we kill them?" the sergeant asked.

"I don't think that's necessary, unless you are attacked. Just disarm them and tie them up," he replied. "The most important task is taking care of our wounded. But we have to do this fast; it'll be dark soon."

They finally arrived back at the road on foot. What horses they could catch were being used to carry the wounded.

"Where's the wagon?" one of the defenders called, looking down the road.

"It's gone," another replied.

Daryan and Kevan slid down the embankment to the road and looked in both directions. Sir Kevan cursed. "They must have taken it. They've beaten us at every turn, damn them. What are we going to do now? All our food, the tents and blankets, everything…"

"Axtya, too, and the men who were guarding the wagon. There's not much we can do now," Daryan replied, "It's too dark. We'll have to make camp here. Sergeant, organize the men to gather firewood. We'll have to light several fires to keep everyone warm. Spread them out along the middle of the road—we don't want to set the trees on fire. Some of you find some small branches with the foliage attached to use as makeshift bedding for the wounded to lie on." He looked around, wondering what else to do. People carrying torches lit the area fairly well. "Would you check the wounded?" he asked Kevan. "We should count our casualties. I'll get Lady Farah to contact Bartony and warn them. They'll have to send us more supplies and two wagons to carry the wounded and bring more supplies."

"I hate this sort of warfare," Kevan said. "Never knowing where the enemy is and where he'll strike next. It looks as if the days of chivalry are gone forever. I hope the others are having better luck than we are."

One of the defenders approached Daryan. "Something strange happened up there, commander," he said. "I thought you might be interested."

"What was that, defender?" Daryan asked, thinking to himself, what wasn't strange about this whole business?

"Some of those enemy bodies looked as if they'd mauled by wild animals. Those were the only wounds on them."

"That is interesting. Could it have been cats do you think?"

"It must have been big cats; whatever they were had powerful jaws and big sharp claws."

62 – Felindra Escapes

Felindra

I've never been so bored in my life, Felindra mused. I always thought being imprisoned would be more scary and disgusting, than boring. There's nothing to do. There isn't even a rat for me talk to. Sometimes Felindra played little games in her head to pass the time, trying to name all the flowers or animals starting with a certain letter, or listing everyone she could think of that she'd met and putting them in categories. She now had an idea how Darson worked. Apart from her family, the person who came most frequently to mind was Lord Varen. She realized that, even though she'd only seen him twice, he'd become important her.

She calculated that she had been in the cell for six days, measuring the time by the number of meals she'd received. Food came regularly, once a day, as far as she could tell. A flat metal pan with a lid, accompanied by a canister of water was usually left for her while she was sleeping, which seemed to be most of the time. The food was always cold and most of the time, consisted of some sort of mush of beans or grains, unflavored apart from the occasional bits of onion. She never got any fruit or vegetables except for one time when someone had included a tiny shriveled apple. She wondered who cooked the food. Probably a former monastery worker like Dominel. She doubted the people who put her here would send anything that was not rancid or stale, although she only had a vague idea of what prisoners were given to eat from books she'd read.

She spent a lot of time thinking about food because she was always hungry. She also dwelled a lot on hygiene. They hadn't provided her any means of keeping herself clean, although they did empty her waste bucket occasionally. Even so, the cell was starting to smell quite rank. Fortunately, her monthly cycle had stopped since she became a prisoner, whether it was something natural or the mercy of the Light, she didn't know, but she was grateful whatever the cause.

She had just woken from one of her frequent naps and was trying to summon the will to get up and move around a bit when the light began to increase and the Messenger appeared, standing in the corner by the door. "It's time for you to go," she said.

"You mean I'll be free?"

"That is up to you, child. We can put certain conditions in place, but it is your will that decides what to do with them."

"I don't understand."

"For example, we can unlock doors and provide light to guide you, but we cannot make you walk out."

"Will I be shown a way to escape?"

"The light will guide you."

"What about these chains?"

"That is not a problem. See, they're unlocked!"

Felindra heard a jangle of metal against rock and felt the shackles loosen their grip on her ankles. She drew her feet out and kicked them away from her, and then she reached for her boots. "Oh thank you, Messenger. I already feel freer." She put on her boots and laced them, and then stood up.

"Now, there is one thing you need to do before leaving this place," the Messenger said. "There is a man locked in one of the other cells. We will make sure the cell is unlocked, but you must persuade him to go with you."

"Who is he?"

"I leave that up to him to reveal. Know that he is important to us and to the monastery. Are you ready?"

"I have some more questions," Felindra said, her heart pounding. "What time of day is it? And what will I do if the man refuses to leave?"

"It is two hours before sunrise. By the time you get outside, the day will be dawning. We believe the man will go willingly, but if he hesitates, you may tell him the Light wills it. Now, it is time to leave. Remember, the Light will guide you." With that, she faded from view.

Felindra heard the lock click, and then the light in the cell faded, leaving only a small disc of light focused on the door. Anxiety over what she was about to do suddenly made her feel weak, as if her legs had become nerveless and she was gasping for breaths. *Calm down,* she admonished herself. *You can do it. Think! You're getting out of this horrible place. That is if nothing goes wrong.* She felt guilty then; was her faith so weak? *I'm sorry, Light, I know you are here with me, but I get scared sometimes.* Before opening the door, she went back and grabbed her cloak.

She pushed the door open slowly, ready to jump back if anyone was there, but when she looked out into the hallway, it was empty; there was not even a guard on watch. Before leaving, she made sure the cell door was closed. The disk of light had moved to the wall opposite, providing enough illumination for her to see her surroundings. When it bobbed slightly to the left, she turned in that direction, peering anxiously over her shoulder a few times as she went. Both sides of the hallway had closed doors, but she could hear no evidence of other presences within the cells. The light came to a stop at one of the doors. Felindra heard a click. She walked towards it and pulled the handle to open it. She was almost overcome by the appalling smell that greeted her.

The light illuminating the inside of the cell revealed a thin figure sitting back on a dirty pallet regarding her warily. *The poor man; he must have been in here a very long time.*

"Excuse me," Felindra said softly. "I think you have to come with me."

The man rose to his feet, but he leaned against the wall for support. His dark hair was long and matted, and his face almost skeletal. She could see his hands trembling, whether from fear or weakness, she wasn't sure. He blinked in the light, obviously unaccustomed to seeing any. His filthy clothes were in rags, barely covering him.

He cleared his throat. "Who...who are you? What are you doing here?" he asked tremulously.

"I'm Felindra from Trethawynd. I'm a prisoner like you, but the Light is helping us to escape." She took off her cape and held it out to him. "Here, you look so cold, wear this."

He didn't reach for it although it was obvious he needed it. "What about you? You'll be cold then."

"I'm all right," she replied. "Come on please, sir. We must hurry before somebody comes."

The man groaned as he stood away from the wall and came towards the door. Felindra wrapped the cape around his shoulders and took his arm to help support him as he left his cell.

The odor coming from his body was overwhelming, but she clamped her mouth shut resolutely and took shallow breaths as she started to lead him slowly down the hall, following the light.

The passage ended with a turn to the right leading to a flight of stairs going up.

"I know the way," the man said. "This stairwell leads to a door to the outside."

"Did you live here … before?" she asked.

"Oh yes, my dear. I've lived here most of my life. I never thought it would come to this, though," he replied, pointing to himself. "I know every nook and cranny. You'll have to be patient with me though; I feel a bit weak."

"Maybe I can help you with that, sir."

"Don't tell me you're a healer too. I'd already decided you're an angel."

"I'm not, sir. I'm just an ordinary girl. The Light has blessed me with some gifts, but I don't think I'm a healer. May I touch you?"

"We should hurry; you never know when someone will come."

"Don't worry, sir, the Light is protecting us. May I try now?" She was not only concerned for his fitness and strength, but also because it would be very humiliating for him to meet others in his current condition.

"Go ahead."

Felindra put her hands on his shoulders and closed her eyes, pleading with the Light to help the man. The light beside them glowed a little stronger and a shudder passed through them both. She opened her eyes and looked at him. "Did it work?"

He straightened up from his stooped posture and held his shoulders back. His face seemed to fill out and his eyes became clear. In addition, the dreadful odor had disappeared and even his hair looked cleaner. Now she could see streaks of grey among the dark hair. He took a deep breath and smiled at her. "Indeed it did, child. I feel much better. Thank you." Even his voice sounded stronger, less tremulous.

"It was the Light, not me."

"Nevertheless, you must be a very special person to be able to use the Light's benefits so easily."

"I know I'm blessed, sir, but it is all from the Light. Should we move on?"

"Of course, my dear."

They climbed the long flight of stairs and arrived at door that opened onto a wider passage. Glancing both ways, they confirmed that there was no one in sight and continued, following the light disk. The air seemed warmer up here, and the floor was paved with smooth tiles. Felindra noticed her companion looking around at the damaged walls and the dirt and litter on the floor, an expression of sadness and dismay on his face. He sighed and continued walking to the end of the hall. Although the hallway came to a dead end, there was one more door on the side.

"We have to be careful here," he said. "Our people might have put a trap on the lock. Let me see if it's safe before we try to open it." He put his ear against the door close to the lock and closed his eyes to concentrate, and then he straightened up and turned to her. "As I suspected, there was a trap, but someone has already sprung it. It should be safe to proceed now." He opened the door to reveal another staircase leading downward. A cold draft of fresh air rose from the bottom of these stairs. "It's only a short flight, and then we have to go through a tunnel that leads to the outside. I'm going to restore the trap on the lock. It will show them how we escaped, but will also slow down anyone trying to follow us."

As they descended the stairs, Felindra thought about her companion, wondering who he was and why he was so important to the Light. She finally gathered the courage. "Do you mind if I ask you a question, sir?"

"What would you like to know, child?"

"Are you a mage?"

"I am."

"An archmage?"

"That too," he replied with a smile.

"Would it be bad manners to ask about your gifts?"

"Before we go into that, tell me something about yourself. How did you come to be in a cell in ValkonenMaa?"

She related her experiences since she'd been abducted by Barengush and his Trethawyndian coconspirator.

"That's quite a story," the old man said when she'd finished. "Your parents must be out of their minds with worry, wondering what's happening to you. You must have a very rare gift if these people went to so much trouble to bring you here. What did they want from you?"

"I'm a whisperer," she replied shyly. She still felt uncomfortable about people's reaction when they heard this.

"Ah! That explains a lot. Yes, I can see how they would want to use you for their own purposes. Have they tried anything, yet?"

"Well, they tested me with some horses in an enclosure." She smiled at the memory and glanced sideways at him. "I opened the gate and let them all out. They were so crowded together they were hurting themselves and one another."

"That must have caused some trouble. What did they do?"

"They tried to round up the horses, but they couldn't catch them all, so they just closed the monastery gates and let them roam free. They took me inside to Monaltor's office and tried something else."

"Monaltor, eh? I've heard of him. A very nasty character, his son too. How did that go?"

"He was going to do something with wires attached to my head, but Barengush, the son, came in with a puppy and he decided to try something else first. I was supposed to hold

509

the little dog and communicate with it while Barengush had his hands on my head, but pressure started to build up in my brain. It felt as if my head exploded and then I passed out. It gave me a terrible headache and I was sick for a while. Monaltor told me his son had been thrown across the room and blacked out too. He was sicker than I was."

The man smiled. "I'm sorry you were hurt, but it sounds to me as if you've developed the gift of Repel."

"Could it come suddenly like that?" Felindra asked.

"Maybe the extreme stress you were being subjected to could have triggered it, but it must have been a latent gift. I've never heard of it coming spontaneously like that, but I suppose it is possible. You have certainly developed a strong relationship with the Light. Were you in the cell all the time, except when they tested you?"

"No, I had a nice clean little room at first. An old man called Dominel took care of me."

"Ah, Dominel. He didn't get away, then. He's one of the best men we had in our employ. I'm glad he's all right. How did you end up in the cells?"

"I made friends with Barengush—you know, Monaltor's son—and started to tell him about the Light. I don't think he's evil like his father and Ogryn ... now he's *really* evil, you can feel it radiating from him. Barengush has been treated so badly by his father; he's always criticizing and humiliating him—he even killed his mother. Monaltor was really mad because I told him about the Light so he had me locked in the dungeons to punish me."

"I see," the man said. "It's their loss. How did you get along with the son? Did he sound as if he was genuinely interested?"

"I'm not sure, but at least he listened." She took a deep breath and rubbed her arms. They'd reached the bottom of the stairs and the draft of fresh air had become stronger.

"You're cold. I should give you back your cloak." He started to remove it from his shoulders.

"No, please don't. You need it more than I do, and I don't like to see you in those ragged clothes." This was her way of hinting that he would be half-naked if he didn't have the cloak.

"Very well," he said. "We're almost there now and there might be some clothing stored in those containers."

The tunnel widened, forming a cavern. The old man looked around. "Some of our people escaped this way," he told Felindra. "We usually keep a few supplies down here for emergencies, but I see most of the containers have been opened and emptied. Let's see what's left."

They both started to search the bins and sacks that littered the cavern. "Here's something," Felindra said, holding up a pair of long culottes. She handed them to him. "Do you think they'll fit?"

The only other thing they found that would be useful was a very small cloak, probably intended for a child. Felindra shook it out, releasing a cloud of dust and a spider. She put it over her shoulders; although it only reached her knees, she'd be warm enough.

"It will soon warm up outside," the old man said. He'd changed into the trousers while she was digging around among the containers and she'd persuaded him to keep her cloak. He'd had to roll the cuffs of the trousers up, but he needed a belt to hold them in place. He recovered the sash from the old rags he'd been wearing and tied it around his waist.

"Where do you think we should go?" she asked him as they exited the cavern into the early morning light.

"I know a safe place we can use while we decide what to do. There might even be food there."

Before they'd gone very far, they heard several people approaching on horseback. "Quickly, we must hide until we know who they are." He grasped her arm and led her into some bushes. As soon as the riders drew close enough to be identified, he stood up and returned to the path. "Captain, it's good to see you got away,"

"Grand Master! We thought...I don't know what we thought ... the worst, I'm afraid." He jumped down from his horse and rushed to embrace the old man. "I can't tell you how good it is to see you."

The Grand Master! Felindra was astonished. She was even more convinced the Light was with them. This man was obviously important in the League's struggle against the Dark Brethren. She became aware of a young defender watching her closely, as if wondering who she was. He caught her looking and smiled.

"And who is this?" the captain asked the Grand Master, looking at Felindra.

"This is Felindra of Trethawynd...let me see...she's a whisperer, and has many more gifts, thanks to the Light. Oh, and she rescued me from the dungeons. I don't know how she managed it, but here we both are. I think she is uniquely blessed by the Light."

Felindra felt her face heating up and looked at her scuffed boots.

"That's quite a spectacular recommendation," the defender said, smiling at her. "I'm Captain Arendt of the League of Light," he added with a small bow. He went on to introduce the other members of his party, but the only one Felindra could recall afterwards was Vertan D'Alcona, the young defender.

"Where were you heading, Grand Master?" Arendt inquired.

"I was thinking of the sanctuary, but if you have a better idea.... I haven't much knowledge of what's been happening outside. They kept me in a warded cell down in the old dungeons, so I couldn't communicate. The guards wouldn't tell me anything. How are things going out here?"

"Before I tell you that and, based on the current situation, I think it would be best to go to the sanctuary. Are you hungry?" he asked, suddenly remembering they'd just escaped from the dungeons.

"We are," the Grand Master replied. "They didn't feed us very well in there."

Arendt went to one of the saddlebags and retrieved several cloth-wrapped packages. "Here's a little something to tide you over until we can get you something more substantial." He handed two to the Grand Master and two to Felindra who immediately unwrapped a package containing some bread and cooked meat. She closed her eyes ecstatically as she savored the aroma of solid food. She quickly made a sandwich roll and took a bite.

"Thank you," she said with her mouth full. Then, after a final chew, she swallowed the food in her mouth. "That was wonderful!"

"I should have thought of it sooner," Arendt replied. "Vertan, how about letting Felindra ride your horse?" he turned to address the Grand Master. "You can take mine."

"There might be some horses wandering around in the woods," Felindra said. "Do you want me to try to locate some?"

"How would you do that?" Vertan asked.

Felindra shrugged. "I just try to sense them. I don't even know of it will work, but I can try,"

She closed her eyes and concentrated for a few seconds. "Sorry, I couldn't find any. They must have rounded them up and taken back them inside the wall. I do sense someone, though, and he seems to be coming our way."

"Do you know who it is?"

"I think it's the wizard, Barengush."

"Is he alone?"

"Yes."

"Let's take cover and wait for him, with your consent, Grand Master. Maybe we can capture him and get some answers."

"Don't threaten him," Felindra said hastily. "He has some very nasty destructive powers. Maybe I should meet him. He knows me."

"I don't like that idea, Felindra. I don't want to put you at risk."

"Don't worry, commander, we're almost friends, as much as you can be with such a person. He tried to help me escape once."

"All right. But we'll be covering you." He turned to the defenders. "We'll use bows. We won't have time to reach him with swords. If he used his powers, the effect would be instantaneous."

Felindra and the Grand Master found cover in some shrubbery while the four defenders moved farther back, spreading out on both sides of the path.

After a few minutes, Barengush appeared around the bend. He wasn't wearing his wizard's costume. He was dressed in a black tunic over an ordinary pair of beige culottes. He didn't appear to be armed, but he had a satchel hanging from his shoulder and there was a saddlebag on the horse.

Felindra strolled casually out of the bushes and stood in the path waiting for him. He frowned when he saw her, but kept coming. "You got out, I see," he said in a neutral tone. "What are you planning to do now?"

"What are you doing here?" she asked.

"I thought you might need some help."

"You mean you want to help me escape again?"

He shrugged. "Don't you want any help?"

"But why are you doing this?"

"I've been doing a lot of thinking since our talk, and I'm sick of all the things they make me do. I want to see what it's like in the real world."

"I wish I could believe you," Felindra replied. "I know you're unhappy about the way your father treats you, but I can't see you leaving everything behind. Where would you go?"

He looked down at his hands on the reins. "I want to go with you."

"Barengush, I have to tell you something and I don't want you to get excited. Promise me you won't do anything rash."

"It depends," he replied. "I will protect myself if I'm threatened."

"That's good enough." She paused for a moment, wondering how to introduce him to the others without everything turning sour. "I'm not alone."

Before she could go on, Barengush jumped from his horse and grabbed her. "Is this a trap?" he snarled.

The Grand Master and the four defenders stepped out onto the path, arrows nocked in the bows of the defenders. Barengush pulled her to him, turning her around to face away, and held her with one arm tight against her neck. She tried to shake her head but couldn't move it. "It's all right. They won't hurt you. Just let me go and they'll lower their weapons." She coughed from the effects of trying to talk through a limited airway.

"She's right," Arendt added. "Just let go of her. None of us wants to hurt you. At least we're willing to give you a chance." He turned to the other defenders. "Lower your bows."

The arm that was holding Felindra relaxed and his hand moved to her shoulder. He sighed heavily. "I hope you really mean it," he said. "All right, you can go," he added as he took his hand from her shoulder and allowed her to move at will.

Felindra looked at the Grand Master and Arendt, hoping they would keep their promise. Arendt nodded. "We'll need your horse," he said to Barengush. The first test of the wizard's sincerity.

Barengush reluctantly offered Felindra the reins.

"Where are you going?" Barengush asked.

Felindra looked to Arendt to respond. "Second test," he said. "Don't ask questions. If you come with us, we expect you to follow some rules, one of which is mind your own business, the second one is don't try to escape; if you do, we'll have to kill you. For all we know, you could be a spy for the Dark Brethren. And we'll know if you try to send any messengers. At least two of us are sensors."

63 – New Wagons

Daryan

By the time the fires were started, it was completely dark. The troops made themselves as comfortable as they could without tents, blankets or food. *Maybe we should have tried to catch something for to cook, but we're too tired,* Dayan mused as he shifted his position once more. *We made some foolish decisions today ... I made foolish decisions. We underestimated them, expecting they'd be disorganized.* The pain in his stomach had become a permanent fixture, and now he'd run out of medicine.

Just as he thought he was finally going to fall asleep, he heard some rustling in the bushes behind his head. He grabbed the sword that was lying by his side and looked up. "Show yourself!" he ordered. He was hopeful that an animal would be scared off by his voice. It was doubtful an enemy would come near so many armed men and women, but you never knew. His curiosity was put to rest when an unlovely face with huge eyes poked through the foliage.

"Axtya!"

"Yes." The werman slid down the embankment and came to rest close to where Daryan had been lying. He gazed soulfully at Daryan as if waiting for him to decide his fate.

"These people are trying to sleep so let's walk and you can tell me what happened."

Daryan walked slowly down the road away from the sleepers, so that the little man could keep up. Not everyone was sleeping. They could hear the moans of the wounded still, and one person was crying. Daryan saw a healer tending to one of the wounded defenders. *I should ask him if he has anything for my stomach,* Daryan thought, but continued walking. Some of the defenders were tossing about and muttering curses, unable to sleep.

"Tell me what happened?" Daryan asked as soon as they were far enough away from the camp.

"Man people come. Axtya not want find him. Hide in trees." He waved his stump towards the forest on the opposite side of the road.

"Did you see what happened to the men guarding the wagon?"

"Bad men stop them, no move, tie with rope."

Daryan scratched his head, trying to figure out what he meant by 'stop, no move'. Maybe a wizard cast some kind of spell to paralyze them. After he'd seen what wizards are capable of, he was relieved they hadn't done worse.

"How are we going to find them?" Daryan said, as much to himself as to Axtya.

"That way," Axtya said, pointing towards the northeast.

"To the border?"

Axtya shrugged and nodded.

Does that mean maybe? Daryan yawned. *I really should get some sleep.* "Find somewhere to sleep. We'll discuss this in the morning." He walked back to the place where he'd been lying and sat down again, leaning his back against the bank.

***

"Look who's turned up," Daryan announced the next morning. He beckoned to Axtya to join him, ignoring scowls and grimaces of distaste from the Trethawynd defenders. "Axtya may be able to help us find our wagon."

"How's that?" Sir Kevan asked.

"He hid when he heard them approaching, and watched them."

"What about the men guarding the wagon?" a defender asked.

"According to Axtya, the wizard put some sort of spell on them, making it so they couldn't move, and then tied them up."

"Will they still be paralyzed?" Kevan asked.

"I doubt it," Daryan replied. "If they were taking them with them, they'd have to be able to walk. There wasn't enough room in the wagon for everyone." Daryan looked around at the remaining defenders who were still on their feet "I'm sure everyone is as hungry as I am, so we had better start moving. Axtya thinks they are going north east, so we'll have to backtrack and use the other road." He thought for a moment and added to Lady Farah, "Any news from Bartony?"

"Yes, commander. A response from the duke came a few minutes ago. He's sending another wagonload of supplies and one for the wounded. He wants to know if we need any more defenders."

"Thank you, Farah. I'll think about that once we find out how many casualties we have."

"We have an estimate of casualties," Sir Kevan said. "I'll fill you in as we walk."

Daryan ordered half the able-bodied to start walking, and the rest to stay behind to guard the wounded. "Would you stay with us, Farah?" he asked the sender. "We may need to send another message." When she nodded consent, he turned back to Kevan

"How many have we lost?" he asked Kevan.

"Seven dead, and two or three more who won't make it unless they have medical attention soon. The healers are doing the best they can, but most of their medicines were in the wagon. They only carried emergency packs in the field."

Daryan sighed and shook his head. "What else? Can any of the injured walk?"

"One or two at the most. There were twenty-two wounded; some have burns, nasty cuts that needed suturing, one man lost his leg below the knee, and a woman her hand. In addition to that, there are broken bones—legs, shoulders, arms, everything. The healers have applied splints, but they are running out of pain medicine."

"Let's take a look." Daryan led the way along a row of men and a few women who were lying on pallets made of vegetation. Four were standing, supporting themselves with staves made from slender trunks of saplings.

One of the men standing caught sight of Axtya who was trailing behind Daryan. "I bet it was that thing," he said, glaring at the werman. "He's probably a spy. He gave then some sort of signal to tell them where we were."

"That's nonsense, Firinci," Kevan snapped. "I don't want you inciting hatred. We have enough trouble as it is."

"But how do we know he's not working for them?" the man persisted.

"I'll tell you why," Dayan said. "He's working for me and he's already provided us with some useful information. Besides, he'd be the first one they'd kill if they caught him. Now, let's continue with the matter in hand."

The man, Firinci, looked a bit crestfallen, and it was obvious he wasn't happy having accept a creature he'd been taught to hate.

They continued to visit the casualties, trying to give them comfort and encouragement. "I'm going to stay with you until help arrives. It's on its way, but it might take a while to get here. We'll do everything in our power to help you, so if you have any concerns, let us know.

"I'd like a nice hot mug of tea," a defender with his arm in a sling quipped.

"Me, I'd rather have ale," another added.

"Me too." Daryan said with a smile. "I wish there was a way to get them for you."

"Sir," one of the uninjured defenders said. "If we're going to wait for the wagons, why don't some of us hunt up some game and at least get everyone something to eat?"

"A brilliant idea," Daryan replied. "I don't know why I didn't think of it myself."

"You've got a lot on your mind, sir," the man said.

"You've no idea," Daryan replied, unconsciously putting his palm over his stomach. "Very well, take another couple of defenders and go hunt."

"I'll be off, now to meet the wagons," Sir Kevan announced. Walking back towards his horse.

"Wait," Daryan called after him. Kevan stopped and turned to face him. Take Axtya with you. He might be able to help find the people who stole our wagon."

"I'll try,' Kevan replied. "He may not want to go with us."

"Tell him I said so."

After about half an hour, the hunters returned with the carcass of a young doe. Daryan winced, knowing how this would upset his tenderhearted daughter would be, but he didn't say anything. At least it had had a quick death and not been torn apart by cougars or wolves. The hunters quickly dressed out the animal while others gathered firewood and started a fire.

Daryan leaned back on the embankment and left them to it while he closed his eyes and tried to make up some of the sleep he'd lost during the night.

A hand on his shoulder brought Daryan awake instantly. He rubbed his eyes and stood up. "Farah! News?"

"Yes commander. I've just heard from Toma. I'd like to tell you what he sent."

"Ashavan! I hope it's good news for once." The smile on her face told him it was. "All right, tell me."

"Very good news," Farah replied. "Your daughter has escaped from the dungeons of the ValkonenMaa monastery."

Daryan's heart lurched. "What? Truly?" Farah smiled and nodded. "Thank the Light!" he suddenly felt as if a great weight had been lifted from him.

"Not only that," Farah continued. "She's rescued the Grand Master who was also in one of the cells. She wants you to know she's safe and is currently in a sanctuary with a League defender. Toma said you might be amused to know that the wizard who abducted her is with them."

"They've taken him prisoner?" Daryan exclaimed in astonishment. "That must have been quite a feat."

"No. Apparently, she's been teaching him about the Light and he wants to get away from his father and the rest of the Dark Brethren."

"That girl grows more amazing every day! Thank you, Farah. That news takes away some of the bitterness of our current situation. Anything else?"

"He says that your wife and son miss you and send their love, and everything else there is fine."

Daryan thanked her, and then leaned back and closed his eyes.

"Are you hungry, commander?" Daryan opened his eyes and saw one of the hunters. "Food's ready. There's not much to go around, but it should take the edge off while we're waiting for the wagons, then we'll be able to have a real feast.

***

It was almost dark when the wagon arrived for the casualties. Fires had been lit along the roadway again to keep them warm and give them some light. It could be quite hot on a sunny day in the mountains, but the temperature fell rapidly once the sun went down.

It took a couple of hours to get the wounded ready for moving. Now the healers had more supplies, they were able to treat their injuries properly, suturing wounds, dispensing pain and anti-infection medications, setting and immobilizing broken bones, all the procedures that gave hope of a good recovery.

While they were working, Daryan supervised the distribution of food and blankets to the defenders who'd stayed behind. The healers had to take turns eating the bread with cheese and cooked meat slices, in order that their work wouldn't be interrupted too much.

While Daryan was eating, he sat down with the wagon master. "How were things along the road?"

"Your other people are camping at a junction with another road north. By now, they should be well-fed and sleeping comfortably."

"Any more incidents?"

"A few things: We passed a couple of burning villages with no sign of the people who lived there. And there was a rockslide close to where your people are camped. Fortunately for us, it didn't completely block the road and we were able to get by."

"You and your men must be tired, and the horses probably need rest. I think we should stay here until dawn."

"That would suit us fine," the man replied. "I'll go and see how they're getting on, and tell them to make themselves comfortable."

Daryan slept well now that he had less worries, and was able to forget about his unpredictable stomach for a time.

64 – Sanctuary

Felindra

Vertan walked beside Felindra, who was riding his horse, while the Grand Master rode the one Barengush had been riding.

"I don't see why we can't double up on the horses," Vertan said. "Some of us are not heavy enough to strain them."

"Yes, but who would want to share a horse with Barengush?" she glanced back over her shoulder and saw him with hands tied with rope in front of him and secured to the saddle of one of the defenders.

"I see your point," Vertan admitted, and then changed the subject. "You must miss your home and family a lot, and they must be worried sick about you. How long have you been here?"

She looked at Vertan, sadness and yearning reflected in her eyes. He looked very downcast, too, as if he had also experienced a recent tragedy. "I don't really know. It seems like weeks. Has the autumn equinox passed?"

"Yes, that was five days ago. How is it you don't know?"

"It's impossible to tell how much time passes when you're in a dark cell, and I slept a lot more than usual." She sighed and looked away at the trees. "My anniversary was two days ago and I didn't even know it. What about your parents? Are they safe?"

He looked down at the ground and put his hand on the horse's side, as if seeking solace. "They didn't survive the attacks," he said and cleared his throat. "I miss them, but I know they are journeying together towards the Light."

They were silent for a while. Felindra had a feeling he wanted to say more, but for some reason, held back. She didn't want to press him. He would tell her whatever it was in his own good time.

Finally, he asked her, "How did you meet Barengush?"

"He's the one who abducted me and brought me to ValkonenMaa."

"How can you make friends with someone who's done that to you?"

"I was very angry, especially after what he did to Ashala."

"Ashala?"

"She's my wolf-sister. I love her as much, as if she were my own blood kin. He hurt her very badly, using her as bait to trap me. There are lots of other dreadful things he did on top of that."

"So what happened to change your mind?"

"I guess I saw how unhappy he was. His father treats him like a dog. He's so cold and doesn't have a trace of love in his heart. One day, Barengush took me for a walk outside; he knew how cooped up and restless I was feeling. It was after I did something that helped him; I guess that was his way of thanking me. Anyway, I started telling him about the Light, and how hopeless darkness was. He didn't seem to be very interested, but he must have told his father something because that's when the old man had me thrown in the dungeons. Barengush came to visit me there once and got into trouble for that as well."

"He must have taken in some of what you told him. Now he wants to leave the Brethren behind and go with us? I'd say that's a pretty good commitment. That is if he's not fooling us and is just here to spy."

"We'll see, won't we? I hope he isn't a spy. He already has to pay for the crimes he committed against Trethawynd, but if his conversion is genuine, I'm sure that would go in his favor."

The sun was at its zenith and the air was quite hot. This was the first time she'd felt really warm since before she'd been sent to the dungeons. "Is it much farther to the sanctuary?"

"I don't think so. I've only been there once and I don't remember much about that time. It was just after the attack and everyone was so frightened; it was confusing." Vertan shook his head and looked down at his feet. "We'll talk later," he said and ran ahead to catch up with the captain.

Felindra fell back until she was riding next to Barengush. "Do you think they'll come after you when they find out you're gone?" she asked him.

"I don't think they know I've gone yet. I told the guards at the gate I was going hunting. That should give me a few hours. They'd try to force me to go back. My father likes to use *the voice* when he wants me. I'm sick of hearing it." He gave her a sour look and glanced up at the defender whose horse he was tied to. "I hope I can trust your people."

"I hope you mean what you say," Felindra replied.

"So it all boils down to trust," he said. "Don't worry, little girl, you'll be all right and I'm sorry I hurt you ... before."

"It's not the way you hurt me that infuriates me, it's what you did to my wolf. You're lucky she still lives, otherwise, I'd make sure you paid for it."

They arrived at the sanctuary in the late afternoon, thankful to be able to dismount and stretch their leg. "What do we do with the horses, captain?" a defender asked.

"We'll have to picket them by the stream," Arendt replied. "Come on, I'll show you the way. It's a bit hard to find if you don't know it's there."

"The horses would know," another defender said. "They can smell water from a good way off."

Arendt nodded and turned to Vertan. "Would you go into the cave and find some rope. There should be some in the outer chamber. Bring it to the stream when you have it." He addressed the others. "Leave your packs inside the cave while we take care of this. Just follow Vertan."

Arendt led them through the trees until they reached a thicket of prickly bushes and ferns. The glitter of water illuminated a narrow opening in the bush. Arendt led his horse through first and the others followed. The stream widened at this point into a pond surrounded by rushes and ornamented with lily pads and water hyacinth.

"What a beautiful place," Felindra said to the Grand Master.

"Indeed. Being out here in such beautiful and peaceful surroundings is a balm for the soul."

Vertan arrived with the rope and the men quickly stretched a generous length between two trees and then looped the reins on it. "That should keep them," Arendt said when they'd finished.

"What happens if they're attacked by predators?" Felindra asked.

"Have you ever seen a horse fight for its life?" Arendt replied. "They put up a fearsome defense. A kick in the head from a horse can stun a wolf ... kill it even. And they can easily break free if they need to; the ropes aren't tied too securely. We can go back to the cave now and see what there is to eat, once everyone's re filled his water container."

"We should gather some firewood on the way back," the Grand Master suggested. "I know how dank and cold it can be in that cavern."

Once inside the cave, they gathered around the fire to eat and discuss what to do next.

"I conferred with Archmage Solvang while we were travelling," the Grand Master said. "I'm afraid I couldn't resist using my gift once I was free of that ward." He smiled around at everyone and shrugged one shoulder. "She advised me to travel immediately to the capital, and I'm afraid she wants you to escort me. The crown prince has arrived in Mainio and is deploying his forces around the duchy to deal with the Dark Brethren."

"Would it be all right for me to go back to my family in Trethawynd?" Felindra asked.

"You couldn't go all that way alone, my dear," the Grand Master objected. "It's very dangerous in these woods, even without the Dark Brethren." He glanced at Barengush.

"I could protect her," Barengush offered.

"And lead her right back to the monastery," Arendt said sharply.

"I wouldn't, I swear," Barengush replied. "You can scan me and see for yourselves I'm truthful." He was starting to sound desperate.

"Why this obsession with Felindra?" the Grand Master asked him.

"I don't know. Maybe it has something to do with the Light. She told me about it, you know. Or maybe I want to make amends for what I did to her. I could protect her."

"I would not permit you to go alone," the Grand Master replied. "If we could get one of these defenders to go with you, I might consider allowing it."

Felindra wasn't sure what to think. She certainly didn't want to be alone with him for days, possibly weeks, but he would know the way, and be able to protect her.

"I could go with them," Vertan offered. "With your permission, captain," he added to Arendt.

"There's something else I haven't told anyone yet: my wolf is coming to find me. She's the best protection anyone could have. Not only that, she has alerted the Guardian of the Forest to what's happening, and he will ask the animals of the forest to watch over us."

"That's quite remarkable," the Grand Master said, looking at her penetratingly. "I'd almost forgotten what the gift of whispering could achieve." He turned to Barengush. "You realize, young man, that if you go to Trethawynd, you will have to face retribution for your deeds and the damage you have done there. I don't sense any desire to betray our trust in you, so, with all the protection that seems to be available to you, young lady, I have no objection to the plan. What about you, captain? Would you release this young man ... what's your name, son? ... right, Vertan, to accompany them?"

"He's only a recent recruit, not fully trained in defender skills, yet." Arendt replied.

"What do you think, Vertan?"

"I will abide by the will of the Light," Vertan replied. "And I think this is something He would want me to do, Grand Master. I'm not concerned about failing because I know the Light will be with us."

"Your faith and confidence are remarkable, Vertan." The Grand Master looked from him to Felindra, a bemused expression on his face. Then he turned to Arendt. "What do you say, Captain? Shall we give him a chance to prove himself?"

"How can I resist such powerful persuasion? I hope you will be safe, Vertan and, as you say, the Light will protect all of you." Arendt added a few more sticks to the fire and looked around at his companions. "I think it's time we got some sleep. We'll discuss in the morning how we are going to equip them for their journey."

65 –Lost Wagon

Daryan

The team carrying the wounded men and women arrived at the junction around noon the next day. Daryan and Sir Kevan decided to send only the worst cases—those with severe injuries that would take time to heal and those who were immobilized, around twenty-six in all—to Bartony to receive further treatment and recuperate. The remaining five casualties, those who could get around and would be ready for action after taking it easy for a while, would travel in the new supply wagon or ride horses, if they were able. Daryan also sent a message to Duke Valdor asking for some reinforcements.

Axtya looked relieved to see him and followed him around everywhere, making Daryan wonder what had happened while he was away. Although the League defenders were relatively tolerant, the duchy defenders were not as understanding of his role and the reason he was with them.

"What's our next move?" Daryan asked Kevan, once the ambulance wagons had departed.

"I think we should go after our wagon, and catch the fiends who caused us all this trouble. We're well rested now and have an idea what we're up against."

"I agree. Let's get started while we still have some daylight. Is Nadi around? I'd like to talk to him."

"The last time I saw him, he was helping pack the wagon."

"I'll find him," Daryan replied. "Do you want to get everyone together?"

Daryan went to the supply wagon and saw Nadi folding blankets and storing them away.

"Well met, Commander," he said when he saw Daryan.

"Well met, Nadi. They're keeping you busy I see." Daryan didn't object to being called commander when they were among the troops. He didn't want to make Nadi uncomfortable in their company. Defenders could be a bit guarded when they were around friends of their commanding officers. "We're leaving now and I want you to ride with me and Sir Kevan so that you can warn us if you sense anything dangerous." He hesitated a moment. "Oh, by the way, I heard from Ashavan that Felindra has escaped from her captors."

"Praise the Light," Nadi replied. "Is she well?"

"I think so. She's probably out asking every animal she meets to help in our struggle. I believe she may be heading this way."

"Perhaps we'll meet her; I hope so. I'm happy for you, Daryan. I know how I'd feel if anything happened to Lis or Vanelda."

Once everyone was ready to move, they started north on a narrow trail. In places, it became so narrow, they could barely force the wagon through. The passage of their stolen wagon was evident in the damaged foliage and gauged embankments. The Dark Brethren had had plenty of time to get away and Daryan wondered if they were going to be able to catch up with them. They examined carefully the entrances to every side road and trail for signs of their turning off, but by nightfall, it appeared they were still on this same road.

They'd sent a couple of scouts ahead to look for a place to camp. It was difficult on such a narrow road between dense foliage for them to find a suitable site, especially one close to water. They kept going, lighting their way with torches until they met the scouts returning.

"There's a place up ahead that might do," one of them reported. "There's not much open space, so it'll be a bit crowded, but there is a stream."

"Lead the way, defender, we'll take a look."

It ended up being a matter of necessity—they had to stop with everyone exhausted and hungry. The horses needed water and a place to rest and graze. Fires were lit for warmth wherever it was possible without setting the woods on fire. There wasn't room to erect tents, so they had to sleep in their bedrolls—waterproof groundsheets and blankets—using their packs as pillows.

During the night, they heard wolves calling in the distance. Daryan wondered if Ashala was involved. He wouldn't be surprised if she'd raised a whole pack to help her search for Felindra. This was his second night of sleeping without cinders smoldering in his stomach. It was good to be doing something after the attack and the long wait for rescue, but he put his sense of well-being down to the news of Felindra's escape.

The following day, the road rose steeply until it passed over a ridge and began to descend into a wooded valley. There were signs of habitation among the trees, the occasional glimpse of stone and wood buildings with wood smoke rising from some of them, but there was no trace of the Dark Brethren. They must have been taking advantage of the delay they'd caused to get as far away as possible. As they drew closer to a small settlement whose major occupation appeared to be logging, they saw a group of people waving to them.

"They look as if they know us," Kevan commented.

"That's because they're our agents. One of the groups we sent out earlier to survey the situation," Daryan replied. "We thought it would be safer if they dressed like the local inhabitants so they wouldn't stand out.

When they reached the group, Daryan stopped and dismounted. "Well met," he greeted them.

"Well met, indeed, commander," a tall woman replied. "We heard you were in the area, but we didn't expect you to use this back road."

"Ah well, we couldn't get by the roadblock our adversaries set on the other route, so we had to turn back and come this way." He looked at her three companions, noticing how tired and strained they seemed. "It's time for a break, so why don't we sit down and have something to eat." He indicated his intentions to Kevan, who immediately gave the order to the others.

While they were eating, Daryan related their encounter with the Dark Brethren. "I don't suppose you saw any sign of them in the last couple of days," he asked.

"We were up in the hills investigating an incident at a lumber camp. We just got back this morning," one of the men replied.

"But the villagers here said a group of strangers went by yesterday. They didn't stop or try to make contact with the villagers, but they helped themselves to a goat and a few chickens as they passed."

"Did they by any chance have a wagon?"

The woman, a healer, answered. "I think someone did mention a wagon. The people here didn't think it odd given the number of people in the group."

"That's our supply wagon," Daryan told them. "They took it while we were engaged in fighting off their brothers. They also took several of our people who were guarding the wagon. We were hoping to catch the thieves and rescue our defenders. Where does this road come out?"

"It meets the east-west road just over the next ridge. It's not much of a road; if the rain isn't washing it out, the snow is obliterating it, but the local people depend on it and try to keep it clear as much as possible. Theirs is not an easy life," she added.

"So it seems," Daryan replied. "I don't envy them. Have there been any incidents around here lately?"

"We heard of something happening up there." She nodded towards the hills to the east. "There was a fire which we thought might be an attack, but it turned out to have been caused by a fight between two loggers. They knocked over a lamp and set fire to one of the cabins. No one was badly hurt, but they were glad to have some salve for their burns."

"There was that attack down the south road," one of the men added. "But you probably passed that on your way from Bartony."

"Aye, we did. Sadly, we arrived too late to do anything." Daryan sighed and looked around to see if everyone was ready to move on. "Before we leave, is there anything you need?"

"We were going to take a trip to Bartony soon to replenish our supplies, but if you could leave some bread and maybe some nuts and dried fruit, it would help tide us over. Do you still want us to continue our activities now that the offensive has started?"

"It looks as if you're ready for some leave," Daryan replied. "The duke is stationed in Bartony now, coordinating everything, so I suggest you report to him and see if he has anything you could help with, but I strongly recommend you take a break and go back to your families for a while. I'll have the quartermaster pack up the things you need, and I wish you good fortune. Your contribution to the effort has not gone unnoticed and we are grateful for everything you've done."

"It's an honor to serve," the healer said as she stood up from the log she'd been resting on. "But I can't deny it would be wonderful to have a break. Thank you, commander. Light protect you, and good fortune."

"And you."

Daryan stood up and shook the crumbs from his tunic, and then went over to the supply wagon and spoke to the man in charge, asking him to pack a few food supplies for them.

Later that day, the road became even narrower in order to pass through a canyon. The commanders called a halt before entering the canyon.

"This is too great an opportunity for them to set an ambush, so we need to look around a bit before we continue. We'll send scouts up both sides to survey." He stopped and spoke to Kevan. "Would you like to ask your sergeant to pick a few men to scout?" he asked. It was awkward having two men in charge; Daryan always seemed to make the decisions, being the older and more experienced, but he didn't want his Sir Kevan to lose face because of this. Kevan's personality was less assertive than Daryan's, which made him more a follower than a leader, and he didn't seem to resent Daryan taking the lead.

"My pleasure," Kevan said. "I'll get him working on it."

Daryan and Kevan sat on boulders at the entrance to the canyon while the defenders gave some water and fodder to the horses, before sitting down to eat some of their rations.

Nadi came over to the commanders, his brows wrinkled with worry. "I sense something, commander," he said glancing down the canyon.

"Could you be more specific, Nadi?" Dayan said.

"Dark life, but it's diffuse. I can't pinpoint any particular place; it seems to be spread out in that area." He waved his arm from one side of the canyon to the other. "Almost like the last ambush."

"Thank you, Nadi. The scouts do seem to be taking a long time," Daryan added to Kevan. "I hope they haven't fallen into a trap. Nadi's senses are usually quite accurate, so there must be something amiss." He turned to Nadi. "Would you ask the mages to come over here, please?"

Before the mages arrived, men and women started coughing and began to stagger aimlessly. Daryan's own throat was irritated and he was starting to feel a bit woozy. He stood up and used all his willpower to remain standing. Get back," he shouted, between coughs waving his hand shakily down the road. "Come on, quickly!" he staggered over to his horse, grabbed its reins and led it back down the road. Even the horses were unsteady. It *must be some sort of gas*, he thought, *but I can't smell anything. How could they deliver it out in the open like this?* He looked behind him at the other defenders, some of them staggering slowly on, but others were already sitting or lying in the road and several of the horses had collapsed. He couldn't leave them, but what good would it do if he succumbed as well. *Damn their rotting souls!*

He noticed movement in the brush above the road and dragged his sword from its scabbard in slow motion. It felt as if it was made of lead and he wasn't sure he would be able to wield it effectively. *Light save us, I'm....* the last thing he remembered was the clang of his sword falling on the ground.

When Daryan opened his eyes a short time later, he saw a wizard standing over him, wielding his sword. "You're awake, at last," the man said. "I've been looking forward to meeting the famous Commander Peshanar. And look here, I've found one of his famous enchanted swords." He placed the tip of the sword on Daryan's cheek.

Daryan cleared his throat and coughed. Adrenalin coursed through his system, washing away the lethargy. "I wouldn't use that if I were you," he growled. He wanted to sit up, but the sword in his face prevented his moving.

The wizard laughed and pressed the point harder until Daryan felt it cut into his skin. "Don't think you can fool me with that trick. I tell you what; let's try and see what happens."

"Don't say I didn't warn you," Daryan gasped quickly. In a way, he hoped the wizard would try something. He wasn't too afraid of the pain and it would be worthwhile to see how powerful the effects of the enchantment would be.

"Oh, now you've really got me frightened," the wizard sneered. He raised the sword and slashed it against Daryan's cheek. A sharp searing pain shot through his face, but it was not as spectacular as was what happened to the wizard. A powerful current shot through the sword into its wielder, throwing him back several paces until his smoking body landed in the middle of the road, lifeless. *You wouldn't listen,* Daryan thought as he sat up and reached for the fallen sword. *I did warn you.*

Until this point, Daryan had barely been aware of the chaos around him. Horses neighing, bucking and kicking; Dark Brethren running around grabbing weapons and anything else they might find useful, striking out at defenders and mages who were coming out of their stupors. But the dominant sound was the howls of wolves coming from the forest above the road. As the attackers became aware of the wolves, they started to retreat into the canyon, terrified as they tried to get away and still hold onto their loot. The snarling grey creatures flashed from the brush and went for the dark brothers, latching onto whatever part of their bodies presented itself. Screams rent the air as limbs were severed and throat slashed, adding to the frantic uproar from the terrified horses. The Trethawynd forces backed away from the fray, almost as frightened as those being attacked by wolves, and tried to calm their horses, the ones that hadn't bolted.

Daryan sat stunned, not knowing what to do. *They're only attacking the dark ones: how do they tell the difference?* His thoughts were interrupted by something soft poking his back followed by a gentle yip. He turned quickly to make sure. "Ashala?"

She whined and started to lick the blood off the cut on his cheek. "Hey, girl, it's all right, you don't have to do that." He gently pushed her away and put his arm around her neck, hugging her close.

"What the ...?" a woman's voice exclaimed. "What are you doing with that wolf?"

Daryan looked up at the defender. "This is not just any wolf," he said. "Don't you remember her? She was always wandering around the Monastery grounds."

"Oh." The woman looked as dazed as he felt. "That wolf. How did she get up here?"

"She's going to find my daughter."

"That's good, I suppose." She looked at his face. "You should get that cut seen to, Commander. Shall I find a healer?"

"You could do that, defender, and thank you." When she was gone, he turned his attention to Ashala. "You can call them off now," he said, stroking her head. "I think we can handle it from here." The fighting and noise had died down, leaving the moaning and cries of the wounded. "Thank you for helping. I hope your friends weren't hurt. You can go and find Felindra now." *I hope she understood. It felt so good to be close to her.*

Ashala whined and wagged her tail, and then she howled at the rest of the wolves, who began to merge back into the bushes.

Kevan found Daryan and together, they walked around the site to assess the damage. "I saw what happened with the wizard," Kevan said as they walked. "How did you manage that?"

"He made the mistake of trying to use my own sword against me. This sword won't allow that." Daryan tried to smile, but the pain from the cut made it lopsided and not very convincing.

"I take it that's one of the enchantments," Kevan said, glancing at the sword, which was now back in its scabbard. "I wouldn't mind having one of those myself."

"It could be arranged, when this is over and I get back to work." He paused and looked around. "Let's take stock and see if we can carry on."

They looked around at the carnage among the brethren, many with serious wounds: chunks of flesh torn from their bodies, amputated hands. Blood lay in pools on the roadway and already scavengers—crows, small carnivores, and flies— were starting to assemble to squabble over the remains.

"We'll have to do what we can for their wounded, after we take care of our own casualties," Daryan said. "How many healers do we have now?" he looked around to see who was working on the wounded. "It looks as if we have more than we started out with."

"Yes, the duke sent a couple more. We don't seem to have many casualties of our own, but I don't understand why we have to help the attackers."

"Information," Daryan replied. "We need prisoners to interrogate. I want to get our cart back and they are bound to know its whereabouts. Not only that, they know the area better than we do and we might get some information about the terrain and trouble spots to watch out for. I wonder how many of them got away."

"Not many, I'm sure. Those wolves were pretty efficient."

"I think we should get these bodies off the road, come on, let's round up a few men to do that."

Once he was sure all the work was progressing, Daryan went to speak to Nadi. "You were right about the danger," he said. "Has it gone now?"

Nadi closed his eyes for a moment while he probed their surroundings. "It seems to be clear, although I do sense fear ... coming from over there."

"It must be some who escaped. Can you tell how many?"

"Only one as far as I can tell."

"Hold on while I get some men to reconnoiter."

"One thing I don't understand," Nadi said when Daryan returned. "Why there were no wizard attacks on the wolves. They always use their dark magic when they're attacked."

"We killed a couple of wizards." *I killed*, he thought. Daryan was never happy at the thought of taking a life, in spite of it being part of his profession. "Maybe they only had two with them."

Two defenders had been killed by the Brethren while they were still affected by the sedative and three more injured, mainly cuts from knife slashes. Once the wolves came on the scene, their attack was so intense, the remaining defenders had escaped while the Brethren were occupied defending themselves.

"We still need to send a couple of scouts up each side of the canyon," Daryan said. They may have set booby traps to drop rocks on us. We can eat here while the healers finish their work and the bodies are moved."

"What about our two fatalities?" Kevan asked. "We can't leave them for scavengers."

"We'll have to bury them, the ground is probably too hard for digging deeply so we'll cover the graves with stones," Daryan replied. "Could you organize that while I talk to the scouts?"

The scouts returned with a very irate prisoner who had been hiding among some ferns.

"Tie him up with the others," Daryan instructed them. "No wizards, then?"

"Afraid not, sir," one of the scouts replied. "They must have been the first to disappear, unless we've killed all of them."

It was almost sunset by the time they got through the canyon. The road widened slightly once they were past and they were able to reach the junction before it was completely dark.

"What a day!" Daryan said as he leaned back against a boulder and took a sip of water. "Two in a row. Did you expect anything like this?" he asked Kevan.

"Not in my most fantastic dreams. This is a new kind of warfare for us; we're not trained for it." Kevan said with a shake of his head.

"It's certainly not like the last time, army facing army on a battlefield. I think they learned something from that defeat and decided to try a different approach this time. Their problem, apart from the evil they subscribe to, is that there aren't many of them, so this is an effective strategy; it's much harder to root all the scattered groups that disappear so fast. At least we got something out of the prisoners. We know where the wagon is now and where they're keeping our people they abducted when they stole it."

"If they're telling the truth," Kevan said. "And none of them would talk about how the prisoners are being treated.

For all we know, they could be wounded, or they may have been tortured by the brutes. Let's pray they still live."

"They don't know much to give away. These prisoners are foot soldiers; they're not privy to everything their leaders plan and do. They don't give the impression of being evil men; in fact, they seem quite ordinary. They must have been in pretty dismal straits to be mixed up with the Brethren like this."

"Did they tell you how they managed to put everyone to sleep?"

"They didn't seem to know very much about it, but one of them suggested it was a spell that ordered our brains to go to sleep."

"But what about the coughing? That's more like gas, although I was doubtful it could be that over such a wide-open area. I wonder what they have up their sleeves next."

66 – Felindra on the Road

The following morning, everyone left the cave sanctuary and went down to the stream to check the horses and wash themselves.

"We're still short two horses," Arendt said. "Barengush can take his horse, Vertan too, but you will have to double up on one of them," he told Felindra.

"I don't mind," Vertan said. "Felindra isn't very heavy and I'm not either. She can ride behind me."

Barengush's eyebrows drew together; he didn't seem very pleased with the arrangement. "I might be able to release another horse from the monastery without being seen," he offered.

"We can take turns, all right? I don't want to go anywhere near the monastery again."

"Let's go," Barengush replied. "We're wasting time."

"Which way are you going?" Arendt asked.

"I think we should..." "There's a trail..." Barengush and Vertan started at the same time.

"You first," Vertan said.

Barengush shrugged. "I think we should head to the southeast, the pass. There must be a road somewhere around here."

"That's what I was going to say. I grew up here and I know the area pretty well. A trail heads south from here so we can circumvent the monastery. It joins a road that runs south east."

"I wish I had some clean clothes to put on," Felindra said as they prepared to mount their horses. "I've been wearing these for weeks and they smell really foul."

"I could loan you some spares while you wash them," Vertan offered. "They may be a bit large, but you can roll up the trouser legs and sleeves."

"You seem to have everything under control," Arendt said. "I think we'll head out. Oh, before we leave let me give you some coins so you can buy food." He opened the leather purse attached to his belt and dug out a handful of silver and dropped it Vertan's outstretched palm. "That should be good for a few days. You can supplement it with a bit of hunting and fishing." He looked at Barengush. "Did you bring any coin, wizard?"

"I have some, yes. I can support my own upkeep, don't worry," he grumbled. "And maybe have some left over to share."

"All right, then. Time for us to go. Stay safe and the Light protect you."

"Felindra," the Grand Master said, putting his hands on her shoulders. "Thank you, my dear for helping me to get out of that dreadful place. I never thought I'd be glad to leave my own home, but under circumstances ..." He grimaced. "I'll be

541

just as happy to return when it's liberated though." He squeezed her shoulders. "I can sense you are a special person, Felindra, and predict you have a remarkable future in front of you. Be safe and walk in the Light. And you young men, don't let anything happen to her," He added as he let go of her and turned towards his horse.

When they had gone, Felindra went to speak to Vertan. "I'd like to take you up on your offer of some clothes. Could you and Barengush leave me alone for a few minutes while I wash and change? I'll call you when I'm ready."

Vertan rummaged in his saddle pack and brought out a wrinkled tunic and pair of culottes. "Sorry they're a bit crumpled, I'm not very good at packing, but they are clean. Do you want some soap as well?"

Felindra nodded. "Yes please. I won't be too long. Thank you, Vertan."

Not to be outdone, Barengush brought out a thickly woven cotton sheet. "Towel," he said as he handed it to her.

"Thank you, Barengush. Now I won't have to stay wet for half the morning."

"Come on. Wizard. Let's go back to the cave and see if there's anything we can use."

As soon as she was sure they'd gone, Felindra stripped off her dirty clothes and dropped them in the water, among the reeds so they wouldn't be washed away. She grabbed the soap and walked slowly into the stream, trying to ignore the freezing temperature of the water. *Let's get it over with; it's this or stay dirty.* Once her hair and body were clean, she grabbed her clothes and gave them a good scrubbing, and then she threw them onto the bank and climbed out to grab the towel.

After dressing in the borrowed clothes, which still smelled of laundry soap, she wrapped the towel around her head so she wouldn't have cold water dripping down her neck. She wrung out her wet clothes and lay them on the grass. She whistled loudly to let her companions know she was ready, and then began to saddle the horses. They arrived just as she was finishing.

"What am I going to do with my wet clothes?" she wondered rhetorically. "Maybe I could hang them from the saddles. Let's see how that would work."

"We'd better get moving, so make up your mind quickly," Barengush urged. "It'll be noon before we even get started."

"I'm sorry to inconvenience you," she replied with a frown. "I'm ready." She picked up her culottes and tunic and hung them, one on each side, from his saddle. She decided to keep her undergarments to herself and hung them behind Vertan's saddle, then climbed up behind him.

At first, she felt a little uncomfortable. She's never been this close to any male her own age before—apart from the awful man on the road to the monastery—but after a while she began to relax, convincing herself it was no different from riding with her brother. She was glad of the warmth from his body, being dressed only in a cotton tunic and culottes. She hadn't washed the cloak knowing the wool would take much longer to dry than cotton, and she might need it later when the sun went down.

"Comfortable?" Vertan asked.

"Yes," she replied. "Now I know how my little brother felt when he had to ride behind me. It's warm."

"Not too hot, I hope."

"No, just comfortable."

Vertan rode in front because the path was narrow and he knew the way. She could almost feel Barengush scowling behind them. She couldn't really like him, but she did feel some compassion. *If the Light can forgive him*, she thought, *I suppose I'll have to try, but it's hard.* What he did to Ashala was hard to ignore. *I'll try, Light, I will try, I promise.* Felindra began to feel as if she was blanketed in a cloud of warmth.

"What did you just do," Vertan asked.

"Why, did it bother you?"

"No, on the contrary, it felt good."

"I was just thinking about the Light."

"Does that always happen when you think of Him?"

"Not always, mostly when I'm talking to Him. I think it's his way of reassuring me. What did it feel like to you?"

"Just warm and comforting."

"Me too."

"What are you two mumbling about?" Barengush asked grumpily from behind.

"The Light, if you're concerned. We aren't plotting against you," Vertan answered.

"You can join us if you're interested," Felindra said. *Poor Barengush; he's so insecure.*

"Do you think we could stop now and have something to eat?" Barengush said.

"That's not a bad idea," Vertan answered. "Next place we find where there's some water. I seem to recall there's a stream a little way ahead. Although with the amount of food we have, we could eat it in the saddle."

"But we do need water," Felindra reminded them. "And the horses might be thirsty."

They found the rock strew mountain stream about half an hour later and settled down to eat bread and cheese, both rock solid, and a handful of dried fruit each while the two horses quenched their thirst.

"Is it far to the border?" Felindra asked.

"About two days' journey," Vertan replied. "That's if there are no obstacles."

"Is there a town where we can buy some more food?" Barengush asked.

"We could reach one by sundown if we left now," Vertan replied.

"Well, let's go then."

Vertan came and mounted his horse, waiting for Felindra to jump up behind him, but she had other ideas. "I think I should ride with Barengush for a while and give your horse a rest." It was not that she wanted to ride with the wizard, but she didn't want either of them to feel left out or jealous. She was not comfortable riding behind Barengush. He seemed to emanate an air of inner conflict, hurt pride and fear. She could understand his feelings, given his background and recent deeds. She tried to send soothing thoughts to him and after a while, he relaxed a little.

The sun was close to setting when they saw its rosy light reflecting from the windows of some buildings ahead. "There's the place I was telling you about," Vertan said. "We should be able to get something to eat there."

"Do you think we have enough coin to rent a room for the night?" Barengush asked. "It would be nice not having to sleep on the cold ground for one night."

"I don't know," Vertan replied. "I think we ought to save what we have to buy food and for emergencies. We could warm up at the inn while we're eating."

The inn was rather small and only had a few customers when they entered. The customers, mostly working men by the look of their clothes, watched them for a moment or two and then went back to their drinks. The trio found a small table squeezed in a corner close to the fire. Felindra had brought her damp clothes and hung them over the back of her chair facing the fire. As soon as they were settled, a young woman came over and asked them if they wanted to order something.

"What have you got cooking tonight?" Vertan asked.

"You're in luck," the woman replied. "My husband killed a deer today, so we have some roast venison. Would you like some?"

"That would be grand," Vertan replied. "And could we have bread and some vegetables with it?"

After they'd finished eating, Felindra went over to the doorway where the serving woman had disappeared and saw it led to the kitchen. The woman was sitting at a table with a man she presumed to be her husband. They were both eating their supper, but looked up when she appeared in the doorway. "Is there something you need?" the man asked.

Felindra heard a baby's murmur and noticed a cradle near the stove with a pair of tiny hands waving over it and a pair of kicking feet. "I'm sorry to disturb you, lady. I can wait 'til you're finished; it's not urgent. I was just wondering if you have a place where I could change my clothes. They got wet and I had to borrow these." She pulled at the overlarge tunic. "I'd like to change into my own things now that they're dry."

"We have rooms for rent, if you'd like to stay the night," the man said.

Knowing they couldn't afford it, but being reluctant to admit it, she replied, "It's all right, we have a place to sleep." *The cold ground.*

The woman stood up and pushed back her chair. "Don't worry, love, you can change in our room. Fetch your clothes and I'll show you the way."

When Felindra returned with her pack and dried clothing, the woman led her through a door on the opposite side of the kitchen which let into a cozy little bedroom. "Are you and the young men related?" she asked.

"We only met yesterday, but we are going the same way, so we joined up for company on the road," Felindra replied. "But we are friends."

"Forgive me if I'm intruding, but I am wondering where you are planning to sleep. Not outside on the ground, I hope."

Felindra hated to lie to the kind hostess, but was ashamed to admit the truth. *What would the Light do?* She wondered.

"It's all right, we're used to it, and we can build a fire to keep us warm."

"I have a better idea," the woman said. "I can let you have a room with a bed, and the young men can lie on the floor in the common room near the fire, once all the customers are gone. They won't be staying late tonight; they have to work tomorrow."

"You are very kind," Felindra replied. "I'll talk to them and see what they say."

The woman nodded. "I'll leave you to dress now." She went out, closing the door behind her.

It only took Felindra a few moments to put her own clothes on. She decided to keep Vertan's tunic on top of her own for extra warmth. Her culottes were still a little damp, but they would soon dry if she stayed by the fire. She rolled up Vertan's culottes and stuffed them in her pack before leaving the room. The hostess was sitting on a chair with the baby on her lap, looking serenely content, but her husband was nowhere in sight. "Feel better now?" she asked.

"Much better,"

"Sit down for a few minutes. My husband is out there talking to your friends, so they won't miss you." Felindra sat on the chair vacated by the husband. "You're from Trethawynd, aren't you? I can tell by your accent."

"I am. My name is Felindra Peshanar."

"I'm Arland. Aren't you a bit young to be travelling alone?"

Felindra nodded. "It's not by choice," she said. "I'd much rather be home with my mother." She blinked her eyes, hoping to dispel the tears that threatened to form.

Arland reach over and patted her hand. "What brought you here, if I'm not intruding on a private matter?"

Felindra sighed and looked down at the table. "I was abducted by the Dark Brethren. They brought me to ValkonenMaa. They kept me at the monastery, but I escaped two days ago and I am trying to get back home. Those two boys are helping me."

"That's terrible! Why would they abduct you? Are you someone important? Sorry, that doesn't sound right. Everybody's important."

"Well, my father is the Commander of the League of Light in Trethawynd, but they seemed more interested in testing my gift. I think they wanted to figure out if they could use it as a weapon," Felindra replied with a shrug.

"How did that go?"

"I think they got more than they bargained for. Someone got hurt when they started poking into my head. They weren't very pleased with that." Felindra smiled at the memory.

"Why would they want your gift? Is it so unusual?"

Felindra nodded. "I can communicate with animals."

"I've never heard of that," Arland replied. "It must be interesting."

Their conversation was interrupted by the return of her husband with a tray load of empty drinking vessels and bowls.

"Has everyone gone?" Arland asked him.

"All but the young lads," he replied. He turned to Felindra who was now standing up. "I think they are worried about where you've got to."

"I'd better go and reassure them," Felindra said. "Thank you for your help, Arland."

"Remember what I said," Arland replied. "I'll be out in a minute, as soon as I've changed this little fellow's wraps."

Felindra joined her friends at the table. "The hostess has made us an offer of accommodation for the night. I don't know if her husband will approve, but it sounds good. She wants to give me a room to sleep in, and you two can sleep down here by the fire, if you want to. What do you think?

"I say take it," Barengush replied.

"It wouldn't be fair to take advantage of them like that," Vertan said. He dug his fingers into his belt purse and brought out a handful of coins. "I think we could afford a silver for your room. If they'll accept that, we should stay."

"How did she know we have nowhere to sleep? Did you tell her?" Barengush asked her.

"She guessed, I think. But I couldn't lie to her after she had been so kind."

They were on the road early the next morning after buying some supplies for the journey from the innkeeper. Felindra was satisfied that both parties had benefitted from their meeting.

"Why did you get all these vegetables?" Barengush asked as he tried to stuff some carrots and beans into his pack. "They're heavy and they take up too much room."

"Don't you know? Vegetables carry the essences of life," she replied. "You should eat some once in a while; they might improve your attitude. Isn't that right, Vertan?"

Vertan grinned. "I suppose so."

"Men! All you think about is stuffing yourselves full of meat and bread."

"And ale," Barengush added.

They stopped for a meal shortly after midday. The weather was turning cold and clouds were rolling in so they lit a fire. "How do you plan to cook these?" Barengush asked when he opened his pack. "We're using the kettle to heat water."

"You don't have to cook them. They're just as good raw. You should try one." She walked over to his pack and retrieved a carrot, wiped it with a cloth to remove the dirt, and took a bite. "Mm, that tastes good," she said.

Barengush looked at her as if she'd just swallowed a worm.

The trio sat around the fire for a while, eating sparingly in case they didn't come across another place to buy food. "I've been meaning to ask you something," Barengush said to Vertan. "Why don't you League defenders use your powers to kill your enemies? It seems to me that the minute you stop the attack, you stop fighting, instead of finishing everyone off."

"Sure, we want to stop you doing the damage you do, but we don't enjoy killing people. We just want to keep you from hurting them."

"Like you did at the Castle in DarSolas," Felindra added. "All that destruction was unnecessary, killing hundreds of innocent people who weren't able to defend themselves. We'd rather try to persuade you to turn to the Light and away from the evils of the Dark Brethren."

"Bravo! Nice speech," a voice said. The words were followed by the sound of clapping hands as several people broke through the surrounding bushes. The three friends jumped to their feet, the two men grabbing their weapons.

"I wouldn't if I were you," the familiar voice warned. "We've got you completely surrounded and you'll only get hurt if you try to resist."

"Father!" Barengush was the first to recover from the shock. "What are you ...?"

"Quiet boy! Yes, it is me. Because of you and your little friends, I had to leave important work to come and find you. Thought you could get away with your newfound friends, did you? You forget, I can find you anywhere you go. You can't hide from me."

Disappointment sank so hard into Felindra, it made her dizzy; her knees became so weak, she felt as if they would collapse if she didn't hold on to something. She grasped Vertan's arm for support. *I'm sorry,* she sent to him.

Not your fault, he sent back.

"You can stop that," Monaltor snarled, spinning to face them. He turned to the three wizards accompanying him. "Tie them up and guard them so they don't start using their magic. But watch out for the girl. Don't try to read her; she has a powerful repelling power. Take them to their horses! Put the two of them together and make sure they're their well secured. This girl is very tricky."

Felindra could feel the rage building up inside herself, the disappointment of being caught again, the sheer injustice of it after all they'd gone through. She had expected to be home in a few days, back with her family and Ashala. Now all her hopes were shattered, again. Her eyes filled with tears. How could this happen to her twice? *Light?* The pressure inside her head diminished slightly, though she still wanted to hurt somebody. *If it's your will, so be it, but I still wish they hadn't caught us. I'm frightened."*

Be patient. All will become clear.

Once they were on the horse, her arms were pulled around Vertan's body and were bound together in front of him. Their feet were fastened to the stirrups. Barengush was also tied up and secured to his horse. "Bring everything they were carrying," Monaltor ordered. He then picked up their cooking pot and poured the water over their fire, stamped on the ashes and then tossed it away into the bush.

"How did you find us?" Barengush asked sullenly once they were moving.

"We have eyes everywhere; you should know that. Once I sensed the direction you'd taken, all I had to do was make some inquiries in the area. I know you stayed at the inn last night. Someone saw you there. You can get all kinds of information for a little coin. Hardly need to use magic at all, unless you want to have some fun. You were careless, all three of you. But your little adventure wasn't completely without compensation; now we have a bonus prize, the boy. A League defender yet! We should be able to get some useful information from him."

"You can try," Vertan mumbled so that only Felindra could hear.

"Don't worry about him," she murmured. "I think he's a bit scared of me after what happened to his son." She didn't feel as confident as she sounded, but there was no need to make Vertan feel worse than he already did.

"Barengush? What happened?"

She gave him a brief account of the power she'd suddenly acquired that blasted both of them into unconsciousness.

"Speak up, girl! If you have something to say, share it with everyone."

She just glared at him without replying.

"Don't think it is going to be as easy for you this time. I was too permissive with you last time, but that's going to change. This time you are going to find out who's in charge."

"I'm not afraid of your threats," Felindra replied. "I have the Light on my side and he will protect me."

"Stupid, deluded girl. Do you think you can defy the power of Oglestra?"

"Don't worry," she whispered into Vertan's ear. "He's watching over us and He won't let anything bad happen to us."

"I know," Vertan murmured back."

They arrived back at the monastery after dark. The clouds that had threatened early finally released their load, adding to their misery by making everyone cold and wet.

Felindra and Vertan were taken directly to the dungeons and thrown into two cells, one at each end of the hallway. "So you won't be able to talk to each other," Monaltor told them.

When Felindra was in the cell, Monaltor said to her, "Take all your clothes off and throw them out here."

"No." she was terrified. Of all the things he could do to her, this was the worst. She wouldn't even have imagined that anyone would take her clothes and leave her naked in a dark and freezing cell.

"Stop wasting time. If you don't do as I say, my friend here will be happy to help you. You'll think twice about escaping if you don't have clothes."

The thought of having a strange man strip her was even worse. It made her feel sick. Reluctantly, she started to peel off her sodden clothes and throw them out into the hallway, all but her under garments and stockings. She started to tremble violently, tears of shame and humiliation streaming down her face as she reached her hands across her body and tried to rub some warmth into her upper arms.

"EVERYTHING! Monaltor demanded.

She reluctantly peeled off her stockings and tossed them to the doorway.

"Is that everything?"

She saw a man's shadow advance through the doorway. "NO! STOP IT!" she screamed. "LEAVE ME ALONE! GO AWAY!" she added, hoping he would believe she was close to breaking point—and he knew what that meant—but she wasn't able to prevent a sob escaping, even though she didn't want him to know how much this latest humiliation was demoralizing her.

The wizard stepped back quickly, driven by her rage. Apparently, he'd heard about the incident in Monaltor's workshop. The cell door slammed and the familiar grating of the key in the lock followed.

Felindra slid down the wall and sat on the cold stones of the floor, weeping bitterly. She didn't even have a cloak to keep her warm as she had last time. *Oh, Light! What am I going to do?*

67 – The Cave

"We should split up here," Daryan said to Don Kevan the next morning. "There's a lot of territory to cover and it'll be faster if we do it separately."

"And if one of us is attacked." Kevan smiled. "There'll still be someone left to carry on the mission. How do you suggest we do it?"

"I'll take the west direction and you can go east towards the border crossing. "I'll look for other the wagon while we're at it. They said it had been stashed this way somewhere. I'll take a couple of the prisoners with me, and Axtya to help us explore the cave they mentioned. We can split up the defenders and mages so that each of us has enough protection. You take the new wagon, after we unload some of the supplies to take with us. How does that sound?"

"Suits me," Kevan replied. "It seems to me you've given me the easier road."

"I hope so, Kevan. That's why I'm going to take the most experienced people. From what the prisoners say, they are concentrating their efforts towards the west, so I hope you don't run into any trouble. I'm afraid I'll have to keep Lady Farah with me, too, so you won't have a sender, but you'll have some gifted defenders with you to compensate. I'll try to find one with a telepathic gift."

"That seems more than fair," Kevan said. "Shall we start getting them organized?"

Daryan found Nadi next. "Are you up for some more adventure?" he asked. "I'm giving you a choice; you can come with us, which might be more hazardous, or go with Sir Kevan on route I hope is less dangerous."

"It's a hard choice," Nadi responded. "I want to survive for the sake of my family, but I feel my duty lies in getting rid of the Brethren. I suppose that, ultimately, whichever I choose will be for the good, so I'll trust in the light and go with you."

He grinned at Daryan. "That sounded a bit pompous, didn't it? I'm ready when you are."

"I think you summed it up quite succinctly, Nadi. I feel the same way. Now, let's get on the road!"

Axtya wouldn't have the wagon to ride in, so he had to ride on horseback and, since no one wanted to ride with him, he was forced to manage alone. His feet wouldn't reach the stirrups whatever level they were set at, so Daryan contrived to tie his feet to the stirrup straps. "Don't worry, you won't fall off. You have to use the reins, pull when you want her to stop and steer her by pulling to the side you want to go. Just kick her sides when you want her to start moving. Don't worry, Axtya; she'll follow the other horses and she's very gentle. All right?"

Axtya turned his downcast eyes on Daryan and nodded his head.

"Think of the story you'll be able to tell your children." At this, Axtya straightened his shoulders and looked ahead.

The things I have to do for that one creature, and I still don't know if he'll be of any use to us. Daryan sighed and mounted his own horse, and then gave Axtya's mount a slap on the rump as he passed to get her going.

After they'd gone about a league, Daryan asked the sergeant to bring, the most cooperative of the new prisoners. "Now, show me this cave where you left the wagon." Daryan demanded when he arrived.

"You have to look out for a landmark," the man replied.

"What landmark?"

"Let me think a minute." The prisoner wrinkled his brows to convince Daryan he was thinking hard. "Yeah, now I remember, there's a rock sticking out from the mountain like a big nose." The right side of the road was bounded by woodland sloping up to steep, almost vertical mountainside. This was the final boundary between Trethawynd and

ValkonenMaa. "It's just past there. There's a trail leading up to it. You can't miss it."

"I hope not," Daryan replied. "Stay behind me in case I want to ask you anything else. Oh, by the way, how many wizards were there with your group?"

"Two," the prisoner replied. "There was three, but one of them, the youngest, killed himself in an accident." He smiled at the memory.

Daryan was curious. "What kind of accident?"

"He was one of them people who think they're smarter than anyone else, you know what I mean?" Daryan did. It put him in mind of the one who'd abducted Felindra. "Anyway, we was clearing the trees around the entrance to make more room and he had the bright idea of using his powers to knock them down instead of us from having to cut them all. He decided to demonstrate by picking one of the biggest trees and blasting it. The only thing he didn't take into account was which way it would fall. It squashed him like a bug, the young fool."

"You don't sound too sorry about the mishap."

"Good riddance, I say. He was nothing but a weasel's arsehole. They all were." The prisoner spat on the ground.

Daryan looked at the man with new eyes. "Why did you join them in the first place if you don't like them?"

"I was a logger. That's another thing I didn't like, them attacking honest working men and destroying their livelihood. There was a forest fire in the heat of summer where I was working. I managed to escape, but it travelled so fast, it destroyed not only the camp, but also the village where our families lived. I lost everything, my family—wife, children—and my job. There was no work for us and the lumber company sent us packing, the survivors."

"How did you get involved with the Dark Brethren?"

"They was going around the duchy looking for people like me, men who'd lost their jobs through acts of fate and so on.

556

They promised us if we joined them, we'd get rich with the loot we captured. I didn't like the idea, but what was I to do? I had nothing, not even a change of clothes."

"How did that work out?"

"Well, none of us got rich, that's for sure. The places we attacked hardly had anything themselves and I would have felt tainted if I robbed them of anything."

"What's your name again?"

"Bertold, Bertold Einton."

"Didn't you ever feel like running away and going back to ValkonenMaa?"

"We was too scared. You wouldn't want to see what they did to anyone who deserted. They seemed to be able to find them, no matter how far they went or how well they hid. They made us watch the punishment." He gulped. "They burnt them to a crisp. You wouldn't even know they were men when they were finished."

"Yes I've seen what they can do. There's one in particular I'd like to get my hands on for what he did to our defenders." Daryan checked on the other riders then continued. "How would you like to join us, Bertold? I think you would be an asset to us, knowing the terrain so well."

"What's in it for me?"

"Is that the reason you would join us, for the advantages you'd have? I thought you might want to do it because it would be the right thing to do. We're the defenders of the Light. Don't you believe in the Light?"

Bertold turned way, bowing his head. "I'm sorry, sir. I didn't mean it that way. It's just that I don't know where I'll get my next bite, or change of clothes. I guess I'm a bit desperate. Yes, I'll join you. You've treated me fair, and got me away from that evil lot. I appreciate that. I seem to have lost faith in the Light lately, after all that's happened to me and mine. So many terrible things happening and where is He when we need him?"

"You'll find out if you join us," Daryan replied. "I'm not going to give you a sermon, but I assure you, you'll receive food and clothing, plus some coin, and when we are sure we can trust you, you'll be provided with a weapon. For now, you'll have to make do with your belt knife. How does that sound?"

"Very fair, Sir." He looked down at the shackles holding his wrists in place.

"We'll take those off when we stop. Are we getting close?"

"Not far now, just beyond the next bend if I remember rightly."

"What about your comrade?"

Bertold looked around to see if the other prisoner was within hearing range. Satisfied, he said to Daryan, "I hate to speak ill of a comrade, but he's a bit of a fanatic. He seemed to enjoy the things we were ordered to do, especially when the wizards went into action. Like it didn't bother him to see people being hurt."

"Fair enough. I'm glad to know that and we'll take it into consideration when we decide what to do with him." Daryan already had something in mind. The man could be useful, in spite of his inclinations.

They reached the turnoff at about noon, just as the prisoner had described it. After they'd made the turn onto the trail, Daryan turned his head and looked at the man. "You must know this way quite well."

Bertold nodded, and then changed his mind. "Not that well," he said. "I've just got a good memory, that's all. It's safe as far as I know; I don't think there's anybody there except a few demons."

The trail was difficult to navigate, constantly changing direction as they climbed. Daryan was surprised they'd managed to get the wagon up the trail at all, but the damaged vegetation and debris on either side were testament that they had. At the top of the trial, they found a spacious area around the cave mouth had been cleared of trees and brush.

"Would you bring me the other prisoner, please," Daryan said to the sergeant. "And then you have time, remove this man's manacles."

He looked around while he waited for the prisoner, noting the features of the site and its defensibility. He didn't have to wait long before the surly prisoner was brought before him, still on horseback. "You must have been here a long time," Daryan commented. "Was this some sort of storage depot used by the Brethren?"

"I guess so."

"You mean you don't know?"

The man shrugged his shoulders, looking even more sullen than when he'd arrived. "Where would your comrades have gone, the ones who escaped the wolf attack?" Daryan continued.

"How would I know? Can I get down now? Me leg's killing me." Daryan remembered he'd been bitten by one of the wolves, but had managed to get away.

"Let's stick to the subject, shall we? Would they have come back here?"

He shrugged again, not seeming to care very much about anything. "Might have."

"Are there any spells or anything to keep out intruders?"

The prisoner shook his head. "I wouldn't know."

Daryan gave him a piercing look and called over one of the defenders. "Get him down," he ordered. "He's going to lead us inside."

The prisoner turned visibly paler; he looked terrified. "Don't make me go in there," he pleaded.

"You weren't telling me the truth were you? You'd better tell us everything if you want to live."

"I wasn't lying; I just kept back a few things. How can you expect me to betray my friends?"

"What are you afraid of?"

"Traps. The wizard laid traps in case anyone tried to get at our stuff."

"What kind of traps?"

"I don't know how he did it, but one day a bear tried to get in and it was blown to pieces. There was … you know … bits of meat and fur and blood all over the place." He seemed to brighten up a little as he recalled the incident.

Daryan called the sergeant. "Tell everyone to stand down, have something to eat and drink, but don't go near the cave."

Daryan thought about the traps for a moment. How could they create a trap like that? *It would mean enchanting some object I suppose. Trust wizards to think of even more revolting ways to use their powers.* The gift of enchanting he used for his swords was the same power, but his enchantments were mostly designed for defensive purposes, not deliberate destruction. The fact that his sword had killed the wizard who attacked him the day before was not because of the lethal enchantment; the man had been free to choose whether to use it or not, and he had been warned of the danger. He knew what he was doing. *What would I use for the enchantment?* Daryan wondered. It would have to be something innocuous, an object that wouldn't attract notice. The only things he could think of were pieces of wood or stones. All the victim would need to do to activate it would be to step on it or kick it out of the way. Another way would be to bury it in a hole and cover it with soil or leaves.

He went back to the prisoner who was now sitting with his back to the rock wall, eating some bread. "How far into the cavern did these traps go?"

"Just the entrance, the first room, I think. I never saw him doing anything farther in where we kept our stuff."

"You saw him set them up?" Daryan asked hopefully.

"Nah. He sent is away when he did that, but I did see him deactivating them one time. At least I suppose that's what he was doing, going along waving his hands at the ground and muttering something."

"Is that what he did when you wanted to go inside?"

"Yeah." The prisoner snorted and spat on the ground.

"I see. So we'll have to sweep the first cavern. Is that where the wagon is?"

"It was," the prisoner replied.

"What do you mean was?"

"Last time I saw it. We've been away for a few days. Somebody might have moved it." He shrugged. "I don't know."

"Did you ever see any of them using black powder?" Daryan had heard of black powder a few years ago. Apparently it was invented in some country in the northwest, and created powerful explosions when in contact with fire."

"What do you mean?"

"Never mind. It wouldn't apply here anyway." He'd realized they would have needed a way to ignite it.

Daryan went to sit down among the defenders and eat some bread and cold meat from his pack. "We have a problem," he said. "Apparently, the wizards laid enchanted traps in the cavern, so we daren't go in. According to the prisoner, they must be on the floor where any unwary person or animal could step on them. They produce a violent explosion, guaranteed to be lethal. Now we have to think of a way to deactivate them, and I'm asking for suggestions. The main thing is that we cannot risk entering the cave, so we would have to find a way to clear it remotely."

"Do we have anyone that could sense the enchantment?" Captain Moro, one of the Trethawynd defenders asked.

"Anyone?" Daryan queried.

"I could try," Nadi said. "I'm not sure I could because I usually only sense life."

"I'm not going to risk you, Nadi. I think we need to consider a more mechanical approach."

The sergeant raised his hand. "I have an idea, sir," he said. "We've got plenty of rope. Why don't we throw something into the back of the cave and then shoot an arrow attached to rope into it and drag it back?"

"That might work. Let's try it, unless anyone else can think of something."

"We could throw stones in," a defender mumbled.

"A bit haphazard," Daryan said. "And no guarantee of success, unless setting off one triggered the others. Let's try Sergeant Perini's idea and see how we get on. If it works, we could at least cut a pathway to the back. I want to see what they have stored here."

After a little experimenting and many other suggestions, a method was agreed upon. They piled a collection of debris, pieces of wood, leaves and a few stones on a ground sheet and then tied it to form a bag. A burly Trethawynd defender was chosen to throw it in, standing well back from the entrance. The first throw landed on one of the traps and the bag was blown to bits, but it did succeed in setting off two others close to it, sending a cloud of debris and dust out of the opening.

"Well, that's three down," Daryan said encouragingly. "Prepare another package."

The second try was more successful, probably because the traps closer to the back had been destroyed. Daryan had decided that they would use two ropes so that the people pulling it could stand to the sides of the entrance and be sheltered from the blasts.

Once the arrows were securely implanted, they pulled the bundle rapidly along the ground in the hope that it would be moving fast enough to avoid being blown up by the trap it had just activated. After three more explosions that shook the ground and sent the horses into a frenzy of bucking, snorting, and pulling against their hitches. The last blast had severed the ropes attached to the bag. Just to make sure, they repeated the exercise once more running another weighted bundle from the site of the last explosion. It was a good thing they did, because it activated another one close to the entrance.

"We'll wait for the dust to clear and then take a look. If everything went according to plan, we should now have a clear path to the back."

"I hope we didn't blow up our wagon," someone said.

"I hope so too," Daryan replied. "Or the hurt our defenders they captured."

68 – Back to Prison

Felindra

Felindra had been sitting by the wall adjacent to the door, but she remembered there was a pallet of sorts by the wall opposite. Even though it might be damp and not very clean, it wouldn't be as bad as sitting on the cold stones. She crossed the cell and dropped down onto it, then lay down and curled herself into a tight ball, leaving as little surface as possible exposed to the chilly dampness of the air. *Oh, Light, what am I going to do? I'm so cold.*

A faint light began to fill the cell, increasing gradually to a gentle twilight. The air was warming up too and soon reached a comfortable level comparable to being near a fire. *Thank you, Light.*

Sleep, child.

She was woken by the sound of a key in the lock. She dashed across the room so that she wouldn't be visible from the door. The lights in the cell faded and the temperature dropped. The door opened a little way, and a hand reached in to deposit a bundle on the floor. She reached out and touched it and felt the warm texture of a wool blanket.

"Who is it?" she asked softly.

"It's me, Dominel."

"How did you know I was here?" she asked.

"I don't know," he replied. "I was just having my supper when I got this urge to bring these things to the dungeons. I was even shown where to find the key."

"Bless the Light! What about my friend in the cell at the other end? Did you get the urge to visit him as well?"

"I'm going there now," he replied softly. "I have to hurry before anybody finds out. Light protect you, child."

"Thank you, Dominel, you may have saved my life, Light bless you."

The door lock clicked and he was gone. She didn't even hear his footsteps as he walked away. The light returned as soon as the door closed. She picked up the bundle Dominel had left and took it over to the pallet. Something fell out of it onto the floor as she crossed. She bent down and picked up a soft package wrapped in paper. From the warmth and smell of it, she knew it was food. *What a brave man! The Light knows how to pick His servants. I hope he doesn't get into trouble.* The blanket held one more surprise: a wool shirt. She dropped the blanket on the pallet and donned the shirt, quickly tying the laces to close it. It came down to her knees and felt wonderful even though it was large.

She decided to move the pallet to the wall beside the door so that if anyone opened the door, she wouldn't be the first thing he saw. Then she wrapped the blanket around her and ate the food Dominel had brought—some warm chicken wrapped in flatbread, a tomato and an apple. She folded the wrapping paper and put it on the mattress, intending to use it for toilet paper should the need arise. The last time she'd been here, she'd been forced to use straw she'd pulled out of her mattress. When she'd finished her meal, she looked around the cell, assessing everything. There was the slop bucket, over in the corner and ... what's that? She reached out and picked up the metal canister standing on the floor just inside the door. Water! She took off the lid and sniffed it. It didn't smell bad so she took a sip—nice and fresh—she took a few mouthfuls and replaced the lid. She'd have to ration it carefully.

She leaned back and closed her eyes. *I wonder how Vertan is feeling. Did they take his clothes away too? I wonder what's happening to Barengush. He was so brave to run away from the monastery and his horrible father, but now he's in even worse trouble than he was before.*

Barengush

Barengush lay on the bed in the cell-like room he'd been assigned to when his father had finished with him. They'd even locked the door on him! He was so angry, he was almost in tears, but for once, he was able to control himself. *He keeps harping on my lack of self-control, but I'll show him! I'll be very controlled while I plan how to make him pay for everything he's done to me. My powers ... how could he?* He'd gone over the events repeatedly since they'd brought him back, trying to think of how he could have avoided such a terrible punishment.

When they'd arrived at the monastery, Monaltor had ordered a mage and a guard to take him directly up to his office while he took care of the other two prisoners. There had been no doubt in his mind about his status now; he was a prisoner too. When Monaltor returned from the dungeons, he'd dropped a bundle of damp clothes on the floor, which Barengush recognized as belonging to Felindra and Vertan.

"Take these away and put them with the trash," he'd said offhandedly to the guard.

Once the guard had left, his father launched into a harangue, detailing everything Barengush had done in his life to disappoint him from the time he'd learned to walk, or so it seemed. And to make his humiliation complete, he'd kept the other wizard in the room listening to it all. Barengush clenched his fists. He wanted to smash something to smithereens even now, remembering it.

"You are the disappointment of my life, a failure, and to teach you a lesson," he'd said once he'd finished the monologue. "We're going to confiscate your powers."

"You can't do that!"

"Oh can't I? We'll see how well you can do without them. Maybe your new friends can help you, if you ever see them again. Or maybe the Light will give you one of his pathetic abilities." He'd nodded to the wizard. "Are you ready? Just his will, I'll do the rest.

Barengush felt strong pressure in his head and suddenly he couldn't move, couldn't even speak—his tongue was frozen—and then it felt as if a fire was washing through his brain burning up everything he knew. After that, he felt nothing until he awoke on the bed in this room, with a furious headache, and an intense feeling of loss and emptiness.

Vertan

Vertan sat on the soggy straw filled mattress, completely naked, knees up to his chin and arms wrapped round his legs. He was shivering uncontrollably in the frigid atmosphere. *I don't know if I can survive this,* he thought. *Maybe they mean to freeze us to death if we don't starve first*—he hadn't eaten anything since the aborted meal when they were captured. *Now I'm whining. You're not supposed to whine and complain, only trust in the Light. Everything will be all right. I just have to endure this. It won't last forever.* He sensed the change through his eyelids and opened his eyes. The cell was filled with a faint but discernable glow and he gradually realized he was starting to feel a bit warmer. It could only be the Light. He took some deep breaths then rubbed his arms and legs to encourage circulation. *Thank you, Light. I should have known you wouldn't fail us. Now maybe I can sleep for a while.* He did manage to sleep for a short time, until he was interrupted by the key being turned in the lock. The light faded just before the door opened. He saw the silhouette of a small man bend down and place something on the floor then take hold of the edge of the door to close it. "Wait!" Vertan called. "Who are you?"

"Only a servant, sir. The girl knows me." He closed and locked the door.

69 – Exploring the Cave

Daryan

Daryan looked around for Nadi and Farah, nodded to both of them to attend him. "Let's go to the mouth of the cavern and see if either of you can sense anything."

A little dust was still filtering out from the cave, carrying the smell of smoke and something bitter and acrid. "Turn your backs so you won't be forced to breathe it," Daryan suggested. "Can you feel anything?"

"People, scared and in pain," Nadi replied.

"They seem confused and are wondering what's happening," Farah added.

"Anything that suggests danger?"

"I wouldn't be able to sense that," Farah said.

"All I can feel is the dark magic. I don't know if it's the residue from the traps, of more problems we have yet to discover," Nadi said.

"All right. Your observations were helpful, thank you both. At least we know there's someone alive in there, and now I know what we must do." He left the cave mouth and went to the uncooperative prisoner. "Bring him," he said to the defender guarding the man. "Now, you're going to lead us through this cavern to the back. We want to be sure that we've cleared all the traps. You should be quite safe if you follow the path we've cleared."

"I'm not going in there. No, not me." The prisoner shook his head forcefully.

"Some soldier you are. Are you the sort of coward who can only prey on the weak and helpless and leave other people to take the risks? That's typical of cowards, isn't it? Now, get in there." Daryan pushed the man's back, driving him into the entrance.

The prisoner stopped as soon as he caught his balance and stood where he was.

"I see you need a little persuasion," Daryan said, beckoning to one of the archers. "I want you to aim an arrow at his back and if he doesn't move, shoot him. Don't kill him; just shoot his arm or leg."

The man looked over his shoulder to see if Daryan was bluffing and saw the defender raising his bow, an arrow already nocked and ready to shoot. He looked terrified, but he turned round and took a tentative step forward.

"That's better," Daryan said encouragingly. Watch the floor; if you only walk where explosions were, you should be all right."

The prisoner made it to the back of the cavern without incident, but seemed reluctant to retrace his steps.

"It's all right, let him stay there," Daryan said to the archer when he looked for further instructions. "We're going to have to find a place to hold him and it might as well be back there." Daryan took a tentative step into the cavern, and then turned around to face his troops. "Ten of you follow me, and include the healers. He looked right at Axtya. "You too, Axtya. This is your chance to do something useful. The rest of you set up camp. We'll stay here for the night and decide how we'll proceed on the morrow."

The little werman stared at him blank-faced, reflexively rubbing the stump of his right arm, but he moved in behind the others. He knew by now not to fool with Daryan.

Daryan led the way after warning everyone not to stray from the path. As they went, they saw their supply wagon in a far corner, surrounded by a heap of sacks and boxes—their own supplies? he wondered. The wagon seemed to be undamaged, apart from some scrapes along the side. Now they'd have to find a way to reach it without destroying it or the supplies. There was probably a safe path leading to it, but he wasn't going to risk guessing where it was. Most of the cavern was empty. "Go back and get Bertold," he said to the nearest defender. "He's the cooperative prisoner." To the rest of the group he said, "You go on, but make sure this prisoner goes ahead of you and give him some space. Right now, the important thing is to find our comrades. Call them as you go and let them know it's us."

When Bertold arrived, he was able to confirm that this area was used as a stable, although it was not hard to guess; the place reeked of manure and there were straw and leaves scattered all over the floor. "Make yourself useful," he told Bertold. "You can show us around. We have a captive Werman who is working for us and he'll deal with any werfolk who might be farther in."

One of the defenders came back to report. "We've found them," he said. "I think you should come and see. It's safe in the next area. We're making the prisoner go around and check everything first."

"Are they in a bad way?" Daryan asked.

"Sort of, sir. Come and see."

Daryan followed him through the main tunnel to a side tunnel. "Give me the torch," he said to one of the defenders. He wanted to see for himself, although he could tell from the odor it was not good. The tunnel was cold and damp, filled with a pall of smells, the most dominant being feces and the ammonia smell of stale urine. The four men were all naked and chained to the walls. They all looked as if they hadn't eaten in a while and many of them were covered in cuts and bruises.

"By the Light!" he exclaimed. "No man should have to suffer such indignity. We'll get you out as fast as we can," he added to the four men. "You three ..." he chose three of the defenders "... go back and get some water and clean clothes. The rest of you, get these manacles off immediately, and give what aid you can until we can get them cleaned up." He went to help release them himself, and try to reassure them. As soon as they were freed of the manacles, they were taken out of the stinking place. Two of them needed medical attention and help moving, the other two managed to stagger along slowly on their own.

Within minutes, the three defenders were back with two buckets of water, soap and washrags, and clean dry clothes, which they placed on a clean box near the wall. "We'll wait for you outside," Daryan said, to give them some privacy. "The rest of you can go on exploring the caves."

Once the released men were cleaned up and dressed, they were led outside to eat. They were reluctant to talk about their ordeal, though. Daryan understood. It would be very painful for them to reveal their humiliation at the hands of the Dark Brethren and have to relive it again, it in public this time. "Leave them alone," he told the other defenders after the four men had left the group and gone to rest in some of the tents. "If they want to talk about it, they will, but don't try to force them. They need all the support we can give them right now. It was a very traumatic experience for them and they need time to recover."

While they were finishing their midday meal, Axtya arrived accompanied by two other wermen armed with knives. As soon as the defenders saw them, they stood up and took out their swords.

"NO," Axtya shouted. "They friends."

"It's all right," Daryan said. "Let them pass. We'll see what they have to say. Bring your friends over here," he told Axtya.

As soon as he and the two strange wermen were seated near the fire, Daryan said, "Are you hungry? Help yourselves if you are."

Axtya gave a smug grin. "No. Friend have rat." He rubbed his stomach to show his satisfaction.

"You must have enjoyed that," Daryan said with a smile. *Axtya and his rats!* "So, what have you got to report?"

"Big home for people there," he pointed back over his shoulder into the cave.

"A big settlement? Are they friends with your people?"

"No. Help us some time, we help them some time."

"Sort of like allies." Axtya nodded, although Daryan wasn't sure he understood. "What do they have to say about the wizards and Dark Brethren?"

"No like. Take many people. Kill many people. Babies and mothers." Axtya's big eyes shone with unshed tears.

"So, they will help us?"

Axtya stroked his stump. "All man bad, but they more bad." He wasn't exactly coming around to trusting any humans yet. "Help you find way in wall."

"Do they know a shortcut, a quick way to go?"

Axtya nodded and pointed behind him at the cavern entrance.

"You mean there's a way through the mountain?"

"Yes. Long, long way."

"Can we get the horses through?" Daryan was excited by this information. If they could get through the mountain, he would be a lot closer to finding Felindra.

"Yes," Axtya replied. "Big cave."

"How about the wagon?"

Axtya shook his head.

"Well, we'll have to improvise, I suppose. Is there anything else you'd like to tell us?"

"Mother sick, need medicine," the little man replied.

Daryan wondered if this were a test to get their cooperation. "We can send a healer to look at her. What's wrong with her?"

"Baby no come. Mother die, much pain. Medicine man not know what to do. She die! Baby die!"

"That sounds serious. Would it be better to send a female healer?"

Axtya shrugged. "All right. Come now?"

"Yes, let me just fill her in and you can be on your way."

After the men they'd just released came out of their tents, he was able to take them aside. "Would you like to tell me what happened?" he asked the wagon master.

"They came on us all of a sudden, while we were having something to eat," the wagon master said. He was one of the injured men. He had a sprained ankle, which he was happy to discover wasn't broken, although it was very swollen and painful. "We didn't even hear them. Before we knew it, we were all paralyzed, couldn't even blink our eyes. It was one of them damned wizards put a spell on us."

"Well, he won't be doing that any more," Daryan said. "He no longer lives."

"Good riddance, I say. Anyway, they dragged me down from the wagon—that's how I got this." he dipped his head to indicate the heavily wrapped ankle. Hurt like the blazes; and they made me walk on it! It swelled up like a watermelon. The only thing I can say in favor of that hole they put us in, is that it was cold, so the swelling went down a bit."

"How did you get your injury?" Daryan asked the injured defender who'd been guarding the wagon.

"I'd gone into the woods ... call of nature ... when somebody crept up on me ... while I was at a bit of a disadvantage, you might say. I was hit over the head with something heavy and hard. I didn't hear him coming, and I didn't see who it was. When I woke up, it was all over. I was lying on the road and the others were tied up tight. Head hurt like it was being pounded on by demons. They tied me up and threw me in the back of the wagon. That's how this happened..." he indicated a cut on his face that ran across his cheek from ear to mouth. "Hit against the edge of a box as I landed." The cut had been cleaned and sutured by a League healer and left without a dressing to heal in the air.

"So then what happened?"

"When we came round, we was all trussed up like fowls ready for roasting." The wagon master continued the account. "They made me sit on the driver's box and drive the wagon with wizard next to me. Fedor and Landri was tied to the sides of the wagon and had to jog along with it. We went back down the way we'd come and turned into this other road, a bit narrow for a cart."

The wagon master continued to talk about the journey to the cave. Daryan shut him off after he'd heard enough. They still looked exhausted and could hardly keep their heads up. "I should get on with my work." He stood up and dusted the seat of his trousers. "You've been very helpful. Now try to get some more sleep."

Daryan returned to the rest of his team and set them to work. "We have to pack everything we can carry, and I suggest you make some travois to carry extra supplies. I'm going to see if we can get to those boxes they've unloaded from the wagon. Five of you come with me and the rest of you start preparing for a march."

"May I make a suggestion, commander?" a corporal said to Daryan.

"By all means, Bela. I'd welcome anything that would make things easier.

"It could take a while," she apologized. "But it might be worth it. I thought maybe we could take the wheels of the wagon and turn them into carts to carry stuff."

"It's a good idea, Bela, but I understand the passage is too narrow to for the chassis to go through, and we haven't had a chance to check the wagon yet, make sure there are no more traps."

"We might be able to do something about the chassis, sir. My grandfather was a wagon maker and he had a little trick to make chassis reusable when the upper structure was discarded. I could take a look and see if this wagon has that feature. The axletree has to be adjustable. It would be made of two iron shanks that are held together in the middle by heavy bolts. You just remove the bolts and adjust the width." She waited for his reaction, red-faced, hoping she wasn't making a fool of herself.

"It might be worth a try," Daryan replied. "You mentioned carts. How do you make two carts from wheels made for one?"

"It's not too hard, sir," Corporal Bela replied. "We could make them into a pair of two-wheeled carts, providing they have the proper axles."

"Let's see what we can do. Go ahead, after we find out whether we can get to the wagon without being blown to pieces. We're going to take a look now. I'll send someone to let you know as soon as we have an answer. I appreciate your initiative, but for the time being, help with the packing. If it's the style you think will work, go ahead, and get some of the men to help you with the heavy work; I don't expect you to do it all by yourself. And I'll find our how narrow it has to be to get through the tunnel as well while you're waiting."

What would be the mostly likely place for them to set a trap? Daryan pondered. Probably leading to the wagon from the entrance. He went back into cavern with his team and scanned the area. They'd have to leave room for the horses that were stabled here, couldn't have them blowing themselves up. "Where do you think they might lay other traps?" he asked the men.

"If they kept the horses in here," one of the defenders said. "They might not have laid any others."

574

"That makes sense to us, but nothing they do is simple. How are we going to find out?"

"How about making the prisoner walk around and see what happens?" One of the duchy defenders suggested, obviously not having the sensibility that League-trained defenders usually had.

"Don't you think that's a bit brutal?"

"Look what *they* do to people. I've got no pity for them."

"Well let's start with another option. I doubt they would set traps near the supplies, so first we'll examine that area."

Not more traps were discovered and they were able to proceed with their plans. They recovered most of their stolen supplies and started work on converting the wagon.

The healer returned shortly before sunset and reported to Daryan. "That poor creature," she said. "I can't believe she was old enough to bear a child, she looked like a child herself. I couldn't save them; she was too weak." She wiped her face with the back of her wrist. "I tried everything in my compendium, drugs, analgesics, manipulation of the fetus in the birth canal, but to no avail. It was coming feet first and one foot was caught on her pelvic bone. I wanted to try to remove it surgically, but the women—at least twenty of them crowded into the cavern room—all shrieked at the tops of their voices every time I time I touched her. They were putting up such a commotion, I didn't dare try anything more drastic. At least I was able to relieve her pain with an infusion of poppy."

"Poor creature indeed. You look exhausted, lady," Daryan said. "Get cleaned up and eat something, then have a rest, if you can find a quiet place."

"Thank you, commander. I'll do that."

They wouldn't be ready to leave until the next day, but the time had been put to good use. They had two travois, and two makeshift carts from the old wagon were nearing completion.

70 – Those who Wait

Parvana

Darson threw open the door and entered with an armload of books. "Mami, what's the matter? Have you heard some bad news?"

Parvana massaged her forehead to wipe the worry wrinkles on her brow and smiled at her son. "No, nothing since we heard that Felindra had escaped, and your father was all right the last I heard. I'm just tired, I suppose. How was your day? I see you've been to the library."

"My day was very interesting, I worked in the palace for a while. They wanted me do some more calculations."

"Anything interesting?" she asked.

"Mami, you know I'm not supposed to talk about it. It's secret."

"You mean even to the commander's wife?" she hugged him and kissed the top of his head. "I'm glad you're taking your responsibility seriously. Now, are you hungry?"

"Mami, do you think they'll be all right?"

Knowing whom he meant, she replied, "I'm sure they'll come back to us good as new and they'll have plenty of exciting stories to tell us. Now, is there something you know that you can't tell me?" she asked as she walked into the Kitchen alcove.

Darson frowned and bowed his head. He seemed to be having an internal debate over how much he could reveal. He followed her and stood watching as she took out items from the shelves to make a meal. "I'm not supposed to tell anyone, but I can't help it. I think you have a right to know. Dadi's company was ambushed, but he wasn't hurt."

Parvana felt the blood leave her face. "Light preserve us. That's it? Did they win the battle? Were there casualties?"

Darson nodded. "I shouldn't be talking about this, mami, but I can't..."

"What is it? She put down the knife she was using to cut carrots and went to him. "I understand how you feel and wish I hadn't talked you into this, but I could see it has you upset, so you might as well finish, otherwise we'll both be in a state."

"They killed a wizard," Darson blurted. "But some of our people were hurt, and the Dark Brethren stole their supply wagon. That's all I know about it."

"Maybe you aren't supposed to talk about your work, but, as your mother, I think it's best to talk about it. I don't want you holding in things that upset you like this, and if anyone complains, I'll tell them it's too much for a boy of eleven to deal with alone. We'll probably hear all about it from Ashavan anyway. Now, help me take the dishes to the table."

"Thank you, mother. I appreciate what you say," Darson said with a weak smile, falling unconsciously into formal mode. "Should I continue to tell you things that involve father?"

"If you want to talk anything over with me, I want you to feel free to do so, Darson, but only if it's something that is upsetting you so much that you cannot deal with it alone. If I find you losing sleep or having nightmares, I shall ask them to relieve you from these duties. You're too young and don't have the experience to know what everything means and how to deal with stressful news."

"Please don't do that, mami. I want to do it—I like the work—and think of all the experience I'm getting. That must be good for something." He looked at her anxiously. "What is there to drink?"

Parvana smiled. *Oh to be so young and able to change focus so quickly!* "The usual selection, buttermilk, apple juice, and water."

Valdor

"Let's walk; we can talk about this outside just as easily as in here." Valdor said to Sir Arvand and Imali. "It's a warm day out there; we need to take advantage of the weather before the rain starts again."

The three men descended the stairs from their command post in the castle of Bartony. Behind the castle was a pleasant garden with shade trees and autumn flowers, chrysanthemums, purple asters, and late-blooming roses, which spread an enchanting aroma over the area. A path paved with stones separated the flower garden from the lawns in the center. Even though the borders were weedy, the lawn needed trimming, and tufts of grass, and weeds peeked up between the paving stones, it was a restful place. The fountain in the center of the lawn was dry and filled with autumn leaves that had blown down from the trees during the last rainstorm.

Valdor picked up a handful of dead leaves from the bowl of the fountain. "Look at this mess!"

"Looks as if it needs a bit of work," Imali commented.

"I suppose everyone is too busy with the war," Valdor said. He continued walking along the path, hands behind his back in his thinking pose. "What do you think of this idea, Arvand? There must be people around who have nothing to do. What about the wounded who are almost ready to return to the field, for example? It might be good for them to get some exercise with a little light work."

"If they are recovered enough to work in a garden, they should be fit enough to return to their posts," Arvand replied.

"What if we asked those who are not *quite* fit yet if they would like to spend some time out here. It's not going to kill them to rake some leaves or pull a few weeds. They would be able to quit if they found it too much, but some of them might enjoy it. After all, there's nothing better than exercise and fresh air to encourage a return to health. We could ask them if they'd like to do it."

"You make a persuasive argument, Your Grace. I'll look into it and have a word with the healers."

"Make a note of that please, Imali." Valdor looked down at the paper in his hand, "The news about the tunnel through the mountains is encouraging, don't you think? It would come out closer to the monastery than going all the way round through the pass."

"I agree," Arvand replied. "But I'd like to wait until Commander Peshanar reaches the other side before sending anyone else that way."

Valdor decided to change the subject. "The prince seems to be making good progress in ValkonenMaa, apart from that setback when they tried to reach the monastery." The duke was referring to a company of mixed forces that attempted to get through to the monastery a few days ago on a road that ran through a mountainous region and was ambushed in a narrow gorge, losing about a quarter of their number.

"They managed to kill a wizard and take some prisoners," Arvand replied. "I expect everybody will be wary of being trapped in narrow passes from now on."

"How's Commander Haro doing?"

"He seems to be mopping up quite handily. The local people up there have begun to act in their own defense as well. They've had enough and aren't willing to take these attacks submissively any more. Many of the villages and camps are arming themselves and putting on watches day and night to warn them of hostiles in the area. Haro is providing them with some weapons and tips on how to organize their defense. We just can't be everywhere, and not knowing from where or when the next attack will come, this seems to be a reasonable way of handling it. He has also been advising families to leave the remotest communities and go to places that have defensive watches and other protections."

They turned in unison when they heard footsteps hurrying towards them and saw one of the senders. "I'm sorry to interrupt, Your Grace, but I've just received an important message," he said. I thought you'd like to see it right away."

"That's all right, Kellen, bring it here. From the look on your face, it's not good news."

"No Your Grace. Shall I read it?"

"Yes, go on, don't keep us in suspense."

It's from Captain Ladyl." The sender looked at the three men. "He's Commander Haro's second-in-command."

"Get on with it, man," Sir Arvand said.

"Sorry, sir," Kellen cleared his throat. Although he seemed reluctant to give them the message, he straightened his shoulders and began. "Captain Ladyl regrets to inform you that Commander Haro was killed in action during the night when the camp was attacked while we were sleeping. By the time the sentries alerted us, the commander had already been injured. The attack began when their wizard directed a power blast at the camp and destroyed several trees, as well as killing some of the horses. Commander Haro was injured when a large limb fell from a tree and crushed him. He succumbed to his injuries two hours later. Nothing could be done to save him as his spine had been shattered, and in addition, a broken branch had pierced his lung."

"Light preserve us," Valdor gasped. "That's devastating news! He was such a good man, and a dear friend. The world will be an emptier place without him in it." He looked down at the ground and wiped the corner of his eye with his finger, needing a moment to compose himself. He sighed deeply and continued, "Is that all?"

"Yes, Your Grace"

"I'll have to send a message to his family immediately. They'll be shattered." He started towards the building, fists clenched. *Damn their evil souls!* He turned round to make sure

Imali was following him. "I'll need you as well, Kellen," he added. "We have some arrangements to make."

71 – Felindra meets Ogryn

Felindra

The key scraped in the lock of Felindra's cell door. As the light faded in the cell and the door opened, new illumination came from a torch. "What have you done with the mattress?" The guard poked his head into the cell and looked around. Felindra pulled the blanket around her. "Where did you get that blanket?"

"It was cold in here, so I asked for a blanket, and here it is."

"Don't give me that girl. And how could you ask someone, no one's allowed down here but us guards and we wouldn't give it to you. We aren't allowed to talk to you even. Somebody brought it to you and I want to know who it was."

"How come you're talking to me now if you're not allowed?"

"Because I've been sent to get you. And stop changing the subject. Who gave you the blanket?"

"If you really want to know, I'll tell you, but you probably won't believe me if I do."

"Who was it?"

"It was the Light."

"We'll get it out of you eventually, you mark my words. But right now, the grand wizard wants to see you."

An icy feeling of dread settled around her stomach. "I'm not going anywhere without some clothes, and if you try to make me, you'll regret it."

"You can't use your magic in here, girl, it's warded."

"Not against the Light it isn't."

"Here, I brought these." He threw a bundle into the cell.

Felindra scampered to the other end of her mattress and reached for it, wondering what they'd sent. She unfolded the bundle and found a pair of loose cotton culottes and a sleeveless tunic. They smelled a bit musty, probably from being in storage for a long time, but otherwise they seemed clean. She pulled up the culottes under the blanket and quickly pulled the tunic over her head, and then she stood up. "Some shoes would be nice," she called. "Especially with these wet floors."

"Stop wasting time, he's waiting and he doesn't like being held up."

Felindra let out a breath and stood up, tucking the blanket under the mattress, hoping he would forget about it. She left the cell, closing the door behind her to keep in the warmth.

"What sort of a mood is he in?" she asked the guard.

"Same as usual," he replied. "Not that it's any of your business."

"What time is it?"

"You'll find out. Now keep your mouth shut. I'm not paid to listen to complaints or to answer questions." He gave her a shove in the back to get her moving.

Felindra didn't know what to expect, daytime or night. Her feet began to feel as cold as the stone under them as they climbed the steps to ground level. "How's my friend in the other cell?"

"I told you to shut up. You're asking for trouble, girl, if you keep it up." He opened the door to the grounds and pulled her outside. It was much warmer out here and she was gratified to see it was daytime, and the sun was shining. She stood for a moment, basking in the sunlight until he grabbed her arm and hurried her along.

"Why do you keep trying to make trouble for us?"

"Neither of us has anything better to do," she replied. She squinted sideways at him. "You know, you don't seem such a bad person. Why do you work for these evil people?"

The guard didn't answer.

He delivered her to Monaltor's office and went out, closing the door behind him. She was surprised he hadn't told the grand wizard about the blanket. Maybe it would have got him into trouble for allowing it. She stood about half a pace from the desk and looked at her jailor. He stared back at her without blinking. *Are you afraid of me?* She thought

"You've given us a lot of trouble for a little girl. What are we going to do with you?"

"I think the best answer to that question would be to let me go."

He scowled and slapped his hand down on the desk. "Silence! Come closer!"

She shuffled a couple of short steps closer to him and waited.

He shook his head. "I don't understand you at all," he said. "You don't seem to appreciate the seriousness of your situation. How can I convince you? You must cooperate with us; if you are no use to us, we'll have to dispose of you. We haven't abused you, have we? Yet you continue to defy us." He stopped and waited for her to say something.

Felindra thought over what he'd said and for some reason, wasn't intimidated by it. "You said you hadn't hurt me, but keeping me against my will hurts. It hurts a lot. I can't see my family or live in my own house, and I can't be with my friends, or go to school. I think that's bad enough. And putting me in that horrible dungeon..."

"SILENCE! Do you have any concept of what I could do to you? You should be punished for what you did to my son, and for enticing him to escape with you." She started to reply, but he put up his hand. "No, don't bother to answer. Barengush has been punished for his part in your little adventure, and we could do the same to you if you don't start to behave and cooperate."

"I don't know what you want me to do. All you've done so far is ask me about my gift."

"We haven't had time because of your shenanigans, but starting now, you are going to help us."

"I'll never help you. You people are evil."

"Enough!" His hand slammed down on the desktop. "I'll decide what you are going to do, not you. You would be advised to think about what could be in store for you if you don't cooperate."

"What have you done to Barengush?"

"Would you like to see him?"

"Why?"

"You can find out how he feels about disobeying me and the consequences of doing so." He went to the door and summoned the guard. "Take her down to the boy's room, but don't leave them alone; there's no telling what they'd get up to. Here's the key."

The guard escorted her outside and back to the building above the dungeons. She was surprised. Barengush was housed here ... and locked in! She almost felt sorry for him. He had shown some backbone when he'd run away with her. She dreaded finding out what his evil father had done to him. When the guard unlocked the door, she heard a raspy voice say, "Go away. Whatever you want, leave me alone."

"I've brought you a visitor, wizard." The guard pushed the door open, but she couldn't see Barengush; his bed must have been moved behind the door.

"I'm not a wizard, damn you!" he screeched. "And whoever is here, I don't want to see him, either. I don't want to see anybody or hear anything ever again. Now leave me alone." His voice became muffled at the end of his declaration, as if he'd covered his face with something.

Not a wizard? What did he mean by that?

"Come on, Barengush, she'll be very disappointed if you send her away." The guard nodded to her and pushed her forward into the room. The room was dark and stuffy and fetid with the odor of unwashed body.

She poked her head back into the hallway and took a deep breath, then closed her mouth and went inside. "It's me, Barengush. I want to talk to you."

He was lying on his face, but at the sound of her voice, he turned over and squinted at her. "How did you get out? Don't tell me you tried to escape again."

She shook her head and leaned back against the wall across the room from Barengush from where she could see him and the guard in the doorway at the same time. "No, nothing like that. Your father sent me."

"He's not my father," Barengush snarled. "I've disowned him."

"Can you do that?"

"I don't care whether you can or not. He's not my father anymore." He coughed weakly and cleared his throat, and then he dragged himself laboriously into sitting position with his bare legs over the side if the bed. He seemed listless, enervated without even a spark of life.

Felindra was shocked at how much he had changed in the few days since she'd seen him last. His hair was lank and greasy, his skin pasty, but worse than anything else, his whole body seemed to have shrunk. She could see every bone in his bare arms and legs, and the skull clearly defined under the skin of his face. "Dear Light, what has he done to you? You look half dead."

"I might as well be." He began to gasp for breath and coughed to clear his throat. "The sooner I'm gone, the better."

Oh my, he is in a sorry state. What could be so bad that he'd want to die? Light, is the anything we can we do to help him?

"Why?" she asked Barengush.

He shrugged feebly. "Do you know what he's done to me?

"That's what I came to find out. He's threatening to do the same to me if I don't do what he asks of me."

He made an effort and raised his head to look at her. She could see the melancholy and bleakness in his eyes, and an undercurrent of horror. He sighed. "He's taken my powers." He fell back on the bed; he'd obviously used up all his energy.

Felindra gasped. What a monster! It's no wonder Barengush wanted to disown him. What could she say? It would be fruitless to drag out meaningless clichés ... you'll get over it ... it's not the end of the world.... *Oh, Light, please help me.* "Barengush," she walked closer to the bed and put her hand lightly on his body. She felt a current of warmth pass through her and into him. "Barengush, listen to me. Don't forget about the Light. With him, anything is possible. You just have to trust him and have faith." He stirred slightly under her hand, but didn't reply. I can help you, but you have to start by helping yourself. I want you to bathe and put on some clean clothes, and then you must eat something. Will you do that for me?"

"What's the use?" he moaned.

She withdrew her hand, but stayed close. "Stop feeling sorry for yourself. Isn't it obvious to you that the Light wants you? Didn't you feel His warmth when I touched you?"

His eyes flicked open to look at her, and then closed again as if keeping them open took too much effort. "So what? What can he do? Can he give me my powers back?"

"You must realize that all our gifts come from Him in the first place. If he wills it, He will return your gifts, but only if you undertake to use them for good. Now, let's get started."

She heard the guard clear his throat. She looked at him and saw him scowling. "I'm not sure that's what the grand wizard wanted. You were just supposed to see what he could do to you," he said

"It's all right," Felindra said. "If this man is not going to die soon, we have to help him. He has to want to live. I won't take more than a few minutes, and you can help too. I want you to see Dominel—you know, the old monastery servant— ask him to bring some hot water and clean clothes, then some food. And this room needs some light. Anyone would be depressed in this gloom."

"In case you may have forgotten, you're the prisoner. I tell you what to do; you don't give orders."

"I wasn't giving you an order; I was just telling you what you can do to help a fellow human being. It's not much, but if you don't want him to die, I think you can find it in your heart to carry a simple message."

He shook his head. "You've got some pluck, I'll give you that. I don't know how you keep it up in your position. Hurry now; he'll be wondering what we're doing."

"It's my trust in the Light. I have complete faith in Him, so there's nothing to be afraid of. Just a few more seconds, then I'm ready to go back." Before he could offer more objections, she returned to Barengush's bedside and touched his shoulder. "Listen to me, Barengush. The Light will never let you down; you just have to meet Him halfway. Promise me you'll try to help Him make you better. Clean yourself up and eat. I'll be concentrating on helping you as well, so don't despair."

He grunted something, but she couldn't interpret his meaning. "I'm going now, but I'll see you again soon, and next time, I want you to be strong and healthy. There's still much to be done."

Once the door was closed, she let out a whoosh of breath. *Poor Barengush. I hope he pulls himself together. I wonder how his father will react when he hears about this conversation.*

"I have orders to take you back to your cell, now," the guard said, grasping her arm and guiding her to the stairs. He paused to light up a torch before descending into the dank gloom of the dungeons.

I hope he doesn't take my clothes, she wished fervently. *Light, please make him forget.* She felt no response but hoped for the best. When they reached her cell, she saw no sign that anyone had been inside. "Don't forget to talk to Dominel," she reminded him hoping this would distract him enough to make him forget about her clothes. It must have worked, because he shoved her inside, pushed the door shut and locked it. She stood still inside for a moment until she heard his footsteps retreat and was sure he was gone, and then she sat down on her mattress.

Poor Barengush; what a vicious monster to have for a father. I can't imagine dadi even thinking of doing anything so cruel.

The light glowed softly and the cell became so warm, she didn't even need the blanket. She folded it neatly and arranged it on the floor under her mattress, and then lay down. *Are they ever going to bring me some food? I'm starving.*

She sat up when she heard the key in the lock, eagerly anticipating having something to eat, but was bitterly disappointed when the door slammed open and Monaltor entered in a raging temper.

"Get up!" he shrieked at her. She stood up from the mattress and looked at him, waiting for him to have his say.

"What did I tell you about interfering with my son?"

"Someone needs to take care of him after what you did to him, and I don't see you trying to help him. He's dying, in case you care."

She watched his eyes and saw something awful peering out from them, something dark and evil. His fist struck the side of her head like lightening, throwing her sideways into the stone wall. "I've had enough of your interference." He raged, spittle spraying from his mouth. "I don't want you near him ever again, enchanting him with your spells, infecting his mind with your rubbish."

Felindra straightened up, swaying on her feet for a moment until the dizziness subsided. The shock stunned her. It was the second time he'd struck her in the same place. The side of her face ached and burned, but she was determined not to cry. When she touched her cheekbone, the most painful spot, there a lump. Her fingers traced the other side of her head where it had hit the wall and came away sticky with blood.

She refrained from answering him, but the look she gave him was condemning enough to relay how she felt. It would be futile to answer anyway; their views and reasoning were diametrically opposed and she knew they would never find common ground. But there was hope for Barengush; a comforting thought.

"Nothing to say?" he asked mockingly. "Your precious Light abandoned you? Now, come with me; I'm taking you to see the master himself. Hurry up; don't waste my time."

She staggered to the door, still reeling from the blow. He pushed her in the back to drive her into the passage. "Bring her," he ordered the guard. The guard, a new one she hadn't seen before, took her arm. "And watch her. She's full of tricks."

If only that were true, she thought to herself. *I'm terrified, all the time, but I won't let them see it.* A warm feeling passed through her like a caress. *If it weren't for you, Light, I don't know what I'd do. I'll stand up to them, I promise.*

They took her to an old door halfway along the passage. The door was locked and required a large, old-fashioned key to open it. A blast of cold air carrying the stench of mold hit them as the door swung open on creaking hinges. Inside was a stone staircase leading downward. Felindra had thought until now that the dungeons were on the lowest level, but she was obviously mistaken. *It's like entering the abyss of the damned,* she thought. She hesitated for a second. *I hope...*

"Why have you stopped?" Monaltor sneered. "Scared? Move!" He thumped her in the back hurling her forward so that she almost lost her balance; if the guard hadn't been holding her arm, she would have plunged down the steps into the darkness below.

"Where are you taking me?" she asked timidly.

"Frightened? You are right to be afraid. The person we are going to see now is our supreme leader, Oglestra's disciple himself. We'll see what he has to say about your tricks."

The passage at the bottom of the stairs was narrower than the one above, and the ceiling was so low, she would have been able to touch it easily had she the urge, but even thinking about doing so made her shudder. The walls, floor and ceiling were all covered in a patchwork of greenish black slime. The smell was rancid and bitter. They reached a door made of thick dark wood and reinforced with strips of roughcast iron. The door had neither a latch nor a keyhole, but there was a cast iron knocker. Monaltor rapped twice with the knocker and, after a long pause, the door creaked open.

Monolta entered first, beckoning her to follow, but leaving the guard outside. *Not good enough to be admitted into the presence of such an illustrious being,* Felindra thought derisively, although she was quaking with fear inwardly. He was the lucky one, not having to face whatever was in store for her. This was the Enemy, the malevolent creature responsible for every evil thing that happened, and now she was going to be face to face with him. She kept her eyes directed at the floor, not wanting to look at him.

"What is it now, Monaltor? Can't you handle things yourself without having to constantly interrupt me? I have important work, as you well know. Hurry up; let's get it over with."

Felindra sneaked a quick peek before averting her eyes again. In the weak illumination provided by the single candle in the room, she saw the small gnome-like creature who had visited her in her cell. He was sitting scrunched up on a high chair behind a large stone table. His head was hairless. He had tiny malevolent black eyes, and a loose, thick-lipped mouth (*made for slobbering,* she thought). If it weren't for the eyes and bald head, he could have been a werman, but no werman would radiate the hatred that this creature exuded, although she understood why people called wermen demons.

"Get to the point! I've got work to do."

"It's this girl, esteemed leader," Monaltor said quickly. "Ever since she arrived here, she's caused all kinds of problems. I don't know what to do with her. She doesn't seem to be frightened of anything and she's completely corrupted my son. She's been filling his head with nonsense about the Light. He even helped her escape ..."

"That's not true," Felindra interrupted him. "It was the Light who helped me escape."

"Quiet, Girl!" Monaltor raged.

"Ah, your son again. What's he done this time?" he glanced up at her. "And you keep your mouth shut. I won't hear that kind of language in my presence."

Ah, he's afraid of the Light.

"He escaped with her and was heading for Trethawynd when we intercepted them. There was another boy with them. He's in the cells now.

"If you can't handle your own son, don't come to me with your failures."

"Oh, I've fixed him all right. He won't be making any more trouble. It's her that's the problem."

"I didn't ask to be abducted and brought to this evil place. I'd be quite ..."

"Quiet girl! Don't you dare interrupt!" Ogryn snarled. "Or you'll rue the day you were born."

She looked around the room to avoid looking at him. Another table close by held a collection of skulls, some of which looked human. She shivered involuntarily.

"You mean she continues to flout our authority? What's she done now?"

"I allowed her to see Barengush just to show her what would happen to her if she didn't cooperate. I don't know what she did to him, but he's changed again. She started ordering the guard who was watching them to bring food and clothes, and water for bathing. The guard said she was making him promises about what the Light would do for him. The boy's besotted." He stopped and glared at her. "I just came to ask if you have any suggestions."

"Refresh my memory, why did you bring her here exactly?"

"She has a very rare ability, talking with animals. I thought if we could harness this power, it would prove useful to us."

"And have you tried?"

"Yes, I thought we could transfer it to my son, but the attempt was a complete failure. As soon as we started to probe her mind, she manifested a very powerful Repel that rendered my son and her unconscious and very ill. It took several days for them to recover."

"I suppose you could dispose of her if she's of no use to us anymore," Ogryn said sounding quite indifferent about the matter. "We have to show her precious Light who is really in charge of this universe. We will conquer them eventually, never fear, then her kind will be dealt with summarily. These stupid people can't be fooled forever with fairytales and wishful thinking; they'll find out the truth eventually."

"You're wrong," Felindra said impulsively. "You can fool some people, but you can't fool the Light. He will destroy you and all your evil activities eventually." *Light?*

"Silence!" Ogryn screeched. He jumped from his chair, his black robes flaring, making him look like an angry bat, stretched out his clawed fingers towards her and let go of a powerful bolt that threw her back into the wall.

She was stunned momentarily, but soon regained her wits. To her amazement, she saw the room gradually fill with light.

"What have you done? Stop it, STOP IT!" he screeched. He flung himself out of his chair and turned tail, scurrying through a small door behind his table, allowing it to slam behind him. *So he's vulnerable to something*, Felindra thought triumphantly. *They'll be pleased to know that at home.*

"What did you do?" Monaltor was very agitated.

"I didn't do anything," Felindra asserted. "That was the Light. He takes care of his faithful servants."

Ogryn

Oglestra help me! His eyes were burning and the pain in his head throbbed like a hammer. *Damn my father! Why did he do this to me?* Ogryn was the fruit of a drunken human's rape of a werwoman. Their mating shouldn't have borne fruit, but he knew you couldn't always trust nature; it sometimes had nasty surprises for the unsuspecting. His mother had been banished from her tribe. She'd taken him to an isolated cave to raise as best she could by herself. She'd been killed by a bear when he was in his eighth year and from then on, he was on his own, despised and victimized by both humans and werfolk. He would never forgive his father.

For years, he'd roamed the mountains and forests of Albasiny, friendless, unable to find work to support himself, shunned by everyone, both wermen and humans, a complete outcast. For years, he'd looked at every man he encountered of a certain age, smoldering with hatred, wondering if he was his father. He'd survived by trapping small animals and birds, eating them, raw most of the time because he couldn't tolerate the light of a fire to cook them. He'd also gathered herbs and experimented with them on himself, before trying to sell them to medicine practitioners.

One night, after consuming a new herb, he'd had a vivid dream in which Oglestra came to him. "I've been waiting a long time for you," the Fallen One had told him. "You will be my disciple and lead my followers. I will endow you with gifts and guide you, and you will do what I will." These words had been followed by a current infusing his body with a feeling of exhilarating darkness and icy coolness.

It had taken him centuries to gather followers from among the discontented, the angry, and those naturally drawn to cruelty and evil. Several attempts to spread his message in other parts of the world had ended in failure, but he had time; after all, he was immortal now. The number of his followers had gradually increased, especially among the Nordics of ValkonenMaa at a time when they were reeling from their persecution by the League of the Light. In fact, he felt he owed much of his success to those historic followers of the Light. Eventually, he'd settled in a cave in the mountains of ValkonenMaa, where his followers, who'd named themselves the Dark Brotherhood, had come to receive their instructions and make their tributes. He was especially gratified that many gifted people sought his guidance and become powerful wizards.

This was his latest and, he hoped, his final and most successful assault on the forces of the Light. So far, he was feeling optimistic, in spite of a few setbacks. They'd taken the monastery with ease to make it their headquarters, and he'd moved to his current location in order to be at the Brotherhood's center of power.

***

No one was ever allowed past the barricaded door from his receiving room. He staggered down the passage that led to his private quarters and let himself in. He had to bathe his eyes with an astringent wash to sooth them, and then he took a draft of a healing elixir for the pain. After that, he lay down in his leather reclining couch and closed his eyes. It would take a moment or two for the effects of the blinding light to wear off, and then he would be able to get back to his favorite occupation, destroying living creatures by the varied methods he'd acquired or invented during his long lifetime. He sighed contentedly as the pain receded and opened his eyes. Low-level indigo light was the one he found most soothing on stressful occasions and that's what he summoned now. He opened his eyes and looked around at the luxuries he'd acquired over the centuries. Shelves of leather-bound books, precious sculptures and ornamental rugs from all over the world. He had a set of gold chalices, crystal dishes and carafes, and one of the most complete sets of instruments of torture ever assembled. He smiled to himself. *If only the fools knew. This is what it means to be a disciple! The power. Forget about the pathetic Light. He has no power over me. I'm in a class by myself. This is what I work for, all the contributions from fools like Monaltor and his underlings only consolidate my wealth and comfort. Little do they realize there's nothing in it for them! I have to get some sort of satisfaction after the life my stupid father ... curse his soul ... made for me.* Ogryn got up and walked across the room. *Now for some fun! I think we'll do a rabbit today; they're so pathetic. Let me see ... shall I cut out its beating heart, or maybe drive hot nails into its eyes?* He rubbed his hands together as he made for the door of what he called his recreation room. *Oh how I hate being interrupted by those fools.*

While he was busy torturing the poor rabbit, Ogryn's thoughts turned to Felindra. That girl! She has a strange power; how did she do that? Maybe I should examine her further. It might be fun to bring her here and play with her. Her and her stupid Light. We'll see what the Light can do for her when she's in the hands of a true master.

With his tongue between his lips to aid his concentration, he put the final touches to his latest victim and grinned idiotically when it let out its final squeal.

72 – Through the Tunnel

Daryan had found a place to erect his small tent under the sheltering boughs of a large cedar tree. After such a strenuous day, he was able to fall asleep easily, until he was roused from a deep sleep by a poke at his shoulder. He opened his eyes and saw that it was still dark outside, but he could see the yellow eyes peering at him through the opening in the tent. A soft whine confirmed his suspicion. "Ashala!" He sat up and ruffled her fur affectionately. She ducked his hand and licked it. Although he couldn't see it, he could hear her tail slapping against the canvas of the tent.

Daryan found it amazing that she had come all this way by herself. She could have had help from the Guardian of the Forest, he supposed. "What are you doing here?" he asked, as if she would understand.

She responded with a moaning kind of howl, so clearly tinged with melancholy, he was immediately alarmed. *Felindra!* "Has something happened to her?" The wolf's responding whine did nothing to allay his fears. He got up from his ground sheet onto his knees, picked up his knife, and crawled out of the tent.

"Commander! I thought I heard a wolf. Are you all right, sir?" then he caught sight of Ashala. "By the light...." He drew his sword, but Daryan forestalled him.

"Be easy, Italo; she's a family friend."

"Yes, sir, but it's so big. She could rip someone's throat out. Are you sure it's safe?"

"Absolutely. She belongs to my daughter." The icy bolus of fear arose in his chest and traveled down his torso when he spoke of Felindra. What could have happened? "Carry on, defender." He barely managed to get the words out and was thankful when the man left.

"Go into the woods and wait for me," he said to Ashala. "Don't frighten the people." He gave her a comforting hug—

to comfort himself—and pushed her from behind in the direction of the trees. He stood for a moment outside his tent, thinking. *I have to know. I can't bear the suspense of not knowing. Pray the Light she hasn't been....* He couldn't finish that thought. *I'll have to wake Farah.*

Daryan lit a torch from the smoldering remains of the previous evening's fire and looked around the campsite. He recognized her tent by the communicator emblem painted in yellow on the side of it. Not all communicators used this method of identification, but Farah thought it would make it easier to find her in an emergency.

He knelt on the ground outside and shook the flap, then called her name softly. He didn't want to wake up the whole camp; the defenders needed their rest after the exertion of the past few days. He heard rustling inside the tent. "Who is it?" she asked.

"It's me, Daryan, I need you to send a message for me."

"I'll be right out."

After a bit more rustling, Farah's head emerged from the tent. Daryan stood up and put out his hand to help her to her feet. When he saw her bleary eyes and tousled hair, he felt guilty for waking her, but then she smiled at him, not looking the least bothered.

"I'm sorry I woke you," Daryan said. "I should have waited until morning."

"Well, I'm awake now, what can I do for you?

"I want to send a message," he replied. He noticed her shiver and rub her arms. "It's cold, isn't it? Why don't you get your cloak, then we can go somewhere to talk."

She ducked back into the tent, grabbed her cloak, and put it around her shoulders. They moved away from the other tents and found a small dell in which they could talk freely. "Whom do you wish to communicate with?"

"Ashavan. He should know everything that's going on. Tell him I'm concerned about Felindra and have reason to believe she's in danger. But before we do, I'd like you to see if you can get anything from Ashala."

"You mean she's here?" Farah exclaimed.

"Yes. She's the one who woke me. Just a second." Daryan gave a soft whistle and waited. A moment later, the wolf came out of the bushes to his side. "This is a friend," he said, introducing Farah. "Come over here and let her get your scent," he added to the Farah.

Once the introduction was complete, Daryan said, "Put your hand on her head while I try to talk to her." Then he turned his attention to the wolf. "Where's Felindra?" Ashala let out a pitiful howl in response.

"Did you get anything?" Daryan asked Farah.

"Only that Ashala is very upset and afraid. I got an image of your daughter being dragged away by some men, but that's all." She took her hand away from the wolf. How does she know?" she asked Daryan.

"I don't really know, but I believe she gets news from other animals. They seem to have a network." He gave Ashala a hug. "You're a good girl, Ashala. We'll find her, don't worry." With a pat on the head, he signaled her back into the trees.

"I think she understood what you said; at least she brightened up a bit when you spoke."

"I hope so. Now how about Ashavan?"

"It may take a while to find him," she said. "But I'll get started."

"Sit down while we wait," Daryan advised her. He sat down on the mossy bank by a tree and leaned his back against the trunk, sitting on his cloak to protect him from the dampness. Farah did the same. He watched her sitting with her head back against the tree trunk and her eyes closed in concentration. Farah wasn't traditionally beautiful, but there was a special warmth about her as if she genuinely enjoyed being with people. She seemed to like everyone and never hid the fact. It was her smile that made her attractive; it was like sunshine.

He looked away, feeling he was invading her privacy by staring at her while she was working. She looked vulnerable somehow.

A short time later, she opened her eyes and spoke to him. "I got him. He was awake … trust Toma. He always did keep strange hours. Now we have to wait for him to try to find out where she is and what happening."

"Good. I know what you mean about Ashavan," Daryan said. "I've known him for years and he always seems to pop up when he's needed. You rarely have to search for him. It's almost as if he has foresight."

"Maybe he does," she said with a fond smile. "I've often wondered about that myself. His gift is certainly more complex than mere telepathy." Her eyelids dropped, and then opened again. "Here he is now. Do you want me to speak what he is sending?"

"That would be good."

Farah closed her eyes again and after a few seconds, began to speak as Ashavan. "As far as I can ascertain, she is back at the monastery. She is alive and unhurt, but there is a strong sense of evil around her. I haven't been able to make contact with her at all. Maybe they're continuing to keep her warded, but when I was trying to contact her earlier, she came into range occasionally, as if she were moving from one place to another where the ward was not active.

Daryan felt as if an enormous weight had been lifted from him, although he was very upset that she had been recaptured. *Damn them to the deepest pit.* "So you are sure she's all right,"

"He says that is the most likely conclusion, given the facts.' Farida smiled as she relayed this.

Daryan smiled too; the formality of wording reminded him of his son, Darson. "Ask him if there's any more news."

He saw tears seep between her closed eyelids. "Oh no!" she uttered involuntarily, and then she looked up at Daryan, wiping her eyes. "It's bad news, I'm afraid," she said shakily.

Another flare of ice took up residence in his stomach. He dreaded the answer, but he had to ask. "What is it?"

"Your friend, Commander Haro, has been killed. I'm so sorry, Daryan. He was a very special person."

Daryan managed to utter one terse phrase, "that's all, thank you." and then he stood up and pushed his way into the trees with tears in his eyes. *My friend, probably the best friend I'll ever have ... always there when I needed him, always cheerful and thoughtful. I took it for granted that he always would be, now ... what am I going to do without you, Andro? You've left a great emptiness; the world doesn't feel complete without you. What will Valina do, and the little ones? I should send them a message, but not now. I'll wait until tomorrow. Farewell, my friend. Light be with you on your journey. I know we'll meet again one day.*

And Felindra in the hands of those monsters. Who knows what's happening to her? Light protect her.

Andro! Daryan dashed tears from his eyes. *Gone. I can't believe I'll never see you again, or hear your voice, not in this life.*

He wiped his eyes, straightened his shoulders, and walked back to his tent, knowing he wouldn't sleep now. *It's almost dawn anyway; I might as well start getting ready to move out.*

When everything was packed and ready to move, horses harnessed, carts and travois loaded. Daryan took a last look around before leading his horse into the cavern. The horse didn't seem to like entering the cave; it didn't actually baulk, but it put its head down and had to be prodded a second time to get it moving. As he entered the inner tunnel, he felt a tug on his trouser leg. He looked down and saw Axtya's big eyes looking up at him.

"What do you need, Axtya? Aren't you coming with us?

"Come, yes. Find home. People live here say bad passage."

"What do you mean, bad?"

"No go that way. People show you safe way. Other way not safe."

Daryan looked back at the caravan waiting to move on. He found Farah among the defenders directly behind him and spoke to her. "Do you know what he's talking about?"

"I get an image of rocks falling in the tunnel. Apparently, the werfolk who live here have told him about it and have offered to guide us through. I also read a loathing for the Dark Brethren."

"Is that right, Axtya?"

"Yes. They show good way."

"All right. Are they ready?"

"Ready." He beckoned to two wermen waiting farther into the tunnel. "We go now."

"Do you want to ride?" Daryan asked him.

"Not horse. Walk."

Independent little man, Dayan thought. "All right, let's go. Oh, Axtya, Felindra's wolf is behind us. She won't hurt anyone unless she's attacked. She's just trying to get to Felindra. I know they're afraid of wolves, but tell them she won't hurt them. She's part of my family. Will you do that?"

Axtya scowled. "No like wolf. Like girl. I tell. Yes."

Dayan looked questioningly at Farah. "The werfolk don't like wolves, but he likes your daughter, so he will warn them. I think he means it."

Daryan sighed. "I can't really blame him. It was Ashala who caused the loss of his hand, although it was his fault." He looked around to make sure everyone was ready. "Move on."

The pace was very slow, dependent on the wermen leading them. Finally, they reached the place where the tunnel branched. The two wermen guiding indicated that the right hand one was safer.

"Thank you," Daryan said. He turned to Axtya. "Ask them if it's safe now or are there any more things we should watch for?"

Axtya went into a long conversation with the two guides with much gesturing and pointing. "Safe." He replied. "Only water now."

Water! What does that mean? He turned to Farah for clarification.

"He seems to be talking about a place where the tunnel dips and water drips down from the walls, pooling in the sunken level. That's the picture I got from their conversation."

"How deep does it get?" Daryan asked Axtya. "Can we get through it?"

Axtya held another brief discourse with the guides and gave his usual succinct reply. "Here," he said, leveling his left hand just above his waist. *Just above my knee,* Daryan thought. *I suppose we can manage that.*

After travelling through the caves for about four hours and not encountering anything too disturbing, Daryan called for a rest stop. They'd arrived at a place where the tunnel widened into a substantial chamber with room for them to spread out and eat some of the food they'd brought. "Go easy on the water," Daryan warned them. "We may not find any drinkable water until we reach the other side."

"How far do you think it is?" a junior office asked.

"I really don't know," Daryan replied. "In the worst case, we have to be prepared for several days, three at least, but I'm hopeful it will be less. And, if we reach a point where we can go no farther with our baggage carts, we'll have to abandon them and carry what we can on our backs."

Later that day, they came upon one of the flooded areas they'd been warned about. The horse drank the water readily, which they would not have done had it been tainted. "Next time," Daryan said, "if there is another pool, make sure we get to it before the horses so that we can fill out water bottles."

"We could use this pool for washing," the sergeant suggested.

"Certainly."

Cut off from the sun and sky, they had no natural way of telling the time, so when everyone began to slow down and drag their feet, Daryan decided to stop for the night at the next widening of the tunnel. It wasn't as cold this far into the tunnel as it had been closer to the outside. The wind didn't penetrate this deep and warmth from the earth provided a small amount of heat. Even so, it was a restless night for most of the group, sleeping on the uneven ground, all crowded into a not very large cavern. The horses had been connected together with rope in the narrower part of the tunnel to prevent their wandering off.

What was I thinking of? This is worse than I expected. Did I think we would be able to prance through a short tunnel and arrive in ValkonenMaa in a day? Ah well, this will pass. We'll get there eventually. Daryan shifted once more, brushed a small stone from under his ground sheet, and tried to relax.

The next day they made an early start, having decided not to light a fire to heat their food. Daryan was not the only one who wanted to move on; everyone was up and ready to go in no time. They could eat their rations as they walked.

"I wonder what time it is," a defender mumbled to his neighbor.

"Who cares?" the other man replied. "We're moving; that's all that matters."

"But it feels strange, not knowing if it's day or night."

"Don't make any difference to me."

After they'd been travelling for what Daryan estimated was the best part of a day, they came to a section of tunnel littered with fallen rocks. "This is going to be tricky; we won't be able to get the carts through if we don't move some of these rocks." Daryan said. "I can see you're all too tired for more work, so here's what we'll do: We'll have something to eat, rest for a little while, and then we'll started moving the stones."

By the time they finished clearing a passage, they were so exhausted and they lay down on the tunnel floor to sleep, regardless of comfort.

The sleepers were roused during the sleep period by the restlessness of the horses that were stabled farther back in the tunnel. There was a great deal of neighing, snorting, and stamping hooves, but it died down before anyone could be bothered to investigate. Finally, one of the defenders lit a torch and went to check on them, make sure they could reach the water trough and had enough fodder, then after a few reassuring pats, he went back to his ground sheet and returned to sleep.

Ashala

Ashala slunk quietly through the tunnels, following the scent trail left by Daryan's people. Another, more disturbing odor hung in the air, but she didn't stop to investigate it. The creatures she was scenting could be difficult and she didn't want to arouse them. She had purposely waited until dark before venturing into the cavern, hoping that all the day creatures would be sleeping. The horses didn't like her presence, so she squeezed by, keeping close to the opposite wall. She had one purpose in her mind that far outweighed everything else, even hunting for food, and that was her girl. The girl was in danger and Ashala was going to find her and help her. She didn't even stop to greet Daryan.

Daryan

Daryan was surprised when he awoke and realized he had actually slept for a while, and was feeling refreshed. Then the memory of Andro's death swept into his mind like the bitter kiss of a winter dawn. He sank back on his bedroll and closed his eyes, forcing himself not to weep. *I can't think about that now. I'll honor his memory and avenge him by ridding the*

604

world of the fiends who took away his life, but right now, I have a job to do and people depending on me.

He groaned and sat up to put his boots on. Most of the company was already eating and packing up equipment. He stood up and stretched, then bent to pick up his ground sheet and roll it up. Once he'd completed his ablutions and found something to chew on, he went to get his horse.

"Is everyone ready?" he asked Captain Moro.

"Yes, all ready to go."

"Well let's be on our way. You take the rear and I'll lead."

It was a tight squeeze through the stretch where the rock fall had been cleared. About half way through, they had to stop and chip away some protruding rock with a pick, which started another, minor slide. They wasted almost an hour clearing the space before they could move on.

"I'm starting to wonder if this is all worthwhile, Daryan said to Lieutenant Larine who was walking beside him.

"It probably is," the lieutenant replied. "It's like being explorers, finding new routes to travel."

Daryan smiled. *He's so young,* he thought. "I hope...What was that?"

They heard the rumbling of falling rock, the screams of horses and men. Everyone already through was now pressing forward, fearing the fall would spread and trap them. The carts were stuck in the crush of pushing bodies; the terrified horses whinnied in panic. Daryan tried to force his way back through the pack, and finally had to shout. "Make way. Keep going, but slow down and stop panicking. Let me get through to check the damage."

"It must be another rock fall." The lieutenant, who was trying to keep up behind him, stated the obvious. Daryan managed not to roll his eyes. *He's just a youngster.*

"Good, you're with me," he replied. "We're going to need some help. I want you to send telepaths and healers back here. Ask the league defenders to help you find them." Daryan looked around at the crush of people. "We have to get all these people out of the way. If you see any officers or a sergeant, ask them to keep everyone moving, out of the way." *What else?* He resumed his push against the advancing herd and finally entered the space in front of the rockslide. A few other defenders, those who'd barely escaped being trapped themselves, were trying to remove some of the rocks. "Before you go on," he said to them. "I want to wait for Nadi and a telepath to find out if anyone still lives under the rocks.

He heard distant human cries and the screams of horse from the piled up rocks and clenched his fists. A woman was moaning not very far away. There is nothing more disturbing than the screams of an injured horse, unless it's the cries of a wounded human, trapped and unable to move.

A horse was imprisoned under the pile of rocks with only its head free. Its cries faded to gasps and groans as its eyes clouded over. The rider was standing by it with tears streaming down his face. "End its suffering, defender!" Daryan ordered. The man looked at him, confused. "Do you want me to do it?" the man nodded, still not seeming to understand what was happening. *Shock*, Daryan thought. He took out his sharp dagger, and went to the poor horse. *It's almost dead already*, he thought as he quickly slashed the artery in its neck, and then jumped sideways to avoid the spurting blood.

One of the healers arrived. "Take him," Daryan said. "He needs a hot drink and something to keep him warm. Come right back; you might still be needed here." The defender who had just seen his horse die was shivering and pale as the healer led him away.

Nadi arrived with a telepath close behind.

"Good, you're here," Daryan said. "What do you sense?"

Nadi took a deep breath. This wasn't a very pleasant task to perform, but he closed his eyes and concentrated, turning pale as he listened with his mind. "Several alive, maybe three or four, but they are in severe pain and very frightened," he reported. "The horses are just as bad, but there are only two of them still living."

"I was able to contact two of our defenders," the telepathic defender said. "One of them is not too badly hurt because he's in a sort of pocket trapped between two large rocks. The other is a woman. She's badly injured and barely able to maintain consciousness." He took a deep breath. "Do you want me to keep trying?"

"Yes, of course. I want to know all about what is happening in there before we start moving debris."

"I just contacted Captain Moro," the telepath said. "He's conscious, but his legs are crushed and his horse is dead. It seems he was just entering the slide area when it happened."

Daryan groaned. He knew they wouldn't be able to rescue the captain in time. He tried not to think of those who would be bereaved by his death. He didn't even know if he had a family, children. *And I sent him to die*, he thought. He shook his head. *I should pull myself together.*

"All right, people," he said to the waiting defenders. "We have to try to rescue as many as we can, but keep in mind that this is a very unstable area and any move you make could cause another slide, so be careful. At the least sign of movement, back out! Don't risk your lives trying to be heroes."

Dear Light, what have I brought us to? So many dead already. Did I make the wrong decision? He snorted. *That's obvious; I don't need to ask. This whole campaign is turning into a complete disaster. I'm not cut out for this kind of warfare. Everything that could go wrong has done so. We are down to less than half the number that left Bartony.* He sighed and rubbed his forehead to release the tension. He was starting to develop a headache, and the fire in his stomach was flaring up again.

"Is there anything I can do, commander?" the lieutenant asked. His former enthusiasm over the discovery of this tunnel had disappeared and he now looked very strained and a little helpless.

I have to start thinking. What should they be doing? Everyone needs something to do. He looked back down the tunnel and saw that one of the carts still standing by. It had been the last to pass through before the slide. "Leave that cart here," he called to the driver. "We may need some supplies for the wounded. I'd like you to walk down to the front of the column and tell them to keep on moving. We'll just keep a few defenders back to help with the rescue. Tell them to keep going until everyone is tired and hungry, and then take a break. We'll catch up with them."

Daryan followed the driver halfway along the line, picking out ten of the strongest-looking men to help clear the rocks and the remaining healers in case they were able to rescue some of the injured before they died of their injuries. As he walked back to the rock fall, Daryan realized that all the injured horses had stopped screaming, and he couldn't hear any sound from the people who were trapped either. He called Nadi and Rhodi, the telepathic defender. "Keep monitoring," he told them. "I want to know how many still live. Rhodi, can you tell the difference between unconsciousness and lifelessness?"

"Yes, commander. Even when unconscious, the brain still keeps active with the automatic functions of life."

Daryan stepped back as the men began to pull rocks out of the pile, drawing the other two with him. "I'm telling you this in confidence," he said to Nadi and Rhodi. "We'll have to abandon the rescue attempt when no one remains alive. We can't risk losing more lives trying to recover bodies. I know it sounds harsh, but you must understand the necessity of continuing with the mission and preserving as many lives as we can. Believe me, it's a hard decision to make. Do you understand what I'm saying?" The two men nodded unhappily. "Tell me the moment you no longer detect life."

Just then, there was the rumble of falling rocks and a shout, "Watch out!" Men came running down the tunnel as rocks from the top of the heap started to roll down, burying the dead horse under the new slide.

"Was anyone hurt?" Daryan asked.

One man held up a bleeding arm, and another was limping from foot injury, but the rest seemed fine. They were wearing their gauntlets to protect their hands and most of them wore helmets, but they'd dispensed with the rest of their armor.

Daryan looked back at the rock pile blocking the passage. He saw blood puddled outside place where the horse was now buried, and bloody the footprints of defenders trampled through it. He hooked his thumbs in his belt and thought about the situation. *What do we do now? We can't abandon anyone who still lives, but this seems to be a time-wasting effort. We have to be sure though before we can leave.* He caught the eyes of Nadi and Rhodi, the telepath, and raised his eyebrows. Nadi shook his head and Rhodi came towards him so he wouldn't have to shout.

"I only sense one life now," he said, turning away from Daryan, unable to look him in the eyes with the raw emotion he was feeling.

Daryan nodded. "Can you tell how far away he is?"

"She seems fairly close. Maybe a pace or two."

"A woman! Is she badly hurt?" Daryan asked.

"I think she is. She seems to be hurt everywhere, her head, all her limbs, and she finds it very painful to breathe, so I assume she has chest injuries as well." Rhodi stopped talking, holding out his hand towards Daryan. He looked down at the ground and took a deep breath, shaking his head. "She...she just..." he shook his head again unable to continue. Tears filled his eyes.

"Has she gone?" Daryan asked softly, placing his hand on the telepath's shoulder.

Rhodi nodded. He sniffed and wiped his nose on a cotton rag. "Sorry."

"There's nothing to be sorry about, Rhodi. Am I right in thinking you have a special connection with this woman?"

"She...she's...was, my cousin." Unable to contain his grief any longer, the telepath walked down the tunnel and rested his head against the side of his horse, his shoulders heaving.

This is a hateful business, Daryan thought. *All this loss of so many young lives, the pain of bereavement, all the families...*

He turned to the men surrounding him. "No one lives," he said, rubbing his forehead with his fingertips. "I'm devastated by this, but I have to tell you that everyone trapped in the rock slide has expired. They are in the care of the Light now. We won't dig any further. We'll just carry on and hope to get out of this wretched tunnel without any more disasters. Before we go, would any of you like to say a memorial prayer for our lost brothers and sisters?"

They probably blame me, but I didn't know this would happen. I'd never have started this journey if I'd had any inkling it was so dangerous. I thought it would save time. He massaged his flaming stomach.

73 – Felindra and Vertan

Monaltor and the guard took Felindra back up to her cell. After shoving her inside, Monaltor ordered her, "The clothes. Throw them out."

"Why do you always want to take my clothes?" she asked.

"Because you don't like it," he replied. "Now, hurry up or I'll get the guard to do it."

She took off the shirt and culottes he'd given her earlier and threw them towards the door. The guard scooped them up, and Monaltor said, "You are giving me far too much trouble. I expect Ogryn will have a few ideas for making you more cooperative. He loves that sort of a challenge. He's softened up quite a few reluctant workers. And you don't even want to know how he did it."

Felindra huddled on her pallet hugging her knees against her chest. "He seemed like a pitiful creature to me," she replied. "He didn't do too well against the Light just now, did he?"

"You'd better control your mouth, girl. You have no idea what he is capable of."

"I do know is that he's helpless against the Light."

Monaltor slammed the cell door and left. Once she heard the key, she felt under her mattress and took out the clothes Dominel had brought and the blanket. Even though they were a bit damp, she put on the clothes she wrapped the blanket around herself. The light in the cell brightened and the air warmed up.

Felindra sighed. *Thank you, Light.* She wasn't half as confident as she pretended to be, in fact, she was quite apprehensive about what they might have be planning for her. She was putting on an act, chiefly to annoy Monaltor. He was a nasty man—but that ugly little creature who called himself 'The Disciple'—he was a monster filled with pure evil. *His blood, if he has any, is probably black.* She could very well believe that he was connected to Oglestra, but she had been taught that even Oglestra, a celestial being who had descended into sin, had been defeated and held no power at all now. So from where did these evil people get their power? It was puzzling. She believed what she had said about the Light being the only source of gifts, but could His gifts be perverted and used for evil? *Oh light, I hope you'll give me an answer so that I can understand what is happening.*

Vertan

Vertan spent most of his time sleeping, although he also did regular exercises to keep himself strong. It wasn't easy to feel strong with the paucity of food they provided. As far as he could work out, they only brought food once a day, although he couldn't be sure, not being able to observe the cycle of days. The food was usually bread and a broth flavored with vegetables, with a few beans floating in it. Sometimes they brought him a porridgy mush of beans and grain. Neither meal had much flavor nor was it warm, but he relished every bite when it came, eating it slowly to make it last. The bread and cheese the old man had brought had been much better, but he'd never returned.

He sighed and got up from his pallet. *Might as well do some exercise. It's time someone emptied the slop bucket, the stink is getting really bad.*

He half-heartedly began his warmup. It was something to do to alleviate the boredom for a few minutes. Falling into his usual routine, he continued the more strenuous moves while he thought about his situation. *It's strange they didn't bother to chain us up. They must be very confident that we can't escape. Maybe they have some sort of spell to prevent it, like the warding spell.* He stopped moving and wiped the sweat off his face and arms with the shirt the old man had provided. *The problem with exercise is it makes you sweat, and that makes you thirsty. They don't leave enough water, so you're always thirsty.*

He sat down on the mattress, not bothering to put the shirt back on. It seemed hotter in the cell after the activity. He noticed the light was fading and quickly removed the pants and shoved them under the mattress along with the blanket. He had become accustomed to this routine after a while. The light fading usually meant someone was coming. Sure enough, he heard footsteps approaching. By the time the key scraped in the lock, he was sitting innocently, arms wrapped around his knees.

The door opened and a guard looked in. "Here, put these on," he ordered, throwing a bundle of clothes at him. The guard looked around the cell suspiciously. "Why is it so warm in here?"

"I've just been exercising," Vertan replied. "Are we going somewhere?" he asked, picking up the garments, a tunic and pair of cotton culottes, no undergarments.

"Just do what you're told and don't ask questions."

Vertan picked up the pants and pulled them on, tying the drawstrings around his waist, then donned the tunic. Both garments were a bit damp and had a musty smell, but they were better than being naked.

"Hurry up. We haven't got all day."

"I'm ready," Vertan replied cheerfully. "Where are we going?"

"The chief want to see you," the guard replied. "Before we go, put this on." He handed Vertan a piece of chain with a manacle at each end. *I wonder,* Vertan thought when he had the manacle in his hand. *Could I take him?* His mistake was looking at the guard.

"Don't even think about it." The guard touched the pommel of a short sword at his waist.

Vertan sighed and clamped the manacles over his wrists, and then watched the guard lock them. Once secured, he took the hold chain and led Vertan up the stairs.

Moving from the dungeons to the office of the Grand Wizard involved going outside the building. The sun was shining and Vertan breathed his first lungful of fresh air in several days. The warmth of the sun and the piney smell of the woods were like a balm to his troubled spirit. They walked through the yard and entered the former administration building. It was hard to believe this was the same place he'd lived most of his life, everything was so grimy and neglected. It was like walking through a ruin. Vertan had one consoling thought: The Grand Master had escaped.

"Do you think I could have some water?" Vertan asked the guard.

"Just keep walking. We're nearly there."

"I know," Vertan replied. "This was my home, and that was the Grand Master's study," he added as the guard approached the door.

"Come in and sit down," the man who had led their capture said.

"I was asking the guard if I could have some water to drink," Vertan said. "They never seem to bring us enough to drink and I get very thirsty."

"I didn't bring you here to listen to complaints" The wizard scowled at him, but nodded at the guard. "Just do as you're told and sit down."

Peevish man, Vertan thought. *I wonder what's biting his tail.* He sat down on the chair in front of the Grand Master's beautiful mahogany table, which was now scratched and covered in dust and water rings. *They really are disgusting people. Not to worry, though, they'll be gone soon.*

"Let's get to the point right away. You are a member of the League defenders, are you not?"

"Just a recruit. I was only accepted into the league after your raid on our monastery, so I don't have much experience."

"But you know something about the operations of the League."

Before Vertan could answer, the guard came in. He came over to the desk and laid a tin mug in front of Vertan. He'd brought him water! He could barely believe it and wondered of there was an ulterior motive behind it; maybe it contained some sort of drug to make him talk about things he shouldn't reveal. "Thank you," he said to the guard as he returned to the door. *The thing is I have nothing to reveal. I can't tell them about anything because I don't know anything. I'd be glad to tell them about the Light though, but that would probably make him mad. I wonder how Felindra deals with them.* He picked up the mug and took a sip. It tasted all right, not very fresh, but not tainted either.

"Let's get back to the question," the wizard snapped. "If you've finished your little diversion."

"What was the question again?

"Oglestra damn you! This isn't a game. You're as bad as that girl. I was asking you about the operations of the League."

"I assume you want to know its history. They recruit new members from among the students of the ..."

"Damn it boy! That's not what I'm asking you. To put it more bluntly, how are they organizing their defense?"

Vertan blew out a stream of air through his pursed lips. "That's a tough one. I don't really know much about it. Mostly what my unit did was patrols. I heard that the prince consort is on his way from the capital with an army, and Trethawynd is also sending forces." Vertan knew he wasn't revealing anything they didn't know already. "I couldn't say what their plans are, but I'm sure there will be an early victory with all those forces united against you." He watched the wizard's face turn brick red and his knuckles whiten as he clenched his fists. *Uh, oh, that really got to him.*

Monaltor slammed his fists down on the tabletop, shaking the bottles and candleholders, and sending papers flying. "I can see you are determined to be obstructive. I won't tolerate it! I want some concrete information, not the ramblings of your fantasies. What I want to know is where and when they will attack and how many fighters they have."

"I told you. I can't tell you things I don't know. Do you think the commanders discuss their plans with me? All I can do is guess. They will attack as soon as they get organized and in places where your people are causing the most trouble. As for how many, hundreds I would guess. Probably more than a thousand."

Monaltor stood up and paced towards the window, which was curtained off. He pulled aside the curtain and peered outside. He seemed more disappointed than angry. *He must know he can't win.* "Look, you're a wizard. Can't you read my mind? I have nothing to hide. *Not even my contempt for you.*

"I did," the grand wizard replied, turning back to face him. "What can you tell me about the girl?"

"You mean Felindra? I only met her the day she escaped with the Grand Master. *Good chance to rub it in about the Grand Master's escape.* She's a whisperer, but I expect you know that already. She's a nice girl, very brave. I have a feeling that the Light has a special interest in her. That's about it."

"How do you feel about her?"

"I just told you; she's very nice, kind and brave."

"I'm not asking you for a characterization, damn it! Do have any, should I say, romantic feelings?"

"I've only just met her," Vertan protested. "I was with her for less than two days."

"Very well." The grand wizard came back to the table and sat down. "What can you do?"

"I don't understand."

"I already told you; don't play games with me. What powers do you have?"

"Relocation and some telepathy. That's all."

"I see. Well, it looks as if you're not much use to us. I've probed your mind. It seems to be empty of anything that would be useful to us. So what am I to do with you?"

"You could let me go." He caught his breath as his heart started to pound. This meeting wasn't going well. *What else could I say?*

"That was a rhetorical question." Monaltor stood up. "That's all. I'm sending you back to your cell while I make a decision. Maybe our leader, the Disciple, will have a suggestion." He beckoned to the guard.

"How's Felindra?" Vertan asked before the guard could take him away.

"She lives," Monaltor said with a scowl. "For now. I'm still trying to find a use for her, too. Now leave. I'm tired of looking at you."

Mean bastard. I don't like his insinuations one bit.

74 – Out of the Cave

It took another day and night to reach the end of the cave system. With everyone brooding about the tragedy of the rockslide, it was a sorry band of warriors that emerged from the caves into the forest of ValkonenMaa. A brief survey of position of the sun and the shadows on the ground told them it was a little before noon. They found a narrow trail down the mountainside, obviously trodden by animals and werfolk, but it was too narrow to accommodate their carts.

Daryan allotted two defenders to scout the trial ahead, and two more to hunt for game, and put the rest to work unloading the carts and packing the supplies into bundles that the horses could carry. Once everyone was occupied, he took Nadi and Farah aside.

"Nadi, you know the names of all the defenders, don't you?"

Nadi nodded. "I think so. What is it you require?"

"I need a list of all the casualties so that I can include them in my report." He took a large, leather-bound notebook out of the satchel he always carried, and tore out some blank pages. Here's something to write on. Do you need a graphite stick? Here."

After handing the graphite and paper to Nadi, he took Farah to the other side of the clearing. "I need to send two messages, one to the Monastery and one to Duke Valdor. Here's what I need to send, Farah." He opened his notebook and reread the notes he'd been working on during breaks.

Once he was satisfied, he tore out the pages and handed them to her. "I've marked the recipient of each one."

"Do you want me to wait for replies, Commander?"

"Yes, please, unless the recipient is not immediately available. Now that we're out of the mountain, we can receive it any time. You might also try to get some updates on the general situation while you're at it. Tell them I'll have some more to report after we finish this list." He nodded towards Nadi, who was frowning with concentration, biting the wooden end of the graphite.

While she was sending, he went to the other side of the clearing and sat down beside Nadi. How's it going?" he asked.

Nadi handed him the list he'd compiled so far. "I can't remember the name of that little fellow who drove the wagon."

"Zhiff! Was he killed as well?"

"I'm afraid so. In the cave-in," he replied with a nod. "How do you spell that?"

After spelling the name, Daryan shook his head despondently. There was nothing he could say that would make it any easier. *I think I'll retire permanently after this is over. That's if I'm still alive. I'm just not up to it anymore.* "How many?" he asked.

"You wanted all the casualties?" Nadi asked. "From the other two incidents as well as the cave-in?"

"Not the first attack, but the second one at the rock slide and the ambush at the canyon, yes."

When they'd finished compiling the list, Daryan gave it to Farah to send to the duke and the Monastery. He leaned back against a tree trunk and buried his face in his hands. Twenty-five deaths in last two incidents. It added up to a fifth of their original complement. He wondered how the other groups were faring, hoping it was better than his team.

When Farah had finished sending, Daryan roused himself. "Let's go back and see how things are going. The scouts
618

should be back by now. You can tell me what you learned on the way back."

Duke Valdor reported that the Dark Brethren had been virtually cleared out of Trethawynd, and from the Monastery, he learned that everything there was quiet, and Ashavan was still trying to locate Felindra.

Ashala

Ashala woke up and sniffed the air. She was still becoming used to the different smell of this new forest, and steered her way around other wolves when she sensed them. There was a strong indication that there was more than one pack in the area. She'd heard them howling in the night, but had refrained from answering until she could feel confident that they would accept her and not try to drive her off or attack her. She knew she *needed* to be in this area and could allow nothing to prevent her reaching her goal.

It was late afternoon, not too early for her to hunt. She had to be careful not to trespass into the territory of one pack or another, although she was fortunate that the game in this forest was plentiful. After testing the air in every direction, she detected a family of rabbits, without any of the scent markers of other wolves. She crouched until her belly almost touched the ground and crept forward silently as a shadow. When she saw them, she stopped for a moment. Like rabbits everywhere, they were highly alert, noses twitching and ears erect, heads darting in every direction—at least the adults were; the four babies were more intent on their play. After making her assessment, she decided on the large buck, knowing she wouldn't be able to get more than one. Once alerted, they moved too fast, even the babies, but the buck would make an adequate meal.

After she'd finished eating, Ashala licked her muzzle and paws, then went in search of water. Although she couldn't sense Felindra directly, she was conscious of her being somewhere ahead. She would find her and she knew she was getting closer.

Daryan

Although the two hunters had spotted a deer, it had vanished too quickly for them to get a shot at it, so they had to make do with their regular rations. The response from Duke Valdor arrived just as they were finishing their meal. Farah brought him the message as soon as she received it. In addition to condolences, it contained orders from Valdor to join up with the ValkonenMaa League defenders in a town called Tuulinen, on the road between the capital, Mainio, and the monastery.

75 – Felindra Makes a Scene.

Felindra opened her eyes. That's funny, it's dark, and cold. Light! What's happening? Where've you gone? She felt a soft caress of warm air.

There were voices outside her cell. What was going on? The key scraped in the lock and the door opened, letting in the light of a torch. "Get up!" The guard's voice grated on her. *What now?* "Come on, hurry up we haven't got all night."

She sat up. "Aren't you going to give me something to wear?"

"Never mind that. You won't need clothes where you're going."

An icy hand gripped her insides. What was this, some new form of torture? She straightened her garments and stepped to the door. There was no way she was going out there without clothes.

"Where did you get those?" the guard asked suspiciously.

"The last person that brought me back must have forgotten to take them."

"Well come on. They're waiting for us."

"Who's waiting?"

"You'll find out. The grand wizard has a special treat in store for you." He smirked at her.

He drove her forward to the door that led downstairs. *Oh no, not that again!* Her pulse began to accelerate and a feeling of dread washed over her.

They descended the damp steps into what she thought of as the Dark Underworld. She could see the light from another torch flickering in the tunnel just out of sight. When they reached the bottom, she turned the corner and saw Vertan standing shivering between Monaltor and another guard. He had no clothes on apart from a loincloth and his skin looked blue under the accumulated dirt on his body.

"It's about time," Monaltor said peevishly. "Hurry, he's waiting for you."

Felindra felt her anger building at their treatment of her poor friend. She clenched her fists and tried to calm down, but when she thought that it could be her standing there naked, it only increased. "Why haven't you given him some clothes?" she yelled. "Damn you for your insensitivity. Are you monsters? Get him some clothes!" she glared at Monaltor and then the guard. "GO ON; YOU HEARD ME!"

Monaltor's mouth was open as if he couldn't believe her outburst. She saw fear in his eyes. "This is not for you to say," he said. 'Now let's get moving; we've work to do!"

"It's all right, Felindra," Vertan said. "Don't make trouble for yourself."

"I'm not going anywhere until he has some warm clothes," Felindra said, ignoring Vertan. "I'm warning you, I won't be responsible for what I might do IF YOU DON'T." Her voice rose in pitch and volume towards the end of her warning.

There it was again ... fear. Monaltor nodded to one of the guards. "Go! And don't take all day."

Felindra went and stood next to Vertan, trying to keep her eyes off him and not make him feel more humiliated than he already was. "Give me your arm," she murmured. "I'll try to give you some of my warmth, such as it is in this evil place." She wound her arm through his and pressed herself close to his side.

"You are amazing," Vertan said softly.

"It's not me," she replied in a whisper. "I'm scared out of my mind. I'm shocked when this happens, but I know we have the support of the Light to protect us. You wouldn't believe what a timid little thing I really am. But I've changed a lot since I came here."

"What are you two whispering about?" Monaltor growled. "If you have something to say, say it out loud."

"We were talking about the Light," Felindra replied. "I didn't think you would be interested, but I can share it with you if you like." She saw the guard come round the corner from the stairs. "Ah, here are your clothes," she said to Vertan, letting go of his arm. She leaned over and whispered in his ear, "The creature is afraid of light; don't forget that." Then she added aloud. "Cloaks would be nice. I see you have a warm one, wizard."

Monaltor had obviously had enough. "Shut up and don't say another word until we tell you to speak." He stamped off down the passage, not waiting for Vertan to finish dressing. "Bring them!"

The clothes the guard had brought—pair of culottes and a short tunic—were made of flimsy cotton and not very cleans ... summer clothes. At least he would be more comfortable.

They entered the disciple's room together, and then the guards closed the door behind them, remaining outside. The room was just as dismal as the last time with a single candle for light.

"You kept me waiting." Ogryn said with a dangerous glint in his black eyes

She felt like commenting, but didn't want to make either of them any angrier than they were already.

"That's all, wizard. You may go."

Felindra saw Monaltor's fists clench at his sides and his shoulders hunch. When he turned to face them, it was obvious, even in the dim light, that he was furious at being dismissed like a servant. He went out and slammed the door behind him.

Felindra stood close to Vertan for comfort, apprehensive about what was about to happen.

"Well aren't you a pretty pair?" Ogryn sneered.

They didn't bother to answer, but stood before him, determined not to show any fear.

"Aren't you curious about why I sent for you?"

Once more, they didn't answer.

"Speechless, eh? Are you so awed by my magnificence?" He giggled, although Felindra found no humor in his utterance.

"Very well, if that's how you feel, I'll do the talking. I will tell you why I'm gracing you with my presence, whether you are interested or not. I intend to grant you an honor even friend Monaltor has not had. Come with me. I want to show you my inner sanctum." He climbed down from his high chair and waddled to the low door behind it. "Follow me. You're not frightened are you?" He giggled at his dubious attempt to be funny.

Grotesque, Felindra thought. *Yes, I'm afraid, but I'm not going to let it show. I wonder what he's up to.* She was intrigued, in spite of her fear. She reached out and took Vertan's hand. "Come on, we don't have any choice. Don't forget what I told you."

Vertan had to stoop to get through the door. It led into a short, dank passage excavated through the bedrock to another door. In the light from the single candle, they could see an identical door at the other end. Ogryn manipulated some sort of locking device to open it and bid them to follow him inside. Felindra stopped in the doorway, unable to control a gasp at what lay before them. The richness and elegance of the décor were so out of character for this evil little creature, it left her speechless. Even the bluish purple lighting that made it possible to see everything surprised her, although it was gloomy and depressing. *Why is he letting us see this? He must have some ulterior motive if even Monaltor isn't allowed in here. He obviously doesn't want his followers to see the splendor he lives in. There's more going on here than we suspected.*

"Well, what do you think?" he asked, rubbing his hands together.

"It's very..." she looked at Vertan to see if he wanted to comment.

"It's opulent," Vertan said. "You've got a ... rich collection. How did you manage to assemble such treasures?"

"Ah, the privileges of leadership! Gifts and bequests from various admirers and grateful seekers of my unique wisdom." He giggled again, very pleased with himself. *He's nervous,* Felindra thought. "And some who were not so grateful. Before we get started, can I offer you some refreshment?"

Felindra spotted the shelf loaded with unusual implements. "What are those?" she asked, ignoring his offer. *He'd probably offer us a choice between blood and something poisonous, anyway.*

Ogryn went to the shelf and picked up something. I'm so glad you asked," he said. "They are instruments of persuasion. Very useful in interrogations. This one for example..." he held out the instrument, which consisted of a corkscrew arrangement of a thin spiral blade set in a rounded wooden hilt with a turning handle at the top. "It can make a real mess of someone's eyes, or any other part of the body. Very painful, I can assure you."

Sickened, Felindra turned her eyes away in disgust.

Ogryn returned it to the shelf and turned to face them. "But we won't need to use any of them on you, will we? You didn't answer my question; would you like something to drink?"

"We're fine," Vertan said. "Perhaps we can get to the point of this little exercise."

"Of course. Actually, the reason I brought you here is to show you my recreation room. I thought maybe one of you could help me with a little experiment. One of my hobbies." Another giggle.

Here it comes. The foreplay is coming to an end; now we'll see what he really wants. Not really expecting a favorable answer, Felindra said, "I think we've seen enough. May we go back now?" *Even a cell would be preferable to this.*

"No, no, my dear. You disappoint me. I was looking forward to showing you my pets."

Pets? Oh Light, what's he up to now? I might have known animals would be involved. It's my gift he wants. But why? What for? She stood silently, waiting for his next move, clinging to Vertan's arm. *Now I am scared.*

"I know, let's take this one with us. You should find this interesting." He pricked up the screw blade and carried it to one of the other doors in the room.

Felindra gasped at what was revealed when the door opened. First the noise: terrified bleating, whining, hissing, and squeaking; then the smell: the strong odor of stale urine and animal feces, and the iron smell of blood; finally, the sight: stacks of small cages containing several varieties of mammals, particularly rodents. There was even a snake in one cage. The room was a shambles, a slaughterhouse that was never cleaned. The animals cowered in their cages, which were too small for them to be able to change position. Their coats were plastered in their own feces and uneaten food.

She looked at the creature who was responsible for this, her skin crawling with horror. "I can't believe any human being could be responsible for such ... cruelty. But then, you're not human are you?"

He shrugged and smirked at her. "I thought you would enjoy communicating with my pets," he said blandly. "That's why I invited you here."

"You're a monster." Vertan said, his voice quivering with rage.

"Now, now, children, let's not get carried away." He turned to Felindra. "As I already told you, I want you to help me with something. I want to know how they feel."

She staggered, unable to cope with the mass of torment she was absorbing from the poor caged creatures. Vertan put out a hand to steady her and she clung to him, but she couldn't block out the tremendous waves of misery that were invading her mind. She shouldn't block out their suffering; they were the Light's creatures. She needed to do something. "Light, help me," she murmured.

"Stop the drama," Ogryn said. "Pick a pet. Go on; the cages aren't locked. Just open one and take it out."

Felindra stood, helpless. She couldn't think properly with all the noise in her brain, much less move.

"I'll do it," Vertan offered. He went to the wall of cages and looked inside them one by one. The animals became even more alarmed, but they stopped their noise, as if they could avoid notice by being silent. They cowered as far back as they could from the mesh, which had barely a finger's width to spare. They obviously knew what would happen when someone opened a cage, and it obviously would be extremely unpleasant. He finally decided on a rat and opened the cage. The rodent didn't give him a chance to pick it up; it bolted the moment the cage door opened and disappeared behind a box on the floor.

"Not like that, you clumsy fool. Here, let me show you." Ogryn went to a cage containing a mother cat and two kittens and opened the door just wide enough to grab one of the kittens, but he wasn't fast enough to escape the claws of the hissing mother. Enraged by her attack, he threw the baby animal at the wall with such force that it fell dead on the floor, leaving behind a trail of blood.

"Stop it!" Felindra screamed. "Light?"

The light in the room increased slowly. It was a warm light, an improvement on the ghastly indigo hue to which the Disciple was accustomed. He tried to shut it out by covering his eyes, but it didn't help much.

"Stop what you're doing!" he screeched. "Stop it!

"I'm not doing anything," Felindra replied. "That's the Light. He obviously doesn't approve of your activities."

Ogryn rushed to the door and disappeared into the main room, the light of which had remained his preferred color. The animals in their cages remained quiescent, as if they sensed the presence of their creator.

"What are we going to do?" Vertan asked.

"I don't know. We should rescue these poor creatures, but I don't know how we'd get them out."

"Let's open all the cages and see what happens," Vertan suggested.

"What are you doing," Ogryn croaked from the doorway, still in the throes of the disability caused by the light. His eyes were turning red and oozing a sticky fluid.

The light in the room increased again, driving him back. They could hear him groaning and stumbling around blindly.

"It must really hurt him," Vertan commented as he began to open cage doors.

Felindra started to help him release the animals. They jumped down from their cages, but wouldn't go past the doorway into the room to which Ogryn had retreated. "I have an idea," she said. "If the light could illuminate his other room, it would disable him enough to get out the other door with the animals."

"Look at them; they're afraid to go near him. I doubt they'd follow us."

"I could talk to them and tell them we're taking them somewhere safe." As she spoke, the snake, which was about a span in length and almost as thick as her wrist, dropped from its cage to the floor. The other animals immediately started shrieking and backing away from it. "I hope that's not a poisonous snake," she said. "I think I should talk to it first. Can you catch it for me?"

Vertan looked at her dubiously, but made a quick grab and caught the creature by the neck. It was probably weak from lack of food because it didn't struggle very much. Felindra put her hand on its head. She'd never communicated with a reptile before. Its mind was strange, like a cold fog, but she did manage to pick up its need for food, specifically small animals. She sent it a message telling it that it could find food outside and not to touch the animals here, hoping she was getting through to it. Ogryn's poor victims had suffered enough already and didn't need to be hunted by a hungry snake. "All right, put it down gently near the door. It might leave by itself. I didn't feel the fear of the monster that the others have."

Felindra found the mother cat sniffing the corpse of her kitten, licking it as if trying to revive it. Felindra approached it cautiously, sending out waves of compassion and comfort. In a way, it reminded her of her first contact with Ashala, a frightened animal that needed reassurance and love. The hair on the cat's neck was still erect, but she stared at Felindra with more curiosity than fear. She held her hand out and creature sniffed it, then she moved her hand slowly up towards the top of its head. It flinched, but didn't pull away, so she stroked it gently. A puppy came over to her and poked her arm with its nose. "You too, eh?" she said to it and put her other hand on its neck. The cat hissed at the puppy, but still allowed Felindra to touch her. "Two at once; that'll make it easier." She went through her practiced message, hoping to reassure them and make them cooperative. The main feature of the message was not to get into a fight with the other creatures.

They could hear Ogryn groaning and cursing in the other room and once, the sound of breaking glass, but he never returned to the doorway. She didn't have time to talk to all the animals—there must have been at least a dozen of various species, the largest being a small fox—but she covered a selection of prey and predatory creatures, hoping the others would catch on. Small ones, like the mice, had already escaped and gone into hiding in some obscure cranny.

"Now for the hard part," Vertan said when she stood and looked through the doorway. "I feel like destroying this awful place," he added, looking around the abysmal room.

"Do you know how to summon fire?" Felindra replied, half meaning it.

Vertan shook his head. "But I could overturn that candle on top of the cages; they're mostly wood.

"I'll go and try to find the way out of here. We'd have to get the animals out before you start lighting fires."

Light? She watched the light increase in the room where Ogryn was lurking. He let out a screech of pain, stumbled across the room, holding his robe over his eyes, and disappeared through another door, slamming it behind him. "All right. He's out of the way. I just hope we can get the outer door open." As she walked into the main room, she saw it in full light and realized how shabby it really was, dust everywhere, patches of mildew on walls and rugs, and worn and faded areas on the upholstery and drapery. *Why would he need drapery when there are no windows?* The animals started after her, with some minor balking and snarling between traditional enemies, but no outright attacks. "Good children," Felindra said gently, still sending reassuring and peaceful thoughts. It took her few minutes to get the door open, but once she'd figured out the trick to it—it required the sliding of some catches in addition to turning the knob—the lock clicked and it opened. She shook her head. *How ridiculous! A child could figure it out,* she thought with an ironic grin. The animals fled from the room into the hallway, smelling freedom. But they were stymied by the door blocking the other end of the hall.

She smelled smoke from inside and turned to see Vertan in the doorway. "I see you managed to start a fire." She grinned at him. "How did you do it?"

"Oh I found some more candles and some sheets of paper. It seems the monster kept notes on his so-called experiments. What a vile creature! Let's get out of here before he wakes up, or recovers, whichever."

"What about the guards waiting outside the door?" Felindra asked.

"I guess they'll take us back to our cells. Thanks for what you did about the clothes, by the way."

"It was the decent thing to do, besides, you already thanked me once. Now, I hope they let the animals through. I guess I'll have to talk to them. Let's go." She turned the doorknob, but it wouldn't budge. Vertan had brought one of the lit candles with him and shone it on the knob. "It looks the same as the other," she said. "We just have to wiggle these things a bit." The sequence wasn't the same as the other door, but it was close enough and she finally managed to get it open. "He's consistent at least; probably doesn't have the mental power for anything too complicated."

The outer door of Ogryn's 'office' opened without any difficulty, but the startled guards jumped away when the animals rushed out. "What the ...?" one of them gasped. "What in helvetti happened in there?"

"You'll probably hear about it soon enough, but I wouldn't advise you to be around when Ogryn appears. Now, we have to get these creatures outside. Could you take care of it? All you have to do is lead the way and open doors; they'll follow." she asked one of the guards. "I'm sure your comrade can take us wherever we are going."

The guards blustered for a moment, so Felindra added, "I don't think the grand wizard would want wild animals roaming around the building. Oh, and before you go, I want to say something to these creatures." Before they could object, she grabbed the fox. It lay in her arms seeming quite calm and unafraid, although she could feel its little heart beating rapidly. "Follow this man and he'll set you free," she whispered audibly enough for them to hear, projecting an image of him out in the forest, free. She hoped the other animals would take their cue from the fox. "All right," she said to the guard. "They're as ready as I can make them; now it's up to you. And don't do anything to frighten them!"

"Let them go ahead," Felindra said to the other guard. "Then you can take us wherever we're supposed to go."

A mixture of feelings passed over the guard's face, anger at being given orders by a prisoner, and then bemusement at her audacity. "When did you suddenly become the boss?" he asked. "I thought you were our prisoner, not the other way around."

Felindra smiled at him. "You have complete control over us," she said mildly. "We go where you tell us to go, and do whatever you command. You know that. I was only trying to help you and your friend out of a difficult situation. It's up to you whether you want to report it to the Grand Wizard or not."

The guard shook his head. "Come on; let's get you back to your cells and no more shenanigans."

Felindra was intrigued by the strange word he used. It must be a Valkonen thing, she thought. *Shenanigans; I must remember that and try it on Darson when I get home.*

As they were climbing up the staircase, Felindra sent a trial message to Vertan. *Slow down.* She saw him start. *Did you hear what I sent?*

"You two are very quiet," the guard said, looking over his shoulder at them. "We're almost there."

"Thought we'd give you a break," Felindra said. "I realize we sometimes annoy you. And didn't want you to be mad with us." *Forgive me, Light, for the untruth, but it might make him feel better.*

She took Vertan's hand after they exited the stairwell and came into the cell level. *Take heart, Vertan. We will soon be out of here. Nothing can harm us with the Light protecting us.*

What about that monster down in his hellish lair. He's going to be furious when he recovers.

Maybe the fire you lit will finish him off. Felindra smiled at him.

No such luck, but I wish it would. Have to go; he's getting suspicious. Be well.

I'm glad we had a chance to talk, Felindra replied. *Farewell.*

"What are you two up to now?" the irate guard said. "Back to your cells and don't forget to throw out the clothes."

"Do we really need to?" Felindra objected. "It's cold down here without any clothes."

"Orders," was all he said. "Now, get going."

The two prisoners went obediently to their cells at opposite ends of the corridor and after a moment, each threw out a small bundle of clothing. "It's like minding a bunch of unruly children," Felindra heard the guard mutter as he closed the door.

When he was gone, she quickly donned her warm shirt, sat down on the mattress, wrapping herself in the blanket.

76 – Meet an Ally

While everyone was packing up and preparing to leave for Tuulinen, Daryan went in search of Axtya. They had a map of ValkonenMaa, but it didn't give many details about roads and byways, nor did it show obstacles that might hinder their progress, so he needed to get some information from the werman.

"Has anyone seen Axtya?" he asked a group of defenders who were saddling their horses.

"He disappeared into the trees over there a few minutes ago," one replied.

Daryan hurried after Axtya, calling his name several times. He finally caught up with him standing in some bushes, looking back at him apprehensively.

"Where are you going?" Daryan asked. "I need your help with something."

"Go my home," the werman replied.

"I understand you want to get back to your family, Axtya, but can you wait a little while longer? You shouldn't have to sneak off like this. I have something I want to give you when you go. Payment for your help to us."

Axtya lost his sullen look and replaced it with surprise. "You give me ... "

"It's your pay. Everyone is paid who serves the League, including you. It will help your family. Will you come back with me so that we can discuss the problem we need help with?"

Axtya nodded reluctantly and started walking back towards the camp. Daryan had to take shorter steps so he could remain level with the smaller creature. "We have to go to the town of Tuulinen, but we don't know how to get there. Do you know the area?"

"Not much."

Daryan and his people didn't even know where they were exactly; the cave they'd come from not being on the map. "Which direction is it?" he asked.

"That way." Axtya point to the northwest.

"Is it far?"

"Far?"

"A long way," Daryan clarified.

"One day, two," Axtya replied.

"All right, I'm going to take you to the woman who understands." Daryan was reluctant to say 'reads minds' for fear of frightening him off, but Farah might be able to get an image from his mind of what he was explaining.

They entered the clearing and found the sender standing by her horse. "I'm going to ask Axtya some questions about the route to our destination, and then I'm going to pay him and send him off home to his family," he explained to her. "Could you monitor us and tell me his thoughts?" He unfolded the map against the horse's back. "Now, Axtya, you say Tuulinen is in that direction, right?"

Axtya nodded.

"So we must be about here." Daryan marked a place on the map about halfway up the mountain, just a guess, but that's all they had to go on. "Now Axtya, is there a road?"

"There?" he pointed due north.

"How do we reach it? Is there a trail we can follow?"

Axtya pointed off to the left where the trees seemed to thin out a little.

They continued like this for a while, trying to find out as much as they could about clearways and obstacles. They found out about numerous streams running down the mountains to join a sizeable river farther down, which was marked on the map. The road appeared to follow the south side of the river. Farah added a comment from time to time throughout the process.

Once they felt they had all the information Axtya could provide, Daryan led the werman over to his horse and removed a bundle from his saddle. Although it was rather heavy, he thought Axtya would be able to manage it with the leather sling he'd fashioned for carrying; if not, he could always drag it. "Here's your payment," Daryan said, handing it to Axtya. "I did not think coin would be much use to you, so I've put together a collection of tools and appliances you might find useful, unfortunately, most of the things are made of iron, so it's a bit heavy. Do you have to go far?"

"Two days." Axtya hefted the bundle, testing its weight. He grinned at Daryan, his wide mouth stretching to the edges of his face. "I go."

"Farewell, Axtya. I hope you find your family well. Thank you for your help. Good fortune to you."

"Now I go," Axtya repeated as he turned away and started walking.

Funny little fellow, Daryan thought. *No goodbye, no thank you, just leave. We have a lot to learn about their customs. I don't even know what he thinks about everything he's been through.*

They reached Tuulinen a day and a half later, just as the sun was setting. The ValkonenMaa League troops had set up a camp to the south of the island city, near the road on which the Trethawynd contingent was travelling. There was enough space in the field for them to raise their own tents close by and settle down for the night, so Daryan left his people to prepare a meal and went in search of the ValkonenMaa commander.

He asked one of the ValkonenMaa defenders and was directed to a fire near the center of the camp. He found the commander sitting on a log eating. "Captain Arendt?" he said when he recognized the insignia on the officer's cloak. "No, don't get up," he said when Arendt put down his dish and started to raise himself. "I'm Daryan Peshanar of Trethawynd. Well met, captain."

"Well met, indeed," Arendt replied. "Join me; we've plenty of food." He beckoned to a cook and signaled him to bring another bowl.

Daryan sat on the other end of the log and was soon feasting on a fine bowl of stewed meat with vegetables. "Thank you. This is very tasty. What kind of meat is it?"

"Venison," Arendt replied. He looked at Daryan with a faint smile on his lips. "You wouldn't believe how hard it is to get these people to eat vegetables—they're so used to eating nothing but meat and bread—they don't realize the nutritional value of fresh vegetables. I've trained the cook—not an easy job by the way—to make stews and soups instead of roasting the meat on a spit."

"I know what you mean; my wife feels the same way. And then I have to contend with my daughter who abhors harming any animal and is turning into a vegetarian." Daryan mopped the bowl with a piece of bread, popped it in his mouth. After putting the bowl on the ground, he picked up the mug of water to wash down the food. "I suppose we should get down to business now. What exactly is our mission?"

"The Grand Master—did you realize he was set free from the monastery dungeons by a young girl from Trethawynd...?

Daryan interrupted. "That was my daughter."

"Really? That's amazing. I didn't realize... I knew she was a whisperer, but I didn't realize she was your daughter. You must be relieved now she's free. How did she come to be there in the first place?"

"She was abducted by one of their wizards and taken there."

"What's she doing now? Has she gone home to Trethawynd?"

Daryan clasped his hands between his knees. "She and her two companions were recaptured before they'd gone very far. To the best of my knowledge, she's back in the dungeons. We can't reach her telepathically, so I assume there's a ward around her. At least, I hope that's the reason." Daryan raised his hands and massaged the hollows of his temples with his thumbs. *If it's not fire in my stomach, it's these damned spikes in my head. I'm really going to retire as soon as we get home.* With a sigh, he continued, "I should let you tell me about the mission."

"Before we go on, any news about my trainee, Vertan? He was travelling with her."

"He must have been captured along with Felindra and the wizard."

"I might have known they'd jump at the chance to capture one of us." Arendt sighed. "They'll pay dearly if he's harmed ... if either of them is." He threw another piece of wood onto the fire, raising sparks like a swarm of fireflies.

"Now, to business. The Grand Master wants us to reclaim the monastery and clean out the Brethren. We stopped here this morning to allow you to catch up with us. We'll continue tomorrow."

"How long will it take to get there?"

"A day's travel should bring us close enough to make camp, and then we can start surveillance, and action the following day, we hope."

"What's the strategy?"

"We've been detecting some sort of disturbance there the last couple of days. It's possible that all is not going well for the occupiers. We hope they will be otherwise distracted so we can take advantage of it. In addition, our probes tell us there aren't many people inside the walls. Our major fear is the devastating power of the wizards."

"We've been successful in destroying several wizards in Trethawynd. There can't be that many left. Do you have any estimate of their number?"

"Not an accurate one, but I can't imagine their having more than about twenty-five or so. Considering they've spread all over the duchy creating havoc, or at least they were—we've been able to put several out of action. The duchy defenders, along with the prince's forces, are still out there chasing them down. Unless they go to ground, or leave the duchy, we should be able to finish them off in no time. That leaves the monastery. According to the information we received from Barengush—the wizard captured with your daughter—and my recruit, there are only two other wizards left inside the walls, apart from the Grand Wizard, Monaltor. Although that's not to say more haven't arrived."

"Were they able to provide any information about the other personnel: defenders and guards?"

"Barengush puts the number of guards at around seventeen—there aren't that many prisoners, as far as he knew. He says the guards come and go, so the number fluctuates. As for the number of fighting men, he thinks there are less than a hundred. He seems to believe they are becoming disaffected, so they may not put up much of a fight. Their main defense, as I see it, is hostages and the wizards."

77 – The Messenger Visits Felindra

Felindra woke from a deep sleep, feeling warmer and better rested than she'd felt in a long time. It was almost like being in her own bed at home. Her eyes snapped open when she sensed extra light in the room and she saw the messenger looking down at her. Felindra sat up and looked quizzically at the celestial being, relishing the feeling of goodwill she radiated.

"Well, Felindra, we see you have been busy recently," she said in her musical voice.

Felindra felt momentary alarm. "Did I do something wrong?"

"No, child. You would not have the support of the Light if you were not doing his will. You've been a very courageous girl, and we want you to know that your actions have greatly increased the chance of success in the battle against Oglestra's followers.

"I am here to warn you that you are about to face a dangerous situation that will require you to use all your courage and faith. Remember, the Light is always beside you and will not allow you to be harmed, but you will have to use your own strength and wisdom, and your courage, to prevail in the coming events. The Light is not testing your faith in a dangerous situation, but is giving you the opportunity to grow and develop your strength. Do you understand?"

A feeling of dread overcame Felindra. "C...can you tell me anything about it?" she asked.

"It is a situation that is arising from your recent activities, particularly with the foul Disciple of Oglestra. He will not sit still for the insult to his self-assumed importance and power. We were gratified to see how well you stood up to him and dealt with his foulness, but we fear he will retaliate. We do not know the nature of his retaliation; at this moment, he's still licking his wounds, so to speak, and hasn't decided yet what action he will take, but we know it will come, and it will be brutal. During your encounter, he discovered certain things about your nature which we are sure he will use against you and the young man."

The more the messenger told, the more her dread increased. "What shall I do?"

"You must choose the course you take, child. If you choose the will of the Creator, He will not fail you."

"But how do I know what is His will?"

"Your instinct will tell you. He is always with you, in your mind, guiding you. You may not always be aware of his presence, but you may feel it and act according to his guidance."

"I'm too young for this. It's too much for me. I don't know if I can handle it, the responsibility."

"You can handle what is required of you, child. That's why you were chosen. Remember, He loves you and is always there for you."

"I hope so, but I'm still frightened. Will Vertan be with me?"

"Of course. The two of you will support each other."

"Are you like an angel. Messenger?"

"Something like that. The angels are our sisters and assist us greatly in our work." She reached out her hand and placed it on Felindra's head. She could feel warmth and comfort flowing into her, but not the actual touch of a physical hand. "I will leave you now. The Blessings of the Light are with you always."

Before Felindra could begin to ask the questions she wanted to ask, the Messenger faded and the intensity of the light in the cell decreased. She realized her anxiety had diminished a little and she was more relaxed.

78 – Ogryn Receives a Gift

Ogryn was eating his supper which consisted of the raw flesh of the animal he'd tortured to death that afternoon. Although he didn't recall what sort of animal it was, he found out the moment he tasted it: one of his all-time favorites, a wolf cub. Once he'd cleaned the meat from the bones, he cracked them one by one and sucked out the marrow. Ecstasy! He felt his energy building up immediately. It even did away with the remnants of the headache he'd had since his encounter with the girl.

As always since the last encounter with her, he ended up brooding about the girl. She was a veritable thorn in his side, or more accurately, a light in his darkness. *Damn her to eternal light ...no, that's what she wants...make that darkness, eternal darkness.* How could a mere human child get the better of him? He picked up a sliver of bone and started to clean pieces of meat fiber from between his teeth. For the first time in several days, he felt ... what? Satisfied? No, he wouldn't be satisfied until he had her under his control. Maybe ready ... that's it, he felt ready to do something, to act. But first, he had to plan, and this time, he wouldn't make the mistake of allowing her to get the upper hand.

The door to his lab was open and through it, he heard a scratching sound on the outer door, followed by a knock. He knew who it was. Nobody else knew about the secret entrance from the forest. "All right, I'm coming." He got up and went through the lab, kicking aside the offal from his latest kill, and undid the complex fastenings that secured the door and protected him from intruders. His heart began to pound with anticipation. *I hope he's brought me something good ... more interesting than the last lot.* He rubbed his hands together with glee at the thought of getting new material to experiment on. When he saw who was out there, he was suffused with rage.

"Bog, who did you bring with you?" he screeched. "You know I told you never to bring anyone here."

The werman backed away, trembling. "I'm sorry, master. I couldn't carry her by myself and I didn't want to damage her by dragging her. You're going to like this one. Remember the last time, how you were so angry about that girl? Well look what I've got for you." The little man wrung his hands together nervously and beckoned to the other two. They dragged a squirming bundle towards Ogryn.

"Let me see ... oh yes." He closed his eyes and pressed his hands together in anticipation of working with the new prize. Bring it inside."

The three wermen manhandled the struggling girl into the lab and dropped her on the floor. The sound of her terrified voice was audible, shrieking through the strip of leather they'd tied around her mouth.

"Be quiet girl!" Ogryn snapped. The girl's muffled shrieks became a whimper. Her whole body shook with fear. From the wet culottes and smell coming from her, fear had made her void her bladder. He saw she was a dark-skinned Trethawyndian type like the prisoner, although this one's black hair was straight. He was becoming aroused at the thought of what he could do with her. She was perfect and so young.

"You're an imbecile, Bog, bringing those two here. Now I'm going to have to take their tongues so they won't tell anyone about this."

"Please, master, don't hurt them. They're my brothers. They won't tell, I guarantee. And if you're afraid of their talking, even without tongues, they could still lead someone here if they wanted to, but they don't. Please, I beg you. Don't you like the prize we brought you?" His two brothers began sidling towards the door.

"Maybe I should kill them instead, that would guarantee they wouldn't reveal this place." Ogryn removed a sharp tool from the shelf by the door. The two wermen had already reached the tunnel outside. The moment they saw the tool, they both bolted. Ogryn sighed and pointed the spike at Bog's eye. "You will stand guarantor of those two?"

"Of course master," he said, closing his eyes. "They are too afraid of you to do anything, but I will make sure they don't."

"Be quiet," Ogryn said to the girl on the floor and kicked her in the stomach. She screamed through the gag, but stopped wailing and curled up to protect herself from further blows. "All right you can go," he said to Bog."

"But, master, aren't you going to...?" he held out his hand for his payment, but all he got from Ogryn was a slash across his palm. He howled in pain and curled his hand, cradling it in the other.

"You disobeyed me, so you get nothing. Next time, remember that. Go on, get out." Truth be told, he was almost bursting with excitement and desire and couldn't wait to get rid of them. They'd wasted too much of his time.

He reverted to Albasinian to talk to his newest treasure. This one was by far the best he'd received in a long time. He's almost forgotten the joy of being able to work on a human. He knelt on the floor and cut the ropes binding her with the metal spike.

"Now let me take a look at you. First we need to get rid of these wet clothes so I can see you better." He knelt down on the floor beside her. She'd stopped struggling, frozen in terror.

79 – Outside the Monastery.

Daryan is pushing his way through a forest, searching for something in the dark with just the moon to light his way. He doesn't know what he seeks, but he feels compelled to keep going, although his mind is filled with dread over what he might find. The forest is strangely silent, not even the peep of a bird or the rustle of leaves disturbed by a passing animal. He doesn't understand why he is walking instead of riding his horse. He wonders where his comrades are. After a while, he becomes aware of a smell—that combination of odors ... body fluids, feces, and decaying animal matter—that spells death.

What am I doing here? What's that smell? Something's dead. Is that what I'm looking for?

He keeps going. The way is easy, even in the darkness, as if obstacles are moving out of his way as he comes to them. Eventually, as the putrid odor gets stronger, he reaches a clearing. The moon chooses that moment to find a gap in the foliage and illuminate the area as bright as day. It's a body, and he can tell from the bloody rags still clinging to it that it's human. He goes closer and peers down, keeping his hand over his mouth and nose to filter the smell. It's a girl with black curly hair matted with blood. He looks closer and sees empty pits where the eyes should be. "Felindra!" he shrieks.

He woke with a start, sweat pouring from his body, and terror filling his mind. The little tent felt claustrophobic and he thrashed around, trying to get free of it. Once outside, he wiped his face with his tunic sleeve, took a deep breath and shook his head as it to purge his mind of the dream. *That was the worst one I've ever had. My poor little girl. Horrifying beyond belief ... I hope it wasn't an omen. They say that really vivid dreams warnings of things to come. No, it can't be that. Not Felindra! Light, you will protect her won't you?* His stomach and gullet were on fire; that must be what caused the dream.

He sat on the ground with his back to a tree. The thought of returning to that tent was repugnant to him in his current state. A watchman on his rounds saw him as he approached.

"Is everything all right, Commander?"

"Yes, I'm fine, thank you. Just wanted to get some fresh air."

"Could I get you a hot drink; the water's hot."

"That would be nice ... Biel, isn't it? Do we have any mint?"

"I could check, sir. I won't be a minute."

"I'll come with you. It's chilly out here, but I can't face that tent for a while."

He got up and followed the defender to the fire, which, although small, was still burning brightly in its hearth of stones. As Biel searched for the mint among the jars of various teas they packed with them, Daryan moved the water pan over the coals to bring it to a boil. "Quiet night, defender?"

"Yes sir. Too quiet if you ask me. Here, I've found some."

The mention of the quietness of the night brought the dream back to him. What if it was real? He shook his head again, determined to stop thinking about it. "Here." He held out his hand to take the jar of mint leaves. "I'll take it from here and let you get back to your rounds."

The sun came up eventually and the camp came to life again. With daylight, the dream became hazier, and by the time they were ready to leave, he'd almost forgotten it, almost, but it still nagged faintly in the back of his mind, like a phantom pain.

Daryan and Arendt rode together at the head of the column so that they could become better acquainted and discuss how they would proceed once they arrived at the monastery.

"I have a suggestion," Arendt said.

"Tell me," Daryan replied.

"We should organize our forces so each Trethawyndian has a Valkonen partner. My men and women are familiar with the area around the monastery so they could help your people find their way around."

"That's an excellent idea. We have no idea what to expect over here, so we'd be glad of some guidance. It would also keep us from straying into areas that might be dangerous."

By midday, when they stopped for rest, they were within an hour's ride of the monastery.

"I'm going to send out some scouts," Arendt told Daryan. "Do you want to include a couple or yours?"

"Of course. It would give them an opportunity to get to know the area a bit better."

"What I want them to do, is move around the area and scan for ... anything really, movement, where the people are, and so on. I'd like to get an idea how things are inside the walls. Do you have a couple of gifted who can sense life, or read people?"

"Yes. I'll tell them to get ready, now. I assume you're sending them immediately," Daryan replied.

"Yes, as soon as they finish eating."

When Daryan came back from talking to Farah and Nadi, he returned to sit beside Arendt. He couldn't keep from yawning, although he tried to stifle it. "Have a bad night?" Arendt asked

"Nightmares," Daryan replied. "Must be something I ate. No, no, not the dinner; that was excellent. I meant earlier in the day. We've been on rations for the past five or six days."

"I know what that's like. Why don't you lie down for a while? We won't be moving until the scouts return."

'I might just do that. Now that everything is in such good hands, I may be able to stop worrying so much and relax."

80 – Felindra Has a Surprise

Two guards came for Felindra and Vertan, but without Monaltor this time.

"Come on, hurry!" one guard said nervously. "You know he gets upset if we keep him waiting."

"So he's recovered from his last encounter with us, has he? What does he want this time?" Felindra asked, not really expecting an answer, even if the guards knew the reason. She sighed. He's probably got some sort of revenge planned."

"Probably," Vertan with a nod.

"What did you do to him, anyway? We feared he would explode with rage. We've never heard so much fury before, even from him."

Felindra shrugged one shoulder. "Nothing," she replied innocently. "We just showed him the Light." She turned and winked at Vertan.

The first guard led them down the stairs and into the tunnel towards Ogryn's audience chamber. "What I don't understand is how you can be so cool about it. Why aren't you quaking with fear?"

Little does he know, Felindra thought. *I'm falling apart inside, I'm terrified, and I wager Vertan is too.*

She looked at Vertan who walked with his body held rigid, as if he had to hold himself in to keep his fear under control. He nodded at her. *How did you guess?*

"Go in; it's open," the guard said, pushing the door. "We'll wait for you out here."

"Good luck," the other one added, earning a nasty look from his partner.

I think he likes us, Felindra thought.

I think he does. Did you notice they said nothing about our clothes?

They walked into the dismal room so close together their arms were touching.

There he was, perched behind his table, gazing at them menacingly, although he couldn't conceal the excitement in his demeanor. "Well, here you are, my little friends. I have a big surprise for you today. You're going to love it ... pardon the obscenity."

The two young people looked at each other, both thinking the same thought, *if you thought it up, it's bound to be something truly vile*. Neither of them felt like answering, so they just stood, waiting for him to go on.

"Spiders tied your tongues, did they? Oh well, never mind. Let's get on with it. Follow me." He opened the door behind his chair and gestured for them to enter. "I should warn you," he said as they passed him. "I have protection now against your light trick, so don't try anything."

"I should warn you," Vertan replied. "We have the power of the Light with us."

"Pfah! We'll see about that. Don't *you* forget, I have the power of Oglestra with me. He hasn't lost a battle yet with your precious Light."

"There's always a first time," Felindra replied.

"He only survives because of the infinite mercy of the Light, waiting for him to repent his evil." Vertan added.

Ogryn finished fumbling with the lock on the door to his inner sanctum and threw it open. He nodded towards the room and they entered, gasping at the awful smell inside. This was worse than anything they'd ever encountered. It was almost palpable, a mixture of body wastes, vomit and blood, with undercurrents of extreme pain and fear. Something horrendous had happened here recently. Felindra raised the hem of her tunic to cover her nose and mouth, but it did little to lessen the smell. Vertan's stomach heaved. Felindra could see he was trying very hard not to vomit, holding his hand over his lower face. They couldn't see anything that gave a clue to the source of the stench because the lighting was too dim, but she was sure it was all round them.

"Sorry about the mess," Ogryn said jovially. "My servant didn't come today and I had to clean up myself." He gave a little giggle. "Not very good at domestic matters, as you may have observed. Let's go through into the other room, shall we?" Without waiting for an answer, he opened the door to his so-called recreation room.

They had no choice but to follow him and find out what he was up to. The smell in there was just as bad, if not worse because there was also the residual smell of smoke from their previous visit. Before she'd taken more than two steps, she trod on something soft and squishy. She looked at the floor, dreading what she would see under her foot. It was hair, long human hair, still attached to a piece of scalp, obviously torn off the ill-fated victim with some force. Feeling herself growing dizzy, she reached out to Vertan for support as the room began to spin. He put his arms around her and held her close, gently patting her back with one hand. "I've got you," he said. "I feel just as bad. I know I'm going to vomit if we don't get out of this abattoir soon."

He looked at Ogryn who was watching them with gleeful interest, as if they were specimens. "Whatever you're up to, it has to stop now!" Vertan managed to keep his voice steady and assertive, but only just.

"Oh you poor babies, can't take a little fun?"

Adrenalin surged through Felindra. She turned her head so she could see him. "You call this fun, you monster?" She had to stop shouting because she was too close to crying. Trembling, she turned her face back to the warmth of Vertan's body.

"Don't you want to see the surprise I have for you?"

Neither of them responded, although they let go of each other and watched the monster. He moved some boxes aside and revealed door. It was of very old wood, but looked solid. In height, it came to just below the top of Vertan's head. Ogryn lifted a thick bar from the slots that held it, and pushed it open. "In there," he said.

They looked through the door and saw pitch-blackness, but a chill wind blew in, so it must open to the outside. They looked at him, not trusting him, expecting to be confronted by some other atrocity, unless they were the intended victims of the next one. What was out there? Felindra wondered. Her mind went through a list of possibilities, wolves, bears, maybe snakes, or another demon like him?

Ogryn walked towards them threateningly, a spike covered in dry blood raised in his hand. "This is my surprise," he said in mock sadness. "And you don't even want it. I am disappointed. Don't you want to be free?"

"What do you mean, free?" Vertan asked suspiciously.

Ogryn gave a ghastly grin, revealing blackened teeth and releasing his putrid breath. "I'm letting you go. I had such a good time last night, I'm feeling benevolent. Since I have no further use for you, you're free to leave, and as a token of my sincerity, I'll even give you a weapon to protect yourselves against the predators of the forest." He offered Vertan the spike he held in his hand. It was just a piece of metal, about the length of a man's foot, sharpened to a point at one end.

Vertan took the thing reluctantly, looking around for something to clean it, but there was nothing that was not already fouled. He held it by the blunt end with the tips of his finger, making sure it didn't touch him.

"Go on! The tunnel leads outside into the forest. I'm afraid I don't have any torches to light your way. I could give you a candle, but the wind would probably blow it out. I'm sure you'll think of something. Now go, get out of my sight, both of you!" His voice rose in anger as he uttered the final words, almost compelling Felindra to believe him.

Ogryn

Once he'd slammed the door after them, rubbed his hands together and almost danced with glee. *Oh, this is going to be so much fun!*

Felindra

Light? Felindra thought. The air became warmer and at the same time, the tunnel was illuminated with dim light. It was enough to show their surroundings, what appeared to be natural cave.

"Did you know this cave was here?" she asked Vertan.

He shook his head. "It's new to me. Come on, I think we should go before he changes his mind."

"Do you mean you trust him? You think he's really setting us free?" Felindra asked as they started down the claustrophobic tunnel, which was barely high enough to stand upright, and the walls crowded in on them from both sides.

"Not a chance," Vertan replied. "I trust him as much as I'd trust an angry scorpion not to sting me."

"So what do you think he's up to?"

"No idea, but whatever he has planned, you can wager your life it's nothing pleasant."

"Perhaps he'll come after us."

"You know he can't hurt us, Felindra, not with the Light's protection."

"I know, but I'm still frightened." She rubbed her arms. "It's getting colder. I wish we'd brought our blankets. I don't fancy being out in the forest at night dressed like this."

"Me neither," he saw an opening ahead. "I think this is the exit." The light in the cave faded, to be replaced by the partial daylight coming from the opening.

"It must be sunset," Felindra said.

"Or sunrise," Vertan replied.

"I hope it is ... sunrise I mean. He won't come out of his lair if it's getting lighter."

"He might have helpers. I don't think he would be able to collect all those animals by himself."

They stepped out into a thicket of prickly shrubs. "There must be a way through," Vertan said. "You stay back and I'll try to find a gap." He shook his head. "It's like the obstacle courses we used to run when I was in school. But somebody comes through here, so there must be a way."

Vertan found a broken branch on the ground and used it to poke at the bushes to see if he could find a place where they weren't packed so tightly. "Here," he said. "I think we can get through this way. We're still going to get scratched, but there seems to be more space to move in." He held out his hand for her and realized he could barely see her now. That meant night was fast approaching.

Great, Felindra thought, *scratched skin and freezing air. But I shouldn't complain. At least we're out of the dungeons.*

Once they got through the thicket, Vertan looked around, trying to ascertain where they were and which way they should go. It was obvious that, if Ogryn did come after them, he would have some way of sensing their direction, so it was essential they find something defensible. The spike he'd given them was a joke, but it was better than nothing. Finally, he came to a decision. "This way," he said holding out his hand for Felindra.

"Why this way?" she asked, grateful for the warmth of his hand.

"I don't know," he replied. "It just feels right. It's as good as any other direction, I suppose, but it seems more ... I don't know ... inviting, perhaps."

They walked for about half an hour before it was completely dark. "Do you sense anything?" Vertan asked.

"Like what?"

"I don't know," he replied. "It's like that sensation you get when you're being watched, but can't see anyone."

"No, I can't feel anything except the night creatures, you know, owls and foxes and so on. Oh, wait, now I feel it, something intelligent, but not friendly. Do you think it's him?"

"I think we'd smell the stench of him if it was."

"We should hurry."

"I wish we could ... we should get away from here as fast as we can ... but I can barely distinguish the trees from the darkness around them." As if in answer to his wishes, a glow of soft light formed around them. It wasn't as strong as a torch, but it was more powerful and less fluttery than a candle.

"Won't this make it easier for him to find us?" said Felindra, although she was grateful for the light. It even made her feel a bit warmer.

"If it's a gift of the Light, it must be all right. Light repels him, remember?"

As they proceeded, small things like rustling in the bushes and the snap of trodden twigs, finally convinced Felindra that they were being watched and followed. "What can we do?" Felindra asked in a whisper.

"Not much, I'm afraid," Vertan answered softly. "Just be prepared. It seems to me that if they were going to attack us, they've had plenty of opportunity."

"That means they must be tracking us for another reason."

"Exactly. And who would set them on us? The only person who knows where we are."

"Him." Felindra shivered. "I don't like this at all."

A wolf howled in the distance, answered shortly by several others. "I hope they're not going to attack us as well," Vertan said.

"I doubt it, unless they've been enchanted," she said, recalling the time her family been attacked on the way to the Monastery. "Let me see if I can find out." She closed her eyes and sent her senses roving through the forest. She sensed many creatures closer, and some very close to them and clearly hostile. Suddenly, she encountered a familiar mind. *Ashala!* Her eyes filled with tears. *Where are you, my sweet girl? Can you howl for me and tell me if you're close?*

Another wolf call echoed through the forest. Felindra was sure she recognized it. It seems quite a distance away, but if they hurried towards it, she calculated they might meet within hours. *Ashala, my precious love, hurry, we're coming.* She almost jumped for joy. Now that monster wouldn't dare attack them. And she had Ashala back; nothing short of being reunited with her family could bring her greater joy.

"What happened," Vertan asked as if he'd sensed a change in her.

"Ashala is coming. She's not far away. We'll be safer with her to protect us. I'm so happy, Vertan. I've missed her so much." Another round of wolf howls rang through the trees.

"There they go again," Vertan said. "Are you sure they won't come after us?"

"Quite sure. If Ashala is around, they'll probably help us. That might have been her rallying them."

"She must be a pretty intelligent wolf," Vertan offered.

"She's not only intelligent," Felindra said. "She seems to have an inborn goodness. I would trust her with my own baby, if I had one."

"That's a pretty good recommendation. I'd like to meet her."

"You will."

The rustling in the bushes around them became more agitated. The watchers didn't seem to care if they were heard. But something had obviously happened because the noises they made were retreating. After a few minutes, they couldn't hear them at all.

"How auspicious," a snide voice said. "We meet again, so soon."

"You!" Vertan exclaimed. "We knew we hadn't seen the last of you, monster."

"Are you ready for some fun now?" Ogryn said, ignoring the insult.

81 – The Monastery of ValkonenMaa

Daryan

When the scouts returned, Daryan joined Arendt to their reports. Arendt's sensor reported first. "It feels empty, as if there aren't many people inside the walls. Some of them are our own people who've been forced to serve the Brethren. I recognized old Dominel among them, plus a cook and a laundry woman."

Arendt interrupted to explain. "Dominel was one of our handymen. A gentle, kind old fellow; everyone loved him. If your daughter came into contact with him, he would see she was comfortable, if he could." He turned back to the sensor. "Continue."

The telepath joined in. "There seems to be some confusion in the minds of those inside. Even some dissatisfaction among their guards, especially the ones without powers."

"I sensed that too," Farah commented. "And fear."

"I wonder what they're afraid of," Daryan said.

"They probably know the game's up. We've destroyed so many of their followers, they must know by now they can't win," Arendt explained. "What else?"

"I felt the dark life," Nadi reported. "—that's what I call the aura they give off—but it doesn't seem as powerful as it was before when they first started the attacks."

"How many do you estimate inside the walls, and how many will fight us?" Arendt asked.

"Not much more than a hundred. Less than sixty will resist, and most of those don't have powers. I'd say at the most, a dozen with powers," the Valkonen replied.

Daryan turned to the other scouts. "What about defenses?"

"Nothing much has changed structurally since we left. Vegetation has grown up closer to the walls, filling the spaces we always kept clear, so we'll be able to get a lot closer without being seen, unless they have some sort of warning system."

"There was some damage to the gate when they attacked us," another defender added. "It's hanging crooked on its hinges and they don't seem to have done anything to repair it, so we might be able to break in quite easily."

Daryan was amazed at how few obstacles were in their way, but even so, there were about a dozen powerful wizards to contend with. It had taken fewer to bring down the Castle in DarSolas.

"Any sign that they are using wermen?" he asked.

"We didn't sense any inside, but there are quite a lot in the surrounding woods," the Valkonen sensor said.

"Hostile? To us I mean," Daryan asked.

"A little," he replied. "They don't seem to like humans in general, and I don't blame them after the way the Brethren treat them. I get the impression that they expected to gain something by working for them, poor creatures. So, I can't say they'll help us, and I wouldn't wager they're not spying for them either."

"So the situation is dubious," Darian summed up. "I wish we had Axtya with us."

Arendt raised his eyebrows quizzically. "Axtya?"

Daryan laughed. "He was a special project of mine. One of the wermen brought to Trethawynd by the brethren to create havoc. We caught him and took him back to the Monastery. I managed to persuade him to work for us. He provided some help and useful information, but he's gone back to his family now."

"That would have been useful. I'll have to mention it to our commander," Arendt replied. He stood up. "Well, I suppose we should be on our way."

Daryan deferred to Arendt when it came to organizing their plan of attack. Arendt continued to form the troops into small bands of ten defenders each, a mix of Trethawynd and Valkonen. "We'll wait until morning to attack. Right now, we're going to get as close to the walls as we can, without attracting attention. Then we'll settle down for the night. Spread out so that we have defenders all around the wall. Remember, no fire and no torches. You'll have to find your way in the dark. Be as quiet as you can. Leave the horses by the stream on the west side, and remove their harnesses so they don't make a noise. Don't attack anyone or anything unless you are attacked first." He looked at Daryan. "Can you think of anything else?"

"No, I think you've covered the essentials. You might remind everyone to draw dry rations and water, if they don't already have them."

It took them another two hours to reach the environs of the monastery and settle the horses. Daryan, leading half the defenders, took the south and west sides of the monastery wall and Arendt the north and east. The teams dropped off at what they estimated were equally spaced locations—the Valkonens had to decide the distances since Daryan was unfamiliar with the area. He found a place to wait about halfway along the line and took his bedroll out of his pack, then settled down to wait and watch. It was not a very comfortable position to be in; for one thing, the mosquitoes were out in force, ravenous for blood. *Their damned whining must be the most irritating sound in the world,* he fumed. *You can't get away from them; they're* incessant. *I'll never get any sleep now.* But he did, after covering his head with his ground sheet.

He awoke with a start. Wolves! They howled again; there seemed to be a fair number of them from the sound of it, maybe two packs. Mosquitoes forgotten, he sat up and leaned against his pack. He was about to get up and patrol the line when he heard a lone howl. It sounded as if it were at least two hours away. He stood up and walked south along the line, checking in with the defenders, most of whom complained about the wolves and the mosquitoes, all in whispers. But the local people were used to hearing wolves in the night. He returned to his starting place and went north. It was the same story there.

When he returned to his own bedroll, he started to feel uneasy. Nothing specific, just that something was very wrong. *Maybe it's the wolves,* he thought. *But surely...*

The wolf call came again, a little closer now. Could that really be Ashala? *I should have warned everyone not to be afraid of her. I hope the people from Trethawynd will tell them so they don't attack her. Other wolves responded in a chorus circling the forest around the monastery.*

82 – The Hunter Gets His Prey

Felindra looked towards Ogryn, but all she could see was a stunted shadowy figure with a foul smell. She shuddered. *What do we do now?* She quickly sent out a mental probe for her father. Before she could finish the message, she was cut off. "That's enough of that. I don't mind if someone is trying to find you, though. It'll be more prey for me to play with, but I won't have you leading them to us." He rounded on Vertan. "You too, boy."

Vertan moved closer to Felindra and whispered, "I told your father where we are." He took her hand. "Get ready!"

"And no talking!"

Ready for what? Felindra thought.

"Shall we begin?" Ogryn said gleefully. "You run, and I'll chase you."

Vertan let go of her hand and leapt at Ogryn with the spike. "You evil monster," he shouted. "I'll..." But before he could get close enough to hurt him, the creature raised his hand and released a power blast at him, throwing him back several paces into a tree trunk.

"There, you see how generous I can be. I even gave you a weapon, but you weren't supposed to use it on me. Now let's get on with this. Start running! I'm starting to get hungry for your tender flesh."

"You really are an evil demon, aren't you?" Felindra moved closer to where Vertan was standing by the tree rubbing his shoulder. She was followed by Ogryn's menacing laughter. "Are you hurt?" she asked.

"It's nothing, only a bruise. Are we going to play his game? It's our best chance to get away."

"Yes. Don't worry, he won't get us."

"And trust in the Light?" Vertan said.

"Of course." She took his hand. "Let's go! We'll run towards the wolves. Make sure we don't get separated."

They heard Ogryn's malevolent chuckle behind them as they started to run through the trees.

"I don't know how he hopes to keep up with us with his stumpy legs," Vertan said.

"Maybe he has some magic power for speed."

"More likely he has others out here ready to catch us," Vertan replied.

"Probably."

They ran as best they could in the dark forest, tracking the small candle of light that led them south.

"You'd better run faster than that." The snide voice of their tormentor came from close by. "There won't be any sport in this if you don't try harder to escape. If you try really hard, you just might get away."

"And demons might change into angels," Vertan replied angrily.

"Don't let him get to you," Felindra said. "Come on, let's speed up."

By following the light, they managed to avoid obstacles that might trip them and were able to run much faster.

"That's much better," the voice said. "Much more fun. I just love the chase."

"What are you going to do when the sun rises?" Vertan gasped breathlessly.

"Oh we'll be finished long before dawn. If you really make an effort, you might get away in time."

"I already detect a glow in east," Felindra said.

"Pooh, it's just your imagination. There's lots of time yet."

"I wonder where he is," Felindra said softly. "Let's stop and see if we can see him."

The pair slowed down, filling their lungs with the fresh air of the forest. "I don't smell him," Vertan said. "Where are you, monster?"

"I'm right behind you."

"I don't believe you. Show yourself."

"Just keep running."

"I was right," Felindra said. "He's just projecting his voice at us."

"He must have another scheme under his robe," Vertan said. "Anyway, let's go on."

They started to run again, but it didn't take long for them to become short of breath. They were weakened by their incarceration and neither of them was used to strenuous exercise after being cooped up for so long, nor had they eaten anything recently. They entered a small clearing and paused to get their breaths. Rustling in the foliage alerted them, but too late. They spun around and found they were surrounded by a pack of wermen.

"Got you!" Ogryn crowed softly, his voice so close, it seemed as if he was standing beside them. "Wasn't that fun?" He gave an inane snicker. "Now for the part I like best." He began to speak in a language they didn't understand, but it was obvious the wermen did for they moved in and several of them grabbed Felindra and led her away from Vertan.

Use your gift, Felindra sent to Vertan as they dragged her away.

Suddenly, the wermen let go of her and started looking around as if lost. She rubbed her arms and ran back to him. *It's working! They look completely lost. Let's go!*

They started to run south again, but the monster's voice shattered their hopes. "Very clever, but it won't do you any good. You think I can't override your pathetic illusion magic?"

The werfolk came after them again and, in spite of their shorter legs, soon caught up. *I'd use my Repel on them, but I don't know what it would do to us,* Felindra thought.

"Wise choice," the voice gloated. "It's no use trying your pitiful magic; I can nullify it in a flash."

The wermen were on them again. Before they could grab Vertan, he managed to get the spike into his hand and he lashed out at the closest one and buried it in his chest. The creature screeched and fell backwards, blood gushing from the wound. Before Vertan could retrieve the weapon, the rest were on him, punching, scratching, and biting him in their rage. They kept a tight hold on his arms as he struggled. He kicked out at them, managing to land a few blows before they wrestled him to the ground.

Felindra still couldn't detect Ogryn's presence, no dreadful odor, no emanations of evil.

The cries of wolves rang through the forest again and the wermen holding her to tense. "Do they scare you?" she asked, baiting them. "They'll tear you to pieces if they catch you." She saw their eyes bulge with terror, and their grips relaxed slightly. They glanced around as if expecting to see wolves popping out of the bushes. "They're getting closer, coming fast," she added to ratchet up their fear.

"I suppose you think you're being clever," Ogryn said, appearing suddenly in the clearing, trailing clouds of putrescence. "No more of that!" he addressed the wermen in the language he'd used earlier, which she assumed was their tongue.

Now she saw Ogryn among the wermen, she was able to see how like them he was, although he was taller than they were, and was bald in contrast with their fuzzy heads; his eyes were smaller too. It was almost as if he carried parts of both races, human and wer in his blood.

Apparently, Ogryn had been issuing instructions to the wermen because they held her tighter and started to pull her northward out of the clearing. She wondered if he was having them taken back to his charnel house of a den. He wouldn't have been able to take them alone, unless he had other magic than that which he'd already displayed.

Vertan cried out in pain, but she couldn't see what they were doing to him, they were crowded in to closely. "Don't damage him," Ogryn cried. "I want that pleasure for myself." Then he said something in the wer language.

Suddenly the whole thing became too much. Why were she and Vertan being manipulated by this crazed monster? The pressure began to build up to unbearable proportions, and then it exploded in a surge of force that sent werfolk flying in all directions. Those who were holding Vertan felt the shock and looked around for its source. Seeing their fellows lying unconscious, they let go of Vertan and started to back away into the bush.

"That will be enough of that!" Ogryn screeched madly. He held up his hands, pointing one at Felindra, the other at Vertan, and started to chant in a strange tongue that sounded different from Wer. Although she hadn't been knocked out by her power bolt, she was very groggy, swaying on her feet, her head spinning, but as soon as Ogryn had finished his spell, or whatever it was, she froze, totally paralyzed. She couldn't even move her eyes, although she was relieved she could still breathe, albeit shallowly. She tried to say something, but found she couldn't talk either. Panic set in and terror surged through her leaving her heart pounding and closing her throat, making breathing even more difficult. She felt as if ice water was running through her insides. *Light?*

A feeling of calmness fell over her, although she was still paralyzed.

Ogryn walked around her, running his hands over her body. His foul breath was choking her and his touch sending waves of nausea through her. *Oh, Light, I can't stand this. Help me, please, help me.*

Nothing happened, except she began to feel calmer. He continued to paw her, feeling every part of her body. "So tender," he crooned. "So delicious." He stood back and looked at her. "Oh, I'm going to enjoy this so much. Although it's too bad they didn't feed you better in that dungeon."

She tried to communicate with someone, with Ashala or Vertan, but to no avail; it seemed as if the airwaves, or spirit waves, were dead. *Where are you, girl? Dadi?* No answer. She felt tears pressing painfully against her eyes, but was unable to shed them. She saw Ogryn take a long sharp blade from inside his robe. *Light, please!* She had never felt so terrified or helpless in her life. Was there no one out there who could help her? He held up the knife and came to within touching distance. "Now, where shall we start?" He touched her with the point. "These lovely soft little breasts? That's what I love about young girls, so tender and tasty."

Nausea and terror swept through her in waves. The effort of her eyes to shed tears became more painful.

He moved the blade again. "These arms look as if they would be delicious, or even these round little buttocks. Ooh, I can almost taste them." He made a little jigging motion. "There's enough meat on you to last me for several days, and then the boy over there … I think I'll keep him alive until I've fully enjoyed you. Now I have to decide whether to eat you raw or cooked. Even though fire hurts my eyes, I suppose I might make an exception… we'll see."

83 – Ogryn Meets his Match

Ashala

The wolf sniffed the air, whined, and then let out a howl that reverberated through the forest. The sense of urgency overwhelmed her and sent her running with all her might. She knew she was too far away, but she persisted even when each breath burned her lungs. She could sense the evil in the air, the danger to her sister.

Felindra

"I suppose we'll have to carry you back. Don't move!" Ogryn said with a giggle. "I'm going to have to get help." He poured out stream of alien words, not shouting, just in his normal voice, as if he could project the words at whatever he was summoning.

You are utterly despicable, she thought, *but this is your last day of tormenting the Light's creatures and spreading your evil. Take it from me; you're finished.*

He looked over his shoulder at her and smiled, the sickly movement of his gross lips bearing no trace of humor or humanity. He shook his head. "Poor little girl, so deluded by her ridiculous Light worship. He has no power over me while Oglestra protects me."

Felindra couldn't move her eyes or turn her head to look at Vertan, but she could imagine what he was thinking. *You're the deluded one, monster.*

A wolf call rang through the air. It sounded desperate. Felindra's heart missed a beat. Could that be her? Oh, pray the Light it is Ashala. If only she gets here in time, but she sounds so far away.

"Are you hoping for rescue?" the monster taunted her. "Too bad it's not coming. Besides, a puny wolf can't hurt me. I could destroy it with a wave of my hand. Ah, here they are!" Eight wermen emerged from the bushes. Ogryn gave them some instructions in their own tongue and half of them approached her and picked her up, one on each limb. It was not a comfortable way to be picked up, but she couldn't feel their hands touching her skin, only the dizziness caused by the blood rushing to her head, which was almost touching the ground. A few more words from Ogryn, and they started moving north towards his den. Her fear was so overwhelming, she could barely breathe. Her body felt as if it was freezing from the inside, and her heartbeat became so fast, it felt like one continuous vibration. *Light, how much longer?*

Several more wolf calls echoed through the night. She could feel the wermen trembling. They were terrified. One of them dropped her arm and ran into the bushes, leaving it and her head dangling on the ground. Ogryn saw him and sent a blast of energy after him. There was a loud boom and a single terrified scream, then silence. He snarled several words at the remaining porters, leaving little doubt as to what he was saying to them. He pointed to the three carrying her body and said it so she could understand, "One of you take both her arms and keep her head off the ground. I don't want my banquet to be spoiled by rough handling." Then spoke a few words in their language. *Good, anything to delay them.*

The werman holding her arms suddenly collapsed on the ground, moaning, leaving her head to fall onto the forest floor. Ogryn started ranting about another delay. He came over to her and kicked the fallen werman in the head. He moaned with pain, but didn't get up. Ogryn screeched in the wer tongue. He seemed to be addressing all of them, as he turned from her and moved to the group carrying Vertan. She heard another couple of screams from them and a thud. She couldn't see what was happening, but she could guess.

From her position on the ground, she could look up at the sky. *Am I imagining it, or is it getting a bit lighter?*

Ogryn brought one of Vertan's porters over to her and ordered him to hold her under her arms, but after a couple of steps, he tripped over a root and fell down. *So stupid, telling him to walk backwards in the dark. But it's giving us a bit more time.* Her head was lying between the werman's legs, not a very comfortable position being so close to the rank, sour odor of his body, but she couldn't move. She tried to will him to move back, but by the time she got the thought out, Ogryn had come along and started to berate and kick him so that he moved of his own accord, to escape the abuse.

She could feel the fury radiating from Ogryn. Time was passing, slowly, and it was a long way back to his lair. She wondered if he was beginning to realize that and thinking of a new plan.

"It looks as if we'll have to try another way of getting you home," he said silkily, as if he didn't have a care. "Because of the incompetence of my helpers, I'll have to speed up my plan by dismembering you both and just taking the juiciest portions home. Too bad I'm forced to hurry. I much prefer doing it slowly so that I can relish each pain to the limit." He sighed and withdrew a knife from his cloak. "Put her down!" he yelled at the two wermen who were holding her legs.

Daryan

Daryan woke suddenly, feeling he'd only just fallen asleep. Something was wrong; a cold sinking feeling filled his gut. Looking at the sky, he saw that the sun would be up soon, so he might as well get up. He heard a wolf call in the distance. *Maybe that's what woke me.* He stood up and folded his groundsheet.

The other defenders were stirring now. When he saw Daryan standing nearby, one of them spoke to him. "Lot of wolves around last night!"

"They obviously weren't interested in us," another said. "They were over that way as far as I could make out." He pointed towards the southeast.

"Something's up to get them that excited."

Nadi rushed into the campsite. "Daryan," he said breathlessly. "I sense something terrible happening over there," he gasped waving in the same direction the defender had indicated.

"Slow down and get your breath, Nadi, then tell us about it."

Nadi put his hands on his knees and took a couple of deep breaths, then straightened up and continued. "I feel a powerful presence of dark life, extreme evil. I also sense some young humans. I can't identify them, but one feels familiar. They're terrified. They must be in danger. We have to hurry!" he finished. Taking Daryan's arm as if to pull him into action.

Daryan's heart sank. Someone familiar ... wolves ... danger? It could only be.... He looked at the defenders who were all on their feet now. "Get some horses from the picket. We have to leave now. Come with us, Nadi." He grabbed his sword and put it in its sheath, then took off in the direction of their mounts.

Felindra

He knelt down beside her and started to cut her tunic away with his knife, starting at the neck. "Might as well see what I'm doing," he murmured softly. "Don't worry, my dear; I'll have to do it quickly. It'll all be over in no time, unfortunately." He sighed as if he were making a hard decision, sending another cloud of foulness her way.

She couldn't move a muscle, she couldn't even move her eyes to see what he was doing, but she could feel the adrenalin surging through her body, pumping her heart up and freezing her internal organs. Her breath came in small rapid puffs. *Light! Somebody help me!* her mind shrieked in panic.

Vertan

Light! Help us ... please!

I'm here.

We have to help her. What can I do?

Find the wolf.

?

Vertan cast his mind around until he became aware of the animal's essence. He could feel her exhaustion as she kept pushing herself forward, forcing her legs to keep moving, front, then back, front then back, over and over. She was so desperate.

What do I do now?

Give her your strength.

How?

You'll know.

Vertan concentrated on Ashala. He entered her tired muscles and burning lungs, and pushed with all his might to force his own energy into her. He pictured it entering her body and filling her with new strength; he felt the fatigue drain out of her as she was revitalized. Then she was able to make the extra effort needed to speed up the race to save her beloved sister.

But Vertan felt drained. *Thank you light.*

Felindra

A grey shadow came into her line of sight, flying towards her. Before he knew what was happening, it had a firm grip on Ogryn's throat. As its teeth sank deeper, Felindra could feel the paralysis leave her. "Ashala! Oh, my good girl!" she sat up and scooted back to give her room.

The wolf managed to utter a short whine of acknowledgement without loosening her grip, and then she started to shake Ogryn, growling low in her own throat as her teeth sank deeper into the cartilage and blood vessels. Felindra could see the monster's terrified bulging eyes watching her, but she felt no pity, only relief. "Now you're getting a taste of what you dish out!" she taunted him. "Don't worry, it'll soon be over. Unfortunately, this wolf is merciful and prefers the quick kill." But the life had already gone out of Ogryn. All that remained was the puny body and dreadful smell. Ashala moved away from the body and automatically started to lick his blood off her snout. She started choking when the blood entered her mouth. She tried to force it out with her tongue, and then with her paws, scraping her jaws, first with her hind paw and then with the front ones. Finally, she collapsed on the ground and stopped moving.

Daryan

Nadi flinched. Daryan saw it from the corner of his eye. "What is it?" he asked in alarm.

"Something happened. The dark life seemed to flare for a moment, and then it stopped abruptly."

"What do you mean stopped?"

"It just vanished, died out completely."

"Could the creature be dead?"

"That's the only conclusion I can draw," Nadi replied.

"What about the other life?"

"It's still there, but there's an animal with them now as well. One person is very upset."

"Nadi, would you mind going back to bring a healer and Lady Farah? I think we're going to need them. Also, bring two more horses." He turned to one of the Valkonen defenders. "Go with him, defender, to help with the horses"

"At your service, commander." Nadi and the defender turn back the way they had come and galloped away.

"We'd better hurry and find out what's going on," Daryan spurred his horse into a gallop now that dawn was approaching and they could see obstacles better. After a while, he saw a light ahead among the trees.

He saw them huddled together in a clearing, Felindra kneeling, bending over something on the ground. There was a boy kneeling close to her with his hand on her back. Then foul, sulfurous odor reached him. He pulled back on the reins to stop the horse and jumped to the ground. She was so involved in what she was doing, she didn't notice he was there, so Daryan had a brief moment to look at her.

My little girl. My poor baby, she looks so... Oh Light, how she must have suffered.

"Felindra!" he said softly and took a step towards her.

She turned and looked over her shoulder. "Dadi!" she shouted as she stood up, clutching the torn edges of her tunic together. He looked at her more closely, barely believing his eyes. Her face was wet with tears, both her arms scratched and bleeding, her skin had a ghostly yellowish pallor, and her hair was a knotted tangle. She looked so thin, he could almost see the bones poking through her skin. Her scant clothing was nothing but rags and she looked frozen.

He took off his cloak and held it out for her "Come here, my daughter," he said. "Put this around you, you must be freezing." She moved hesitantly towards him at first, as though she couldn't believe he was there, then rushed and buried her face in his chest, sobbing uncontrollably. He put the cloak around her shoulders and hugged her tightly. "I've got you, my precious girl. You've been through some terrible experiences, but you're safe now. Don't cry." He took a piece of cotton from his belt and gently wiped her face.

"Dadi, you have to help us." Felindra pulled free of her father's arms and went back to the wolf lying motionless on the ground, its face and paws covered in a black, tarry substance. "It's Ashala, dadi," she said, her voice hitched with a sob. "I can't wake her up. She killed him, but his blood ... We have to do something or she'll die," she cried through her tears. She stood up and looked around in panic.

Daryan dashed away and gathered some water containers from the defenders' horses. "We have to get the poison out of her. She must have swallowed some of it. Can you get her mouth open?"

Felindra knelt and forced Ashala's jaws apart. Daryan leaned in and started to pour water slowly into her mouth. Most of it trickled out, but some must have gone in because her throat spasmed as if she was trying to swallow. "Put her head back so we get more into her mouth.

"What's that awful smell?" he asked.

"It's him," Felindra cried with a shudder. "Ashala killed the monster. It's his body that stinks."

"Who is this monster?"

"It's was Ogryn," a young male voice answered his question.

Daryan looked around when a shadow fell over them and saw the boy standing behind him. The boy looked exhausted, as if all his energy had drained away.

"Solas Naofa! Are you sure. That's the disciple?" Daryan shook his head. It was unbelievable.

"Yes, dadi. Ashala killed him," Felindra replied

"Do you want me to show you?" the boy asked.

Daryan looked at his daughter. She obviously still needed help with Ashala. "Thank you, but I can find it myself." Daryan said, rising to his feet. "You're Vertan, aren't you?"

"Yes commander. It's an honor to meet you, sir."

"Would you help Felindra, while I look around?" Daryan thought for a moment. "Is there anything you need right now?"

"Some water, more than anything," Vertan replied as he knelt down and picked up a water bag.

"Both of you, use the water in these water bags; I'll fetch some more for you. Is there a stream around here?" He bent and gathered up the empty bags from the ground.

"Can I do anything to help, sir?" It was one of the duchy defenders. "I was going to give the boy my cloak; he looks half frozen." She held out the cloak, which she'd just taken off her own shoulders.

"That's very kind of you, defender. Would you like to take his place and help my daughter? While I take Vertan to show me the way to a stream. Just keep pouring water into her, but don't touch the black stuff."

"Vertan stood up and allowed the defender to wrap the cloak around his shoulders." Thank you, lady," he said shyly, avoiding her eyes. He looked uncomfortable about having people see him in such a pathetic condition.

"Captain Arendt will be happy to hear you're safe. He's been worried about you." Daryan said as they walked away.

"Is he here?" Vertan asked.

"He is. We're part of a team sent to liberate the monastery. With Ogryn dead, it should be a much easier undertaking. I'll send a messenger to tell him the good news when we get back."

"The body's over here by these bushes," Vertan said.

"What an awful stench. It's the worst thing I've ever smelled."

"Light save us!" Vertan exclaimed. "Look at it; it's melting. It's burning the grass." He turned away, took a few steps, and then bent over and vomited."

Daryan looked at the smoldering bundle of rags on the ground; the body was rapidly turning into black sludge, emitting a powerful smell of sulfur. He turned away, pulling his tunic up over his lower face and then took a few deep breaths to allay his nausea.

"Are you feeling better now?" he asked Vertan when the boy looked back.

"I bit. I really need some water though."

"Here, finish off this bag." Daryan handed an almost empty water bag to the boy and led him back to the clearing.

"Defender!" He beckoned the one closest to him. "Take someone and gather some dry leaves and twigs and burn that thing in there." He turned and pointed to the body. "And don't touch it, whatever you do. We've got to get rid of it as fast as we can."

When they'd gone, Daryan rounded up the rest of the people in his team and told them to start a cook fire and see if they could rustle up some food for the young pair. "I'd like one of the Valkonen defenders to find Captain Arendt and bring him back. Tell him that Ogryn is dead." He stood up and followed Vertan.

Vertan washed himself downstream while Daryan filled the water bags.

Having Vertan alone gave Daryan the opportunity to ask about the events of the previous night.

"He said he was letting us go. He showed us a way out of the Monastery through a cave, and told us we were free to leave."

"You mean Ogryn?" The boy was obviously reluctant to say the name.

"Yes," Vertan replied. "The demon monster."

Vertan continued to tell him about the hunt and its aftermath, stumbling over the final episode.

"He was going to eat us!" Vertan cried, his voice rising in indignation. "Cut us up and eat us!" Tears ran down Vertan's face unchecked. "He was just starting on Felindra when the wolf jumped out of the bushes. He knew the sun would be up soon, and he was going to cut up our bodies and take pieces back ...." He choked on a sob.

Daryan put the full water bags on the ground and put his arm across the boy's shoulder. *Those poor kids,* he thought. He'd never heard of anything so awful and could barely imagine what it had been like for them. Vertan turned and pressed his face into Daryan's chest, sobbing uncontrollably. Daryan put his other arm around him and patted his back. "You're safe now, son."

When they got back with the water, Nadi was back with Farah and the healer.

"Would you see if there's anything you can do for the wolf? He asked the healer. "Talk to my daughter; she'll tell you about what happened."

The healer's expression clearly reflected what he was thinking: 'are you serious?', but he replied, "As you wish, commander."

"Don't worry, defender, she's a very special wolf and it would break my daughter's heart if she died."

Felindra

Felindra looked up as a man approached her. She saw he wore a healer's crystal on a chain around his neck.

"What is the problem?" he asked, crouching beside her.

"It's this stuff," she pointed to the black matter clinging to Ashala's coat. "It's the demon's blood she got in her mouth when she killed him. I think it's poisoning her." She continued to dribble water down Ashala's throat.

"Let me see what I can find," the healer said.

"Be careful! Don't get any of it on you."

He nodded and placed his hands on Ashala's abdomen, which was free of the blood. After closing his eyes and waiting for a while, the healer nodded his head and drew back his hands. He then scanned her whole torso without touching her. "Her heart is strong," he told Felindra, "so I think she will live, but we need to get rid of this noxious substance. You're doing the right thing, but maybe I can hasten the process with some herbs." He stood up. "I'll just get my satchel from the horse. Don't give her any more water." He looked closely at Felindra. "You look as if you need some healing yourself. Try to drink some of the water for a start.

Felindra looked down at Ashala, fighting back more tears. "I know you've got a strong heart," she whispered. "You're going to live, my precious girl, I know you are." *I couldn't live without you.*

She picked up one of the refilled water bags her father had just dropped off and gulped a few mouthfuls.

"Here we are," the healer knelt down beside her. "The problem with washing poison out this way is it can damage her kidneys. What we need to do is make her vomit. I'm going

674

to mix these herbs in some water and feed it to her. I have a tube here to get it into her."

"Will it hurt her?" Felindra asked.

"No more than she's already hurt," he replied. He took a small beaker from his satchel and poured in some water, and then he opened two small bottles of dark fluid. "One of these will help ease the pain of the damage caused by the tainted blood, the other should make her vomit." After mixing one of the herbal tinctures with the water, he dug into his satchel brought out a strange contraption, a glass tube, about the length of a hand, with one end shaped like a conical funnel. "Now, hold her head back as firmly as you can."

He slowly poured the medicine down Ashala's throat, managing to get most of it into her. By the time he was halfway through, Ashala began to struggle, as if she was choking. The healer moved back as she started to buck. "Get back!" he warned Felindra. "I think it's working."

Ashala's body began to convulse and then gag. Finally, she raised her head sent forth a mass of watery fluid, tinted with the black poison and her own blood. When she had finished, she whined piteously and lowered her head. Her legs twitched, but she seemed helpless to move them further. She hadn't opened her eyes the entire time.

Felindra crouched beside her and stroked her head. "I'm sorry, my precious. You deserve a better reward than this after saving our lives. You're going to get better and I'm going to stay you all the time."

"Miss Felindra, can I have a word?" She looked up at the healer. "She's going to have a lot of pain now. You'll need to cook her food and make it into a soup, and I'm going to give you these herbal tinctures to give her to help with the healing." He handed her two bottles. "But first, let's get this one into her to sooth her pain.

"Thank you, healer," she said. "Is there anything else I can do?"

"Yes, two things: have something to eat and get some sleep; if you don't, you're going to be in trouble yourself."

"I'll second that."

"Dadi!" She hadn't seen him arrive. She stood up and wiped her hands down the cloak he given her. "She's going to be all right, but she's very sick. We still have to wash her fur, and can someone move her away from this mess?" The ground around them was fouled by all the smelly fluids produced by their attempts to revive her.

"All in good time. For now, I want you to come with me. You need to wash up and put on some clean clothes, and then you can eat something. I'll get someone to wash the mess from her fur, and then move her away from here."

Felindra smiled at her father. "I know she's going to be all right. If only she'd wake up."

"She must rest so she can recover. If it could consume his body, it must be a powerful poison. As a matter of fact, my hands are tingling. How about you?"

She looked down at her hands. They were bright red, almost as if they'd been dipped in paint, and they were starting to burn and tingle. "Wash them, quickly. There's a bowl of water and some clean clothes over there in the bushes." Felindra swayed and staggered as her father led her away. "I'll take you there now. Will you need some help?"

"No, dadi, I c...can manage. I'll c...call if I d...."

Felindra opened her eyes and looked at the foliage directly above her. She turned her head and looked around, and then she did a quick survey of herself. Under the clean blanket that covered her, she felt clean and her clothes were softer and more comfortable. *How?* "You're awake," a female voice said behind her. "How do you feel?" Lady Farah came into view on her left side.

Felindra sat up and looked down at herself. Someone had bather her and put on clean clothes, a soft wool shirt and culottes. "Who did this," she asked.

"After you collapsed, you father sent for me and asked me to help you. He carried you over here, and I bathed and dressed you. Do you feel better now?"

Felindra nodded and started to stand up. "I'll help you up." Farah took her arm and gave Felindra a boost. "Are you hungry?"

"Starving," she replied. "How's Ashala. Is she all right?"

"She seems to be much better. They got all the blood off and moved her to a clean place. She got up a while ago and went into the bush, but she came back and lay down again. She's sleeping now."

Felindra's heart gave a little jump of joy. "How long was I asleep?"

Farah glanced at the sky. "Oh, about three hours. Now, let's go and find something to eat."

Daryan

By the time Arendt and the others returned, Ogryn's remains had been consumed by fire.

"I'll take everyone's word that it was Ogryn," Arendt said, glancing as the ashes with a look of disgust. "I've never actually seen him, anyway, so I wouldn't have any reference to identify him from." He then spoke to Vertan, "I understand you spent some time with him. What was he like? Foolish question; I know he was an evil monster, but how did he act, what did he look like?"

Vertan squinted when a beam of sunlight broke through the trees. "He wasn't very big," he started. "Sort of between a werman and a human. He looked a bit like a werman." He stopped, plucked some grass and wove it through his fingers. Then he looked up at his commander, revulsion written in his expression. "He enjoyed torturing animals to death and I think he ate them, probably before they were completely dead. Humans too. We saw some human hair on the floor in his den. It was like a charnel house where he lived. And he said he was going to eat us, too. He was just starting on

Felindra when the wolf arrived and killed him." He turned away and gazed into the trees as his eyes filled with tears.

"We'll have to explore his lair," Arendt said. "I didn't know there was another way into the Monastery. Do you think you could find it?"

"I think so. You'll probably find piles of bones outside the entrance from all the things he's killed. I don't know where else he could put them. Oh, I almost forgot; he was terrified of light. It had a disabling effect on him, making him helpless."

"That's interesting," Daryan said. "Fitting in a way. It's no wonder he turned against the Light."

"It was the Light that saved us," Felindra said. "Without His...." She put her face in her hands, her shoulders shaking in time to her sobs.

Daryan went over to fire where she was sitting and enfolded her in his arms. For the first time in weeks, his heart felt lighter.

84 – Liberating the Monastery

Felindra

When Felindra woke up, the sun was approaching the western horizon. She sat up and stretched her arms above her head, and then looked around. The clearing was empty apart from two defenders, one she recognized from the Trethawynd monastery. "Where is everyone?" she asked.

"They've gone to do some reconnaissance," a defender she assumed was from ValkonenMaa replied.

"What about Vertan; did he go too?"

"No. He went off into the bush. He's probably gone to wash himself in the stream."

"Are you well rested?" the Trethawynd defender asked.

"I feel much better now, thank you." She looked around again and realized someone else was missing. "Where's my wolf?"

"She woke up a while ago and took off into the woods."

"Thank the light! Did she look all right?"

"She was a bit wobbly on her feet, but she got steadier as she moved."

"I'm so glad she's better." Felindra stood up. "I think I need to do a few things in the woods. I won't be long." She started walking away, and then turned back. "Oh, if you hear a loud whistle, don't worry, it's only me calling her."

Daryan

"Let's talk about our next move," Daryan said. "Any ideas about how to proceed?"

"How about sending six people to find a way into the monastery through Ogryn's cave, and the rest of us prepare to take the monastery from the outside?" Arendt said.

"A two pronged attack; that could work," Daryan replied "What do you plan to do when you get there?"

"A few of us could go right to the gate and speak to whoever they have guarding it. Tell them we want to speak to their leader and inform him that Ogryn is dead. With him gone, I might be able to talk them into surrendering."

"You'd have to give them some incentive to surrender," Daryan said.

"Oh, I've plenty of incentive to offer them under current circumstances. Perhaps we could offer them amnesty to everyone but the wizards if they surrender. Do you think our leaders would consider that?"

"We could probably talk them into it; it would save more lives. I know they wouldn't agree to amnesty for the wizards, though."

"How about you? What are you going to do?"

"I'll have to take one of the young people to help us find the entrance." He glanced across at his daughter who was sitting on the grass with one arm around Ashala's neck, a look of bliss on her face. *She looks so thin and wasted. We'll have to make sure she eats plenty before her mother sees her.* "I would prefer not to put my daughter through that again, though. I doubt she would consent to being separated from her wolf anyway."

"Of course she can't go back into—what was it Vertan called it? ... that charnel house. Besides, she's a non-combatant. I think Vertan should handle it."

They called the two young people over. "We need a guide to help us find the cave," Daryan explained.

"I'll go," Felindra volunteered without thought. "I need to set the animals free."

Daryan shook his head. "Not you, my girl. This is a military operation and we can't have non-combatants involved." He turned to Arendt for confirmation.

"That's right," Arendt said with a nod of his head. "Vertan can go."

"But what about the locks?" Felindra said.

"I can open them," Vertan asserted. "I saw what you did, and besides, you said yourself it didn't need an engineer to figure them out."

"Oh all right," Felindra agreed. "What am I going to do?"

"Is Ashala fit to travel?" Daryan asked.

"She seems to be all right," Felindra replied, stroking the wolf's head. "I don't feel anything wrong, except she's very tired and her insides hurt. I'll give her some more of the healer's medicine."

"Good. You're going to get on a horse and go back with Commander Arendt. He'll find a safe place for you to wait. And you are to stay there! I don't want to have to worry about you getting hurt again. Promise me!"

"I promise, father. I won't get in the way. You be careful, as well!"

Vertan

On horseback, it took hardly any time to reach Ogryn's den. Even before they arrived there, the horses had started to become restless, tossing their heads and snorting, trying to veer away. It took all his strength and persuasiveness to keep his on track. He could see that the others were struggling too.

"It's obvious they don't like it here and I don't see why we should make them suffer needlessly," Daryan said. "Two of you take the horses take back to the monastery and join Captain Arendt. The rest of us will go in this way."

Vertan shivered, rubbing his upper arms. The sun was close to setting and already there was a chill in the air. This was the part he was dreading, having to go back into that appalling place. *At least I'm still living, thank the Light. I hope we can get this over with fast.*

"Let's get some torches ready," Commander Peshanar said. "You lead the way, Vertan."

They followed him towards the cave mouth, where sure enough, they found piles of bones among the rocks that had been concealed with bushes. Large bones and small, many of the bones smashed into fragments. Some were fresh, giving off the odor of decaying flesh. "Look here, Commander. A human skull!" one of the defenders pointed out.

Vertan shuddered. *I wonder who that poor soul had been. It could have been me, or Felindra, if her wolf hadn't arrived in time.* He didn't want to look at the bones ... to be reminded of the fate he'd barely escaped.

"There's more over here," someone else called. "Small ones. Probably wermen. Poor little sods."

Vertan lit his torch from someone else's and walked towards the cave entrance. "Let's get this over with," he muttered to himself.

As Vertan led them through the narrow passage, the stench of evil and decay grew stronger. He turned to the commander. "There's a little door leading into his den. We'll have to stoop to get through it."

"Light help us!" the commander cried when he saw the carnage that had taken place in there. "It's like a slaughterhouse."

"He called this his recreation room," Vertan said with a grimace.

The animals in the cages began to show their fear, hissing, screeching, and cowering away from the front. The monster had somehow managed to replace those he and Felindra had freed, probably by having the wermen hunt for him. He'd also managed to get some new cages built to hold them, although not as many as before.

"The other door leads to his living quarters," Vertan said, eager to get out of the place.

Some of the defenders went through, but the commander held back a couple. "Set these animals loose, for Light's sake. And then follow us."

They spent several minutes examining the living and sleeping quarters, marveling at the valuable collection of objects he'd amassed, but the commander wanted to keep going, so Vertan went to the door that exited from the quarters into the monastery. He looked at the locking mechanism for a moment, trying to recall exactly how Felindra had opened it. He had to try several times before he got it open.

"There's another one at the end of the passage," he told the commander. "It leads into the room he called his receiving room."

"Did he always keep everything so dark?" the commander asked.

"Yes. He couldn't tolerate light. The first time we were brought down here to meet him, Felindra summoned the

Light, and the whole room filled with bright light. He nearly went crazy. He vanished through that door as if his eyeballs were on fire. That's when he began to take an interest in us." Vertan finished opening the next door and they entered the office.

"She seems to have developed some extra gifts while she was here," the commander said.

"I don't know if they are her gifts, or if the Light just responds to her in a special way."

"Whatever it is, it saved her life, both your lives, and I thank the Light for that mercy." He walked over to the other door. "Does this door lead into the monastery?" he asked.

"Actually, it leads into the dungeons. That's where they kept us."

"Were you in the same cell?"

"No; they put us both at opposite ends of the hallway. We couldn't even talk to each other."

They went through into the next passage and up a long flight of stairs. "We should be careful here, there might be some guards through this door." Vertan cautioned.

"Let me take a look," the commander said. He slowly opened the door a crack, although caution was futile; the hinges of the old door creaked loudly at the slightest movement, so he abandoned caution and opened it wider, pulling his sword free before he moved out into the hallway. This passage was completely dark and there was no sign of any guards. "Let's get some lights out here," he called back to his followers.

Daryan

Daryan looked down the hall. "Which was her cell?" he asked the boy.

"That one, at the end." Vertan pointed left. "Mine was this one," he added, pointing right.

"Let's take a look; I'm curious to get an idea what it was like for her." Daryan walked quickly to the end of the hallway and through the open door into the cell. At least it was clean and the straw mattress on the floor didn't look too bad. He lifted it and looked underneath. "A blanket. So they did they give you blankets," he said. "It's very cold in here."

"No," the boy replied. "No blankets and they took our clothes as well."

"By the Light!" Daryan exclaimed. "That's an outrage. It's a wonder you didn't both freeze to death."

"It was thanks to the Light, and to one of the old monastery servants who brought us some clothes and blankets. That's why she hid it under the mattress, so the guards wouldn't find it. She didn't want old Dominel to be punished."

"I'll have to thank him personally," Daryan said. "It must have been dark in here with the door closed."

Vertan looked undecided for a moment, gazing down at the floor and scuffling it with his foot. "The Light kept us warm and gave us light to see by." He looked Daryan in the eye as if to say, 'please don't ask me any more about it.'

"Well, we have a task to complete," Daryan said, leaving the empty cell. "I take it the stairs we passed lead to ground level."

85 – Prisoners Discovered

This time when they reached the top of the stairs, Daryan was prepared, although this door was newer and shouldn't have such squeaky hinges as the old one. Before they had a chance to try it, they heard shouts and running feet on the other side. Daryan backed down a step and murmured softly to Vertan, "What's on the other side of that door?"

"It's mostly the guards' quarters and there are a few rooms that were occupied by staff members. It's a separate building from the rest of the monastery."

"That's good to know. They seem to have gone, so let's take a look." He opened the door and peered out. "All clear, but go quietly. We don't know if there are more people in the rooms here."

Once everyone was in the hallway, he asked Vertan, "Which way to the gate?"

"This way, commander." He led the way down the hall towards the main door of the building. "If we go out this door, it's to the left."

As they were walking down the hallway, they heard a weak voice calling from inside one of the rooms. "Help! Let me out. Don't leave me in here."

"Should we see who it is?" Vertan asked. "It might be another of their prisoners."

"Go ahead, but be careful," Daryan replied.

Vertan tried the latch on the door, but it wouldn't open. "It's locked," he announced.

"Ask who it is?" Daryan suggested.

"Who are you?"

The speaker was now close to the door. "Evanar of Trethawynd. Who are you?"

Daryan was stunned. He went closer to the door. "My lord, is it really you?" *He sounds like an old man,* Daryan thought.

"It is I," came the reply. "Who are you?"

"I'm Commander Peshanar of the Trethawynd League of Light"

"Truly? I think I met you once at the Castle when my father was still alive. Can you get me out?

"We can try, but we don't have a key."

"Commander," Vertan interrupted. "There's a board in the common room where they keep some keys. Do you want me to look?"

"Go ahead. Wait!" Daryan examined the lock. "It looks like a fairly new lock, so only bring keys that look newer."

Daryan turned back to the door. "My lord, we are in the middle of liberating the monastery from the Dark Brethren, so I have to continue with our action. Be patient and we will get you out. The young man who went for the keys is a Valkonen defender cadet; I'll leave him here to help you."

Vertan returned with a handful of keys. "Shall I try these, sir?"

"Go ahead, but first tell me how far it is to the gate."

Vertan's eyes turned up to the left as he calculated. "About thirty, thirty-five paces."

"Is there any cover between here and the gate?"

"Not this way," Vertan replied, "but there's a back exit that leads out to the garden. I'd say there is less likelihood of anyone being out there. There are some shrubs and trees we could use for cover."

"Thank you Vertan. Take good care of Lord Evanar. I'll be back as soon as we've finished mopping up, My Lord." he added to Evanar.

"Light go with you, Commander!"

A loud boom rent the air outside the building, followed by screams and the sound of splintering wood. Then they heard shouts and the clash of weapons. Some horses galloped past, but the noise of their hooves and their startled cries faded after a moment.

"Well, I suppose that decides it." Daryan said. "We'll leave this way instead of sneaking through the garden. They won't be expecting an attack from their rear. Draw your weapons! Ready? Let's go!"

Felindra

Felindra lay curled up in a sunny glade, covered with a blanket. Her hand rested on Ashala, who was also sleeping. Two Trethawynd defenders were sitting nearby, guarding her. Suddenly, Ashala raised her head and growled softly. Felindra woke instantly and looked around. "What is it, girl?" she murmured. She discovered from Ashala's mind that someone was out there in the woods, trying to creep through the fallen leaves without being detected.

Felindra glanced across at the man and woman guarding her. Realizing she was awake, they looked over at her and saw Ashala stand up and slink away into the trees. The female defender got up and came over. Felindra put her finger over her mouth, the sign for silence. "She heard something, a human, creeping around in the woods," she said very softly.

The defender nodded and beckoned her partner to join them. "There's someone out there," she told him. "Think we should take a look?"

"Can't leave her unguarded," he replied. "I'll go; you stay with her." He drew his belt knife and crept in the direction Ashala had taken. He had gone barely three strides when a terrified scream echoed through the trees. The defender rushed towards the scream that had now turned into a moan of pain, accompanied by the deep growl of the wolf.

He returned moments later leading a man by the arm, holding his belt knife in the other hand. Ashala followed them, licking blood off her jaws.

"Who is it?" the female defender asked.

"I can tell you that," Felindra answered. "It's the Grand Wizard, Monaltor."

"Here, girl," she called Ashala. "Good girl. That's twice today you've helped us. You should get a citation." She ruffled the wolf's hair affectionately and then turned her attention to Monaltor. "What are you doing out here?" she asked. She saw blood running down from his arm over his hand, although he seemed oblivious to it. "Shouldn't you be inside, leading your people?"

Monaltor scowled at her, but refused to say anything.

"What do you think we should do with him?" the woman asked.

"We should let Captain Arendt know. Let's all go and take him in. It sounds a bit quieter back there. The battle must be almost over. If it isn't, they won't have the will left to fight once they see we've captured their leader."

They'd been hearing the sound of combat for a while, and one loud boom that must have been a wizard using his powers, but it seemed to have quieted down within the last few minutes.

On the way back to the monastery, Felindra couldn't resist asking the grand wizard about Ogryn. "Have you heard from your friend Ogryn recently?"

"Of course not. I've been much too busy."

"Did you know he's dead?"

He stopped in his tracks and turned to look at her. "What are you talking about? Of course he's not dead. Nobody can kill the Disciple, you foolish girl. He's lived hundreds of years; he's Immortal"

Felindra was delighted to continue baiting him. "Oh, he wasn't killed by a person; she killed him," she said gleefully, patting Ashala on the head. "And you'll never believe what happened when he was dead." She paused, waiting for his response, but he kept his silence, refusing to look at her. The male defender pushed Monaltor's back to get him moving again and they continued on their way. The two defenders were as interested in her account as the wizard should have been.

"What happened?" the female defender prompted.

"His body just melted into a horrible stinking black goo."

"Nonsense!" that was the only utterance she could get out of Monaltor.

"You'll see," she continued. "You'll be able to see his den as well when we get back. You have to see that. It's really quite amazing. I wager you didn't have any idea what he was up to down there." *Let him chew on that for a while,* she thought. After a few moments, she had another thought. "Where's Barengush?"

'That failure. As far as I know, he's still locked up in his room."

"I wonder what he'll think about his dadi running away from a battle."

Daryan

It wasn't much of a battle, once they had the Brethren forces surrounded and convinced that their leader was dead, they caved in like a house of straw. Even the wizards, the two that remained, gave up the fight, once they realized the Grand Wizard had disappeared.

"Take the wizards to the cells," Arendt ordered four of the defenders as they began rounding up the remnants of the Brethren. "Put them together in the same cell. That way, if they start trying to use their powers to escape, they will be more likely to hurt each other."

The two wizards in question glared at everyone, but submitted themselves meekly to the inevitable and went without a struggle. Neither looked as if he had more than eighteen years.

"I'd like to question them later," Daryan said. "Find out how they got into this mess with the Brethren. I feel we might be able to rehabilitate them and teach them how to put their powers to good uses instead of destructive."

Activity at the gate turned their attention away from the prisoners. It was the arrival of Felindra and Ashala. They were accompanied by the two defenders who'd been guarding her, and a forlorn-looking figure in a black robe.

"Look what we found in the woods," Felindra said when she got close enough for them to hear. "Actually, it was Ashala who found him, but here he is, the Grand Wizard. We think he may have been running away."

Monaltor gave her a scathing look, but said nothing. It was as if all the spirit had gone out of him, leaving him a shrunken, empty shell of his former self.

"Why were you outside the walls?" Arendt asked.

"I went out to pick some herbs for my experiments."

"Didn't you know the monastery was being attacked? Didn't you hear anything?" Daryan asked him.

"I wasn't paying much attention. I was thinking about other things."

"A likely story," Arendt said. "I think you were trying to escape."

"Believe what you like. What about my son?"

"I thought you said he was locked in his room," Felindra retorted.

"Is that the young wizard who caused such havoc in Trethawynd?" Daryan asked.

"Yes," Felindra replied. "I think I know where he is. Do you want me to find him for you?"

"It would be better if you left that to us." Daryan said. "I don't want you getting into any more dangerous situations."

"He won't hurt me," Felindra said. "He's sort of a friend now." She glared at the grand wizard. "That one, his loving father, had his powers removed because he escaped with us and helped us. Besides, he is interested in the Light now and wants to make amends for what he did. You can send someone with me if you like," she added with an impish smile.

"Oh very well," Daryan replied. "But I have some serious questions for him and he'll have to face charges in Trethawynd for his crimes. You two go with her, and watch out for him. He may not be as friendly as my daughter believes."

"According to his father, he's locked in. We'll need the key to his room."

"The key," Daryan demanded, holding out his hand to Monaltor.

"Any of the guards can open the door," the grand wizard snarled.

"Anyone?" Daryan asked, looking around at the prisoners. One of them stepped forward. He took a key chain from his belt that held numerous keys and handed it to the commander. Daryan passed it on to one of the defenders who was to accompany Felindra. "She's only going to show you the way," he added to the defenders. "You are to take charge of securing the prisoner."

"Now I have to go and talk to another of their prisoners, if you'll excuse me," Daryan said. He turned and followed Felindra. It appeared that Lord Evanar and the grand wizard's son were in the same building.

Felindra

Felindra led them into the building that contained the dungeons and along a hallway to a door near the end. Before anyone could stop her, she called through the door, "It's me, Barengush. Felindra. We've come to let you out." When one of the defenders gently moved her aside, she said softly, "it's better if I am the first person he sees. He trusts me. And please don't hurt him; he's suffered enough at the hands of his father."

"If I had my way," the defender said angrily. "I would have him burned alive like he did to those poor people in DarSolas. I lost my sister in that attack on the castle."

"I'm sorry, I feel your sorrow and understand why you feel that way, but we have to start changing things and the first step would be to understand him."

"What's to understand? He's a monster who should be eliminated."

Felindra sighed. "All right, but will you let me be the first person he sees when you open the door?"

"Very well, but don't go near him."

The defender looked at the lock and then at the assortment of keys on the chain, assessing each one to see which was likely to be the one to use. "May I?" Felindra asked. "I know which it is; I saw a guard unlock the door once." Before he could reply, or do anything else, she lifted one of the keys. "This one."

He unlocked the door and quickly looked inside, then backed away and let Felindra stand in the doorway.

She saw an almost indistinguishable mound lying on the cot across the room, unmoving. "Barengush, it's Felindra. Can you hear me?"

The bundle moved and a hand appeared to pull the blanket higher. "Go away. I don't want to talk to anyone."

She felt the defender preparing to move, but she shook her head at him. "Let me talk to him first," she murmured.

He rolled his eyes, but stayed out of sight.

"I have some good news to tell you," she said to Barengush. "Ogryn is dead. The league has taken the monastery and…"

The bundle on the cot came apart and Barengush became almost visible in the murky room. "What did you say? I don't believe you. He can't be dead. Nobody can kill him." He sounded a bit more alert now.

"It's true. I was there and I saw it with my own eyes. And your father is a prisoner of the League of Light." She held her arms out from the sides to prevent the defender barging in before she'd finished. "Some people are with me. They're going to take you to the captain. Don't worry; they're not going to hurt you. I'll tell them how you've changed and are with the Light now. Do you want to come out now?"

692

He stood up. "Is this some trick? Are they using you to get at me?"

"No, Barengush, I insisted on coming to make sure they don't hurt you."

"All right, that's enough!" the defender pushed her aside and led his partner into the dingy room. "Light, it stinks in here! How can you live like this?" the first defender said, pinching his nose. "All right, come with us." Barengush made no resistance and allowed himself to be grabbed by the arms and led from the room.

Felindra was shocked by his appearance. She would have believed anyone who told her he hadn't eaten anything since she last saw him. He looked like a walking skeleton inside a skin. His hair and beard were tangled and greasy, and his fingernails grown long. The clothes he wore were filthy and torn, and he smelled terrible.

As they guided him down the hallway, Felindra asked, "Can't you let him wash and get some clean clothes before you take him out there?"

"We were only told to detain him, not to be nursemaids."

"Wait here," she urged them. "I'll run and find out if he can get cleaned up first."

"I don't know why you're so concerned about this killer. You should have more sympathy for the people he's massacred."

"I do, but isn't it better if he has repented and wants to be led by the Light?"

The defender blew out a gush of air. "All right, don't waste too much time!"

As she ran towards the door, she heard her father talking to someone in the next hallway. She ran round and saw him outside one of the rooms with Vertan. "Dadi, we've got Barengush, but he's a real mess. Is it all right if he gets cleaned up before he goes outside?"

"As you wish," he replied, smiling. "If it's important to you."

"Thank you dadi. What are you doing here?"

"Releasing another prisoner."

The subject of clean clothes and water for bathing, reminded Felindra of Dominel. She hadn't seen him around and wondered what had become of him. She wanted to thank him for his kindness. She ran back to Barengush's room and told the two defenders what her father has said, and then she went in search of the old man.

First, she went to the yard outside and asked Captain Arendt. "Have you seen Dominel? I want to thank him."

Arendt wiped his brow and looked down at his boots, then up at her. He had tears in his eyes. "He's gone," he replied. "I've known that old man since I was a baby and ..." He couldn't continue.

"You mean he's been killed?" Felindra asked, horrified. "How did it happen?" Tears ran down her nose and she wiped it with the heel of her hand.

Arendt cleared his throat. "He was caught in the wizard's power blast. It stopped his heart."

Felindra turned to run back to the building to find her father, tears streaming down her face.

86 – Lord Evanar

Daryan

The door opened and Daryan received another shock. The person who faced him only vaguely resembled the light-hearted young man he remembered from his visits to the Castle. His hair was long and streaked with grey and his once neat beard was straggly and almost completely grey. His body was emaciated, with sagging, parched-looking skin. In all, he looked like an elderly man in poor health. His eyes had lost their bright sparkle and seemed to have sunk into their darkened sockets. The clothes he was wearing, although clean, were wrinkled and sagged on his lean frame.

"By the look on your face," Evanar said, "I must look pretty awful. Believe me when I tell you, I probably look a lot worse than I feel at this moment." He held out his arms to Daryan who grasped his upper arms gently, almost afraid of crushing them. In return, Lord Evanar gripped him fiercely. "It's so good to see you, Daryan. I never thought I'd see anyone...." He stopped, released his hands, and wiped tears from his eyes.

Daryan's eyes welled. "I'm glad we found you, My Lord. Your brother will be very relieved to hear that you're safe, but I think we should fatten you up a bit before he sees you." He said with a smile. "Now, let's go to meet the others. There's going to be a conference, and a good meal, I hope.

87 – Going Home

Felindra

"We're going home." Her father held out his open arms; Felindra rushed into his embrace, a feeling of relief coursing through her, although her joy was tainted by the sadness of Dominel's death.

"When?" she asked.

"As soon as we tie up some loose ends here. The Grand Master wants us to come to the Monastery—our Monastery—and give him a report of recent events. He wants to talk to you as well, and has asked us to bring Barengush with us to face a board of inquiry."

"What will they do to him?" she asked, hoping his punishment would not be too harsh.

"That depends on what we have to report about his activities and what sort of account he makes of himself. It would be nice if he could be rehabilitated and learn how to use his gifts properly. That goes for the other young wizards too. It would appear that they have all been adversely influenced while they were too young to form their own judgement of what they were being taught. We might be able to do something with them. For now, we just have to wait and see."

"But Barengush's father had his gifts taken away. How can he learn to use them if he doesn't have them?"

"I think there was a bit of deception there on the part of Monaltor. He convinced the boy that he could no longer use his powers by some kind of deep hypnosis. He will need a great deal of help if he is to recover from his present mood, though, but it is possible. Right now, believing he no longer has gifts, he's fallen into a deep depression and has given up."

"What about his father?"

"Oh, he'll be dealt with separately. The prince wants him sent to the Sola Regis to face a royal tribunal, so we're leaving it up to the crown to settle that matter. If you're willing, we'd like you to talk to Barengush. You don't have to if you don't want to, but you seem to have developed some rapport with him"

"I will, of course. We seemed to have been making good progress before his father caught us and brought us back here. I know he has done some terrible things to our people, but I feel he's not all bad."

"You realize that Duke Valdor will probably want to try him for the destruction of the castle and for participating in the assassination of his wife and daughter?"

Felindra sighed. "I know. There's so much against him, but both of those were Gremulkin's doing. I mean Gremulkin planned the events and was in control of them. Do you think they will want to execute Barengush for that?"

"It's possible," her father replied. "Although there might be some opposition to that from the Monastery. We've been trying to abolish the death penalty for years. It would be better if he could make reparations for his crimes, but they are so heinous, the people might not accept that solution."

"They should blame his father; he's the one who led the Dark Brethren. I wouldn't object to *him* being executed."

"It may come to that in the end. We'll have to wait and see how it plays out."

"I wonder what Vertan will do now."

"I suppose he'll go on with his defender training. You were close to him, weren't you?"

Felindra went over the question in her mind, nibbling her bottom lip as she thought. *How do I feel about him? I liked him, he's nice and kind, but nothing more.* "I think we have a lot in common and I'll miss him, but...." She shrugged. "Which reminds me, I should say goodbye and thank him before we leave. He was as responsible as Ashala for killing that creature; he gave her his strength so that she could keep going."

It took them two weeks to reach the Monastery. Ashala had refused to ride in one of the wagons. Although Felindra was a little hurt by her rejection, she realized it was nothing personal. She was still a wild animal, more at home in the forests with her own kind. Being around a lot of people and skittish horses was stressful for her.

They arrived early in the evening, welcomed by lanterns and torches illuminating the Monastery courtyard, and what looked like the entire population of the Monastery. Duke Valdor was there with his knights to greet them.

The entire company and the horses were exhausted after travelling since sunrise, so the festivities were quickly over and the men and women of the League were freed to go to their own quarters. Barengush was taken to a detention cell in the defenders' building. It was the one Axtya had occupied with a few moderations. It now contained man-sized furniture, bars had been placed on the windows, and a lock installed on the door.

Before he was taken away, Felindra managed to have a few words with him. "Don't be afraid. These are good people, they won't hurt you, and I think you will find the cell quite comfortable. I'll come and see you tomorrow." She squeezed his hand and turned her attention to finding her mother. When she saw her and Darson struggling to cut a pathway through the mob, her eyes filled with tears. She almost failed to recognize Darson. He seemed to have grown taller, and his eyes were now covered by a pair of lenses that reflected the torch light.

After hugging him she asked, "When did you get the spectacles?"

"They're not spectacles, they're lenses," he replied pedantically. "I've had them for about a month. Do you like them?"

"I do. They make you look quite ... distinguished and learned. Why do you have them?"

"I was having a bit of trouble seeing small writing. They're wonderful. I can see fine details and everything now." His new lenses had obviously done wonders for his self-esteem.

When Parvana finished greeting her husband, she turned to Felindra and hugged her breathless, smothering her with kisses. She put her arm around Felindra's shoulder and started to lead them all back to their home. "Are you sure you're all right?" she asked for the second time. "I was so worried about you, I couldn't function. I barely slept the whole time you were gone, and kept forgetting what I was doing and everything else, just worrying about you. Now, thank the Light you're back safe and unharmed, well, relatively.... You must be hungry; I've made some of your favorite dishes, so I hope you have a good appetite."

Felindra was surprised by her mother's verbosity; she didn't usually have so much to say. It reminded her of Haro and brought tears to her eyes. *He was such a good man. I can't believe I'll never see him again....*

Daryan

The next morning, Daryan donned his ceremonial uniform and reported at the Palace of Trethawynd. The meeting was being held in the large committee room on the third floor. Among those present were several of the duke's knights, the Grand Master, Ashavan, and, to his surprise, Lord Evanar, looking a little healthier, although he still had shadows around his eyes. His hair would never be the glossy black again, but it had been trimmed and washed. He'd shaved off the beard and looked more like his old self.

"Shall we get started?" the duke said. "Grand Master?" he indicated the slightly larger chair at the end of the long table. He took the one at the other end for himself. "Would you like to start, Grand Master?"

The Grand Master had a pile of papers, which he placed on the table in front of him. He spent a moment checking the first document and then looked up. "Welcome home, everyone. Sadly, there were many casualties, those brave men and women who will never return. We may console ourselves with the thought that they are now with the Light, embarking on their progress through eternity. However, this is little consolation for the loved ones of the fallen. They will have to continue their remaining days without someone who is dear to their hearts, one with whom they expected to share the rest of their lives." He cleared his throat and continued: "Tomorrow, we will be having an open memorial service for the fallen, which I hope you will all attend to show support for the bereaved.

"Next, we come to another matter, but before I start, I would like you to join me in giving Lord Evanar a heartfelt welcome home." The people around the table drummed on it with their palms and called, "Welcome home!"

Evanar smiled back at them and nodded. He seemed somewhat dazed, as if he couldn't get used to being free after all the time he'd spent in a solitary cell.

"Now we come to the matter of the former chancellor Gremulkin. We have been seeking him for several months, ever since the destruction of the Castle, but we are hardly any closer to finding him than when we started. There were reports of his being seen embarking on ship from the southwest port of Espea, but there the trail stops. The ship he allegedly left on was traced to its destination, but he wasn't on board when it arrived. He could have changed ships anywhere along the trade route. It's strange that we lost track of him; we had some of the most powerful telepaths in Albasiny searching for him. Our allies have been warned to look out for him, but I doubt he would go to roost with any of them. It's more likely he's gone to some non-treaty nation." The Grand Master realized the duke anted to say something. "Yes, Your Grace?"

"My brother had a bit more contact with Gremulkin that most of us, I'll let him tell you. Evanar..."

"First let me say that it shames me that I was forced to be in his presence so much, but I assure you, it was not by choice. Gremulkin and Charnwell turned up for a meeting once in the middle of the night. They were sitting by the fireplace, whispering to each other. My cot was in an alcove at the opposite end of the room. They'd checked to make sure I was sleeping before they sat down. I couldn't hear everything they said, but I did catch the name 'Mosfel' several times, for example, I heard them say, 'have you contacted Mosfel?' and 'when you see Mosfel'. I don't know if it's a place or a person. I hope this helps." Evanar sat down.

Duke Valdor looked around the table. "Does anyone recognize the name?"

Ashavan raised his hand. "There is a wizard called 'Mosfel' in the Nevasin Islands; it might be to him they were referring."

"Very good," the Grand Master said. "We'll look into it immediately, Your Grace. If we find anything through our methods, we'll turn it over to you for action. That's all I have to discuss for now."

Valdor, without referring to any notes, took the chair. "Are we to assume that Gremulkin and Charnwell are together, then?"

"It's a distinct possibility," the Grand Master replied.

"My people have been searching for Charnwell as well," Valdor said. "All we could discover was that he took everything of value from his home and his business, and embarked on a voyage to who-knows-where. The ship he took from DarSolas was a merchant vessel heading west towards..." he paused to look at his notes "...Braston. We talked to the captain, when he returned to Trethawynd, and he reported that Charnwell had changed to another ship about halfway through the voyage at a port in Sayir, but he couldn't name its destination, or where it was registered, so we hit another dead end. It sounds likely to me that they are planning to meet somewhere and carry on together. Let's pray no other unsuspecting ruler falls prey to their scheming."

Valdor paused and took a drink from the glass in front of him. "Now to what I consider is the most important and gratifying event of this conflict, the contribution Commander Peshanar's daughter made to our victory. If it hadn't been for the courage of Felindra Peshanar ... and her wolf ... we might still be out there fighting." He continued by giving a brief outline of Felindra's activities in ValkonenMaa, then he looked at Daryan with a gleam in his eye. "I have news for you, Commander. The queen has already contacted us and has invited you and your family to the capital where she plans to award your daughter with a special citation."

"Oh, she'll love that." Daryan said ironically. "You know how she dislikes being singled out for attention. I'll have my work cut out trying to persuade her when she hears about it." The rest of those around the table laughed.

"Oh, she'll come around," the duke said, smiling.

***

When Daryan told her about it later that day, first she looked distressed, then thoughtful. She took his arm and led him into the kitchen alcove where she whispered in his ear. "I have something to tell you," she said. "Can we go outside and walk?"

"If it's that important, why not tell everyone?"

"I cannot. I'm sorry, dadi. I didn't really want to tell even you, but I want you to understand why I don't deserve such an honor."

"Very well. I can't imagine what you could tell me that would make me believe you don't deserve it. Now you have me really mystified." He returned to the sitting area and told Parvana and Darson they were going out for a walk.

"Can we come?" Darson asked.

"You stay here," Daryan replied. "We have to discuss secret League business."

"But I've..." Daryan looked at his son, put a finger cross his lips and shook his head. Darson understood and sat back with a sigh.

When they reached the garden behind the white palace, Felindra chose a bench to sit on near the fountain. Within seconds of sitting down, Ashala was there, giving them licks and tail wags, showing her pleasure in their company. "Sit still, girl," Felindra said, putting her arm over the wolf's shoulder.

"All right, out with it!" Daryan said.

"It's something that happened when I was at the Valkonen monastery," she said. She gave him a quick glance and then looked off into the trees. "I hope you will believe what I'm going to tell you, because it is very ... strange? ... unusual." She looked at him again and he nodded, giving her an encouraging smile. "It's the truth, I swear it. It wasn't a dream." She took her hand off Ashala and twisted it in the

702

one that was resting in her lap. "I didn't want to tell anyone about it. I thought they might say I was crazy or having delusions, but...." She took a deep breath and continued. "All right, here goes: I developed another gift when I was there at the monastery, the gift of Repel. Monaltor was trying to do something to my brain with Barengush helping and I got really scared. I could feel the pressure building up inside my head until it exploded, and the next thing I knew, I was lying on the bed in my room feeling very sick. The pain in my head was so bad, I couldn't even move."

"My poor girl." Daryan moved closer and took her hand in his. "Was this what you were afraid to tell me?"

"Oh, no. It's what happened next. As I was lying there, feeling terribly sick, someone came into my room without opening the door. It wasn't a person, more like an angel, although she said she wasn't an angel. She told me she was a Messenger of the Light. She touched my head and made me feel better, then she told me I'd been chosen to serve the Light and the Light would always protect me and I should never be afraid. She told me many other things, then she left, she just faded away. You do believe me, don't you, dadi?"

Daryan squeezed her hands. "You're sure it wasn't a dream? You were sick and sometimes sickness does things to our minds and makes us have strange dreams."

Felindra took her hand away from him and bowed her head. "I knew you wouldn't believe me. You think I'm just a silly girl trying to make myself look important, but it's true, I swear by the Light, it really happened." Her voice started to take on a desperate edge. "After that, other things started to happen. I was able to cure Barengush by touching him and asking the Light for help. You know I'm not a healer. He was as sick as I was from my power blast. Then, when Monaltor sent me to the dungeons, light came from the cell walls and the air became warmer. Then *she* came again and told me it was time to escape. She told me what to do and which way to go, and how to rescue the Grand Master. The doors were unlocked for me and no guards were around when we got away. Lots of things like that. The second time, after we had been caught again and they took away our clothes, the old man, Dominel, brought me some food and clothes, and a blanket. He said he just got the urge to bring them, but I know it was the Light working through him." She paused for breath, giving him a quick, pleading glance.

"Go on; I'm listening." Her father glanced at her, and then leaned forward on the bench with his elbows on his knees and his hands clasped.

"Dadi, I was so scared. All the time ... that monster Ogryn terrified me. How can anyone think I'm brave if I was scared all the time?"

Her father straightened up and took her hand again. "It's not the lack of fear that makes someone courageous; it's doing what must be done in spite of being afraid. And that's what you did, my love. You're a hero by anyone's definition, and I'm very proud of you."

"But do you believe me about the Messenger?"

"Let's say I'm reserving judgement. I do believe something very profound happened to you and that it's related to your faith in the Light. Will that do?" he took her hand and stood up "Let's go back. Your mother and brother will be wondering if we got lost. So, are you looking forward to going to Sola Regis to get your award?"

"Sort of. I am excited about seeing the capital and the queen, but I still don't think I deserve a medal. Will mami be going and Darson?"

"Of course. I think they deserve some sort of treat after waiting for us at home all those weeks, not knowing what was happening to us."

"You know, dadi, I never thought I'd become a warrior. Isn't it amazing, the things that happen? I know one person who will not be pleased to hear about what happened to me: my classmate, Arnaz Pashin. He'll be so envious."

"Is that the son of Captain Pashin?"

"Yes; why?"

"He was seriously injured in the same encounter that killed our friend Andro Haro. He lives, but he may not walk again."

"Oh, no. Poor man. Poor Arnaz. War is such a terrible thing. I don't know why people want to do such awful things to one another. Can't the Light stop it?"

"That's what free will is about, my sweet, it's up to us to follow His will, but he won't compel us to do so. One day, maybe.... Well we're here. I enjoyed our little talk." Daryan pushed the door open.

"Me too, dadi. Thank you for listening."

88 – Felindra Meets the Queen

A special ship was sent to bring the guests to the capital, a vessel of the Royal Transport Service. It was luxuriously appointed with comfortable staterooms and cabins for the guests, and a sumptuous dining salon where first-class food was served. Duke Valdor occupied the royal suite with his son, while Commander Peshanar and his family had the one next to it as the second ranking family among the passengers. Felindra was surprised to see the Haro family on the ship, until she thought about it. Commander Haro was a war hero who had given his life for the Children of Light.

Felindra met Valina Haro walking on the deck the day they embarked on the voyage. She looked a lot smaller and thinner than Felindra remembered her. She was wearing a long grey cotton tunic over her black culottes and a black shawl around her shoulders that, along with the dark stains under her eyes, seemed to age her considerably. "Lady Haro, I feel your loss so much. It was like losing a member of my own family."

"I know, Felindra, thank you." She seemed about to hold out her hands to Felindra, but took a cotton handkerchief from her pocket to dab her eyes instead. "I'm sorry; it's still hard to cope with the loss. I don't know if we will ever recover, but we must keep going somehow."

"How are the children?" Felindra asked, at a loss for anything else to say.

"Sometimes, they seem to be coping fairly well, but they have their moments. Children seem to be more resilient than grownups. Sleep doesn't come easily for me now and I've heard young Micah crying at night on a couple of occasions. Ivana is devastated. Girls always take the loss of their father harder. Olin's the one I worry about. He's become silent and withdrawn, and he's always angry." She stopped talking and put her hand on Felindra's arm. "I'm sorry to ramble on like that. How about you? I understand you're a hero."

"You don't have to apologize for talking about your family's loss, lady," Felindra replied, ignoring the question. "I'll be glad to talk with you any time you feel like it. It's hard to imagine how I would feel if anything happened to my father. Have you decided what you are going to do now?"

Valina sighed. "I'd like to go back to Cavalcitas and continue his work. Olin will be old enough soon to take more responsibility, unless he decided to stay at the Monastery and continue his education."

"I hope it works out for you all," Felindra replied. "As for being a hero, I'm not. Really. All I did was follow the Light and trust Him that everything would be all right. And Ashala helped a lot too. I feel like a fraud, getting an award, but it looks as if I have no choice about it."

"I'm sure you've earned the citation," Valina replied. "From what I've heard about your captivity, it must have been a terrifying experience. I don't know how you got through it. But I can well believe what you said about Ashala. She's the most remarkable animal I've ever met." She smiled.

"I think she's gifted," Felindra said with a grin.

***

After the evening meal the next day, Lord Varen invited her to walk on the upper deck with him. "I missed you while you were gone," he said once they were outside. "I was so scared about what the black wizard might do to you. I imagined all sorts of horrors. Did he hurt you?"

"Not really. Not physically at least, but it hurt me to be taken from my home, and I hated him for what he did to Ashala."

"I don't blame you. I'm glad you came back safely." He reached out and took her hand. "You know I care for you, Felindra," he said in a rush.

Felindra felt a hot current flow down through her body and her face flushed. She gently released her hand. "I care about you, too." Felindra didn't know how to react to his comment. *What does he mean?* she wondered. *We wouldn't be able to...* she knew she shouldn't take this line of thought any further. "It's good to be back and see you and all my friends again."

Lord Evanar turned towards the ship's rail and looked at the trail of moonlight on the surface of the ocean, and then up at the sky. "Do you know anything about the stars?" he asked.

"No, not much, except that they're distant suns and some of them might have worlds with them. That's more my brother's field. He can't make up his mind whether to be a scientist—he hasn't decided which science yet—or a mathematician."

"Lucky boy, to have a choice."

"Can't you choose what you want to be?"

"Not really. Anything I choose to study, apart from learning to be a duke, would be looked on as a hobby." He leaned over the rail and watched the sea swells rushing by as the ship plowed through the water.

"Don't you want to be a duke?" she asked.

"I suppose I do, but I don't want my father to die, and that's the only way I can become one."

"What would you do if you could choose?"

Evanar shrugged and turned to face her, leaning back with his elbows on the rail. "I must be like your brother, I can't decide. I'm drawn towards astronomy and ... promise not to laugh ... I'd like to be an architect and design buildings."

"I think that's wonderful. How about becoming an architect as a profession, and studying astronomy as hobby?" she said with a grin.

"Sounds like the ideal solution. I'll have think about it; see if I can fit them in with my training in the art of dukemanship," he replied, smiling. "That's enough about me. What about you? Do you have anything in mind, apart from working with animals?"

"Not really. It's true what you say about animals, but I can learn a lot about them just by being with them. I thought about studying languages, but I don't know what use that would be to me."

"That's interesting. Do you like to travel?"

Felindra chuckled. "I don't have much to judge by apart from being dragged against my will onto a creaky old barge and taken to Valkonen."

"Sorry, that was not a very sensible question, was it? Why do you call it Valkonen?"

"That's what they call it most of the time. You have to admit, ValkonenMaa is a bit of a mouthful."

"Are you coming back to school when we get back?"

"Of course. I still have to learn how to control my gifts." The moment she said that, she regretted it. As far as everyone knew, she only had one gift and she hated discussing the new ones. She was saved from the questions by the arrival of her father and mother, accompanied by Duke Valdor.

"I thought we'd find you out here," her father said.

"Are you warm enough?" her mother asked.

Back to normal.

***

When they arrived at Sola Regis, several carriages waited at the royal dock to transport the guests to the palace where they were to be accommodated during their stay. Felindra couldn't resist reading the horses, and found they were quite content being out with the carriages.

When they arrived at the palace, they were shown to the guest suites on the third level and left to themselves to freshen up and change their clothes for the banquet Queen Zenobia was hosting in their honor.

Felindra's mother helped her dress while a maid provided by the palace arranged her hair. "I hate all this fussing," Felindra said as she watched the maid rub fragrant oil into the hair to control the curls.

"Apologies, lady, it will soon be finished and you will look even more beautiful." She took strands of hair and wound them around her fingers, patting each strand in place as she finished it. Finally, she took all the strands in a bunch and pinned them on top of Felindra's head, then added some jeweled ornaments. "What do you think?" the maid asked when she'd finished.

Felindra was impressed with the skill of the young woman and agreed she did look different, more grown up, but hardly beautiful. She couldn't understand why people thought she was. "I like it," she replied. "You did a wonderful job. Thank you."

The woman bowed and left, carrying her basket of supplies under her arm.

"You look gorgeous, darling," her mother said when she arrived with a shawl for her shoulders.

Felindra stood up, scowling. "I hate dressing up like this. I feel so restricted. You know I never wear fancy culottes.

They're so inconvenient. And this hair." She looked critically at herself in the mirror afraid to touch her hair lest it fall down from its precarious position. "It's not me."

Her mother smiled. "Yes, I can't imagine you romping in the garden with Ashala dressed like that, but this is different. It is a great honor to be received by the queen, so the least we can do is follow protocol. Do you know what good taste means?"

Felindra shook her head.

"It can apply to many things, not just clothing. Basically, it's knowing and doing what is appropriate for the occasion. For example, you wouldn't go to a banquet in the overalls you wear to clean the stables."

"Interesting." Felindra stroked her hands over the flimsy pale yellow culottes and tunic she was wearing. The tunic was a slender silk garment decorated at the neck with turquoise beads. "Actually I like this color," she said. "But don't blame me if I trip over the culottes. They're so long and loose, I'm sure my shoes will get tangled in the hems."

"Oh stop fretting. All you have to do is take smaller steps, and you can lift the legs when you walk, but only above the ankles, not too high. Remember, you're in a royal palace, not chasing wolves across fields. Here, put on the shawl." She smiled as she handed Felindra a white lace shawl. "Now the shoes."

"These things are going to kill my feet," Felindra complained, picking up one of the shoes. They were pretty shoes covered in white satin and decorated with sparkling crystals, but to her, used to wearing sandals and boots, or going barefoot, they represented a form of torture, especially the elevated heels that increased her height by two finger-breadths, making her feel as if she would topple over at any moment. She sighed and put them on. They weren't too uncomfortable; it was just that they made her feel insecure, off balance.

"You're just nervous, love. Don't think about it; take things slowly and you'll be fine. You look so beautiful, no one will be paying attention to anything else, and remember to smile. This is a celebration, not a wake."

A knock came on the door. Her mother went to open it and admit her father. He stopped in the doorway and looked around. "Where's Felindra? It's time to go."

"Oh, dadi, you know I'm here."

'You! But I thought I was escorting my daughter to a banquet. Who's this stranger I see before me?"

"Come on let's go," her mother said, holding out her hand for Felindra.

"You mean that beautiful, elegant young maiden is Felindra. I didn't recognize her. And you look ravishing, my love," he added to his wife.

"You don't look so bad yourself," Parvana replied, looking him up and down.

He was dressed in his full League regalia, white tunic with gold trim over fitted dark blue trousers tucked into shiny black boots. He even wore the ceremonial headdress, a square of white silk held in place with a circlet of gold braid.

"This is so exciting," Darson said as they followed a footman down the carpeted hallway. "We're going to see the queen, even sit at the same table. I wager the food will be fabulous."

"Better than mine?" his mother said, taking his hand. Darson was wearing a miniature variation of his father's costume without the headdress or League decorations.

I'm so nervous, I might be sick if I try to eat anything. Felindra thought.

They passed the Duke's suite and heard voices inside, but the door didn't open until they had passed. Felindra was afraid to look around to see who was fallowing them, but her father did. He stopped and turned back. "Good evening, Your Grace, and Lord Varen."

As if that was an invitation, the duke and his son hurried to catch up with them. *Oh no. I don't want him to see me like this.* But Varen came to her side. She felt her skin flushing as he looked at her.

"Sola Naofa! I almost didn't recognize you. You look so lovely. I like your hair like that. May I walk with you?" He held up his arm for her.

"Thank you," she replied, putting her hand on his forearm. *What am I going to say to him?* Her mind had gone completely blank. *I hope he can't feel me quaking.* "You can catch me if I trip," she blurted, her face burning with mortification. *Oh, Light, I'm not cut out for this.*

"Gladly," Varen replied.

"I mean ... these shoes ... I'm not used to wearing them." Light! How much worse can I make it? I should keep my mouth shut, or I'll come off sounding like a complete idiot.

***

The next morning, the day she was dreading, the royal protocol officer appeared at their door shortly after they had finished breaking their fast. As soon as the maids had straightened the bed in Felindra's room, the woman started pulling out garments from the chest at the foot. She held up pair of gold-colored culottes, long, of course. "This should be fine, and this white tunic to go with it, but I don't see a mantle. Do you have one?"

"No, lady. I didn't realize I'd need one. I'm sorry."

"It's all right," the woman said. She was a stern looking woman with about thirty-five years. "I can get one for you. Wait here. I'll return shortly and finish coaching you on the protocol."

The nightmare begins. Light, if I get through this, I promise I'll never complain about anything ever again. By the time the woman returned, Felindra was sweating and wringing her hands nervously, while trying to slow her fluttering heart. *Take a deep breath,* she told herself. *And stop whining!*

Everything will be fine; it will soon be over. The thought of running barefoot in the meadow with Ashala would be bliss compared with what she was doing now.

Felindra sat on the edge of the bed and listened to a long string of rules for this type of ceremony. Luckily, her mother was there with her. She knew she would immediately forget everything the protocol officer said and she was relying on Parvana to help her.

"That's about it then," the woman said as she stood up to leave. "Do you have any questions?

Felindra looked at her mother. "When I walk up to the throne, can my father walk with me?"

The woman looked astonished by the question. "Let me think," the woman said. "First, tell me why you want him with you."

Felindra looked down at her hands, fighting back tears. "I'm so nervous; I'm afraid I might trip and fall."

"Hm. We do allow elders and people with disabilities to be escorted, but I don't know about a healthy young person like you. What makes you feel you might trip?"

"I'm not used to wearing long culottes and shoes with heels."

The protocol officer offered some ideas for overcoming her fear, but would not agree to her to having an escort. "Now, is your speech ready?"

"Speech?" Felindra's voice rose to a high-pitched squeak.

"It is traditional for the awardee to say a few words after receiving the award. You mean you didn't know?"

"No. Do I have to?" Felindra was close to tears.

"As I said, it's traditional. It is a courtesy to her majesty. You only need a few short sentences to say how you feel about receiving the award. Two or three. Speak slowly when you deliver them."

"I'll help you, darling," her mother said, taking Felindra's hand. "Don't worry, it will soon be over," she added in a whisper as the door closed on the protocol officer. "I never realized these functions could be so complicated and have so many rules."

"I think I need a glass of wine," Felindra said. "Or something to relax me."

***

Felindra walked between her parents to the grand assembly hall. Rehearsing the words in her mind that she and her mother had worked out. *Oh, Light, please don't let me forget what I have to say.*

Fortunately, she was one of the first to be called to accept her citation. The queen stood in front of her throne and said a few words about Felindra's contribution to the victory over the Dark Brethren and then placed a blue ribbon around her neck supporting a gold medallion, and handed her a vellum scroll with the royal seal. She patted Felindra on the wrist and whispered in her ear, "don't be nervous dear; it's almost over. You're a very courageous young lady." And then she returned to her seat next to Prince Felidorn.

Felindra rolled up the scroll with trembling hands, and then faced the throne: *Help me!* She was suffused with warmth. "You … your majesty, Prince Consort, honorable guests, I feel deeply honored and privileged to be here today to accept this award. I would not be here at all without the support and leading of the Light, who made it possible for me to survive." Here she paused to think, and then made a decision. "And my dear friend, Ashala, the wolf," she added in a rush.

The audience broke into applause, with a few laughs and some murmurs throughout the crowded hall.

She was about to turn and leave when the Queen spoke up again. "Have you given any thought to your future career, Felindra?"

"Not really, your majesty. I'll be continuing my education when I get back."

"Study well and choose your path carefully. We think you have a great future ahead of you and we will be following you with interest."

Felindra was stunned. "Your majesty, I'm unworthy of such attention, but thank you for..." She couldn't think how to finish.

"On the contrary, my dear. It is your humility and your faith that make you so worthy. We'll meet again; until then, farewell, and the Light guide you."

About the Author

Vicki was born and grew up in England. She now lives in British Columbia, where she wrote *The Whisperer.*

Having read between 5,000 and 6,000 books, she's decided to make her own contribution and now writes full-time.

She has had jobs too numerous to count, but her favorite was law office accountant, and the worst was filing tax returns at the Revenue Agency—five days a week of excruciating headaches.

Vicki loves peace, her four kids, classic rock and classical music, trees, animals, people, gardening, RPG and Adventure games; she also likes washing dishes, and couldn't live without color. She loathes cruelty, injustice, television, filing, and noise.

She is a Jesusonian, a pacifist, and a vegetarian.

If you have any comments about this book or just want to say hello, she can be contacted at *vickiwriteson@gmail.com.*

A review on Amazon would be greatly appreciated.